THE COLLECTED

JOHN CARTER OF MARS

VOLUME THREE

Swords of Mars was first published in *The Blue Book Magazine* as a six-part serial,
November 1934 through April 1935. Copyright © 1934, 1935 Edgar Rice Burroughs,
Inc. All rights reserved. *Synthetic Men of Mars* was first published in *Argosy Magazine* as
a six-part serial, January through February 1939. Copyright © 1938, 1939 Edgar Rice
Burroughs, Inc. All rights reserved. *Llana of Gathol* was first published as four novelettes
in *Amazing Stories* magazine under the following names: "The City of Mummies" in
March 1941, "Black Pirates of Barsoom" in June 1941, "Yellow Men of Mars" in August
1941, and "Invisible Men of Mars" in October 1941. Copyright © 1941 Ziff-Davis
Publishing Company. All rights reserved. *John Carter of Mars* was first published as two
novelettes in *Amazing Stories* magazine. The first part was published under the name
"John Carter and the Giant of Mars" in January 1941. Copyright © 1940 Ziff-Davis
Publishing Company. All rights reserved. The second part was published under the
name "Skeleton Men of Jupiter" in February 1943. Copyright © 1942 Ziff-Davis
Publishing Company. All rights reserved. These authorized editions are published by
Disney Editions in arrangement with Edgar Rice Burroughs, Inc.

Printed in the United States of America

First Disney Editions paperback edition
10 9 8 7 6 5 4 3 2 1
ISBN 978-1-4231-6559-0
G475-5664-5-11349

Visit www.disneybooks.com

SUSTAINABLE FORESTRY INITIATIVE Certified Fiber Sourcing
www.sfiprogram.org

THIS LABEL APPLIES TO TEXT STOCK

THE COLLECTED

JOHN CARTER OF MARS

VOLUME THREE

Swords of Mars
Synthetic Men of Mars
Llana of Gathol
John Carter of Mars

BY EDGAR RICE BURROUGHS

EDITIONS
NEW YORK

contents

SWORDS OF MARS

LLANA OF GATHOL

Part 1: The Ancient Dead

Part 2: The Black Pirates of Barsoom

Part 3: Escape on Mars

Part 4: Invisible Men of Mars

JOHN CARTER OF MARS

Part 1: John Carter and the Giant of Mars

Part 2: Skeleton Men of Jupiter

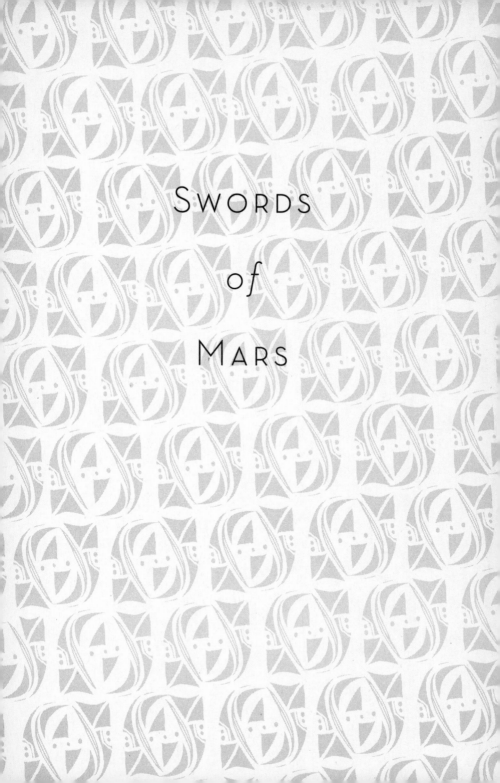

Swords

of

Mars

THE MOON had risen above the rim of the canyon near the headwaters of the Little Colorado. It bathed in soft light the willows that line the bank of the little mountain torrent and the cottonwood trees beneath which stood the tiny cabin where I had been camping for a few weeks in the White Mountains of Arizona.

I stood upon the little porch of the cabin enjoying the soft beauties of this Arizona night; and as I contemplated the peace and serenity of the scene, it did not seem possible that but a few years before the fierce and terrible Geronimo had stood in this same spot before this self-same cabin, or that generations before that this seemingly deserted canyon had been peopled by a race now extinct.

I had been seeking in their ruined cities for the secret of their genesis and the even stranger secret of their extinction. How I wished that those crumbling lava cliffs might speak and tell me of all that they had witnessed since they poured out in a molten stream from the cold and silent cones that dot the mesa land beyond the canyon.

My thoughts returned again to Geronimo and his fierce Apache warriors; and these vagrant musings engendered memories of Captain John Carter of Virginia, whose dead body had lain for ten long years in some forgotten cave in the mountains not far south of this very spot—the cave in which he had sought shelter from pursuing Apaches.

My eyes, following the pathway of my thoughts, searched the heavens until they rested upon the red eye of Mars shining there in the blue-black void; and so it was that Mars was uppermost in my mind as I turned into my cabin and prepared for a good night's rest beneath the rustling leaves of the cottonwoods, with whose soft and soothing lullaby was mingled the rippling and the gurgling of the waters of the Little Colorado.

I was not sleepy; and so, after I had undressed, I arranged a kerosene lamp near the head of my bunk and settled myself for the enjoyment of a gangster story of assassination and kidnaping.

My cabin consists of two rooms. The smaller back room is my bedroom. The larger room in front of it serves all other purposes, being dining room, kitchen, and living room combined. From my bunk, I cannot see directly into the front room. A flimsy partition separates the bedroom from the living room. It consists of rough-hewn boards that in the process of shrinking have left wide cracks in the wall, and in addition to this the door between the two rooms is seldom closed; so that while I could not see into the adjoining room, I could hear anything that might go on within it.

I do not know that I am more susceptible to suggestion than the average man; but the fact remains that murder, mystery, and gangster stories always seem more vivid when I read them alone in the stilly watches of the night.

I had just reached the point in the story where an assassin was creeping upon the victim of kidnapers when I heard the front door of my cabin open and close and, distinctly, the clank of metal upon metal.

Now, insofar as I knew, there was no one other than myself camped upon the headwaters of the Little Colorado; and certainly no one who had the right to enter my cabin without knocking.

I sat up in my bunk and reached under my pillow for the .45 Colt automatic that I keep there.

The oil lamp faintly illuminated my bedroom, but its main strength was concentrated upon me. The outer room was in darkness, as I could see by leaning from my bunk and peering through the doorway.

"Who's there?" I demanded, releasing the safety catch on my automatic and sliding my feet out of bed to the floor. Then, without waiting for a reply, I blew out the lamp.

A low laugh came from the adjoining room. "It is a good thing your wall is full of cracks," said a deep voice, "or otherwise I might have stumbled into trouble. That is a mean-looking gun I saw before you blew out your lamp."

The voice was familiar, but I could not definitely place it. "Who are you?" I demanded.

"Light your lamp and I'll come in," replied my nocturnal visitor. "If you're nervous, you can keep your gun on the doorway, but please don't squeeze the trigger until you have had a chance to recognize me."

"Damn!" I exclaimed under my breath, as I started to relight the lamp.

"Chimney still hot?" inquired the deep voice from the outer room.

"Plenty hot," I replied, as I succeeded at last in igniting the wick and replacing the hot chimney. "Come in."

I remained seated on the edge of the bunk, but I kept the doorway covered with my gun. I heard again the clanking of metal upon metal, and then a man stepped into the light of my feeble lamp and halted in the doorway. He was a tall man apparently between twenty-five and thirty with grey eyes and black hair. He was naked but for leather trappings that supported weapons of unearthly design—a short-sword, a long-sword, a dagger, and a pistol; but my eyes did not need to inventory all these details before I recognized him. The instant that I saw him, I tossed my gun aside and sprang to my feet.

"John Carter!" I exclaimed.

"None other," he replied, with one of his rare smiles.

We grasped hands. "You haven't changed much," he said.

"Nor you at all," I replied.

He sighed and then smiled again. "God alone knows how old I am. I can recall no childhood, nor have I ever looked other than I look tonight; but come," he added, "you mustn't stand here in your bare feet. Hop back into bed again. These Arizona nights are none too warm."

He drew up a chair and sat down. "What were you reading?" he asked, as he picked up the magazine that had fallen to the floor and glanced at the illustration. "It looks like a lurid tale."

"A pretty little bedtime story of assassination and kidnaping," I explained.

"Haven't you enough of that on earth without reading about it for entertainment?" he inquired. "We have on Mars."

"It is an expression of the normal morbid interest in the horrifying," I said. "There is really no justification, but the fact remains that I enjoy such tales. However, I have lost my interest now. I want to hear about you and Dejah Thoris and Carthoris, and what brought you here. It has been years since you have been back. I had given up all hope of ever seeing you again."

He shook his head, a little sadly I thought. "It is a long story, a story of love and loyalty, of hate and crime, a story of dripping swords, of strange places and strange people upon a stranger world. The living of it might have driven a weaker man to madness. To have one you love taken from you and not to know her fate!"

I did not have to ask whom he meant. It could be none other than the incomparable Dejah Thoris, Princess of Helium, and consort of John Carter, Warlord of Mars—the woman for whose deathless beauty a million swords had been kept red with blood on the dying planet for many a long year.

For a long time John Carter sat in silence staring at the floor. I knew that his thoughts were forty-three million miles away, and I was loath to interrupt them.

At last he spoke. "Human nature is alike everywhere," he said. He flicked the edge of the magazine lying on my bunk. "We think that we want to forget the tragedies of life, but we do not. If they momentarily pass us by and leave us in peace, we must conjure them again, either in our thoughts or through some such medium as you have adopted. As you find a grim pleasure in reading about them, so I find a grim pleasure in thinking about them.

"But my memories of that great tragedy are not all sad. There was high adventure, there was noble fighting; and in the end there was— but perhaps you would like to hear about it."

I told him that I would, so he told me the story that I have set down here in his own words, as nearly as I can recall them.

chapter 1

RAPAS THE ULSIO

OVER NINETEEN HUNDRED miles east of The Twin Cities of Helium, at about Lat. 30° S., Lon. 172° E., lies Zodanga. It has ever been a hotbed of sedition since the day that I led the fierce green hordes of Thark against it and, reducing it, added it to the Empire of Helium.

Within its frowning walls lives many a Zodangan who feels no loyalty for Helium; and here, too, have gathered numbers of the malcontents of the great empire ruled over by Tardos Mors, Jeddak of Helium. To Zodanga have migrated not a few of the personal and political enemies of the house of Tardos Mors and of his son-in-law, John Carter, Prince of Helium.

I visited the city as seldom as possible, as I had little love either for it or its people; but my duties called me there occasionally, principally because it was the headquarters of one of the most powerful guilds of assassins on Mars.

The land of my birth is cursed with its gangsters, its killers, and its kidnapers; but these constitute but a slight menace as compared with the highly efficient organizations that flourish upon Mars. Here assassination is a profession; kidnaping, a fine art. Each has its guild, its laws, its customs, and its code of ethics; and so widespread are their ramifications that they seem inextricably interwoven into the entire social and political life of the planet.

For years I have been seeking to extirpate this noxious system, but the job has seemed a thankless and hopeless one. Entrenched behind age-old ramparts of habit and tradition, they occupy a position in the public consciousness that has cast a certain glamour of romance and honor upon them.

The kidnapers are not in such good odor, but among the more notorious assassins are men who hold much the same position in the esteem of the masses as do your great heroes of the prize ring and the baseball diamond.

Furthermore, in the war that I was waging upon them, I was also handicapped by the fact that I must fight almost alone, as even those of the red men of Mars who felt as I did upon the subject also believed that to take sides with me against the assassins would prove but another means for committing suicide. Yet I know that even this would not have deterred them, had they felt that there was any hope of eventual success.

That I had for so long escaped the keen blade of the assassin seemed little less than a miracle to them, and I presume that only my extreme self-confidence in my ability to take care of myself prevented me from holding the same view.

Dejah Thoris and my son, Carthoris, often counseled me to abandon the fight; but all my life I have been loath to admit defeat, nor ever have I willingly abandoned the chance for a good fight.

Certain types of killings upon Mars are punishable by death, and most of the killings of the assassins fell in such categories. So far, this was the only weapon that I had been able to use against them, and then not always successfully, for it was usually difficult to prove their crime, since even eyewitnesses feared to testify against them.

But I had gradually evolved and organized another means of combating them. This consisted of a secret organization of super-assassins. In other words, I had elected to fight the devil with fire.

When an assassination was reported, my organization acted in the rôle of detective to ferret out the murderer. Then it acted as judge and jury and eventually as executioner. Its every move was made in secret, but over the heart of each of its victims an "X" was cut with the sharp point of a dagger.

We usually struck quickly, if we could strike at all; and soon the public and the assassins learned to connect that "X" over the heart as the mark of the hand of justice falling upon the guilty; and I know that in a number of the larger cities of Helium we greatly reduced the death rate by assassination. Otherwise, however, we seemed as far from our goal as when we first started.

Our poorest results had been gained in Zodanga; and the assassins of that city openly boasted that they were too smart for me, for although they did not know positively, they guessed that the X's upon the breasts of their dead comrades were made by an organization headed by me.

I hope that I have not bored you with this exposition of these dry facts, but it seemed necessary to me that I do so as an introduction to the adventures that befell me, taking me to a strange world in an effort to thwart the malign forces that had brought tragedy into my life.

In my fight against the assassins of Barsoom, I had never been able to enlist many agents to serve in Zodanga; and those stationed there worked only in a half-hearted manner, so that our enemies had good reason to taunt us with our failure.

To say that such a condition annoyed me would be putting it mildly; and so I decided to go in person to Zodanga, not only for the purpose of making a thorough investigation, but to give the Zodangan assassins a lesson that would cause them to laugh out of the other side of their mouths.

I decided to go secretly and in disguise, for I knew that if I were to go there as John Carter, Warlord of Mars, I could learn nothing more than I already knew.

Disguise for me is a relatively simple matter. My white skin and black hair have made me a marked man upon Mars, where only the auburn-haired Lotharians and the totally bald Therns have skin as light colored as mine.

Although I had every confidence in the loyalty of my retainers, one never knows when a spy may insinuate himself into the most carefully selected organization. For this reason, I kept my plans and preparations secret from even the most trusted members of my entourage.

In the hangars on the roof of my palace are fliers of various models, and I selected from among them a one-arm scout flier from which I surreptitiously removed the insignia of my house. Finding a pretext to send the hangar guard away for a short time early one evening, I smuggled aboard the flier those articles that I needed to insure a satisfactory disguise. In addition to a red pigment for my own skin and paints for the body of the flier, I included a complete set of Zodangan harness, metal, and weapons.

That evening I spent alone with Dejah Thoris; and about twenty-five xats past the eighth zode, or at midnight earth time, I changed to a plain leather harness without insignia, and prepared to leave upon my adventure.

"I wish you were not going, my prince; I have a premonition that—well—that we are both going to regret it."

"The assassins must be taught a lesson," I replied, "or no one's life will be safe upon Barsoom. By their acts, they have issued a definite challenge; and that I cannot permit to go unnoticed."

"I suppose not," she replied. "You won your high position here with your sword; and by your sword I suppose you must maintain it, but I wish it were otherwise."

I took her in my arms and kissed her and told her not to worry— that I would not be gone long. Then I went to the hangar on the roof.

The hangar guard may have thought that it was an unusual time of night for me to be going abroad, but he could have had no suspicion as to my destination. I took off toward the West and presently was cutting the thin air of Mars beneath the myriad stars and the two gorgeous satellites of the red planet.

The moons of Mars have always intrigued me; and tonight, as I gazed upon them, I felt the lure of the mystery that surrounds them. Thuria, the nearer moon, known to earth men as Phobos, is the larger; and as it circles Barsoom at a distance of only 5800 miles, it presents a most gorgeous sight. Cluros, the farther moon, though only a little smaller in diameter than Thuria, appears to be much smaller because of the greater distance of its orbit from the planet, lying as it does, 14,500 miles away.

For ages, there was a Martian legend, which remained for me to explode, that the black race, the so-called First-born of Barsoom, lived upon Thuria, the nearer moon; but at the time I exposed the false gods of Mars, I demonstrated conclusively that the black race lived in the Valley Dor, near the south pole of the planet.

Thuria, seemingly hanging low above me, presented a gorgeous spectacle, which was rendered still more remarkable by the fact that she apparently moved through the heavens from west to east, due to the fact that her orbit is so near the planet she performs a revolution in less than one-third of that of the diurnal rotation of Mars. But as I watched her this night in dreamy fascination, little could I guess the part that she was so soon to play in the thrilling adventures and the great tragedy that lay just beyond my horizon.

When I was well beyond The Twin Cities of Helium, I cut off my running lights and circled to the South, gradually heading toward the East until I held a true course for Zodanga. Setting my destination compass, I was free to turn my attention to other matters, knowing that this clever invention would carry the ship safely to its destination.

My first task was to repaint the hull of the flier. I buckled straps onto my harness and onto rings in the gunwale of the craft; and then, lowering myself over the side, I proceeded to my work. It was slow work, for after painting as far as I could reach in all directions, I had to come on deck and change the position of the straps, so that I could cover another portion of the hull. But toward morning it was finally accomplished, though I cannot say that I looked with pride upon the result as anything of an artistic achievement. However, I had succeeded in covering the old paint and thus disguising the craft insofar as color was concerned. This accomplished, I threw my brush and the balance of the paint overboard, following them with the leather harness that I had worn from home.

As I had gotten almost as much paint upon myself as upon the hull of the boat, it took me some little time to erase the last vestige of this evidence that would acquaint a discerning observer with the fact that I had recently repainted my craft.

This done, I applied the red pigment evenly to every square inch of my naked body; so that after I had finished, I could have passed anywhere on Mars as a member of the dominant red race of Martians; and when I had donned the Zodangan harness, metal, and weapons, I felt that my disguise was complete.

It was now mid-forenoon; and, after eating, I lay down to snatch a few hours of sleep.

Entering a Martian city after dark is likely to be fraught with embarrassment for one whose mission may not be readily explained. It was, of course, possible that I might sneak in without lights; but the chances of detection by one of the numerous patrol boats was too great; and as I could not safely have explained my mission or revealed my identity, I should most certainly be sent to the pits and, doubtless, receive the punishment that is meted to spies—long imprisonment in the pits, followed by death in the arena.

Were I to enter with lights, I should most certainly be apprehended; and as I should not be able to answer questions satisfactorily, and as there would be no one to sponsor me, my predicament would be almost equally difficult; so as I approached the city before dawn of the second day, I cut out my motor and drifted idly well out of range of the searchlights of the patrol boats.

Even after daylight had come, I did not approach the city until the middle of the forenoon at a time when other ships were moving freely back and forth across the walls.

By day, and unless a city is actively at war, there are few restrictions placed upon the coming and going of small craft. Occasionally the patrol boats stop and question one of these; and as fines are heavy for operating without licenses, a semblance of regulation is maintained by the government.

In my case, it was not a question of a license to fly a ship but of my right to be in Zodanga at all; so my approach to the city was not without its spice of adventure.

At last the city wall lay almost directly beneath me; and I was congratulating myself upon my good fortune, as there was no patrol boat in sight; but I had congratulated myself too soon, for almost immediately there appeared from behind a lofty tower one of those swift little cruisers that are commonly used in all Martian cities for patrol service, and it was headed directly toward me.

I was moving slowly, so as not to attract unfavorable attention; but I can assure you that my mind was working rapidly. The one-man scout flier that I was using is very fast, and I might easily have turned and outdistanced the patrol boat; however, there were two very important objections to such a plan. One was that, unquestionably, the patrol boat would immediately open fire on me with the chances excellent that they would bring me down. The other was, that should I escape, it would be practically impossible for me to enter the city again in this way, as my boat would be marked; and the entire patrol system would be on the lookout for it.

The cruiser was steadily approaching me, and I was preparing to bluff my way through with a cock-and-bull story of having been long absent from Zodanga and having lost my papers while I was away. The best that I could hope from this was that I should merely be fined for not having my papers, and as I was well supplied with money, such a solution of my difficulties would be a most welcome one.

This, however, was a very slim hope, as it was almost a foregone conclusion that they would insist upon knowing who my sponsor was at the time my lost papers were issued; and without a sponsor I would be in a bad way.

Just as they got within hailing distance, and I was sure that they were about to order me to stop, I heard a loud crash above me; and glancing up, I saw two small ships in collision. I could see the officer in command of the patrol boat plainly now; and as I glanced at him, I saw him looking up. He barked a short command; the nose of the patrol boat was elevated; and it circled rapidly upward, its attention diverted from me by a matter of vastly greater importance. While it was thus engaged, I slipped quietly on into the city of Zodanga.

At the time, many years ago, that Zodanga was looted by the green hordes of Thark, it had been almost completely razed. It was the old city with which I had been most familiar, and I had visited the rebuilt Zodanga upon but one or two occasions since.

Cruising idly about, I finally found that for which I sought—an unpretentious public hangar in a shabby quarter of the city. There are quarters in every city with which I am familiar where one may go without being subjected to curious questioning, so long as one does not run afoul of the officers of the law. This hangar and this quarter of Zodanga looked such a place to me.

The hangar was located on the roof of a very old building that had evidently escaped the ravages of the Tharks. The landing space was small, and the hangars themselves dingy and unkempt.

As my craft settled to the roof, a fat man, well smeared with black grease, appeared from behind a flier upon the engine of which he was evidently working.

He looked at me questioningly, and I thought with none too friendly an expression. "What do you want?" he demanded.

"Is this a public hangar?"

"Yes."

"I want space for my craft."

"Have you got any money?" he demanded.

"I have a little. I will pay a month's rental in advance," I replied.

The frown melted from his face. "That hangar there is vacant," he said, pointing. "Run her in there."

Having housed my flier and locked the controls, I returned to the man and paid him.

"Is there a good public house near by?" I asked, "one that is cheap and not too dirty."

"There is one right in this building," he replied, "as good as any that you will find around here."

This suited me perfectly, as when one is on an adventure of this nature, one never knows how quickly a flier may be required or how soon it may be all that stands between one and death.

Leaving the surly hangar proprietor, I descended the ramp that opened onto the roof.

The elevators ran only to the floor below the roof, and here I found one standing with its door open. The operator was a dissipated looking young fellow in shabby harness.

"Ground floor?" he asked.

"I am looking for lodgings," I replied. "I want to go to the office of the public house in this building."

He nodded, and the elevator started down. The building appeared even older and more dilapidated from the inside than the out, and the upper floors seemed practically untenanted.

"Here you are," he said presently, stopping the elevator and opening the door.

In Martian cities, public houses such as this are merely places to sleep. There are seldom but few, if any, private rooms. Along the side walls of long rooms are low platforms upon which each guest places his sleeping silks and furs in a numbered space allotted to him.

Owing to the prevalence of assassination, these rooms are patrolled night and day by armed guards furnished by the proprietor; and it is largely because of this fact that private rooms are not in demand. In houses that cater to women, these guests are segregated; and there are more private rooms and no guards in their quarters, as the men of Barsoom seldom, if ever, kill a woman, or I may qualify that by saying that they do not employ assassins to kill them, ordinarily.

The public house to which chance had led me catered only to men. There were no women in it.

The proprietor, a burly man whom I later learned was formerly a famous panthan, or soldier of fortune, assigned me a sleeping place and collected his fee for a day's lodging; and after directing me to an eating-place in response to my inquiries, left me.

Scarcely any of the other guests were in the house at this hour of the day. Their personal belongings, their sleeping silks and furs, were in the spaces allotted to them; and even though there had been no guards patrolling the room, they would have been safe, as thievery is practically unknown upon Mars.

I had brought with me some old and very ordinary sleeping silks and furs and these I deposited upon the platform. Sprawled in the adjoining space was a shifty-eyed individual with an evil face. I had noticed that he had been eyeing me surreptitiously ever since I had entered. At last he spoke to me.

"Kaor!" he said, using the familiar form of Martian greeting.

I nodded and replied in kind.

"We are to be neighbors," he ventured.

"So it would seem," I replied.

"You are evidently a stranger, at least in this part of the city," he continued. "I overheard you asking the proprietor where you could find an eating-place. The one he directed you to is not as good as the one that I go to. I am going there now; if you'd like to come along, I'll be glad to take you."

There was a furtiveness about the man that, in connection with his evil face, assured me that he was of the criminal class; and as it was among this class that I expected to work, his suggestion dovetailed nicely with my plans; so I quickly accepted.

"My name is Rapas," he said, "they call me Rapas the Ulsio," he added, not without a touch of pride.

Now I was sure that I had judged him correctly, for Ulsio means rat.

"My name is Vandor," I told him, giving him the alias I had selected for this adventure.

"By your metal, I see that you are a Zodangan," he said, as we walked from the room to the elevators.

"Yes," I replied, "but I have been absent from the city for years. In fact, I have not been here since it was burned by the Tharks. There have been so many changes that it is like coming to a strange city."

"From your looks, I'd take you to be a fighting man by profession," he suggested.

I nodded. "I am a panthan. I have served for many years in another country, but recently I killed a man and had to leave." I knew that if he were a criminal, as I had guessed, this admission of a murder upon my part would make him freer with me.

His shifty eyes glanced quickly at me and then away; and I saw that he was impressed, one way or another, by my admission. On the way to the eating-place, which lay in another avenue a short distance from our public house, we carried on a desultory conversation.

When we had seated ourselves at a table, Rapas ordered drinks; and immediately after he had downed the first one his tongue loosened.

"Are you going to remain in Zodanga?" he asked.

"That depends upon whether or not I can find a living here," I replied. "My money won't last long; and, of course, leaving my last employer under the circumstances that I did, I have no papers; so I may have trouble in finding a place at all."

While we were eating our meal, Rapas continued to drink; and the more he drank the more talkative he became.

"I have taken a liking to you, Vandor," he announced presently; "and if you are the right kind, as I think you are, I can find you employment." Finally he leaned close to me and whispered in my ear. "I am a gorthan," he said.

Here was an incredible piece of good fortune. I had hoped to contact the assassins, and the first man whose acquaintance I had made admitted that he was one.

I shrugged, deprecatively.

"Not much money in that," I said.

"There is plenty, if you are well connected," he assured me.

"But I am not connected well, or otherwise, here in Zodanga," I argued, "I don't belong to the Zodangan guild; and, as I told you, I had to come away without any papers."

He looked around him furtively to see if any were near who might overhear him. "The guild is not necessary," he whispered; "we do not all belong to the guild."

"A good way to commit suicide," I suggested.

"Not for a man with a good head on him. Look at me; I am an assassin, and I don't belong to the guild. I make good money too, and I don't have to divide up with anyone." He took another drink. "There are not many with as good heads on them as Rapas the Ulsio."

He leaned closer to me. "I like you, Vandor," he said; "you are a good fellow." His voice was getting thick from drink. "I have one very rich client; he has lots of work, and he pays well. I can get you an odd job with him now and again. Perhaps I can find steady employment for you. How would you like that?"

I shrugged. "A man must live," I said; "he can't be too particular about his job when he hasn't very much money."

"Well, you come along with me; I am going there tonight. While Fal Sivas talks to you, I will tell him that you are just the man that he needs."

"But how about you?" I inquired. "It is your job; certainly no man needs two assassins."

"Never mind about me," said Rapas; "I have other ideas in my head." He stopped suddenly and gave me a quick, suspicious look. It was almost as though what he had said had sobered him. He shook his head, evidently in an effort to clear it. "What did I say?" he demanded. "I must be getting drunk."

"You said that you had other plans. I suppose you mean that you have a better job in view."

"Is that all I said?" he demanded.

"You said that you would take me to a man called Fal Sivas who would give me employment."

Rapas seemed relieved. "Yes, I will take you to see him tonight."

chapter II

FAL SIVAS

FOR THE BALANCE of the day Rapas slept, while I occupied my time puttering around my flier in the public hangar on the roof of the hostelry. This was a far more secluded spot than the public sleeping room or the streets of the city, where some accident might pierce my disguise and reveal my identity.

As I worked over my motor, I recalled Rapas's sudden fear that he had revealed something to me in his drunken conversation; and I wondered idly what it might be. It had come following his statement that he had other plans. What plans? Whatever they were, they were evidently nefarious, or he would not have been so concerned when he feared that he had revealed them.

My short acquaintance with Rapas had convinced me that my first appraisal of his character was correct and that his sobriquet of Rapas the Rat was well deserved.

I chafed under the enforced inactivity of the long day; but at last evening came, and Rapas the Ulsio and I left our quarters and made our way once more to the eating-place.

Rapas was sober now, nor did he take but a single drink with his meal. "You've got to have a clear head when you talk to old Fal Sivas," he said. "By my first ancestor, no shrewder brain was ever hatched of a woman's egg."

After we had eaten, we went out into the night; and Rapas led me through broad avenues and down narrow alleyways until we came to a large building that stood near the eastern wall of Zodanga.

It was a dark and gloomy pile, and the avenue that ran before it was unlighted. It stood in a district given over to warehouses, and at this time of night its surroundings were deserted.

Rapas approached a small doorway hidden in an angle of a buttress. I saw him groping with his hands at one side of the door, and presently he stepped back and waited.

"Not everyone can gain admission to old Fal Sivas's place," he remarked, with a tinge of boastfulness. "You have to know the right signal, and that means that you have to be pretty well in the confidence of the old man."

We waited in silence then for perhaps two or three minutes. No sound came from beyond the door; but presently a very small, round port in its surface opened; and in the dim light of the farther moon I saw an eye appraising us. Then a voice spoke.

"Ah, the noble Rapas!" The words were whispered; and following them, the door swung in.

The passage beyond was narrow, and the man who had opened the door flattened himself against the wall that we might pass. Then he closed the door behind us and followed us along a dark corridor, until we finally emerged into a small, dimly lighted room.

Here our guide halted. "The master did not say that you were bringing another with you," he said to Rapas.

"He did not know it," replied Rapas. "In fact, I did not know it myself until today; but it is all right. Your master will be glad to receive him when I have explained why I brought him."

"That is a matter that Fal Sivas will have to decide for himself," replied the slave. "Perhaps you had better go first and speak to him, leaving the stranger here with me."

"Very well, then," agreed my companion. "Remain here until I return, Vandor."

The slave unlocked the door in the far side of the ante-room; and after Rapas had passed through, he followed him and closed it.

It occurred to me that his action was a little strange, as I had just heard him say that he would remain with me, but I would have thought nothing more of the matter had I not presently become impressed with the very definite sensation that I was being watched.

I cannot explain this feeling that I occasionally have. Earth men who should know say that this form of telepathy is scientifically impossible, yet upon many occasions I have definitely sensed this secret surveillance, later to discover that I really was being watched.

As my eyes wandered casually about the room, they came to rest again upon the door beyond which Rapas and the slave had disappeared. They were held momentarily by a small round hole in the paneling and the glint of something that might have been an eye shining in the darkness. I knew that it was an eye.

Just why I should be watched, I did not know; but if my observer hoped to discover anything suspicious about me, he was disappointed; for as soon as I realized that an eye was upon me, I walked to a bench at one side of the room and sat down, instantly determined not to reveal the slightest curiosity concerning my surroundings.

Such surveillance probably meant little in itself, but taken in connection with the gloomy and forbidding appearance of the building and the great stealth and secrecy with which we had been admitted, it crystallized a most unpleasant impression of the place and its master that had already started to form in my mind.

From beyond the walls of the room there came no sound, nor did any of the night noises of the city penetrate to the little ante-room. Thus I sat in utter silence for about ten minutes; then the door opened, and the same slave beckoned to me.

"Follow me," he said. "The master will see you. I am to take you to him."

I followed him along a gloomy corridor and up a winding ramp to the next higher level of the building. A moment later he ushered me into a softly lighted room furnished with Sybaritic luxury, where I saw Rapas standing before a couch on which a man reclined, or I should say, crouched. Somehow he reminded me of a great cat watching its prey, always ready to spring.

"This is Vandor, Fal Sivas," said Rapas, by way of introduction.

I inclined my head in acknowledgment and stood before the man, waiting.

"Rapas has told me about you," said Fal Sivas. "Where are you from?"

"Originally I was from Zodanga," I replied, "but that was years ago before the sacking of the city."

"And where have you been since?" he asked. "Whom have you served?"

"That," I replied, "is a matter of no consequence to anyone but myself. It is sufficient that I have not been in Zodanga, and that I cannot return to the country that I have just fled."

"You have no friends or acquaintances in Zodanga, then?" he asked.

"Of course, some of my acquaintances may still be living; that I do not know," I replied, "but my people and most of my friends were killed at the time that the green hordes overran the city."

"And you have had no intercourse with Zodanga since you left?" he asked.

"None whatsoever."

"Perhaps you are just the man I need. Rapas is sure of it, but I am never sure. No man can be trusted."

"Ah, but master," interrupted Rapas, "have I not always served you well and faithfully?"

I thought I saw a slight sneer curl the lip of Fal Sivas.

"You are a paragon, Rapas," he said, "the soul of honor."

Rapas swelled with importance. He was too egotistical to note the flavor of sarcasm in Fal Sivas's voice.

"And I may consider myself employed?" I asked.

"You understand that you may be called upon to use a dagger more often than a sword," he asked, "and that poisons are sometimes preferred to pistols?"

"I understand."

He looked at me intently.

"There may come a time," he continued, "when you may have to draw your long-sword or your short-sword in my defense. Are you a capable swordsman?"

"I am a panthan," I replied; "and as panthans live by the sword, the very fact that I am here answers your question."

"Not entirely. I must have a master swordsman. Rapas, here, is handy with the short-sword. Let us see what you can do against him."

"To the death?" I asked.

Rapas guffawed loudly. "I did not bring you here to kill you," he said.

"No, not to the death, of course," said Fal Sivas. "Just a short passage. Let us see which one can scratch the other first."

I did not like the idea. I do not ordinarily draw my sword unless I intend to kill, but I realized that I was playing a part and that before I got through I might have to do many things of which I did not approve; so I nodded my assent and waited for Rapas to draw.

His short-sword flashed from its scabbard. "I shall not hurt you badly, Vandor," he said; "for I am very fond of you."

I thanked him and drew my own weapon.

Rapas stepped forward to engage me, a confident smile upon his lips. The next instant his weapon was flying across the room. I had disarmed him, and he was at my mercy. He backed away, a sickly grin upon his face. Fal Sivas laughed.

"It was an accident," said Rapas. "I was not ready."

"I am sorry," I told him; "go and recover your weapon."

He got it and came back, and this time he lunged at me viciously. There would have been no mere scratch that time if his thrust had succeeded. He would have spitted me straight through the heart. I parried and stepped in, and again his sword hurtled through the air and clanked against the opposite wall.

Fal Sivas laughed uproariously. Rapas was furious. "That is enough," said the former. "I am satisfied. Sheath your swords."

I knew that I had made an enemy of Rapas; but that did not concern me greatly, since being forewarned I could always be watchful of him. Anyway, I had never trusted him.

"You are prepared to enter my service at once?" asked Fal Sivas.

"I am in your service now," I replied.

He smiled. "I think you are going to make me a good man. Rapas wants to go away for a while to attend to business of his own. While he is away, you will remain here as my bodyguard. When he returns, I may still find use for you in one way or another. The fact that you are unknown in Zodanga may make you very valuable to me." He turned to Rapas. "You may go now, Rapas," he said, "and while you are away, you might take some lessons in swordsmanship."

When Fal Sivas said that, he grinned; but Rapas did not. He looked very sour, and he did not say good-by to me as he left the room.

"I am afraid that you offended his dignity," said Fal Sivas after the door had closed behind the assassin.

"I shall lose no sleep over it," I replied, "and anyway it was not my fault. It was his."

"What do you mean?" demanded Fal Sivas.

"Rapas is not a good swordsman."

"He is considered an excellent one," Fal Sivas assured me.

"I imagine that as a killer he is more adept with the dagger and poison."

"And how about you?" he asked.

"Naturally, as a fighting man, I prefer the sword," I replied.

Fal Sivas shrugged. "That is a matter of small concern to me," he said. "If you prefer to kill my enemies with a sword, use a sword. All I ask is that you kill them."

"You have many enemies?" I asked.

"There are many who would like to see me put out of the way," he replied. "I am an inventor, and there are those who would steal my inventions. Many of these I have had to destroy. Their people suspect me and seek revenge; but there is one who, above all others, seeks to destroy me. He also is an inventor, and he has employed an agent of the assassins' guild to make away with me.

"This guild is headed by Ur Jan, and he personally has threatened my life because I have employed another than a member of his guild to do my killing."

We talked for a short time, and then Fal Sivas summoned a slave to show me to my quarters. "They are below mine," he said; "if I call, you are to come to me immediately. Good night."

The slave led me to another room on the same level. In fact, to a little suite of three rooms. They were plainly but comfortably furnished.

"Is there anything that you require, master?" the slave inquired, as he turned to leave me.

"Nothing," I replied.

"Tomorrow a slave will be assigned to serve you." With that he left me, and I listened to see if he locked the door from the outside; but he did not, though I would not have been surprised had he done so, so sinister and secretive seemed everything connected with this gloomy pile.

I occupied myself for a few moments inspecting my quarters. They consisted of a living room, two small bedrooms, and a bath. A single door opened from the living room onto the corridor. There were no windows in any of the rooms. There were small ventilators in the floors and in the ceilings, and draughts of air entering the former indicated that the apartment was ventilated mechanically. The rooms were lighted by radium bulbs similar to those generally used throughout Barsoom.

In the living room was a table, a bench, and several chairs, and a shelf upon which were a number of books. Glancing at some of these, I discovered that they were all scientific works. There were books on medicine, on surgery, chemistry, mechanics, and electricity.

From time to time, I heard what appeared to be stealthy noises in the corridor; but I did not investigate, as I wanted to establish myself in the confidence of Fal Sivas and his people before I ventured to take it upon myself to learn any more than they desired me to know. I did not even know that I wanted to know anything more about the household of Fal Sivas; for, after all, my business in Zodanga had nothing to do with him. I had come to undermine and, if possible, overthrow the strength of Ur Jan and his guild of assassins; and all I needed was a base from which to work. I was, in fact, a little disappointed to find that Fate had thrown me in with those opposed to Ur Jan. I would have preferred and, in fact, had hoped to be able to join Ur Jan's organization, as I felt that I could accomplish much more from the inside than from the out.

If I could join the guild, I could soon learn the identity of its principal members; and that, above all other things, was what I wished to do, that I might either bring them to justice or put the cross upon their hearts with the point of my own sword.

Occupied with these thoughts, I was about to remove my harness and turn into my sleeping silks and furs when I heard sounds of what might have been a scuffle on the level above and then a thud, as of a body falling.

The former preternatural silence of the great house accentuated the significance of the sounds that I was hearing, imparting to them a mystery that I realized might be wholly out of proportion to their true importance. I smiled as I realized the effect that my surroundings seemed to be having upon my ordinarily steady nerves; and had resumed my preparations for the night when a shrill scream rang through the building.

I paused again and listened, and now I distinctly heard the sound of feet running rapidly. They seemed to be approaching, and I guessed that they were coming down the ramp from the level above to the corridor that ran before my quarters.

Perhaps what went on in the house of Fal Sivas was none of my affair, but I have never yet heard a woman scream without investigating; so now I stepped to the door of my living room and threw it open, and as I did so I saw a girl running rapidly toward me. Her hair was disheveled; and from her wide, frightened eyes she cast frequent glances backward over her shoulder.

She was almost upon me before she discovered me; and when she did she paused for a moment with a gasp of astonishment or fear, I could not tell which; then she darted past me through the open door into my living room.

"Close the door," she whispered, her voice tense with suppressed emotion. "Don't let him get me! Don't let him find me!"

No one seemed to be pursuing her, but I closed the door as she had requested and turned toward her for an explanation.

"What is the matter?" I demanded. "From whom were you running?"

"From him." She shuddered. "Oh, he is horrible. Hide me; don't let him get me, please!"

"Whom do you mean? Who is horrible?"

She stood there trembling and wide-eyed, staring past me at the door, like one whom terror had demented.

"Him," she whispered. "Who else could it be?"

"You mean—?"

She came close and started to speak; then she hesitated. "But why should I trust you? You are one of his creatures. You are all alike in this terrible place."

She was standing very close to me now, trembling like a leaf. "I cannot stand it!" she cried. "I will not let him!" And then, so quickly that I could not prevent her, she snatched the dagger from my harness and turned it upon herself.

But there I was too quick for her, seizing her wrist before she could carry out her designs.

She was a delicate-looking creature, but her appearance belied her strength. However, I had little difficulty in disarming her; and then I backed her toward the bench and forced her down upon it.

"Calm yourself," I said; "you have nothing to fear from me— nothing to fear from anybody while I am with you. Tell me what has happened. Tell me whom you fear."

She sat there staring into my eyes for a long moment, and presently she commenced to regain control of herself. "Yes," she said presently, "perhaps I can trust you. You make me feel that way—your voice, your looks."

I laid my hand upon her shoulder as one might who would quiet a frightened child. "Do not be afraid," I said; "tell me something of yourself. What is your name?"

"Zanda," she replied.

"You live here?"

"I am a slave, a prisoner."

"What made you scream?" I asked.

"I did not scream," she replied; "that was another. He tried to get me, but I eluded him, and so he took another. My turn will come. He will get me. He gets us all."

"Who? Who will get you?"

She shuddered as she spoke the name. "Fal Sivas," she said, and there was horror in her tone.

I sat down on the bench beside her and laid my hand on hers. "Quiet yourself," I said; "tell me what all this means. I am a stranger here. I just entered the service of Fal Sivas tonight."

"You know nothing, then, about Fal Sivas?" she demanded.

"Only that he is a wealthy inventor and fears for his life."

"Yes, he is rich; and he is an inventor, but not so great an inventor as he is a murderer and a thief. He steals ideas from other inventors and then has them murdered in order to safeguard what he has stolen. Those who learn too much of his inventions die. They never leave this house. He always has an assassin ready to do his bidding; sometimes here, sometimes out in the city; and he is always afraid of his life.

"Rapas the Ulsio is his assassin now; but they are both afraid of Ur Jan, chief of the guild of assassins; for Ur Jan has learned that Rapas is killing for Fal Sivas for a price far lower than that charged by the guild."

"But what are these wonderful inventions that Fal Sivas works upon?" I asked.

"I do not know all of the things that he does, but there is the ship. That would be wonderful, were it not born of blood and treachery."

"What sort of a ship?" I asked.

"A ship that will travel safely through interplanetary space. He says that in a short time we shall be able to travel back and forth between the planets as easily as we travel now from one city to another."

"Interesting," I said, "and not so very horrible, that I can see."

"But he does other things—horrible things. One of them is a mechanical brain."

"A mechanical brain?"

"Yes, but of course I cannot explain it. I have so little learning. I have heard him speak of it often, but I do not understand.

"He says that all life, all matter, are the result of mechanical action, not primarily, chemical action. He holds that all chemical action is mechanical.

"Oh, I am probably not explaining it right. It is all so confusing to me, because I do not understand it; but anyway he is working on a mechanical brain, a brain that will think clearly and logically, absolutely uninfluenced by any of the extraneous media that affect human judgments."

"It seems rather a weird idea," I said, "but I can see nothing so horrible about it."

"It is not the idea that is horrible," she said; "it is the method that he employs to perfect his invention. In his effort to duplicate the human brain, he must examine it. For this reason he needs many slaves. A few he buys, but most of them are kidnaped for him."

She commenced to tremble, and her voice came in little broken gasps. "I do not know; I have not really seen it; but they say that he straps his victims so that they cannot move and then removes the skull until he has exposed the brain; and so, by means of rays that penetrate the tissue, he watches the brain function."

"But his victims cannot suffer long," I said; "they would lose consciousness and die quickly."

She shook her head. "No, he has perfected drugs that he injects into their veins so that they remain alive and are conscious for a long time. For long hours he applies various stimuli and watches the reaction of the brain. Imagine if you can, the suffering of his poor victims.

"Many slaves are brought here, but they do not remain long. There are only two doors leading from the building, and there are no windows in the outer walls. The slaves that disappear do not leave through either of the two doorways. I see them today; tomorrow they are gone, gone through the little doorway that leads into the room of horror next to Fal Sivas's sleeping quarters.

"Tonight Fal Sivas sent for two of us, another girl and myself. He purposed using only one of us. He always examines a couple and then selects the one that he thinks is the best specimen, but his selection is not determined wholly by scientific requirements. He always selects the more attractive of the girls that are summoned.

"He examined us, and then finally he selected me. I was terrified. I tried to fight him off. He chased me about the room, and then he slipped and fell; and before he could regain his feet, I opened the door and escaped. Then I heard the other girl scream, and I knew that he had seized her, but I have won only a reprieve. He will get me; there is no escape. Neither you nor I will ever leave this place alive."

"What makes you think that?" I inquired.

"No one ever does."

"How about Rapas?" I asked. "He comes and goes apparently as he wishes."

"Yes, Rapas comes and goes. He is Fal Sivas's assassin. He also aids in the kidnaping of new victims. Under the circumstances he would have to be free to leave the building. Then there are a few others, old and trusted retainers, really partners in crime, whose lives Fal Sivas holds in the palm of his hand; but you may rest assured that none of these know too much about his inventions. The moment that one is taken into Fal Sivas's confidence, his days are numbered.

"The man seems to have a mania for talking about his inventions. He must explain them to someone. I think that is because of his great egotism. He loves to boast. That is the reason he tells us who are doomed so much about his work. You may rest assured that Rapas knows nothing of importance. In fact, I have heard Fal Sivas say that one thing that endeared Rapas to him is the assassin's utter stupidity. Fal Sivas says that if he explained every detail of an invention to him, Rapas wouldn't have brains enough to understand it."

By this time the girl had regained control of herself; and as she ceased speaking, she started toward the doorway. "Thank you so much," she said, "for letting me come in here. I shall probably never see you again, but I should like to know who it is who has befriended me."

"My name is Vandor," I replied, "but what makes you think you will never see me again, and where are you going now?"

"I am going back to my quarters to wait for the next summons. It may come tomorrow."

"You are going to stay right here," I replied; "we may find a way of getting you out of this, yet."

She looked at me in surprise and was about to reply when suddenly she cocked her head on one side and listened. "Someone is coming," she said; "they are searching for me."

I took her by the hand and drew her toward the doorway to my sleeping apartment. "Come in here," I said. "Let's see if we can't hide you."

"No, no," she demurred; "they would kill us both then, if they found me. You have been kind to me. I do not want them to kill you."

"Don't worry about me," I replied; "I can take care of myself. Do as I tell you."

I took her into my room and made her lie down on the little platform that serves in Barsoom as a bed. Then I threw the sleeping silks and furs over her in a jumbled heap. Only by close examination could anyone have discovered that her little form lay hidden beneath them.

Stepping into the living room, I took a book at random from the shelf; and seating myself in a chair, opened it. I had scarcely done so, when I heard a scratching on the outside of the door leading to the corridor.

"Come in," I called.

The door opened, and Fal Sivas stepped into the room.

Lowering my book, I looked up as Fal Sivas entered. He glanced quickly and suspiciously about the apartment. I had purposely left the door to my sleeping room open, so as not to arouse suspicion should anyone come in to investigate. The doors to the other sleeping room and bath were also open. Fal Sivas glanced at the book in my hand. "Rather heavy reading for a panthan," he remarked.

I smiled. "I recently read his Theoretical Mechanics. This is an earlier work, I believe, and not quite so authoritative. I was merely glancing through it."

Fal Sivas studied me intently for a moment. "Are you not a little too well educated for your calling?" he asked.

"One may never know too much," I replied.

"One may know too much here," he said, and I recalled what the girl had told me.

His tone changed. "I stopped in to see if everything was all right with you, if you were comfortable."

"Very," I replied.

"You have not been disturbed? No one has been here?"

"The house seems very quiet," I replied. "I heard someone laughing a short time ago, but that was all. It did not disturb me."

"Has anyone come to your quarters?" he asked.

"Why, was someone supposed to come?"

"No one, of course," he said shortly, and then he commenced to question me in an evident effort to ascertain the extent of my mechanical and chemical knowledge.

"I really know little of either subject," I told him. "I am a fighting man by profession, not a scientist. Of course, familiarity with fliers connotes some mechanical knowledge, but after all I am only a tyro."

He was studying me quizzically. "I wish that I knew you better," he said at last; "I wish that I knew that I could trust you. You are an intelligent man. In the matter of brains, I am entirely alone here. I need an assistant. I need such a man as you." He shook his head, rather disgustedly. "But what is the use? I can trust no one."

"You employed me as your bodyguard. For that work I am fitted. Let it go at that."

"You are right," he agreed. "Time will tell what else you are fitted for."

"And if I am to protect you," I continued, "I must know more about your enemies. I must know who they are, and I must learn their plans."

"There are many who would like to see me destroyed, or destroy me themselves; but there is one who, above all others, would profit by my death. He is Gar Nal, the inventor." He looked up at me questioningly.

"I have never heard of him," I said. "You must remember that I have been absent from Zodanga for many years."

He nodded. "I am perfecting a ship that will traverse space. So is Gar Nal. He would like not only to have me destroyed, but also to steal the secrets of my invention that would permit him to perfect his; but Ur Jan is the one I most fear, because Gar Nal has employed him to destroy me."

"I am unknown in Zodanga. I will hunt out this Ur Jan and see what I can learn."

There was one thing that I wanted to learn right then, and that was whether or not Fal Sivas would permit me to leave his house on any pretext.

"You could learn nothing," he said; "their meetings are secret.

Even if you could gain admission, which is doubtful, you would be killed before you could get out again."

"Perhaps not," I said; "it is worth trying, anyway. Do you know where they hold their meetings?"

"Yes, but if you want to try that, I will have Rapas guide you to the building."

"If I am to go, I do not want Rapas to know anything about it," I said.

"Why?" he demanded.

"Because I do not trust him," I replied. "I would not trust anyone with knowledge of my plans."

"You are quite right. When you are ready to go, I can give you directions so that you can find their meeting place."

"I will go tomorrow," I said, "after dark."

He nodded his approval. He was standing where he could look directly into the bedroom where the girl was hidden. "Have you plenty of sleeping silks and furs?" he asked.

"Plenty," I replied, "but I will bring my own tomorrow."

"That will not be necessary. I will furnish you all that you require." He still stood staring into that other room. I wondered if he suspected the truth, or if the girl had moved or her breathing were noticeable under the pile of materials beneath which she was hidden.

I did not dare to turn and look for myself for fear of arousing his suspicions further. I just sat there waiting, my hands close to the hilt of my short-sword. Perhaps the girl was near discovery; but, if so, Fal Sivas was also near death that moment.

At last he turned toward the outer doorway. "I will give you directions tomorrow for reaching the headquarters of the gorthans, and also tomorrow I will send you a slave. Do you wish a man or a woman?"

I preferred a man, but I thought that I detected here a possible opportunity for protecting the girl. "A woman," I said.

He smiled. "And a pretty one, eh?"

"I should like to select her myself, if I may."

"As you wish," he replied. "I shall let you look them over tomorrow. May you sleep well."

He left the room and closed the door behind him; but I knew that he stood outside for a long time, listening.

I picked I up the book once more and commenced to read it; but not a word registered on my consciousness, for all my faculties were centered on listening.

After what seemed a long time, I heard him move away; and shortly after I distinctly heard a door close on the level above me. Not until then did I move, but now I arose and went to the door. It was equipped with a heavy bar on the inside, and this I slid silently into its keeper.

Crossing the room, I entered the chamber where the girl lay and threw back the covers that concealed her. She had not moved. As she looked up at me, I placed a finger across my lips.

"You heard?" I asked in a low whisper.

She nodded.

"Tomorrow I will select you as my slave. Perhaps later I shall find a way to liberate you."

"You are kind," she said.

I reached down and took her by the hand. "Come," I said, "into the other room. You can sleep there safely tonight, and in the morning we will plan how we may carry out the rest of our scheme."

"I think that will not be difficult," she said. "Early in the morning everyone but Fal Sivas goes to a large dining room on this level. Many of them will pass along this corridor. I can slip out, unseen, and join them. At breakfast you will have an opportunity of seeing all the slaves. Then you may select me if you still wish to do so."

There were sleeping silks and furs in the room that I had assigned to her, and I knew that she would be comfortable; so I left her, and returning to my own room completed my preparations for the night that had been so strangely interrupted.

Early the next morning Zanda awoke me. "It will soon be time for them to go to breakfast," she said. "You must go before I do, leaving the door open. Then when there is no one in the corridor, I will slip out."

As I left my quarters, I saw two or three people moving along the corridor in the direction that Zanda had told me the dining room lay; and so I followed them, finally entering a large room in which there was a table that would seat about twenty. It was already over half filled. Most of the slaves were women—young women, and many of them were beautiful.

With the exception of two men, one sitting at either end of the table, all the occupants of the room were without weapons.

The man sitting at the head of the table was the same who had admitted Rapas and me the evening before. I learned later that his name was Hamas, and that he was the major-domo of the establishment.

The other armed man was Phystal. He was in charge of the slaves in the establishment. He also, as I was to learn later, attended to the procuring of many of them, usually by bribery or abduction.

As I entered the room, Hamas discovered me and motioned me to come to him. "You will sit here, next to me, Vandor," he said.

I could not but note the difference in his manner from the night before, when he had seemed more or less an obsequious slave. I gathered that he played two rôles for purposes known best to himself or his master. In his present rôle, he was obviously a person of importance.

"You slept well?" he asked.

"Quite," I replied; "the house seems very quiet and peaceful at night."

He grunted. "If you should hear any unusual sounds at night," he said, "you will not investigate, unless the master or I call you." And then, as though he felt that that needed some explanation, he added, "Fal Sivas sometimes works upon his experiments late at night. You must not disturb him no matter what you may hear."

Some more slaves were entering the room now, and just behind them came Zanda. I glanced at Hamas and saw his eyes narrow as they alighted upon her.

"Here she is now, Phystal," he said.

The man at the far end of the table turned in his seat and looked at the girl approaching from behind him. He was scowling angrily.

"Where were you last night, Zanda?" he demanded, as the girl approached the table.

"I was frightened, and I hid," she replied.

"Where did you hide?" demanded Phystal.

"Ask Hamas," she replied.

Phystal glanced at Hamas. "How should I know where you were?" demanded the latter.

Zanda elevated her arched brows. "Oh, I am sorry," she exclaimed; "I did not know that you cared who knew."

Hamas scowled angrily. "What do you mean by that?" he demanded; "what are you driving at?"

"Oh," she said, "I wouldn't have said anything about it at all but I thought, of course, that Fal Sivas knew."

Phystal was eyeing Hamas suspiciously. All the slaves were looking at him, and you could almost read their thoughts in the expressions on their faces.

Hamas was furious, Phystal suspicious; and all the time the girl stood there with the most innocent and angelic expression on her face.

"What do you mean by saying such a thing?" shouted Hamas.

"What did I say?" she asked, innocently.

"You said—you said—"

"I just said, 'ask Hamas.' Is there anything wrong in that?"

"But what do I know about it?" demanded the major-domo.

Zanda shrugged her slim shoulders. "I am afraid to say anything more. I do not want to get you in trouble."

"Perhaps the less said about it, the better," said Phystal.

Hamas started to speak, but evidently thought better of it. He glowered at Zanda for a moment and then fell to eating his breakfast.

Just before the meal was over, I told Hamas that Fal Sivas had instructed me to select a slave.

"Yes, he told me," replied the major-domo. "See Phystal about it; he is in charge of the slaves."

"But does he know that Fal Sivas gave me permission to select anyone that I chose?"

"I will tell him."

A moment later he finished his breakfast; and as he was leaving the dining room, he paused and spoke to Phystal.

Seeing that Phystal also was about ready to leave the table, I went to him and told him that I would like to select a slave.

"Which one do you want?" he asked.

I glanced around the table, apparently examining each of the slaves carefully until at last my eyes rested upon Zanda.

"I will take this one," I said.

Phystal's brows contracted, and he hesitated.

"Fal Sivas said that I might select whomever I wished," I reminded him.

"But why do you want this one?" he demanded.

"She seems intelligent, and she is good-looking," I replied. "She will do as well as another until I am better acquainted here." And so it was that Zanda was appointed to serve me. Her duties would consist of keeping my apartments clean, running errands for me, cleaning my harness, shining my metal, sharpening my swords and daggers, and otherwise making herself useful.

I would much rather have had a man slave, but events had so ordered themselves that I had been forced into the rôle of the girl's protector, and this seemed the only plan by which I could accomplish anything along that line; but whether or not Fal Sivas would permit me to keep her, I did not know. That was a contingency which remained for future solution when, and if, it eventuated.

I took Zanda back to my quarters; and while she was busying herself with her duties there, I received a call summoning me to Fal Sivas.

A slave led me to the same room in which Fal Sivas had received Rapas and me the night before, and as I entered the old inventor greeted me with a nod. I expected him to immediately question me concerning Zanda, for both Hamas and Phystal were with him; and I had no doubt but that they had reported all that had occurred at the breakfast table.

However, I was agreeably disappointed, for he did not mention the incident at all, but merely gave me instructions as to my duties.

I was to remain on duty in the corridor outside his door and accompany him when he left the room. I was to permit no one to enter the room, other than Hamas or Phystal, without obtaining permission from Fal Sivas. When he left the room, I was to accompany him. Under no circumstances was I ever to go to the level above, except with his permission or by his express command. He was very insistent in impressing this point upon my mind; and though I am not overly curious, I must admit that now that I had been forbidden to go to any of the levels above, I wanted to do so.

"When you have been in my service longer and I know you better," explained Fal Sivas, "I hope to be able to trust you; but for the present you are on probation."

That was the longest day I have ever spent, just standing around outside that door, doing nothing; but at last it drew to a close, and when I had the opportunity, I reminded Fal Sivas that he had promised to direct me to Ur Jan's headquarters, so that I might try to gain entrance to them that night.

He gave me very accurate directions to a building in another quarter of the city.

"You are free to start whenever you wish," he said, in conclusion; "I have given Hamas instructions that you may come and go as you please. He will furnish you with a pass signal whereby you may gain admission to the house. I wish you luck," he said, "but I think that the best you will get will be a sword through your heart. You are pitting yourself against the fiercest and most unscrupulous gang of men in Zodanga."

"It is a chance that I shall have to take," I said. "Good night."

I went to my quarters and told Zanda to lock herself in after I had left and to open the door only in answer to a certain signal which I imparted to her. She was only too glad to obey my injunction.

When I was ready to leave the building, Hamas conducted me to the outer doorway. Here he showed me a hidden button set in the masonry and explained to me how I might use it to announce my return.

I had gone but a short distance from the house of Fal Sivas when I met Rapas the Ulsio. He seemed to have forgotten his anger toward me, or else he was dissimulating, for he greeted me cordially.

"Where to?" he asked.

"Off for the evening," I replied.

"Where are you going, and what are you going to do?"

"I am going to the public house to get my things together and store them, and then I shall look around for a little entertainment."

"Suppose we get together later in the evening," he suggested.

"All right," I replied; "when and where?"

"I will be through with my business about half after the eighth zode. Suppose we meet at the eating-place I took you to yesterday."

"All right," I said, "but do not wait long for me. I may get tired of looking for pleasure and return to my quarters long before that."

After leaving Rapas, I went to the public house where I had left my things; and gathering them up I took them to the hangar on the roof and stored them in my flier. This done, I returned to the street and made my way toward the address that Fal Sivas had given me.

The way led me through a brilliantly lighted shopping district and into a gloomy section of the old town. It was a residential district, but of the meaner sort. Some of the houses still rested upon the ground, but most of them were elevated on their steel shafts twenty or thirty feet above the pavement.

I heard laughter and song and occasional brawling—the sounds of the night life of a great Martian city, and then I passed on into another and seemingly deserted quarter.

I was approaching the headquarters of the assassins. I kept in the shadows of the buildings, and I avoided the few people that were upon the avenue by slipping into doorways and alleys. I did not wish anyone to see me here who might be able afterward to recognize or identify me. I was playing a game with Death, and I must give him no advantage.

When finally I reached the building for which I was seeking, I found a doorway on the opposite side of the avenue from which I could observe my goal without being seen.

The farther moon cast a faint light upon the face of the building but revealed to me nothing of importance.

At first, I could discern no lights in the building; but after closer observation I saw a dim reflection behind the windows of the upper floor. There, doubtless, was the meeting-place of the assassins; but how was I to reach it?

That the doors to the building would be securely locked and every approach to the meeting-place well guarded, seemed a foregone conclusion.

There were balconies before the windows at several levels, and I noticed particularly that there were three of these in front of windows on the upper story. These balconies offered me a means of ingress to the upper floor if I could but reach them.

The great strength and agility which the lesser gravitation of Mars imparts to my earthly muscles might have sufficed to permit me to climb the exterior of the building, except for the fact that this particular building seemed to offer no foothold up to the fifth story, above which its carved ornamentation commenced.

Mentally debating every possibility, by a process of elimination, I was forced to the conclusion that my best approach would be by way of the roof.

However, I determined to investigate the possibilities of the main entrance on the ground floor; and was about to cross the avenue for that purpose when I saw two men approaching. Stepping back into the shadows of my hiding-place, I waited for them to pass; but instead of doing so they stopped before the entrance to the building I was watching. They were there but a moment when I saw the door open and the men admitted. This incident convinced me that someone was on guard at the main entrance to the building, and that it would be futile for me to attempt to enter there.

There now remained to me only the roof as a means of entrance to the building, and I quickly decided upon a plan to accomplish my design.

Leaving my hiding-place, I quickly retraced my steps to the public house in which I had been lodging, and went immediately to the hangar on the roof.

The place was deserted, and I was soon at the controls of my flier. I had now to run the chance of being stopped by a patrol boat, but this was a more or less remote contingency; as, except in cases of public emergency, little attention is paid to private fliers within the walls of the city.

However, to be on the safe side, I flew low, following dark avenues below the level of the roof tops; and in a short time I reached the vicinity of the building that was my goal.

Here I rose above the level of the roofs and, having located the building, settled gently to its roof.

The building had not been intended for this purpose, and there was neither hangar nor mooring rings; but there are seldom high winds on Mars, and this was a particularly quiet and windless night.

Leaving the deck of the flier, I searched the roof for some means of ingress to the building. I found a single small scuttle, but it was strongly secured from within, and I could not budge it—at least without making far too much noise.

Going to the edge of the building, overlooking the avenue, I looked down upon one of the balconies directly below me. I could have lowered myself from the eaves and, hanging by my hands, dropped directly onto it; but here again I faced the danger of attracting attention by the noise that I must make in alighting.

I examined the face of the building just below me and discovered that, in common with most Martian buildings, the carved ornamentation offered handholds and footholds sufficient to my need.

Slipping quietly over the eaves, I felt around with my toes until I found a projection that would support me. Then, releasing one hand, I felt for a new hold; and so, very slowly and carefully, I descended to the balcony.

I had selected the place of my descent so that I was opposite an unlighted window. For a moment I stood there listening. Somewhere within the interior of the building I heard subdued voices. Then I threw a leg over the sill and entered the darkness of the apartment beyond.

Slowly I groped my way to a wall and then followed along it until I came to a door at the end of the room opposite the window. Stealthily I felt for the latch and lifted it. I pulled gently; the door was not locked; it swung in toward me without noise.

Beyond the door was a corridor. It was very faintly illuminated, as though by reflected light from an open doorway or from another corridor. Now the sound of voices was more distinct. Silently I crept in the direction from which they came.

Presently I came to another corridor running at right angles to the one I was following. The light was stronger here, and I saw that it came from an open doorway farther along the corridor which I was about to enter. I was sure, however, that the voices did not come from this room that I could see, as they would have been far more clear and distinct had they.

My position was a precarious one. I knew nothing at all about the interior arrangements of the building. I did not know along which corridor its inmates came and went. If I were to approach the open doorway, I might place myself in a position where discovery would be certain.

I knew that I was dealing with killers, expert swordsmen all; and I did not try to deceive myself into believing that I would be any match for a dozen or more of them.

However, men who live by the sword are not unaccustomed to taking chances, sometimes far more desperate chances than their mission may seem to warrant.

Perhaps such was the case now, but I had come to Zodanga to learn what I could about the guild of assassins headed by the notorious Ur Jan; and now that fortune had placed me in a position where I might gain a great deal of useful information, I had no thought of retreating because a little danger confronted me.

Stealthily I crept forward, and at last I reached the door. Very cautiously I surveyed the interior of the room beyond, as I moved, inch by inch, across the doorway.

It was a small room, evidently an ante-room; and it was untenanted. There was some furniture in it—a table, some benches; and I noticed particularly an old-fashioned cupboard that stood diagonally across one corner of the room, one of its sides about a foot from the wall.

From where I stood in the doorway, I could now hear the voices quite distinctly; and I was confident that the men I sought were in the adjoining room just beyond.

I crept into the ante-room and approached the door at the opposite end. Just to the left of the door was the cupboard that I have mentioned.

I placed my ear close to the panels of the door in an effort to overhear what was being said in the room beyond, but the words came to me indistinct and muffled. This would never do. I could neither see nor hear anything under these conditions.

I decided that I must find some other point of approach and was turning to leave the room when I heard footsteps approaching along the corridor. I was trapped!

chapter IV

DEATH BY NIGHT

ON MORE THAN ONE occasion in my life have I been in tight places, but it seemed to me at the time that I had seldom before blundered into such a trap. The footsteps were approaching rapidly along the corridor. I could tell by their sound that they were made by more than one person.

If there were only two men, I might fight my way past them; but the noise of the encounter would attract those in the room behind me, and certainly any sort of a fight whatever would delay me long enough so that those who were attracted by it would be upon me before I could escape.

Escape! How could I escape if I were detected? Even if I could reach the balcony, they would be directly behind me; and I could not climb out of reach toward the roof before they could drag me down.

My position seemed rather hopeless, and then my eye fell upon the cupboard standing in the corner just beside me and the little foot-wide crack between it and the wall.

The footsteps were almost opposite the doorway. There was no time to be lost. Quickly I slipped behind the cupboard and waited.

Nor was I a moment too soon. The men in the corridor turned into the room almost immediately, so soon, in fact, that it seemed to me that they must have seen me; but evidently they had not, for they crossed directly to the door to the inner chamber, which one of them threw open.

From my hiding-place I could see this man plainly and also into the room beyond, while the shadow of the cupboard hid me from detection.

What I saw beyond that door gave me something to think about. There was a large room in the center of which was a great table, around which were seated at least fifty men—fifty of the toughest-looking customers that I have ever seen gathered together. At the head of the table was a huge man whom I knew at once to be Ur Jan. He was a very large man, but well proportioned; and I could tell at a glance that he must be a most formidable fighter.

The man who had thrown open the door I could see also, but I could not see his companion or companions as they were hidden from me by the cupboard.

Ur Jan had looked up as the door opened. "What now?" he demanded. "Who have you with you?" and then, "Oh, I recognize him."

"He has a message for you, Ur Jan," said the man at the door. "He said it was a most urgent message, or I would not have brought him here."

"Let him come in," said Ur Jan. "We will see what he wants, and you return to your post."

"Go on in," said the man, turning to his companion behind him, "and pray to your first ancestor that your message interests Ur Jan; as otherwise you will not come out of that room again on your own feet."

He stood aside and I saw a man pass him and enter the room. It was Rapas the Rat.

Just seeing his back as he approached Ur Jan told me that he was nervous and terrified. I wondered what could have brought him here, for it was evident that he was not one of the guild. The same question evidently puzzled Ur Jan, as his next words indicated.

"What does Rapas the Ulsio want here?" he demanded.

"I have come as a friend," replied Rapas. "I have brought word to Ur Jan that he has long wanted."

"The best word that you could bring to me would be that someone had slit your dirty throat," growled Ur Jan.

Rapas laughed—it was a rather weak and nervous laugh.

"The great Ur Jan likes his little joke," mumbled Rapas meekly.

The brute at the head of the table leaped to his feet and brought his clenched fist down heavily upon the solid sorapus wood top.

"What makes you think I joke, you miserable little slit-throat? But you had better laugh while you can, for if you haven't some important word for me, if you have come here where it is forbidden that outsiders come, if you have interrupted this meeting for no good reason, I'll put a new mouth in your throat; but you won't be able to laugh through it."

"I just wanted to do you a favor," pleaded Rapas. "I was sure that you would like to have the information that I bring, or I would not have come."

"Well, quick! out with it, what is it?"

"I know who does Fal Sivas's killing."

Ur Jan laughed. It was rather a nasty laugh. "So do I," he bellowed; "it is Rapas the Ulsio."

"No, no, Ur Jan," cried Rapas, "you wrong me. Listen, Ur Jan."

"You have been seen entering and leaving the house of Fal Sivas," accused the assassin chief. "You are in his employ; and for what purpose would he employ such as you, unless it was to do his killing for him?"

"Yes, I went to the house of Fal Sivas. I went there often. He employed me as his bodyguard, but I only took the position so that I might spy upon him. Now that I have learned what I went there to learn, I have come straight to you."

"Well, what did you learn?"

"I have told you. I have learned who does his killing."

"Well, who is it, if it isn't you?"

"He has in his employ a stranger to Zodanga—a panthan named Vandor. It is this man who does the killing."

I could not repress a smile. Every man thinks that he is a great character reader; and when something like this occurs to substantiate his belief, he has reason to be pleased; and the more so because few men are really good judges of character, and it is therefore very seldom that one of us is open to self-congratulation on this score.

I had never trusted Rapas, and from the first I had set him down as a sneak and a traitor. Evidently he was all these.

Ur Jan glowered at him skeptically. "And why do you bring me this information? You are not my friend. You are not one of my people, and as far as I know you are the friend of none of us."

"But I wish to be," begged Rapas. "I risked my life to get this information for you because I want to join the guild and serve under the great Ur Jan. If that came to pass, it would be the proudest day of my life. Ur Jan is the greatest man in Zodanga—he is the greatest man on all Barsoom. I want to serve him, and I will serve him faithfully."

All men are susceptible to flattery, and oftentimes the more ignorant they are, the more susceptible. Ur Jan was no exception. One could almost see him preening himself. He squared his great shoulders and threw out his chest.

"Well," he said in a milder voice, "we'll think it over. Perhaps we can use you, but first you will have to arrange it so that we can dispose of this Vandor." He glanced quickly around the table. "Do any of you men know him?"

There was a chorus of denials—no one admitted to knowing me.

"I can point him out to you," said Rapas the Ulsio. "I can point him out this very night."

"What makes you think so?" asked Ur Jan.

"Because I have an engagement to meet him later on at an eating-place that he frequents."

"Not a bad idea," said Ur Jan. "At what time is this meeting?"

"About half after the eighth zode," replied Rapas.

Ur Jan glanced quickly around the table. "Uldak," he said, "you go with Rapas; and don't return while this Vandor still lives."

I got a good look at Uldak as Ur Jan singled him out; and as I watched him come toward the door with Rapas on his way to kill me, I fixed every detail of the man's outward appearance indelibly upon my mind, even to his carriage as he walked; and though I saw him for but a moment then, I knew that I should never forget him.

As the two men left the larger chamber and crossed the ante-room in which I was concealed, Rapas explained to his companion the plan that he had in mind.

"I will take you now and show you the location of the eating-place in which I am to meet him. Then you can return later and you will know that the man who is with me is the man whom you seek."

I could not but smile as the two men turned into the corridor and passed out of earshot. What would they and Ur Jan have thought, had they known that the object of their criminal purpose was within a few yards of them?

I wanted to follow Rapas and Uldak, for I had a plan that it would have been amusing to carry out; but I could not escape from behind the cupboard without passing directly in front of the doorway leading into the room where sat Ur Jan and his fifty assassins.

It looked as though I would have to wait until the meeting ended and the company had dispersed before I could make my way to the roof and my flier.

Although I was inclined to chafe at the thought of this enforced inactivity, I nevertheless took advantage of the open door to familiarize myself with the faces of all of the assassins that I could see. Some of them sat with their backs toward me, but even these occasionally revealed a glimpse of a profile.

It was fortunate that I took early advantage of this opportunity to implant the faces of my enemies upon my memory, for but a moment or two after Rapas and Uldak had left the room, Ur Jan looked up and noticed the open door and directed one of the assassins sitting near it to close it.

Scarcely had the lock clicked when I was out from behind the cupboard and into the corridor.

I saw no one and heard no sound in the direction that the assassins had used in coming into and going from the ante-room; and as my way led in the opposite direction, I had little fear of being apprehended. I moved rapidly toward the apartment through the window of which I had entered the building, as the success of the plan I had in mind depended upon my being able to reach the eating-place ahead of Rapas and Uldak.

I reached the balcony and clambered to the roof of the building without mishap, and very shortly thereafter I was running my flier into the hangar on the roof of the public house where I stored it. Descending to the street, I made my way to the vicinity of the eating-place to which Rapas was conducting Uldak, reasonably certain that I should arrive there before that precious pair.

I found a place where I could watch the entrance in comparative safety from discovery, and there I waited. My vigil was not of long duration, for presently I saw the two approaching. They stopped at the intersection of two avenues a short distance from the place; and after Rapas had pointed it out to Uldak, the two separated, Rapas continuing on in the direction of the public house where I had first met him, while Uldak turned back into the avenue along which they had come from the rendezvous of the assassins.

It still lacked half a zode of the time that I was to meet Rapas, and for the moment at least I was not concerned with him—my business was with Uldak.

As soon as Rapas had passed me upon the opposite side of the street, I came out of my hiding-place and walked rapidly in the direction that Uldak had taken.

As I reached the intersection of the two streets, I saw the assassin a little distance ahead of me. He was walking slowly, evidently merely killing time until he might be certain that the hour had arrived when I was to meet Rapas at the eating-place.

Keeping to the opposite side of the street, I followed the man for a considerable distance until he entered a quarter that seemed to be deserted—I did not wish an audience for what I was about to do.

Crossing the avenue, I increased my gait; and the distance between us rapidly lessened until I was but a few paces behind him. I had moved very quietly, and he was not aware that anyone was near him. Only a few paces separated us when I spoke.

"You are looking for me?" I inquired.

He wheeled instantly, and his right hand flew to the hilt of his sword. He eyed me narrowly. "Who are you?" he demanded.

"Perhaps I have made a mistake," I said; "you are Uldak, are you not?"

"What of it?" he demanded.

I shrugged. "Nothing much, except that I understand that you have been sent to kill me. My name is Vandor."

As I ceased speaking, I whipped out my sword. He looked utterly astonished as I announced my identity, but there was nothing for him to do but defend himself, and as he drew his weapon he gave a nasty little laugh.

"You must be a fool," he said. "Anyone who is not a fool would run away and hide if he knew that Uldak was looking for him."

Evidently the man thought himself a great swordsman. I might have confused him by revealing my identity to him, for it might take the heart out of any Barsoomian warrior to know that he was facing John Carter; but I did not tell him. I merely engaged him and felt him out for a moment to ascertain if he could make good his boast.

He was, indeed, an excellent swordsman and, as I had expected, tricky and entirely unscrupulous. Most of these assassins are entirely without honor; they are merely killers.

At the very first he fought fairly enough because he thought that he could easily overcome me; but when he saw that he could not, he tried various shady expedients and finally he attempted the unpardonable thing—with his free hand, he sought to draw his pistol.

Knowing his kind, I had naturally expected something of the sort; and in the instant that his fingers closed upon the butt of the weapon I struck his sword aside and brought the point of my own heavily upon his left wrist, nearly severing his hand.

With a scream of rage and pain, he fell back; and then I was upon him in earnest.

He yelled for mercy now and cried that he was not Uldak; that I had made a mistake, and begged me to let him go. Then the coward turned to flee, and I was forced to do that which I most disliked to do; but if I were to carry out my plan I could not let him live, and so I leaped close and ran my sword through his heart from behind.

Uldak lay dead upon his face.

As I drew my sword from his body, I looked quickly about me. No one was within sight. I turned the man over upon his back and with the point of my sword made a cross upon his breast above his heart.

chapter V
THE BRAIN

RAPAS WAS WAITING for me when I entered the eating-place. He looked very self-satisfied and contented.

"You are right on time," he said. "Did you find anything to amuse you in the night life of Zodanga?"

"Yes," I assured him. "I enjoyed myself immensely. And you?"

"I spent a most profitable evening. I made excellent connections; and, my dear Vandor, I did not forget you."

"How nice of you," I said.

"Yes, you shall have reason to remember this evening as long as you live," he exclaimed, and then he burst into laughter.

"You must tell me about it," I said.

"No, not now," he replied. "It must remain a secret for a time. You will know all about it soon enough, and now let us eat. It is my treat tonight. I shall pay for everything."

The miserable rat of a man seemed to have swelled with importance now that he felt himself almost a full-fledged member of Ur Jan's guild of assassins.

"Very well," I said, "this shall be your treat," for I thought it would add to my enjoyment of the joke to let the poor fool foot the bill, and to make it still more amusing I ordered the most expensive dishes that I could find.

When I had entered the eating-place, Rapas had already seated himself facing the entrance; and he was continually glancing at it. Whenever anyone entered, I could see the look of expectation on his face change to one of disappointment.

We spoke of various unimportant things as we ate; and as the meal progressed, I could not but note his growing impatience and concern.

"What is the matter, Rapas?" I inquired after a while. "You seem suddenly nervous. You are always watching the entrance. Are you expecting someone?"

He got himself in hand then, very quickly; but he cast a single searching glance at me through narrowed lids. "No, no," he said, "I was expecting no one; but I have enemies. It is always necessary for me to be watchful."

His explanation was plausible enough, though I knew of course that it was not the right one. I could have told him that he was watching for someone who would never come, but I did not.

Rapas dragged the meal out as long as he could, and the later it grew, the more nervous he became and the more often his glance remained upon the entrance. At last I made a move to go, but he detained me. "Let us stop a little longer," he said. "You are in no hurry, are you?"

"I should be getting back," I replied. "Fal Sivas may require my services."

"No," he told me, "not before morning."

"But I must have some sleep," I insisted.

"You will get plenty of sleep," he said; "don't worry."

"Well, if I am going to, I had better start for bed," I said, and with that I arose.

He tried to detain me, but I had extracted about all the pleasure out of the evening that I thought it held for me, and so I insisted upon leaving.

Reluctantly he arose from the table. "I will walk a little way with you," he said.

We were near the door leading to the avenue when two men

entered. They were discussing something rather excitedly as they greeted the proprietor.

"The Warlord's agents are at work again," said one of them.

"How is that?" asked the proprietor.

"They have just found the body of one of Ur Jan's assassins in the Avenue of the Green Throat—the cross of the Warlord was above his heart."

"More power to the Warlord," said the proprietor. "Zodanga would be better off if we were rid of all of them."

"By what name was the dead man known?" asked Rapas, with considerable more concern, I imagine, than he would have cared to reveal.

"Why, some man in the crowd said that he believed his name was Uldak," replied one of the two men who had brought the news.

Rapas paled.

"Was he a friend of yours, Rapas?" I asked.

The Ulsio started. "Oh, no," he said. "I did not know him. Let us be going."

Together we walked out into the avenue and started in the direction of the house of Fal Sivas. We walked shoulder to shoulder through the lighted district near the eating-place. Rapas was very quiet and seemed nervous. I watched him out of the corner of my eye and tried to read his mind, but he was on guard and had closed it against me.

Oftentimes I have an advantage over Martians in that I can read their minds, though they can never read mine. Why that is, I do not know. Mind reading is a very commonplace accomplishment on Mars, but to safeguard themselves against its dangers, all Martians have cultivated the ability to close their minds to others at will—a defense mechanism of such long standing as to have become almost a universal characteristic; so that only occasionally can one be caught off his guard.

As we entered the darker avenues, however, it became apparent that Rapas was trying to drop behind me; and then I did not have to read his mind to know what was in it—Uldak had failed, and now The Rat had an opportunity to cover himself with glory and win the esteem of Ur Jan by carrying out the assignment of Uldak.

If a man has a sense of humor, a situation such as this can be very enjoyable, as, indeed, it was to me. Here I was walking along a dark avenue with a man who intended to murder me at the first opportunity, and it was necessary for me to thwart his plans without letting him know that I suspected them; for I did not want to kill Rapas the Ulsio, at least not at present. I felt that I could make use of him in one way or another without his ever suspecting that he was aiding me.

"Come," I said, at last, "why do you lag? Are you getting tired?" And I linked my left arm through his sword arm, and thus we continued on toward the house of Fal Sivas.

After a short distance, at the intersection of two avenues, Rapas disengaged himself. "I am leaving you here," he said; "I am not going back to the house of Fal Sivas tonight."

"Very well, my friend," I said; "but I shall be seeing you soon again, I hope."

"Yes," he replied, "soon."

"Tomorrow night, possibly," I suggested, "or if not tomorrow night, the night after. Whenever I am at liberty, I shall come to the eating-house; and perhaps I shall find you there."

"Very well," he said; "I eat there every night."

"May you sleep well, Rapas."

"May you sleep well, Vandor." Then he turned into the avenue at our left, and I proceeded on my way.

I thought that he might follow me, but he did not, and so I came at last to the house of Fal Sivas.

Hamas admitted me, and after passing a few words with him I went directly to my quarters where, in answer to my signal, Zanda admitted me.

The girl told me that the house had been very quiet during the night, and that no one had disturbed her or attempted to enter our quarters. She had prepared my sleeping silks and furs; and, as I was rather tired, I soon sought them.

Immediately after breakfast the next morning, I went on duty again at the door of Fal Sivas's study. I had been there but a short time when he summoned me to his person.

"What of last night?" he asked. "What luck did you have? I see that you are here alive; so I take it that you did not succeed in reaching the meeting-place of the assassins."

"On the contrary, I did," I told him. "I was in the room next to them and saw them all."

"What did you learn?"

"Not much. When the door was closed, I could hear nothing. It was open only a short time."

"What did you hear while it was open?" he asked.

"They knew that you had employed me as your bodyguard."

"What!" he demanded. "How could they have known that?"

I shook my head. "There must be a leak," I told him.

"A traitor!" he exclaimed.

I did not tell him about Rapas. I was afraid that he would have him killed, and I did not want him killed while he might be of use to me.

"What else did you hear?" he demanded.

"Ur Jan ordered that I be killed."

"You must be careful," said Fal Sivas. "Perhaps you had better not go out again at night."

"I can take care of myself," I replied, "and I can be of more service if I can get about at night and talk to people on the outside than I can by remaining cooped up here when I am off duty."

He nodded. "I guess you are right," he said, and then for a moment he sat in deep thought. Finally he raised his head. "I have it!" he exclaimed. "I know who the traitor is."

"Yes?" I asked politely.

"It is Rapas the Ulsio—Ulsio! He is well named."

"You are sure?" I asked.

"It could be no one else," replied Fal Sivas emphatically. "No one else has left the premises but you two since you came. But we will put an end to that as soon as he returns. When he comes back, you will destroy him. Do you understand?"

I nodded.

"It is a command," he said; "see that it is obeyed." For some time he sat in silence, and I could see that he was studying me intently. At last he spoke. "You have a smattering of the sciences I judge from the fact of your interest in the books in your quarters."

"Only a smattering," I assured him.

"I need such a man as you," he said, "if I could only find someone whom I might trust. But who can one trust?" He seemed to be thinking aloud. "I am seldom wrong," he continued musingly. "I read Rapas like a book. I knew that he was mean and ignorant and at heart a traitor."

He wheeled suddenly upon me. "But you are different. I believe that I can take a chance with you, but if you fail me—" he stood up and faced me, and I never saw such a malevolent expression upon a human face before. "If you fail me, Vandor, you shall die such a death as only the mind of Fal Sivas can conceive."

I could not help but smile. "I can die but once," I said.

"But you can be a long time at the dying, if it is done scientifically." But now he had relaxed, and his tone was a little bantering. I could imagine that Fal Sivas might enjoy seeing an enemy die horribly.

"I am going to take you into my confidence—a little, just a little," he said.

"Remember that I have not asked it," I replied, "that I have not sought to learn any of your secrets."

"The risk will be mutual," he said, "your life against my secrets. Come, I have something to show you."

He led me from the room, along the corridor past my quarters, and up the ramp to the forbidden level above. Here we passed through a magnificently appointed suite of living quarters and then through a little door hidden behind hangings, and came at last into an enormous loft that extended upward to the roof of the building, evidently several levels above us.

Supported by scaffolding and occupying nearly the entire length of the enormous chamber, was the strangest-looking craft that I have ever seen. The nose was ellipsoidal; and from the greatest diameter of the craft, which was just back of the nose, it sloped gradually to a point at the stern.

"There it is," said Fal Sivas, proudly; "the work of a lifetime, and almost completed."

"An entirely new type of ship," I commented. "In what respect is it superior to present types?"

"It is built to achieve results that no other ship can achieve," replied

Fal Sivas. "It is designed to attain speed beyond the wildest imaginings of man. It will travel routes that no man or ship has ever traveled.

"In that craft, Vandor, I can visit Thuria and Cluros. I can travel the far reaches of space to other planets."

"Marvellous," I said.

"But that is not all. You see that it is built for speed. I can assure you that it is built to withstand the most terrific pressure, that it is insulated against the extremes of heat and cold. Perhaps, Vandor, other inventors could have accomplished the same end. In fact, I believe Gar Nal has already done so, but there is only one man upon Barsoom, doubtless there is only one brain in the entire Solar System, that could have done what Fal Sivas has done. I have given that seemingly insensate mechanism a brain with which to think. I have perfected my mechanical brain, Vandor, and with just a little more time, just a few refinements I can send this ship out alone; and it will go where I wish it to go and come back again.

"Doubtless, you think that impossible. You think Fal Sivas is mad; but look! watch closely."

He centered his gaze upon the nose of the strange-looking craft, and presently I saw it rise slowly from its scaffolding for about ten feet and hang there poised in mid-air. Then it elevated its nose a few feet, and then its tail, and finally it settled again and rested evenly upon its scaffolding.

I was certainly astonished. Never in all my life had I seen anything so marvellous, nor did I seek to hide my admiration from Fal Sivas.

"You see," he said, "I did not even have to speak to it. The mechanical mind that I have installed in the ship responds to thought waves. I merely have to impart to it the impulse of the thought that I wish it to act upon. The mechanical brain then functions precisely as my brain would, and directs the mechanism that operates the craft precisely as the brain of the pilot would direct his hand to move levers, press buttons, open or close throttles.

"Vandor, it has been a long and terrible battle that I have had to wage to perfect this marvellous mechanism. I have been compelled to do things which would revolt the finer sensibilities of mankind; but I believe that it has all been well worthwhile. I believe that my greatest achievement warrants all that it has cost in lives and suffering.

"I, too, have paid a price. It has taken something out of me that can never be replaced. I believe, Vandor, that it has robbed me of every human instinct. Except that I am mortal, I am as much a creature of cold insensate formulas as that thing which you see resting there before you. Sometimes, because of that, I hate it; and yet I would die for it. I would see others die for it, countless others, in the future, as I have in the past. It must live. It is the greatest achievement of the human mind."

chapter VI

THE SHIP

EVERY ONE OF US, I believe, is possessed of two characters. Oftentimes they are so much alike that this duality is not noticeable, but again there is a divergence so great that we have the phenomenon of a Dr. Jekyll and Mr. Hyde in a single individual. The brief illuminating self-revealment of Fal Sivas suggested that he might be an example of such wide divergence in character.

He seemed immediately to regret this emotional outburst and turned again to an explanation of his invention.

"Would you like to see the inside of it?" he asked.

"Very much," I replied.

He concentrated his attention again upon the nose of the ship, and presently a door in its side opened and a rope ladder was lowered to the floor of the room. It was an uncanny procedure—just as though ghostly hands had performed the work.

Fal Sivas motioned me to precede him up the ladder. It was a habit of his to see that no one ever got behind him that bespoke the nervous strain under which he lived, always in fear of assassination.

The doorway led directly into a small, comfortably, even luxuriously furnished cabin.

"The stern is devoted to storerooms where food may be carried for long voyages," explained Fal Sivas. "Also aft are the motors, the oxygen and water-generating machines, and the temperature-regulating plant. Forward is the control room. I believe that that will interest you greatly," and he motioned me to precede him through a small door in the forward bulkhead of the cabin.

The interior of the control room, which occupied the entire nose of the ship, was a mass of intricate mechanical and electrical devices.

On either side of the nose were two large, round ports in which were securely set thick slabs of crystal.

From the exterior of the ship these two ports appeared like the huge eyes of some gigantic monster; and, in truth, this was the purpose they served.

Fal Sivas called my attention to a small, round metal object about the size of a large grapefruit that was fastened securely just above and between the two eyes. From it ran a large cable composed of a vast number of very small insulated wires. I could see that some of these wires connected with the many devices in the control room, and that others were carried through conduits to the after part of the craft.

Fal Sivas reached up and laid a hand almost affectionately upon the spherical object to which he had called my attention. "This," he said, "is the brain." Then he called my attention to two spots, one in the exact center of each crystal of the forward ports. I had not noticed them at first, but now I saw that they were ground differently from the balance of the crystals.

"These lenses," explained Fal Sivas, "focus upon this aperture in the lower part of the brain," and he called my attention to a small hole at the base of the sphere, "that they may transmit to the brain what the eyes of the ship see. The brain then functions mechanically precisely as the human brain does, except with greater accuracy."

"It is incredible!" I exclaimed.

"But, nevertheless, true," he replied. "In one respect, however, the brain lacks human power. It cannot originate thoughts. Perhaps that is just as well, for could it, I might have loosed upon myself and Barsoom an insensate monster that could wreak incalculable havoc before it could be destroyed, for this ship is equipped with high-power radium rifles which the brain has the power to discharge with far more deadly accuracy than may be achieved by man."

"I saw no rifles," I said.

"No," he replied. "They are encased in the bulkheads, and nothing of them is visible except small round holes in the hull of the ship. But, as I was saying, the one weakness of the mechanical brain is the very thing that makes it so effective for the use of man. Before it can function, it must be charged by human thought-waves. In other words, I must project into the mechanism the originating thoughts that are the food for its functioning.

"For example, I charge it with the thought that it is to rise straight up ten feet, pause there for a couple of seconds, and then come to rest again upon its scaffolding.

"To carry the idea into a more complex domain, I might impart to it the actuating thought that it is to travel to Thuria, seek a suitable landing place, and come to the ground. I could carry this idea even further, warning it that if it were attacked it should repel its enemies with rifle fire and maneuver so as to avoid disaster, returning immediately to Barsoom, rather than suffer destruction.

"It is also equipped with cameras, with which I could instruct it to take pictures while it was on the surface of Thuria."

"And you think it will do these things, Fal Sivas?" I asked.

He growled at me impatiently. "Of course it will. Just a few more days and I will have the last detail perfected. It is a minor matter of motor gearing with which I am not wholly satisfied."

"Perhaps I can help you there," I said. "I have learned several tricks in gearing during my long life in the air."

He became immediately interested and directed me to return to the floor of his hangar. He followed me down, and presently we were pouring over the drawings of his motor.

I soon found what was wrong with it and how it might be improved. Fal Sivas was delighted. He immediately recognized the value of the points I had made.

"Come with me," he said; "we will start work on these changes at once."

He led me to a door at one end of the hangar and, throwing it open, followed me into the room beyond.

Here, and in a series of adjoining rooms, I saw the most marvellously equipped mechanical and electrical shops that I have ever seen; and I saw something else, something that made me shudder as I considered the malignity of this man's abnormal obsession for secrecy in the development of his inventions.

The shops were well manned by mechanics, and every one of them was manacled to his bench or to his machine. Their complexions were pasty from long confinement, and in their eyes was the hopelessness of despair.

Fal Sivas must have noted the expression upon my face; for he said quite suddenly, and apropos of nothing else than my own thoughts, "I have to do it, Vandor; I cannot take the risk of one of them escaping and revealing my secrets to the world before I am ready."

"And when will that time come?" I asked.

"Never," he exclaimed, with a snarl. "When Fal Sivas dies, his secrets die with him. While he lives, they will make him the most powerful man in the universe. Why, even John Carter, Warlord of Mars, will have to bend the knee to Fal Sivas."

"And these poor devils, then, will remain here all their lives?" I asked.

"They should be proud and happy," he said, "for are they not dedicating themselves to the most glorious achievement that the mind of man has ever conceived?"

"There is nothing, Fal Sivas, more glorious than freedom," I told him.

"Keep your silly sentimentalism to yourself," he snapped. "There is no place for sentiment in the house of Fal Sivas. If you are to be of value to me, you must think only of the goal, forgetting the means whereby we attain it."

Well, I saw that I could accomplish nothing for myself or his poor victims by antagonizing him, and so I deferred with a shrug. "Of course, you are right, Fal Sivas," I agreed.

"That is better," he said, and then he called a foreman and together we explained the changes that were to be made in the motor.

As we turned away and left the chamber, Fal Sivas sighed. "Ah," he said, "if I could but produce my mechanical brain in quantities. I could do away with all these stupid humans. One brain in each room could perform all the operations that it now takes from five to twenty men to perform and perform them better, too—much better."

Fal Sivas went to his laboratory on the same level then, and told me that he would not require me for a while but that I should remain in my quarters and keep the door open, seeing that no unauthorized person passed along the corridor toward the ramp leading to his laboratories.

When I reached my quarters, I found Zanda polishing the metal on an extra set of harness that she said Fal Sivas had sent to me for my use.

"I was talking with Hamas's slave a little while ago," she remarked, presently. "She says that Hamas is worried about you."

"And why?" I asked.

"He thinks that the master has taken a fancy to you, and he fears for his own authority. He has been a very powerful man here for many years."

I laughed. "I don't aspire to his laurels," I told her.

"But he does not know that," said Zanda. "He would not believe it, if he were told. He is your enemy and a very powerful enemy. I just wanted to warn you."

"Thanks, Zanda," I said. "I shall be watchful of him, but I have a great many enemies; and I am so accustomed to having them that another, more or less, makes little difference to me."

"Hamas may make a great difference to you," she said. "He has the ear of Fal Sivas. I am so worried about you, Vandor."

"You mustn't worry; but if it will make you feel any better, do not forget that you have the ear of Hamas through his slave. You can let her know that I have no ambition to displace Hamas."

"That is a good idea," she said, "but I am afraid that it will not accomplish much; and if I were you, the next time I went out of the building, I should not return. You went last night, so I suppose that you are free to come and go as you will."

"Yes," I replied, "I am."

"Just as long as Fal Sivas does not take you to the floor above and reveal any of his secrets to you, you will probably be allowed to go out, unless Hamas makes it a point to prevail upon Fal Sivas to take that privilege away from you."

"But I have already been to the level above," I said, "and I have seen many of the wonders of Fal Sivas's inventions."

She gave little cry of alarm, then. "Oh, Vandor, you are lost!" she cried. "Now you will never leave this terrible place."

"On the contrary, I shall leave it tonight, Zanda," I told her. "Fal Sivas has agreed that I should do so."

She shook her head. "I cannot understand it," she said, "and I shall not believe it until after you have gone."

Toward evening Fal Sivas sent for me. He said that he wanted to talk to me about some further changes in the gearing of the motor, and so I did not get out that night, and the next day he had me in the shops directing the mechanics who were working on the new gears, and again he made it impossible for me to leave the premises.

In one way or another, he prevented it night after night; and though he didn't actually refuse permission, I began to feel that I was, indeed, a prisoner.

However, I was much interested in the work in the shops and did not mind much whether I went out or not.

Ever since I had seen Fal Sivas's wonder-craft and had listened to his explanation of the marvellous mechanical brain that controlled it, it had been constantly in my thoughts. I saw in it all the possibilities of power for good or evil that Fal Sivas had visualized, and I was intrigued by the thought of what the man who controlled it could accomplish.

If that man had the welfare of humanity at heart, his invention might prove a priceless boon to Barsoom; but I feared that Fal Sivas was too selfish and too mad for power to use his invention solely for the public good.

Such meditation naturally led me to wonder if another than Fal Sivas could control the brain. The speculation intrigued me, and I determined to ascertain at the first opportunity if the insensate thing would respond to my will.

That afternoon Fal Sivas was in his laboratory, and I was working in the shops with the poor manacled artisans. The great ship lay in the adjoining room. Now, I thought, presented as good a time as any to make my experiment.

The creatures in the room with me were all slaves. Furthermore, they hated Fal Sivas; so it made no difference to them what I did.

I had been kind to them and had even encouraged them to hope, though they could not believe that there was any hope. They had seen too many of their number die in their chains to permit them to entertain a thought of escape. They were apathetic in all matters, and I doubt that any of them noticed when I left the shop and entered the hangar where the ship rested upon its scaffolding.

Closing the door behind me, I approached the nose of the craft and focused my thoughts upon the brain within. I imparted to it the will to rise from its scaffolding as I had seen Fal Sivas cause it to do and then to settle down again in its place. I thought that if I could cause it to do that, I could cause it to do anything that Fal Sivas could.

I am not easily excited; but I must confess that my every nerve was tense as I watched that great thing above me, wondering if it would respond to those invisible thought-waves that I was projecting into it.

Concentrating thus upon this one thing naturally curtailed the other activities of my mind, but even so I had visions of what I might accomplish if my experiment proved successful.

I presume that I had been there but a moment, yet it seemed a long while; and then slowly the great craft rose as though lifted by an invisible hand. It hovered for a moment ten feet above its scaffolding, and then it settled down to rest again.

As it did so, I heard a noise behind me; and, turning quickly, I saw Fal Sivas standing in the doorway of the shop.

chapter VII

THE FACE IN THE DOORWAY

NONCHALANCE IS A corollary of poise. I was thankful at that moment that the poise gene of some ancient forebear had been preserved in my line and handed down to me. Whether or not Fal Sivas had entered the room before the ship came to rest again upon its scaffolding, I did not know. If not, he had only missed the sight by a matter of a split second. My best momentary defense was to act on the assumption that he had not seen, and this I determined to do.

Standing there in the doorway, the old inventor was eyeing me sternly. "What are you doing in here?" he demanded.

"The invention fascinates me; it intrigues my imagination," I replied. "I stepped in from the shop to have another look at it. You had not told me that I should not do so."

He knitted his brows in thought. "Perhaps, I didn't," he said at last; "but I tell you now. No one is supposed to enter this room, unless by my express command."

"I will bear that in mind," I said.

"It will be well for you if you do, Vandor."

I walked then toward the door where he stood, with the intention of returning to the shop; but Fal Sivas barred my way.

"Wait a moment," he said, "perhaps you have been wondering if the brain would respond to your thought-impulses."

"Frankly, I have," I replied.

I wondered how much he knew, how much he had seen. Perhaps he was playing with me, secure in his own knowledge; or perhaps he was merely suspicious and was seeking confirmation of his suspicion.

However that might be, I was determined not to be trapped out of my assumption that he had not seen and did not know.

"You were not, by any chance, attempting to see if it would respond?" he asked.

"Who, other than a stupid dolt, once having seen this invention, would not naturally harbor such a thought?" I asked.

"Quite right, quite right," he admitted; "it would only be natural, but did you succeed?" The pupils of his eyes contracted; his lids narrowed to two ominous slits. He seemed to be trying to bore into my soul; and, unquestionably, he was attempting to read my mind; but that, I knew, he could not accomplish.

I waved my hand in the direction of the ship. "Has it moved?" I asked with a laugh.

I thought that I saw just a faint hint of relief in his expression, and I felt sure then that he had not seen.

"It would be interesting, however, to know whether the mind of another than myself could control the mechanism," he said. "Suppose you try it."

"It would be a most interesting experiment. I should be glad to do so. What shall I try to have it do?"

"It will have to be an original idea of your own," he told me; "for if it is my idea, and I impart it to you, we cannot be definitely sure whether the impulse that actuates it originated in your brain or mine."

"Is there no danger that I might unintentionally harm it?" I asked.

"I think not," he replied. "It is probably difficult for you to realize that that ship sees and reasons. Of course, its vision and its mental functioning are purely mechanical but none the less accurate. In fact, I should rather say, because of that, more accurate. You might attempt to will the ship to leave the room. It cannot do so because the great doors through which it will eventually pass out of this building are closed and locked. It might approach the wall of the building, but the eyes would see that it could not pass through without damage; or, rather, the eyes would see the obstacle, transmit the impression to the brain, and the brain would reason to a logical conclusion. It would, therefore, stop the ship or, more likely, cause it to turn the nose about so that the eyes could seek a safe avenue of exit. But let us see what you can do."

I had no intention of letting Fal Sivas know that I could operate his invention, if he did not already know it; and so I tried to keep my thoughts as far from it as possible. I recalled football games that I had seen, a five-ring circus, and the Congress of Beauties on the Midway of the 1893 Chicago World's Fair. In fact, I tried to think of anything under the sun rather than Fal Sivas and his mechanical brain.

Finally, I turned to him with a gesture of resignation. "Nothing seems to happen," I said.

He appeared vastly relieved. "You are a man of intelligence," he said. "If it will not obey you, it is reasonably safe to assume that it will obey no one but me."

For several moments he was lost in thought, and then he straightened up and looked at me, and his eyes burned with demoniac fire. "I can be master of a world," he said; "perhaps I can even be master of the universe."

"With that?" I asked, nodding toward the ship.

"With the idea that it symbolizes," he replied; "with the idea of an inanimate object energized by scientific means and motivated by a mechanical brain. If I but had the means to do so—the wealth—I could manufacture these brains in great quantities, and I could put them into small fliers weighing less than a man weighs. I could give them means of locomotion in the air or upon the ground. I could give them arms and hands. I could furnish them with weapons. I could send them out in great hordes to conquer the world. I could send them to other planets. They would know neither pain nor fear. They would have no hopes, no aspirations, no ambitions that might wean them from my service. They would be the creatures of my will alone, and the things that I sent them to do they would persist in until they were destroyed.

"But destroying them would serve my enemies no purpose; for faster than they could destroy them, my great factories would turn out more.

"You see," he said, "how it would work?" and he came close and spoke almost in a whisper. "The first of these mechanical men I would make with my own hands, and as I created them I would impel them to create others of their kind. They would become my mechanics, the workmen in my factories; and they would work day and night without rest, always turning out more and more of their kind. Think how rapidly they would multiply."

I was thinking of this. The possibilities astounded and stunned me. "But it would take vast wealth," I told him.

"Yes, vast wealth," he repeated; "and it was for the purpose of obtaining this vast wealth that I built this ship."

"You intend to raid the treasure houses of the great cities of Barsoom?" I asked, smiling.

"By no means," he replied. "Treasures vastly richer lie at the disposal of the man who controls this ship. Do you not know what the spectroscope tells us of the riches of Thuria?"

"I have heard," I said, "but I never took much stock in it. The story was too fabulous."

"It is true, nevertheless," he said. "There must be mountains of gold and platinum on Thuria and vast plains carpeted with precious stones."

It was a bold enterprise; but after having seen this craft, and knowing the remarkable genius of Fal Sivas, I had little doubt but that it was feasible.

Suddenly, as was his way, he seemed to regret that he had confided in me and brusquely directed me to return to my duties in the shop.

The old man had told me so much now that I naturally began to wonder if he would consider it safe to permit me to live, and I was constantly on my guard. It seemed highly improbable that he would consent to my leaving the premises, but I determined to settle this question immediately; for I wanted to see Rapas before he could visit the establishment of Fal Sivas again, thereby compelling me to destroy him. Day after day had passed and Fal Sivas had contrived to prevent my leaving the house, though he had accomplished it so adroitly that it was never actually apparent that he did not wish me to leave.

As he dismissed me that evening, I told him that I was going out to try to locate Rapas and attempt again to contact the assassins of Ur Jan.

He hesitated so long before he replied that I thought he was going to forbid me going out, but at last he nodded in acquiescence. "Perhaps it will be as well," he said. "Rapas does not come here any more, and he knows too much to be at large, unless he is in my service and loyal to me. If I must trust one of you, I prefer that it be you, rather than Rapas."

I did not go to the evening meal with the others, as I intended eating at the place that Rapas frequented and where we had planned to meet when I was at liberty.

It was necessary to acquaint Hamas with the fact that I was

leaving, as only he could open the outer door for me. His manner toward me was not quite as surly as it had been the past few days. In fact, he was almost affable; and the change in his manner put me even more on my guard, for I felt that it boded me no good—there was no reason why Hamas should love me any more today than he had yesterday. If I induced pleasant anticipations in him, it must be because he visualized something unpleasant befalling me.

From the house of Fal Sivas, I went directly to the eating-place; and there I inquired of the proprietor regarding Rapas.

"He has been in every evening," replied the man. "He usually comes about this time and again about half after the eighth zode, and he always asks me if you have been here."

"I will wait for him," I said, and I went to the table The Rat and I usually occupied.

I had scarcely seated myself before Rapas entered. He came directly to the table and seated himself opposite me.

"Where have you been keeping yourself?" he demanded. "I was commencing to think that old Fal Sivas had made away with you or that you were a prisoner in his house. I had about made up my mind to go there tonight and call on the old man, so that I could learn what had happened to you."

"It is just as well that I got out tonight before you came," I said.

"Why?" he demanded.

"Because it is not safe for you to go to the house of Fal Sivas," I told him. "If you value your life, you will never go there again."

"What makes you think that?" he demanded.

"I can't tell you," I replied, "but just take my word for it, and keep away." I did not want him to know that I had been commissioned to kill him. It might have made him so suspicious and fearful of me that he would be of no value to me in the future.

"Well, it is strange," he said; "Fal Sivas was friendly enough before I took you there."

I saw that he was harboring in his mind the thought that, for some reason, I was trying to keep him away from Fal Sivas; but I couldn't help it, and so I changed the subject.

"Has everything been going well with you, Rapas, since I saw you?" I asked.

"Yes, quite well," he replied.

"What is the news of the city? I have not been out since I saw you last, and of course we hear little or nothing in the house of Fal Sivas."

"They say that the Warlord is in Zodanga," he replied. "Uldak, one of Ur Jan's men, was killed the last night I saw you, as you will recall. The mark of the Warlord's agent was above his heart, but Ur Jan believes that no ordinary swordsman could have bested Uldak. Also he has learned from his agent in Helium that John Carter is not there; so, putting the two facts together, Ur Jan is convinced that he must be in Zodanga."

"How interesting," I commented. "And what is Ur Jan going to do about it?"

"Oh, he'll get his revenge," said The Rat; "if not in one way, then in another. He is already planning; and when he strikes, John Carter will wish that he had attended to his own affairs and left Ur Jan alone."

Shortly before we finished our meal, a customer entered the place and took a seat alone at a table across the room. I could see him in a mirror in front of me. I saw him glance in our direction, and then I looked quickly at Rapas and saw his eyes flash a message as he nodded his head very slightly; but without that, I would have known why the man was there, for I recognized him as one of the assassins that had sat at the council with Ur Jan. I pretended not to notice anything; and my glance wandered idly to the doorway, attracted by two customers who were leaving the place at the time.

Then I saw something else of interest—of vital interest. As the door swung open, I saw a man outside looking in. It was Hamas.

The assassin at the table across the room ordered only a glass of wine; and when he had drunk it, he arose and left. Shortly after his departure, Rapas got up.

"I must be going," he said; "I have an important engagement."

"Shall I see you tomorrow night?" I asked.

I could see him attempt to suppress a grin. "I shall be here tomorrow night," he said.

We went out then onto the avenue; and Rapas left me, while I turned my steps in the direction of the house of Fal Sivas. Through the lighted districts I did not have to be particularly on my guard; but when I entered the darker sections of the city, I was watchful; and presently I saw a figure lurking in a dark doorway. I knew it was the assassin waiting to kill me.

chapter VIII

SUSPICION

CLUROS, the farther moon, rode high in the heavens, lighting dimly the streets of Zodanga like a dusty bulb in a huge loft; but I needed no better light to see the shadowy form of the man awaiting my coming.

I knew precisely what was in the man's mind, and I must have smiled. He thought that I was coming along in total ignorance of his presence or the fact that anyone was planning upon murdering me that night. He was saying to himself that after I had passed he would spring out and run his sword through my back; it would be a very simple matter, and then he would go back and report to Ur Jan.

As I approached the doorway, I paused and cast a hasty glance behind me. I wanted to make sure, if I could, that Rapas had not followed me. If I killed this man, I did not want Rapas to know that it was I.

Now I resumed my way, keeping a few paces from the building so that I would not be too close to the assassin when I came opposite his hiding place.

When I did come opposite it, I turned suddenly and faced it. "Come out of there, you fool," I said in a low voice.

For a moment the man did not move. He seemed utterly stunned by his discovery and by my words.

"You and Rapas thought that you could fool me, didn't you?" I inquired. "You and Rapas and Ur Jan! Well, I will tell you a secret— something that Rapas and Ur Jan do not dream. Because you are trying to kill the wrong man, you are not using the right method. You think that you are attempting to kill Vandor, but you are not. There is no such person as Vandor. The man who faces you is John Carter, Warlord of Mars." I whipped out my sword. "And now if you are quite ready, you may come out and be killed."

At that, he came forth slowly, his long-sword in his hand. I thought that his eyes showed a trace of astonishment and his voice certainly did, as he whispered, "John Carter!"

He did not show any fear, and I was glad of that, for I dislike fighting with a man who is really terrified of me, as he starts his fight with a terrible handicap that he can never overcome.

"So you are John Carter!" he said, as he stepped out into the open, and then he commenced to laugh. "You think you can frighten me, do you? You are a first-class liar, Vandor; but if you were all the first-class liars on Barsoom rolled into one, you could not frighten Povak."

Evidently he did not believe me, and I was rather glad of it, for the encounter would now afford me far richer sport as there was gradually revealed to my antagonist the fact that he was pitted against a master swordsman.

As he engaged me, I saw that, while in no respect a mean swordsman, he was not as proficient as had been Uldak. I should have been glad to have played with him for a while, but I could not risk the consequences of being discovered.

So vicious was my attack that I soon pressed him back against the wall of the building. He had had no opportunity to do more than defend himself, and now he was absolutely at my mercy.

I could have run him through on the instant, but instead I reached out quickly with my point and made a short cut upon his breast and then I made another across it.

I stepped back then and lowered my point. "Look at your breast, Povak," I said. "What do you see there?"

He glanced down at his breast, and I saw him shudder. "The mark of the Warlord," he gasped, and then, "Have mercy upon me; I did not know that it was you."

"I told you," I said, "but you wouldn't believe me; and if you had believed me, you would have been all the more anxious to kill me. Ur Jan would have rewarded you handsomely."

"Let me go," he begged. "Spare my life, and I will be your slave forever."

I saw then that he was a craven coward, and I felt no pity for him but only contempt.

"Raise your point," I snapped, "and defend yourself, or I shall run you through in your tracks."

Suddenly, with death staring him in the face, he seemed to go mad. He rushed at me with the fury of a maniac, and the impetuosity of his attack sent me back a few steps, and then I parried a terrific thrust and ran him through the heart.

At a little distance from me, I saw some people coming, attracted by the clash of steel.

A few steps took me to the entrance of a dark alleyway into which I darted; and by a circuitous route, I continued on my way to the house of Fal Sivas.

Hamas admitted me. He was very cordial. In fact, far too cordial. I felt like laughing in his face because of what I knew that he did not know that I knew, but I returned his greeting civilly and passed on to my quarters.

Zanda was waiting up for me. I drew my sword and handed it to her.

"Rapas?" she asked. I had told her that Fal Sivas had commanded me to kill The Rat.

"No, not Rapas," I replied. "Another of Ur Jan's men."

"That makes two," she said.

"Yes," I replied; "but remember, you must not tell anyone that it was I who killed them."

"I shall not tell anyone, my master," she replied. "You may always trust Zanda."

She cleaned the blood from the blade and then dried and polished it.

I watched her as she worked, noticing her shapely hands and graceful fingers. I had never paid very much attention to her before. Of course, I had known that she was young and well-formed and good-looking; but suddenly I was impressed by the fact that Zanda was very beautiful and that with the harness and jewels and hair-dressing of a great lady, she would have been more than noticeable in any company.

"Zanda," I remarked at last, "you were not born a slave, were you?"

"No, master."

"Did Fal Sivas buy you or abduct you?" I asked.

"Phystal and two slaves took me one night when I was on the avenues with an escort. They killed him and brought me here."

"Your people," I asked, "are they still living?"

"No," she replied; "my father was an officer in the old Zodangan Navy. He was of the lesser nobility. He was killed when John Carter led the green hordes of Thark upon the city. In grief, my mother took the last long journey on the bosom of the sacred Iss to the Valley Dor and the Lost Sea of Korus.

"John Carter!" she said, musingly, and her voice was tinged with loathing. "He was the author of all my sorrows, of all my misfortune. Had it not been for John Carter robbing me of my parents I should not be here now, for I should have had their watchful care and protection to shield me from all danger."

"You feel very bitterly toward John Carter, don't you?" I asked.

"I hate him," she replied.

"You would be glad to see him dead, I suppose."

"Yes."

"You know, I presume, that Ur Jan has sworn to destroy him?"

"Yes, I know that," she replied; "and I constantly pray that he will be successful. Were I a man, I should enlist under the banner of Ur Jan. I should be an assassin and search out John Carter myself."

"They say he is a formidable swordsman," I suggested.

"I should find a way to kill him, even if I had to descend to the dagger or poison."

I laughed. "I hope, for John Carter's sake, that you do not recognize him when you meet him."

"I shall know him all right," she said. "His white skin will betray him."

"Well, let us hope that he escapes you," I said laughingly, as I bade her good night and went to my sleeping silks and furs.

The next morning, immediately after breakfast, Fal Sivas sent for me. As I entered his study, I saw Hamas and two slaves standing near him.

Fal Sivas looked up at me from beneath lowering brows. He did not greet me pleasantly as was his wont.

"Well," he snapped, "did you destroy Rapas last night?"

"No," I replied; "I did not."

"Did you see him?"

"Yes, I saw him and talked with him. In fact, I ate the evening meal with him."

I could see that this admission surprised both Fal Sivas and Hamas.

It was evident that it rather upset their calculations, for I judged that they had expected me to deny having seen Rapas, which I might have done had it not been for the fortunate circumstance that had permitted me to discover Hamas spying upon me.

"Why didn't you kill him?" demanded Fal Sivas. "Did I not order you to do so?"

"You employed me to protect you, Fal Sivas," I replied; "and you must rely upon my judgment to do it in my own way. I am neither a child nor a slave. I believe that Rapas has made connections that will be far more harmful to you than Rapas, himself; and by permitting him to live and keeping in touch with him, I shall be able to learn much that will be to your advantage that I could never learn if I destroyed Rapas. If you are not satisfied with my methods, get someone else to protect you; and if you have decided to destroy me, I suggest that you enlist some warriors. These slaves would be no match for me."

I could see Hamas trembling with suppressed rage at that, but he did not dare say anything or do anything until Fal Sivas gave him the word. He just stood there fingering the hilt of his sword and watching Fal Sivas questioningly, as though he awaited a signal.

But Fal Sivas gave him no signal. Instead, the old inventor sat there studying me intently for several minutes. At last he sighed and shook his head. "You are a very courageous man, Vandor," he said; "but perhaps a little overconfident and foolish. No one speaks to Fal Sivas like that. They are all afraid. Do you not realize that I have it within my power to destroy you at any moment?"

"If you were a fool, Fal Sivas, I might expect death this moment; but you are no fool. You know that I can serve you better alive than dead, and perhaps you also suspect what I know—that if I went out I should not go alone. You would go with me."

Hamas looked horrified and grasped the hilt of his sword firmly, as though about to draw it; but Fal Sivas leaned back in his chair and smiled.

"You are quite right, Vandor," he said; "and you may rest assured that if I ever decide that you must die, I shall not be within reach of your sword when that sad event occurs. And now tell me what you expect to learn from Rapas and what makes you believe that he has information that will be of value to me?"

"That will be for your ears, alone, Fal Sivas," I said, glancing at Hamas and the two slaves.

Fal Sivas nodded to them. "You may go," he said.

"But, master," objected Hamas, "you will be left alone with this man. He may kill you."

"I shall be no safer from his sword if you are present, Hamas," replied the master. "I have seen and you have seen how deftly he wields his blade."

Hamas's red skin darkened at that; and without another word he left the room, followed by the two slaves.

"And now," said Fal Sivas, "tell me what you have learned or what you suspect."

"I have reason to believe," I replied, "that Rapas has made connections with Ur Jan. Ur Jan, as you have told me, has been employed by Gar Nal to assassinate you. By keeping in touch with Rapas, it is possible that I may be able to learn some of Ur Jan's plans. I do not know of course, but it is the only contact we have with the assassins, and it would be poor strategy to destroy it."

"You are absolutely right, Vandor," he replied. "Contact Rapas as often as you can, and do not destroy him until he can be of no more value to us. Then—" his face was contorted by a fiendish grimace.

"I thought that you would concur in my judgment," I replied. "I am particularly anxious to see Rapas again tonight."

"Very well," he said, "and now let us go to the shop. The work on the new motor is progressing nicely, but I want you to check over what has been done."

Together we went to the shop; and after inspecting the work, I told Fal Sivas that I wanted to go to the motor room of the ship to take some measurements.

He accompanied me, and together we entered the hull. When I had completed my investigation I sought an excuse to remain longer in the hangar, as there was half-formed in my mind a plan that would necessitate more intimate knowledge of the room in the event that I found it necessary or feasible to carry out my designs.

In pretended admiration of the ship, I walked all around it, viewing it from every angle; and at the same time viewing the hangar from every angle. My particular attention was riveted upon the great doorway through which the ship was to eventually pass out of the building. I saw how the doors were constructed and how they were secured; and when I had done that, I lost interest in the ship for the time being at least.

I spent the balance of the day in the shop with the mechanics, and that night found me again in the eating-place on the Avenue of Warriors.

Rapas was not there. I ordered my meal and had nearly finished it, though I was eating very slowly; and still he had not come. Still I loitered on, as I was very anxious to see him tonight.

But at last, when I had about given him up, he came. It was evident that he was very nervous, and he appeared even more sly and furtive than ordinarily.

"Kaor!" I said, as he approached the table; "you are late tonight."

"Yes," he said; "I was detained."

He ordered his meal and fidgeted about, uneasily.

"Did you reach home last night all right?" he said.

"Why, yes, of course."

"I was a little bit worried about you," he said. "I heard that a man was killed on the very avenue through which you must have passed."

"Is that so?" I exclaimed. "It must have happened after I had passed by."

"It is very strange," he said; "it was one of Ur Jan's assassins, and again he had the mark of John Carter upon his breast."

He was eyeing me very suspiciously, but I could see that he was afraid even to voice what was in his mind. In fact, I think it frightened him even to entertain the thought.

"Ur Jan is certain now that John Carter, himself, is in the city."

"Well," I said, "why be so upset about it? I am sure that it does not concern either you or me."

chapter IX

ON THE BALCONY

EYES SPEAK THE TRUTH more often than the lips. The eyes of Rapas the Ulsio told me that he did not agree with me that the killing of one of Ur Jan's assassins was of no concern to either him or me, but his lips spoke otherwise.

"Of course," he said, "it is nothing to me; but Ur Jan is furious. He has offered an immense reward for the positive identification of the man who killed Uldak and Povak. Tonight he meets with his principal lieutenants to perfect the details of a plan which, they believe, will definitely and for all time end the activities of John Carter against the guild of assassins. They—"

He stopped suddenly, and his eyes registered a combination of suspicion and terror. It was as though for a moment his stupid mind had forgotten the suspicion that it had held that I might be John Carter and then, after exposing some of the secrets of his master, he had recalled the fact and was terrified.

"You seem to know a great deal about Ur Jan," I remarked, casually. "One would think that you are a full-fledged member of his guild."

For a moment he was confused. He cleared his throat several times as though about to speak, but evidently he could not think of anything to say, nor could his eyes hold steadily to mine. I enjoyed his discomfiture greatly.

"No," he disclaimed, presently; "it is nothing like that. These are merely things that I have heard upon the street. They are merely gossip. It is not strange that I should repeat them to a friend."

Friend! The idea was most amusing. I knew that Rapas was now a creature of Ur Jan's and that, with his fellows, he had been commissioned to kill me; and I had been commissioned by Fal Sivas to kill Rapas; yet here we were, dining and gossiping together. It was a most amusing situation.

As our meal drew to an end, two villainous-looking fellows entered and seated themselves at a table. No sign passed between them and Rapas, but I recognized them both and knew why they were there. I had seen them both at the meeting of the assassins, and I seldom forget a face. Their presence was a compliment to me and an admission that Ur Jan realized that it would take more than one swordsman to account for me.

I should have been glad to put my mark upon their breasts, but I knew that if I killed them, the suspicion that Ur Jan harbored that I might be John Carter would be definitely confirmed. The killing of Uldak and Povak and the marking of their breasts with the sign of the Warlord might have been a coincidence; but if two more men, sent to destroy me, met a similar fate, no doubt could remain even in a stupid mind but that all four had come to their end at the hands of John Carter himself.

The men had but scarcely seated themselves when I arose. "I must be getting along, Rapas," I said; "I have some important work to do tonight. I hope you will forgive me for running off like this, but perhaps I shall see you again tomorrow night."

He tried to detain me. "Don't hurry away," he exclaimed; "wait just a few moments. There are a number of things I should like to talk to you about."

"They will have to wait until tomorrow," I told him. "May you sleep well, Rapas," and with that I turned and left the building.

I went only a short distance along the avenue in the opposite direction to that which led toward the house of Fal Sivas. I concealed myself in the shadows of a doorway then and waited, nor had I long to wait before the two assassins emerged and hurried off in the direction in which they supposed I had gone. A moment or two later Rapas came out of the building. He hesitated momentarily and then he started walking slowly in the direction taken by the assassins.

When all three were out of sight, I came from my hiding-place and went at once to the building on the top of which my flier was stored.

The proprietor was puttering around one of the hangars when I came onto the roof. I could have wished him elsewhere, as I did not particularly care to have my comings and goings known.

"I don't see much of you," he said.

"No," I replied; "I have been very busy." I continued in the direction of the hangar where my ship was stored.

"Going to take your flier out tonight?" he asked.

"Yes."

"Watch out for the patrol boats," he said, "if you are on any business you wouldn't want the authorities to know about. They have been awfully busy the last couple of nights."

I didn't know whether he was just giving me a friendly tip, or if he were trying to get some information from me. There are many organizations, including the government, that employ secret agents. For aught I knew, the fellow might be a member of the assassins' guild.

"Well," I said, "I hope the police don't follow me tonight." He pricked up his ears. "I don't need any help; and, incidentally, she is extremely good-looking." I winked at him and nudged him with my elbow as I passed, in a fashion that I thought his low mentality would grasp. And it did.

He laughed and slapped me on the back. "I guess you're worried more about her father than you are the police," he said.

"Say," he called after me, as I was climbing to the deck of my flier, "ain't she got a sister?"

As I slipped silently out over the city, I heard the hangar man laughing at his own witticism; and I knew that if he had had any suspicions I had lulled them.

It was quite dark, neither moon being in the heavens; but this very fact would make me all the more noticeable to patrol boats above me when I was passing over the more brilliantly lighted portions of the city, and so I quickly sought dark avenues and flew low among the dense shadows of the buildings.

It was a matter of only a few minutes before I reached my destination and dropped my flier gently to the roof of the building that housed the headquarters of the assassins' guild of Zodanga.

Rapas' statement that Ur Jan and his lieutenants were perfecting a plan aimed at my activities against them was the magnet that had lured me here this night.

I had decided that I would not again attempt to use the ante-room off their meeting-place, as not only was the way to it fraught with too much danger but even were I to safely reach the shadowed niche behind the cupboard, I still would be unable to hear anything of their proceedings through the closed door.

I had another plan, and this I put into immediate execution.

I brought my flier to rest at the edge of the roof directly above the room in which the assassins met; then I made a rope fast to one of the rings in her gunwale.

Lying on my belly, I looked over the edge of the roof to make sure of my position and found that I had gauged it to a nicety. Directly below me was the edge of a balcony before a lighted window. My rope hung slightly to one side of the window where it was not visible to those within the room.

Carefully I set the controls of my ship and then tied the end of a light cord to the starting lever. These matters attended to, I grasped the rope and slipped over the eaves of the roof, carrying the light cord in one hand.

I descended quietly, as I had left my weapons on my flier lest they clank against one another or scrape against the side of the building as I descended and thus attract attention to me.

Very cautiously I descended; and when I had come opposite the window, I found that I could reach out with one hand and grasp the rail of the balcony. I drew myself slowly to it and into a position where I could stand securely.

Shortly after I had dropped below the edge of the roof, I had heard voices; and now that I was close to the window, I was delighted to discover that it was open and that I could hear quite well nearly all that was going on within the room. I recognized Ur Jan's voice. He was speaking as I drew myself to the balcony.

"Even if we get him tonight," he said, "and he is the man I think he is, we can still collect ransom from the girl's father or grandfather."

"And it should be a fat ransom," said another voice.

"All that a great ship will carry," replied Ur Jan, "and with it a promise of immunity for all the assassins of Zodanga and their promise that they will not persecute us further."

I could not but wonder whom they were plotting against now—probably some wealthy noble; but what connection there was between my death and the kidnaping of the girl, I could not fathom, unless, perhaps, they were not speaking of me at all but of another.

At this point, I heard a rapping sound and Ur Jan's voice saying, "Come in."

I heard a door open and the sound of men entering the room.

"Ah," exclaimed Ur Jan, clapping his hands together, "you got him tonight! Two of you were too many for him, eh?"

"We did not get him," replied a surly voice.

"What?" demanded Ur Jan. "Did he not come to the eating-place tonight?"

"He was there all right," said another voice, which I recognized instantly as that of Rapas. "I had him there, as I promised."

"Well, why didn't you get him?" demanded Ur Jan angrily.

"When he left the eating-place," explained one of the other men, "we followed him immediately; but he had disappeared when we reached the avenue. He was nowhere in sight; and though we walked rapidly all the way to the house of Fal Sivas, we saw nothing of him."

"Was he suspicious?" asked Ur Jan. "Do you think that he guessed that you had come there for him?"

"No, I am sure he did not. He did not seem to notice us at all. I did not even see him look at us."

"I cannot understand how he disappeared so quickly," said Rapas, "but we can get him tomorrow night. He has promised to meet me there then."

"Listen," said Ur Jan; "you must not fail me tomorrow. I am sure that this man is John Carter. After all, though, I am glad that we did not kill him. I have just thought of a better plan. I will send four of you tomorrow night to wait near the house of Fal Sivas. I want you to take John Carter alive and bring him to me. With him alive, we can collect two shiploads of treasure for his princess."

"And then we will have to hide in the pits of Zodanga all the rest of our lives," demurred one of the assassins.

Ur Jan laughed. "After we collect the ransom, John Carter will never bother us again," he said.

"You mean—?"

"I am an assassin, am I not?" demanded Ur Jan. "Do you think that an assassin will let a dangerous enemy live?"

Now I understood the connection between my death and the abduction of the girl they had mentioned. She was none other than my divine princess, Dejah Thoris. From Mors Kajak, Tardos Mors, and myself, the scoundrels expected to collect two shiploads of ransom; and they well knew, and I knew, that they had not figured amiss. We three would gladly have exchanged many shiploads of treasure for the safety of the incomparable Princess of Helium.

I realized now that I must return immediately to Helium and insure the safety of my princess, but I lingered there on the balcony a moment longer listening to the plans of the conspirators.

"But," objected one of Ur Jan's lieutenants, "even if you succeed in getting Dejah Thoris—"

"There is no 'even' about it," snapped Ur Jan. "It is already as good as accomplished. I have been preparing for this for a long time. I have done it very secretly so that there would be no leak; but now that we are ready to strike, it makes no difference. I can tell you that two of my men are guards in the palace of the princess, Dejah Thoris."

"Well, granted that you can get her," objected the former speaker skeptically, "where can you hide her? Where, upon all Barsoom, can you hide the Princess of Helium from the great Tardos Mors, even if you are successful in putting John Carter out of the way?"

"I shall not hide her on Barsoom," replied Ur Jan.

"What, not upon Barsoom? Where, then?"

"Thuria," replied Ur Jan.

"Thuria!" The speaker laughed. "You will hide her on the nearer moon. That is good, Ur Jan. That would be a splendid hiding-place— if you could get her there."

"I can get her there all right. I am not acquainted with Gar Nal for nothing."

"Oh, you mean that fool ship he is working on? The one in which he expects to go visiting around among the planets? You don't think that thing will work, even after he gets it finished, do you—if he ever does get it finished?"

"It *is* finished," replied Ur Jan, "and it will fly to Thuria."

"Well, even if it will, we do not know how to run it."

"Gar Nal will run it for us. He needs a vast amount of treasure to complete other boats, and for a share of the ransom he has agreed to pilot the ship for us."

Now, indeed, I realized all too well how carefully Ur Jan had made his plans and how great was the danger to my princess. Any day now they might succeed in abducting Dejah Thoris, and I knew that it would not be impossible with two traitors in her guard.

I decided that I could not waste another moment. I must leave for Helium at once, and then Fate intervened and nearly made an end of me.

As I started to climb the rope and swung away from the balcony, a part of my harness caught upon one of its iron ornaments; and when I attempted to disengage it, the thing broke loose and fell upon the balcony.

"What was that?" I heard Ur Jan's voice demand, and then I heard footsteps coming toward the window. They came fast, and an instant later the figure of Ur Jan loomed before me.

"A spy," he yelled, and leaped onto the balcony.

chapter X

Jat Or

WERE I PRONE to seek excuses outside of myself to explain the causes of misfortunes which overtake me, I might, at that moment, have inquired why Fate should throw her weight in favor of evildoers and against me. My cause was, unquestionably, a cause of righteousness, yet the trifling fact that an iron ornament upon a balcony in the city of Zodanga had been loose and that my harness had accidently caught upon it had placed me in a situation from which it seemed likely that I could not escape with my life.

However, I was not dead yet; and I had no intention of resigning myself to the dictates of an unkind and unjust Fate without a struggle. Furthermore, in the idiom of a famous American game, I had an ace in the hole.

As Ur Jan clambered out onto the balcony, I had swung away from it, clinging to the rope attached to my flier above; and, at the same time, I started to climb.

Like a pendulum, I swung; and, having reached the end of my arc, I swung back again, seemingly directly into the arms of Ur Jan.

It all happened very quickly, much more quickly than I can tell it. Ur Jan laid hold of the hilt of his sword; I drew my knees well up against my body; I swung toward him; then, as I was almost upon him, I kicked him with both feet full in the chest and with all my strength.

Ur Jan staggered back against another of the assassins who was following him onto the balcony, and they both went down in a heap.

Simultaneously, I pulled on the light cord that I had attached to the starting lever of my motor. In response, the ship rose; and I rose with it, dangling at the end of my rope.

My situation was anything but an enviable one. I could not, of course, guide the ship; and if it failed to rise rapidly enough, I stood an excellent chance of being dashed to death against some building as I was dragged across the city; but even this menace was by no means the greatest which threatened me, for now I heard a shot, and a bullet whirred past me—the assassins were attempting to shoot me down.

I climbed as rapidly as I could toward my flier; but climbing a small rope, while swinging beneath a rising airship, is not an enviable situation, even without the added hazard of being fired at by a band of assassins.

The ship carried me diagonally across the avenue upon which stood the building that harbored Ur Jan's band. I thought surely that I must hit the eaves of the opposite building; and, believe me, I put every ounce of my strength and agility into climbing that rope, as I swung rapidly across the avenue.

In this instance, however, Fate favored me; and I skimmed just above the roof of the building.

The assassins were still firing at me, but I imagine that most of their hits in the past had been scored with daggers of poison, for their pistol practice was execrable.

At last my fingers closed over the gunwale of my ship, and a moment later I had drawn myself to her deck. Reaching for her controls, I opened the throttle wide and set her nose for Helium.

Perhaps I was reckless, for I ignored the threat of the patrol boats and made no effort to escape their vigilance. Nothing mattered to me now but to reach Helium in time to safeguard my princess.

How well my enemies knew where to strike at me! How well

they knew my vulnerable parts! They knew that nothing I possessed, including my life, would I refuse to give for the preservation of Dejah Thoris. They must have known, too, the price that they would have to pay if harm befell her; and this fact marked them for the desperate men that they were. I had threatened their security and their lives, and they were risking all in this attempt to defeat me.

I wondered if any of them had recognized me. I had not seen Rapas at the window; and, in the darkness of the night, there seemed little likelihood that the other two assassins, who had seen me but momentarily in the eating-place, could have been sure that it was I whom they saw for a second dangling at the end of a twirling rope. I felt that they might have suspected that it was Vandor, but I hoped that they were not sure that it was John Carter.

My swift craft moved rapidly across the city of Zodanga; and I thought that I was going to get away without difficulty, when suddenly I heard the warning wail of a patrol boat, signalling me to stop.

It was considerably above me, and slightly ahead and to the starboard, when it discovered me. My throttle was open wide, and I was racing through the thin air of the dying planet at full speed.

The patrol boat must have realized instantly that I had no intention of stopping, for it shot forward in a burst of speed, at the same time diving for me. Its velocity in that long dive was tremendous; and though it was, normally, not as fast a craft as mine, its terrific speed in the dive was far greater than my craft could attain.

I was already too low to gain speed by diving, nor could I thus have equalled the great speed of the larger craft, the weight of which added to its momentum.

It was coming right down on top of me and overhauling me rapidly—coming diagonally from my starboard side.

It seemed futile to hope that I could escape it; and when it opened up on me with its bow guns, I almost had it in my mind to give up the fight and surrender, for at least then I should be alive. Otherwise, I should be dead; and dead I could be of no help to Dejah Thoris. But I was faced then with the fact that I would be delayed, that I might not be able to reach Helium in time. I was sure to be arrested, and almost certainly I would be imprisoned for attempting to escape the patrol boat. I had no papers, and that would make it all the harder for me. I stood an excellent chance of being thrown into slavery, or into the pits beneath the city to await the coming games.

The risk was too great. I must reach Helium without delay.

Suddenly I swung my helm to starboard; and, so quickly the little craft obeyed my will, I came very near to being catapulted from her deck as she swung suddenly into the new course.

I tacked directly beneath the hull of the patrol boat as she hurtled close above me; and thus she could not fire upon me, as her guns were masked by her own hull.

Now it was that her greater weight and the speed of her dive worked to my advantage. They could not check the velocity of this larger ship and turn her onto the new course with the same facility with which I had maneuvered my lighter one-man craft.

The result was that before she was on my trail again, I had passed far beyond the outer walls of Zodanga; and, running as I was without lights, the patrol boat could not pick me up.

I saw her own lights for a few moments, but I could tell that she was not upon the right course; and then, with a sigh of relief, I settled myself for the long journey to Helium.

As I sped through the thin air of dying Mars, Thuria rose above the Western horizon ahead, flooding with her brilliant light the vast expanse of dead sea bottoms where once rolled mighty oceans bearing on their bosoms the great ships of the glorious race that then dominated the young planet.

I passed their ruined cities upon the verges of these ancient seas; and in my imagination I peopled them with happy, carefree throngs. There again were the great jeddaks who ruled them and the warrior clans that defended them. Now all were gone, and doubtless the dark recesses of their stately buildings housed some wild tribe of cruel and mirthless green men.

And so I sped across the vast expanse of waste land toward The Twin Cities of Helium and the woman I loved—the woman whose deathless beauty was the toast of a world.

I had set my destination compass on my goal, and now I stretched myself upon the deck of my flier and slept.

It is a long and lonely journey from Zodanga to Helium, and this time it seemed stretched to interminable length because of my anxiety for the safety of my princess, but at last it was ended, and I saw the scarlet tower of greater Helium looming before me.

As I approached the city, a patrol boat stopped me and ordered me alongside.

During the day, I had removed the red pigment from my skin; and even before I gave my name, the officer in command of the patrol boat recognized me.

I thought I noticed some restraint and embarrassment in his manner, but he said nothing other than to greet me respectfully and ask if his ship might escort me to my palace.

I thanked him and asked him to follow me so that I would not be detained by other patrol boats; and when I was safely above my own hangars, he dipped his bow and left.

As I alighted on the roof, the hangar guard ran forward to take the ship and run her into her hangar.

These men were old and loyal retainers who had been in my service for years. Ordinarily, they greeted me with enthusiasm when I returned from an absence, their manner toward me, while always respectful, being more that of old servants than strictly military retainers; but tonight they greeted me with averted eyes and seemed ill at ease.

I did not question them, though I felt intuitively that something was amiss. Instead, I hastened down the ramp into my palace and made my way immediately toward the quarters of my princess.

As I approached them, I met a young officer of her personal guard; and when he saw me he came rapidly to meet me. His face looked lined and careworn, and I could see that he was laboring under suppressed emotions.

"What is wrong, Jat Or?" I demanded; "first the commander of the patrol boat, then the hangar guard, and now you all look as though you had lost your last friend."

"We have lost our best friend," he replied.

I knew what he meant, but I hesitated to demand a direct explanation. I did not want to hear it. I shrank from hearing the words that I knew he would speak, as I had never shrunk from anything before in my life, not even a rendezvous with death.

But Jat Or was a soldier, and so was I; and however painful a duty may be, a soldier must face it bravely.

"When did they take her?" I asked.

He looked at me in wide-eyed astonishment. "You know, sir?" he exclaimed.

I nodded. "It is what I hastened from Zodanga to prevent; and now, Jat Or, I am too late; am I not?"

He nodded.

"Tell me about it," I said.

"It happened last night, my prince—just when, we do not know. Two men were on guard before her door. They were new men, but they had successfully passed the same careful examination and investigation that all must who enter your service, sir. This morning when two female slaves came to relieve the two that were on duty with the princess last night, they found her gone. The two slave women lay dead in their sleeping silks and furs; they had been killed in their sleep. The two guards were gone. We do not know; but we believe, of course, that it was they who took the princess."

"It was," I said. "They were agents of Ur Jan, the assassin of Zodanga. What has been done?"

"Tardos Mors, the jeddak, her grandfather, and Mors Kajak, her father, have dispatched a thousand ships in search of her."

"It is strange," I said; "I saw not a single ship on my entire flight from Zodanga."

"But they were sent out, my prince," insisted Jat Or. "I know because I begged to be permitted to accompany one of them; I felt that the responsibility was mine, that in some way it was my fault that my princess was taken."

"Wherever they are searching, they are wasting their time," I said. "Carry that word from me to Tardos Mors. Tell him to call back his ships. There is only one ship that can follow where they have taken Dejah Thoris, and only two men in the world who can operate that ship. One of them is an enemy; the other is myself. Therefore, I must return to Zodanga at once. There is no time to be lost; otherwise, I would see the Jeddak myself before I leave."

"But is there nothing that we can do here?" he demanded. "Is there nothing that I can do? If I had been more watchful, this would not have happened. I should have slept always before the door of my princess. Let me go with you. I have a good sword; and there may come a time when even the Warlord, himself, would be glad of another to back up his own."

I considered his appeal for a moment. Why not take him? I have been on my own so much during my long life that I have come to rely only upon my own powers, yet on the occasions when I have fought with good men at my side, I have been glad that they were there—such men as Carthoris, Kantos Kan, and Tars Tarkas. This young padwar I knew to be clever with the sword; and I knew, too, that he was loyal to my princess and myself. At least, he would be no hindrance, even if he were no help.

"Very well, Jat Or," I said. "Change into a plain harness. You are no longer a padwar in the navy of Helium; you are a panthan without a country, at the service of any who will take you. Ask the Officer of the Guard to come to my quarters at once; and when you have changed, come there also. Do not be long."

The Officer of the Guard reached my quarters shortly after I did. I told him that I was going in search of Dejah Thoris and that he would be in charge of the household until I returned.

"While I am waiting for Jat Or," I said, "I wish that you would go to the landing deck and signal for a patrol boat. I want it to escort me beyond the walls of the city, so that I shall not be delayed."

He saluted and left, and after he had gone I wrote a short note to Tardos Mors and others to Mors Kajak and Carthoris.

As I completed the last of these, Jat Or entered. He was a trim and efficient-looking fighting man, and I was pleased with his appearance. Although he had been in our service for some time I had not known him intimately in the past, as he was only a minor padwar attached to the retinue of Dejah Thoris. A padwar, incidentally, holds a rank corresponding closely to that of lieutenant in an earthly military organization.

I motioned Jat Or to follow me, and together we went to the landing deck. Here I selected a fast two-man flier; and as I was running it out of its hangar, the patrol boat that the Officer of the Guard had summoned settled toward the deck.

A moment later we were moving toward the outer walls of greater Helium under escort of the patrol boat; and when we had passed beyond, we dipped our bows to one another in parting salute. I set the nose of my flier in the direction of Zodanga and opened the throttle wide, while the patrol boat turned back over the city.

The return journey to Zodanga was uneventful. I took advantage of the time at my disposal to acquaint Jat Or with all that had occurred while I was in Zodanga and of all that I had learned there, so that he might be well prepared in advance for any emergency which might arise. I also again tinted my flesh with the red pigment which was my only disguise.

Naturally, I was much concerned regarding the fate of Dejah Thoris, and devoted much time to useless conjecture as to where her abductors had taken her.

I could not believe that Gar Nal's interplanetary ship could have approached Helium without being discovered. It seemed, therefore, far more reasonable to assume that Dejah Thoris had been taken to Zodanga and that from that city the attempt would be made to transport her to Thuria.

My state of mind during this long journey is indescribable. I visualized my princess in the power of Ur Jan's ruffians; and I pictured her mental suffering, though I knew that outwardly she would remain calm and courageous. To what insults and indignities would they subject her? A blood-red mist swam before my eyes as thoughts like these raced through my brain, and the blood-lust of the killer dominated me completely, so that I am afraid I was a rather surly and uncommunicative companion that Jat Or sailed with during the last hours of that flight.

But at last we approached Zodanga. It was night again.

It might have been safer to have waited until daylight, as I had on a previous occasion, before entering the city; but time was an all-important factor now.

Showing no lights, we nosed slowly toward the city's walls; and keeping constant watch for a patrol boat, we edged over the outer wall and into a dark avenue beyond.

Keeping to unlighted thoroughfares, we came at last in safety to the same public hangar that I had patronized before.

The first step in the search for Dejah Thoris had been taken.

chapter XI

IN THE HOUSE OF GAR NAL

IGNORANCE AND STUPIDITY occasionally reveal advantages that raise them to the dignity of virtues. The ignorant and stupid are seldom sufficiently imaginative to be intelligently curious.

The hangar man had seen me depart in a one-man flier and alone. Now he saw me return in a two-man flier, with a companion. Yet, he evidenced no embarrassing curiosity on the subject.

Storing our craft in a hangar and instructing the hangar man that he was to permit either one of us to take it out when we chose, I conducted Jat Or to the public house in the same building; and after introducing him to the proprietor, I left him, as the investigation that I now purposed conducting could be carried on to better advantage by one man than two.

My first objective was to learn if Gar Nal's ship had left Zodanga. Unfortunately, I did not know the location of the hangar in which Gar Nal had built his ship. I was quite sure that I could not get this information from Rapas, as he was already suspicious of me, and so my only hope lay in Fal Sivas. I was quite sure that he must know, as from remarks that he had dropped, I was convinced that the two inventors had constantly spied upon one another; and so I set out in the direction of the house of Fal Sivas, after instructing Jat Or to remain at the public house where I could find him without delay should I require his services.

It was still not very late in the evening when I reached the house of the old inventor. At my signal, Hamas admitted me. He appeared a little surprised and not overly pleased when he recognized me.

"We thought that Ur Jan had finally done away with you," he said.

"No such luck, Hamas," I replied. "Where is Fal Sivas?"

"He is in his laboratory on the level above," replied the major-domo. "I do not know that he will want to be disturbed, though I believe that he will be anxious to see you."

He added this last with a nasty inflection that I did not like.

"I will go up to his quarters, at once," I said.

"No," said Hamas; "you will wait here. I will go to the master and ask his pleasure."

I brushed past him into the corridor. "You may come with me, if you will, Hamas," I said; "but whether you come or not, I must see Fal Sivas at once."

He grumbled at this disregard of his authority and hastened along the corridor a pace or two ahead of me.

As I passed my former quarters, I noticed that the door was open; but though I saw nothing of Zanda within, I gave the matter no thought.

We passed on up the ramp to the level above, and there Hamas knocked on the door of Fal Sivas's apartment.

For a moment there was no answer; and I was about to enter the room when I heard Fal Sivas's voice demand querulously, "Who's there?"

"It is Hamas," replied the major-domo, "and the man, Vandor, who has returned."

"Send him in, send him in," directed Fal Sivas.

As Hamas opened the door, I brushed past him and, turning, pushed him out into the corridor. "He said, 'Send him in,'" I said. Then I closed the door in his face.

Fal Sivas had evidently come out of one of the other rooms of his suite in answer to our knock, for he stood now facing me with his hand still on the latch of a door in the opposite wall of the room, an angry frown contracting his brows.

"Where have you been?" he demanded.

Naturally, I have not been accustomed to being spoken to in the manner that Fal Sivas had adopted; and I did not relish it. I am a fighting man, not an actor; and, for a moment, I had a little difficulty in remembering that I was playing a part.

I did even go so far as to take a couple of steps toward Fal Sivas with the intention of taking him by the scruff of the neck and shaking some manners into him, but I caught myself in time; and as I paused, I could not but smile.

"Why don't you answer me?" cried Fal Sivas, "You are laughing; do you dare to laugh at me?"

"Why shouldn't I laugh at my own stupidity?" I demanded.

"Your own stupidity? I do not understand. What do you mean?"

"I took you for an intelligent man, Fal Sivas; and now I find that I was mistaken. It makes me smile."

I thought he was going to explode, but he managed to control himself. "Just what do you mean by that?" he demanded angrily.

"I mean that no intelligent man would speak to a lieutenant in the tone of voice in which you have just addressed me, no matter what he suspected, until he had thoroughly investigated. You have probably been listening to Hamas during my absence; so I am naturally condemned without a hearing."

He blinked at me for a moment and then said in a slightly more civil voice, "Well, go ahead, explain where you have been and what you have been doing."

"I have been investigating some of Ur Jan's activities," I replied, "but I have no time now to go into an explanation of that. The important thing for me to do now is to go to Gar Nal's hangar, and I do not know where it is. I have come here to you for that information."

"Why do you want to go to Gar Nal's hangar?" he demanded.

"Because I have word that Gar Nal's ship has left Zodanga on a mission in which both he and Ur Jan are connected."

This information threw Fal Sivas into a state of excitement bordering on apoplexy. "The calot!" he exclaimed, "the thief, the scoundrel; he has stolen all my ideas and now he has launched his ship ahead of mine. I—I—"

"Calm yourself, Fal Sivas," I urged him. "We do not know yet that Gar Nal's ship has sailed. Tell me where he was building it, and I will go and investigate."

"Yes, yes," he exclaimed, "at once; but Vandor, do you know where Gar Nal was going? Did you find that out?"

"To Thuria, I believe," I replied.

Now, indeed, was Fal Sivas convulsed with rage. By comparison with this, his first outburst appeared almost like enthusiastic approval of his competitor for inventive laurels. He called Gar Nal every foul thing he could lay his tongue to and all his ancestors back to the original tree of life from which all animate things on Mars are supposed to have sprung.

"He is going to Thuria after the treasure!" he screamed in conclusion. "He has even stolen that idea from me."

"This is no time for lamentation, Fal Sivas," I snapped. "We are getting no place. Tell me where Gar Nal's hangar is, so that we may know definitely whether or not he has sailed."

With an effort, he gained control of himself; and then he gave me minute directions for finding Gar Nal's hangar, and even told me how I might gain entrance to it, revealing a familiarity with his enemy's stronghold which indicated that his own spies had not been idle.

As Fal Sivas concluded his directions, I thought that I heard sounds coming from the room behind him—muffled sounds—a gasp, a sob, perhaps. I could not tell. The sounds were faint; they might have been almost anything; and now Fal Sivas crossed the room toward me and ushered me out into the corridor, a little hurriedly, I thought; but that may have been my imagination. I wondered if he, too, had heard the sounds.

"You had better go, now," he said; "and when you have discovered the truth, return at once and report to me."

On my way from the quarters of Fal Sivas, I stopped at my own to speak to Zanda; but she was not there, and I continued on to the little doorway through which I came and went from the house of Fal Sivas.

Hamas was there in the ante-room. He looked disappointed when he saw me. "You are going out?" he asked.

"Yes," I replied.

"Are you returning again tonight?"

"I expect to," I replied; "and by the way, Hamas, where is Zanda? She was not in my quarters when I stopped in."

"We thought you were not returning," explained the major-domo, "and Fal Sivas found other duties for Zanda. Tomorrow I shall have Phystal give you another slave."

"I want Zanda again," I said. "She performs her duties satisfactorily, and I prefer her."

"That is something you will have to discuss with Fal Sivas," he replied.

I passed out then into the night and gave the matter no further thought, my mind being occupied with far more important considerations.

My way led past the public house where I had left Jat Or and on into another quarter of the city. Here, without difficulty, I located the building that Fal Sivas had described.

At one side of it was a dark narrow alley. I entered this and groped my way to the far end, where I found a low wall, as Fal Sivas had explained that I would.

I paused there a moment and listened intently, but no sound came from the interior of the building. Then I vaulted easily to the top of the wall, and from there to the roof of a low annex. Across this roof appeared the end of the hangar in which Gar Nal had built his ship. I recognized it for what it was by the great doors set in the wall.

Fal Sivas had told me that through the crack between the two doors, I could see the interior of the hangar and quickly determine if the ship were still there. But there was no light within; the hangar was completely dark, and I could see nothing as I glued an eye to the crack.

I attempted to move the doors, but they were securely locked. Then I moved cautiously along the wall in search of another opening.

About forty feet to the right of the doors, I discovered a small window some ten feet above the roof upon which I was standing. I sprang up to it and grasped the sill with my fingers and drew myself up in the hope that I might be able to see something from this vantage point.

To my surprise and delight, I found the window open. All was quiet inside the hangar—quiet and as dark as Erebus.

Sitting on the sill, I swung my legs through the window, turned over on my belly, and lowered myself into the interior of the hangar; then I let go of the sill and dropped.

Such a maneuver, naturally, is fraught with danger, as one never knows upon what he may alight.

I alighted upon a moveable bench, loaded with metal parts and tools. My weight upset it, and it crashed to the floor with a terrific din.

Scrambling to my feet, I stood there in the darkness waiting, listening. If there were anyone anywhere in the building, large as it appeared to be, it seemed unlikely that the racket I had made could pass unnoticed, nor did it.

Presently I heard footsteps. They seemed at a considerable distance, but they approached rapidly at first and then more slowly. Whoever was coming appeared to grow more cautious as he neared the hangar.

Presently a door at the far end was thrown open, and I saw two armed men silhouetted against the light of the room beyond.

It was not a very brilliant light that came from the adjoining chamber, but it was sufficient to partially dispel the gloom of the cavernous interior of the hangar and reveal the fact that there was no ship here. Gar Nal had sailed!

I had evidently been hoping against hope, for the discovery stunned me. Gar Nal was gone; and, unquestionably, Dejah Thoris was with him.

The two men were advancing cautiously into the hangar. "Do you see anyone?" I heard the man in the rear demand.

"No," replied the leader, and then, in a loud voice, "who is here?"

The floor of the hangar had a most untidy appearance. Barrels, crates, carboys, tools, parts—a thousand and one things—were scattered indiscriminately about it. Perhaps this was fortunate for me; as, among so many things, it would be difficult to discover me as long as I did not move, unless the men stumbled directly upon me.

I was kneeling in the shadow of a large box, planning upon my next move in the event that I was discovered.

The two men came slowly along the center of the room. They

came opposite my hiding-place. They passed me. I glanced at the open door through which they had come. There seemed to be no one there. Evidently these two men had been on guard; and they, alone, had heard the noise that I had made.

Suddenly a plan flashed to my mind. I stepped out of my hiding-place and stood between them and the open door through which they had entered.

I had moved quietly, and they had not heard me. Then I spoke. "Do not move," I said, "and you will be safe."

They stopped as though they had been shot, and wheeled about. "Stand where you are," I commanded.

"Who are you?" asked one of the men.

"Never mind who I am. Answer my questions, and no harm will befall you."

Suddenly one of the men laughed. "No harm *will* befall us," he said. "You are alone, and we are two. Come!" he whispered to his companion; and drawing their swords, the two rushed upon me.

I backed away from them, my own sword ready to parry their thrusts and cuts. "Wait!" I cried. "I do not want to kill you. Listen to me. I only want some information from you, and then I will go."

"Oh, ho! He does not want to kill us," shouted one of the men. "Come now," he directed his fellow, "get on his left side, and I will take him on the right. So he does not want to kill us, eh?"

Sometimes I feel that I am entitled to very little credit for my countless successes in mortal combat. Always, it seems to me, and it certainly must appear even more so to my opponents, my flashing blade is a living thing inspired to its marvellous feats by a power beyond that of mortal man. It was so tonight.

As the two men charged me from opposite sides, my steel flashed so rapidly in parries, cuts, and thrusts that I am confident that the eyes of my opponents could not follow it.

The first man went down with a cloven skull the instant that he came within reach of my blade, and almost in the same second I ran his companion through the shoulder. Then I stepped back.

His sword arm was useless; it hung limp at his side. He could not escape. I was between him and the door; and he stood there, waiting for me to run him through the heart.

"I have no desire to kill you," I told him. "Answer my questions truthfully, and I will let you live."

"Who are you, and what do you want to know?" he growled.

"Never mind who I am. Answer my questions, and see that you answer them truthfully. When did Gar Nal's ship sail?"

"Two nights ago."

"Who was on board?"

"Gar Nal and Ur Jan."

"No one else?" I demanded.

"No," he replied.

"Where were they going?"

"How should I know?"

"It will be well for you, if you do know. Come now, where were they going; and who were they taking with them?"

"They were going to meet another ship somewhere near Helium, and there they were going to take aboard someone whose name I never heard mentioned."

"Were they kidnaping someone for ransom?" I demanded.

He nodded. "I guess that was it," he said.

"And you don't know who it was?"

"No."

"Where are they going to hide this person they are kidnaping?"

"Some place where no one will ever find her," he said.

"Where is that?"

"I heard Gar Nal say he was going to Thuria."

I had gained about all the information that this man could give me that would be of any value; so I made him lead me to a small door that opened onto the roof from which I had gained entrance to the hangar. I stepped out and waited until he had closed the door; then I crossed the roof and dropped to the top of the wall below, and from there into the alleyway.

As I made my way toward the house of Fal Sivas, I planned rapidly. I realized that I must take desperate chances, and that whatever the outcome of my adventure, its success or failure rested wholly upon my own shoulders.

I stopped at the public house where I had left Jat Or, and found him anxiously awaiting my return.

The place was now so filled with guests that we could not talk with privacy, and so I took him with me over to the eating-place that Rapas and I had frequented. Here we found a table, and I narrated to him all that had occurred since I had left him after our arrival in Zodanga.

"And now," I said, "tonight I hope that we may start for Thuria. When we separate here, go at once to the hangar and take out the flier. Keep an eye out for patrol boats; and if you succeed in leaving the city, go directly west on the thirtieth parallel for one hundred haads. Wait for me there. If I do not come in two days, you are free to act as you wish."

chapter XII

"We Must Both Die!"

THURIA! She had always intrigued my imagination; and now as I saw her swinging low through the sky above me, as Jat Or and I separated on the avenue in front of the eating-place, she dominated my entire being.

Somewhere between that blazing orb and Mars, a strange ship was bearing my lost love to some unknown fate.

How hopeless her situation must appear to her, who could not guess that any who loved her were even vaguely aware of her situation or whither her abductors were taking her. It was quite possible that she, herself, did not know. How I wished that I might transmit a message of hope to her.

With such thoughts was my mind occupied as I made my way in the direction of the house of Fal Sivas; but even though I was thus engrossed, my faculties, habituated to long years of danger, were fully alert, so that sounds of footsteps emerging from an avenue I had just crossed did not pass unnoticed. Presently, I was aware that they had turned into the avenue that I was traversing and were following behind me, but I gave no outward indication that I heard them until it became evident that they were rapidly overtaking me.

I swung around then, my hand upon the hilt of my sword; and as I did so, the man who was following addressed me.

"I thought it was you," he said, "but I was not certain."

"It is I, Rapas," I replied.

"Where have you been?" he asked. "I have been looking for you for the past two days."

"Yes?" I inquired. "What do you want of me? You will have to be quick, Rapas; I am in a hurry."

He hesitated. I could see that he was nervous. He acted as though he had something to say, but did not know how to begin, or else was afraid to broach the subject.

"Well, you see," he commenced, lamely, "we haven't seen each other for several days, and I just wanted to have a visit with you—just gossip a little, you know. Let's go back and have a bite to eat."

"I have just eaten," I replied.

"How is old Fal Sivas?" he asked. "Do you know anything new?"

"Not a thing," I lied. "Do you?"

"Oh, just gossip," he replied. "They say that Ur Jan has kidnaped the Princess of Helium." I could see him looking at me narrowly for my reaction.

"Is that so?" I inquired. "I should hate to be in Ur Jan's shoes when the men of Helium lay hold of him."

"They won't lay hold of him," said Rapas. "He has taken her where they will never find her."

"I hope that he gets all that is coming to him, if he harms her," I said; "and he probably will." Then I turned as though to move away.

"Ur Jan won't harm her, if the ransom is paid," said Rapas.

"Ransom?" I inquired. "And what do they consider the Princess of Helium worth to the men of Helium?"

"Ur Jan is letting them off easy," volunteered Rapas. "He is asking only two shiploads of treasure—all the gold and platinum and jewels that two great ships will carry."

"Have they notified her people of their demand?" I asked.

"A friend of mine knows a man who is acquainted with one of Ur

Jan's assassins," explained Rapas; "communication with the assassins could be opened up in this way."

So he had finally gotten it out of his system. I could have laughed if I had not been so worried about Dejah Thoris. The situation was self-evident. Ur Jan and Rapas were both confident that I was either John Carter or one of his agents, and Rapas had been delegated to act as intermediary between the kidnapers and myself.

"It is all very interesting," I said; "but, of course, it is nothing to me. I must be getting along. May you sleep well, Rapas."

I venture to say that I left The Rat in a quandary as I turned on my heel and continued on my way toward the house of Fal Sivas. I imagine that he was not so sure as he had been that I was John Carter or even that I was an agent of the Warlord; for certainly either one or the other should have evinced more interest in his information than I had. Of course, he had told me nothing that I did not already know; and therefore there had been nothing to induce within me either surprise or excitement.

Perhaps it would have made no difference either one way or the other had Rapas known that I was John Carter; but it pleased me, in combating the activities of such men, to keep them mystified and always to know a little more than they did.

Again Hamas admitted me when I reached the gloomy pile that Fal Sivas inhabited; and as I passed him and started along the corridor toward the ramp that leads up to Fal Sivas's quarters on the next level, he followed after me.

"Where are you going?" he asked, "to your quarters?"

"No, I am going to the quarters of Fal Sivas," I replied.

"He is very busy now. He cannot be disturbed," said Hamas.

"I have information for him," I said.

"It will have to wait until tomorrow morning."

I turned and looked at him. "You annoy me, Hamas," I said; "run along and mind your own business."

He was furious then, and took hold of my arm. "I am major-domo here," he cried, "and you must obey me. You are only a—a—"

"An assassin," I prompted him meaningly, and laid my hand upon the hilt of my sword.

He backed away. "You wouldn't dare," he cried. "You wouldn't dare!"

"Oh, wouldn't I? You don't know me, Hamas. I am in the employ of Fal Sivas; and when I am in a man's employ, I obey him. He told me to report back to him at once. If it is necessary to kill you to do so, I shall have to kill you."

His manner altered then, and I could see that he was afraid of me. "I only warned you for your own good," he said. "Fal Sivas is in his laboratory now. If he is interrupted in the work that he is doing, he will be furious—he may kill you himself. If you are wise, you will wait until he sends for you."

"Thank you, Hamas," I said; "I am going to see Fal Sivas now. May you sleep well," and I turned and continued on up the corridor toward the ramp. He did not follow me.

I went at once to the quarters of Fal Sivas, knocked once upon the door, and then opened it. Fal Sivas was not there, but I heard his voice coming from beyond the little door at the opposite end of the room.

"Who's that? What do you want? Get out of here and do not disturb me," he cried.

"It is I, Vandor," I replied. "I must see you at once."

"No, no, go away; I will see you in the morning."

"You will see me now," I said; "I am coming in there."

I was halfway across the room, when the door opened and Fal Sivas, livid with rage, stepped into the room and closed the door behind him.

"You dare? You dare?" he cried.

"Gar Nal's ship is not in its hangar," I said.

That seemed to bring him to his senses, but it did not lessen his rage; it only turned it in another direction.

"The calot!" he exclaimed, "the son of a thousand million calots! He has beaten me. He will go to Thuria. With the great wealth that he will bring back, he will do all that I had hoped to do."

"Yes," I said. "Ur Jan is with him, and what such a combination as Ur Jan and a great and unscrupulous scientist could do is incalculable; but you too have a ship, Fal Sivas. It is ready. You and I could go to Thuria. They would not suspect that we were coming. We would have all the advantage. We could destroy Gar Nal and his ship, and then you would be master."

He paled. "No, no," he said, "I can't. I can't do it."

"Why not?" I demanded.

"Thuria is a long way. No one knows what might happen. Perhaps something would go wrong with the ship. It might not work in practice as it should in theory. There might be strange beasts and terrible men on Thuria."

"But you built this ship to go to Thuria," I cried. "You told me so, yourself."

"It was a dream," he mumbled; "I am always dreaming, for in dreams nothing bad can happen to me; but in Thuria—oh, it is so far, so high above Barsoom. What if something happened?"

And now I understood. The man was an arrant coward. He was

allowing his great dream to collapse about his ears because he did not have the courage to undertake the great adventure.

What was I to do? I had been depending upon Fal Sivas, and now he had failed me. "I cannot understand you," I said; "with your own arguments, you convinced me that it would be a simple thing to go to Thuria in your ship. What possible danger can confront us there that we may not overcome? We shall be veritable giants on Thuria. No creature that lives there could withstand us. With the stamp of a foot, we could crush the lives from the greatest beasts that Thuria could support."

I had been giving this matter considerable thought ever since there first appeared a likelihood that I might go to Thuria. I am no scientist, and my figures may not be accurate, but they are approximately true. I knew that the diameter of Thuria was supposed to be about seven miles, so that its volume could be only about two per cent of that of, let us say, the Earth, that you may have a comparison that will be more understandable to you.

I estimated that if there were human beings on Thuria and they were proportioned to their environment as man on Earth is to his, they would be but about nine and a half inches tall and weigh between four and five pounds; and that an earth-man transported to Mars would be able to jump 225 feet into the air, make a standing broad jump of 450 feet and a running broad jump of 725 feet, and that a strong man could lift a mass equivalent to a weight of 4½ tons on earth. Against such a Titan, the tiny creatures of Thuria would be helpless—provided, of course, that Thuria were inhabited.

I suggested all this to Fal Sivas, but he shook his head impatiently. "There is something that you do not know," he said. "Perhaps Gar Nal, himself, does not know it. There is a peculiar relationship between Barsoom and her moons that does not exist between any of the other planets in the solar system and their satellites. The suggestion was made by an obscure scientist thousands of years ago, and then it seemed to have been forgotten. I discovered it in an ancient manuscript that I came upon by accident. It is in the original handwriting of the investigator and may have had no distribution whatsoever.

"However, the idea intrigued me; and over a period of twenty years I sought either to prove or disprove it. Eventually, I proved it conclusively."

"And what is it?" I asked.

"There exists between Barsoom and her satellites a peculiar relation which I have called a compensatory adjustment of masses. For example, let us consider a mass travelling from Barsoom to Thuria. As it approaches the nearer moon, it varies directly as the influences of the planet and the satellite vary. The ratio of the mass to the mass of Barsoom at the surface of Barsoom, therefore, would be the same as the ratio of the mass to the mass of Thuria, at the surface of Thuria.

"You were about right in assuming that an inhabitant of Thuria, if such exists, if he were of the same proportion to Thuria as you are to Barsoom, would be about eight sofs tall; and consequently, if my theory is correct, and I have no reason to doubt it, were you to travel from Barsoom to Thuria you would be but eight sofs tall when you reached the surface of the moon."

"Preposterous!" I exclaimed.

He flushed angrily. "You are nothing but an ignorant assassin," he cried. "How dare you question the knowledge of Fal Sivas? But enough of this; return to your quarters. I must get on with my work."

"I am going to Thuria," I said; "and if you won't go with me, I shall go alone."

He had turned back to enter his little laboratory, but I had followed him and was close behind him.

"Go away from here," he said; "keep out, or I will have you killed."

Just then I heard a cry from the room behind him, and a woman's voice calling, "Vandor! Vandor, save me!"

Fal Sivas went livid and tried to dash into the room and close the door in my face, but I was too quick for him. I leaped to the door and pushed him aside as I stepped in.

A terrible sight met my eyes. On marble slabs, raised about four feet from the floor, several women were securely strapped, so that they could not move a limb or raise their heads. There were four of them. Portions of the skulls of three had been removed, but they were still conscious. I could see their frightened, horrified eyes turn toward us.

I turned upon Fal Sivas. "What is the meaning of this?" I cried. "What hellish business are you up to?"

"Get out! Get out!" he screamed. "How dare you invade the holy precincts of science? Who are you, dog, worm, to question what Fal Sivas does; to interfere with the work of a brain the magnitude of which you cannot conceive? Get out! Get out! or I will have you killed."

"And who will kill me?" I demanded. "Put these poor creatures out of their misery, and then I will attend to you."

So great was either his rage or his terror, or both, that he trembled all over like a man with the palsy; and then, before I could stop him, he turned and darted from the room.

I knew that he had gone for help; that presently I should probably have all the inmates of his hellish abode upon me.

I might have pursued him, but I was afraid that something might happen here while I was gone, and so I turned back to the girl on the fourth slab. It was Zanda.

I stepped quickly to her side. I saw that she had not yet been subjected to Fal Sivas's horrid operation, and drawing my dagger I cut the bonds that held her. She slipped from the table and threw her arms about my neck. "Oh, Vandor, Vandor," she cried, "now we must both die. They come! I hear them."

chapter XIII

PURSUED

HERALDING THE APPROACH of armed men was the clank of metal on metal. How many were coming, I did not know; but here I was with only my own sword between me and death and my back against the wall.

Zanda was without hope, but she remained cool and did not lose her head. In those few brief moments I could see that she was courageous.

"Give me your dagger, Vandor," she said.

"Why?" I asked.

"They will kill you, but Fal Sivas shall not have me nor these others to torture further."

"I am not dead, yet," I reminded her.

"I shall not kill myself until you are dead; but these others, there is no hope for them. They pray for merciful death. Let me put them out of their misery."

I winced at the thought, but I knew that she was right, and I handed her my dagger. It was a thing that I should have had to have done myself. It took much more courage than facing armed men, and I was glad to be relieved of the ghastly job.

Zanda was behind me now. I could not see what she was doing, and I never asked her what she did.

Our enemies had paused in the outer room. I could hear them whispering together. Then Fal Sivas raised his voice and shouted to me.

"Come out of there and give yourself up," he screamed, "or we will come in and kill you."

I did not reply; I just stood there, waiting. Presently Zanda came close to me and whispered, "There is a door on the opposite side of this room, hidden behind a large screen. If you wait here, Fal Sivas will send men to that door; and they will attack you from in front and behind."

"I shall not wait, then," I said, moving toward the door leading into the outer room where I had heard my enemies whispering.

Zanda laid a hand upon my arm, "Just a moment, Vandor," she said. "You remain where you are, facing the door; and I will go to it and swing it open suddenly. Then they cannot take you by surprise, as they could if you were to open it."

The door was hinged so that it swung in, and thus Zanda would be protected as she drew it inward and stepped behind it.

Zanda stepped forward and grasped the handle while I stood directly in front of the door and a few paces from it, my long-sword in my hand.

As she opened the door, a sword flashed inward in a terrific cut that would have split my skull had I been there.

The man who wielded the sword was Hamas. Just behind him, I saw Phystal and another armed man, while in the rear was Fal Sivas.

Now the old inventor commenced to scream at them and urge them on; but they held back, for only one man could pass through the doorway at a time; and none of them seemed to relish the idea of being the first. In fact, Hamas had leaped back immediately following his cut; and now his voice joined with that of Fal Sivas in exhorting the other two to enter the laboratory and destroy me.

"On, men!" cried Hamas. "We are three, and he is only one. Onward, you, Phystal! Kill the calot!"

"In with you, yourself, Hamas," growled Phystal.

"Go in! Go in and get him!" shrieked Fal Sivas. "Go in, you cowards." But no one came in; they just stood there, each urging the other to be first.

I did not relish this waste of time, and for two reasons. In the first place, I could not abide the thought of even a moment's unnecessary delay in starting out upon my quest for Dejah Thoris; and, secondly, there was always the danger that reinforcements might arrive. Therefore, if they would not come in to me, I would have to go out to them.

And I did go out to them, and so suddenly that it threw them into confusion. Hamas and Phystal, in their efforts to avoid me, fell back upon the man behind them. He was only a slave, but he was a brave man—the bravest of the four that faced me.

He pushed Phystal and Hamas roughly aside and sprang at me with his long-sword.

Fal Sivas shouted encouragement to him.

"Kill him, Wolak!" he shrieked; "kill him and you shall have your freedom."

At that, Wolak rushed me determinedly. I was fighting for my life, but he was fighting for that and something even sweeter than life; and now Hamas and Phystal were creeping in on me—like two cowardly jackals, they hovered at the edge of the fight, waiting to rush in when they might do so without endangering themselves.

"Your weight in gold, Wolak, if you kill him," screamed Fal Sivas.

Freedom and wealth! Now, indeed, did my antagonist seem inspired. Life, liberty, and riches! What a princely reward for which to strive; but I, too, was fighting for a priceless treasure, for my incomparable Dejah Thoris.

The impetuosity of the man's attack had driven me back a couple of paces, so that I now stood at the doorway, which was really a most strategic position in that it prevented either Hamas or Phystal from attacking me from the side.

Just behind me stood Zanda, spurring me on with low words of encouragement; but though I appreciated them, I did not need them. I was already set to terminate the affair as quickly as possible.

The edge of a Martian long-sword is just as keen as a razor, and the point needle-like in sharpness. It is a trick to preserve this keen edge during a combat, taking the blows of your adversary's weapon on the back of your blade; and I prided myself upon my ability to do this, saving the keen cutting edge for the purpose for which it is intended. I needed a sharp edge now, for I was preparing to execute a little trick that I had successfully used many times before.

My adversary was a good swordsman and exceptionally strong on defense; so that, in ordinary swordplay, he might have prolonged the duel for a considerable time. For this, I had no mind. I wished to end it at once.

In preparation, I pushed him back; then I thrust at his face. He did the very thing that I knew he would do. He threw his head back, involuntarily, to avoid my point; and this brought his chin up exposing his throat. With my blade still extended, I cut quickly from right to left. The point of my sword moved but a few inches, but its keen edge opened his throat almost from ear to ear.

I shall never forget the look of horror in his eyes as he staggered back and crumpled to the floor.

Then I turned my attention to Hamas and Phystal.

Each of them wanted the other to have the honor of engaging me. As they retreated, they made futile passes at me with their points; and I was steadily pushing them into a corner when Fal Sivas took a hand in the affair.

Heretofore, he had contented himself with screaming shrill encouragement and commands to his men. Now he picked up a vase and hurled it at my head.

Just by chance, I saw it coming and dodged it; and it broke into a thousand fragments against the wall. Then he picked up something else and threw at me, and this time he hit my sword hand, and Phystal nearly got me then.

As I jumped back to avoid his thrust, Fal Sivas hurled another small object; and from the corner of my eye I saw Zanda catch it.

Neither Phystal nor Hamas was a good swordsman, and I could easily have overcome them in fair fight, but I could see that these new tactics of Fal Sivas were almost certain to prove my undoing. If I turned upon him, the others would be behind me; and how they would have taken advantage of such a God-given opportunity!

I tried to work them around so that they were between Fal Sivas and myself. In this way, they would shield me from his missiles, but that is something easier said than done when you are fighting two men in a comparatively small room.

I was terribly handicapped by the fact that I had to watch three men; and now, as I drove Hamas back with a cut, I cast a quick glance in the direction of Fal Sivas; and as I did so, I saw a missile strike him between the eyes. He fell to the floor like a log. Zanda had hoisted him with his own petard.

I could not repress a smile as I turned my undivided attention upon Hamas and Phystal.

As I drove them into a corner, Hamas surprised me by throwing his sword aside and falling upon his knees.

"Spare me, spare me, Vandor!" he cried; "I did not want to attack you. Fal Sivas made me." And then Phystal cast his weapon to the floor; and he, too, went upon his marrow bones. It was the most revolting exhibition of cowardice that I had ever witnessed. I felt like running them through, but I did not want to foul my blade with their putrid blood.

"Kill them," counseled Zanda; "you cannot trust either of them."

I shook my head. "We cannot kill unarmed men in cold blood," I said.

"Unless you do, they will prevent our escape," she said, "even if we can escape. There are others who will stop us on the lower level."

"I have a better plan, Zanda," I said, and forthwith I bound Hamas and Phystal securely in their own harness and then did the same with Fal Sivas, for he was not dead but only stunned. I also gagged all three of them so that they could not cry out.

This done, I told Zanda to follow me and went at once to the hangar where the ship rested on her scaffolding.

"Why did you come here?" asked Zanda. "We ought to be getting out of the building as quickly as possible—you are going to take me with you, aren't you, Vandor?"

"Certainly I am," I said, "and we are going out of the building very shortly. Come, perhaps I shall need your help with these doors," and I led the way to the two great doors in the end of the hangar. They were well hung, however, and after being unlatched, slid easily to the sides of the opening.

Zanda stepped to the threshold and looked out. "We cannot escape this way," she said; "it is fifty feet to the ground, and there is no ladder or other means of descent."

"Nevertheless, we are going to escape through that doorway," I told her, amused at her mystification. "Just come with me, and you will see how."

We returned to the side of the ship, and I must say that I was far from being as assured of success as I tried to pretend, as I concentrated my thoughts upon the little metal sphere that held the mechanical brain in the nose of the craft.

I think my heart stopped beating as I waited, and then a great wave of relief surged through me as I saw the door open and the ladder lowering itself toward the floor.

Zanda looked on in wide-eyed amazement. "Who is in there?" she demanded.

"No one," I said. "Now up with you, and be quick about it. We have no time to loiter here."

She was evidently afraid, but she obeyed me like a good soldier, and I followed her up the ladder into the cabin. Then I directed the brain to hoist the ladder and close the door, as I went forward into the control room, followed by the girl.

Here I again focused my thoughts upon the mechanical brain just above my head. Even with the demonstration that I had already had, I could not yet convince myself of the reality of what I was doing. It seemed impossible that that insensate thing could raise the craft from its scaffolding and guide it safely through the doorway, yet scarcely had I supplied that motivating thought when the ship rose a few feet and moved almost silently toward the aperture.

As we passed out into the still night, Zanda threw her arms about my neck. "Oh, Vandor, Vandor!" she cried; "you have saved me from the clutches of that horrible creature. I am free! I am free again!" she cried, hysterically. "Oh, Vandor, I am yours; I shall be your slave forever. Do with me whatever you will."

I could see that she was distraught and hysterical.

"You are excited, Zanda," I said, soothingly. "You owe me nothing.

You are a free woman. You do not have to be my slave or the slave of any other."

"I want to be your slave, Vandor," she said, and then in a very low voice, "I love you."

Gently I disengaged her arms from about my neck. "You do not know what you are saying, Zanda," I told her; "your gratitude has carried you away. You must not love me; my heart belongs to someone else, and there is another reason why you must not say that you love me—a reason that you will learn sooner or later, and then you will wish that you had been stricken dumb before you ever told me that you loved me."

I was thinking of her hatred of John Carter and her avowed desire to kill him.

"I do not know what you mean," she said; "but if you tell me not to love you, I will try to obey you, for no matter what you say, I am your slave. I owe my life to you, and I shall always be your slave."

"We will talk about that some other time," I said; "just now I have something to tell you that may make you wish that I had left you in the house of Fal Sivas."

She knitted her brows and looked at me questioningly. "Another mystery?" she asked. "Again you speak in riddles."

"We are going on a long and dangerous journey in this ship, Zanda. I am forced to take you with me because I cannot risk detection by landing you anywhere in Zodanga; and, of course, it would be signing your death warrant to set you down far beyond the walls of the city."

"I do not want to be set down in Zodanga or outside it," she replied. "Wherever you are going, I want to go with you. Some day you may need me, Vandor; and then you will be glad that I am along."

"Do you know where we are going, Zanda?" I asked.

"No," she said, "and I do not care. It would make no difference to me, even if you were going to Thuria."

I smiled at that, and turned my attention again to the mechanical brain, directing it to take us to the spot where Jat Or waited; and just then I heard the wailing signal of a patrol boat above us.

ALTHOUGH I had realized the likelihood of our strange craft being discovered by a patrol boat, I had hoped that we might escape from the city without detection. I knew that if we did not obey their command they would open fire on us, and a single hit might put an end to all my plans to reach Thuria and save Dejah Thoris.

While the armament of the ship, as described to me by Fal Sivas, would have given me an overwhelming advantage in an encounter with any patrol boat, I hesitated to stand and fight, because of the chance that a lucky shot from the enemy's ship might disable us.

Fal Sivas had boasted of the high potential speed of his brain conception; and I decided that however much I might dislike to flee from an enemy, flight was the safest course to pursue.

Zanda had her face pressed to one of the numerous ports in the hull of the ship. The wail of the patrol boat siren was now continuous— an eerie, menacing voice in the night, that pierced the air like sharp daggers.

"They are overhauling us, Vandor," said Zanda; "and they are signalling other patrol boats to their aid."

"They have probably noticed the strange lines of this craft; and not only their curiosity, but their suspicion has been aroused."

"What are you going to do?" she asked.

"We are going to put the speed of Fal Sivas's motor to a test," I replied.

I glanced up at the insensate metal sphere above my head. "Speed up! Faster! Escape the pursuing patrol boat!" Such were the directing thoughts that I imparted to the silent thing above me; then I waited.

I did not, however, have long to wait. No sooner had my thoughts impinged upon the sensitive mechanism than the accelerated whirr of the almost noiseless motor told me that my directions had been obeyed.

"She is no longer gaining on us," cried Zanda excitedly. "We have leaped ahead; we are outdistancing her."

The swift staccato of rapid fire burst upon our ears. Our enemy had opened fire upon us, and almost simultaneously, intermingling with the shots, we heard in the distance the wail of other sirens apprising us of the fact that reinforcements were closing in upon us.

The swift rush of the thin air of Mars along the sides of our ship attested our terrific speed. The lights of the city faded swiftly behind us. The searchlights of the patrol boats were rapidly diminishing bands of light across the starlit sky.

I do not know how fast we were going but probably in the neighborhood of 1350 haads an hour.

We sped low above the ancient sea bottom that lies west of Zodanga; and then, in a matter of about five minutes—it could not have been much more—our speed slackened rapidly, and I saw a small flier floating idly in the still air just ahead of us.

I knew that it must be the flier upon which Jat Or awaited me, and I directed the brain to bring our ship alongside it and stop.

The response of the ship to my every thought direction was uncanny; and when we came alongside of Jat Or's craft and seemingly ghostly hands opened the door in the side of our ship, I experienced a brief sensation of terror, as though I were in the power of some soulless Frankenstein; and this notwithstanding the fact that every move of the ship had been in response to my own direction.

Jat Or stood on the narrow deck of his small flier gazing in astonishment at the strange craft that had drawn alongside.

"Had I not been expecting this," he said, "I should have been streaking it for Helium by now. It is a sinister-looking affair with those great eyes giving it the appearance of some unworldly monster."

"You will find that impression intensified when you have been aboard her for a while," I told him. "She is very 'unworldly' in many respects."

"Do you want me to come aboard now?" he asked.

"Yes," I replied, "after we make disposition of your flier."

"What shall we do with it?" he asked. "Are you going to abandon it?"

"Set your destination compass on Helium, and open your throttle to half speed. When you are under way, we will come alongside again and take you aboard. One of the patrol boats at Helium will pick up the flier and return it to my hangar."

He did as I had bid, and I directed the brain to take us alongside of him after he had gotten under way. A moment later he stepped into the cabin of Fal Sivas's craft.

"Comfortable," he commented; "the old boy must be something of a Sybarite."

"He believed in being comfortable," I replied, "but love of luxury has softened his fibre to such an extent that he was afraid to venture abroad in his ship after he had completed it."

Jat Or turned to look about the cabin, and it chanced that his eyes fell upon the doors in the side of the ship just as I directed the brain to close them. He voiced an ejaculation of astonishment.

"In the name of my first ancestor," he exclaimed, "who is closing those doors? I don't see anyone, and you have not moved or touched any sort of operating device since I came aboard."

"Come forward into the control room," I said, "and you shall see the entire crew of this craft reposing in a metal case not much larger than your fist."

As we entered the control room, Jat Or saw Zanda for the first time. I could see his surprise reflected in his eyes, but he was too well bred to offer any comment.

"This is Zanda, Jat Or," I said. "Fal Sivas was about to remove her skull in the interests of science when I interrupted him this evening. The poor girl was forced to choose between the lesser of two evils; that is why she is with me."

"That statement is a little misleading," said Zanda. "Even if my life had not been in danger and I had been surrounded by every safe-guard and luxury, I would still have chosen to go with Vandor, even to the end of the universe."

"You see, Jat Or," I remarked, with a smile, "the young lady does not know me very well; when she does, she will very probably change her mind."

"Never," said Zanda.

"Wait and see," I cautioned her.

On our trip from Helium to Zodanga, I had explained to Jat Or the marvellous mechanism that Fal Sivas called a mechanical brain; and I could see the young padwar's eyes searching the interior of the control room for this marvellous invention.

"There it is," I said, pointing at the metal sphere slightly above his head in the nose of the craft.

"And that little thing drives the ship and opens the doors?" he asked.

"The motors drive the ship, Jat Or," I told him, "and other motors operate the doors and perform various other mechanical duties aboard the craft. The mechanical brain merely operates them as our brains would direct our hands to certain duties."

"That thing thinks?" he demanded.

"To all intents and purposes, it functions as would a human brain, the only difference being that it cannot originate thought."

The padwar stood gazing at the thing in silence for several moments. "It gives me a strange feeling," he said at last, "a helpless feeling, as though I were in the power of some creature that was omnipotent and yet could not reason."

"I have much the same sensation," I admitted, "and I cannot help but speculate upon what it might do if it could reason."

"I, too, tremble to think of it," said Zanda, "if Fal Sivas has imparted to it any of the heartless ruthlessness of his own mind."

"It is his creature," I reminded her.

"Then let us hope that it may never originate a thought."

"That, of course, would be impossible," said Jat Or.

"I do not know about that," replied Zanda. "Such a thing was in Fal Sivas's mind. He was, I know, working to that end; but whether he succeeded in imparting the power of original thought to this thing, I do not know. I know that he not only hoped to accomplish this miracle eventually, but that he was planning also to impart powers of speech to this horrible invention."

"Why do you call it horrible?" asked Jat Or.

"Because it is inhuman and unnatural," replied the girl. "Nothing good could come out of the mind of Fal Sivas. The thing you see there was conceived in hate and lust and greed, and it was contrived for the satisfaction of such characteristics in Fal Sivas. No ennobling or lofty thoughts went into its fabrication; and none could emanate from it, had it the power of original thought."

"But our purpose is lofty and honorable," I reminded her; "and if it serves us in the consummation of our hope, it will have accomplished good."

"Nevertheless, I fear it," replied Zanda. "I hate it because it reminds me of Fal Sivas."

"I hope that it is not meditating upon these candid avowals," remarked Jat Or.

Zanda slapped an open palm across her lips, her wide eyes reflecting a new terror. "I had not thought of that," she whispered. "Perhaps this very minute it is planning its revenge."

I could not but laugh at her fear. "If any harm befalls us through that brain, Zanda," I said, "you may lay the blame at my door, for it is my mind that shall actuate it as long as the ship remains in my possession."

"I hope you are right," she said, "and that it will bear us safely wherever you wish to go."

"And suppose we get to Thuria alive?" interjected Jat Or. "You know I have been wondering about that. I have been giving the matter considerable thought, naturally, since you said that that was to be our destination; and I am wondering how we will fare on that tiny satellite. We shall be so out of proportion in size to anything that we may find there."

"Perhaps we shall not be," I said, and then I explained to him the theory of compensatory adjustment of masses as Fal Sivas had expounded it to me.

"It sounds preposterous," said Jat Or.

I shrugged. "It does to me, too," I admitted; "but no matter how much we may abhor Fal Sivas's character, we cannot deny the fact that he has a marvellous scientific brain; and I am going to hold my opinion in abeyance until we reach the surface of Thuria."

"At least," said Jat Or, "no matter what the conditions there may be, the abductors of the princess will have no advantage over us if we find them there."

"Do you doubt that we shall find them?" I asked.

"It is merely a matter of conjecture, one way or another," he replied; "but it does not seem within the realms of possibility that two inventors, working independently of one another, could each have conceived and built two identical ships capable of crossing the airless void between here and Thuria, under the guidance of mechanical brains."

"But as far as I know," I replied, "Gar Nal's craft is not so operated. Fal Sivas does not believe that Gar Nal has produced such a brain. He does not believe that the man has even conceived the possibility of one, and so we may assume that Gar Nal's craft is operated by Gar Nal, or at least wholly by human means."

"Then which ship has the better chance to reach Thuria?" asked Jat Or.

"According to Fal Sivas," I replied, "there can be no question about that. This mechanical brain of his cannot make mistakes."

"If we accept that," said Jat Or, "then we must also accept the possibility of Gar Nal's human brain erring in some respects in its calculations."

"What do you mean by that?" I asked.

"It just occurred to me that through some error in calculations Gar Nal might not reach Thuria; whereas, directed by an errorless brain, we are certain to."

"I had not thought of that," I said. "I was so obsessed by the thought that Gar Nal and Ur Jan were taking their victim to Thuria that I never gave a thought to the possibility that they might not be able to get there."

The idea distressed me, for I realized how hopeless my quest must be if we reached Thuria only to find that Dejah Thoris was not there. Where could I look for her? Where could I hope to find her in the illimitable reaches of space? But I soon cast these thoughts from me, for worry is a destructive force that I have tried to eliminate from my philosophy of life.

Zanda looked at me with a puzzled expression. "We are really going to Thuria?" she asked. "I do not understand why anyone should want to go to Thuria; but I am content to go, if you go. When do we start, Vandor?"

"We are well on our way, now," I replied. "The moment that Jat Or came aboard, I directed the brain to head for Thuria at full speed."

chapter XV

THURIA

LATER, as we hurtled on through the cold, dark reaches of space, I urged Zanda and Jat Or to lie down and rest.

Although we had no sleeping silks and furs we should not suffer, as the temperature of the cabin was comfortable. I had directed the brain to control this, as well as the oxygen supply, after we left the surface of Barsoom.

There were narrow but comfortable divans in the cabin, as well as a number of soft pillows; so there was no occasion for any of us suffering during the trip.

We had left Barsoom about the middle of the eighth zode, which is equivalent to midnight earthtime; and a rather rough computation of the distance to be travelled and our estimated speed, suggested that we should arrive on Thuria about noon of the following day.

Jat Or wanted to stand watch the full time, but I insisted that we must each get some sleep; so, on my promise to awaken him at the end of five hours, he lay down.

While my two companions slept, I made a more careful examination of the interior of the ship than I had been able to do at the time that Fal Sivas had conducted me through it.

I found it well supplied with food, and in a chest in the storeroom I also discovered sleeping silks and furs; but, of course, what interested me most of all were the weapons. There were long-swords, short-swords, and daggers, as well as a number of the remarkable Barsoomian radium rifles and pistols, together with a considerable quantity of ammunition for both.

Fal Sivas seemed to have forgotten nothing, yet all his thought and care and efficiency would have gone for nothing had I not been able to seize the ship. His own cowardice would have prevented him from using it; and of course he would not have permitted another to take it out, even had he believed that another brain than his could have operated it, which he had been confident was not possible.

My inspection of the ship completed, I went into the control room and looked out through one of the great eyes. The heavens were a black void shot with cold and glittering points of light. How different the stars looked when one had passed beyond the atmosphere of the planet.

I looked for Thuria. She was nowhere in sight. The discovery was a distinct shock. Had the mechanical brain failed us? While I was wasting my time inspecting the ship, was it bearing us off into some remote corner of space?

I am not inclined to lose my head and become hysterical when confronted by an emergency; nor, except when instant action is required, do I take snap judgment. I am more inclined to think things out carefully, and so I sat down on a bench in the control room to work out my problem.

Just then Jat Or came in. "How long have I been sleeping?" he asked.

"Not long," I replied; "you had better go back and get all the rest that you can."

"I am not sleepy," he said. "In fact it is rather difficult to contemplate sleep when one is in the midst of such a thrilling adventure. Think of it, my prince—"

"Vandor," I reminded him.

"Sometimes I forget," he said; "but, anyway, as I was saying, think of the possibilities; think of the tremendous possibilities of this adventure; think of our situation."

"I have been thinking of it," I replied a little gloomily.

"In a few hours we shall be where no other Barsoomian has ever been—upon Thuria."

"I am not so sure of that," I replied.

"What do you mean?" he asked.

"Take a look ahead," I told him. "Do you see anything of Thuria?"

He looked out of one of the round ports and then turned to the other. "I don't see Thuria," he said.

"Neither do I," I replied. "And do you realize what that suggests?"

He looked stunned for a moment. "You mean that we are not bound for Thuria—that the brain has erred?"

"I don't know," I replied.

"How far is it from Barsoom to Thuria?" he asked.

"A little over 15,700 haads," I replied. "I estimated that we should complete the trip in about five zodes."

Just then Thuria hurtled into view upon our right, and Jat Or voiced an exclamation of relief. "I have it," he exclaimed.

"What?" I asked.

"Your mechanical brain is functioning better than ours," he replied. "During the ten zodes of a Barsoomian day, Thuria revolves about our planet over three times; so while we were travelling to the path of her orbit she would encircle Barsoom one and a half times."

"And you think the mechanical brain has reasoned that out?"

"Unquestionably," he said; "and it will time our arrival to meet the satellite in its path."

I scratched my head. "This raises another question that I had not thought of before," I said.

"What is that?" asked Jat Or.

"The speed of our ship is approximately 3250 haads per zode, whereas Thuria is travelling at a rate of over 41,250 haads during the same period."

Jat Or whistled. "Over twelve and a half times our speed," he exclaimed. "How in the name of our first ancestor are we going to catch her?"

I made a gesture of resignation. "I imagine we shall have to leave that to the brain," I said.

"I hope it doesn't get us in the path of that hurtling mass of destruction," said Jat Or.

"Just how would you make a landing if you were operating the ship with your own brain?" I asked.

"We've got to take Thuria's force of gravity into consideration," he said.

"That is just it," I replied. "When we get into the sphere of her influence, we shall be pulled along at the same rate she is going; and then we can make a natural landing."

Jat Or was looking out at the great orb of Thuria on our right. "How perfectly tremendous she looks," he said. "It doesn't seem possible that we have come close enough to make her look as large as that."

"You forget," I said, "that as we approached her, we commenced to grow smaller—to proportion ourselves to her size. When we reach her surface, if we ever do, she will seem as large to us as Barsoom does when we are on its surface."

"It all sounds like a mad dream to me," said Jat Or.

"I fully agree with you," I replied, "but you will have to admit that it is going to be a most interesting dream."

As we sped on through space, Thuria hurtled across our bow and eventually disappeared below the Eastern rim of the planet that lay now so far below us. Doubtless, when she completed another revolution, we should be within the sphere of her influence. Then, and not until then, would we know the outcome of this phase of our adventure.

I insisted now that Jat Or return to the cabin and get a few hours' sleep, for none of us knew what lay in the future and to what extent our reserves of strength, both physical and mental, might be called upon.

Later on, I called Jat Or and lay down myself to rest. Through it all, Zanda slept peacefully; nor did she awaken until after I had had my sleep and returned to the control room.

Jat Or was sitting with his face glued to the starboard eye. He did not look back at me, but evidently he heard me enter the cabin.

"She is coming," he said in a tense whisper. "Issus! What a magnificent and inspiring sight!"

I went to the port and looked out over his shoulder. There before me was a great world, one crescent edge illuminated by the sun beyond it. Vaguely I thought that I saw the contour of mountains and valleys, lighter expanses that might have been sandy desert or dead sea bottom, and dark masses that could have been forests. A new world! A world that no earthman nor any Barsoomian had ever visited.

I could have been thrilled beyond the power of words to express at the thought of the adventure that lay before me had my mind not been so overcast by fear for the fate of my princess. Thoughts of her dominated all others, yet they did not crowd out entirely the sense of magnificent mystery that the sight of this new world aroused within me.

Zanda joined us now; and as she saw Thuria looming ahead, she voiced a little exclamation of thrilled excitement. "We are very close," she said.

I nodded. "It will not be long now before we know our fate," I said. "Are you afraid?"

"Not while you are with me," she answered simply.

Presently I realized that we had changed our course. Thuria seemed directly beneath us now instead of straight ahead. We were within the sphere of her influence, and were being dragged through space at her own tremendous velocity. Now we were spiralling downward; the brain was functioning perfectly.

"I don't like the idea of landing on a strange world at night," said Jat Or.

"I am not so enthusiastic about it myself," I agreed. "I think we had better wait until morning."

I then directed the brain to drop to within about two hundred haads of the surface of the satellite and cruise slowly in the direction of the coming dawn.

"And now, suppose we eat while we are waiting for daylight," I suggested.

"Is there food on board, master?" inquired Zanda.

"Yes," I replied, "you will find it in the storeroom abaft the cabin."

"I will prepare it, master, and serve you in the cabin," she said.

As she left the control room, Jat Or's eyes followed her. "She does not seem like a slave," he said, "and yet she addresses you as though she were your slave."

"I have told her that she is not," I said, "but she insists upon maintaining that attitude. She was a prisoner in the house of Fal Sivas, and she was assigned to me there to be my slave. She really is the daughter of a lesser noble—a well-bred, intelligent, cultured girl."

"And very beautiful," said Jat Or. "I think she loves you, my prince."

"Perhaps she thinks it is love," I said, "but it is only gratitude. If she knew who I were, even her gratitude would be turned to hate. She has sworn to kill John Carter."

"But why?" demanded Jat Or.

"Because he conquered Zodanga; because all her sorrows resulted from the fall of the city. Her father was killed; and, in grief, her mother took the last long journey upon the bosom of Iss; so you see she has good reason to hate John Carter, or at least she thinks she has."

Presently Zanda called us, and we went into the cabin where she had a meal spread upon a folding table.

She stood to wait upon us, but I insisted that she sit with us and eat.

"It is not seemly," she said, "that a slave should sit with her master."

"Again I tell you that you are not my slave, Zanda," I said. "If you insist upon retaining this ridiculous attitude, I shall have to give you away. Perhaps I shall give you to Jat Or. How would you like that?"

She looked up at the handsome young padwar seated opposite her. "Perhaps he would make a good master," she said, "but I shall be slave to no one but Vandor."

"But how could you help it if I gave you to him?" I asked. "What would you do about it?"

"I would kill either Jat Or or myself," she replied.

I laughed and stroked her hand. "I would not give you away if I could," I said.

"If you could?" she demanded. "Why can't you?"

"Because I cannot give away a free woman. I told you once that you were free, and now I tell you again in the presence of a witness. You know the customs of Barsoom, Zanda. You are free now, whether you wish to be or not."

"I do not wish to be free," she said; "but if it is your will, Vandor, so be it." She was silent for a moment, and then she looked up at me. "If I am not your slave," she asked, "what am I?"

"Just at present, you are a fellow adventurer," I replied, "an equal, to share in the joys and sorrows of whatever may lie before us."

"I am afraid that I shall be more of a hindrance than a help," she said, "but of course I can cook for you and minister to you. At least I can do those things which are a woman's province."

"Then you will be more of a help than a hindrance," I told her. "And to make sure that we shall not lose you, I shall detail Jat Or to be your protector. He shall be responsible for your safety."

I could see that this pleased Jat Or, but I could not tell about Zanda. I thought she looked a little hurt; but she flashed a quick sweet smile at the young padwar, as though she were afraid he might have guessed her disappointment and did not wish to hurt him.

As we cruised low over Thuria, I saw forests below us and meandering lines of a lighter color that I took to be brooks or rivers; and in the distance there were mountains. It seemed a most beautiful and intriguing world.

I could not be sure about the water because it was generally believed on Barsoom that her satellites were practically without moisture. However, I have known scientists to be mistaken.

I was becoming impatient. It seemed that daylight would never arrive, but at last the first rosy flush of dawn crept up behind the mountain tops ahead of us; and slowly the details of this strange world took form below us, as the scene in a photographic print takes magic form beneath the developer.

We were looking down upon a forested valley, beyond which low foothills, carpeted with lush vegetation, ran back to higher mountains in the distance.

The colors were similar to those upon Barsoom—the scarlet grasses, the gorgeous, strange-hued trees; but as far as our vision reached, we saw no living thing.

"There must be life there," said Zanda, when Jat Or commented upon this fact. "In all that wealth of beauty, there must be living eyes to see and to admire."

"Are we going to land?" asked Jat Or.

"We came here to find Gar Nal's ship," I replied, "and we must search for that first."

"It will be like looking for a tiny bead among the moss of a dead sea bottom," said Jat Or.

I nodded. "I am afraid so," I said, "but we have come for that purpose and that purpose alone."

"Look!" exclaimed Zanda. "What is that—there, ahead?"

LOOKING DOWN in the direction that Zanda had indicated, I saw what appeared to be a large building on the bank of a river. The structure nestled in a clearing in the forest, and where the rising sun touched its towers they sent back scintillant rays of many-hued light.

One section of the building faced upon what appeared to be a walled court, and it was an object lying in this court which aroused our interest and excitement to a far greater extent than the building itself.

"What do you think it is, Zanda?" I asked, for it was she who had discovered it.

"I think that it is Gar Nal's ship," replied the girl.

"What makes you think that?" asked Jat Or.

"Because it is so much like this one," she replied. "Both Gar Nal and Fal Sivas stole ideas from one another whenever they could, and I should be surprised indeed if their ships did not closely resemble one another."

"I am sure that you are right, Zanda," I said. "It is not reasonable to assume that the inhabitants of Thuria have, by some miraculous coincidence, constructed a ship so similar to that of Fal Sivas's; and the possibility is equally remote that a third Barsoomian ship has landed on the satellite."

I directed the brain to spiral downward, and presently we were flying at an altitude that gave us a clear view of the details of the building and the surrounding terrain.

The more closely we approached the ship in the courtyard the more certain we became that it was Gar Nal's; but nowhere did we see any sign of Gar Nal, Ur Jan, or Dejah Thoris; nor, indeed, was there any sign of life about the building or its grounds. The place might have been the abode of the dead.

"I am going to ground the ship beside Gar Nal's," I said. "Look to your weapons, Jat Or."

"They are ready, my—Vandor," he replied.

"I do not know how many fighting men are aboard that ship," I continued. "There may be only Gar Nal and Ur Jan, or there may be more. If the fight goes our way, we must not kill them all until we are positive that the princess is with them.

"They left Barsoom at least a full day ahead of us; and while it is only a remote possibility, still they may have made some disposition of their prisoner already. Therefore, we must leave at least one of them alive to direct us to her."

We were descending slowly. Every eye was on the alert. Zanda had stepped from the control room a moment before, and now she returned with the harness and weapons of a Martian warrior strapped to her slender form.

"Why those?" I asked.

"You may need an extra sword hand," she replied. "You do not know against how many foemen you will be pitted."

"Wear them, if you like," I said, "but remain in the ship where you will be safe. Jat Or and I will take care of the fighting."

"I shall go with you and fight with you," said Zanda, quietly but emphatically.

I shook my head. "No," I said; "you must do as I say and remain on this ship."

She looked me steadily in the eye. "Against my will, you insisted upon making me a free woman," she reminded me. "Now I shall act as a free woman and not as a slave. I shall do as I please."

I had to smile at that. "Very well," I said; "but if you come with us, you will have to take your chances like any other fighting man. Jat Or and I may be too busy with our own antagonists to be able to protect you."

"I can take care of myself," said Zanda, simply.

"Please stay on board," pleaded Jat Or solicitously; but Zanda only shook her head.

Our ship had settled quietly to the ground beside that of Gar Nal. I caused the door in the port side to be opened and the ladder lowered. Still there was no sign of life either on the other craft or elsewhere about the castle. A deathly silence hung like a heavy mantle over the entire scene.

Just a moment I stood in the doorway looking about; and then I descended to the ground, followed by Jat Or and Zanda.

Before us loomed the castle, a strange weird building of unearthly architecture, a building of many towers of various types, some of them standing alone and some engaged in groups.

Partially verifying Fal Sivas's theory of the tremendous mineral wealth of the satellite, the walls of the structure before us were constructed of blocks of precious stones so arranged that their gorgeous hues blended and harmonized into a mass of color that defies description.

At the moment, however, I gave but cursory attention to the beauties of the pile, turning my attention instead to Gar Nal's ship. A door in its side, similar to that in our ship, was open; and a ladder depended to the ground.

I knew that in ascending that ladder, a man would be at great disadvantage if attacked from above; but there was no alternative. I must discover if there were anyone on board.

I asked Zanda to stand at a little distance, so that she could see into the interior of the ship and warn me if an enemy exhibited himself. Then I mounted quickly.

As the ship was already resting on the ground, I had only to ascend a few rungs of the ladder before my eyes were above the level of the cabin floor. A quick glance showed me that no one was in sight, and a moment later I stood inside the cabin of Gar Nal's ship.

The interior arrangement was slightly different from that of Fal Sivas's, nor was the cabin as richly furnished.

From the cabin, I stepped into the control room. No one was there. Then I searched the after part of the ship. The entire craft was deserted.

Returning to the ground, I reported my findings to Jat Or and Zanda.

"It is strange," remarked Jat Or, "that no one has challenged us or paid any attention to our presence. Can it be possible that the whole castle is deserted?"

"There is something eerie about the place," said Zanda, in low, tense tones. "Even the silence seems fraught with suppressed sound. I see no one, I hear no one, and yet I feel—I know not what."

"It *is* mysterious," I agreed. "The deserted appearance of the castle is belied by the well-kept grounds. If there is no one here now, it has not been deserted long."

"I have a feeling that it is not deserted now," said Jat Or. "I seem to feel presences all around us. I could swear that eyes were on us— many eyes, watching our every move."

I was conscious of much the same sensation myself. I looked up at the windows of the castle, fully expecting to see eyes gazing down upon us; but in none of the many windows was there a sign of life. Then I called aloud, voicing the common peace greeting of Barsoom.

"Kaor!" I shouted in tones that could have been heard anywhere upon that side of the castle. "We are travellers from Barsoom. We wish to speak to the lord of the castle."

Silence was my only answer.

"How uncanny!" cried Zanda. "Why don't they answer us? There must be someone here; there *is* someone here. I know it! I cannot see them, but there are people here. They are all around us."

"I am sure that you are right, Zanda," I said. "There must be someone in that castle, and I am going to have a look inside it. Jat Or, you and Zanda wait here."

"I think we should all go together," said the girl.

"Yes," agreed Jat Or; "we must not separate."

I saw no valid objection to the plan, and so I nodded my acquiescence; then I approached a closed door in the face of the castle wall. Behind me came Jat Or and Zanda.

We had crossed about half the distance from the ship to the door, when at last suddenly, startlingly, the silence was shattered by a voice, terror-ridden, coming from above, apparently from one of the lofty towers overlooking the courtyard.

"Escape, my chieftain!" it cried. "Escape from this horrible place while you may."

I halted, momentarily stunned—it was the voice of Dejah Thoris.

"The princess!" exclaimed Jat Or.

"Yes," I said, "the princess. Come!" Then I started on a run toward the door of the castle; but I had taken scarce a half dozen steps, when just behind me Zanda voiced a piercing scream of terror.

I wheeled instantly to see what danger confronted her.

She was struggling as though in the throes of convulsions. Her face was contorted in horror; her staring eyes and the motions of her

arms and legs were such as they might have been had she been battling
with a foe, but she was alone. There was no one near her.

Jat Or and I sprang toward her; but she retreated quickly, still
struggling. Darting to our right, and then doubling back, she moved
in the direction of the doorway in the castle wall.

She seemed not to move by the power of her own muscles but
rather as though she were being dragged away, yet still I saw no one
near her.

All that I take so long to tell, occurred in a few brief seconds—
before I could cover the short distance to her side.

Jat Or had been closer to her; and he had almost overtaken her
when I heard him shout, "Issus! It has me, too."

He went to the ground then as though in a faint, but he was struggling as Zanda struggled—as one who gives battle to an assailant.

As I raced after Zanda my long-sword was out, though I saw no
enemy whose blood it might drink.

Scarcely ever before in my life have I felt so futile, so impotent.
Here was I, the greatest swordsman of two worlds, helpless in defense
of my friends because I could not see their foes.

In the grip of what malign power could they be that could seemingly reach out through space from the concealment of some hidden
vantage point and hold them down or drag them about as it wished?

How helpless we all were, our helplessness all the more accentuated by the psychological effect of this mysterious and uncanny attack.

My earthly muscles quickly brought me to Zanda's side. As I
reached out to seize her and stop her progress toward the castle door,
something seized one of my ankles; and I went down. I felt hands
upon me—many hands. My sword was torn from my grasp; my other
weapons were snatched away.

I fought, perhaps never as I have fought before. I felt the bodies of my antagonists pressing against me. I felt their hands as they touched me and their fists as they struck me; but I saw no one, yet my own blows landed upon solid flesh. That was something. It gave me a little greater sense of equality than before; but I could not understand why, if I felt these creatures, I could not see them.

At least, however, it partially explained the strange actions of Zanda. Her seeming convulsions had been her struggles against these unseen assailants. Now they were carrying her toward the doorway; and as I battled futilely against great odds, I saw her disappear within the castle.

Then the things, whatever they were that assailed me, overpowered me by numbers. I knew that there were very many of them, because there were so many, many hands upon me.

They bound my wrists behind my back and jerked me roughly to my feet.

I cannot accurately describe my sensations; the unreality of all that had occurred in those few moments left me dazed and uncertain. For at least once in my life, I seemed wholly deprived of the power to reason, possibly because the emergency was so utterly foreign to anything that I had ever before experienced. Not even the phantom bowmen of Lothar could have presented so unique a situation, for these were visible when they attacked.

As I was jerked to my feet, I glanced about for Jat Or and saw him near me, his hands similarly trussed behind his back.

Now I felt myself being pushed toward the doorway through which Zanda had disappeared, and near me was Jat Or moving in the same direction.

"Can you see anyone, my prince?" he asked.

"I can see you," I replied.

"What diabolical force is this that has seized us?" he demanded.

"I don't know," I replied, "but I feel hands upon me and the warmth of bodies around me."

"I guess we are done for, my prince," he said.

"Done for?" I exclaimed. "We still live."

"No, I do not mean that," he said; "I mean that as far as ever returning to Barsoom is concerned, we might as well give up all hope. They have our ship. Do you think that even if we escape them, we shall ever see it again, or at least be able to repossess it? No, my friend, as far as Barsoom is concerned we are as good as dead."

The ship! In the excitement of what I had just passed through I had momentarily forgotten the ship. I glanced toward it. I thought that I saw the rope ladder move as though to the weight of an unseen body ascending it.

The ship! It was our only hope of ever again returning to Barsoom, and it was in the hands of this mysterious unseen foe. It must be saved.

There was a way! I centered my thoughts upon the mechanical brain—I directed it to rise and wait above the castle, out of harm's way, until I gave it further commands.

Then the invisible menace dragged me through the doorway into the interior of the castle. I could not know if the brain had responded to my directions.

Was I never to know?

MY THOUGHTS were still centered upon the brain in the nose of Fal Sivas's ship as I was being conducted through a wide corridor in the castle. I was depressed by the fear that I might not have been able to impart my controlling directions to it at so great a distance or while my brain was laboring under the stress and excitement of the moment. The ship meant so much to us all, and was so necessary to the rescue of Dejah Thoris, that the thought of losing it was a stunning blow; yet presently I realized that worrying about it would do no good, and so I expelled these subversive thoughts from my mind.

Raising my eyes, I saw Jat Or moving along the corridor near me. As he caught my eyes upon him, he shook his head and smiled ruefully.

"It looks as though our adventure on Thuria might be short-lived," he said.

I nodded. "The future doesn't look any too bright," I admitted. "I have never been in such a situation before, where I could neither see my enemy nor communicate with him."

"Nor hear him," added Jat Or. "Except for the feel of hands on my arms and the knowledge that some force is dragging me along this corridor, I am not conscious of the presence of any but ourselves here. The mystery of it leaves me with a sense of utter futility."

"But eventually we must find someone whom we can see and against whom we can pit our own brain and fighting ability on a more equable basis, for this castle and what we see about us indicate the presence of creatures not unlike ourselves. Notice, for instance, the benches and divans along the walls of this corridor. They must have been intended for creatures like ourselves. The beautiful mosaics that decorate the walls, the gorgeous rugs and skins upon the floor—these things are here to satisfy a love of beauty that is a peculiar attribute of the human mind, nor could they have been conceived or produced except by human hands under the guidance of human brains."

"Your deductions are faultless," replied Jat Or, "but where are the people?"

"There lies the mystery," I replied. "I can well believe that our future depends upon its solution."

"While I am concerned with all these questions," said Jat Or presently, "I am more concerned with the fate of Zanda. I wonder what they have done with her."

That, of course, I could not answer, although the fact that she had been separated from us caused me no little concern.

At the end of the corridor, we were conducted up a wide and ornate staircase to the next level of the castle; and presently we were led into a large room—a vast chamber in which we saw at the far end a single, lonely figure.

It was Zanda. She was standing before a dais upon which were two large ornate throne chairs.

The room was gorgeous, almost barbaric in its decoration. Gold and precious stones encrusted floor and walls. They had been fabricated into an amazing design by some master artist who had had at his disposal rare gems such as I had never seen either upon earth or upon Barsoom.

The invisible force that propelled us conducted us to Zanda's side; and there the three of us stood, facing the dais and the empty throne chairs.

But I wondered if they were empty. I had that same strange feeling that I had noticed in the courtyard, of being surrounded by a multitude of people, of having many eyes fixed upon me; yet I saw none and I heard no sound.

We stood there before the dais for several minutes, and then we were dragged away and conducted from the room. Along another corridor we were taken, a narrower corridor, and up a winding stairway which Jat Or had some little difficulty in negotiating. Such contrivances were new to him, as stairways are not used on Mars, where inclined ramps lead from one level of a building to another.

I had once tried to introduce stairways in my palace in Helium; but so many of my household and my friends came near breaking their necks on them, that I eventually replaced them with ramps.

After ascending several levels, Zanda was separated from us and taken along a diverging corridor; and at another level above, Jat Or was dragged away from me.

None of us had spoken since we had entered the great throne room, and I think that now that we were being separated words seemed wholly inadequate in the hopelessness of our situation.

Now I was quite alone; but yet up and up I climbed, guided by those invisible hands upon my arms. Where were they taking me? To what fate had they taken my companions? Somewhere in this great castle was the princess whom I had crossed the void to find, yet never had she seemed farther away from me than at this minute; never had our separation seemed so utterly complete and final.

I do not know why I should have felt this way, unless again it was the effect of this seemingly unfathomable mystery that surrounded me.

We had ascended to such a great height that I was confident that I was being conducted into one of the loftier towers in the castle that I had seen from the courtyard. Something in this fact and the fact that we had been separated suggested that whatever the power that held us, it was not entirely certain of itself; for only fear that we might escape or that, banded together, we might inflict harm upon it, could have suggested the necessity for separating us; but whether or not I reasoned from a correct premise was only conjecture. Time alone could solve the mystery and answer the many questions that presented themselves to my mind.

My mind was thus occupied when I was halted before a door. It had a peculiar latch which attracted my attention, and while I was watching it I saw it move as though a hand turned it; then the door swung in, and I was dragged into the room beyond.

Here the bonds were cut from my wrists. I turned quickly intending to make a bolt for the door; but before I could reach it, it closed in my face. I tried to open it, but it was securely locked; and then, disgusted, I turned away from it.

As I turned to inspect my prison, my eyes fell upon a figure seated upon a bench at the far side of the room.

For want of a better word, I may describe the figure that I saw as that of a man; but what a man!

The creature was naked except for a short leather skirt held about its hips by a broad belt fastened by a huge golden buckle set with precious stones.

He was seated upon a red bench against a panel of grey wall; and his skin was exactly the color of the wall, except that portion of his legs which touched the bench. They were red.

The shape of his skull was similar to that of a human being, but his features were most inhuman. In the center of his forehead was a single, large eye about three inches in diameter; the pupil a vertical slit, like the pupils of a cat's eyes. He sat there eyeing me with that great eye, apparently appraising me as I was appraising him; and I could not but wonder if I presented as strange an appearance to him as he did to me.

During those few moments that we remained motionless, staring at one another, I hurriedly took note of several of his other strange physical characteristics.

The fingers of his hands and four of the toes of each of his feet were much longer than in the human race, while his thumbs and large toes were considerably shorter than his other digits and extended laterally at right angles to his hands and feet.

This fact and the vertical pupils of his eye suggested that he might be wholly arboreal or at least accustomed to finding his food or his prey in trees.

But perhaps the most outstanding features of his hideous countenance were his mouths. He had two of them, one directly above the other. The lower mouth, which was the larger, was lipless, the skin of the face forming the gums in which the teeth were set, with the result that his powerful white teeth were always exposed in a hideous, death-like grin.

The upper mouth was round, with slightly protruding lips controlled by a sphincter-like muscle. This mouth was toothless.

His nose was wide and flat, with upturned nostrils. At first I detected no ears, but later discovered that two small orifices near the top of the head and at opposite sides served the purposes of audition.

Starting slightly above his eye, a stiff yellowish mane about two inches wide ran back along the center of his cranium.

All in all, he was a most unlovely spectacle; and that grinning mouth of his and those powerful teeth, taken in connection with his very noticeable muscular development, suggested that he might be no mean antagonist.

I wondered if he were as ferocious as he looked, and it occurred to me that I might have been locked in here with this thing that it might destroy me. It even seemed possible that I might be intended to serve as its food.

Not once since I had entered the room had the creature taken that single, awful eye from me, nor in fact had I looked elsewhere than at it; but now, having partially satisfied my curiosity insofar as that could be accomplished by vision, I let my eyes wander about the room.

It was circular and evidently occupied the entire area and evidently the highest level of a tower. The walls were panelled in different colors; and even here in this high-flung prison cell was evidence of the artistic sensibilities of the builder of the castle, for the room was indeed strangely beautiful.

The circular wall was pierced by half a dozen tall, narrow windows. They were unglazed, but they were barred.

On the floor, against one portion of the wall, was a pile of rugs and skins—probably the bedding of the creature imprisoned here.

I walked toward one of the windows to look out, and as I did so the creature rose from the bench and moved to the side of the room farthest from me. It moved noiselessly with the stealthy tread of a cat; and always it transfixed me with that terrible, lidless eye.

Its silence, its stealth, its horrible appearance, made me wary lest it leap upon my back should I turn my face away from it. Yet I cast a hasty glance through the window and caught a glimpse of distant hills and, below me, just outside the castle wall, a river and beyond that a dense forest.

What little I saw suggested that the tower did not overlook the courtyard in which the ship lay, and I was anxious to see that part of the castle grounds to ascertain if I had been successful in directing the brain to take the ship to a point of safety.

I thought that perhaps I might be able to discover this from one of the windows on the opposite side of the tower; and so, keeping my eyes on my cell-mate, I crossed the room; and as I did so he quickly changed his position, keeping as far from me as possible.

I wondered if he were afraid of me or if, cat-like, he were just awaiting an opportunity to pounce on me when he could take me at a disadvantage.

I reached the opposite window and looked out, but I could see nothing of the courtyard, as others of the numerous towers of the castle obstructed my view on this side. In fact, another loftier tower rose directly in front of me in this direction and not more than ten or fifteen feet distant from the one in which I was incarcerated.

Similarly, I moved from window to window searching in vain for a glimpse of the courtyard; and always my weird and terrible cell-mate kept his distance from me.

Having convinced myself that I could not see the courtyard nor discover what success I had had in saving the ship, I turned my attention again to my companion.

I felt that I must learn something of what his attitude toward me might be. If he were to prove dangerous, I must ascertain the fact before night fell; for something seemed to tell me that that great eye could see by night; and inasmuch as I could not remain awake forever, I must fall easy prey to him in the darkness of the night, if his intentions were lethal.

As I glanced at him again, I noticed a surprising change in his appearance. His skin was no longer grey but vivid yellow, and then I noted that he was standing directly in front of a yellow panel. This was interesting in the extreme.

I moved toward him, and again he changed his position. This time he placed himself in front of a blue panel, and I saw the yellow tint of his skin fade away and turn to blue.

On Barsoom there is a little reptile called a darseen which changes its colors to harmonize with its background, just as do our earthly chameleons; but I had never seen any creature even remotely resembling a human being endowed with this faculty of protective coloration. Here, indeed, was the most amazing of all the amazing creatures that I have ever seen.

I wondered if it were endowed with speech, and so I addressed it. "Kaor!" I said; "let's be friends," and I raised my sword hand above my head with the palm toward him, indicating my friendly intentions.

He looked at me for a moment; and then from his upper mouth issued strange sounds, like the purring and meowing of a cat.

He was trying to speak to me, but I could not understand him any more than he could understand me.

How was I to learn his intentions toward me before night fell?

It seemed hopeless, and I resigned myself to wait with composure whatever might occur. I therefore decided to ignore the presence of the creature until it made advances, either hostile or otherwise; and so I walked over and seated myself on the bench that it had quitted.

Immediately it took up a new position as far from me as possible and this time in front of a green panel, whereupon its color immediately changed to green. I could not but wonder what kaleidoscopic result would be obtained were I to chase the thing around this multicolored apartment. The thought caused me to smile, and as I did so I saw an immediate reaction in my cell-mate. He made a strange purring sound and stretched his upper mouth laterally in what might have been an attempt at an answering smile. At the same time he rubbed his palms up and down his thighs.

It occurred to me that the stretching of the mouth and the rubbing of the thighs might constitute the outward expression of an inner emotion and be intended to denote its attitude toward me; but whether that attitude were friendly or hostile, I could not know. Perhaps my smile had conveyed to the creature a meaning wholly at variance with what a smile is usually intended to convey among the human inhabitants of Earth or Mars.

I recalled that I had discovered this to be a fact among the green men of Barsoom, who laugh the loudest when they are inflicting the most diabolical tortures upon their victims; although that is scarcely analogous to what I mean, as in the case of the green Martians, it is the result of a highly specialized perversion of the sense of humor.

Perhaps, on the other hand, the grimace and the gesture of the creature constituted a challenge. If that were true, the sooner I discovered it the better. In fact, it was far more necessary to know the truth at once, if he were unfriendly, than if he were friendly. If the former were true, I wanted to know it before darkness fell.

It occurred to me that I might gain some knowledge of his intentions by repeating his own gestures, and so I smiled at him and rubbed my palms up and down my thighs.

His reaction was immediate. His upper mouth stretched sideways; he came toward me. I stood up as he approached, and when he came quite close to me, he stopped; and reaching forth one of his hands stroked my upper arm.

I could not but believe that this was an overture of friendship, and so I similarly stroked one of his arms.

The result astounded me. The creature leaped back from me, that strange purring noise issuing from its lips; and then it broke into a wild dance. With cat-like springs, it leaped and cavorted about the room in wild abandon.

Hideous and grotesque as was its physical appearance, yet was I impressed by the consummate grace of all its movements.

Three turns about the room it took, as I seated myself again upon the bench and watched it; then, its dance completed, it came and sat down beside me.

Once again it purred and meowed in an evident attempt to communicate with me; but I could only shake my head, to indicate that I did not understand, and speak to it in the tongue of Barsoom.

Presently it ceased its meowing and addressed me in a language that seemed far more human—a language that employed almost the same vowel and consonant sounds as those languages of the human race to which I am accustomed.

Here, at last, I detected a common ground upon which we might discover mutual understanding.

It was obvious that the creature could not understand any language that I could speak, and it would serve no purpose to attempt to teach him any of them; but if I could learn his language I would then be able to communicate with some of the inhabitants of Thuria; and if the creatures of Thuria had a common language as did the inhabitants of Mars, then my existence upon this tiny satellite would be fraught with fewer difficulties.

But how to learn his language? That was the question. My captors might not permit me to live long enough to learn anything; but if I were to accept such an assumption as final, it would preclude me from making any attempt to escape or to alleviate my condition here. Therefore I must assume that I had plenty of time to learn one of the languages of Thuria, and I immediately set about to do so.

I commenced in the usual way that one learns a new language. I pointed to various articles in the room and to various parts of our bodies, repeating their names in my own language. My companion seemed to understand immediately what I was attempting to do; and pointing to the same articles himself, he repeated their names several times in the more human of the two languages which he seemed to command, if his meowings and purrings could be called a language, a question which, at that time, I should have been unable to answer.

We were thus engaged when the door to the room opened; and several vessels appeared to float in and settle themselves on the floor just inside the door, which was immediately closed.

My companion commenced to purr excitedly, and ran over to them. He returned immediately with a jar of water and a bowl of food which he set on the bench beside me. He pointed to the food and then to me, as though indicating that it was mine.

Crossing the room once more, he returned with another jar of water and a cage containing a most remarkable-appearing bird.

I call the thing a bird because it had wings; but to what family it belonged, your guess is as good as mine. It had four legs and the scales of a fish, but its beak and comb gave its strange face a bird-like appearance.

The food in the bowl set before me was a mixture of vegetables, fruit, and meat. I imagine that it was very nutritious, and it was quite palatable.

As I quenched my thirst from the jar and sampled the food that had been brought me, I watched my companion. For a moment or two he played with the bird in the cage. He inserted a finger between the bars, whereat the creature flapped its wings, voiced a shrill scream, and tried to seize the finger with its beak. It never quite succeeded, however, as my cell-mate always withdrew his finger in time. He seemed to derive a great deal of pleasure from this, as he purred constantly.

Finally he opened the door in the cage and liberated the captive. Immediately the creature fluttered about the room, seeking to escape through the windows; but the bars were too close together. Then my companion commenced to stalk it, for all the world like a cat stalking its prey. When the thing alighted, he would creep stealthily upon it; and when he was close enough, pounce for it.

For some time it succeeded in eluding him; but finally he struck it down heavily to the floor, partially stunning it. After this he played with it, pawing it around. Occasionally he would leave it and move about the room pretending that he did not see it. Presently he would seem to discover it anew, and then he would rush for it and pounce upon it.

At last, with a hideous coughing roar that sounded like the roar of a lion, he leaped ferociously upon it and severed its head with a single bite of his powerful jaws. Immediately he transferred the neck to his upper mouth and sucked the blood from the carcass. It was not a pretty sight.

When the blood had been drained, he devoured his prey with his lower jaws; and as he tore at it he growled like a feeding lion.

I finished my own meal slowly, while across the room from me my cell-mate tore at the carcass of his kill, swallowing in great gulps until he devoured every last vestige of it.

His meal completed, he crossed to the bench and drained his water jar, drinking through his upper mouth.

He paid no attention to me during all these proceedings; and now, purring lazily, he walked over to the pile of skins and cloths upon the floor and lying down upon them curled up and went to sleep.

chapter XVIII

CONDEMNED TO DEATH

YOUTH ADAPTS itself easily to new conditions and learns quickly; and, though only my Creator knows how old I am, I still retain the characteristics of youth. Aided by this fact, as well as by a sincere desire to avail myself of every means of self-preservation, I learned the language of my companion quickly and easily.

The monotony of the days that followed my capture was thus broken, and time did not hang so heavily upon my hands as it would otherwise.

I shall never forget the elation that I felt when I realized that my cell-mate and myself were at last able to communicate our thoughts to one another, but even before that time arrived we had learned one another's name. His was Umka.

The very first day that I discovered that I could express myself well enough for him to understand me, I asked him who it was that held us prisoners.

"The Tarids," he replied.

"What are they?" I asked. "What do they look like? Why do we never see them?"

"I do see them," he replied. "Don't you?"

"No; what do they look like?"

"They look very much like you," he replied; "at least they are the same sort of creature. They have two eyes and a nose and only one mouth, and their ears are big things stuck on the sides of their heads like yours. They are not beautiful like we Masenas."

"But why do I not see them?" I demanded.

"You don't know how," he replied. "If you knew how, you could see them as plainly as I do."

"I should like very much to see them," I told him. "Can you tell me how I may do so?"

"I can tell you," he said, "but that does not mean that you will be able to see them. Whether you do or not will depend upon your own mental ability. The reason you do not see them is because by the power of their own minds they have willed that you shall not see them. If you can free your mind of this inhibition, you can see them as plainly as you see me."

"But I don't know just how to go about it."

"You must direct your mind upon theirs in an effort to overcome their wish by a wish of your own. They wish that you should not see them. You must wish that you should see them. They were easily successful with you, because, not expecting such a thing, your mind had set up no defense mechanism against it. Now you have the advantage upon your side, because they have willed an unnatural condition, whereas you will have nature's forces behind you, against which, if your mind is sufficiently powerful, they can erect no adequate mental barrier."

Well, it sounded simple enough; but I am no hypnotist, and naturally I had considerable doubt as to my ability along these lines.

When I explained this to Umka, he growled impatiently.

"You can never succeed," he said, "if you harbor such doubts. Put them aside. Believe that you will succeed, and you will have a very much greater chance for success."

"But how can I hope to accomplish anything when I cannot see them?" I asked. "And even if I could see them, aside from a brief moment that the door is open when food is brought us, I have no opportunity to see them."

"That is not necessary," he replied. "You think of your friends, do you not, although you cannot see them now?"

"Yes, of course, I think of them; but what has that to do with it?"

"It merely shows that your thoughts can travel anywhere. Direct your thoughts, therefore, upon these Tarids. You know that the castle is full of them, because I have told you so. Just direct your mind upon the minds of all the inhabitants of the castle, and your thoughts will reach them all even though they may not be cognizant of it."

"Well, here goes," I said; "wish me luck."

"It may take some time," he explained. "It was a long time after I learned the secret before I could pierce their invisibility."

I set my mind at once upon the task before me, and kept it there when it was not otherwise occupied; but Umka was a loquacious creature; and having long been denied an opportunity for speech, he was now making up for lost time.

He asked me many questions about myself and the land from which I came, and seemed surprised to think that there were living creatures upon the great world that he saw floating in the night sky.

He told me that his people, the Masenas, lived in the forest in houses built high among the trees. They were not a numerous people, and so they sought districts far from the other inhabitants of Thuria.

The Tarids, he said, had once been a powerful people; but they had been overcome in war by another nation and almost exterminated.

Their enemies still hunted them down, and there would long since have been none of them left had not one of their wisest men developed among them the hypnotic power which made it possible for them to seemingly render themselves invisible to their enemies.

"All that remain of the Tarids," said Umka, "live here in this castle. There are about a thousand of them altogether, men, women, and children.

"Hiding here, in this remote part of the world, in an effort to escape their enemies, they feel that all other creatures are their foes. Whoever comes to the castle of the Tarids is an enemy to be destroyed."

"They will destroy us, you think?" I asked.

"Certainly," he replied.

"But when, and how?" I demanded.

"They are governed by some strange belief," explained Umka; "I do not understand it, but every important act in their lives is regulated by it. They say that they are guided by the sun and the moon and the stars.

"It is all very foolish, but they will not kill us until the sun tells them to, and then they will not kill us for their own pleasure but because they believe that it will make the sun happy."

"You think, then, that my friends, who are also prisoners here, are still alive and safe?"

"I don't know, but I think so," he replied. "The fact that you are alive indicates that they have not sacrificed the others, for I know it is usually their custom to save their captives and destroy them all in a single ceremony."

"Will they destroy you at the same time?"

"I think they will."

"And you are resigned to your fate, or would you escape if you could?"

"I should certainly escape, if I had the chance," he replied; "but I shall not have the chance; neither will you."

"If I could only see these people and talk to them," I said, "I might find the way whereby we could escape. I might even convince them that I and my friends are not their enemies, and persuade them to treat us as friends. But what can I do? I cannot see them; and even if I could see them, I could not hear them. The obstacles seem insuperable."

"If you can succeed in overcoming the suggestion of their invisibility which they have implanted in your mind," said Umka, "you can also overcome the other suggestion which renders them inaudible to you. Have you been making any efforts along these lines?"

"Yes; I am almost constantly endeavoring to throw off the hypnotic spell."

Each day, near noon, our single meal was served to us. It was always the same. We each received a large jar of water, I a bowl of food, and Umka a cage containing one of the strange bird-like animals which apparently formed his sole diet.

After Umka had explained how I might overcome the hypnotic spell that had been placed upon me and thus be able to see and hear my captors, I had daily placed myself in a position where, when the door was opened to permit our food to be placed within the room, I could see out and discover if the Tarid who brought our food to us was visible to me.

It was always with a disheartening sense of frustration that I saw the receptacles containing the food and water placed upon the floor just inside the door by invisible hands.

Hopeless as my efforts seemed, I still persisted in them, hoping stubbornly against hope.

I was sitting one day thinking of the hopelessness of Dejah Thoris's situation, when I heard the sound of footsteps in the corridor beyond our door and the scraping of metal against metal, such as the metal of a warrior makes when it scrapes against the buckles of his harness and against his other weapons.

These were the first sounds that I had heard, other than those made by Umka and myself—the first signs of life within the great castle of the Tarids since I had been made a captive there. The inferences to be drawn from these sounds were so momentous that I scarcely breathed as I waited for the door to open.

I was standing where I could look directly out into the corridor when the door was opened.

I heard the lock click. Slowly the door swung in upon its hinges; and there, distinctly visible, were two men of flesh and blood. In conformation they were quite human. Their skins were very fair and white, and in strange contrast were their blue hair and blue eyebrows. They wore short close-fitting skirts of heavy gold mesh and breastplates similarly fabricated of gold. For weapons, each wore a long-sword and a dagger. Their features were strong, their expressions stern and somewhat forbidding.

I noted all these things in the few moments that the door remained open. I saw both men glance at me and at Umka, and I was quite sure that neither of them was aware of the fact that they were quite visible to me. Had they known it, I am sure that their facial expressions would have betrayed the fact.

I was tremendously delighted to find that I had been able to throw off the strange spell that had been cast upon me; and after they had gone, I told Umka that I had been able to both see and hear them.

He asked me to describe them; and when I had done so, he agreed that I had told the truth.

"Sometimes people imagine things," he said, in explanation of his seeming doubt as to my veracity.

The next day, in the middle of the forenoon, I heard a considerable commotion in the corridor and on the stairway leading to our prison. Presently the door was opened and fully twenty-five men filed into the room.

As I saw them, a plan occurred to me that I thought might

possibly give me an advantage over these people if an opportunity to escape presented itself later on; and therefore I pretended that I did not see them. When looking in their direction, I focused my eyes beyond them; but to lessen the difficulty of this playacting I sought to concentrate my attention on Umka, whom they knew to be visible to me.

I regretted that I had not thought of this plan before, in time to have explained it to Umka, for it was very possible that he might inadvertently betray the fact that the Tarids were no longer invisible to me.

Twelve of the men came close to me, just out of reach. One man stood near the door and issued commands; the others approached Umka, ordering him to place his hands behind his back.

Umka backed away and looked questioningly at me. I could see that he was wondering if we might not make a break for liberty.

I tried to look as though I were unaware of the presence of the warriors. I did not wish them to know that I could see them. Looking blankly past them, I turned indifferently around until my back was toward them and I faced Umka; then I winked at him.

I prayed to God that if he didn't know what a wink was some miracle would enlighten him in this instance. As an added precaution, I placed a finger against my lips, enjoining silence.

Umka looked dumb, and fortunately he remained dumb.

"Half of you get the Masena," ordered the officer in charge of the detachment; "the rest of you take the black-haired one. As you can see, he does not know that we are in the room; so he may be surprised and struggle when you touch him. Seize him firmly."

I guess Umka must have thought that I was again under the influence of the hypnotic spell, for he was looking at me blankly when the warriors surrounded and took him in hand.

Then twelve of them leaped upon me. I might have put up a fight, but I saw nothing to be gained by doing so. As a matter of fact, I was anxious to leave this room. I could accomplish nothing while I remained in it; but once out, some whim of Fate might present an opportunity to me; so I did not struggle much, but pretended that I was startled when they seized me.

They then led us from the room and down the long series of stairways up which I had climbed weeks before and finally into the same great throne room through which Zanda, Jat Or, and I had been conducted the morning of our capture. But what a different scene it presented now that I had cast off the hypnotic spell under which I had labored at that time.

No longer was the great room empty, no longer the two throne chairs untenanted; instead the audience chamber was a mass of light and color and humanity.

Men, women, and children lined the wide aisle down which Umka and I were escorted toward the dais upon which stood the two throne chairs. Between solid ranks of warriors, resplendent in gorgeous trappings, our escort marched us to a little open space before the throne.

Congregated there under guard, their hands bound, were Jat Or, Zanda, Ur Jan, another whom I knew must be Gar Nal, and my beloved princess, Dejah Thoris.

"My chieftain!" she exclaimed. "Fate is a little kind in that she has permitted me to see you once again before we die."

"We still live," I reminded her, and she smiled as she recognized this, my long-time challenge to whatever malign fate might seem to threaten me.

Ur Jan's expression revealed his surprise when his eyes fell upon me. "You!" he exclaimed.

"Yes, I, Ur Jan."

"What are you doing here?"

"One of the pleasures of the trip I am to be robbed of by our captors," I replied.

"What do you mean?" he asked.

"The pleasure of killing you, Ur Jan," I replied.

He nodded understandingly, with a wry smile.

My attention was now attracted to the man on the throne. He was demanding that we be silent.

He was a very fat man, with an arrogant expression; and I noted in him those signs of age that are so seldom apparent among the red men of Barsoom. I had also noted similar indications of age among other members of the throng that filled the audience chamber, a fact which indicated that these people did not enjoy the almost perpetual youth of the Martians.

Occupying the throne at the man's side was a young and very beautiful woman. She was gazing at me dreamily through the heavy lashes of her half-closed lids. I could only assume that the woman's attention was attracted to me because of the fact that my skin differed in color from that of my companions as, after leaving Zodanga, I had removed the disguising pigment.

"Splendid!" she whispered, languidly.

"What is that?" demanded the man. "What is splendid?"

She looked up with a start, as one awakened from a dream. "Oh!" she exclaimed nervously; "I said that it would be splendid if you could make them keep still; but how can you if we are invisible and inaudible to them, unless," she shrugged, "you silence them with the sword."

"You know, Ozara," demurred the man, "that we are saving them for the Fire God—we may not kill them now."

The woman shrugged. "Why kill them at all?" she asked. "They look like intelligent creatures. It might be interesting to preserve them."

I turned to my companions. "Can any of you see or hear anything that is going on in this room?" I asked.

"Except for ourselves, I can see no one and hear no one," said Gar Nal, and the others answered similarly.

"We are all the victims of a form of hypnosis," I explained, "which makes it impossible for us either to see or hear our captors. By the exercise of the powers of your own minds you can free yourselves from this condition. It is not difficult. I succeeded in doing it. If the rest of you are also successful, our chances of escape will be much better, if an opportunity to escape arises. Believing that they are invisible to us, they will never be on their guard against us. As a matter of fact, I could, this moment, snatch a sword from the fellow at my side and kill the Jeddak and his Jeddara upon their thrones before anyone could prevent me."

"We cannot work together," said Gar Nal, "while half of us have it in our hearts to kill the other half."

"Let us call a truce on our own quarrels, then," I said, "until we have escaped from these people."

"That is fair," said Gar Nal.

"Do you agree?" I asked.

"Yes," he replied.

"And you, Ur Jan?" I asked.

"It suits me," said the assassin of Zodanga.

"And you?" demanded Gar Nal, looking at Jat Or.

"Whatever the—Vandor commands, I shall do," replied the padwar.

Ur Jan bestowed a quick glance of sudden comprehension upon me. "Ah," he exclaimed; "so you are also Vandor. Now I understand much that I did not understand before. Did that rat of a Rapas know?"

I ignored his question. "And now," I said, "let us raise our hands and swear to abide by this truce until we have all escaped from the Tarids and, further, that each of us will do all in his power to save the others."

Gar Nal, Ur Jan, Jat Or, and I raised our hands to swear.

"The women, too," said Ur Jan; and then Dejah Thoris and Zanda raised their hands, and thus we six swore to fight for one another to the death until we should be free from these enemies.

It was a strange situation, for I had been commissioned to kill Gar Nal; and Ur Jan had sworn to kill me, while I was intent upon killing him; and Zanda, who hated them both, was but awaiting the opportunity to destroy me when she should learn my identity.

"Come, come," exclaimed the fat man on the throne, irritably, "what are they jabbering about in that strange language? We must silence them; we did not bring them here to listen to them."

"Remove the spell from them," suggested the girl he had called Ozara. "Let them see and hear us. There are only four men among them; they cannot harm us."

"They shall see us and they shall hear us when they are led out to die," replied the man, "and not before."

"I have an idea that the light-skinned man among them can see us and hear us now," said the girl.

"What makes you think so?" demanded the man.

"I sense it when his eyes rest upon mine," she replied dreamily. "Then, too, when you speak, Ul Vas, his eyes travel to your face; and when I speak, they return to mine. He hears us, Ul Vas, and he sees us."

I was indeed looking at the woman as she spoke, and now I realized that I might have difficulty in carrying on my deception; but this time, when the man she had called Ul Vas replied to her, I focused my eyes beyond the girl and did not look at him.

"It is impossible," he said. "He can neither see nor hear us." Then he looked down at the officer in command of the detachment that had brought us from our cells to the audience chamber. "Zamak," he demanded, "what do you think? Can this creature either see or hear us?"

"I think not, All-highest," replied the man. "When we went to fetch him, he asked this Masena, who was imprisoned with him, if there were anyone in the room, although twenty-five of us were all about him."

"I thought you were wrong," said Ul Vas to his jeddara; "you are always imagining things."

The girl shrugged her shapely shoulders and turned away with a bored yawn, but presently her eyes came back to me; and though I tried not to meet them squarely thereafter, I was aware during all the rest of the time that I was in the audience chamber that she was watching me.

"Let us proceed," said Ul Vas.

Thereupon an old man stepped to the front and placed himself directly before the throne. "All-highest," he intoned in a sing-song voice, "the day is good, the occasion is good, the time has come. We bring before you, most august son of the Fire God, seven enemies of the Tarids. Through you, your father speaks, letting his people know his wishes. You have talked with the Fire God, your father. Tell us, All-highest, if these offerings look good in his eyes; make known to us his wishes, almighty one."

Ever since we had come into the audience chamber, Ul Vas had been inspecting us carefully; and especially had his attention been centered upon Dejah Thoris and Zanda. Now he cleared his throat.

"My father, the Fire God, wishes to know who these enemies are," he said.

"One of them," replied the old man who had spoken before, and whom I took to be a priest, "is a Masena that your warriors captured while he was hunting outside our walls. The other six are strange creatures. We know not from whence they came. They arrived in two unheard-of contraptions that moved through the air like birds, though they had no wings. In each of these were two men and a woman. They alighted inside our walls; but from whence they came or why, we do not know, though doubtless it was their intention to do us harm, as is the intention of all men who come to the castle of the Tarids. As you will note, All-highest, five of these six have red skins, while the sixth had a skin only a little darker than our own. He seems to be of a different race, with his white skin, his black hair, and his grey eyes. These things we know and nothing more. We await the wishes of the Fire God from the lips of his son, Ul Vas."

The man on the throne pursed his lips, as though in thought, while his eyes travelled again along the line of prisoners facing him, lingering long upon Dejah Thoris and Zanda. Presently, he spoke.

"My father, the Fire God, demands that the Masena and the four strange men be destroyed in his honor at this same hour, after he has encircled Ladan seven times."

There were a few moments of expectant silence after he had ceased speaking—a silence that was finally broken by the old priest.

"And the women, All-highest?" he asked; "what are the wishes of the Fire God, your father, in relation to them?"

"The Fire God, to show his great love," replied the jeddak, "has presented the two women to his son, Ul Vas, to do with as he chooses."

chapter XIX

OZARA

LIFE IS SWEET; and when I heard the words of doom fall from the lips of the jeddak, Ul Vas, the words that condemned five of us to die on the seventh day, I must naturally have experienced some depressing reaction; but I was not conscious of it, in view of the far greater mental perturbation induced by the knowledge that Dejah Thoris's fate was to be worse than death.

I was glad that she was mercifully deaf to what I had heard. It could not help her to know the fate that was being reserved for her, and it could only cause her needless anguish had she heard the death sentence pronounced upon me.

All my companions, having seen nothing and heard nothing, stood like dumb cattle before the throne of their cruel judge. To them it was only an empty chair; for me it held a creature of flesh and blood—a mortal whose vitals the point of a keen blade might reach.

Again Ul Vas was speaking. "Remove them now," he commanded. "Confine the men in the Turquoise Tower, and take the women to the Tower of Diamonds."

I thought then to leap upon him and strangle him with my bare hands, but my better judgment told me that that would not save Dejah Thoris from the fate for which she was being reserved. It could only result in my own death, and thus would be removed her greatest, perhaps her only, hope of eventual succor; and so I went quietly, as they led me away with my fellow-prisoners, my last memory of the audience chamber being the veiled gaze of Ozara, Jeddara of the Tarids.

Umka and I were not returned to the cell in which we had previously been incarcerated; but were taken with Jat Or, Gar Nal, and Ur Jan to a large room in the Turquoise Tower.

We did not speak until the door had closed behind the escort that had been invisible to all but Umka and myself. The others seemed mystified; I could read it in the puzzled expressions upon their faces.

"What was it all about, Vandor?" demanded Jat Or. "Why did we stand there in silence in that empty chamber before those vacant thrones?"

"There was no silence," I replied; "and the room was crowded with people. The Jeddak and his Jeddara sat upon the thrones that seemed vacant to you, and the Jeddak passed the sentence of death upon all of us—we are to die on the seventh day."

"And the princess and Zanda, too?" he demanded.

I shook my head. "No, unfortunately, no."

"Why do you say unfortunately?" he asked, puzzled.

"Because they would prefer death to what is in store for them. The Jeddak, Ul Vas, is keeping them for himself."

Jat Or scowled. "We must do something," he said; "we must save them."

"I know it," I replied; "but how?"

"You have given up hope?" he demanded. "You will go to your death calmly, knowing what is in store for them?"

"You know me better than that, Jat Or," I said. "I am hoping that something will occur that will suggest a plan of rescue; although I see no hope at present, I am not hopeless. If no opportunity occurs before, then in the last moment, I shall at least avenge her, if I cannot save her; for I have an advantage over these people that they do not know I possess."

"What is that?" he asked.

"They are neither invisible nor inaudible to me," I replied.

He nodded. "Yes, I had forgotten," he said; "but it seemed impossible that you could see and hear where there was nothing to be seen nor heard."

"Why are they going to kill us?" demanded Gar Nal, who had overheard my conversation with Jat Or.

"We are to be offered as sacrifices to the Fire God whom they worship," I replied.

"The Fire God?" demanded Ur Jan. "Who is he?"

"The sun," I explained.

"But how could you understand their language?" asked Gar Nal. "It cannot be possible that they speak the same tongue that is spoken upon Barsoom."

"No," I replied, "they do not; but Umka, with whom I have been imprisoned ever since we were captured, has taught me the language of the Tarids."

"What are Tarids?" asked Jat Or.

"It is the name of the people in whose power we are," I explained.

"What is their name for Thuria?" asked Gar Nal.

"I am not sure," I replied; "but I will ask Umka. Umka," I said, in his own language, "what does the word *Ladan* mean?"

"That is the name of this world we live on," he replied. "You heard Ul Vas say that we should die when the Fire God had encircled Ladan seven times."

We Barsoomians fell into a general conversation after this, and I had an opportunity to study Gar Nal and Ur Jan more carefully.

The former was, like most Martians, of indeterminate age. He was not of such extreme age that he commenced to show it, as did

Fal Sivas. Gar Nal might have been anywhere from a hundred to a thousand years old. He had a high forehead and rather thin hair for a Martian, and there was nothing peculiarly distinctive about his features, except his eyes. I did not like them; they were crafty, deceitful, and cruel.

Ur Jan, whom of course I had seen before, was just what one might have expected—a burly, brutal fighting man of the lowest type; but of the two, I thought then that I should have trusted Ur Jan farther than Gar Nal.

It seemed strange to me to be confined here in such small quarters with two such bitter enemies; but I realized, as they must have also, that it would profit us nothing to carry on our quarrel under such circumstances, whereas if an opportunity to escape presented itself, four men who could wield swords would have a very much better chance to effect the liberty of all than if there were only two of us. There would not have been more than two, had we dared to continue our quarrel; for at least two of us, and possibly three, must have died in order to insure peace.

Umka seemed rather neglected as we four talked in our own tongue. He and I had grown to be on very friendly terms, and I counted on him to assist us if an opportunity arose whereby we might attempt escape. I was therefore particularly anxious that he remain friendly, and so I drew him into the conversation occasionally, acting as interpreter for him.

For days, day after day, I had watched Umka play with the hapless creatures that were brought to him for his food, so that the sight no longer affected me; but when the food was brought us this day, the Barsoomians watched the Masena in fascinated horror; and I could see that Gar Nal grew actually to fear the man.

Shortly after we had completed our meal, the door opened again and several warriors entered. Zamak, the officer who had conducted Umka and me to the audience chamber, was again in command.

Only Umka and I could see that anyone had entered the room; and I, with difficulty, pretended that I was not conscious of the fact.

"There he is," said Zamak, pointing to me; "fetch him along."

The soldiers approached and seized my arms on either side; then they hustled me toward the door.

"What is it?" cried Jat Or. "What has happened to you?" he shouted. "Where are you going?" The door was still ajar, and he saw that I was headed toward it.

"I do not know where I am going, Jat Or," I replied. "They are taking me away again."

"My prince, my prince," he cried, and sprang after me, as though to drag me back; but the soldiers hustled me out of the chamber, and the door was slammed in Jat Or's face between us.

"It's a good thing these fellows can't see us," remarked one of the warriors escorting me. "I think we should have had a good fight on our hands just now, had they been able to."

"I think this one could put up a good fight," said one of the fellows who was pushing me along; "the muscles in his arms are like bands of silver."

"Even the best of men can't fight antagonists that are invisible to them," remarked another.

"This one did pretty well in the courtyard the day that we captured him; he bruised a lot of the Jeddak's guard with his bare hands, and killed two of them."

This was the first intimation that I had had any success whatsoever in that encounter, and it rather pleased me. I could imagine how they would feel if they knew that I could not only see them but hear them and understand them.

They were so lax, because of their fancied security, that I could have snatched a weapon from almost any of them; and I know that I should have given a good account of myself, but I could not see how it would avail either me or my fellow-prisoners.

I was conducted to a part of the palace that was entirely different from any portion that I had hitherto seen. It was even more gorgeous in its lavish and luxurious decorations and appointments than the splendid throne room.

Presently we came to a doorway before which several warriors stood on guard.

"We have come, as was commanded," said Zamak, "and brought the white-skinned prisoner with us."

"You are expected," replied one of the guardsmen; "you may enter," and he threw open the large double doors.

Beyond them was an apartment of such exquisite beauty and richness that, in my poor vocabulary, I find no words to describe it. There were hangings in colors unknown to earthly eyes, against a background of walls that seemed to be of solid ivory, though what the material was of which they were composed, I did not know. It was rather the richness and elegance of the room's appointments that made it seem so beautiful, for after all, when I come to describe it, I find that, in a sense, simplicity was its dominant note.

There was no one else in the room when we entered. My guard led me to the center of the floor and halted.

Presently a door in the opposite side of the room opened, and a woman appeared. She was a very good-looking young woman. Later I was to learn that she was a slave.

"You will wait in the corridor, Zamak," she said; "the prisoner will follow me."

"What, alone, without a guard?" demanded Zamak in surprise.

"Such are my commands," replied the girl.

"But how can he follow you," asked Zamak, "when he can neither see nor hear us; and if he could hear us, he could not understand us?"

"I will lead him," she replied.

As she approached me, the soldiers relinquished their grasp upon my arms; and taking one of my hands, she led me from the apartment.

The room into which I was now conducted, though slightly smaller, was far more beautiful than the other. However, I did not immediately take note of its appointments, my attention being immediately and wholly attracted by its single occupant.

I am not easily surprised; but in this instance I must confess that I was when I recognized the woman reclining upon a divan, and watching me intently through long lashes, as Ozara, Jeddara of the Tarids.

The slave girl led me to the center of the room and halted. There she waited, looking questioningly at the Jeddara; while I, recalling that I was supposed to be deaf and blind to these people, sought to focus my gaze beyond the beautiful empress whose veiled eyes seemed to read my very soul.

"You may retire, Ulah," she said presently.

The slave girl bowed low and backed from the room.

For several moments after she departed, no sound broke the silence of the room; but always I felt the eyes of Ozara upon me.

Presently she laughed, a silvery musical laugh. "What is your name?" she demanded.

I pretended that I did not hear her, as I found occupation for my eyes in examination of the beauties of the chamber. It appeared to be the boudoir of the empress, and it made a lovely setting for her unquestionable loveliness.

"Listen," she said, presently; "you fooled Ul Vas and Zamak and the High Priest and all the rest of them; but you did not fool me. I will admit that you have splendid control, but your eyes betrayed you. They betrayed you in the audience chamber; and they betrayed you again just now as you entered this room, just as I knew they would betray you. They showed surprise when they rested upon me, and that can mean only one thing; that you saw and recognized me.

"I knew, too, in the audience chamber, that you understood what was being said. You are a highly intelligent creature, and the changing lights in your eyes reflected your reaction to what you heard in the audience chamber.

"Let us be honest with one another, you and I, for we have more in common than you guess. I am not unfriendly to you. I understand why you think it to your advantage to conceal the fact that you can see and hear us; but I can assure you that you will be no worse off if you trust me, for I already know that we are neither invisible nor inaudible to you."

I could not fathom what she meant by saying we had much in common, unless it were merely a ruse to lure me into an admission that I could both see and hear the Tarids; yet on the other hand, I could see no reason to believe that either she or the others would profit by this knowledge. I was absolutely in their power, and apparently it made little difference whether I could see and hear them or not. Furthermore, I was convinced that this girl was extremely clever and that I could not deceive her into believing that she was invisible to me. On the whole, I saw no reason to attempt to carry the deception further with her; and so I looked her squarely in the eyes and smiled.

"I shall be honored by the friendship of the Jeddara, Ozara," I said.

"There!" she exclaimed; "I knew that I was right."

"Yet perhaps you had a little doubt."

"If I did, it is because you are a past master in the art of deception."

"I felt that the lives and liberty of my companions and myself might depend upon my ability to keep your people from knowing that I can see and understand them."

"You do not speak our language very well," she said. "How did you learn it?"

"The Masena with whom I was imprisoned taught me it," I explained.

"Tell me about yourself," she demanded; "your name, your country, the strange contrivances in which you came to the last stronghold of the Tarids, and your reason for coming."

"I am John Carter," I replied, "Prince of the house of Tardos Mors, Jeddak of Helium."

"Helium?" she questioned. "Where is Helium? I never heard of it."

"It is on another world," I explained, "on Barsoom, the great planet that you call your larger moon."

"You are, then, a prince in your own country?" she said. "I thought as much. I am seldom mistaken in my estimate of people. The two women and one of the other men among your companions are well-bred," she continued; "the other two men are not. One of them, however, has a brilliant mind, while the other is a stupid lout, a low brute of a man."

I could not but smile at her accurate appraisal of my companions. Here, indeed, was a brilliant woman. If she really cared to befriend me, I felt that she might accomplish much for us; but I did not allow my hopes to rise too high, for after all she was the mate of Ul Vas, the Jeddak who had condemned us to death.

"You have read them accurately, Jeddara," I told her.

"And you," she continued; "you are a great man in your own world. You would be a great man in any world; but you have not told me why you came to our country."

"The two men that you last described abducted a princess of the reigning house of my country."

"She must be the very beautiful one," mused Ozara.

"Yes," I said. "With the other man and the girl, I pursued them in another ship. Shortly after we reached Ladan, we saw their ship in the courtyard of your castle. We landed beside it to rescue the princess and punish her abductors. It was then that your people captured us."

"Then you did not come to harm us?" she asked.

"Certainly not," I replied. "We did not even know of your existence."

She nodded. "I was quite sure that you intended us no harm," she said, "for enemies would never have placed themselves thus absolutely in our power; but I could not convince Ul Vas and the others."

"I appreciate your belief in me," I said; "but I cannot understand why you have taken this interest in me, an alien and a stranger."

She contemplated me in silence for a moment, her beautiful eyes momentarily dreamy.

"Perhaps it is because we have so much in common," she said; "and again perhaps because of a force that is greater than all others and that seizes and dominates us without our volition."

She paused and regarded me intently, and then she shook her head impatiently.

"The thing that we have in common," she said, "is that we are both prisoners in the castle of Ul Vas. The reason that I have taken this interest in you, you would understand if you are one-tenth as intelligent as I gave you credit for."

chapter XX

We Attempt Escape

OZARA MAY HAVE overestimated my intelligence, but she underestimated my caution. I could not admit that I understood the inference that I was supposed to draw from what she had said to me. As a matter of fact, the implication was so preposterous that at first I was inclined to believe that it was a ruse intended to trap me into some sort of an admission of ulterior designs upon her people, after she had wholly won my confidence; and so I sought to ignore the possible confession in her final statement by appearing to be dumbfounded by her first statement, which really was a surprise to me.

"You, a prisoner?" I demanded. "I thought that you were the Jeddara of the Tarids."

"I am," she said, "but I am no less a prisoner."

"But are not these your people?" I asked.

"No," she replied; "I am a Domnian. My country, Domnia, lies far away across the mountains that lie beyond the forest that surrounds the castle of Ul Vas."

"And your people married you to Ul Vas, Jeddak of the Tarids?" I asked.

"No," she replied; "he stole me from them. My people do not know what has become of me. They would never willingly have sent me to the court of Ul Vas, nor would I remain here, could I escape. Ul Vas is a beast. He changes his jeddaras often. His agents are constantly searching other countries for beautiful young women. When they find one more beautiful than I, I shall go the way of my predecessors; but I think that he has found one to his liking already, and that my days are numbered."

"You think that his agents have found another more beautiful than you?" I asked; "it seems incredible."

"Thank you for the compliment," she said, "but his agents have not found another more beautiful than I. Ul Vas has found her himself. In the audience chamber, did you not see him looking at your beautiful compatriot? He could scarcely keep his eyes from her, and you will recall that her life was spared."

"So was the life of the girl, Zanda," I reminded her. "Is he going to take her also to be his jeddara?"

"No, he may only have one at a time," replied Ozara. "The girl whom you call Zanda is for the High Priest. It is thus that Ul Vas propitiates the gods."

"If he takes this other woman," I said, "she will kill him."

"But that will not help me," said Ozara.

"Why?" I asked.

"Because while one jeddara lives, he cannot take another," she explained.

"You will be destroyed?" I asked.

"I shall disappear," she replied. "Strange things happen in the castle of Ul Vas, strange and terrible things."

"I commence to understand why you sent for me," I said; "you would like to escape; and you think if you can help us to escape, we will take you with us."

"You are commencing to understand at least a part of my reasons," she said. "The rest," she added, "I shall see that you learn in time."

"You think there is a chance for us to escape?" I asked.

"Just a bare chance," she said; "but inasmuch as we are to die anyway, there is no chance that we may not take."

"Have you any plans?"

"We might escape in the ship, the one that is still in the courtyard."

Now I was interested. "One of the ships is still in the courtyard?" I demanded. "Only one? They have not destroyed it?"

"They would have destroyed it, but they are afraid of it; they are afraid to go near it. When you were captured, two of Ul Vas's warriors entered one of the ships, whereupon it immediately flew away with them. It did not fly away before the first one who had entered it had called back to his companion that it was deserted. Now they think that these ships are under a magic spell, and they will not go near the one that lies in the courtyard."

"Do you know what became of the other ship?" I asked. "Do you know where it went?"

"It lies in the sky, far above the castle. It just floats there, as though it were waiting—waiting for something, we know not what. Ul Vas is afraid of it. That is one reason why you have not been destroyed before. He was waiting to see what the ship would do; and he was also waiting to screw up his courage to a point where he might order your destruction, for Ul Vas is a great coward."

"Then you think that there is a chance of our reaching the ship?" I asked.

"There is a chance," she said. "I can hide you here in my apartment until nightfall, and the castle sleeps. Then if we can pass the guard at the outer doorway and reach the courtyard, we should succeed. It is worth trying, but you may have to fight your way past the guard. Are you skilled with the sword?"

"I think that I can give a good account of myself," I replied, "but how are we to get the rest of my party into the courtyard?"

"Only you and I are going," she said.

I shook my head. "I cannot go unless all my people go with me."

She eyed me with sudden suspicion. "Why not?" she demanded. "You are in love with one of those women; you will not go without her." Her tone was tinged with resentment; it was the speech of a jealous woman.

If I were to effect the escape of the others, and especially of Dejah Thoris, I must not let her know the truth; so I thought quickly, and two good reasons occurred to me why she and I could not depart alone.

"It is a point of honor in the country from which I come," I told her, "that a man never deserts his comrades. For that reason, I could not, in honor, leave without them; but there is another even more potent reason."

"What is that?" she asked.

"The ship that remains in the courtyard belongs to my enemies, the two men who abducted the princess from my country. My ship is the one that floats above the castle. I know nothing at all about the mechanism of their ship. Even if we succeeded in reaching it, I could not operate it."

She studied this problem for a while, and then she looked up at me. "I wonder if you are telling me the truth," she said.

"Your life depends upon your believing me," I replied, "and so does mine, and so do the lives of all my companions."

She considered this in silence for a moment, and then with a gesture of impatience she said, "I do not know how we can get your friends out into the courtyard and to the ship."

"I think I know how we may escape," I said, "if you will help us."

"How is that?" she demanded.

"If you can get me tools with which we can cut the bars to the windows of their prison cells, and also describe exactly the location of the room in which the girls are imprisoned, I am sure that I can be successful."

"If I did these things, then you could escape without me," she said suspiciously.

"I give you my word, Ozara, that if you do as I ask, I shall not leave without you."

"What else do you want me to do?" she asked.

"Can you gain entrance to the room where the princess and Zanda are imprisoned?"

"Yes, I think that I can do that," she replied, "unless Ul Vas should realize that I suspected his intention and might think that I intended to kill the women; but I am not so sure that I can get the tools with which you may cut the bars to the windows of your prison. I can get them," she corrected herself, "but I do not know how I can get them to you."

"If you could send some food to me, you might conceal a file or saw in the jar with the food," I suggested.

"Just the thing!" she exclaimed; "I can send Ulah to you with a jar of food."

"And how about the bars on the windows of the girls' prison?" I asked.

"They are in the Diamond Tower," she replied, "very high. There are no bars on their windows because no one could escape from the Diamond Tower in that way. There are always guards at its base, for it is the tower in which are the Jeddak's quarters; so if you are planning on your women escaping through a window, you might as well abandon the idea at once."

"I think not," I replied. "If my plan works, they can escape with even greater ease from the Diamond Tower than from the courtyard."

"But how about you and the other men of your party? Even if you are able to lower yourselves from the window of your cell, you will never be able to reach the Diamond Tower to insure our escape."

"Leave that to me," I said; "have confidence in me, and I think that if you do your part, we shall all be able to escape."

"Tonight?" she asked.

"No, I think not," I said; "we had better wait until tomorrow night, for we do not know how long it will take to sever the bars of our window. Perhaps you had better send me back now and smuggle the tools to me as soon thereafter as possible."

She nodded. "You are right."

"Just a moment," I said. "How am I to know the Tower of Diamonds? How am I to find it?"

She appeared puzzled. "It is the central and loftiest tower of the castle," she explained, "but I do not know how you will reach it without a guide and many fighting men."

"Leave that to me, but you must help guide me to the room where the two women are imprisoned."

"How can I do that?" she demanded.

"When you reach their room, hang a colored scarf from a window there—a red scarf."

"How can you see that from inside the castle?" she demanded.

"Never mind; if my plan works, I shall find it. And now, please send me away."

She struck a gong hanging near her and the slave girl, Ulah, entered the apartment. "Take the prisoner back to Zamak," she instructed, "and have him returned to his cell."

Ulah took me by the hand and led me from the presence of the Jeddara, through the adjoining apartment and into the corridor beyond, where Zamak and the guards were waiting. There she turned me over to the warriors who conducted me back to the room in the Turquoise Tower, where my companions were imprisoned.

Jat Or voiced an exclamation of relief when he saw me enter the room. "When they took you away, my prince, I thought that I should never see you again; but now fate is growing kinder to me. She has just given me two proofs of her returning favor—I have you back again, and when the door opened I saw the Tarids who returned with you."

"You could see them?" I exclaimed.

"I could see them and hear them," he replied.

"And I, too," said Gar Nal.

"How about you, Ur Jan?" I asked, for the more of us who could see them, the better chance we would have in the event that there was any fighting during our attempt to rescue the women and escape.

Ur Jan shook his head gloomily. "I could see nothing or hear nothing," he said.

"Don't give up," I urged; "you *must* see them. Persevere, and you shall see them."

"Now," I said, turning to Gar Nal, "I have some good news. Our ships are safe; yours still lies in the courtyard. They are afraid to approach it."

"And yours?" he asked.

"It floats in the sky, high above the castle."

"You brought others with you from Barsoom?" he asked.

"No," I replied.

"But there must be somebody aboard the ship, or it could not get up there and remain under control."

"There is someone aboard it," I replied.

He looked puzzled. "But you just said that you brought no one with you," he challenged.

"There are two Tarid warriors aboard it."

"But how can they handle it? What can they know about the intricate mechanism of Fal Sivas's craft?"

"They know nothing about it and cannot handle it."

"Then how in the name of Issus did it get up there?" he demanded.

"That is something that you need not know, Gar Nal," I told him. "The fact is, that it is there."

"But what good will it do us, hanging up there in the sky?"

"I think that I can get it, when the time comes," I said, although, as a matter of fact, I was not positive that I could control the ship through the mechanical brain at so great a distance. "I am not so much worried about my ship, Gar Nal, as I am about yours. We should recover it, for after we escape from this castle, our truce is off; and it would not be well for us to travel on the same ship."

He acquiesced with a nod, but I saw his eyes narrow craftily. I wondered if that expression reflected some treacherous thought; but I passed the idea off with a mental shrug, as really it did not make much difference what Gar Nal was thinking as long as I could keep my eyes on him until I had Dejah Thoris safely aboard my own craft.

Ur Jan was sitting on a bench, glaring into space; and I knew that he was concentrating his stupid brain in an effort to cast off the hypnotic spell under which the Tarids had placed him. Umka lay curled up on a rug, purring contentedly. Jat Or stood looking out of one of the windows.

The door opened, and we all turned toward it. I saw Ulah, the Jeddara's slave, bearing a large earthen jar of food. She set it down upon the floor inside the door, and stepping back into the corridor, closed and fastened the door after her.

I walked quickly to the jar and picked it up; and as I turned back toward the others, I saw Ur Jan standing wide-eyed staring at the door.

"What's the matter, Ur Jan?" I asked. "You look as though you had seen a ghost."

"I saw her!" he exclaimed. "I saw her. Ghost or no ghost, I saw her."

"Good!" ejaculated Jat Or; "now we are all free from that damnable spell."

"Give me a good sword," growled Ur Jan; "and we'll soon be free of the castle, too."

"We've got to get out of this room first," Gar Nal reminded him.

"I think we have the means of escape here, in this jar," I told them. "Come, we might as well eat the food, as long as we have it, and see what we find in the bottom of the jar."

The others gathered around me, and we started to empty the jar in the most pleasurable fashion; nor had we gone deep into it before I discovered three files, and with these we immediately set to work upon the bars of one of our windows.

"Don't cut them all the way through," I cautioned; "just weaken three of them so that we can pull them aside when the time arrives."

The metal of which the bars were constructed was either some element unknown upon Earth or Barsoom or an equally mysterious alloy. It was very hard. In fact, it seemed at first that it was almost as hard as our files; but at last they commenced to bite into it, yet I saw that it was going to be a long, hard job.

We worked upon those bars all that night and all of the following day.

When slaves brought our food, two of us stood looking out of the window, our hands grasping the bars so as to cover up the evidence of our labors; and thus we succeeded in finishing the undertaking without being apprehended.

Night fell. The time was approaching when I might put to trial the one phase of my plan that was the keystone upon which the success of the entire adventure must rest. If it failed, all our work upon the bars would be set for naught, our hopes of escape practically blasted. I had not let the others know what I purposed attempting, and I did not now acquaint them with the doubts and fears that assailed me.

Ur Jan was at the window looking out. "We can pull these bars away whenever we wish," he said, "but I do not see what good that is going to do us. If we fastened all our harnesses together, they would not reach to the castle roof below us. It looks to me as though we had had all our work for nothing."

"Go over there and sit down," I told him, "and keep still. All of you keep still; do not speak or move until I tell you to."

Of them all, only Jat Or could have guessed what I purposed attempting, yet they all did as I had bid them.

Going to the window, I searched the sky; but I could see nothing of our craft. Nevertheless, I sought to concentrate my thoughts upon the metallic brain wherever it might be. I directed it to drop down and approach the window of the tower where I stood. Never before in my life, I think, had I so concentrated my mind upon a single idea. There seemed to be a reaction that I could feel almost as definitely as when I tensed a muscle. Beads of cold sweat stood out upon my forehead.

Behind me the room was as silent as the grave; and through the open window where I stood, no sound came from the sleeping castle below me.

The slow seconds passed, dragging into a seeming eternity of time.

Could it be that the brain had passed beyond the sphere of my control? Was the ship lost to me forever? These thoughts assailed me as my power of concentration weakened. My mind was swept into a mad riot of conflicting hopes and doubts, fears and sudden swift assurances of success that faded into despond as rapidly as they had grown out of nothing.

And then, across the sky I saw a great black hulk moving slowly toward me out of the night.

For just an instant the reaction left me weak; but I soon regained control of myself and pulled aside the three bars that we had cut.

The others, who had evidently been watching the window from where they either sat or stood, now pressed forward. I could hear smothered exclamations of surprise, relief, elation. Turning quickly, I cautioned them to silence.

I directed the brain to bring the ship close to the window; then I turned again to my companions.

"There are two Tarid warriors aboard her," I said. "If they found the water and food which she carried, they are still alive; and there is no reason to believe that starving men would not find it. We must therefore prepare ourselves for a fight. Each of these men, no doubt, is armed with a long-sword and a dagger. We are unarmed. We shall have to overcome them with our bare hands."

I turned to Ur Jan. "When the door is opened, two of us must leap into the cabin simultaneously on the chance that we may take them by surprise. Will you go first with me, Ur Jan?"

He nodded and a crooked smile twisted his lips. "Yes," he said, "and it will be a strange sight to see Ur Jan and John Carter fighting side by side."

"At least we should put up a good fight," I said.

"It is too bad," he sighed, "that those two Tarids will never have the honor of knowing who killed them."

"Jat Or, you and Gar Nal follow immediately behind Ur Jan and me." And then, in his own language, I told Umka to board the ship immediately after Jat Or and Gar Nal. "And if the fighting is not all over," I told him, "you will know what to do when you see the two Tarid warriors." His upper mouth stretched in one of his strange grins, and he purred contentedly.

I stepped to the sill of the window, and Ur Jan clambered to my side. The hull of the craft was almost scraping the side of the building; the doorway was only a foot from the sill on which we stood.

"Ready, Ur Jan," I whispered, and then I directed the brain to draw the doors aside as rapidly as possible.

Almost instantly, they sprang apart; and in the same instant Ur Jan and I sprang into the cabin. Behind us, came our three companions. In the gloom of the interior, I saw two men facing us; and without waiting to give either of them a chance to draw, I hurled myself at the legs of the nearer.

He crashed to the floor, and before he could draw his dagger I seized both his wrists and pinioned him on his back.

I did not see how Ur Jan handled his man; but a moment later, with the assistance of Jat Or and Umka, we had disarmed them both.

Ur Jan and Gar Nal wanted to kill them offhand, but that I would not listen to. I can kill a man in a fair fight without a single qualm of conscience; but I cannot kill a defenseless man in cold blood, even though he be my enemy.

As a precautionary measure, we bound and gagged them.

"What now?" demanded Gar Nal. "How are you going to get the women?"

"First, I am going to try and get your ship," I replied, "for even if we extend our truce, we shall stand a better chance of returning to Barsoom if we have both ships in our possession, as something might happen to one of them."

"You are right," he said; "and, too, I should hate to lose my ship. It is the fruit of a lifetime of thought and study and labor."

I now caused the ship to rise and cruise away until I thought that it was out of sight of the castle. I adopted this course merely as a strategy to throw the Tarids off our track in the event that any of the guards had seen the ship maneuvering among the towers; but when we had gone some little distance, I dropped low and approached the castle again from the side where Gar Nal's ship lay in the courtyard.

I kept very low above the trees of the forest and moved very slowly without lights. Just beyond the castle wall, I brought the ship to a stop and surveyed the courtyard just ahead and below us.

Plainly I saw the outlines of Gar Nal's ship, but nowhere upon that side of the castle was there any sign of a guard.

This seemed almost too good to be true, and in a whisper I asked Umka if it could be possible that the castle was unguarded at night.

"There are guards within the castle all night," he said, "and upon the outside of the Tower of Diamonds, but these are to guard Ul Vas against assassination by his own people. They do not fear that any enemy will come from beyond the walls at night, for none has ever attacked except by day. The forests of Ladan are full of wild beasts; and if a body of men were to enter them at night, the beasts would set up such a din of howling and roaring that the Tarids would be warned in ample time to defend themselves; so you see, the beasts of the forest are all the guards they need."

Thus assured that there was no one in the courtyard, I took the ship across the wall and dropped it to the ground beside Gar Nal's.

Quickly I gave my instructions for what was to follow. "Gar Nal," I said, "you will go aboard your ship and pilot it, following me. We are going to the window of the room where the girls are confined. As I draw in and stop at their window, both the doors in the sides of my ship will be open. Open the door on the port side of your ship and place it alongside mine, so that if it is necessary you can cross through my ship and enter the room where the women are confined. We may need all the help that we have, if the women are well guarded."

VAGUE MISGIVINGS disturbed me as I saw Gar Nal enter his ship. They seemed a premonition of disaster, of tragedy; but I realized that they were based upon nothing more substantial than my natural dislike for the man, and so I sought to thrust them aside and devote my thoughts to the business in hand.

The night was dark. Neither Mars nor Cluros had risen. It was, indeed, because of the fact that I knew neither of them would be in the sky that I had chosen this hour for my attempt to rescue Dejah Thoris and her companion.

Presently I heard the motors of Gar Nal's ship, which we had decided should be the signal that he was ready to start. Leaving the ground, I rose from the courtyard, crossed the wall and set a course away from the city. This I held until I felt that we were out of sight of any possible watcher who might have discovered us. Trailing us was the dark hulk of Gar Nal's ship.

In a wide spiral, I rose and circled back to the opposite side of the castle; and then, approaching it more closely, I picked out the lofty Tower of Diamonds.

Somewhere in that gleaming shaft were Dejah Thoris and Zanda; and if Ozara had not betrayed me and if no accident had befallen her plan, the Jeddara of the Tarids was with them.

There had been moments when I had been somewhat concerned as to the honesty and loyalty of Ozara. If she had spoken the truth, then there was every reason why she should wish to escape from the clutches of Ul Vas. However, she might not be so enthusiastic about the escape of Dejah Thoris and Zanda.

I confess that I do not understand women. Some of the things that they do, their mental processes, are often inexplicable to me. Yes, I am a fool with women; yet I was not so stupid that I did not sense something in Ozara's manner toward me, something in the very fact that she had sent for me, that indicated an interest on the part of the Jeddara of the Tarids that might prove inimical to the interests of the Princess of Helium.

Ozara, Jeddara of the Tarids, however, was not the only doubtful factor in the problem which confronted me. I did not trust Gar Nal. I doubt that anyone who had once looked into the man's eyes could trust him. Ur Jan was my avowed enemy. His every interest demanded that he either betray or destroy me.

Zanda must have learned by this time from Dejah Thoris that I was John Carter, Prince of Helium. That knowledge would, undoubtedly, free her from all sense of obligation to me; and I could not but recall that she had sworn to kill John Carter if ever the opportunity presented itself. This left only Jat Or and Umka upon whom I could depend; and, as a matter of fact, I was not depending too much upon Umka. His intentions might be good enough, but I knew too little of his fighting heart and ability to be able to definitely assure myself that the cat-man of Ladan would prove an important and effective ally.

As these discouraging thoughts were racing through my brain, I was causing the ship to drop slowly toward the Diamond Tower and circle it; and presently I saw a red scarf across the sill of a lighted window.

Silently the ship drew closer. The doors in both sides of the cabin were open to permit Gar Nal to cross from his ship to the window in the tower.

I stood upon the threshold of the port doorway, ready to leap into the room the instant that the ship drew close enough.

The interior of the room beyond the window was not brilliantly lighted, but in the dim illumination I could see the figures of three women, and my heart leaped with renewed hope.

The discovery of the scarlet scarf flying from the window had not wholly reassured me, as I was fully conscious of the fact that it might have been placed there as a lure; but the presence of the three women in the chamber appeared reasonable evidence that Ozara had carried out her part of the agreement loyally.

As the ship came closer to the sill, I prepared to leap into the room beyond; and just as I jumped I heard a voice raised in alarm and warning far below me at the base of the tower. We had been discovered.

As I alighted from the floor of the chamber, Dejah Thoris voiced a little exclamation of happiness. "My chieftain!" she cried. "I knew that you would come. Wherever they might have taken me, I knew that you would follow."

"To the end of the universe, my Princess," I replied.

The warning cry from below that told me that we had been discovered left no time now for greeting or explanation, nor would either Dejah Thoris or myself reveal to strangers the emotions that were in our breasts. I wanted to take her to my heart, to crush her beautiful body to mine, to cover her lips with kisses; but instead I only said, "Come, we must board the ship at once. The guard below has raised the alarm."

Zanda came and clutched my arm. "I knew you would come, Vandor," she said.

I could not understand her use of that name. Could it be that Dejah Thoris had not told her who I was? Ozara also knew my name. It seemed incredible that she should not have mentioned it when she came to the room to explain to the two women imprisoned there that a rescue had been planned and who was to execute it.

The Jeddara of the Tarids did not greet me. She scrutinized me beneath narrowed lids through the silky fringe of her long lashes; and as my eyes rested for a moment on hers, I thought that I recognized in her glance a hint of malice; but perhaps that was only my imagination, and certainly I had no time now to analyze or question her emotions.

As I turned toward the window with Dejah Thoris, I was filled with consternation. The ships were gone!

Running to the opening, I looked out; and to the left I saw both crafts moving off into the night.

What had happened to thus wreck my plans in the very instant of success?

The three women shared my consternation. "The ship!" exclaimed Dejah Thoris.

"Where has it gone?" cried Ozara.

"We are lost," said Zanda, quite simply. "I can hear armed men running up the stairway."

Suddenly I realized what had happened. I had directed the brain to approach the window, but I had not told it to stop. I had jumped, and it had gone on before my companions could follow me; and Gar Nal, not knowing what had occurred, had continued on with it, following me as I had directed.

Instantly, I centered my thoughts upon the mechanical brain and directed it to bring the ship back to the window and stop there. Self-reproach now was useless but I could not help but be cognizant of the fact that my carelessness had jeopardized the safety of my princess and those others who had looked to me for protection.

I could now plainly hear the warriors approaching. They were coming swiftly. From the window, I could see both ships turning now. Would they reach us before it was too late? I commanded the brain to return at the highest speed compatible with safety. It leaped forward in response to my wishes. The warriors were very close now. I judged that they were approaching the next level below. In another moment they would be at the door.

I carried the long-sword of one of the Tarid warriors that we had overpowered in the cabin of the craft, but could a single sword for long prevail over the many that I knew must be coming?

The ships drew closer, Gar Nal's almost abreast of mine. I saw Jat Or and Ur Jan standing in the doorway of Fal Sivas's ship.

"The alarm has been raised and warriors are almost at the door," I called to them. "I will try to hold them off while you get the women aboard."

Even as I spoke, I heard the enemy just outside the door of the chamber. "Stay close to the window," I directed the three women, "and board the boat the moment it touches the sill;" then I crossed the room quickly to the door, the Tarid long-sword ready in my hand.

I had scarcely reached it, when it was thrown open; a dozen warriors crowded in the corridor beyond. The first one to leap into the room leaped full upon the point of my blade. With a single, piercing scream he died; and as I jerked my steel from his heart, he lunged forward at my feet.

In the brief instant that my weapon was thus engaged, three men forced themselves into the room, pushed forward by those behind.

One thrust at me, and another swung a terrific cut at my head. I parried the thrust and dodged the cut, and then my blade clove the skull of one of them.

For a moment I forgot everything in the joy of battle. I felt my lips tense in the fighting smile that is famous in two worlds. Again, as upon so many other fields, my sword seemed inspired; but the Tarids were no mean swordsmen, nor were they cowards. They pushed forward into the room over the bodies of their dead companions.

I think that I could have accounted for them all single-handed, with such fierce enthusiasm did I throw my whole being into the defense of my princess; but now from below I heard the tramp of many feet and the rattling of accouterments. Reinforcements were coming!

It had been a glorious fight so far. Six lay dead upon the floor about me; but now the other six were all in the room, yet I would have felt no discouragement had I not heard the thunderous pounding of those many feet leaping rapidly upward from below.

I was engaged with a strapping fellow who sought to push me back, when one of his companions attempted to reach my side and distract my attention, while another edged to my opposite side.

My situation at that moment was embarrassing, to say the least, for the man who engaged me in front was not only a powerful fellow but a splendid swordsman; and then I saw a sword flash at my right and another at my left. Two of my adversaries went down, and in the next instant a quick glance showed me that Ur Jan and Jat Or were fighting at my side.

As the three remaining Tarids bravely leaped in to take the places of their fallen comrades, the van of their reinforcements arrived; and a perfect avalanche of yelling warriors burst into the apartment.

As I finally succeeded in spitting my antagonist, I snatched a momentary opportunity to glance behind me.

I saw the three women and Umka in the room and Gar Nal standing upon the sill of the window.

"Quick, Gar Nal," I cried, "get the women aboard."

For the next few minutes I was about as busy as I can remember ever having been before in my life. The Tarids were all around us. They had succeeded in encircling us. I was engaged constantly with two or three swordsmen at a time. I could not see what was taking place elsewhere in the room, but my thoughts were always of Dejah Thoris and her safety; and suddenly it occurred to me that if all of us who were fighting there in the room should be destroyed, she would be left in the power of Gar Nal without a defender.

Jat Or was fighting near me. "The princess!" I called to him; "she is alone on the ship with Gar Nal. If we are both killed, she is lost. Go to her at once."

"And leave you, my prince?" he demanded.

"It is not a request, Jat Or," I said; "it is a command."

"Yes, my prince," he replied, and fought his way to the window.

"Help him, Ur Jan," I commanded.

The three of us managed to cut a path for Jat Or to the window, and as we stood with our backs to it, I saw something which filled me with consternation. At one side, struggling in the grip of two warriors, was Ozara, the Jeddara of the Tarids.

"Save me, John Carter," she cried. "Save me, or I shall be killed."

There was nothing else that I could do. No other path would be honorable. Ozara had made it possible for us to escape. Perhaps her deed had already succeeded in saving Dejah Thoris. My own stupidity had placed us in this position, which now had become a definite threat to the life of the Jeddara.

Jat Or, Ur Jan, and I had succeeded in cutting down the warriors that immediately faced us; and the others, probably the least courageous of the band, seemed to hesitate to engage us again immediately.

I turned to my companions. "On board with you, quick," I cried, "and hold the entrance to the ship until I bring the Jeddara aboard."

As I started toward the warriors holding Ozara, I saw Umka at my side. He had given a good account of himself in the fight, although he had carried no sword, which, at the time, I did not understand because there was a plentiful supply of weapons aboard the craft; but later I was to learn that it is not the manner of the Masenas to fight with swords or daggers, with the use of which they are wholly unfamiliar.

I had seen in this encounter how he fought; and I realized that his powerful muscles and the terrible jaws of his lower mouth were adequate weapons even against a swordsman, aided as they were by the catlike agility of the Masena.

Umka had received a number of wounds; and was bleeding profusely, as, in fact, were all of us; but I thought that he looked about finished and ordered him back to the ship. He demurred at first, but finally he went, and I was alone in the room with the remaining Tarids.

I knew that my position was hopeless, but I could not leave to her death this girl who had aided me.

As I sprang forward to attack her captors, I saw another contingent of reinforcements burst into the room.

My case was now, indeed, hopeless.

The newcomers paid no attention to me; they ran straight for the window where the ship lay. If they succeeded in boarding her, the doom of Dejah Thoris would be sealed.

There was only one way in which I could circumvent them, though it definitely spelled the end for me.

The two men holding Ozara were waiting for me to attack them, but I paused long enough to hurl a mental order at the mechanical brain in the nose of Fal Sivas's ship.

I cast a glance back at the craft. Ur Jan and Umka stood in the doorway; Jat Or was not there; but at the very instant that the ship started to move away in obedience to my command, the young padwar sprang into view.

"My prince," he cried, "we have been betrayed. Gar Nal has fled with Dejah Thoris in his own ship."

Then the Tarids were upon me. A blow upon my head sent me down to merciful unconsciousness.

chapter XXII

IN THE DARK CELL

ENVELOPED IN DARKNESS, surrounded by the silence of the grave, I regained consciousness. I was lying on a cold, stone floor; my head ached; and when I felt it with my palms, it was stiff with dried blood; and my hair was matted.

Dizzily, I dragged myself to a sitting posture and then to my feet. Then came realization that I probably was not seriously injured, and I commenced to investigate my surroundings.

Moving cautiously, groping through the darkness with outstretched hands before me, I soon came in contact with a stone wall. This I followed for a short distance, when I discovered a door. It was a very substantial door, and it was securely fastened from the opposite side.

I moved on; I encircled the room and came to the door again. It was a small room, this new cell of mine. It had nothing to offer to either my eyes or to my ears. I commenced to realize the sort of world that the blind and the deaf must live in.

There were left to me then, only the senses of taste and smell and touch.

The first, of course, was useless to me under the circumstances; my nose, at first, identified a stale and musty odor; but presently becoming accustomed to it, it did not react at all. There was left to me then only the sense of touch. A strong wall broken by a wooden door—this was my world.

I wondered how long they would leave me here. It was like being buried alive. I knew that I must steel my will against the horrible monotony of it, with only the stone wall and that wooden door and my thoughts for company.

My thoughts! They were not pleasant. I thought of Dejah Thoris alone in the power of Gar Nal; I thought of poor Jat Or imprisoned in a ship that he could not control, with Ur Jan, the brutal assassin of Zodanga. I knew what his thoughts must be, knowing nothing of my fate, and feeling his sole responsibility for the safety of Dejah Thoris, whom he was helpless either to protect or avenge.

I thought of poor Zanda, to whom fate had been so unkind, condemned now to almost certain death above this distant satellite.

And Umka. Well, Umka had expected to die; and so he was no worse off now than he would have been had he never met me.

But the bitterest thought of all was that my own carelessness had brought disaster upon those who had looked to me for aid and protection.

Thus, futilely, I added mental torture to the monotony of those dragging hours.

The vault-like hole in which I was incarcerated was chill and damp. I surmised that they had placed me in the pits beneath the castle where no ship could reach me. My muscles were stiff; my blood ran sluggishly through my veins; hopelessness engulfed me.

Presently I realized that if I gave way to my morbid reflections, I should indeed be lost. Again and again I reminded myself that I still lived. I told myself that life was sweet; for so long as it persisted, there was still a chance that I might redeem myself and go out into the world again to serve my princess.

Now I commenced to move around my cell, encircling it several times until I knew its dimensions; and then I trotted to and fro, back and forth, around and around; and like a shadow boxer, I lead and feinted and parried, until at last I had my blood flowing again and felt the warmth of life renewing my vitality and flushing the sediment of foul worry from my brain.

I could not keep this up constantly, and so I sought to find other diversions by counting the stones set in the walls of my cell. I started at the door and moved around to the left. It was not the most entertaining pastime in which I had indulged, but at least there was a spice of excitement added to it by the thought that I might find some loose stones and possibly uncover an aperture leading to another apartment and to escape. Thus my imagination helped to alleviate the horrors of the darkness and the silence.

I could not, of course, measure time. I did not know how long I had been imprisoned there, but finally I became sleepy. I lay down upon the cold, damp floor.

When I awoke, I did not know how long I had slept; but I was very much refreshed, and so I concluded that I had passed the normal number of hours in rest.

Again, however, I was numb and cold; and once more I set myself to the exercises that would restore my circulation to normal; and as I was thus engaged, I heard sounds beyond the door of my cell.

I stopped and listened. Yes, someone was approaching. I waited, watching in the direction that I knew the door to be; and presently it opened, and a light flared in.

It was a blinding light to one whose eyes had become accustomed to the total darkness of the cell. I had to turn away my head and shield my eyes with my hand.

When I could look again, I saw a single warrior carrying a torch, a bowl of food, and a jug of water.

He had opened the door only wide enough to permit him to pass the receptacles through and set them on the floor of my cell. I saw that a heavy chain prevented the door from opening farther, as well as preventing me from attacking the bearer of my food and escaping.

The fellow raised his torch above his head and looked at me, inserting it through the crack of the door so that it fully illuminated the entire interior of the cell, or at least as high as some heavy wooden beam that spanned the room about twenty feet from the floor.

"So you weren't killed after all," commented the warrior.

"That is more than you can say for some of the others who fought in the Diamond Tower last night," I replied; "or was it last night?"

"No, it was night before last," he said. "It must have been some fight," he added. "I was not there, but the whole castle has been talking about it ever since. Those who fought against you say you are the greatest swordsman that ever lived. They would like to have you stay here and fight for them instead of against them, but old Ul Vas is so furious that nothing will satisfy him but your death."

"I can imagine that he doesn't feel very kindly toward me," I agreed.

"No, my life on it, he doesn't. It was bad enough letting all his prisoners escape, but planning to take his jeddara with you, phew! By my life, that was something. They say that the reason that you still live is because he hasn't been able to think of any death commensurate with your crime."

"And the Jeddara?" I asked; "what of her?"

"He's got her locked up; she'll be killed, too. I imagine that he is planning to put you both to death at the same time and probably in the same way. It is a shame to kill such a swordsman as you, but I am sure that it is going to be very interesting. I hope that I shall be fortunate enough to see it."

"Yes," I said, "I hope you enjoy it."

"Everyone will enjoy it but you and Ozara," he said, good-naturedly; and then he withdrew the torch, closed and locked the door; and I heard his footsteps receding as he departed.

I groped my way over to the food and water, as I was both hungry and thirsty; and as I ate and drank, I speculated upon what he had told me and upon what I had seen in the light of the flaring torch.

The beams, twenty feet above the floor, intrigued me. Above them there seemed to be nothing but a dark void, as though the ceiling of the cell was much farther above.

As I finished my meal, I determined to investigate what lay above those beams. On Mars, my earthly muscles permitted me to jump to extraordinary heights. I recalled the calculation that a full-sized earth man on Thuria could jump to a height of 225 feet. I realized, of course, that my size had been reduced, so that in proportion to Thuria I was no larger than I had been upon Barsoom; but I was still certain that my earthly muscles would permit me to jump much higher than any inhabitant of Ladan.

As I prepared to put my plan into practice, I was confronted by the very serious obstacle which the total darkness presented. I could not see the beams. In jumping for them, I might strike my head squarely against one of them with highly painful, if not fatal, results.

When you cannot see, it is difficult to tell how high you are jumping; but I had no light and no way of making a light; so all I could do was to be as careful as I could and trust to luck.

I tried springing upward a little way at a time at first, my hands extended above my head; and this proved very successful, for eventually I struck a beam.

I jumped again to place its exact position, and then I leaped for it and caught it. Raising myself onto it, I felt my way along to the wall. There I stood erect and reached upward, but I could feel nothing above me.

Then I went to the opposite end of the beam, and still I found nothing to give me any ray of hope.

It would have been suicidal to have investigated farther by leaping up from the beam, and so I dropped to the floor again. Then I leaped for another beam and made a similar investigation, with the same result.

Thus, one beam at a time, I explored the void above them as far as I could reach; but always the result was the same.

My disappointment was intense. In a situation such as mine, one grasps at such tiny straws. He reposes all his hopes, his future, his very life upon them; and when they are inadequate to support the weight of so much responsibility, he is plunged into the uttermost depths of despair.

But I would not admit defeat. The beams were there; they seemed to have been providentially placed for me to use in some way.

I racked my brain, searching for some plan whereby I might escape. I was like a rat in a trap, a cornered rat; and my mind commenced to function with all the cunning of a wild beast seeking to escape a snare.

Presently an idea came to me. It seemed Heaven-sent; but that was probably more because it was the only plan that had presented itself, rather than because it had any intrinsic merit. It was a wild, hare-brained plan that depended upon many things over which I had no control. Fate must needs be very kind to me if it were to succeed.

I was sitting disconsolately upon the last beam that I had investigated when it came to me. Immediately I dropped to the floor of my cell and went and stood by the door, listening.

How long I remained there, I do not know. When fatigue overcame me, I lay down and slept with my ear against the door. I never left it. I took my exercise jumping about in the same spot there by that fateful door.

At last my ears were rewarded by that for which they had been listening. Footsteps were approaching. I could hear them shuffling in the distance; I could hear the clank of metal upon metal. The sounds were increasing in volume. A warrior was approaching.

I leaped for the beam directly above the door; and crouching there like a beast of prey, I waited.

The footsteps halted just outside my cell. I heard the bars that secured the door sliding from their keepers, and then the door was pushed open and a light appeared. I saw an arm and hand extend into the room and set down jars of food and water. Then a flaming torch was thrust into the room, followed by a man's head. I saw the fellow looking around the interior of the cell.

"Hey, there!" he cried; "where are you?"

The voice was not that of the man who had brought my food on the previous occasion. I did not reply.

"By the crown of the Jeddak," he muttered, "has the fellow escaped?"

I heard him fussing with the chain that held the door from opening but a few inches, and my heart stood still. Could it be that my wild hope was to be realized? Upon this one hoped-for possibility hinged all the rest of my plans and hopes.

The door swung open, and the man stepped cautiously into the room. He was a sturdy warrior. In his left hand he carried the torch, and in his right he gripped a keen long-sword.

He moved cautiously, looking around him at every step.

He was still too close to the door. Very slowly he started across the cell, muttering to himself; and in the darkness above, I followed along the beam, like a panther stalking its prey. Still mumbling surprised exclamations, he started back. He passed beneath me; and as he did so, I sprang.

chapter XXIII

THE SECRET DOOR

ECHOING THROUGH the chamber and the corridor beyond, the screams of the warrior seemed enough to bring every fighting man in the castle upon me, as I launched myself upon him and brought him to the floor.

As the man went down, the light of the torch was extinguished; we fought in total darkness. My first aim was to quiet his screams, and this I did the instant that my fingers found his throat.

It seemed almost in the nature of a miracle that my dream of escape should be materializing, step by step, almost precisely as I had visualized it; and this thought gave me hope that good fortune might continue to attend me until I was safely out of the clutches of Ul Vas.

The warrior with whom I struggled upon the stone floor of that dark cell beneath the castle of the Tarids was a man of only ordinary physical strength, and I soon subdued him.

Possibly I accomplished this sooner than I might have otherwise; for, after I got my fingers on his throat, I promised I would not kill him if he would cease his struggling and his attempted screaming.

With me, time was an all-important factor; for even if the man's outcry had not been heard by his comrades above stairs, it seemed quite reasonable that if he did not return to his other duties within a reasonable time, a search for him would be instituted. If I were to escape, I must get out at once; and so, after I made my offer to the man and he ceased his struggling momentarily, I released my grip upon his throat long enough for him to accept or refuse my proposition.

Being a man of intelligence, he accepted.

I immediately bound him with his own harness and, as an added precaution, stuffed a gag in his mouth. Next I relieved him of his dagger, and after groping around on the floor for some time I found the long-sword that had fallen from his hand when I first attacked him.

"And now good-by, my friend," I said. "You need not feel humiliated at your defeat; far better men than you have gone down before John Carter, Prince of Helium." Then I went out and closed and locked the door of the cell after me.

The corridor was very dark. I had had but one brief glimpse of it, or rather of a portion of it, when my food had been brought to me the previous day.

It had seemed to me then that the corridor led straight away from the entrance to my cell, and now I groped my way through the darkness in that direction. Probably I should have moved slowly along that unknown passageway; but I did not, for I knew that if the warrior's cries had been heard in the castle above, there might be an investigation; and I most certainly did not wish to meet a body of armed men in that cul-de-sac.

Keeping one hand against the wall to guide me, I moved rapidly forward; and I had gone perhaps a hundred yards when I discerned a faint suggestion of light ahead of me. It did not seem to be the yellowish light of a torch, but, rather, diffused daylight.

It increased in volume as I approached it, and presently I came to the foot of the stairway down which it was shining.

All this time, I had heard nothing to indicate that anyone was coming to investigate; so it was with a feeling of at least some security that I ascended the stairway.

With the utmost caution, I entered the level above. Here it was much lighter. I was in a short corridor with a doorway on either side;

ahead of me the passageway ended in a transverse corridor. I moved quickly forward, for I could now see my way quite clearly, as the corridor, although extremely gloomy, was much better lighted than that from which I had emerged.

I was congratulating myself upon my good fortune as I was about to turn into the transverse corridor, when I bumped full into a figure at the turn.

It was a woman. She was probably much more surprised than I, and she started to scream.

I knew that, above all things, I must prevent her from giving an alarm; and so I seized her and clapped a hand across her mouth.

I had just turned the corner into the other corridor when I collided with her; its full length was visible to me; and now, as I silenced the woman, I saw two warriors turn into it at the far end. They were coming in my direction. Evidently I had congratulated myself too soon.

Unencumbered by my captive, I might have found a hiding-place, or, failing that, I could have lain in ambush for them in this darker passageway and killed them both before they could raise an alarm; but here I was with both of my hands occupied, one of them holding the struggling girl and the other effectually silencing her attempt to cry out.

I could not kill her, and if I turned her loose she would have the whole castle on me in a few moments. My case seemed entirely hopeless, but I did not give up hope. I had come this far; I would not, I could not, admit defeat.

Then I recalled the two doors that I had passed in the short corridor. One of them was only a few paces to my rear.

"Keep still, and I will not harm you," I whispered, and then I dragged her along the corridor to the nearest door.

Fortunately, it was unlocked; but what lay beyond it, I did not know. I had to think quickly and decide what I should do if it were occupied. There seemed only one thing to do, push the girl into it and then run back to meet the two warriors that I had seen approaching. In other words, try to fight my way out of the castle of Ul Vas—a mad scheme, with half a thousand warriors to block my way.

But the room was not occupied, as I could see the moment that I entered it; for it was well lighted by several windows.

Closing the door, I stood with my back against it, listening. I had not looked down at the woman in my arms; I was too intent upon listening for the approach of the two warriors I had seen. Would they turn into this corridor? Would they come to this very room?

I must have unconsciously released my pressure upon the girl's lips; for before I could prevent it, she tore my hand away and spoke.

"John Carter!" she exclaimed in a low tone.

I looked down at her in surprise, and then I recognized her. It was Ulah, the slave of Ozara, the Jeddara of the Tarids.

"Ulah," I said, earnestly, "please do not make me harm you. I do not wish to harm anyone in the castle; I only wish to escape. More than my life depends upon that, so very much more that I would break the unwritten law of my caste even to killing a woman, were it necessary to do so to accomplish my purpose."

"You need not fear me," she said; "I will not betray you."

"You are a wise girl," I said; "you have bought your life very cheaply."

"It was not to save my life that I promised," she said. "I would not have betrayed you in any event."

"And why?" I asked. "You owe me nothing."

"I love my mistress, Ozara," she said simply.

"And what has that to do with it?" I asked.

"I would not harm one whom my mistress loves."

Of course, I knew that Ulah was romancing—letting her imagination work overtime; and as it was immaterial what she believed so long as she helped me, I did not contradict her.

"Where is your mistress now?" I asked.

"She is in this very tower," she replied. "She is locked in a room directly above this one, on the next level. Ul Vas is keeping her there until he is ready to destroy her. Oh, save her, John Carter, save her!"

"How did you learn my name, Ulah?" I asked.

"The Jeddara told me," she replied; "she talked about you constantly."

"You are better acquainted with the castle than I am, Ulah," I said; "is there any way in which I can reach the Jeddara? Can you get a message to her? Could we get her out of that room?"

"No," she replied; "the door is locked, and two warriors stand guard outside it day and night."

I walked to the window and looked out. There seemed to be no one in sight. Then I leaned out as far as I could and looked up. Perhaps fifteen feet above me was another window. I turned back into the room.

"You are sure that the Jeddara is in the room directly above this?" I asked.

"I know it," she replied.

"And you want to help her to escape?"

"Yes; there is nothing that I would not do to serve her."

"What is this room used for?" I asked.

"Nothing, now," she replied; "you see everything is covered with dust. It has not been used for a long time."

"You think it is not likely that anyone will come here?" I asked. "You think I might hide here safely until tonight?"

"I am sure that you are perfectly safe," she replied; "I do not know why anyone should come here."

"Good!" I exclaimed. "Do you really want to help your mistress to escape?"

"With all my heart," she replied. "I could not bear to see her die."

"You can help her, then," I said.

"How?"

"Bring me a rope and a strong hook. Do you think you can do it?"

"How long a rope?"

"About twenty feet."

"When do you want them?"

"Whenever you can bring them without danger of detection, but certainly before midnight tonight."

"I can get them," she said. "I will go at once."

I had to trust her; there was no other way, and so I let her depart.

After she had gone and I had closed the door behind her, I found a heavy bar on the inside. I dropped this into its keeper so that no one could enter the room unexpectedly and take me by surprise. Then I sat down to wait.

Those were long hours that dragged themselves slowly by. I could not but constantly question my wisdom in trusting the slave girl, Ulah. What did I know about her? By what loyalty was she bound to me, except by the thin bond engendered by her foolish imagination? Perhaps, already, she had arranged for my capture. It would not be at all surprising that she had a lover among the warriors, as she was quite beautiful. What better turn could she serve him than by divulging the place of my concealment and permitting him to be the means of my capture and perhaps thereby winning promotion?

Toward the end of the afternoon, when I heard footsteps coming along the corridor toward my hiding place—the first sounds that I had heard since Ulah left me—I was certain that warriors were coming to seize me. I determined that I would give a good account of myself; and so I stood by the door, my long-sword ready in my hand; but the footsteps passed by me. They were moving in the direction of the stairway up which I had come from the black corridor leading to my cell.

Not long after, I heard them returning. There were a number of men talking excitedly, but through the heavy door I could not quite catch their words. When they had passed out of hearing, I breathed a sigh of relief; and my confidence in Ulah commenced to take new heart.

Night fell. Light began to shine beyond many of the windows in the castle visible from the room in which I hid.

Why did not Ulah return? Had she been unable to find a rope and a hook? Was something or someone detaining her? What futile questions one propounds in the extremity of despair.

Presently I heard a sound outside the door of the room. I had heard no one approaching; but now I knew that someone was pushing on the door, attempting to enter. I went close to it and put my ear against the panels. Then I heard a voice. "Open, it is Ulah."

Great was my relief as I drew the bar and admitted the slave girl. It was quite dark in the room; we could not see one another.

"Did you think I was never going to return, John Carter?" she asked.

"I was commencing to have my doubts," I replied. "Were you able to get the things I asked for?"

"Yes, here they are," she said, and I felt a rope and a hook pressed into my hand.

"Good!" I exclaimed. "Have you learned anything while you were away that might help me or the Jeddara?"

"No," she said, "nothing that will help you but something that may make it more difficult for you to leave the castle, if that were possible at all, which I doubt."

"What is that?" I demanded.

"They have learned of your escape from the cell," she replied. "The warrior who was sent there with your food did not return; and when other warriors went to investigate, they found him bound and gagged in the cell where you should have been."

"It must have been they I heard passing the door late in the afternoon," I said. "It is strange they have not searched this room."

"They think you went in another direction," she explained. "They are searching another part of the castle."

"But eventually they will come here?" I asked.

"Yes," she said; "eventually they will search every room in the castle, but that will take a long time."

"You have done well, Ulah," I said. "I am sorry that I can offer you nothing more in return than my thanks."

"I shall be glad to do even more," she said; "there is nothing that I would not do to help you and the jeddara."

"There is nothing more that you can do," I told her; "and now you had better go, before they find you here with me."

"You are sure that there is nothing more I can do?" she asked.

"No, nothing, Ulah," and I opened the door, and she went out.

"Good-by, and good luck, John Carter," she whispered, as I closed the door behind her.

I went at once to the window, after rebolting the door. It was very dark outside. I had wanted to wait until after midnight and until the castle was asleep before I attempted to put into practice the plan I contemplated for the rescue of Ozara, but the knowledge that they were searching the castle for me forced me to put aside every consideration except haste.

I fastened one end of the rope securely to the hook that Ulah had brought me. Then I sat on the window sill and leaned far out.

I took one end of the rope in my left hand where I grasped the frame of the window, and held the hook in my right hand, permitting the slack of the rope to fall free beneath me against the side of the tower outside the window.

I gauged the distance upward to the sill of the window above. It seemed too far for me to hope to make a successful cast from the position in which I was sitting, and so I arose and stood on the sill of the window. This brought me a few feet nearer my goal and also gave me a little more freedom of action.

I was very anxious to be successful at the first cast; for I feared that if I missed, the rattling of the metal hook against the side of the tower might attract attention.

I stood there several minutes gauging the distance and going through all the motions of throwing the hook except actually releasing it.

When I felt that I had the timing and the distance as accurately gauged as it was possible to do in this manner, I swung the hook upward and released it.

I could see the sill above me, because a faint light was coming from the room beyond it. I saw the hook swing into this light; I heard it strike the sill with a metallic ring; then I pulled down upon the rope.

The hook had caught! I put considerable weight upon the rope, and still the hook held. I waited a moment to see if I had attracted the attention of Ozara or anyone else who might be in the room with her.

No sign came out of the silence above, and I let my body swing out upon the rope.

I had to ascend very carefully, for I did not know how secure a hold the hook had upon the sill above.

I had not a great distance to climb, yet it seemed an eternity before my hand touched the sill.

First the fingers of one hand closed over it; then I drew myself up until I could grasp it with my other hand. Slowly, by main strength, I raised myself until my eyes were above the level of the sill. Before me was a dimly lighted room, apparently vacant.

I drew myself up farther until I could get one knee upon the sill, and always I was very careful not to dislodge the hook.

When, at last, my position was secure, I entered the room, taking the hook in with me lest it slip and fall to the bottom of the tower on the outside.

Now I saw that the room was occupied. A woman rose from her bed upon the opposite side. She was looking at me with wide, horror-struck eyes. It was Ozara. I thought she was going to scream.

Raising a warning finger to my lips, I approached her. "Make no sound, Ozara," I whispered; "I have come to save you."

"John Carter!" She breathed the name in tones so low that they could not have been heard beyond the door. As she spoke, she came close and threw her arms about my neck.

"Come," I said, "we must get out of here at once. Do not talk; we may be overheard."

Taking her to the window, I drew in the rope and fastened the lower end of it around her waist.

"I am going to lower you to the window of the room just below," I whispered. "As soon as you are safely inside, untie the rope and let it swing out for me."

She nodded, and I lowered her away. Presently the rope went slack, and I knew that she had reached the sill of the room below. I waited for her to unfasten it from her body; then I engaged the hook over the sill upon which I sat, and quickly descended to the room below.

I did not wish to leave the hook and the rope as they were, because, in the event that anyone should enter Ozara's cell above, this evidence would point immediately to the room below; and I did not know how long we might have to wait here.

As gently as possible, I shook the hook loose and was fortunate in catching it as it dropped and before it could scrape against the side of the tower.

As I entered the room, Ozara came close to me and placed her hands upon my breast. She was trembling, and her voice was trembling as she spoke.

"I was so surprised to see you, John Carter," she said. "I thought that you were dead. I saw them strike you down, and Ul Vas told me that they had killed you. What a terrible wound; I do not see how you recovered. When you faced me in the room above and I saw the blood dried upon your skin and in your hair, it was as though a dead man had come back to life."

"I had forgotten what a spectacle I must present," I said. "I have had no opportunity to wash the blood from me since I was wounded. What little water they brought me barely sufficed for drinking purposes; but as far as the wound is concerned, it does not bother me. I am quite recovered; it was only a flesh wound."

"I was so frightened for you," she said; "and to think that you took that risk for me, when you might have escaped with your friends."

"You think they got away all right?" I asked.

"Yes," she replied, "and Ul Vas is very furious about it. He will make you and me pay, if we do not escape."

"Do you know of any way by which we can escape from this castle?" I asked her.

"There is a secret doorway, known only to Ul Vas and two of his most faithful slaves," she replied. "At least, Ul Vas thinks that only those three know of it; but I know. It leads out to the edge of the river where the waters lap the walls of the castle.

"Ul Vas is not well-liked by his people. There are plots and intrigues in the castle. There are factions that would like to overthrow Ul Vas and set up a new jeddak. Some of these enemies are so powerful that Ul Vas does not dare destroy them openly. These, he murders secretly; and he and his two faithful slaves carry the bodies to this secret doorway and cast them into the river.

"Once, suspecting something of the kind, I followed him, thinking that I might discover a way to escape and return to my own people in Domnia; but when I saw where the passage led, I was afraid. I would not dare to jump into the river; and even if I did, beyond the river there is a terrible forest. I do not know, John Carter, that we would be much better off either in the river or the forest than we are here."

"If we remain here, Ozara, we know that we shall meet death and that there will be no escape. In the river or the forest beyond, there will be at least a chance; for often wild beasts are less cruel than men."

"I know that all too well," she replied; "but even in the forest there are men, terrible men."

"Nevertheless, I must take the chance, Ozara," I told her. "Will you come with me?"

"Wherever you take me, John Carter, whatever fate befalls us, I shall be happy as long as I am with you. I was very angry when I learned that you loved that woman from Barsoom," she said; "but now she is gone, and I shall have you all to myself."

"She is my mate, Ozara."

"You love her?" she demanded.

"Of course," I replied.

"That is all right," she said, "but she is gone, and you are mine now."

I had no time to waste on such matters then. It was apparent that the girl was self-willed; that she had always had her own way, had everything that she wished, and could not brook being crossed, no matter how foolish her whim might be. At another time, if we lived, I might bring her to her senses; but now I must bend every effort to escape.

"How can we reach this secret doorway?" I asked. "Do you know the way from here?"

"Yes," she replied; "come with me."

We crossed the room and entered the corridor. It was very dark, but we groped our way to the stairs that I had ascended from the pit earlier in the day. When she started down these, I questioned her.

"Are you sure this is the right way?" I asked. "This leads to the cell in which I was imprisoned."

"Perhaps it does," she said; "but it also leads to a distant part of the castle, close to the river, where we shall find the doorway we are seeking."

I hoped that she knew what she was talking about as I followed her down the stairway and through the Stygian darkness of the corridor below.

When I had come through it before, I had guided myself by pressing my right hand against the wall at my side. Now Ozara followed the opposite wall; and when we had gone a short distance, turned into a corridor at our right that I had passed without knowing of its existence, because I had been following the opposite wall; and of course in the absolute darkness of the corridor, I had not been able to see anything.

We followed this new corridor for a long distance, but finally ascended a circular stairway to the next level above.

Here we came into a lighted corridor.

"If we can reach the other end of this without being discovered," whispered Ozara, "we shall be safe. At the far end is a false door that leads into the secret passageway ending at the door above the river."

We both listened intently. "I hear no one," she said.

"Nor I."

As we started down the long corridor, I saw that there were rooms opening from it on either side; but as we approached each door I was relieved to find that it was closed.

We had covered perhaps half the length of the corridor when a slight noise behind us attracted my attention; and, turning, I saw two men step from one of the rooms we had recently passed. They were turning away from us, toward the opposite end of the corridor; and I was breathing a sigh of relief, when a third man followed them from the room. This one, through some perversity of fate, glanced in our direction; and immediately he voiced an exclamation of surprise and warning.

"The Jeddara!" he cried, "and the black-haired one!"

Instantly the three turned and ran toward us. We were about halfway between them and the door leading to the secret passage that was our goal.

Flight, in the face of an enemy, is something that does not set well upon my stomach; but now there was no alternative, since to stand and fight would have been but to insure disaster; and so Ozara and I fled.

The three men pursuing us were shouting at the tops of their voices for the evident purpose of attracting others to their assistance.

Something prompted me to draw my long-sword as I ran; and it is fortunate that I did so; for just as we were approaching a doorway on our left, a warrior, attracted by the noise in the corridor, stepped out. Ozara dodged past him just as he drew his sword. I did not even slacken my speed but took him in my stride, cleaving his skull as I raced past him.

Now we were at the door, and Ozara was searching for the secret mechanism that would open it to us. The three men were approaching rapidly.

"Take your time, Ozara," I cautioned her, for I knew that in the haste of nervousness her fingers might bungle the job and delay us.

"I am trembling so," she said; "they will reach us before I can open it."

"Don't worry about them," I told her. "I can hold them off until you open it."

Then the three were upon me. I recognized them as officers of the Jeddak's guard, because their trappings were the same as those worn by Zamak; and I surmised, and rightly, that they were good swordsmen.

The one in the lead was too impetuous. He rushed upon me as though he thought he could cut me down with his first stroke, which was not the part of wisdom. I ran him through the heart.

As he fell, the others were upon me but they fought more cautiously; yet, though there were two of them, and their blades were constantly thrusting and cutting in an endeavor to reach me, my own sword, moving with the speed of thought, wove a steel net of defense about me.

But defense alone would not answer my purpose; for if they could keep me on the defensive, they could hold me here until reinforcements came; and then, by force of numbers, I must be overcome.

In the instant, following a parry, my point reached out and pricked one of my adversaries sharply above the heart. Involuntarily, he shrank back; and as he did so I turned upon his companion and opened his chest wide.

Neither wound was mortal, but they slowed my adversaries down. Ozara was still fumbling with the door. Our situation promised to be most unpleasant if she were unable to open it, for now at the far end of the corridor I saw a detachment of warriors racing toward us; but I did not warn her to hurry, fearing that then, in her excitement, she would never be able to open it.

The two wounded men were now pressing me hard again. They were brave warriors and worthy foemen. It is a pleasure to be pitted against such, although there are always regrets when one must kill them. However, I had no choice, for then I heard a sudden cry of relief from Ozara.

"It is open, John Carter," she cried. "Come! Hurry!"

But now the two warriors were engaging me so fiercely that I could not break away from them.

But just for an instant was I held. With a burst of speed and a ferocity such as I imagine they had never beheld before, I took the battle to them. A vicious cut brought down one; and as he fell, I ran the other through the chest.

The reinforcements running toward us had covered half the length of the corridor as I hurried through the doorway after Ozara and closed the door behind me.

Now again we were in complete darkness. "Hurry!" cried Ozara. "The passageway is straight and level all the way to the door."

Through the darkness, we ran. I heard the men behind me open the door, and knew that they were in the passageway at our rear; fully twenty of them there must have been.

Suddenly I ran full upon Ozara. We had come to the end of the passage, and she was standing at the door. This door she opened more quickly; and as it swung in, I saw the dark river flowing beneath us. Upon the opposite shore was the gloomy outline of the forest.

How cold and mysterious this strange river looked. What mysteries, what dangers, what terrors, lay in the sinister wood beyond?

But I was only vaguely conscious of such thoughts. The warriors who would seize us and carry us back to death were almost upon us as I took Ozara in my arms and jumped.

chapter XXIV

Back to Barsoom

DARK, FORBIDDING WATERS closed over our heads and swirled about us as we rose to the surface; and, equally dark and forbidding, the forest frowned upon us. Even the moaning of the wind in the trees seemed an eerie warning, forbidding, threatening. Behind us, the warriors in the doorway shouted curses upon us.

I struck out for the opposite shore, holding Ozara in one arm and keeping her mouth and nose above water. She lay so limp that I thought she had fainted, nor would I have been surprised, for even a woman of the strongest fibre might weaken after having undergone what she had had to during the last two days.

But when we reached the opposite shore, she clambered out on the bank in full possession of all her faculties.

"I thought that you had swooned," I said; "you lay so very still."

"I do not swim," she replied; "and I knew that if I struggled, it would hamper you." There was even more to the erstwhile Jeddara of the Tarids than I had imagined.

"What are we going to do now, John Carter?" she asked. Her teeth were chattering from cold, or terror; and she seemed very miserable.

"You are cold," I said; "if I can find anything dry enough to burn, we shall have a fire."

The girl came close to me. I could feel her body trembling against mine.

"I am a little cold," she said, "but that is nothing; I am terribly afraid."

"But why are you afraid now, Ozara? Do you think that Ul Vas will send men after us?"

"No, it is not that," she replied. "He couldn't make men come into this wood at night, and even by daylight they would hesitate to venture into it on this side of the river. Tomorrow he will know that it will be useless to send after us, for tomorrow we shall be dead."

"What makes you say that?" I demanded.

"The beasts," she said, "the beasts that hunt through the forest by night; we cannot escape them."

"Yet you came here willingly."

"Ul Vas would have tortured us," she replied; "the beasts will be more merciful. Listen! You can hear them now."

In the distance, I heard strange grunts and then a fearsome roar.

"They are not near us," I said.

"They will come," she replied.

"Then I had better get a fire started; that will keep them away."

"Do you think so?" she asked.

"I hope so."

I knew that in any forest there must be deadwood; and so, although it was pitch dark, I commenced to search for fallen branches; and soon I had collected a little pile of these and some dry leaves.

The Tarids had not taken away my pocket pouch, and in it I still had the common Martian appliance for making fire.

"You said that the Tarids would hesitate to enter the forest on this side of the river even by day," I remarked, as I sought to ignite the dry leaves with which I hoped to start my fire. "Why is that?"

"The Masenas," she replied. "They often come up the river in great numbers, hunting the Tarids; and unfortunate is he whom they find outside the castle walls. It is seldom, however, that they cross to the other side of the river."

"Why do they hunt the Tarids?" I asked. "What do they want of them?"

"Food," she replied.

"You don't mean to say that the Masenas eat human flesh?" I demanded.

She nodded. "Yes, they are very fond of it."

I had succeeded in igniting the leaves, and now I busied myself placing small twigs upon my newborn fire and building it up into the semblance of something worthwhile.

"But I was imprisoned for a long time with one of the Masenas," I reminded her. "He seemed very friendly."

"Under those circumstances, of course," she said, "he might not try to eat you. He might even become very friendly; but if you should meet him here in the forest with his own people, you would find him very different. They are hunting beasts, like all of the other creatures that inhabit the forest."

My fire grew to quite a respectable size. It illuminated the forest and the surface of the river and the castle beyond.

When it blazed up and revealed us, the Tarids, called across to us, prophesying our early death.

The warmth of the fire was pleasant after our emersion from the cold water and our exposure to the chill of the forest night. Ozara came close to it, stretching her lithe, young body before it. The yellow flames illuminated her fair skin, imparted a greenish tinge to her blue hair, awakened slumberous fires in her languorous eyes.

Suddenly she tensed, her eyes widened in fright. "Look!" she whispered, and pointed.

I turned in the direction that she indicated. From the dense shadows just beyond the firelight, two blazing eyes were flaming.

"They have come for us," said Ozara.

I picked a blazing brand from the fire and hurled it at the intruder. There was a hideous, bloodcurdling scream as the eyes disappeared.

The girl was trembling again. She cast affrighted glances in all directions.

"There is another," she exclaimed presently, "and there, and there, and there."

I caught a glimpse of a great body slinking in the shadows; and all about us, as I turned, I saw blazing eyes. I threw a few more brands, but the eyes disappeared for only a moment to return again almost immediately, and each time they seemed to come closer; and now, since I had cast the first brand, the beasts were roaring and growling and screaming continuously—a veritable diapason of horror.

I realized that my fire would not last long if I kept throwing it at the beasts, as I had not sufficient wood to keep it replenished.

Something must be done. I cast about me rather hopelessly in search of some avenue of escape and discovered a nearby tree that looked as though it might be easily scaled. Only such a tree would be of any advantage to us, as I had no doubt that the creatures would charge the moment that we started to climb.

I took two brands from the fire and handed them to Ozara, and then selected two for myself.

"What are we going to do?" she asked.

"We are going to try to climb that tree," I replied. "Perhaps some of these brutes can climb, too, but we shall have to take a chance. Those I have seen look too large and heavy for climbing.

"We will walk slowly to the foot of the tree. When we are there, throw your brands at the nearest beasts; and then start to climb. When you are safely out of their reach, I will follow."

Slowly we crossed from the fire to the tree, waving the blazing brands about us.

Here, Ozara did as I had bid her; and when she was safely out of the way, I grasped one of my brands in my teeth, hurled the other, and started to climb.

The beasts charged almost instantly, but I reached a point of safety before they could drag me down, though what with the smoke of the brand in my eyes and the sparks being scraped off against my naked hide, I was lucky to have made it at all; but I felt that we must have the light of the brand, as I did not know what arboreal enemies might be lurking in the branches above.

I immediately examined the tree, climbing to the highest branches that would support my weight. With the aid of my light, I discovered that no creature was in it, other than Ozara and myself; and high among the branches I made a happy find—an enormous nest, carefully woven and lined with soft grasses.

I was about to call down to Ozara to come up, when I saw her already ascending just below me.

When she saw the nest, she told me that it was probably one of those built by the Masenas for temporary use during a raid or expedition into this part of the forest. It was certainly a most providential find, as it afforded us a comfortable place in which to spend the remainder of the night.

It was some time before we could accustom ourselves to the noises of the beasts howling beneath us, but at last we fell asleep; and when we awoke in the morning, they had departed; and the forest was quiet.

Ozara had told me that her country, Domnia, lay across the mountains that rose beyond the forest and that it might be reached by following the river down for a considerable distance to the end of the range, where we could follow another river up to Domnia upon the opposite side.

The most remarkable feature of the following two days was the fact that we survived them. We found food in plenty; and as we were always near the river, we never suffered for lack of water; but by day and by night we were constantly in danger of attack by the roving flesh-eaters.

We always sought to save ourselves by climbing into trees, but upon three occasions we were taken by surprise; and I was forced to fall back upon my sword, which had seemed to me a most inadequate weapon of defense against some of the ferocious beasts that assailed us.

However, in these three instances, I managed to kill our attackers, although, I must confess, that it seemed to me then, and still does, wholly a matter of luck that I succeeded.

By now, Ozara was in a more sanguine frame of mind. Having survived this long, she felt that it was entirely possible that we might live to reach Domnia, although originally she had been confident that we could not come through the first night alive.

She was often quite gay now, and she was really very good company. Especially was this true on the morning of the third day as we were making good progress toward our distant goal.

The forest seemed to be unusually quiet; and we had seen no dangerous beasts all that day, when suddenly a chorus of hideous roars arose all about us; and simultaneously a score or more of creatures dropped from the concealing foliage of the trees about us.

Ozara's happy chatter died on her lips. "The Masenas!" she cried.

As they surrounded us and started to close in on us, their roaring ceased and they commenced to meow and purr. This, to me, seemed far more horrifying. As they came closer, I decided to make our capture cost them dearly, though I knew that eventually they would take us. I had seen Umka fight, and I knew what to expect.

Although they closed about me, they did not seem anxious to engage me. By pushing close to me on one side and then on the other, by giving away here and then there, I was forced to move about considerably; but I did not realize until it was too late that I was moving in the direction that they wished me to move and in accordance with their designs.

Presently they got me where they wanted me, beneath the branches of a great tree; and immediately a Masena dropped upon my shoulders and bore me to earth. Simultaneously, most of the others swarmed on top of me, while a few seized Ozara; and thus they disarmed me before I could strike a blow.

There was a great amount of purring after that, and they seemed to be having some sort of a discussion; but as it was in their own language, I did not understand it. Presently, however, they started down river, dragging us along with them.

After perhaps an hour, we came to a section of the forest from which all the brushwood had been cleared. The ground beneath the trees was almost like a lawn. The branches of the trees were trimmed to a considerable distance about the ground.

As we reached the edge of this park-like space, our captors set up a loud roaring which was presently answered from the trees we were approaching.

We were dragged to the foot of a great tree, up which several of our captors swarmed like cats.

Then came the problem of getting us up. I could see that it puzzled the Masenas, as well it might have. The bole of the tree was so large in diameter that no ordinary man could scale it, and all the branches had been cut off much higher than a man could jump. I could easily have entered it, but I did not tell them so. Ozara, however, could never have succeeded alone.

Presently, after considerable meowing and purring and not a little growling, some of those in the tree above lowered a pliant liana. One of the Masenas on the ground seized Ozara around the waist with one arm and the liana with his free hand and both his feet. Then those above hoisted this human elevator until it could find secure footing for itself and its passenger among the branches above.

In like manner, I was hoisted into the tree, where, thereafter, the climbing was easy.

We ascended only a few feet, however, before we came to a rude platform upon which was built one of the strange, arboreal houses of the Masenas.

Now, in all directions, I could see similar houses as far as my eyes could penetrate through the foliage. I could see that in some places branches had been cut and laid from tree to tree to form walk-ways between the houses. In other places there were only lianas where the Masenas must have crossed hand over hand from one tree to its neighbor.

The house into which we were now conducted was quite large and easily accommodated not only the twenty-odd men that had captured us but fully fifty more that soon congregated.

The Masenas squatted upon their haunches facing the far end of the room where sat, alone, a single male that I took to be their king.

There was a great deal of meowing and purring as they discussed us in their language, and finally I became impatient. Recalling that Umka had spoken the language of the Tarids, I thought it not at all unlikely that some of these others might; and so I addressed them in that tongue.

"Why have you captured us?" I demanded. "We are not your enemies. We were escaping from the Tarids, who are. They had us imprisoned and were about to kill us. Do any of you understand what I am saying?"

"I understand you," replied the creature whom I took to be king. "I understand your words, but your argument is meaningless. When we leave our houses and go down into the forest we may mean harm to no creature, yet that does not protect us from the beasts of prey that feed upon the flesh of their kill. There are few arguments that would satisfactorily overcome the cravings of the belly."

"You mean that you are going to eat us?" I demanded.

"Certainly," he replied.

Ozara shrank closer to me. "So this is the end," she said, "and what a horrible end! It did us no good to escape from Ul Vas."

"We have at least had three days of freedom that we would not otherwise have had," I reminded her; "and, anyway, we must die some time."

The Masena king spoke to his people in their own tongue, and immediately they set up a great meowing and purring, as, with savage growls, a number of them seized Ozara and me and started to drag us toward the entrance.

They had almost reached the doorway with us when a lone Masena entered and paused before us.

"Umka!" I cried.

"John Carter!" he exclaimed. "What are you doing here, and the Jeddara of the Tarids?"

"We escaped from Ul Vas, and now we are about to be eaten by your people," I told him.

Umka spoke to the men who were dragging us from the room; they hesitated a moment; and then they led us back before the Masena king, whom Umka addressed for several minutes.

After he had ceased, the king and others in the room carried on what appeared to be a heated discussion. When they had finished, Umka turned toward me.

"You are to be set free," he said, "in return for what you did for me; but you must leave our country at once."

"Nothing would suit us better," I replied.

"Some of us are going with you to see that none of our people attack you while you are still in the land of the Masenas."

After we had set out with our strange escort, I asked Umka to tell me what he knew of my friends.

"After we left the castle of the Tarids," he explained, "we drifted around idly in the air for a long time. They wanted to follow the man who had taken the woman away in the other ship, but they did not know where to search. Today I looked down and saw that we were over Masena, and I asked them to put me on the ground. This they did, and they are still there for all I know, as they were taking fresh water aboard and were going to gather fruits and hunt for meat."

It developed that the landing had been made at no great distance from where we then were, and at my request he led us to the spot.

As we approached it, the hearts of two of that party almost stopped beating, so great was the suspense. It quite easily might mean the difference between life and death for Ozara and me.

And then we saw it, the strange craft, lying in a little clearing among the trees.

Umka thought it best that he and his fellows should not approach the craft, as he might not be able to restrain them in the presence of these others whom they had not promised to protect; so we thanked him and bade him good-by, and he and his weird companions melted into the forest.

None of the three on the ship had noticed our approach, and we were quite close to her before they discovered us. They greeted us enthusiastically as two returned from the dead. Even Ur Jan was genuinely pleased to see me.

The assassin of Zodanga was furious with Gar Nal because he had broken his oath; and now, to my astonishment, the fellow threw his sword at my feet and swore eternal fealty to me.

"Never in my life," he said, "have I fought shoulder to shoulder with such a swordsman, and never shall it be said that I have drawn sword against him."

I accepted his service, and then I asked them how they had been able to maneuver the ship to this point.

"Zanda was the only one who knew anything about the mechanism or its control," explained Jat Or; "and after a little experimenting, she found that she could operate it." He looked proudly at her, and I read much in the smile that passed between them.

"You seem none the worse off for your experiences, Zanda," I said; "in fact, you appear very happy."

"I am very happy, *Vandor*," she replied, "happier than I ever expected to be in my life."

She emphasized the word Vandor, and I thought that I detected a smile lurking deep in her eyes.

"Is your happiness so great," I asked, "that it has caused you to forget your vow to kill John Carter?"

She returned my bantering smile as she replied. "I do not know anyone by the name of John Carter."

Jat Or and Ur Jan were laughing, but I could see that Ozara did not know what it was all about.

"I hope for his sake that you never meet him, Zanda," I said, "for I am rather fond of him, and I should hate to see him killed."

"Yes," she said, "I should hate to kill him, for I know now that he is the bravest man and the truest friend in the world—with possibly one exception," she added, with a sly glance at Jat Or.

We discussed our situation at length, and tried to make plans for the future, and at last we decided to act upon Ozara's suggestion that we go to Domnia and enlist the aid of her father. From there, she thought, we might more easily conduct the search for Gar Nal and Dejah Thoris.

I shall not take up your time with an account of our journey to Ozara's country or of the welcome that we received at the hands of her father and the strange sights that we saw in this Thurian city.

Ozara's father is the jeddak of Domnia. He is a powerful man, with political affiliations in other cities of the nearer moon. His agents are everywhere among the peoples with whom his country has relations, either amicable or otherwise; and it was not long before word reached him that a strange object that floated in the air had become disabled and had been captured in the country of Ombra. In it were a man and a woman.

The Domnians gave us explicit directions for reaching Ombra; and, exacting a promise from us that we would return and visit them after the conclusion of our adventure, they bid us good-by.

My parting with Ozara was rather painful. She told me quite frankly that she loved me, but that she was resigned to the fact that my heart belonged to another. She exhibited splendid strength of character then that I had not believed she possessed, and when she bid me farewell it was with the wish that I find my princess and enjoy the happiness that I deserved.

As our ship rose above Domnia, my heart was full with a sense of elation, so great was my assurance that I should soon be united with the incomparable Dejah Thoris. I was thus certain of success because of what Ozara's father had told me of the character of the Jeddak of Ombra. He was an arrant coward, and almost any sort of a demonstration would bring him to his knees suing for peace.

Now we were in a position to make a demonstration such as the Ombrans had never witnessed; for, in common with the other inhabitants of Thuria that we had seen thus far, they were entirely ignorant of firearms.

It was my intention to fly low and make my demands for the return of Dejah Thoris and Gar Nal to me, without putting myself in the power of the Ombrans.

If they refused, which I was quite certain that they would, I intended giving them a demonstration of the effectiveness of the fire-arms of Barsoom through the medium of the ship's guns that I have already described. That, I was confident, would bring the Jeddak to terms; and I hoped to accomplish it without unnecessary loss of life.

We were all quite gay as we sailed off toward Ombra. Jat Or and Zanda were planning upon the home they expected to establish in Helium, and Ur Jan was anticipating a position among the fighting men of my retinue and a life of honor and respectability.

Presently, Zanda called my attention to the fact that we were gaining considerable altitude, and complained of dizziness. Almost at the same time I felt a weakness stealing over me, and simultaneously Ur Jan collapsed.

Followed by Jat Or, I staggered to the control room, where a glance at the altimeter showed me that we had risen to dangerous heights. Instantly I directed the brain to regulate the oxygen supply in the interior of the ship, and then I directed it to drop nearer to the surface of the satellite.

It obeyed my directions insofar as the oxygen supply was concerned, but it continued to rise past the point where the altimeter could register our height.

As Thuria faded in the distance astern, I realized that we were flying at tremendous speed, a speed far in excess of that which I had directed.

It was evident that the brain was entirely out of control. There was nothing more that I could do; so I returned to the cabin. Here I found that both Zanda and Ur Jan had recovered, now that the oxygen supply had been replenished.

I told them that the ship was running wild in space and that our eventual fate could be nothing more than a matter of idle speculation—they knew as much about it as I.

My hopes, that had been so high, were now completely dashed; and the farther that we sped from Thuria, the greater became my anguish, though I hid my personal feelings from my companions.

It was not until it became apparent that we were headed for Barsoom that even hope of life was renewed in the breasts of any of us.

As we drew near the surface of the planet, it became evident to me that the ship was fully under control; and I wondered whether or not the brain itself had discovered the power of original thought, for I knew that I was not controlling it nor were any of my companions.

It was night, a very dark night. The ship was approaching a large city. I could see the lights ahead, and as we drew closer I recognized that the city was Zodanga.

As though guided by a human hand and brain, the ship slid silently across the eastern wall of the great city, dropped into the shadows of a dark avenue, and moved steadily toward its unknown destination.

But not for long was the destination to be unknown. Presently the neighborhood became familiar. We were moving very slowly. Zanda was with me in the control room, gazing through one of the forward ports.

"The house of Fal Sivas!" she exclaimed.

I recognized it, too, and then just in front of us I saw the open doors of the great hangar from which I had stolen the ship.

With the utmost precision, the ship turned slowly about until its tail pointed toward the hangar doorway. Then it backed in and settled down upon its scaffolding.

At my direction, the doors opened and the ladder dropped out to the floor; and a moment later I was searching for Fal Sivas, to demand an explanation. Ur Jan and Jat Or accompanied me with drawn swords, and Zanda followed close behind.

I went at once to Fal Sivas's sleeping quarters. They were deserted; but as I was leaving them, I saw a note fastened beside the door. It was addressed to me. I opened it and read the following:

From Fal Sivas

Of Zodanga

To John Carter

Of Helium

Let this be known:

You betrayed me. You stole my ship. You thought that your puny mind could best that of the great Fal Sivas.

Very well, John Carter, it shall be a duel of minds—my mind against yours. Let us see who will win.

I am recalling the ship.

I am directing it to return from wherever it may be and at full speed. It is to allow no other brain to change its course. I am commanding it to return to its hangar and remain there forever unless it receives contrary directions from my brain.

Know you then, John Carter, when you read this note, that

I, Fal Sivas, have won; and that as long as I live, no other brain than mine can ever cause my ship to move.

I might have dashed the ship to pieces against the ground and thus destroyed you; but then I could not have gloated over you, as I now shall.

Do not search for me. I am hidden where you can never find me.

I have written. That is all.

There was a grim finality about that note and a certain authority that seemed to preclude even faint hope. I was crushed.

In silence, I handed it to Jat Or and asked him to read it aloud to the others. When he had finished it, Ur Jan drew his short-sword and offered it to me hilt first.

"It is I who am the cause of your sorrow," he said. "My life belongs to you. I offer it to you now in atonement."

I shook my head and pushed his hand away. "You did not know what you were doing, Ur Jan," I said.

"Perhaps it is not the end," said Zanda. "Where can Fal Sivas hide that determined men may not find him?"

"Let us dedicate our lives to that purpose," said Jat Or; and there, in the quarters of Fal Sivas, we four swore to hunt him down.

As we stepped out into the corridor, I saw a man approaching. He was tiptoeing stealthily in our direction. He did not see me instantly because he was casting an apprehensive glance back across his shoulder, as though fearful of discovery from that direction.

When he faced me, we were both surprised—it was Rapas the Ulsio.

At sight of Ur Jan and me standing side by side, The Rat went ashen grey. He started to turn, as though to run; but evidently he thought better of it, for he immediately faced us again, and stood staring at us as though fascinated.

As we approached him, he affected a silly grin. "Well, Vandor," he said, "this is a surprise. I am glad to see you."

"Yes, you must be," I replied. "What are you doing here?"

"I came to see Fal Sivas."

"Did you expect to find him here?" demanded Ur Jan.

"Yes," replied Rapas.

"Then why were you sneaking in on your tiptoes?" inquired the assassin. "You are lying, Rapas. You knew that Fal Sivas was not here. If you had thought that he was here, you would not have had the nerve to come, for you knew that he knew that you were in my employ."

Ur Jan stepped forward quickly and grasped Rapas by the throat. "Listen, you rat," he growled; "you know where Fal Sivas is. Tell me, or I'll wring your neck."

The fellow commenced to grovel and whine.

"Don't, don't; you are hurting me," he cried. "You will kill me."

"At least you have told the truth for once," growled the assassin. "Quick now; out with it. Where is Fal Sivas?"

"If I tell you, will you promise not to kill me?" asked The Rat.

"We will promise you that and more," I said; "Tell us where Fal Sivas is, and I'll give you your weight in treasure."

"Speak up," said Ur Jan, giving the fellow a shake.

"Fal Sivas is in the house of Gar Nal," whispered Rapas, "but don't tell him that I told you; don't tell him that I told you or he will kill me horribly."

I did not dare turn Rapas loose for fear he would betray us, and furthermore he promised to gain entrance to Gar Nal's for us and lead us to the room where we would find Fal Sivas.

I could not imagine what Fal Sivas was doing in the house of Gar Nal, unless he had gone there in Gar Nal's absence in an attempt to steal some of his secrets; nor did I bother to question Rapas about it, as it did not seem of any great importance to me. It was enough that Fal Sivas was there, and that I should find him.

It was half after the eighth zode, or around midnight earth-time, that we reached Gar Nal's. Rapas admitted us and led us to the third level of the house, up narrow ramps at the rear of the building where we met no one. We moved silently without speaking, and at last our guide halted before a door.

"He is in there," he whispered.

"Open the door," I said.

He tried it, but it was locked. Ur Jan pushed him aside, and then hurled his great bulk against the door. With a loud splintering of wood, it burst in. I leaped across the threshold; and there, seated at a table, I saw Fal Sivas and Gar Nal—Gar Nal, the man whom I had thought to be imprisoned in the city of Ombra on the nearer moon.

As the two men recognized Ur Jan and me, they leaped to their feet; their evil faces were studies in surprise and terror.

I sprang forward and seized Gar Nal before he could draw his sword, and Ur Jan fell upon Fal Sivas. He would have killed him off-hand, but I forbade it. All that I wanted was to learn the fate of Dejah Thoris, and one of these men must know the truth concerning her. They must not die until I knew.

"What are you doing here, Gar Nal?" I demanded. "I thought that you were a prisoner in Ombra."

"I escaped," he replied.

"Do you know where my princess is?"

"Yes."

"Where?"

A cunning look entered his eyes. "You would like to know, wouldn't you?" he asked with a sneer; "but do you think Gar Nal is fool enough to tell you? No, as long as I know and you don't, you will not dare to kill me."

"I'll get the truth out of him," growled Ur Jan. "Here, Rapas, heat a dagger for me. Heat it red-hot." But when we looked around, Rapas was not there. As we had entered the room, he had made good his escape.

"Well," said Ur Jan, "I can heat it myself; but first let me kill Fal Sivas."

"No, no," screamed the old inventor. "I did not steal the Princess of Helium; it was Gar Nal."

And then the two commenced to accuse one another, and presently I discovered that after Gar Nal's return from Thuria, these two master inventors and great scoundrels had patched up a truce and joined forces because of their mutual fear of me. Gar Nal was to hide Fal Sivas, and in return Fal Sivas was to show him the secret of his mechanical brain.

They had both been certain that the last place in the world that I would look for Fal Sivas would be in the house of Gar Nal. Gar Nal had instructed his servants to say that he had never returned from his trip with Ur Jan, giving the impression that he was still upon Thuria; and he was planning to leave that very night for a distant hiding-place.

But all this annoyed me. I did not care about them, or their plans. I wanted to know but one thing, and that was the fate of Dejah Thoris.

"Where is my princess, Gar Nal?" I demanded; "tell me that, and I will spare your life."

"She is still in Ombra," he replied.

Then I turned upon Fal Sivas. "That is your death warrant, Fal Sivas," I told him.

"Why?" he demanded. "What have I to do with it?"

"You keep me from directing the brain that operates your ship, and only thus may I reach Ombra."

Ur Jan raised his sword to cleave Fal Sivas's skull, but the coward went down upon his knees and begged for his life.

"Spare me," he cried, "and I will turn the ship over to you and let you control the brain."

"I can't trust you," I said.

"You can take me with you," he pleaded; "that will be better than death."

"Very well," I said; "but if you interfere with my plans or attempt to betray me, you shall pay for your treachery with your life."

I turned toward the door. "I am returning to Thuria tonight," I said to my companions. "I shall take Fal Sivas with me, and when I return with my princess (and I shall not return without her), I hope to be able to reward you in some material way for your splendid loyalty."

"I am going with you, my prince," said Jat Or; "and I ask for no reward."

"And I, too, am going," said Zanda.

"And I," growled Ur Jan, "but first, my prince, please let me run my sword through the heart of this scoundrel," and as he spoke he advanced upon Gar Nal. "He should die for what he has done. He gave you his word, and he broke it."

I shook my head. "No," I said. "He told me where I could find my princess; and in return for that, I have guaranteed his safety."

Grumbling, Ur Jan returned his sword to its scabbard; and then we four, with Fal Sivas, moved toward the door. The others preceded me. I was the last to pass out into the corridor; and just as I did so, I heard a door open at the opposite end of the room we were just leaving. I turned to glance back; and there, in the doorway across the room, stood Dejah Thoris.

She came toward me with arms outstretched as I ran to meet her.

She was breathing very hard and trembling as I took her in my arms. "Oh, my prince," she cried, "I thought I should not be in time. I heard all that was said in this room, but I was bound and gagged and could not warn you that Gar Nal was deceiving you. It was only just this instant that I succeeded in freeing myself."

My exclamation of surprise when I first saw her had attracted the attention of my companions, and they had all returned to the room; and as I held my princess in my arms, Ur Jan leaped past me and ran his sword through the putrid heart of Gar Nal.

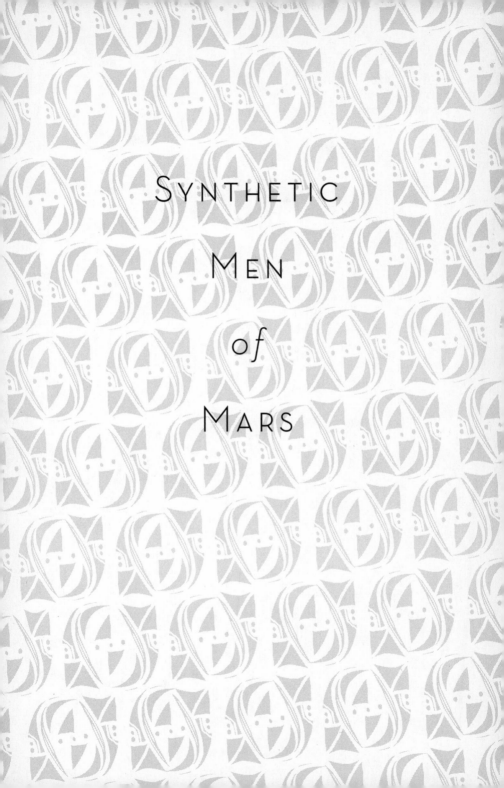

SYNTHETIC

MEN

of

MARS

chapter I

WHERE IS RAS THAVAS?

FROM PHUNDAHL at their western extremity, east to Toonol, the Great Toonolian Marshes stretch across the dying planet for eighteen hundred Earth miles like some unclean, venomous, Gargantuan reptile—an oozy marshland through which wind narrow watercourses connecting occasional bodies of open water, little lakes, the largest of which covers but a few acres. This monotony of marsh and jungle and water is occasionally broken by rocky islands, themselves usually clothed in jungle verdure, the skeletal remains of an ancient mountain range.

Little is known of the Great Toonolian Marshes in other portions of Barsoom, for this inhospitable region is peopled by fierce beasts and terrifying reptiles, by remnants of savage aboriginal tribes long isolated, and is guarded at either extremity by the unfriendly kingdoms of Phundahl and Toonol which discourage intercourse with other nations and are constantly warring upon one another.

Upon an island near Toonol, Ras Thavas, The Master Mind of Mars, had labored in his laboratory for nearly a thousand years until Vobis Kan, Jeddak of Toonol, turned against him and drove him from his island home and later repulsed a force of Phundahlian warriors led by Gor Hajus, the Assassin of Toonol, which had sought to recapture the island and restore Ras Thavas to his laboratory upon his promise to devote his skill and learning to the amelioration of human suffering rather than to prostitute them to the foul purposes of greed and sin.

Following the defeat of his little army, Ras Thavas had disappeared and been all but forgotten as are the dead, among which he was numbered by those who had known him; but there were some who could never forget him. There was Valla Dia, Princess of Duhor, whose brain he had transferred to the head of the hideous old Xaxa, Jeddara of Phundahl, that Xaxa might acquire the young and beautiful body of Valla Dia. There was Vad Varo, her husband, one-time assistant to Ras Thavas, who had restored her brain to her own body— Vad Varo, who had been born Ulysses Paxton in the United States of America and presumably died in a shell hole in France; and there was John Carter, Prince of Helium, Warlord of Mars, whose imagination had been intrigued by the tales Vad Varo had told him of the marvellous skill of a world's greatest scientist and surgeon.

John Carter had not forgotten Ras Thavas, and when an emergency arose in which the skill of this greatest of surgeons was the sole remaining hope, he determined to seek him out and find him if he still lived. Dejah Thoris, his princess, had suffered an appalling injury in a collision between two swift airships; and had lain unconscious for many weeks, her back broken and twisted, until the greatest surgeons of all Helium had at last given up all hope. Their skill had been only sufficient to keep her alive; it could not mend her.

But how to find Ras Thavas? That was the question. And then he recalled that Vad Varo had been the assistant of the great surgeon. Perhaps, if the master could not be found, the skill of the pupil might be adequate. Then, too, of all men upon Barsoom, Vad Varo would be most likely to know the whereabouts of Ras Thavas. And so John Carter determined to go first to Duhor.

He selected from his fleet a small swift cruiser of a new type that had attained a speed of four hundred miles an hour—over twice the speed of the older types which he had first known and flown through the thin air of Mars. He would have gone alone, but Carthoris and Tara and Thuvia pleaded with him not to do so. At last he gave in and consented to take one of the officers of his personal troops, a young padwar named Vor Daj. To him we are indebted for this remarkable tale of strange adventure upon the planet Mars; to him and Jason Gridley whose discovery of the Gridley Wave has made it possible for me to receive this story over the special Gridley radio receiving set which Jason Gridley built out here in Tarzana, and to Ulysses Paxton who translated it into English and sent it across some forty million miles of space.

I shall give you the story as nearly as possible in the words of Vor Daj as is compatible with clarity. Certain Martian words and idioms which are untranslatable, measures of time and of distance will be usually in my own words; and there are occasional interpolations of my own that I have not bothered to assume responsibility for, since their origin will be obvious to the reader. In addition to these, there must undoubtedly have been some editing on the part of Vad Varo.

So now to the strange tale as told by Vor Daj.

chapter II

THE MISSION OF THE WARLORD

I AM VOR DAJ. I am a padwar in The Warlord's Guard. By the standards of Earthmen, for whom I understand I am writing this account of certain adventures, I should long since have been dead of old age; but here on Barsoom I am still a very young man. John Carter has told me that it is a matter worthy of general public interest if an Earthman lives a hundred years. The normal life expectancy of a Martian is a thousand years from the time that he breaks the shell of the egg in which he has incubated for five years and from which he emerges just short of physical maturity, a wild creature that must be tamed and trained as are the young of the lower orders which have been domesticated by man. And so much of that training is martial that it sometimes seems to me that I must have stepped from the egg fully equipped with the harness and weapons of a warrior. Let this, then, serve as my introduction. It is enough that you know my name and that I am a fighting man whose life is dedicated to the service of John Carter of Mars.

Naturally I felt highly honored when The Warlord chose me to accompany him upon his search for Ras Thavas, even though the assignment seemed of a prosaic nature of offering little more than an opportunity to be with The Warlord and to serve him and the incomparable Dejah Thoris, his princess. How little I foresaw what was in store for me!

It was John Carter's intention to fly first to Duhor, which lies some ten thousand five hundred haads, or about four thousand Earth miles, northwest of the Twin Cities of Helium, where he expected to find Vad Varo, from whom he hoped to learn the whereabouts of Ras Thavas, who, with the possible exception of Vad Varo, was the only person in the world whose knowledge and skill might rescue Dejah Thoris from the grave, upon the brink of which she had lain for weeks, and restore her to health.

It was 8:25 (12:13 A.M. Earth Time) when our trim, swift flier rose from the landing stage on the roof of The Warlord's palace. Thuria and Cluros were speeding across a brilliant starlit sky casting constantly changing double shadows across the terrain beneath us that produced an illusion of myriad living things in constant, restless movement or a surging liquid world, eddying and boiling; quite different, John Carter told me, from a similar aspect above Earth, whose single satellite moves at a stately, decorous pace across the vault of heaven.

With our directional compass set for Duhor and our motor functioning in silent perfection there were no navigational problems to occupy our time. Barring some unforeseen emergency, the ship would fly in an air line to Duhor and stop above the city. Our sensitive altimeter was set to maintain an altitude of 300 ads (approximately 3000 feet), with a safety minimum of 50 ads. In other words, the ship would normally maintain an altitude of 300 ads above sea level, but in passing over mountainous country it was assured a clearance of not less than 50 ads (about 490 feet) by a delicate device that actuates the controls as the ship approaches any elevation of the land surface that is less than 50 ads beneath its keel. I think I may best describe this mechanism by asking you to imagine a self-focusing camera which may be set for any distance, beyond which it is always in focus. When it approaches an object within less distance than that for which it has been adjusted it automatically corrects the focus. It is this change that actuates the controls of the ship, causing it to rise until the fixed focus is again achieved. So sensitive is this instrument that it functions as accurately by starlight as by the brightest sunlight. Only in utter darkness would it fail to operate; but even this single limitation is overcome, on the rare occasions that the Martian sky is entirely overcast by clouds, through the medium of a small beam of light which is directed downward from the keel of the ship.

Secure in our belief in the infallibility of our directional compass, we relaxed our vigilance and dozed throughout the night. I have no excuses to offer, nor did John Carter upbraid me; for, as he was prompt to admit, the fault was as much his as mine. As a matter of fact, he took all the blame, saying that the responsibility was wholly his.

It was not until well after sunrise that we discovered that something was radically wrong in either our position or our timing. The snow clad Artolian Hills which surround Duhor should have been plainly visible dead ahead, but they were not—just a vast expanse of dead sea bottom covered with ochre vegetation, and, in the distance, low hills.

We quickly took our position, only to find that we were some 4500 haads southeast of Duhor; or, more accurately, 150° W. Lon., from Exum, and 15° N. Lat. This placed us about 2600 haads southwest of Phundahl, which is situated at the western extremity of The Great Toonolian Marshes.

John Carter was examining the directional compass. I knew how bitterly disappointed he must be because of the delay. Another might have railed at fate; but he only said, "The needle is slightly bent—just enough to carry us off our course. But perhaps it's just as well—the Phundahlians are far more likely to know where Ras Thavas is than anyone in Duhor. I thought of Duhor first, naturally, because we'd be sure of friendly aid there."

"That's more than we can expect in Phundahl, from what I've heard of them."

He nodded. "Nevertheless, we'll go to Phundahl. Dar Tarus, the jeddak, is friendly to Vad Varo; and so may be friendly to Vad Varo's friend. Just to be on the safe side, though, we'll go into the city as panthans."

"They'll think we're flying high," I said, smiling: "—two panthans in a ship of the princely house of The Warlord of Barsoom!"

A panthan is a wandering soldier of fortune, selling his services and his sword to whomever will pay him; and the pay is usually low, for everyone knows that a panthan would rather fight than eat; so they don't pay him very much; and what they do pay him, he spends with prodigality, so that he is quite broke again in short order.

"They won't see the ship," replied John Carter. "We'll find a place to hide it before we get there. You will walk to the gates of Phundahl in plain harness, Vor Daj." He smiled. "I know how well the officers of my ships like to walk."

As we flew on toward Phundahl we removed the insignia and ornaments from our harnesses that we might come to the gates in the plain leather of unattached panthans. Even then, we knew, we might not be admitted to the city, as Martians are always suspicious of strangers and because spies sometimes come in the guise of panthans. With my assistance, John Carter stained the light skin of his body with the reddish copper pigment that he always carries with him against any emergency that requires him to hide his identity and play the role of a native red man of Barsoom.

Sighting Phundahl in the distance, we flew low, just skimming the ground, taking advantage of the hills to hide us from sentries on the city wall; and within a few miles of our destination The Warlord brought the flier to a landing in a little canyon beside a small grove of sompus trees into which we taxied. Removing the control levers, we buried them a short distance from the ship, blazing four surrounding trees in such a manner that we might easily locate the cache when we should return to the ship—if we ever did. Then we set out on foot for Phundahl.

chapter III

THE INVINCIBLE WARRIORS

SHORTLY AFTER the Virginian soldier of fortune had arrived on Mars he had been given the name Dotar Sojat by the green Martian Tharks into whose hands he had fallen; but with the lapse of years the name had been practically forgotten, as it had been used for only a brief period by a few members of that wild horde. The Warlord now decided to adopt it for this adventure, while I retained my own name which was quite unknown in this part of the world; and so it was that Dotar Sojat and Vor Daj, two wandering panthans, trudged through the low hills to the west of Phundahl on this still Barsoomian morning. The mosslike ochre vegetation gave forth no sound beneath our sandalled feet. We moved as silently as our hard, sharp shadows which dogged our footsteps toward the east. Gay plumed voiceless birds watched us from the branches of skeel and sorapus trees, as silent as the beautiful insects which hovered around the gorgeous blooms of the pimalia and gloresta which grew in profusion in every depression of the hills that held Barsoom's scant moisture longest. Mars is a world of vast silences where even voiced creatures are muted as though by the consciousness of impending death, for Mars is a dying world. We abhor noise; and so our voices, like our music, are soft and low; and we are a people of few words. John Carter has told me of the din of Earthly cities and of the brasses and the drums and the cymbals of Earthly music, of the constant, senseless chatter of millions of voices saying nothing. I believe that such as these would drive Martians insane.

We were still in the hills and not yet in sight of the city when our attention was attracted by sounds above and behind us. We turned simultaneously to look back, and the sight that met our eyes was so astonishing that we could scarcely believe the evidence of our own senses. About twenty birds were winging toward us. That in itself was sufficiently astonishing, since they were easily identifiable as malagors, a species long presumed to be extinct; but to add to the incredibility of the sight that met our eyes, a warrior bestrode each of the giant birds. It was quite evident that they must have seen us; so it was quite useless to attempt to hide from them. They were already dropping lower, and presently they were circling us. With this opportunity for closer observation I was impressed by a certain grotesquerie in the appearance of the warriors. There was something a little inhuman about them, and yet they were quite evidently human beings similar to ourselves. One of them carried a woman in front of him on the neck of the great bird that was his mount; but as they were all in constant motion I was unable to obtain a really good look at her; nor, by the same token, of the others.

Presently the twenty malagors alighted in a circle about us, and five of the warriors dismounted and approached us. Now it was that I saw what lent them their strange and unnatural appearance. They seemed the faulty efforts of a poor draftsman, come to life—animated caricatures of man. There was no symmetry of design about them. The left arm of one was scarce a foot long, while his right arm was so long that the hand dragged along the ground as he walked. Four-fifths of the face of one was above the eyes, while another had an equal proportion below the eyes. Eyes, noses, and mouths were usually misplaced; and were either too large or too small to harmonize with contiguous features. But there was one exception—a warrior who now dismounted and followed behind the five who were approaching us. He was a handsome, well formed man, whose trappings and weapons were of excellent quality and design—the serviceable equipment of a fighting man. His harness bore the insignia of a dwar, a rank comparable to that of captain in your Earthly military organizations. At a command from him, the five halted before reaching us; and he addressed us.

"You are Phundahlians?" he asked.

"We are from Helium," John Carter replied. "Our latest employment was there. We are panthans."

"You are my prisoners. Throw down your arms."

The faintest of smiles touched the lips of The Warlord. "Come and take them," he said. It was a challenge.

The other shrugged. "As you will. We outnumber you ten to one. We shall take you, but we may kill you in the taking. I advise you to surrender."

"And you will be wise if you let us go our way, for we have no quarrel with you; and if you pick one, we shall not die alone."

The dwar smiled an inscrutable smile. "As you will," he replied; and then he turned to the five and said, "Take them!" But as they advanced upon us, he did not come with them, but remained behind, quite contrary to the ethics which determine the behavior of Martian officers. He should have led them, engaging us himself and setting an example of courage to his men.

We whipped our long-swords from their scabbards and met the five horrific creatures, standing back to back as they circled us. The blade of The Warlord wove a net of razor-edged steel before him, while I did the best that I could to defend my prince and uphold the honor of my metal; and I did well, for I am accounted a great swordsman by John Carter himself, the greatest of all. Our antagonists were no match for us. They could not pierce our guards, even though they fought with an entire disregard of life, throwing themselves upon our blades and coming in again for further punishment. And that was the disheartening feature of the horrid encounter. Time and again I would run a fellow through, only to have him back away until my blade was out of his body and then come at me again. They seemed to suffer neither from shock nor pain and to know no fear. My blade severed the arm of one of them at the shoulder; and while another engaged me, the fellow stooped and recovered his sword with his other hand and tossed his severed arm to one side. John Carter decapitated one of his antagonists; but the body ran around cutting and slashing in apparent ungovernable fury until the dwar ordered several of his other warriors to capture and disarm it, and all the while the head lay gibbering and grimacing in the dust. This was the first of our antagonists to be rendered permanently *hors de combat*, and suggested the only way that we might be victorious.

"Behead them, Vor Daj!" The Warlord directed, and even as he spoke he lopped the head from another.

I tell you, it was a gruesome sight. The thing kept on fighting, and its head lay on the ground screaming and cursing. John Carter had to disarm it, and then it lunged forward and struck him with the weight of its headless torso just below the knees, throwing him off balance. It was fortunate that I happened to see what was going on, for another of the creatures would have run The Warlord through had I not. I was just in time, and I caught the thing with a clean cut that sent its head toppling to the ground. That left only two of our antagonists, and these the dwar called off.

They withdrew to their mounts, and I saw that the officer was issuing instructions; but what he was saying, I could not overhear. I thought they would give up then and go away, for several of them rose from the ground on their great malagors; but the dwar did not even remount. He just stood there watching. Those who had taken to the air circled just above us, out of reach of our swords; and a number of their fellows dismounted and approached us; but they, too, kept their distance. The three severed heads lay upon the ground, reviling us. The bodies of two of them had been disarmed and trussed up, while that of the third dashed hither and thither pursued by a couple of its fellows who sought to entangle it in nets which they cast at it whenever they could come near enough to it.

These side lights I caught in swift glances, for my attention was more concerned with the action of those who soared above us, in an effort to determine what their next mode of attack would be; nor did I have long to wait before my curiosity was satisfied. Unslinging nets which they wore wrapped about their waists and which I had previously thought were only articles of apparel, they dragged them around and over us in an attempt to entangle us. With a growing sense of futility we slashed at the fabric; and though we cut it in places, we could not escape it; and when they dexterously dropped a couple of them over us we were hopelessly enmeshed. Then those who had surrounded us on foot rushed in and bound us. We fought, but even the great strength of The Warlord was of no avail against the entangling meshes of the nets and the brute strength of the hideous creatures who so greatly outnumbered him. I thought that they would probably kill us now, but at a word of command from their dwar, they fell back. Those in the air alighted and gathered up their nets. Several heads and arms were collected and tied to the backs of malagors, as were the headless bodies; and while these things were being attended to, the officer approached and talked with us. He seemed to bear us no ill will for the damage we had inflicted upon his warriors, and was gracious enough to compliment us upon our courage and swordsmanship.

"However," he added, "you would have been wise to have taken my advice and surrendered in the first place. It is a miracle that you were not killed or at least badly wounded. Only your miraculous swordsmanship saved you."

"The only miracle involved," replied John Carter, "is that any of your men escaped with their heads. Their swordsmanship is abominable."

The dwar smiled. "I quite agree with you, but what they lack in technique they more than make up for in brute strength and fearlessness and the fact that they must be dismembered in order to be rendered harmless. As you may have noticed, they can't be killed."

"And now that we are your prisoners," inquired The Warlord, "what do you intend doing with us?"

"I shall take you to my superiors. They will decide. What are your names?"

"This is Vor Daj. I am Dotar Sojat."

"You are from Helium, and you were going to Phundahl. Why?"

"As I have told you, we are panthans. We are looking for employment."

"You have friends in Phundahl?"

"None. We have never been there. If another city had been in our path, we should have offered our services there. You know how it is with panthans."

The man nodded. "Perhaps you will have fighting yet."

"Would you mind telling me," I asked, "what manner of creatures your warriors are? I have never seen men like them."

"Nor anyone else," he said. "They are called hormads. The less you see of them, the better you will like them. Now that you must admit that you are my prisoners, I have a suggestion to make. Bound as you are, the trip to Morbus will be most uncomfortable; and I do not wish to subject two such courageous fighting men to unnecessary discomfort. Assure me that you will not try to escape before we reach Morbus and I will remove your bonds."

It was evident that the dwar was quite a decent fellow. We accepted his offer gladly, and he removed our bonds himself; then he bade us mount behind a couple of his warriors. It was then that I first had a close view of the woman riding on one of the malagors in front of a hormad. Our eyes met, and I saw terror and helplessness mirrored in hers. I saw, too, that she was beautiful; then the great birds took off with a terrific flapping of giant wings, and we were on our way to Morbus.

chapter IV

THE SECRET OF THE MARSHES

HANGING IN A NET on one side of the malagor upon which I was mounted was one of the heads we had struck off in our fight with the hormads. I wondered why they were preserving such a grisly trophy, and attributed it to some custom or superstition requiring the return of a body to its homeland for final disposal.

Our course lay south of Phundahl, which the leader was evidently seeking to avoid; and ahead I could see the vast Toonolian Marshes stretching away in the distance as far as the eye could see—a labyrinth of winding waterways threading desolate swampland from which rose occasional islands of solid ground, with here and there a darker area of forest and the blue of tiny lakes.

As I watched this panorama unfolding before us, I heard a voice suddenly exclaim, querulously, "Turn me over. I can't see a thing but the belly of this bird." It seemed to come from below me; and, glancing down, I saw that it was the head hanging in the net beneath me that was speaking. It lay in the net, facing upward toward the belly of the malagor, helpless to turn or to move itself. It was a gruesome sight, this dead thing speaking; and I must confess that it made me shudder.

"I can't turn you over," I said, "because I can't reach you; and what difference does it make anyway? What difference does it make whether your eyes are pointed in one direction or another? You are dead, and the dead cannot see."

"Could I talk if I were dead, you brainless idiot? I am not dead, because I cannot die. The life principle is inherent in me—in every tissue of me. Unless it be totally destroyed, as by fire, it lives; and what lives must grow. It is the law of nature. Turn me over, you stupid clod! Shake the net, or pull it up and turn me."

Well, the manners of the thing were very bad; but it occurred to me that I should probably feel irritable if my head had been lopped off; so I shook the net until the head turned upon one side so that it might look out away from the belly of the malagor.

"What are you called?" it asked.

"Vor Daj."

"I shall remember. In Morbus you may need a friend. I shall remember you."

"Thanks," I said. I wondered what good a friend without a body could do me. I also wondered if shaking the net for the thing would outweigh the fact that I had lopped its head off. Just to be polite, I asked what its name might be.

"I am Tor-dur-bar," it replied. "I am Tor-dur-bar, himself. You are very fortunate to have me for a friend. I am really outstanding. You will appreciate this when you come to Morbus and learn to know many of us hormads."

Tor-dur-bar is four-million-eight in the language of you Earthmen. It seemed a peculiar name, but then everything about these hormads was peculiar. The hormad in front of me had evidently been listening to our conversation, for he half turned his head; and said, disparagingly, "Pay no attention to Tor-dur-bar. He is an upstart. It is I who am remarkable. If you wish a powerful friend—well, you need look no farther. I cannot say more; I'm too modest. But if at any time you need a real friend, just come to Teeaytan-ov." (That is eleven-hundred-seven in your language.)

Tor-dur-bar scoffed disgustedly "'Upstart' indeed! I am the finished product of a million cultures, or more than four million cultures, to be exact. Teeaytan-ov is scarcely more than an experiment."

"If I should loosen my net, you would be a finished product," threatened Teeaytan-ov.

Tor-dur-bar commenced to scream, "Sytor! Sytor! Murder!"

The dwar, who had been flying at the head of his strange detachment, wheeled his malagor and flew back alongside us. "What's wrong here?" he demanded.

"Teeaytan-ov threatens to dump me into the Toonolian Marshes," cried Tor-dur-bar. "Take me away from him, Sytor."

"Quarreling again, eh?" demanded Sytor. "If I hear any more out of either of you, you both go to the incinerator when we get back to Morbus; and, Teeaytan-ov, see that nothing happens to Tor-dur-bar. You understand?"

Teeaytan-ov grunted, and Sytor returned to his post. We rode on in silence after this, and I was left to speculate upon the origin of these strange creatures into whose hands I had fallen. The Warlord rode ahead of me and the girl a little to my left. My eyes wandered often in her direction; and my sympathy went out to her, for I was sure she, too, was a prisoner. To what terrible fate was she being borne? Our situation was quite bad enough for a man; I could only guess how much worse it might be for a woman.

The malagors flew swiftly and smoothly. My guess would be that they flew at a speed of more than four hundred haads a zode (about sixty miles an hour). They appeared tireless; and flew on, hour after hour, without rest. After circling Phundahl, we had flown due east; and late in the afternoon approached a large island rising from the surrounding morass. One of the innumerable winding waterways skirted its northern boundary, widening here to form a small lake on the shore of which lay a small walled city which we circled once before descending to a landing before its main gate, which faced the lake. During our descent, I had noticed clusters of small huts scattered about the island outside the walls of the city wherever I could see, suggesting a considerable population; and as I could see only a small portion of the island, which was of considerable extent, I received the impression that it was inhabited by an enormous number of people. I was later to learn that even my wildest guess could not have equalled the truth.

After we had dismounted, we three prisoners were herded together; the arms, legs, heads, and bodies which had been salvaged from our battle earlier in the day were slung in nets so that they could be easily carried; the gates swung open, and we entered into the city of Morbus.

The officer in charge of the gate was a quite normal appearing human being, but his warriors were grotesque, ill-favored hormads. The former exchanged greetings with Sytor, asked him a few questions about us, and then directed the bearers to take their gruesome burdens to "Reclamation Laboratory No. 3," after which Sytor led us away up the avenue that ran south from the gate. At the first intersection, the bearers turned off to the left with the mutilated bodies; and as they were leaving us a voice called out, "Do not forget, Vor Daj, that Tor-dur-bar is your friend and that Teeaytan-ov is little better than an experiment."

I glanced around to see the grisly head of Four-million-eight leering at me from the bottom of a net. "I shall not forget," I said; and I knew that I never should forget the horror of it even though I might wonder in what way a bodiless head might be of service, however friendly its intentions.

Morbus differed from any Martian city I had ever visited. The buildings were substantial and without ornamentation, but there was a certain dignity in the simplicity of their lines that lent them a beauty all their own. It gave the impression of being a new city laid out in accordance with some well conceived plan, every line of which spelled efficiency. I could not but wonder what purpose such a city could serve here in the depths of the Great Toonolian Marshes. Who would, by choice, live in such a remote and depressing environment? How could such a city exist without markets or commerce?

My speculations were interrupted by our arrival before a small doorway in a blank wall. Sytor pounded on the door with the hilt of his sword, whereupon a small panel was opened and a face appeared.

"I am Sytor, Dwar of the 10th Utan, 1st Dar of the 3rd Jed's Guard. I bring prisoners to await the pleasure of The Council of the Seven Jeds."

"How many?" asked the man at the wicket.

"Three—two men and a woman."

The door swung open, and Sytor motioned us to enter. He did not accompany us. We found ourselves in what was evidently a guard-room, as there were about twenty hormad warriors there in addition to the officer who had admitted us, who, like the other officers we had seen, was a normal red man like ourselves. He asked us our names, which he entered in a book with other information such as our vocations and the cities from which we came; and it was during this questioning that I learned the name of the girl. She was Janai; and she said that she came from Amhor, a city about seven hundred miles north of Morbus. It is a small city ruled by a prince named Jal Had who has such a bad reputation that it has reached to far away Helium. That was about all that I knew about Amhor.

After he had finished questioning us, the officer directed one of the hormads to take us away; and we were led down a corridor to a large patio in which there were a number of red Martians. "You will stay here until you are sent for," said the hormad. "Do not try to escape." Then he left us.

"Escape!" said John Carter with a wry smile. "I have escaped from many places; and I can probably escape from this city, but escaping from the Toonolian Marshes is another matter. However, we shall see."

The other prisoners, for such they proved to be, approached us. There were five of them. "Kaor!" they greeted us. We exchanged names; and they asked us many questions about the outside world, as though they had been prisoners for years. But they had not. The fact that Morbus was so isolated seemed to impart to them the feeling that they had been out of the world for a long time. Two of them were Phundahlians, one was from Toonol, one from Ptarth, and one from Duhor.

"For what purpose do they keep prisoners?" asked John Carter.

"They use some as officers to train and command their warriors," explained Pandar, one of the Phundahlians. "The bodies of others are used to house the brains of those of the hormads intelligent enough to serve in high places. The bodies of others go to the culture laboratories, where their tissue is used in the damnable work of Ras Thavas."

"Ras Thavas!" exclaimed The Warlord. "He is here in Morbus?"

"He is that—a prisoner in his own city, the servant of the hideous creatures he has created," replied Gan Had of Toonol.

"I don't follow you," said John Carter.

"After Ras Thavas was driven from his great laboratories by Vobis Kan, Jeddak of Toonol," explained Gan Had, "he came to this island to perfect a discovery he had been working on for years. It was the creation of human beings from human tissue. He had perfected a culture in which tissue grew continuously. The growth from a tiny particle of living tissue filled an entire room in his laboratory, but it was formless.

His problem was to direct this growth. He experimented with various reptiles which reproduce certain parts of their bodies, such as toes, tails, and limbs, when they are cut off; and eventually he discovered the principle. This he has applied to the control of the growth of human tissue in a highly specialized culture. The result of these discoveries and experiments are the hormads. Seventy-five per cent of the buildings in Morbus are devoted to the culture and growth of these horrid creatures which Ras Thavas turns out in enormous numbers.

"Practically all of them are extremely low in intelligence; but a few developed normal brains, and some of these banded together to take over the island and establish a kingdom of their own. On threat of death, they have compelled Ras Thavas to continue to produce these creatures in great numbers; for they have conceived a stupendous plan which is nothing less than to build up an army of millions of hormads and with them conquer the world. They will take Phundahl and Toonol first, and then gradually spread out over the entire surface of the globe."

"Amazing," said John Carter, "but I think they have reckoned without a full understanding of all the problems such an undertaking will involve. It is inconceivable, for instance, that Barsoom could feed such an army in the field; and this little island certainly could not feed the nucleus of such an army."

"There you are mistaken," replied Gan Had. "The food for the hormads is produced by means almost identical with those which produce them—a slightly different culture; that is all. Animal tissue grows with great rapidity in this culture, which can be carried along with an army in tanks, constantly providing sufficient food; and, because of its considerable water content, sufficient water."

"But can these half-humans hope to be victorious over well trained, intelligent troops fitted for modern warfare?" I asked.

"I think so," said Pandar. "They will do it by their overwhelming numbers, their utter fearlessness, and the fact that it is necessary to decapitate them before they can be rendered *hors de combat.*"

"How large an army have they?" inquired John Carter.

"There are several million hormads on the island. Their huts are scattered over the entire area of Morbus. It is estimated that the island can accommodate a hundred million of them; and Ras Thavas claims that he can march them into battle at the rate of two million a year, lose every one of them, and still have his original strength undepleted by as much as a single man. This plant turns them out in enormous quantities. A certain percentage are so grossly malformed as to be utterly useless. These are sliced into hundreds of thousands of tiny pieces that are dumped back into the culture vats, where they grow with such unbelievable rapidity that within nine days each has developed into a full-sized hormad, an amazing number of which have developed into something that can march and wield a weapon."

"The situation would appear serious but for one thing," said John Carter.

"And what is that?" asked Gan Had.

"Transportation. How are they going to transport such an enormous army?"

"That has been their problem, but they believe that Ras Thavas has now solved it. He has been experimenting for a long time with malagor tissue and a special culture medium. If he can produce these birds in sufficient quantities, the problem of transport will have been solved. For the fighting ships which they will need, they are relying on those they expect to capture when they take Phundahl and Toonol as the nucleus of a great fleet which will grow as their conquests take in more and larger cities."

The conversation was interrupted by the arrival of a couple of hormads carrying a vessel which contained animal tissue for our evening meal—a most unappetizing looking mess.

The prisoner from Duhor, who, it seemed, had volunteered to act as cook, built a fire in the oven that formed a part of the twenty-foot wall that closed the only side of the patio that was not surrounded by portions of the building; and presently our dinner was grilling over a hot fire.

I could not contemplate the substance of our meal without a feeling of revulsion, notwithstanding the fact that I was ravenously hungry; and my mind was alive with doubts engendered by all that I had been listening to since entering the compound; so that I turned to Gan Had with a question. "Is this, by any chance, human tissue?" I asked.

He shrugged. "It is not supposed to be; but that is a question we do not even ask ourselves, for we must eat to live; and this is all that they bring us."

chapter V

THE JUDGMENT OF THE JEDS

JANAI, the girl from Amhor, sat apart. Her situation seemed to me pathetic in the extreme—a lone woman incarcerated with seven strange men in a city of hideous enemies. We red men of Barsoom are naturally a chivalrous race; but men are men, and I knew nothing of the five whom we had found here. As long as John Carter and I remained her fellow prisoners she would be safe; that I knew, and I thought that if she knew it, any burden of apprehension she might be carrying would be lightened.

As I approached her, with the intention of entering into conversation with her, the officer who had questioned us in the guard-room entered the compound with two other officers and several hormads. They gathered us together, and the two officers accompanying the officer of the guard looked us over. "Not a bad lot," said one.

The other shrugged. "The jeds will take the best of them, and Ras Thavas will grumble about the material he is getting. He always does."

"They don't want the girl, do they?" asked the officer of the guard.

"Our orders were to bring the prisoners," replied one of the others.

"I should like to keep the girl," said the officer of the guard.

"Who wouldn't?" demanded the other with a laugh. "If she had the face of an ulsio you might get her; but the good looking ones go to the jeds, and she is more than good looking."

Janai was standing next to me, and I could almost feel her shudder. Moved by a sudden impulse, I pressed her hand; and for an instant she clung to mine, instinctively groping for protection; then she dropped it and flushed.

"I wish I might help you," I said.

"You are kind. I understand, but no one can help. You are only better off in that you are a man. The worst they will do to you is kill you."

The hideous hormads surrounded us, and we were marched back through the guard-room and out into the avenue. John Carter asked an officer where we were being taken.

"To the Council of the Seven Jeds," he said. "There it will be determined what disposition is to be made of you. Some of you will go into the culture vats. Those of you who are fortunate will be retained to train and officer troops as I was. It's not much to look forward to, but it's better than death."

"What is the Council of the Seven Jeds?" asked The Warlord.

"They are the rulers of Morbus. They are the seven hormads whose brains developed normally and who wrested control from Ras Thavas. Each one aspired to rule; and as none would give up what he considered his rights, they proclaimed themselves all jeds, and rule conjointly."

At a little distance from our prison we came to a large building before the entrance to which was a guard of hormad warriors commanded by a couple of officers. There was a brief parley here, and then we were taken into the building and along a long corridor to a large chamber before the doorway to which we were detained for a few minutes by another detail of guardsmen. When the door was opened we saw a number of hormads and officers standing about and at the far end of the room a raised dais on which seven red men were seated on carved chairs. These were evidently the seven jeds, but they did not look like the hormads we had previously seen. On the contrary they were quite normal and most of them fine looking men.

We were taken to the foot of the dais; and here they looked us over, asking about the same questions that the officer of the guard had asked us when we were admitted to the prison. They discussed us at some length, as men might discuss a number of thoats or calots they were considering purchasing. Several of them seemed much interested in Janai, and finally three of them laid claim to her. This started an altercation which ended in a vote being taken as to which of them would get her, but as there was never a majority in favor of any one man, it was decided to hold her for a few days and then turn her over to Ras Thavas if the claimants could not come to some agreement among themselves. This decided, one of the jeds addressed us men prisoners.

"How many of you will serve us as officers of our troops if you are permitted to live?" he asked.

The only alternative being death, we all proclaimed our willingness to serve as officers. The jeds nodded. "We shall now determine which of you are best fitted to serve as officers of our fighting men," said one; and, speaking to an officer standing near us: "Fetch seven of our best warriors."

We were then led to one side of the room, where we waited. "It looks like fighting," said John Carter with a smile.

"I am sure that nothing would suit you better," I replied.

"Nor you," he said; then he turned to the officer with whom he had talked on the way from the prison. "I thought you said the seven jeds were hormads," he said.

"They are."

"They don't look like any of the hormads I have seen."

"Ras Thavas fixed them up," said the officer. "Perhaps you don't know that Ras Thavas is the greatest scientist and surgeon on Barsoom."

"I have heard as much."

"You have heard right. He can take your brain out and put it in the skull of another man. He has performed that operation hundreds of times. When the seven jeds heard about it they selected seven of the best looking officers and compelled Ras Thavas to transfer their brains into the skulls of these officers. You see they had been hideous creatures, and they wanted to be handsome."

"And the seven officers?" I asked.

"They went to the culture vats, or rather their brains did—the original bodies of the seven jeds went with them. Here come the seven fighting warriors. In a few minutes you will know which of you are going into the vats."

We were now taken to the center of the room and lined up facing seven huge hormads. These were the least malformed that we had so far seen, but they were still most repulsive looking creatures. We were furnished with swords, and an officer gave us our instructions. Each of us was to engage the hormad facing him, and those of us who survived without a serious wound would be permitted to live and serve as officers in the army of Morbus.

At a command from an officer, the two lines advanced; and in an instant the chamber rang with the clash of steel on steel. We men of Helium believe that we are the best swordsmen on Barsoom, and of us all, none is so great a swordsman as John Carter; so I had no apprehensions as to the outcome of the contest so far as he and I were concerned. The creature attacking me depended upon weight and brute strength to overcome me, which are the tactics most generally adopted by all of them, since they are not endowed with any great amount of intelligence. He evidently hoped to cut through my guard with a single terrific stroke of his heavy weapon, but of course I am too old a hand at fighting to fall victim to any such crude method of attack. As I parried his cut and stepped aside, he rushed past me awkwardly; and I could have run him through easily, but I had learned in my first encounter with these monsters that what would constitute a lethal wound to a mortal man would cause a hormad no inconvenience whatsoever. I should have to sever one of his legs or both his arms or decapitate him to put him out of the fighting. That, of course, gave him a tremendous advantage over me; but it was not insuperable. Or at least that was what I thought at the beginning of our engagement, but I soon commenced to have a suggestion of a doubt. The fellow was a far better swordsman than any of those we had encountered at the time of our capture. As I learned later, these creatures against whom we were pitted were selected for their superior intelligence, which was slightly above the average of their kind, and specially schooled in swordsmanship by red Martian officers.

Of course, had he been a normal man I could have easily dispatched him; but to avoid his mad rushes and his blade and decapitate him presently appeared a much larger job than I had anticipated. Aside from all else, he was a most unpleasant antagonist, for his face was absolutely hideous. One eye was far up at the corner of his forehead and twice as large as its mate. His nose had grown where one of his ears should have been, while his ear occupied the normal position of his nose. His mouth was a large and crooked rent filled with great fangs. His countenance alone might have been quite enough to have unmanned an antagonist.

Occasionally I caught a glimpse of the other duels progressing around me. I saw one of the Phundahlians fall, and almost simultaneously the head of John Carter's antagonist rolled upon the floor where it lay cursing and screaming while its body lunged madly about endangering everyone in the chamber. A number of other hormads and officers pursued it with nooses and nets in an effort to catch and bind it, and while they were thus occupied the thing bumped into my antagonist throwing it off balance and giving me the opening for which I had been waiting. I swung a terrific blow then and caught the fellow square across the neck, sending his head rolling upon the floor. Then there were two headless bodies dashing about hacking right and left with their heavy swords. I tell you, the other hormads and the officers had a busy few minutes before they finally captured and subdued the horrible things; and by the time they had the fighting was over, but there were two more hormads flopping about the floor, each with a leg gone. These had been overcome by Pandar and Gan Had. The man from Ptarth and the man from Duhor had been killed. Only four of us seven were left. The two heads upon the floor reviled us while other hormads gathered up the debris of battle and carried it away in nets.

Now we were taken again before the dais of the Council of the Seven Jeds; and once more they questioned us, but this time more carefully. When they had done with the questioning they whispered among themselves for a while; then one of them addressed us.

"You will serve as officers, obeying your superiors and all orders you may receive from the Council of the Seven Jeds," he said. "You cannot escape from Morbus. If you serve faithfully you will be permitted to live. If you are guilty of disobedience or treason you will be sent to the vats. That will be the end of you." He turned to John Carter and me. "You men from Helium will serve for the present with the laboratory guard. It is the duty of the laboratory guard to see that Ras Thavas does not escape and that no harm befalls him. We have chosen you for this duty for two reasons: you are both extraordinary swordsmen and, being from distant Helium, cannot feel any partiality either for him or for Toonol or for Phundahl. You can therefore act wholly in our interests as against those of these enemies. Ras Thavas would like to escape or regain control of Morbus. Phundahl would like to rescue him. Toonol would like to destroy him. Either one of them would be glad to get him away from us so that he could produce no more hormads. The man from Phundahl and the man from Toonol will be used to train our warriors as they emerge from the vats. The Council of the Seven Jeds has spoken; it is for you to obey." He nodded toward the officer who had brought us in. "Take them away."

I looked toward Janai. She caught my eye and smiled at me. It was a very brave little smile. A pathetic little smile out of a hopeless heart. Then they led us away.

As THEY CONDUCTED us down the corridor toward the main entrance to the building my mind was occupied in reviewing the incredible occurrences of the day. These few hours had encompassed a lifetime. I had passed through such adventures as in my wildest dreams I could not have imagined. I had become an officer in the hideous army of a city the very existence of which I had not dreamed of a few hours ago. I had met a strange girl from far Amhor; and, for the first time in my life, I had fallen in love; and almost within the hour I had lost her. Love is a strange thing. Why it had come to me as it had, how it had come, were quite beyond me to explain. I only knew that I loved Janai, that I should always love her. I should never see her again. I should never know if I might have won her love in return. I should never be able to tell her that I loved her. My whole life hereafter would be colored and saddened by the thought of my love, by my remembrance of her; yet I would not have relinquished my love for her could I have done so. Yes, love is a strange thing.

At the intersection of the main corridor with another, John Carter and I were led to the right. Pandar and Gan Had continued on toward the main entrance. We called good-by to one another and were gone. It is remarkable how quickly friendships are formed in the midst of a common jeopardy. These men were from strange cities commonly enemies of Helium, yet because we had endured danger together I felt a definite friendly attachment toward them; and I did not doubt but that they were inclined similarly toward John Carter and me. I wondered if we should ever meet again.

They led us down this new corridor and across a great courtyard into another building, above the entrance to which were hieroglyphics strange to me. No two nations of Barsoom have the same written language, although there is a common scientific language understood by the savants of all nations; yet there is but one spoken language upon Barsoom, which all peoples use and understand, even the savage green men of the dead sea bottom. But John Carter is very learned and reads many languages. He told me that the hieroglyphics read Laboratory Building.

We were taken into a medium size audience chamber where an officer told us to wait and that he would fetch Ras Thavas, that we might meet the man we were to help guard and watch. He also told us that Ras Thavas was to be treated with respect and consideration as long as he made no effort to escape. He had the freedom of the laboratory and was, in a sense, all powerful there. If he called on us to help him in his work, we were to do so. It was evident that the Council of the Seven Jeds looked with awe upon him although he was their prisoner, and that they had sense enough to make life as easy for him as possible. I was very anxious to see Ras Thavas, of whom I had heard. He was called The Master Mind of Mars, and although he had often turned his remarkable talents to nefarious schemes, he was nevertheless admired because of his great learning and skill. He was known to be over a thousand years old; and because of this fact alone I would have been curious to see him, as the span of life upon Barsoom is seldom so great. A thousand years is supposed to be the limit, but because of our warlike natures and the prevalency of assassination few attain it. He must, indeed, have been a withered little mummy of a man, I thought; and I wondered that he had the strength to carry on the enormous work in which he was engaged.

We had waited but a short time when the officer returned accompanied by an extremely handsome young man who looked at us with a haughty and supercilious air, as though we had been the dregs of humanity and he a god.

"Two more spies to watch me," he sneered.

"Two more fighting men to protect you, Ras Thavas," corrected the officer who had brought us here from the other building.

So this was Ras Thavas! I could not believe my eyes. This was a young man, unquestionably; for while it is true that we Martians show few traces of advancing years until almost the end of our allotted span, at which time decay is rapid, yet there are certain indications of youth that are obvious.

Ras Thavas continued to scrutinize us. I saw his brows contract in thought as his eyes held steadily on John Carter as though he were trying to recall a half remembered face. Yet I knew that these two men had never met. What was in the mind of Ras Thavas?

"How do I know," he suddenly snapped, "that they have not wormed their way into Morbus to assassinate me? How do I know that they are not from Toonol or Phundahl?"

"They are from Helium," replied the officer. I saw Ras Thavas's brow clear as though he had suddenly arrived at the solution of a problem. "They are two panthans whom we found on their way to Phundahl seeking service," concluded the officer.

Ras Thavas nodded. "I shall use them to assist me in the laboratory," he said.

The officer looked surprised. "Had they not better serve in the guard for a while?" he suggested. "That will give you time to have them watched and to determine if it would be safe to have them possibly alone with you in the laboratory."

"I know what I am doing," snapped Ras Thavas. "I don't need the assistance of any fifth-rate brain to decide what is best for me. But perhaps I honor you."

The officer flushed. "My orders were simply to turn these men over to you. How you use them is none of my concern. I merely wished to safeguard you."

"Then carry out your orders and mind your own business. I can take care of myself." His tone was as disagreeable as his words. I had a premonition that he was not going to be a very pleasant person with whom to work.

The officer shrugged, gave a command to the hormad warriors that had accompanied us, and marched them from the audience chamber. Ras Thavas nodded to us. "Come with me," he said. He led us to a small room, the walls of which were entirely lined with shelves packed with books and manuscripts. There was a desk littered with papers and books, at which he seated himself, at the same time motioning us to be seated at a bench nearby.

"By what names do you call yourselves?" he asked.

"I am Dotar Sojat," replied John Carter, "and this is Vor Daj."

"You know Vor Daj well and have implicit confidence in him?" demanded Ras Thavas. It seemed a strange question, since Ras Thavas knew neither of us.

"I have known Vor Daj for years," replied The Warlord. "I would trust to his loyalty and intelligence in any matter and to his skill and courage as a warrior."

"Very well," said Ras Thavas; "then I can trust you both."

"But how do you know you can trust me?" inquired John Carter quizzically.

Ras Thavas smiled. "The integrity of John Carter, Prince of

Helium, Warlord of Barsoom, is a matter of worldwide knowledge," he said.

We looked at him in surprise. "What makes you think I am John Carter?" asked The Warlord. "You have never seen him."

"In the audience chamber I was struck by the fact that you did not appear truly a red Martian. I examined you more closely and discovered that the pigment with which you had stained your skin had worn thin in spots. There are but two inhabitants of Jasoom on Mars. One of them is Vad Varo, whose Earth name was Paxton. I know him well, as he served as my assistant in my laboratories in Toonol. In fact it was he whom I trained to such a degree of skill that he was able to transfer my old brain to this young body. So I knew that you were not Vad Varo. The other Jasoomian being John Carter, the deduction was simple."

"Your suspicions were well founded and your reasoning faultless," said The Warlord. "I am John Carter. I should soon have told you so myself, for I was on my way to Phundahl in search of you when we were captured by the hormads."

"And for what reason did The Warlord of Barsoom search for Ras Thavas?" demanded the great surgeon.

"My princess, Dejah Thoris, was badly injured in a collision between two fliers. She has lain unconscious for many days. The greatest surgeons of Helium are powerless to aid her. I sought Ras Thavas to implore his aid in restoring her to health."

"And now you find me a prisoner on a remote island in the Great Toonolian Marshes—a fellow prisoner with you."

"But I have found you."

"And what good will it do you or your princess?" demanded The Master Mind of Mars.

"You would come with me and help her if you could?" asked John Carter.

"Certainly. I promised Vad Varo and Dar Tarus, Jeddak of Phundahl, that I would dedicate my skill and knowledge to the amelioration of suffering and the betterment of mankind."

"Then we shall find a way," said John Carter.

Ras Thavas shook his head. "It is easy to say, but impossible to accomplish. There can be no escape from Morbus."

"Still we must find a way," replied The Warlord. "I foresee that the difficulties of escaping from the island may not be insuperable. It is travelling the Great Toonolian Marshes that gives me the greatest concern."

Ras Thavas shook his head. "We can never get off the island. It is too well patrolled, for one thing; and there are too many spies and informers. Many of the officers who appear to be red Martians are, in reality, hormads whose brains I have been forced to transfer to the bodies of normal men. Not even I know who these are, as the operations were performed only in the presence of the Council of the Seven Jeds; and the faces of the red men were kept masked. They have cunning minds, some of these seven jeds. They wanted those they could trust to spy upon me, and if I had seen the faces of the red Martians to whom I gave hormad brains their plan would have been ineffective. Now I do not know which of the officers surrounding me are hormads and which are normal men—except two. I am sure of John Carter because I would have known had I performed a brain transfer on a man with the white skin of a Jasoomian; and I have John Carter's word as to you, Vor Daj. Beyond us three there is none we may trust; so be careful with whom you become friendly and what you say in the hearing of others. You will—"

Here he was interrupted by a veritable pandemonium that suddenly broke out in another part of the building. It seemed a horrific medley of screams and bellowings and groans and grunts, as though a horde of wild beasts had suddenly gone berserk.

"Come," said Ras Thavas, "to the spawning of the monsters. We may be needed."

chapter VII

The Vats of Life

Ras Thavas led us to an enormous room where we beheld such a spectacle as probably never had been enacted elsewhere in the entire universe. In the center of the room was a huge tank about four feet high from which were emerging hideous monstrosities almost beyond the powers of human imagination to conceive; and surrounding the tank were a great number of hormad warriors with their officers, rushing upon the terrible creatures, overpowering and binding them, or destroying them if they were too malformed to function successfully as fighting men. At least fifty per centum of them had to be thus destroyed—fearful caricatures of life that were neither beast nor man. One was only a great mass of living flesh with an eye somewhere and a single hand. Another had developed with its arms and legs transposed, so that when it walked it was upside down with its head between its legs. The features of many were grotesquely misplaced. Noses, ears, eyes, mouths might be scattered indiscriminately anywhere over the surfaces of torso or limbs. These were all destroyed; only those were preserved which had two arms and legs and the facial features of which were somewhere upon the head. The nose might be under an ear and the mouth above the eyes, but if they could function appearance was of no importance.

Ras Thavas viewed them with evident pride. "What do you think of them?" he asked The Warlord.

"Quite horrible," replied John Carter.

Ras Thavas appeared hurt. "I have made no attempt as yet to attain beauty," he said; "and I shall have to admit that so far even symmetry has eluded me, but both will come. I have created human beings. Some day I shall create the perfect man, and a new race of supermen will inhabit Barsoom—beautiful, intelligent, deathless."

"And in the meantime these creatures will have spread all over the world and conquered it. They will destroy your supermen. You have created a Frankensteinian host that will not only destroy you but the civilization of a world. Hasn't that possibility ever occurred to you?"

"Yes, it has; but I never intended to create these creatures in any such numbers. That is the idea of the seven jeds. I purposed developing only enough to form a small army with which to conquer Toonol, that I might regain my island and my old laboratory."

The din in the room had now risen to such proportions that further conversation was impossible. Screaming heads rolled upon the floor. Hormad warriors dragged away the newly created creatures that were considered fit to live, and fresh warriors swarmed into the chamber to replace them. New hormads emerged constantly from the culture tank which swarmed with writhing life like an enormous witch's pot. And this same scene was being duplicated in forty similar rooms throughout the city of Morbus, while a stream of new hormads was pouring out of the city to be tamed and trained by officers and the more intelligent hormads.

I was delighted and relieved when Ras Thavas suggested that we inspect another phase of his work and we were permitted to leave that veritable chamber of horrors. He took us to another room where reconstruction work was carried on. Here heads were growing new bodies and headless bodies new heads. Hormads which had lost arms or legs were growing new ones. Sometimes these activities went amiss, when nothing but a single leg sprouted from the neck of a severed head. An identical case was among those that we saw in this room. The head was very angry about it, and became quite abusive, reviling Ras Thavas.

"What good shall I be," he demanded, "with only a head and one leg? They call you The Master Mind of Mars! Phooey! You haven't the brains of a sorak. When they produce their kind they give them a body and six legs, to say nothing of a head. Now what are you going to do about it? That's what I want to know."

"Well," said Ras Thavas, thoughtfully, "I can always redisect you and return the pieces to the culture vat."

"No! No!" screamed the head. "Let me live, but cut off this leg and let me try to grow a body."

"Very well," said Ras Thavas; "tomorrow."

"Why should a thing like that wish to live," I asked, after we had passed along.

"It is a characteristic of life, however low its form," replied Ras Thavas. "Even these poor sexless monstrosities, whose only pleasure in life is eating raw animal tissue, wish to live. They do not even dream of the existence of love or friendship, they have no spiritual or mental resources upon which to draw for satisfaction or enjoyment; yet they wish to live."

"They speak of friendship," I said. "Tor-dur-bar's head told me not to forget that it was my friend."

"They know the word," replied Ras Thavas, "but I am sure they cannot sense its finer connotations. One of the first things they are taught is to obey. Perhaps he meant that he would obey you, serve you. He may not even remember you now. Some of them have practically no memories. All their reactions are purely mechanical. They respond to oft repeated stimuli—the commands to march, to fight, to come, to go, to halt. They also do what they see the majority of their fellows doing. Come! We shall find Tor-dur-bar's head and see if it recalls you. It will be an interesting experiment."

We passed into another chamber where reconstruction work was in progress, and Ras Thavas spoke to an officer in charge there. The man led us to the far end of the room where there was a large vat in which torsos were growing new arms or legs or heads, and several heads growing new bodies.

We had no more than reached the tank when a head cried out, "Kaor, Vor Daj!" It was Four-Million-Eight himself.

"Kaor, Tor-dur-bar!" I replied. "I am glad to see you again."

"Don't forget that you have one friend in Morbus," he said. "Soon I shall have a new body, and then if you need me I shall be ready."

"There is a hormad of unusual intelligence," said Ras Thavas. "I shall have to keep an eye on him."

"You should give such a brain as mine a fine looking body," said Tor-dur-bar. "I should like to be as handsome as Vor Daj or his friend."

"We shall see," said Ras Thavas, and then he leaned close and whispered to the head, "Say no more about it now. Just trust me."

"How long will it take to grow a new body for Tor-dur-bar?" John Carter asked.

"Nine days; but it may be a body he can't use, and then it will have to be done over again. I have accomplished much, but I still cannot control the development of these bodies or any part of them. Ordinarily his head will grow a body. It might be a body so malformed as to be useless, or it might be just a part of a body or even another head. Some day I shall be able to control this. Some day I shall be able to create perfect humans."

"If there is an Almighty God he may resent this usurpation of his prerogatives," remarked The Warlord with a smile.

"The origin of life is an obscure mystery," said Ras Thavas, "and there is quite as much evidence to indicate that it was the result of accident as there is to suggest that it was planned by a supreme being.

I understand that the scientists of your Earth believe that all life on that planet was evolved from a very low form of animal life called amoeba, a microscopic nucleated mass of protoplasm without even a rudimentary form of consciousness or mental life. An omnipotent creator could just as well have produced the highest conceivable form of life in the first place—a perfect creature—whereas no existing life on either planet is perfect or even approximates perfection.

"Now, on Mars, we hold to a very different theory of creation and evolution. We believe that as the planet cooled chemicals combined to form a spore which was the basis of vegetable life from which, after countless ages, the Tree of Life grew and flourished, perhaps in the center of the Valley Dor twenty-three million years ago, as some believe, perhaps elsewhere. For countless ages the fruit of this tree underwent the gradual changes of evolution, passing by degrees from true plant life to a combination of plant and animal. In the first stages, the fruit of the tree possessed only the power of independent muscular action, while the stem remained attached to the parent plant; later, a brain developed in the fruit, so that hanging there by their long stems they thought and moved as individuals. Then, with the development of perception came a comparison of them; judgments were reached and compared, and thus reason and the power to reason were born upon Barsoom.

"Ages passed. Many forms of life came and went upon the Tree of Life, but still all were attached to the parent plant by stems of varying lengths. At length, the fruit upon the tree consisted of tiny plant men, such as may now be found reproduced in huge size in the Valley Dor, but still hanging to the limbs and branches of The Tree by the stems which grew from the tops of their heads.

"The buds from which the plant men blossomed resembled large nuts about a foot in diameter, divided by double partition walls into four sections. In one section grew the plant man, in another a six legged worm, in the third the progenitor of the white ape, and in the fourth the primeval human of Barsoom. When the bud burst, the plant man remained dangling at the end of his stem; but the three other sections fell to the ground, where the efforts of their imprisoned occupants to escape sent them hopping about in all directions.

"Thus, as time went on, these imprisoned creatures were scattered far and wide over the surface of the planet. For ages they lived their long lives within their hard shells, hopping and skipping hither and thither, falling into the rivers, lakes, and seas which then existed upon the surface of Barsoom, to be still further spread across the face of the new world. Countless billions died before the first human broke through his prison walls into the light of day. Prompted by curiosity, he broke open other shells; and the peopling of Barsoom commenced. The Tree of Life is dead, but before it died the plant men learned to detach themselves from it, their bisexuality permitting them to reproduce themselves after the manner of true plants."

"I have seen them in the Valley Dor," said John Carter, "with a tiny plant man growing beneath each arm, dangling like fruit from the stems attached to the tops of their heads."

"Thus, casually, the present forms of life evolved," continued Ras Thavas, "and by studying them all from the lowest forms upward I have learned how to reproduce life."

"Perhaps to your sorrow," I suggested.

"Perhaps," he agreed.

chapter VIII

THE RED ASSASSIN

DAYS PASSED during which Ras Thavas kept us almost constantly with him; but almost invariably there were others around, so that we had few opportunities to plan, as we never knew the friend from the spy. Thoughts of Janai filled me with sorrow, and I was ever watchful for some means whereby I might learn her fate. Ras Thavas warned me not to show too much interest in the girl, as it might result in arousing suspicions that would lead to my destruction; but he assured me that he would aid me in any way that he could that would not lay me open to suspicion, and one day he found the means.

A number of unusually intelligent hormads were to be sent before the Council of the Seven Jeds to be examined as to their fitness to serve in the personal body guards which each jed maintained, and Ras Thavas detailed me with other officers to accompany them. It was the first time I had been outside the laboratory building, as none of us was permitted to leave it other than on some official business such as this.

As I entered the great building, which was in effect the palace of the Seven Jeds, my whole mind was occupied with thoughts of Janai and the hope that I might catch a glimpse of her. I looked down corridors, I peered through open doorways, I even considered leaving the party and concealing myself in one of the rooms we passed and then attempting a search of the palace; but my better judgment came to my rescue, and I continued on with the others to the great chamber where the Council of the Seven Jeds sat.

The examination of the hormads was very thorough, and while listening to it carefully and noting every question and answer and the effect of the answers upon the jeds, the seeds of a plan were planted in my mind. If I could get Tor-dur-bar assigned to the body guard of a jed I might thus learn the fate of Janai. How differently it worked out and what a bizarre plan finally developed, you shall learn in time.

While we were still in the council chamber a number of warriors entered with a prisoner, a swaggering red man, a scarred, hard bitten warrior, whose sneering face and haughty, arrogant manner seemed a deliberate, studied affront to his captors and the seven jeds. He was a powerful man, and despite the efforts of the warriors with him he forced his way almost to the foot of the dais before they could restrain him.

"Who is this man?" demanded one of the jeds.

"I am Gantun Gur, the assassin of Amhor," bellowed the captive in a great voice. "Give me back my sword, you stinking ulsios, and let me show you what a real fighting man can do to these deformed monstrosities of yours and to you, too. They caught me in nets, which is no way for decent men to take a warrior."

"Silence!" commanded a jed, pale with anger, and smarting under the insult of being called an ill smelling rat.

"Silence?" screamed Gantun Gur. "By my first ancestor! There lives no man can make Gantun Gur keep silent. Come down here and try it, man to man, you snivelling worm."

"Off with him!" cried the jed. "Take him to Ras Thavas, and tell Ras Thavas to take out his brain and burn it. He can do what he pleases with the body."

Gantun Gur fought like a demon, knocking hormads to right and left; and they only subdued him at last by entangling him in their nets. Then, bellowing curses and insults, he was dragged away toward the laboratory.

Shortly thereafter the jeds selected the hormads they chose to retain, and we conducted the others out of the chamber, where they were turned over to officers to be assigned to such duties as they were considered equal to. Then I returned to the laboratory building without having had a glimpse of Janai or learning anything concerning her. I was terribly disappointed and despondent.

I found Ras Thavas in his small private study. John Carter and a fairly well formed hormad were with him. The latter was standing with his back toward me as I entered the room. When he heard my voice he turned and greeted me by name. It was Tor-dur-bar with his newly grown body. One arm was a little longer than the other, his torso was out of proportion to his short legs, and he had six toes on one foot and an extra thumb on his left hand; but, altogether, he was a pretty good specimen for a hormad.

"Well, here I am as good as new," he exclaimed, a broad grin splitting his horrid countenance. "What do you think of me?"

"I'm glad to have you as a friend," I said. "I think that new body of yours is very powerful. It's splendidly muscled." And indeed it was.

"I should, however, like a body and face like yours," said Tor-dur-bar. "I was just talking to Ras Thavas about it, and he has promised to get me one, if he can."

Instantly I recalled Gantun Gur, the assassin of Amhor, and the doom that had been pronounced upon him by the jed. "I think a good body is waiting for you in the laboratory," I said; then I told them the story of Gantun Gur. "Now it is up to Ras Thavas. The jed said he could do what he pleased with the body."

"We'll have a look at the man," said The Master Mind of Mars, and led the way out toward the reception room where new victims were held pending his orders.

We found Gantun Gur securely trussed up and heavily guarded. At sight of us he commenced to bellow and rail, insulting all three of us indiscriminately. He appeared to have a most evil disposition. Ras Thavas regarded him for a moment in silence; then he dismissed the warriors and officers who had brought him.

"We will take care of him," he said. "Report to the Council of the Seven Jeds that his brain will be burned and his body put to some good use."

At that, Gantun Gur broke into such a tirade that I thought he had gone mad, and perhaps he had. He gnashed his teeth and foamed at the mouth and called Ras Thavas everything he could lay his tongue to.

Ras Thavas turned to Tor-dur-bar. "Can you carry him?" he asked.

For answer, the hormad picked up the red man as easily as though he had no weight and flung him across one broad shoulder. Tor-dur-bar's new body was indeed a mountain of strength.

Ras Thavas led the way back to his private study and through a small doorway into a chamber that I had not seen before. Here were two tables standing about twenty inches apart, the top of each a beautifully polished slab of solid ersite. At one end of the tables was a shelf on which were two empty glass vessels and two similar vessels filled with a clear, colorless liquid resembling water. Beneath each table was a small motor. There were numerous surgical instruments neatly arranged, various vessels containing colored liquids, and paraphernalia such as one might find in a laboratory or hospital concerning the uses of which I knew nothing, for I am, first and last, a fighting man and nothing else.

Ras Thavas directed Tor-dur-bar to lay Gantun Gur on one of the tables. "Now get on the other one yourself," he said.

"You are really going to do it?" exclaimed Tor-dur-bar. "You are going to give me a beautiful new body and face?"

"I wouldn't call it particularly beautiful," said Ras Thavas, with a slight smile.

"Oh, it is lovely," cried Tor-dur-bar. "I shall be your slave forever if you do this for me."

Although Gantun Gur was securely bound, it took both John Carter and myself to hold him still while Ras Thavas made two incisions in his body, one in a large vein and one in an artery. To these incisions he attached the ends of two tubes, one of which was connected with an empty glass receptacle and the other to the similar receptacle containing the colorless liquid. The connections made, he pressed a button controlling the small motor beneath the table, and Gantun Gur's blood was pumped into the empty jar while the contents of the other jar were forced into the emptying veins and arteries. Of course Gantun Gur lost consciousness almost immediately after the motor was started, and I breathed a sigh of relief when I had heard the last of him. When all the blood had been replaced by the colorless liquid, Ras Thavas removed the tubes and closed the openings in the body with bits of adhesive material; then he turned to Tor-dur-bar.

"You're quite sure you want to be a red man?" he asked.

"I can't wait," replied the hormad.

Ras Thavas repeated the operation he had just performed on Gantun Gur; then he sprayed both bodies with what he told us was a strong antiseptic solution and then himself, scrubbing his hands thoroughly. He now selected a sharp knife from among the instruments and removed the scalps from both bodies, following the hair line entirely around each head. This done, he sawed through the skull of each with a tiny circular saw attached to the end of a flexible, revolving shaft, following the line he had exposed by the removal of the scalps.

It was a long and marvellously skillful operation that followed, and at the end of four hours he had transferred the brain of Tor-dur-bar to the brain pan of him who had been Gantun Gur, deftly connected the severed nerves and ganglia, replaced the skull and scalp and bound the head securely with adhesive material, which was not only antiseptic and healing but locally anaesthetic as well.

He now reheated the blood he had drawn from Gantun Gur's body, adding a few drops of some clear chemical solution, and as he withdrew the liquid from the veins and arteries he pumped the blood back to replace it. Immediately following this he administered a hypodermic injection.

"In an hour," he said, "Tor-dur-bar will awaken to a new life in a new body."

It was while I was watching this marvellous operation that a mad plan occurred to me whereby I might eventually reach the side of Janai, or at least discover what fate had overtaken her. I turned to Ras Thavas. "Could you restore Gantun Gur's brain to his head if you wished to?" I asked.

"Certainly."

"Or could you put it in Tor-dur-bar's abandoned skull?"

"Yes."

"How soon after the removal of a brain do you have to replace it with another?"

"The liquid that I pump into the veins and arteries of a body will preserve it indefinitely. The blood I have withdrawn is also preserved similarly. But what are you driving at?"

"I want you to transfer my brain to the body that was Tor-dur-bar's," I said.

"Are you mad?" demanded John Carter.

"No. Well, perhaps a little, if love is madness. As a hormad I can be sent to the Council of the Seven Jeds and perhaps chosen to serve them. I know I can be chosen, for I know what answers to make to their questions. Once there, I can find the opportunity to discover what has become of Janai. Perhaps I may even rescue her, and when I have either succeeded or failed, Ras Thavas can return my brain to my own body. Will you do it, Ras Thavas?"

Ras Thavas looked questioningly at John Carter. "I have no right to interpose any objections," said The Warlord. "Vor Daj's brain and body are his own."

"Very well," said Ras Thavas. "Help me lift the new Tor-dur-bar from the table and then lie down there yourself."

chapter IX

MAN INTO HORMAD

WHEN I REGAINED consciousness, the first sight that met my eyes was that of my own body lying on an ersite slab a few inches from me. It was rather a ghastly experience, looking at one's own corpse; but when I sat up and looked down at my new body, it was even worse. I hadn't anticipated just how horrible it would be to be a hormad with a hideous face and malformed body. I almost loathed to touch myself with my new hands. Suppose something should happen to Ras Thavas! I broke out in a cold sweat at the thought. John Carter and the great surgeon stood looking at me.

"What is the matter?" demanded the latter. "You look ill."

I told him of the fear that had suddenly assailed me. He shrugged. "It would be just too bad for you," he said. "There is another man in the world, probably the only other man in the entire universe, who could restore your brain to your body were anything to happen to me; but you could never get him to Morbus as long as the hormads rule here."

"Who is he?" I asked.

"Vad Varo, a prince of Duhor now. He was Ulysses Paxton of Jasoom, and he was my assistant in my laboratory at Toonol. It was he who transferred my old brain to this new body. But don't worry. I have lived over a thousand years. The hormads need me. There is no reason why I should not live another thousand years. Before that I shall have trained another assistant, so that he can transfer my brain to a new body. You see, I should live forever."

"I hope you do," I said. Just then I discovered the body of the assassin of Amhor lying on the floor. "What's the matter with Tor-dur-bar?" I asked. "Shouldn't he have regained consciousness before I did?"

"I saw to it that he didn't," said Ras Thavas. "John Carter and I decided that it might be well if none other than he and I knew that your brain had been transferred to the body of a hormad."

"You were right. Let them think that I am all hormad."

"Carry Tor-dur-bar into my study. Let him come to there, but before he does you must be out of sight. Go out into the laboratory and help with the emergence of the new hormads. Tell the officer there that I sent you."

"But won't Tor-dur-bar recognize me when he sees me later?"

"I think not. He never saw his own face often enough to become familiar with it. There are few mirrors in Morbus, and his new body was such a recent acquisition that there is little likelihood that he will recognize it. If he does, we'll have to tell him."

The next several days were extremely unpleasant. I was a hormad. I had to consort with hormads and eat raw animal tissue. Ras Thavas armed me, and I had to destroy the terrible travesties on humanity that wriggled out of his abominable tanks so malformed that they were useless even as hormads. One day I met Teeaytan-ov, with whom I had flown to Morbus on the back of a malagor. He recognized me, or at least he thought he did.

"Kaor, Tor-dur-bar!" he greeted me. "So you have a new body. What has become of my friend, Vor Daj?"

"I do not know," I said. "Perhaps he went into the vats. He spoke of you often before I lost track of him. He was very anxious that you and I be friends."

"Why not?" asked Teeaytan-ov.

"I think it an excellent idea," I said, for I wanted all the friends I could get. "What are you doing now?"

"I am a member of the Third Jed's bodyguard. I live in the palace."

"That is fine," I said, "and I suppose you see everything that goes on there."

"I see a great deal. It makes me want to be a jed. I should like a new body such as they have."

"I wonder what became of the girl who was brought to the palace at the same time Vor Daj was," I ventured.

"What girl?" he asked.

"She was called Janai."

"Oh, Janai. She is still there. Two of the jeds want her, and the others won't let either have her. At least not so far. They are going to take a vote on it soon. I think every one of them wants her. She is the best looking woman they have captured for a long time."

"She is safe for the time being, then?" I asked.

"What do you mean, safe?" he demanded. "She will be very lucky if one of the jeds acquires her. She will have the best of everything and won't have to go to the vats of Ras Thavas. But why are you so interested in her? Perhaps you want her for yourself," and he burst into laughter. He would have been surprised indeed had he known that he had scored a bull's-eye.

"How do you like being a member of a jed's bodyguard?" I asked.

"It is very fine. I am treated well, have plenty to eat and a nice place to sleep, and I do not have to work hard. Also, I have a great deal of freedom. I can go wherever I please on the island of Morbus except into the private quarters of the jeds. You cannot leave this laboratory." He touched a medal hanging from a chain about his neck. "It is this," he said, "that gives me so much freedom. It shows that I am in the service of the Third Jed. No one dares interfere with me. I am a very important person, Tor-dur-bar. I feel quite sorry for you who are only a piece of animal tissue that can walk around and talk."

"It is nice to have such an important friend as you," I said, "especially one who will help me, if he can."

"Help you in what way?" he asked.

"The jeds are constantly calling for new warriors to replace those that are killed. I would make a good warrior for the bodyguard of a jed, and it would be nice if you and I could be together; so, if I am chosen to appear before them for examination, you can put in a good word for me when they ask who knows me."

He thought this over for a minute in his slow-witted way, but finally he said, "Why not? You look very strong; and sometimes, when the members of the guard get to quarrelling among themselves, it is well to have a strong friend. Yes, I'll help you, if I can. Sometimes they ask us if we know a good strong warrior who is intelligent, and then they send for him and examine him. Of course you are not very intelligent, but you might be able to pass because you are so strong. Just how strong are you?"

As a matter of fact, I didn't know, myself. I knew I was quite strong, because I lifted bodies so easily; so I said, "I really don't know."

"Could you lift me?" he asked. "I am a very heavy person."

"I can try," I said. I picked him up very easily. He didn't seem to weigh anything; so I thought I would see if I could toss him up over my head. I succeeded quite beyond my expectations, or his either. I tossed him almost to the ceiling of the room, and caught him as he came down. As I set him on his feet, he looked at me in astonishment.

"You are the strongest person in Morbus," he said. "There never was any one as strong as you. I shall tell the Third Jed about you."

He went away then, leaving me quite hopeful. At best, I had anticipated that Ras Thavas might some day include me with an assignment of hormads to be examined by the jeds; but as the ranks of the bodyguards were often filled by drafts on the villages outside the city, there was no telling how long I should have to wait for such an opportunity.

Ras Thavas had detailed me as the personal servant of John Carter, so we were not separated; and as he worked constantly with Ras Thavas, the three of us were often together. In the presence of others, they treated me as they would have treated any other hormad—like a dumb and ignorant servant, but when we were alone they accepted me once more as an equal. They both marvelled at my enormous strength, which was merely one of the accidents of the growth of Tor-dur-bar's new body; and I was sure that Ras Thavas would have liked to slice me up and return me to the vats in the hope of producing a new strain of super-powerful hormads.

John Carter is one of the most human persons I have ever known. He is in every sense of the word a great man, a statesman, a soldier, perhaps the greatest swordsman that ever lived, grim and terrible in combat; but with it all he is modest and approachable, and he has never lost his sense of humor. When we were alone he would joke with me about my newly acquired "pulchritude," laughing in his quiet way until his sides shook; and I was, indeed, a sight to inspire both laughter and horror. My great torso on its short legs, my right arm reaching below my knees, my left but slightly below my waist line, I was all out of proportion.

"Your face is really your greatest asset," he said, after looking at me for a long time. "I should like to take you back to Helium as you are and present you at the jeddak's next levee. You know, of course, that you were considered one of the handsomest men in Helium. I should say, 'Here is the noble Vor Daj, a padwar of The Warlord's Guard,' and how the women would cluster around you!"

My face really was something to arrest attention. Not a single feature was placed where it should have been, and all were out of proportion, some being too large and some too small. My right eye was way up on my forehead, just below the hair line, and was twice as large as my left eye which was about half an inch in front of my left ear. My mouth started at the bottom of my chin and ran upward at an angle of about 45° to a point slightly below my huge right eye. My nose was scarcely more than a bud and occupied the place that my little left eye should have had. One ear was close set and tiny, the other a pendulous mass that hung almost to my shoulder. It inclined me to believe that the symmetry of normal humans might not be wholly a matter of accident, as Ras Thavas believed.

Tor-dur-bar, with his new body, had wanted a name instead of a number; so John Carter and Ras Thavas had christened him Tun-gan, a transposition of the syllables of Gantun Gur's first name. When I told them of my conversation with Teeaytan-ov they agreed with me that I should keep the name Tor-dur-bar. Ras Thavas said he would tell Tun-gan that he had grafted a new hormad brain into his old body, and this he did at the first opportunity.

Shortly thereafter I met Tun-gan in one of the laboratory corridors. He looked at me searchingly for a moment, and then stopped me. "What is your name?" he demanded.

"Tor-dur-bar," I replied.

He shuddered visibly. "Are you really as hideous as you appear?" he asked; and then, without waiting for me to reply, "Keep out of my sight if you don't want to go to the incinerator or the vats."

When I told John Carter and Ras Thavas about it, they had a good laugh. It was good to have a laugh occasionally, for there was little here that was amusing. I was worried about Janai as well as the possibility that I might never regain my former body; Ras Thavas was dejected because of the failure of his plan to regain his former laboratory in Toonol and avenge himself on Vobis Kan, the jeddak; and John Carter grieved constantly, I knew, over the fate of his princess.

While we were talking there in Ras Thavas's private study an officer from the palace was announced; and without waiting to be invited, he entered the room. "I have come to fetch the hormad called Tor-dur-bar," he said. "Send for him without delay."

"This is an order from the Council of the Seven Jeds," said the officer. He was a sullen, arrogant fellow; doubtless one of the red captives into whose skull the brain of a hormad had been grafted.

Ras Thavas shrugged and pointed at me. "This is Tor-dur-bar," he said.

chapter X

I FIND JANAI

SEVEN OTHER HORMADS were lined up with me before the dais on which sat the seven jeds. I was, perhaps, the ugliest of them all. They asked us many questions. It was, in a way, a crude intelligence test, for they wished hormads above the average in intelligence to serve in this select body of monstrous guardsmen. I was to learn that they were becoming a little appearance conscious, also; for one of the jeds looked long at me, and then waved me aside.

"We do not want such a hideous creature in the guards," he said.

I looked around at the other hormads in the chamber, and really couldn't see much to choose from between them and me. They were all hideous monsters. What difference could it make that I was a little more hideous? Of course there was nothing for me to do; and, much disappointed, I stepped back from the line.

Five of the seven remaining were little better than halfwits, and they were eliminated. The other two might have been high grade morons at the best, but they were accepted. The Third Jed spoke to an officer. "Where is the hormad I sent for?" he demanded. "Tor-dur-bar."

"I am Tor-dur-bar," I said.

"Come here," said the Third Jed, and again I stepped to the foot of the dais.

"One of my guardsmen says you are the strongest person in Morbus," continued the Third Jed. "Are you?"

"I don't know," I replied. "I am very strong."

"He says that you can toss a man to the ceiling and catch him again. Let me see you do it."

I picked up one of the rejected hormads and threw him as high as I could. I learned then that I didn't know my own strength. The room was quite lofty, but the creature hit the ceiling with a dull thud and fell back into my arms unconscious. The seven jeds and the others in the room looked at me with astonishment.

"He may not be beautiful," said the Third Jed, "but I shall take him for my guard."

The jed who had waved me aside objected. "Guardsmen must be intelligent," he said. "This creature looks as though it had no brains at all."

"We shall see," said another jed, and then they commenced to fire questions at me. Of course they were simple questions that the most ignorant of red men could have answered easily, for the questioners had only the brains and experience of hormads after all.

"He is very intelligent," said the Third Jed. "He answers all our questions easily. I insist upon having him."

"We shall draw lots for him," said the First Jed.

"We shall do nothing of the kind," stormed the Third Jed. "He belongs to me. It was I who sent for him. None of the rest of you had ever heard of him."

"We shall take a vote on it," said the Fourth Jed.

The Fifth Jed, who had rejected me, said nothing. He just sat there scowling. I had made a fool of him by proving myself so desirable that many jeds wished me.

"Come," said the Seventh Jed, "let's take a vote to see whether we award him to the Third Jed or draw lots for him."

"Don't waste time," said the Third Jed, "for I am going to take him anyway." He was a big man, larger than any of his fellows.

"You are always making trouble," growled the First Jed.

"It is the rest of you that are making trouble," retorted the Third Jed, "by trying to deprive me of what is rightfully mine."

"The Third Jed is right," said the Second Jed. "None of the rest of us have any claim on this hormad. We were willing to see him rejected until the Third Jed proved that he would make a desirable guardsman."

They wrangled on for a long time, but finally gave in to the Third Jed. Now I had a new master. He put me in charge of one of his own officers and I was taken away to be initiated into the duties of a guardsman in the palace of the seven jeds of Morbus.

The officer conducted me to a large guard-room where there were many other hormad warriors. Teeaytan-ov was among them, and he lost no time in claiming credit for having me chosen for the guards. One of the first things I was taught was that I was to fight and die, if necessary, in defense of the Third Jed. I was given the insignia of the guard to wear around my neck, and then an officer undertook to train me in the use of a long-sword. I had to pretend to a little awkwardness lest he discover that I was more familiar with the weapon than he. He complimented me upon my aptitude, and said that he would give me daily instruction thereafter.

I found my fellow guardsmen a stupid, egotistical lot of morons. They were all jealous of one another and of the seven jeds who were only hormads after all with the bodies of red men. I discovered that only fear held them in leash, for they were just intelligent enough to resent their lot and to envy the officers and jeds who had power and authority. The soil was ripe for mutiny or revolution. It was just an undercurrent that one sensed if he had intelligence, for they feared spies and informers too much to voice their true feeling aloud.

I chafed now at every delay that kept me from searching for Janai. I did not dare make any inquiries concerning her, as that would immediately have aroused suspicion; nor did I dare go poking about the palace until I knew more of its customs and its life.

The following day I was taken with a detachment of guardsmen beyond the walls of the city out among the crowded villages of the common hormads. Here I saw thousands of monstrous creatures, stupid and sullen, with no pleasures beyond eating and sleeping, and just enough intelligence ordinarily to make them dissatisfied with their lot. There were many, of course, with less brains and no more imagination than beasts. These alone were contented.

I saw envy and hate in the glances that many of them cast upon us and our officers, and there were growling murmurs after we had passed that followed us like the low moaning of the wind in the wake of a flier. I came to the conclusion that the Seven Jeds of Morbus were going to find many obstacles in the way of their grandiose plan to conquer a world with these creatures, and the most insurmountable of all would be the creatures themselves.

At last I learned the ways of the palace and how to find my way about, and the first time I was off duty I commenced a systematic search for Janai. I always moved quickly, as though I was on some important errand; so when I met officers or hormads they paid no attention to me.

One day, as I came to the end of a corridor, a hormad stepped from the doorway and confronted me. "What are you doing here?" he demanded. "Don't you know that these are the quarters of the women and that no one is allowed here except those who guard them?"

"You are one of the guards?" I asked.

"Yes; now be on your way, and don't come back here again."

"It must be a very important post, guarding the women," I said.

He swelled perceptibly. "It is, indeed. Only the most trustworthy warriors are chosen."

"Are the women very beautiful?" I asked.

"Very," he said.

"I certainly envy you. I wish that I might be a guard here, too. It would make me happy to see these beautiful women. I have never seen one. Just to get a glimpse of them would be wonderful."

"Well," he said, "perhaps it would do no harm to let you have a little glimpse. You seem to be a very intelligent fellow. What is your name?"

"I am Tor-dur-bar," I said. "I am in the guard of the Third Jed."

"You are Tor-dur-bar, the strongest man in Morbus?" he demanded.

"Yes, I am he."

"I have heard of you. Every one is talking about you, and how you threw a hormad up against the ceiling of the council chamber so hard that you killed him. I shall be very glad to let you have a look at the women, but don't tell anybody that I did so."

"Of course not," I assured him.

He stepped to the door at the end of the corridor and swung it open. Beyond was a large chamber in which were several women and a number of the sexless hormads who were evidently their servants.

"You may step in," said the guard; "they will think you are another guard."

I entered the room and looked quickly about, and as I did so my heart leaped to my throat, for there, at the far end of the room, was Janai. Forgetful of everything else, I started to cross toward her. I forgot the guard. I forgot that I was a hideous monster. I forgot everything but that here was the woman I loved and here was I. The guard overtook me and laid a hand upon my shoulder.

"Hey! Where are you going?" he demanded.

Then I came to myself. "I wanted to get a closer look at them," I said. "I wanted to see what it was that the jeds saw in women."

"Well, you have seen enough. I don't see what they see in them, myself. Come now, you must get out."

As he spoke the door by which we had entered swung open again, and the Third Jed entered. The guard shrivelled in terror. "Quick!" he gasped. "Mingle with the servants. Pretend you are one of them. Perhaps he will not notice you."

I crossed quickly toward Janai and kneeled before her. "What do you want?" she demanded. "What are you doing here, hormad? You are not one of our servants."

"I have a message for you," I whispered. I touched her with my hand. I could not help it. I could scarcely resist the tremendous urge I felt to take her in my arms. She shrank from me, an expression of loathing and disgust upon her face.

"Do not touch me, hormad," she said, "or I shall call the guard."

Then I remembered the hideous monster that I was, and I drew away from her. "Do not call the guard until you have heard my message," I begged.

"There is no one here to send me any message I would care to hear," she said.

"There is Vor Daj," I said. "Have you forgotten him?"

I waited breathlessly to note her reaction.

"Vor Daj!" she breathed in a whisper. "He has sent you to me?"

"Yes. He told me to find you. He did not know but that you were dead. He told me that if I found you I was to tell you that day and night he was searching for some plan whereby he might take you away from Morbus."

"There can be no hope," she said, "but tell him that I have not forgotten him and never shall. Every day I think of him, and now every day I shall bless him for thinking of me and wishing to help me."

I was about to say more to her, to tell her that Vor Daj loved her, so that I might see whether that pleased her or not; but then I heard a loud voice demand, "What are you doing here?" and turning I saw that the First Jed had entered the room and was confronting the Third Jed accusingly.

"I have come after my slave woman," replied the latter. "What are you going to do about it?"

"These women have not been distributed by the Council. You have no right to any of them. If you need more slaves, order some additional hormads. Come on, get out of here!"

For answer, the Third Jed crossed the room and seized Janai by one arm. "Come with me, woman," he ordered, and started to drag her toward the door; then the First Jed whipped out his sword and blocked the way. The sword of the Third Jed flashed from its scabbard, and the two men engaged, which necessitated the Third Jed's relinquishing his hold on Janai.

The duel was a rare spectacle of poor swordsmanship, but they skipped about the room so much and cut and slashed so terrifically in all directions that the other occupants of the chamber had to keep constantly on the move to avoid injury. I tried always to keep between them and Janai, and presently I found myself near the door with the girl close beside me. The attention of the guard as well as all others in the room was riveted upon the two combatants, and the door was just behind us. Nowhere could Janai be in greater danger than here. Perhaps never again would I have such an opportunity to get her out of these quarters in which she was a prisoner. Where I could take her, I did not know; but to get her out of here would be something. If, in some way, I could smuggle her into the laboratory I was sure that John Carter and Ras Thavas would find some place to hide her. Bending my ugly face close to her beautiful one, I whispered, "Come with me," but she shrank away. "Please don't be afraid of me," I begged. "I am doing this for Vor Daj, because he is my friend. I want to try to help you."

"Very well," she said, without further hesitation.

I looked hurriedly about the room. No one was paying any attention to us. Every eye was centered upon the combatants. I took Janai's hand, and together we slipped through the doorway out into the corridor beyond.

Now that we were out of the room where Janai had been imprisoned I hadn't the slightest idea where to take her. The suspicions of the first person who saw us together would be aroused. I asked Janai if she knew any place where I might hide her safely until I could find a way to get her out of the palace. She said that she did not. She knew only the room in which she had been imprisoned.

I hurried her down the corridor along which I had come, but at the head of the ramp leading to the floor below I saw two officers ascending. There was a door at my left; and as we had to get out of sight immediately, I opened it and hurried Janai into the room beyond, which, fortunately, was vacant. It was evidently a storeroom, for there were sacks and boxes piled along the walls. At the far end of the room was a window, and in one of the side walls another door.

I waited until I heard the officers pass along the corridor; then I opened the door in the side wall to see what lay beyond. There was another room in one corner of which was a pile of sleeping silks and furs. Everything was covered with dust, indicating that the room had not been occupied for a considerable time. In a curtained alcove was a bath, and from hooks along the wall hung the trappings of a warrior, even to his weapons. The former occupant must have left, expecting to return; and my guess was that he had been an officer who had gone out on some expedition and been killed, for the trappings and weapons that had been left behind were such as a fighting man wears upon dress occasions.

"We have stumbled upon an excellent place for you to hide," I said. "Keep the door to this room locked; there is a bolt on this side. I shall bring you food when I can, and just as soon as it is possible I'll get you to a safer place."

"Perhaps Vor Daj will come to see me," she suggested. "Be sure to tell him where I am."

"He would come if he could; but he is in the laboratory building, and cannot get out. Would you like to see him very much?" I couldn't resist asking her that.

"Very much, indeed," she said.

"He will be glad to know that, and until he can come I'll do the best I can to help you."

"Why are you so kind to me?" she asked. "You seem very different from the other hormads I have seen."

"I am Vor Daj's friend," I said. "I will do anything I can for him and for you. You are no longer afraid of me?"

"No. I was at first, but not now."

"You need never be afraid of me. There is nothing that I would not do for you, even to laying down my life for you."

"I thank you, even though I do not understand," she said.

"Some day you will understand, but not yet. Now I must be going. Be brave, and don't give up hope."

"Good-by,—Oh, I do not even know your name."

"I am called Tor-dur-bar," I said.

"Oh, now I remember you. Your head was cut off in the fight in which Vor Daj and Dotar Sojat were captured. I remember that then you promised to be Vor Daj's friend. Now you have a new body."

"I wish they might have given me a new face as well," I said, simulating a smile with my hideous great mouth.

"It is enough that you have a good heart," she said.

"It is enough for me that you think so, Janai; and now good-by."

As I passed through the outer room I examined the sacks and boxes piled there, and was overjoyed to discover that they contained food. I hastened to acquaint Janai with this good news; then I left her and returned to the guard-room.

My fellow guardsmen were most uninteresting companions. Like most stupid people they talked principally about themselves and were great braggarts. Food was also a very important topic of conversation with them, and they would spend hours telling of the great quantities of animal tissue they had eaten upon various occasions. When there was no officer around they aired their grievances against the authority of the jeds; but this they did fearfully, as there was always the danger of spies or informers. Promotions to easier berths and larger allowances of animal tissue were the rewards for informing on one's fellows.

I had been back but a short time when an officer entered the room and ordered us to strap on our weapons and accompany him. He marched us to a very large room in the quarters of the Third Jed, to whom we belonged; and there I found that all the armed retainers of the jed were gathered. There was much whispering and speculation. The officers appeared unusually serious, and the atmosphere seemed charged with nervous apprehension.

Presently the Third Jed entered the room accompanied by his four principal dwars. He had been bleeding from several wounds which had been bandaged. I knew where he had acquired them, and I wondered how the First Jed had fared. The Third Jed mounted a dais and addressed us.

"You will accompany me to the Council of the Seven Jeds," he said. "It is your duty to see that no harm befalls me. Obey your officers. If you are loyal, you will receive an extra allowance of food and many privileges. I have spoken."

We were marched to the council chamber which was jammed

with the armed hormads of the personal bodyguards of the seven jeds. The air was tense with suppressed excitement. Even the stupidest hormads seemed infected by it. Six jeds sat upon the dais. The First Jed was swathed in bandages that were red with blood. The throne of the Third Jed was empty. Surrounding our jed, we shouldered our way to the foot of the dais; but he did not mount to the throne. Instead, he stood on the floor facing the six jeds; and his voice and his manner were truculent as he addressed them.

"You sent warriors to arrest me," he said. "They are dead. There is no one in Morbus with the power or authority to arrest me. There are some among you who would like to be jeddak and rule the rest of us. The First Jed would like to be jeddak. The time has come for us to determine which one is fit to be jeddak, for I agree with others of you that seven men cannot rule as well as one. Divided authority is no authority."

"You are under arrest," shouted the First Jed.

The Third Jed laughed at him. "You are giving additional proof that you are not fit to be jeddak, for you can only issue orders—you cannot enforce them."

The First Jed looked down at his followers, addressing his chief dwar. "Seize him!" he commanded. "Take the traitor dead or alive."

The warriors of the First Jed moved toward us, forcing their way slowly through crowds of other warriors. I chanced to be standing in the front row, facing the oncoming hormads. A big warrior was the first to shoulder his way through to us. He made a pass at me with his sword. He was very slow and clumsy, and I had no difficulty stepping quickly to one side and avoiding it. He had put so much into that blow, that, when he missed me, he lost his balance and came tumbling into my arms. That was wonderful! I hoisted him in to the air and threw him fully fifty feet from me, so that he alighted in the midst of his companions, knocking many of them to the floor.

"Good work, Tor-dur-bar!" shouted the Third Jed. "You shall have all the meat you want for that."

A second man reached me and I threw him all the way across the room. I was just beginning to appreciate what enormous strength I had. It seemed absolutely incredible that any creature could be so strong. After that there was a lull during which the Third Jed succeeded in making himself heard again.

"I, the Third Jed," he thundered, "now proclaim myself Jeddak of Morbus. Let the jeds who will swear allegiance to me rise!"

No one rose. It looked bad for the Third Jed, as the chamber was packed with the warriors of the other jeds. It also looked pretty bad for us. I wondered what the Third Jed would do. It seemed to me that his life was forfeit anyway, no matter what he did. He turned and spoke to the dwars clustered about him, and immediately orders were given for us to fall back to the doorway. Then the fighting began as the other jeds ordered their warriors to prevent our escape.

The Third Jed called me by name. "Clear a way to the door, Tor-dur-bar!" he cried. It seemed to me that he was banking rather too heavily upon my strength; but I enjoyed fighting, and this looked like an excellent opportunity to get my fill of it. I forced my way back through our own ranks to what was now the front rank of our attack, and here I found that fate had given me a great advantage in one of my deformities. My enormously long arm was my sword arm, which, backed by my super-human strength and a long-sword, permitted me to cut a swath through the enemy line that opened a path as by magic, for those that I did not mow down turned and fled before the intensity of my attack.

There were heads and arms and legs and halves of bodies writhing and squirming on the floor; there were heads screaming and cursing under foot, and headless bodies dashing about the room colliding with friend and foe indiscriminately. If there ever was a shambles it was there in the great council chamber of the seven jeds of Morbus. The hormads were, for the most part, too stupid to know fear; but when they saw their officers fleeing from me, their morale was shattered; and we won to the door with scarcely a casualty on our side.

From there our officers led us out of the palace into the city and down the long avenue to the city gates. There they knew nothing of what had been going on in the palace, and swung the gates open at the command of the Third Jed. Of course, they couldn't have stopped us anyway, for we greatly outnumbered the guard at the gates.

I wondered where we were going as we marched out of the city of Morbus; but I was soon to discover, for at the first of the outer villages that we came to, the Third Jed demanded its surrender, and announced that he was the Jeddak of Morbus. He swore the officers and warriors into his service, promoted many of the former, promised increased rations to the latter, left a dwar to represent him and marched on to new conquests.

Nowhere did he meet with opposition, and in three days he had conquered all of the island of Morbus except the city itself. The dwars he left behind organized the local warriors to oppose any force that might be sent out by the six jeds remaining in command of the city, but during those three days no army marched out of Morbus to contest the right of the new jeddak to rule.

On the fifth day we marched back to a large village on the coast, near the city; and here Ay-mad, Jeddak of Morbus, established his capital. This is the name he took, the literal translation of which is

One-man, or Number One Man, or First Man. Anyway, he was head man; and I think that of all the seven jeds he was best fitted to be jeddak. He had a physique and face suited to his new role, and he possessed one of the best brains of any of the hormads that I had knowledge of.

Of course all that had happened seemed at the time to have placed me in an utterly hopeless position. Janai was in the city beyond any hope of my succoring her. I was separated from The Warlord and from Ras Thavas. I was only a poor hormad without influence or position. I could do nothing, and by now I must have been so well known in the city that I could not possibly enter it surreptitiously. My hideous features must by this time have become all too well known to the followers of the six jeds to permit me the slightest hope of entering the city unrecognized.

When we finally encamped in the new capital of Ay-mad I threw myself upon the ground with my fellow hormads and awaited the issuance of the slimy animal tissue that was our principal reward for the conquests we had made. It satisfied most of the poor, moronic, half-witted creatures who were my comrades; but it did not satisfy me. I was endowed with more brains, more ability, more experience, more physical strength than any of them. I was by far a better man than the jeddak himself; and yet I was only a hideous, malformed hormad that no self-respecting calot would associate with. I was thus occupied with self-pity when an officer came calling my name aloud. I stood up.

"I am Tor-dur-bar," I said.

"Come with me," he said. "The Jeddak has sent for you."

I accompanied him to where the Jeddak and all his principal officers were gathered, wondering what new task Ay-mad had conceived for the testing of my enormous strength, for I could not believe that he wished to see me for any other purpose. I had acquired the typical inferiority of a true hormad.

They had fixed up a sort of a dais and throne for Ay-mad, and he sat there like a regular jeddak with his officers grouped around him. "Approach, Tor-dur-bar!" he commanded, and so I came forward and stood before the throne. "Kneel," he said, and I kneeled, for I was only a poor hormad. "More than to any other the victory that we won in the council chamber in Morbus was due to you," he said. "You not only have the strength of many men, but you have intelligence. Because of these things I appoint you a dwar, and when we enter Morbus in victory you may select the body of any red man there and I will command Ras Thavas to transfer your brain to it."

So I was a dwar. I thanked Ay-mad, and joined the other dwars clustered about him. They all had the bodies of red men. How many of them had hormad brains, I did not know. I was the only dwar with the body of a hormad. I might, as far as I knew, be the only one with the brains of a human being.

chapter XII

Warrior's Reward

MORBUS IS A walled city. It is practically impregnable to men armed only with swords. For seven days Ay-mad tried to take it, but all his warriors could do was to beat futilely upon the great wooden gates while the defending warriors dropped heavy stones on their heads. At night we withdrew, and the defenders probably went to sleep with a sense of perfect security. On the eighth day Ay-mad called a conference of his dwars. "We are getting nowhere," he said. "We could pound on those gates for a thousand years and do nothing more important than make dents in them. How are we to take Morbus? If we conquer the world we must capture Morbus and Ras Thavas."

"You cannot conquer the world," I said, "but you can take Morbus."

"Why can't we conquer the world?" he demanded.

"It is too large, and there are too many great nations to be overcome."

"What do you know about the world?" he demanded. "You are only a hormad who has never been outside of Morbus."

"You will see that I am right, if you try to conquer the world; but it would be easy to take the city of Morbus."

"And how?" he asked.

I told him in a few words how I should do it were I in command. He looked at me for a long time, thinking the matter out. "It is too simple," he said; then he turned on the others. "Why have none of you thought of this before?" he demanded. "Tor-dur-bar is the only man of brains among you."

All that night a thousand hormads were engaged in building long ladders, all that night and the next day. We had a thousand of them, and when both moons had passed below the horizon on the second night a hundred thousand hormads crept toward the walls of Morbus with their long ladders. In a thousand places all around the city we raised our ladders to the top of the walls, and at a given signal a hundred men scaled each ladder and dropped into the city streets.

The rest was easy. We took the sleeping city with the loss of only a few warriors; and Ay-mad, with his dwars, entered the council chamber. The first thing that he did was to have all but one throne removed from the dais; then, seated there, he had the six jeds dragged before him. They were a sheepish, terrified lot.

"How do you wish to die?" he asked, "or would you rather have your brains returned to the skulls of hormads from whence they came?"

"That cannot be done," said the Fifth Jed, "but if it could, I would rather go to the vats. I do not wish to be a hormad again."

"Why can't it be done?" demanded Ay-mad. "What Ras Thavas has done so many times, he can do again."

"There is no Ras Thavas," said the Fifth Jed. "He has disappeared."

The effect that that statement had upon me may well be imagined. If it were true, I was doomed to lifetime imprisonment in the monstrous carcass of a hormad. There could be no escape, for Vad Varo of Duhor was as far removed from me as though he had been back upon his own planet of Jasoom; and he was the only other man in the world who could restore my brain to its rightful body if Ras Thavas were dead. With the new Jeddak of Morbus seeking to conquer the world, all men would be our enemies. I could not call upon any man to save me.

And what of Janai? I should always be repulsive to her, and so I could never tell her the truth. It were far better that she believe me dead than that she should know that my brain was forever buried behind this loathsome, inhuman mask. How could one with an exterior like mine speak of love? And love was not for hormads.

In a daze, I heard Ay-mad ask what had become of Ras Thavas and the Fifth Jed reply, "No one knows. He has simply disappeared. As he could not escape from the city without detection, we believe that some of the hormads sliced him up and threw him into one of his own culture vats in revenge."

Ay-mad was furious, for without Ras Thavas his dream of world conquest was shattered. "This is the work of my enemies," he cried. "Some of you six jeds had a hand in this. You have destroyed Ras Thavas or hidden him. Take them away! Put them in separate dungeons in the pits. The one who confesses first shall have his life and his liberty. The rest shall die. I give you one day to decide."

After the six jeds had been dragged away Ay-mad offered amnesty to all of their officers who would swear allegiance to him, an invitation which was refused by none, since refusal could mean nothing but death. After this formality, which took a matter of some hours, was completed, Ay-mad publicly acknowledged that the success of his operations against Morbus was due to me; and told me that he would grant me any favor that I might ask and that in addition to that he was appointing me an odwar, a military rank analogous to that of general in the armies of the planet Earth.

"And now," continued Ay-mad, "choose the favor that you would ask."

"That I should like to do in private," I said, "for the favor I wish to ask can be of no interest to any but you and me."

"Very well," he said. "I grant you a private audience immediately upon the conclusion of this one."

It was with some impatience that I awaited the conclusion of the session in the council chamber, and when at last Ay-mad arose and motioned me to follow him I breathed a sigh of relief. He led me into a small apartment directly behind the dais and seated himself behind a large desk.

"Now," he said, "what is the favor you wish to ask?"

"I am going to ask two," I replied. "I should like to be placed in full charge of the laboratory building."

"I see no objection to that," he interrupted. "But why such a strange request?"

"There is the body of a red man there to which I should like to have my brain transferred if Ras Thavas is ever found," I explained, "and if I am in full charge of the laboratory building I can protect the body and make sure that Ras Thavas performs the operation."

"Very well," he said, "your request is granted. What is the other?"

"I want you to give me the girl, Janai."

His face clouded at that. "What do you want of a girl?" he demanded. "You are only a hormad."

"Some day I may be a red man."

"But why the girl, Janai? What do you know of her? I didn't know you had ever seen her."

"I was with the party that captured her. She is the only woman I have ever seen that I wanted."

"I couldn't give her to you if I had a mind to," he said. "She, too, has disappeared. While I was fighting with the First Jed she must have escaped from the room—we were fighting in the apartment in which the women were being held—and she has not been seen since."

"Will you give her to me if she is found?"

"I want her myself."

"But you have the pick of many others. I have seen beautiful women in the palace; and among them there must be one who would make you a splendid wife, a suitable consort for a jeddak. This, of all the favors I might ask, I wish the most."

"She would rather die than belong to a hideous monster like you," he said.

"Well, grant me this, then: that if she is found the decision be left to her."

He laughed. "That I agree to willingly. You don't think, do you, that she would choose you in preference to a jeddak, a monster in preference to a man?"

"I have been told that women are unpredictable. I am willing to take the chance and abide by her decision, if you are."

"Then it is agreed," he said, and he was quite good natured about it, so certain was he of the outcome; "but you are not getting much in the way of reward for the services you have rendered me. I thought you would at least ask for a palace of your own and many servants."

"I asked for the two things I wish most," I said, "and I am content."

"Well, you may have the palace and the servants whenever you wish them, for by your own proposition you will never have the girl, even if she be found."

As soon as he dismissed me I hurried to the apartment where I had left Janai, and my heart was in my mouth for fear that I should not find her there. I had to be careful that no one saw me enter the storeroom that led to her hiding place, for I did not want Ay-mad ever to discover that I had known all along where she was hidden. Fortunately the corridor was empty, and I entered the storeroom unseen. Going to the door of Janai's room, I knocked. There was no answer.

"Janai!" I called. "It is I, Tor-dur-bar. Are you there?"

Then I heard the bolt being withdrawn, and the door swung open. There she stood! My heart almost stopped for very relief. And she was so beautiful! It seemed that each new time I saw her she had become more beautiful.

"You are back," she said. "I began to fear that you would never come. Do you bring word from Vor Daj?"

So she was thinking of Vor Daj! On such slight sustenance does love thrive. I entered the room and closed the door.

"Vor Daj sends greetings," I said. "He thinks of nothing but you and your welfare."

"But he cannot come to me?"

"No. He is a prisoner in the laboratory building, but he has charged me to look after you. Now I can do so better than before for many changes have taken place in Morbus since I last saw you. I am an odwar now, and my influence with the new jeddak is considerable."

"I have been hearing sounds of fighting," she said. "Tell me what has happened."

I told her briefly and that the Third Jed was now jeddak. "Then I am lost," she said, "for he is all powerful."

"Perhaps that is your salvation," I told her. "To reward me for the services I had rendered him, the new jeddak made me an odwar and promised to grant me any favor I asked."

"And what did you ask of him?"

"You."

I could almost feel the shudder that ran through her frame as she looked at my hideous face and deformed body. "Please!" she begged. "You said you were my friend, that you were the friend of Vor Daj. He would not wish you to have me, I am sure."

"I only asked for you that I might protect you for Vor Daj," I said.

"How does Vor Daj know that I would have him?" she demanded.

"He doesn't know. He only hopes that I may protect you from others. I have not said, have I, that Vor Daj wishes you for himself?" I could not resist saying that just to match her seeming indifference to Vor Daj. Her chin went up a little, and that pleased me. I know something of women and their reactions.

"What did the Third Jed say when you asked for me?" she inquired.

"He is jeddak now, and he calls himself Ay-mad," I explained. "He said that you would not have me; so I have come to lay the whole matter before you. It is for you to decide. I think that Vor Daj loves you. You must choose between him and Ay-mad. Ay-mad will ask you to make the choice between him and me; but the choice will really be between him and Vor Daj, only Ay-mad won't know that. If you choose me, Ay-mad will be insulted and angry; but I believe that he will keep his bargain. Then I shall take you to quarters near my own and protect you until such time as you and Vor Daj can escape from Morbus. I can also assure you that Vor Daj will hold you to no promise afterward. His only thought now is to help you."

"I was sure that he would be like that," she said, "and you may be sure that when the choice is given me I shall choose you rather than Ay-mad."

"Even though by choosing him you could become a jeddara?" I asked.

"Even so," she said.

chapter XIII

John Carter Disappears

After leaving Janai I went at once to the laboratory building to find John Carter and learn what he knew of the disappearance of Ras Thavas. Janai and I had decided that she should remain where she was for a few days so that Ay-mad's suspicions would not be aroused by my finding her too easily. I had determined to institute a search during which she should be found by someone else, though I would be close at hand to prevent any miscarriage of our plans.

One of the first persons I met on entering the laboratory building was Tun-gan. At sight of me he flew into a rage. "I thought I told you to keep out of my sight," he blustered. "Do you want to go to the incinerator?"

I pointed to my badge of office, which he evidently had not noticed. "You wouldn't send one of the jeddak's odwars to the incinerator, would you?" I inquired.

He was dumfounded. "You an odwar?" he demanded.

"Why not?" I asked.

"But you are only a hormad."

"Perhaps, but I am also an odwar. I could have you sent to the incinerator or the vats, but I don't intend to. I have your body; so we should be friends. What do you say?"

"All right," he agreed. What else could he do? "But I don't understand how you got to be an odwar with that awful looking face and your deformed body."

"Don't forget that they were your face and body once," I reminded him. "And also don't forget that you couldn't get anywhere with them.

It takes more than a face or body to get places—it takes a brain that is good for something beside thinking of food."

"I still can't understand why you should be made an odwar when there are such fine looking men as I to choose from."

"Well, never mind. That isn't what I came here to discuss. I have been placed in full charge of the laboratory building. I have come to talk with John Carter. Do you know where he is?"

"No. Neither does any one else. He disappeared at the same time Ras Thavas did."

That was a new blow. John Carter gone! But on second thought the fact gave me renewed hope. If they were both gone and nobody knew what had become of them, it seemed to me quite possible that they had found the means to escape together. I was certain John Carter would never desert me. If he were gone of his own free will, he would return. He'd never leave me housed in this awful carcass.

"Has no one any idea of what became of them?" I asked.

"They may have been sliced up and thrown into one of the vats," said Tun-gan. "Some of the older hormads have been getting out of hand, and Ras Thavas had threatened them with the incinerator. They might have done it to save themselves or just to be revenged upon him."

"I'm going to Ras Thavas's study," I said. "Come with me."

I found the study in about the same condition I had last seen it. There was nothing to indicate that a struggle of any kind had taken place, not a clue that pointed to any solution of the mystery. I was completely baffled.

"When were they last seen?"

"About three days ago. One of the hormads said he saw them coming up from the pits. I don't know why they were there. No one goes there any more since they stopped storing bodies, and no prisoners are kept there. They use the pits beneath some of the other buildings for them."

"Were the pits searched?"

"Yes, but no trace of them was found."

"Wait here a minute," I said. I wanted to go into the small laboratory and have a look at my body. I wanted to be sure it was safe, but I didn't wish Tun-gan to see it. I had an idea that he would suspect something if he saw my body. He wasn't very brilliant, but it wouldn't have taken much intelligence to guess what had become of the brain of Vor Daj.

Tun-gan waited for me in the study. I knew where the key to the small laboratory was hidden, because Ras Thavas had shown me; and I was soon turning it in the lock. A moment later I stepped into the room, and then I got another shock—*my body had disappeared!*

My knees became so weak that I collapsed onto a bench, and there I sat with my head in my hands. My body gone! With it had gone my last hope of winning Janai. It was unthinkable that I could win her with this awful face and grotesque body. I wouldn't have wanted to win her like that. I couldn't have had any respect for her or for any other woman who could have chosen such an abominable creature as I.

Presently I gathered myself together and walked over to the table where I had last seen my body. Everything seemed to be in order, except that the container that had held my blood was missing. Could it be possible that Ras Thavas had transferred another brain to my body? He couldn't have done it without John Carter's approval, and if John Carter had approved there must have been a good reason for it. One occurred to me. They might have found an opportunity to escape from the island that had to be taken advantage of on the instant or not at all. In that case, it might have seemed wiser to John Carter to have another brain transferred to my skull and take my body along with him, rather than leave it here in danger of destruction. Of course he would only have done this had he been assured that they could return later and rescue me. But of course this was all idle conjecture. The truth of the matter was that there was no explanation.

As I sat there thinking about the matter, I recalled the case history that Ras Thavas had written and hung at the foot of the table where my body lay. I thought I would take a look at it and see if any further entries had been made, but when I walked to the foot of the table I saw that the history was not there. In its place hung a single sheet on which were written two numbers—"3–17." What did they signify? Nothing, as far as I was concerned.

I returned to the study and directed Tun-gan to accompany me while I made an inspection of the laboratories, for if I were to be in charge I'd have to make some semblance of a gesture in line with my newly acquired authority.

"How have things been going since Ras Thavas disappeared?" I asked Tun-gan.

"Not so well," he replied. "In fact things seem to go all wrong without him," and when I reached the first vat room I realized that that was a crass understatement of fact. Things couldn't well have been much worse. The floor was covered with the remains of hideous monstrosities that the officers had had to have destroyed. The parts still lived. Legs were trying to walk, hands were clutching at whatever came within reach, heads were lying about screaming and moaning. I called the officer in charge to me.

"What is the meaning of this?" I demanded. "Why hasn't something been done with these things?"

"Who are you to question me, hormad?" he demanded.

I touched the insignia of my rank, and his attitude changed sharply. "I am in charge here now," I said. "Answer my questions."

"No one but Ras Thavas knew exactly how to slice them up for the vats," he said, "nor which vats to put them in."

"Have them taken to the incinerator," I said. "Until Ras Thavas returns burn all that are useless."

"Something has gone wrong in No. 4 vat room," he said. "Perhaps you had better have a look in there."

When I reached No. 4 the sight that met my eyes was one of the most horrible I have ever looked upon. Something had evidently gone wrong with the culture medium, and instead of individual hormads being formed, there was a single huge mass of animal tissue emerging from the vat and rolling out over the floor. Various internal and external human parts and organs grew out of it without any relation to other parts, a leg here, a hand there, a head somewhere else; and the heads were mouthing and screaming, which only added to the horror of the scene.

"We tried to do something about it," said the officer, "but when we tried to kill the mess, the hands clutched us and the heads bit us. Even our hormads were afraid to go near it, and if anything is too horrible for them you can't expect human beings to stomach it."

I quite agreed with him. Frankly, I didn't know what to do. I couldn't get near the vat to drain off the culture medium and stop the growth; and with the hormads afraid to approach it, it would be impossible to destroy it.

"Shut the doors and windows," I said. "Eventually it will smother itself or starve to death," but as I was leaving the room I saw one of the heads take a large bite from an adjacent piece of the tissue. At least it wouldn't starve to death.

The scene haunted me for a long time afterward, and I couldn't rid my mind of speculation upon what was transpiring in that chamber of horrors, behind those closed doors and windows.

I spent several days trying to get things straightened out in the laboratory building; and succeeded, largely due to the fact that no one knew just how to prepare the tissue for the culture vats as they were emptied by the development of their horrid spawn. The result was a rapidly decreasing output of hormads, for which I was, of course, thankful. Soon there would be no more of them, and I could have wished that Ras Thavas might never return to renew his obscene labors had it not been for the fact that only through him might I hope to reclaim my own body.

During this time I did not visit Janai, lest her hiding place be discovered and Ay-mad suspicious that he had been tricked; but at last I determined that it would be safe to "find" her; and so I went to Ay-mad, told him that I had been unsuccessful in locating her, and that I was about to institute a thorough search of the palace.

"If you find her," he said, "you will find only a corpse. She could not have left the palace. I think you will agree with me there, for no woman could leave this palace without being seen by a member of the guard or one of our spies."

"But what makes you think her dead?" I asked.

"People cannot live without food or drink, and I have had you and everyone else who might have taken food to her watched. No food has been taken to her. Go on with your search, Tor-dur-bar. Your reward, if there is reward at all, will be the body of a dead woman."

There was something in his expression when he said this that gave me pause. That half smile of his—cunning and self-satisfied. What did it denote? Had he found Janai and had her destroyed? Immediately I began to worry. I conjured all sorts of horrible pictures, and it was with the greatest difficulty that I restrained myself from going at once to Janai's hiding place that I might learn the truth. But my better judgment prevailed; and, instead, I immediately organized a searching party. I put trustworthy officers in charge; and directed each to search a given part of the palace, looking in every room, closet, cubby hole. I accompanied one of the parties. This one was commanded by Sytor, whom I trusted, and included Teeaytan-ov, who often bragged loudly about his friendship for me. The part of the palace it was to search included the room in which Janai was hiding.

I did not direct the search particularly to that apartment, and I became extremely nervous while they searched everywhere but where she was. At last they came to the storeroom. I followed Sytor into it.

"She is not here," I said.

"But there is another door, over there," he replied, and walked over to it.

"Probably just another storeroom," I said, trying to appear indifferent, though my heart was pounding with excitement.

"It's locked," he said—"locked on the other side. This looks suspicious."

I stepped to his side and called, "Janai!" There was no reply. My heart sank. "Janai! Janai!" I repeated.

"She is not there," said Sytor, "but I suppose we'll have to break the door down to make sure."

"Yes, break it down."

He sent for tools, and when they were brought his hormads set to work upon the door. As the panels commenced to splinter, Janai's voice came from the interior of the other room. "I will open," she said. We heard the bolt being withdrawn, and then the door swung open. My heart leaped as I saw her there safe and well. "What do you want of me?" she demanded.

"I am to take you to Ay-mad, the Jeddak," said Sytor.

"I am ready," said Janai. She did not even look at me. I wondered if she had decided at last that it might not be so bad to be a jeddara. She had had many days to think the matter over, during which I had not visited her. Perhaps she had changed her mind. I could understand that the temptation might be great, for what had Vor Daj to offer her? Certainly not security, which is what a woman wants above all things.

Down to the private audience chamber of Ay-mad, Jeddak of Morbus, my heart trailed Sytor and Janai with its tail between its legs.

chapter XIV
WHEN THE MONSTER GROWS

LOVE POSSESSES a morbid imagination which conjures the most appalling pictures. It cannot await the development of eventualities, but must anticipate the worst. Quite often it is clairvoyant. That was what I feared now as Sytor, Janai, and I stood before Ay-mad. Sytor, with his handsome face and fine body; Ay-mad in the trappings of a jeddak; Janai, perfect and beautiful! These I compared with my hideous face and monstrous, malformed body; and my heart sank. How could Janai choose me in preference to any normal man? And if that man were a jeddak, what chance would I have? I insisted on confusing myself with the real Vor Daj, and you must admit that it might be confusing to have one brain and two bodies.

Ay-mad's eyes devoured Janai, and my heart quailed; but if she chose me, and Ay-mad failed to live up to his bargain, I swore to myself that I should kill him. He dismissed Sytor; then he faced Janai.

"This hormad," he said, indicating me, "has been of service to me. To reward him, I told him that I would grant him a favor. He has asked for you. We have decided that we shall abide by your choice. If Ras Thavas is found, the hormad hopes to acquire a new body. If Ras Thavas is not found, he will remain always as he is. If you choose me, you will become jeddara of Morbus. Whom do you choose?"

I could not but feel that Ay-mad had stated the case quite fairly, but I guess he felt that every argument was on his side anyway; so why add embellishments? In weighing the matter, there didn't seem much doubt as to what Janai's answer must be. Ay-mad was offering her marriage and position. Vor Daj had nothing to offer, and there was no more reason to suspect that her heart could be inclined more to one than to the other—she scarcely knew either.

Ay-mad became impatient. "Well," he demanded, "what is your answer?"

"I shall go with Tor-dur-bar," she said.

Ay-mad bit his lip, but he took it rather decently. "Very well," he said, "but I think you are making a mistake. If you change your mind, let me know." Then he dismissed us.

On the way back to the laboratory building I was walking on air. Janai had made her choice, and I should have her with me now and under my protection. She seemed rather happy, too.

"Shall I see Vor Daj right away?" she asked.

"I'm afraid not," I replied.

"Why?" she demanded, and she seemed suddenly depressed.

"It may take a little time," I explained. "In the mean time you will be with me and perfectly safe."

"But I thought that I was going to see Vor Daj. You haven't tricked me into this, have you, hormad?"

"If you think that, you had better go back to Ay-mad," I snapped, prompted by probably the strangest complexity of emotions that any human being had ever been assailed with—I was jealous of myself!

Janai became contrite. "I'm sorry," she said, "but I am terribly upset. Please forgive me. I have been through enough to drive one mad."

I had already selected and arranged quarters for Janai in the laboratory building. They were next to mine and some little distance from the horror of the vat rooms. I had selected several of the more intelligent hormads as her servants and guards, and she seemed quite pleased with the arrangements. When I had seen her safely established, I told her that if she needed me or wished to see me about anything to send for me and I would come; then I left her and went to Ras Thavas's study.

I had accomplished all of my design that required my hideous disguise; but now I could not rid myself of it; and it stood in the way of my aiding Janai to escape from Morbus, for I could not go out into the world in my present monstrous form. Only in Morbus could I hope for any safety.

To occupy my mind I had been looking through Ras Thavas's papers and notes, most of which were utterly meaningless to me; and now I continued idly going through his desk, though my mind was not on anything that I saw. I was thinking of Janai. I was wondering what had become of John Carter and Ras Thavas and what fate had overtaken my poor body. The future could not have looked darker. Presently I came upon what was evidently the plans of a building, and as I examined them casually I saw that they were the plans of the laboratory building, for I easily recognized the two floors with which I was most familiar. At the bottom of the sheets was a floor plan of the pits beneath the building. It was laid out in corridors and cells. There were three long corridors running the length of the pits and five transverse corridors, and they were numbered from 1 to 8. The cells along each corridor were also numbered, even numbers upon one side of each corridor and odd numbers upon the other. It was all very uninteresting, and I rolled the plans up to replace them in the desk. Just then Tun-gan was announced by the guard in the outer room. He was quite excited when he came in.

"What's the matter?" I asked, for I could see by his manner that there was something wrong.

"Come here," he said, "and I'll show you."

He led me out into the main corridor and then into a side room that overlooked a large courtyard that gave light and ventilation to several of the inside rooms of the laboratory, among them No. 4 vat room, the windows of which were directly across from the room in which we were. The sight that met my eyes as I looked out into the courtyard was absolutely appalling. The mass of living tissue had grown so rapidly in the forcing culture medium discovered by Ras Thavas that it had completely filled the room, exerting such pressure in all directions that finally a window had given way; and the horrid mass was billowing out into the courtyard.

"There!" said Tun-gan. "What are you going to do about that?"

"There is nothing I can do about it," I said. "There is nothing that anybody can do about it. I doubt that Ras Thavas could do anything. He has created a force that he probably couldn't control himself, once it got away from him."

"What will be the end of it?" asked Tun-gan.

"If it doesn't stop growing it will crowd every other living thing out of Morbus. It grows and grows and feeds upon itself. It might even envelop the whole world. What is there to stop it?"

Tun-gan shook his head. He didn't know. "Maybe Ay-mad could stop it," he suggested. "He is jeddak."

"Send for him," I said. "Tell him that something has happened here in the laboratory building that I wish him to see for himself." For once in my life I was anxious to shift responsibility to another's shoulders, for I was helpless in the face of such an emergency as had never before confronted any human being since the creation of the world.

Well, in due time Ay-mad came; and when he had looked out of the window and listened to my explanation of the phenomenon he just tossed the whole responsibility back into my lap.

"You wanted to have full charge of the laboratory," he said, "and I put you in charge. This is your problem, not mine." With that he turned away and went back to the palace. By this time the entire floor of the courtyard was covered with the wriggling, jibbering mass; and more was oozing down from the broken window above.

Well, I thought, it will take a long time to fill this courtyard. In the meantime I may think of something to do, and with that I returned to my quarters and sat looking despondently out of the window across the walls of Morbus at the dismal Toonolian Marsh that spread in all directions as far as the eye could see. It reminded me of the spreading mass in the courtyard beneath No. 4 vat room; so I closed my eyes to shut out the sight.

For some reason, the plans of the building, that I had found in Ras Thavas's desk, came to my mind; then I recalled the trip from Helium with The Warlord. That reminded me of my own body, for I could see it now, trapped in the harness of The Warlord's Guards. Where was it? I had last seen it on the ersite slab in the small laboratory of Ras Thavas. That slab was empty now, and at its foot hung a single sheet with the cryptic numbers 3–17 written on it. 3–17! What in the world could that signify?

Suddenly my mind was galvanized into action. Those numbers might have definite significance! I leaped to my feet and hurried to Ras Thavas's little study. Here I dragged out the plans of the building and spread them out, turning back the pages to the floor plan of the pits. I ran my finger quickly down corridor 3 to 17. Could that be the answer? I examined the plans more carefully. In one corner of cell 17 was a tiny circle. There were no circles in any of the other cells. What did that circle mean? Did it mean anything? Did the "3–17" written on the sheet at the foot of the table on which my body had lain have any connection with a corridor and cell number? There was but one way to answer these questions. I rose hurriedly from the desk and went out into the corridor. Passing hormads and officers, I made my way to the ramp that led to the lower floor and the pits. I carried the map of the pits indelibly imprinted upon my memory. I could have found 3–17 with my eyes shut.

The corridors and the cells were plainly numbered; so that I had no difficulty in finding cell 17 in corridor 3. I tried the door. It was locked! How stupid of me. I might have known that it would be locked if it hid the thing for which I sought. I knew where Ras Thavas kept the keys to the various locks in the laboratory building; so now I retraced my steps, but this time I saw several officers look at me in what I imagined was a suspicious manner. Spies, I thought; some of Ay-mad's spies. I should have to be careful. That would mean further delay.

Now I moved listlessly. I pretended to inspect one of the vat rooms. I sent one of the officers I had long suspicioned on an errand. I went to a window and looked out. Eventually I made my leisurely way to the study; and here I had no difficulty in finding the key I sought, as Ras Thavas was meticulously methodical in all he did; and each key had been numbered and marked.

Now I must return to the pits without arousing suspicion. Once again I sauntered out through the corridors and rooms, and finally made my way to the ramp. Unobserved, I descended. At last I stood again before the door to 3–17. I fitted the key, took a last look up and down the corridor to assure myself that I was alone, and then pushed the door open. Like the corridors, the cell was lighted by means of the everlasting radium bulbs commonly used on Barsoom.

Directly before me, on a table, lay my body. I entered the cell and closed the door behind me. Yes, there was my body; and there the vessel containing my blood. We were all together again, my body, my blood, and my brains; but we were still as far apart as the poles. Only Ras Thavas could bring us together as an entity, and Ras Thavas was gone.

I Find My Master

I STOOD FOR A LONG TIME looking at my body. I had never been a vain man, but when I compared it with the horrid thing that my brain now animated it seemed the most beautiful thing I had ever beheld. I thought of Janai in her apartments above, and cursed myself for a fool for ever giving up the body that she might have loved for one that no creature could love.

But such repining was of no avail, and I forced myself to think of other things. The little circle that appeared in the plans of cell 17 came to my mind, and I walked to the corner of the room where it had indicated that something might be found different from what was in the construction of the other cells in the pits. There was something there. It was scarcely visible, but it was there—a faint line marking a circle about two feet in diameter. I got down on my hands and knees and examined it. At one side of it was a small indentation. The thing looked as though it might be a cunningly fitted trap door and the indentation a place to pry it open. I inserted the point of my dagger and pried. The trap rose easily. Presently it was high enough to permit me to get my fingers beneath it, and in another moment I had lifted it to one side revealing a dark void beneath. What lay there? What was the purpose of the opening?

There was only one way to find out. I lowered my body through the aperture which was but barely large enough to accommodate my gross carcass. When I was hanging at the full length of my long right arm my toes just touched something solid. I hoped it was the bottom of the pit, and let go.

I stood now on a solid flooring. The little light that came through the aperture above me showed me a narrow corridor leading away into utter darkness. There was nothing for me to do but explore, now that I had come this far. I wished that I might have returned the cover to its place; so that if any one should come to the cell they might not discover the trap door; then I commenced to wonder just how anyone could get out of this place if the cover were closed above them. Open, a man could jump for the edge of the opening and draw himself up; but closed, he simply couldn't get out.

There was something wrong here. There must be some other way. I commenced to grope about searching for it, whatever it was; and at last I found it—a pole resting on pegs near the top of the corridor. By resting it against the edge of the aperture, I climbed up and dragged the cover almost into position; then I descended and, with the pole, poked the cover into place.

Now I started groping my way through utter darkness along the corridor. I felt ahead with a toe before taking a single step, and I kept my hands on both sides of the corridor lest I miss some forking or crossing corridor that might throw me off my track when I returned— if ever I did return. That thought gave me pause. What would happen to Janai if I failed to return? Perhaps I shouldn't continue on this new adventure. Perhaps I should go back. But no. After all, it was in her interests that I was thus exploring beneath the pits of Morbus. Perhaps here was an avenue to freedom.

On and on I went. The floor of the corridor was level and there were no forks nor cross corridors. It curved a little twice, but not much. I kept thinking, well, I must be nearly to the end of it; but on and on it went. The walls became damp, and the corridor stunk of mold; and then I came to a sharp declivity. For a moment I hesitated, but only for a moment. The floor inclined downward at an angle of some 15°, and by the time I reached level going again I must have been thirty or forty feet below the original level. The walls and ceiling dripped moisture. The floor was slimy with it. I walked on and on along this black, interminable tunnel. I thought it would never end; and when it did, as it must, into what new predicament would I find that it had lured me? Sometimes I thought of turning back, but that was only because I thought of Janai and her dependence upon me.

"Hormad!" I could still hear her calling me that, and I could feel the contempt and loathing that she could not have entirely hidden had she tried. And the way she spoke of Vor Daj in the same breath, and the way her voice changed! Once again a wave of jealousy of myself swept over me; but my sense of humor came to my rescue, and I laughed. That laugh resounded in the corridor, sepulchral and eerie. I didn't laugh again—it was too horrible.

Now the floor of the corridor was rising again. Up and up until I felt that I must have gained the original level; and then, suddenly, I saw light ahead, or rather lesser darkness; and a moment later I stepped out into the open. It was night. Neither moon was in the sky. Where was I? I realized that I had travelled miles, perhaps, through that gloomy corridor. I must be outside the walls of Morbus, but where?

Suddenly a figure loomed before me, and in the dim light I saw that it was a hormad. "Who are you?" it demanded. "What are you doing here?" and without waiting for an answer it came for me with a long-sword.

That was language I understood, and had an answer to. I drew and engaged the thing. It was a better swordsman than any I had previously engaged. It knew some tricks that I thought only the pupils of John Carter knew. When it discovered that I had the solution of all its tricks, it let out a yell; and in a moment or two three other figures came barging out of the night. The leader was no hormad, but a tall red man. He had scarcely engaged me before I recognized him.

"John Carter!" I cried. "It is I, Vor Daj."

Instantly he dropped his point and stepped back. "Vor Daj!" he exclaimed. "In the name of my first ancestor, how did you get here?"

Ras Thavas and a second hormad came up, and I told them briefly how I had discovered the 17th cell and the opening into the corridor.

"And now tell me," I said, "what you are doing here."

"Let Ras Thavas tell you," said The Warlord.

"Morbus is an ancient city," said the great surgeon. "It was built in prehistoric times by a people who are now extinct. In my flight after our defeat at Toonol I discovered it. I have remodeled and rebuilt it, but largely upon the foundations of the old city, which was splendidly built. There is much about it of which I know nothing. There were plans of many of the buildings, including those of the laboratory building. I noticed that circle in cell 17, just as you did. I thought it meant something, but never had the time or inclination to investigate. When we decided to hide your body where it could not be found and destroyed if anything went wrong, I selected cell 17, with the result that we discovered the tunnel to this island which lies fully two miles from Morbus.

"Dur-dan and Il-dur-en carried your body down to cell 17, and we brought them with us. They are two of my best hormads, intelligent and loyal. Having escaped from Morbus, we decided to attempt to make our way to the west end of the Great Toonolian Marsh, recover John Carter's flier, and fly to Helium in the hope that I might arrive in time to save Dejah Thoris from death.

"We have been occupied in building a boat for the long journey through the marsh, and it is about completed. We were in a quandry as to what to do about you. We did not want to desert you; but as the flier will accommodate but two men, you would have to be left somewhere until we could return; and you were safer in Morbus than you would have been in the hills beyond Phundahl."

"You shouldn't have given me a thought," I said. "Our sole objective was to find you and get you back to Helium as quickly as possible. I knew when we set out that I should have to be left behind when you were located, as the flier is not designed for more than two. That would have been a small sacrifice to have made for the Princess of Helium. The Warlord would have sent for me later."

"Naturally," said The Warlord. "Nevertheless, I hated to leave you here; but there was no alternative. We planned to send Il-dur-en back into the city with a message explaining everything to you. Dur-dan is to accompany us. If we manage to escape from the marsh and reach the flier, he will attempt to return to Morbus."

"When do you expect to start?" I asked.

"The boat will be finished tomorrow, and we shall set out as soon as it is dark. We plan to travel by night, resting and hiding during the daylight hours, as Ras Thavas, who is familiar with the marsh, assures me that it would be impossible for any but a large force of warriors to traverse the marsh by day. Many of the islands are inhabited by savage aborigines or by even more savage pirates and outlaws. The Great Toonolian Marshes are the last dregs of the great oceans that once covered a considerable portion of Barsoom, and the creatures which inhabit them are the last dregs of humanity."

"Is there any way in which I can be of help to you?" I asked.

"No," he said. "You have already sacrificed enough."

"Then I shall go back to the city before my absence is noticed. I have responsibilities there almost equal to your own, sir."

"What do you mean?" he asked.

"Janai," I said.

"What of her? Have you found her?"

I then told them of all that had transpired of which they knew nothing, that Ay-mad was jeddak and sole ruler of Morbus, that I was an odwar and in charge of the laboratory building, and that Janai had been given into my protection.

"So you are in charge of the laboratory building," said Ras Thavas. "How does it there in my absence?"

"Horribly," I said. "The only compensation for your absence is the fact that the production of hormads will have to cease, but we are faced now with something that may prove infinitely worse than hormads." Then I told him of what was transpiring in No. 4 vat room.

He appeared deeply concerned. "That is deplorable," he said. "It is something that I have always feared and sedulously guarded against. By all means make every preparation that you can to be prepared to escape from Morbus if you are unable to stem the growth in No. 4 vat room. Eventually it will envelop the entire island if it is not checked. Theoretically, it might cover the entire surface of Barsoom, smothering all other forms of life. It is the original life principal that cannot die, but it must be controlled. Nature controlled it, but I have learned to my sorrow that man cannot. I interfered with the systematic functioning of Nature; and this, perhaps, is to be my punishment."

"But how can I stem the growth? How can I stop this horror from spreading?" I demanded.

He shook his head. "There is but one thing, another phenomenon of Nature, that can check it."

"And that?" I asked.

"Fire," he said, "but evidently it has gone too far for that."

"I am afraid so," I said.

"About all that you can do now is to save yourself and Janai from it and wait for us to return."

"I shall come back with a sufficient force of men and ships to reduce Morbus and rescue you," said The Warlord.

"Until then, sir," I said. "And may you bring me word that the Princess of Helium has been restored to health."

I WAS TERRIBLY depressed as I made my way back through that dark tunnel. It seemed to me that there was little likelihood that John Carter and Ras Thavas would live to reach the western extremity of the marshes. The Warlord would be dead, Dejah Thoris, my beloved princess, would be doomed to death. It seemed to me that then there would be nothing more to live for. Janai was already hopelessly lost to me so long as I was doomed to inhabit this repulsive carcass.

Yes, there was something to live for—Janai. At least I could dedicate my life to her protection. Possibly some day I might be able to engineer her escape from Morbus. Now that I knew of the tunnel my hopes in that direction were a little brighter.

At last I came to cell 17. Once more I delayed to gaze wistfully and admiringly upon my poor corpse. Would my brain ever again animate it? I shrank to give answer to that question, as, with leaden feet, I left the cell and ascended to the upper floors. As I approached the study I was met by Tun-gan.

"I am glad you are back," he said with evident relief.

"Why? What is the matter? Something else gone wrong?"

"I don't know," he replied, "because I don't know where you have been or what you have been doing. Do you know if you were followed, or if anyone has seen you?"

"No one saw me," I said, "but then it would have made no difference if they had. I have merely been inspecting the pits." I wasn't taking any chances with the loyalty of any one. "But why do you ask?"

"Ay-mad's spies have been very active," he said. "I know some of them and suspect others. I think he has sent some new ones to watch you. They say he is furious because the woman chose to come with you rather than remain with him and become Jeddara of Morbus."

"You mean that they have been searching for me?" I asked.

"Yes; everywhere. They have even gone to the apartments of the woman."

"She is all right? They didn't take her away?"

"Not that I know of."

"But you don't know for certain?"

"No."

My heart sank. Could this have happened, too? I hurried toward Janai's apartments, and Tun-gan followed me. The fellow seemed almost as concerned as I. Perhaps he was all right. I hope so, for I needed every loyal ally that I could muster if Ay-mad were planning to take Janai away from me.

When the guard at the door recognized me, he stepped aside and let us enter. At first I did not see Janai. She was sitting with her back toward me, looking out of the window. I called her by name and she rose and turned. She appeared pleased to see me, but when her eyes passed me and alighted on Tun-gan they dilated with terror and she shrank back.

"What is that man doing here?" she demanded.

"He is one of my officers," I said. "What has he done? Has he offered you any harm while I was away?"

"Don't you know who he is?" she demanded.

"Why, he is Tun-gan. He is a good officer."

"He is Gantun Gur, the assassin of Amhor," she said. "He murdered my father."

"I realized at once the natural mistake she had made. "It is only

Gantun Gur's body," I said. "His brain has been burned. The brain he now has is the brain of a friend."

"Oh," she said, relieved. "Some more of the work of Ras Thavas. Forgive me, Tun-gan; I did not know."

"Tell me about the man whose body is now mine," said Tun-gan.

"He was a notorious assassin of Amhor often employed by the prince, Jal Had. Jal Had wanted me, but my father would not give me up. He knew that I would rather die than be the wife of Jal Had; so Jal Had employed Gantun Gur to assassinate my father and abduct me. I managed to escape, and was on my way to Ptarth where my father had friends. Gantun Gur followed me. He had with him a strong party of assassins, all members of the Assassins' Guild. They overtook us and attacked the little party of loyal retainers that had accompanied me into exile. Night came on while they were still fighting, and my party was scattered. I never saw any of them again, and two days later I was captured by hormads. I suppose Gantun Gur was captured later by another party."

"You need never fear him again," I said.

"It seems strange, though, to see him just as I knew him and yet to realize that it is not he."

"There are many strange things in Morbus," I said. "Not all of those you see have the brains or the bodies which originally belonged to them."

It was strange, indeed. Here stood Tun-gan with the body of Gantun Gur and the brain of Tor-dur-bar, and I with the body of Tor-dur-bar and the brain of Vor Daj. I wondered what Janai's reaction would be if she knew the truth. If she had loved Vor Daj, I should have explained everything to her, for it would have been better then for her to know the truth; but not loving him, and there was no reason to believe that she might, my present form might have so revolted her that she could never love me even should I regain my own body. That is the way I reasoned, and so I determined not to tell her.

I explained to her why Tun-gan and I had come to her apartments and that she must be very careful of her every word and act inasmuch as she was doubtless surrounded by the spies and informers of Ay-mad.

She looked at me questioningly for a moment; and then she said, "You have been very good to me. You are the only friend I have. I wish that you would come to see me oftener. You do not have to make excuses or explanations for coming. Do you bring me any word of Vor Daj this time?"

My spirits had risen at the first part of her speech, but with the last sentence I felt that incomprehensible jealousy come over me. Could it be that the body of Tor-dur-bar was so merging with the brain of Vor Daj as to absorb the identity of the latter? Could I be falling in love with Janai as a hormad? And if so what might the outcome be? Might I not come so to hate and fear Vor Daj that I might destroy his body because Janai loved it better than she did the body of Tor-dur-bar? The idea was fantastic, but so were all of the conditions surrounding it.

"I bring you no word of Vor Daj," I said, "because he has disappeared. Perhaps if we knew what had become of Dotar Sojat and Ras Thavas, we might know what has become of Vor Daj."

"You mean that you do not know where Vor Daj is?" she demanded. "Tor-dur-bar, there is something strange about all this. I want to trust you, but you have been very evasive about Vor Daj since first you came to me. I feel that you are trying to keep me from seeing him. Why?"

"You are mistaken," I said. "You will have to trust me, Janai. When I can, I shall bring you and Vor Daj together again. That is all that I can say. But why are you so anxious to see Vor Daj?"

I thought I might surprise her into saying something that would give a hint as to her feelings toward Vor Daj. I didn't know whether I hoped or feared that she might give some indications of affection for him, so confused were all the reactions of my dual personality. But my ruse was of no avail. Her reply suggested nothing.

"He promised to help me escape," she said. That was all. Her interest in Vor Daj was purely selfish. However, that was better than no interest at all. Thus, I thought, love reasons, making a fool of a man, until it occurred to me that my interest in Janai might be purely selfish, too. There was little to choose between the two. She wanted her liberty; I wanted her. The question was, would I risk everything, even my life, to gain her liberty for her, knowing that I should lose her? Well, I knew that I would, so perhaps my love was not entirely selfish. It pleased me to think that it was not.

I noticed, as we talked, that two of the hormad servants were watching us closely, edging nearer and nearer, obviously endeavoring to overhear what we were saying. That they were a couple of Ay-mad's spies, I had no doubt; but their technique was so crude as to render them almost harmless. I cautioned Janai against them in a low tone; and then, as they came within earshot, I said to her, "No, there is no use; I won't permit you to leave your quarters; so don't ask me again. You are much safer here. You see you belong to me now, and I have the right to kill any one who might threaten to harm you. I should do it, too." This was for the benefit of the spies.

I left her then and took Tun-gan with me. Back again in the study, I reached a decision. I must surround myself and Janai with loyal followers, but in order to attempt this I must take some chances. I sounded Tun-gan out. He said he owed everything to Vor Daj and Ras Thavas, and as they were both my friends he would serve me in any way that he could. He had no love for any of the jeds.

During the next two days I talked with Sytor, Pandar, Gan Had, and Teeaytan-ov, and became convinced that I could depend upon their loyalty. I succeeded in having all but Teeaytan-ov transferred to duty in the laboratory building where more officers were needed in an attempt to stem the spread of the horrific growth billowing from No. 4 vat room. Teeaytan-ov was to serve me as a spy in the palace. Sytor was the officer who had been in command of the hormads which had captured The Warlord and me. I had rather liked him, and after talking with him at some length I became convinced that he was a normal red man in possession of his own brain, for he was familiar with places and events of the outer world that no hormad could have had knowledge of. He was from Dusar, and anxious to escape Morbus and return to his own country.

Pandar was the man from Phundahl, and Gan Had the man from Toonol who had been my fellow prisoners; so I knew something about them. They both assured me that if I were truly serving Vor Daj and Dotar Sojat they would work with me willingly.

All of these men thought, of course, that I was only a hormad; but my rank assured them that I had influence and that I was an important person. I explained to them that I had been promised the body of a red man as soon as Ras Thavas was located and that then I should be one of them and anxious to leave Morbus.

The growth of the tissue in No. 4 vat room had now almost filled the large courtyard. I had had all windows and doors opening from the enclosure securely barricaded, so that it could not enter the building, but it threatened to soon top it and flow across the roofs where it would eventually find its way into the city avenues. The production of new hormads had practically ceased, and I had drained all the tanks as they were emptied so that there might be no repetition of what had occurred in No. 4 vat room. This had necessitated my visiting every building in which there were culture tanks, and there were many of them. It was on my return from one of these other buildings that I received a summons to appear before Ay-mad.

As I entered the palace Teeaytan-ov came to meet me. "Be careful," he warned. "Something is afoot. I don't know what it is, but one of Ay-mad's servants said that he was always muttering about you and the woman. Now that he has lost her she seems even more desirable than before. If you want to save yourself trouble, you had better give her back to him; for if you don't he can have you killed and take her anyway, and no woman is worth that."

I thanked him and went on into the audience chamber where all of Ay-mad's principal officers were gathered before the throne. The jeddak greeted me with a scowling countenance as I took my place among the other officers, the only one without the body of a red man. How many hormad brains there were among them, I had no way of knowing; but from what I had heard since coming to Morbus I guessed that most of them were transplanted hormad brains. They would have been surprised, and Ay-mad most of all, could they have known that behind my hideous hormad face lay the brain of a noble of Helium and a trusted aide of The Warlord of Barsoom.

Ay-mad pointed a finger at me. "I trusted you," he said. "I put you in charge of the laboratories, and what have you done? The supply of warriors has ceased."

"I am not Ras Thavas," I reminded him.

"You have permitted the catastrophe of No. 4 vat room, which threatens to overwhelm us."

"Again let me remind you that I am not The Master Mind of Mars," I interrupted.

He paid no attention to that, but went on. "These things threaten the collapse of all our plans to conquer the world and necessitate an immediate attempt to launch our campaign with inadequate forces. You have failed in the laboratory; and I now relieve you of your duties there, but I shall give you another chance to redeem yourself. It is now my intention to conquer Phundahl at once, thus acquiring a fleet of ships with which we can transport warriors to Toonol. The capture of Toonol will give us additional ships and permit us to move on to the capture of other cities. I am placing you in command of the expedition against Phundahl. It will not require a large force to take that city. We have five hundred malagors. They can make two round trips a day. That means that you can transport a thousand warriors a day to a point near Phundahl; or, if the birds can carry double, two thousand. In the same way you can place a thousand warriors inside the city walls to take and open the gates to the main body of your troops. You will first transport the vats and culture medium necessary to produce food for your warriors. With twenty thousand warriors you can make your attack; and I will continue to send you two thousand a day until the campaign is over, for you will lose many. You will immediately give up your quarters in the laboratory building and take quarters here in the palace that I shall assign to you and your retinue."

I saw immediately what he was trying to accomplish. He would get Janai transferred to the palace and then he would send me out on the campaign against Phundahl.

"You will move to the palace immediately and commence the transport of your troops forthwith. I have spoken."

chapter XVII

ESCAPE US NEVER

I NOW FOUND MYSELF faced by a problem for which there seemed no solution. Had I been in possession of my own body I could have escaped with Janai through the tunnel to the island where John Carter and Ras Thavas had hidden and waited there for their return, but I couldn't abandon my body and chance having to go out into the world a hormad. I also felt that it was my duty as a red man to remain and attempt in some way to thwart Ay-mad's plan of world conquest. As I made my way to Janai's quarters to tell her what had befallen us my spirits had reached nadir; they could fall no lower.

As I was passing along a corridor in the laboratory building I was met by Tun-gan who seemed very much perturbed. "The mass from No. 4 vat room has crossed the roof in one place and is overflowing down the side of the building into the avenue," he said. "The growth seems suddenly to have accelerated; and, if it be not stopped, it is only a question of time before it envelops the entire city."

"And the island as well," I said, "but I can do nothing about it; Ay-mad has relieved me of my duties in the laboratory. The responsibility now belongs to my successor."

"But what can we do to save ourselves?" demanded Tun-gan. "We shall all be lost if the growth be not stopped. It has already seized and devoured several of the warriors who were sent to try to destroy it. The hands reach out and seize them, and the heads devour them. Eventually it will eat us all."

Yes, what could we do to save ourselves? For the moment ourselves included only Janai and my two selves in my thoughts, but presently I thought of others—of Pandar and Gan Had and Sytor, yes, even of Tun-gan, the assassin of Amhor, with the brain of a hormad. These men were as near to being friends as any I had in Morbus, and there was poor Teeaytan-ov, too. He had been my friend. I must save them all.

"Tun-gan," I said, "you would like to escape?"

"Of course."

"Will you swear to serve me loyally if I help you to get away from Morbus, forgetting that you are a hormad?"

"I am no hormad now," he said. "I am a red man, and I will serve you loyally if you will help me to escape from the clutches of the horror that is spewing out into the city."

"Very well. Go at once to Pandar and Gan Had and Sytor and Teeaytan-ov and tell them to come to the quarters of Janai. Caution them to secrecy. Let no one overhear what you say to them. And hurry, Tun-gan!"

I went at once to the quarters of Janai, who seemed glad to see me; and told her of Ay-mad's orders that we move to quarters in the palace. The two servants whom I suspected overheard, as I intended they should; and I immediately gave them orders to gather up their mistress's belongings, which gave me an opportunity to talk with Janai privately. I told her what Ay-mad's order portended and that I had a plan which offered some slight hope of escape.

"I will take any risk," she said, "rather than remain in Ay-mad's palace after you are sent away. You are the only person in Morbus that I can trust, my only friend; though why you befriend me, I do not know."

"Because Vor Daj is my friend and Vor Daj loves you," I said. I felt like a coward, adopting this way of avowing a love I might not have had the courage to tell her had I been in possession of my own identity; and now that I had done it I immediately wished that I hadn't. What if she scorned Vor Daj's love? He would not be here in person to press his suit, and certainly a hideous hormad could not do it for him. I held my breath as I waited for her reply.

She was silent for a moment, and then she asked. "What makes you think that Vor Daj loves me?"

"I think it was perfectly obvious. He could not have been so concerned over the fate of any woman if he had not loved her."

"You are probably mistaken. Vor Daj would have been concerned over the fate of any red woman who might have been a prisoner in Morbus. How could there be love between us? We scarcely know one another; we have spoken only a few words together."

I was about to argue the point when Pandar, Gan Had, and Sytor arrived, putting an end to the conversation and leaving me in as much doubt as to the feelings of Janai toward Vor Daj as I had been before. As these three had been employed in the laboratory building, Tun-gan had found them quickly. I sent them to my study to wait for me, as I did not wish to talk to them where we might be overheard by one of Ay-mad's spies.

A few minutes later Tun-gan returned with Teeaytan-ov, and the roster of those whom I hoped would aid me loyally was completed. By this time the servants had gathered Janai's belongings, which I ordered them to take to the palace to our new quarters; and in this way I got rid of them.

As soon as they had gone, I hurried to my study with Janai, Tun-gan, and Teeaytan-ov, where we found the other members of my party awaiting us. We were all together now, and I explained that I planned to escape from Morbus and asked each one if he were willing to accompany me. Each assured me that he did; but Sytor voiced a doubt, which I suppose each of them harbored, that escape would be possible.

"What is your plan?" he asked.

"I have discovered an underground corridor that leads to an island off the shore of Morbus," I said. "It was to this island that Dotar Sojat and Ras Thavas went when they disappeared from the city. They are on their way to Helium now, and you may rest assured that Dotar Sojat will return with a fleet of warships and a sufficient force of warriors to rescue me from Morbus."

Teeaytan-ov appeared skeptical. "Why," he asked, "should Dotar Sojat wish to rescue a hormad from Morbus?"

"And how," inquired Sytor, "can Dotar Sojat, a poor panthan, hope to persuade the jeddak of Helium to send a fleet of warships to the Toonolian Marshes for a hormad?"

"I admit," I replied, "that the idea appears fantastic; but that is because you do not know all the facts, and there are reasons why I do not wish to divulge them all at this time. Upon one point, however, I may set your minds at rest. That is the ability of Dotar Sojat to bring a fleet of warships from Helium. Dotar Sojat is, in reality, John Carter, Warlord of Mars."

This statement rather astounded them; but after I had explained why John Carter had come to Morbus, they believed me. Teeaytan-ov was still at a loss, however, to understand why the great Warlord should be so interested in a hormad as to bring a great fleet all the way from far Helium to rescue him.

I saw that I had made a mistake in speaking as I had, but it was sometimes difficult for me to disassociate my dual personalities. To me, I was always Vor Daj, a noble of the empire of Helium. To others, I was Tor-dur-bar, a hormad of Morbus.

"Perhaps," I said, seeking to explain, "I overemphasized my own importance when I said that he would return to rescue me. It is for Vor Daj that he will return; but for me, too, as both he and Vor Daj are my friends."

"What makes you think that he will rescue any of the rest of us?" asked Pandar of Phundahl.

"He will rescue anyone that Vor Daj asks him too; and that means anyone I suggest, for Vor Daj is my friend."

"But Vor Daj has disappeared," said Gan Had of Toonol. "No one knows what has become of him. It is thought that he is dead."

"You had not told me that, Tor-dur-bar," exclaimed Janai. She turned to Sytor. "Perhaps this is a trick the hormad is playing on us to get us in his power for some reason."

"But I did tell you that he had disappeared, Janai," I said.

"You did not tell me that everyone thought him dead. You say you do not know where he is in the same breath that you say John Carter will return for him. What am I to believe?"

"If you hope to live and escape you will have to believe me," I snapped. "In a few minutes you will see Vor Daj, and then you will understand why he could not come to you." I was commencing to lose my patience with them all, interposing suspicions at a moment when the greatest haste was necessary if we were to escape before the suspicions of Ay-mad were aroused.

"What am I to believe?" demanded Janai. "You do not know where Vor Daj is, yet you say that we shall see him in a few minutes."

"There was a time that I did not know where he was. When I found him it seemed kinder to you, who were depending on him, not to tell you the truth. Vor Daj is helpless to aid you. Only I can help you. Unfortunately, in order to carry out my plan of escape, you will have to learn what has happened to Vor Daj. Now, we have wasted enough time uselessly. I am going, and you are coming with me. I owe it to Vor Daj to help you. The others may do as they see fit."

"I will go with you," said Pandar. "We could not be worse off elsewhere than here."

They all decided to accompany me, Sytor reluctantly. He went and stood near Janai and whispered something to her.

Taking Teeaytan-ov with me, I went into the small laboratory and collected all the instruments necessary to the retransfer of my brain to its own body. These I handed over to Teeaytan-ov; then I disconnected the motor and all its connections, for without the motor my blood could not be pumped back into my veins and arteries. All of this took time, but at last we were ready to depart.

I was quite sure that we could avoid neither notice nor suspicion. The best I could hope for was that we might reach 3–17 before pursuit overtook us. The spectacle of two hormads, four red men, and Janai, together with the burdens Teeaytan-ov and I were carrying, attracted immediate attention; and from no less a figure, among others, than the new governor of the Laboratory Building.

"Where are you going?" he demanded. "What are you going to do with that equipment?"

"I'm going to put it in the pits where it will be safe," I said. "If Ras Thavas returns he will need it."

"It will be safe enough where it was," he replied. "I'm in charge here now, and if I want it moved I'll attend to it myself. Take it back to where you got it."

"Since when did a dwar give orders to an odwar?" I asked. "Stand aside!" Then I moved on again with my companions toward the ramp leading to the pits.

"Wait!" he snapped. "You're going nowhere with that equipment and the girl without an order from Ay-mad. You have your orders to take the girl to the palace, not to the pits; and I have my orders direct from Ay-mad to see that you obey yours." Then he raised his voice and shouted for help. I knew that we would soon be beset by warriors; so I directed my companions to hurry on toward the pits.

We fairly ran down the long winding incline with the Governor of the Laboratory Building at our heels keeping up a continuous bellowing for help; and behind us, presently, we heard the answering shouts of pursuing warriors.

MY WHOLE PLAN now seemed to be doomed to failure, for even though we succeeded in reaching 3–17 I would not dare enter it and reveal the avenue for our escape. We had come this far, however; and there could be no turning back. There was only one solution to our problem: no witness must remain to carry back a report to Ay-mad.

We had reached the pits and were moving along the main corridor. The Governor was dogging our footsteps but keeping a safe distance from us. The shouts of the pursuing warriors evidenced the fact that they were still on our trail. I called to Tun-gan to come to my side where I imparted my instructions to him in a low tone, after which he left me and spoke briefly to Teeaytan-ov and Pandar; then these three turned off into a side corridor. The Governor hesitated a moment, but did not follow them. His interest lay in keeping track of Janai and me, and so he followed on behind us. At the next intersecting corridor I led the remainder of the party to the right, halting immediately and laying aside my burden.

"We will meet them here," I said. "There is just one thing to remember: if we are to escape and live not one of those who are pursuing us must be left alive to lead others after us."

Sytor and Gan Had took their stand beside me. Janai remained a few paces behind us. The Governor stopped well out of sword's reach to await his warriors. There were no firearms among us, as the materials necessary to the fabrications of explosives either did not exist in the Toonolian Marshes or had not as yet been discovered there. We were armed only with long-swords, short-swords, and daggers.

We did not have long to wait before the warriors were upon us. There were nine of them, all hormads. The Governor had the body of a red man and the brain of a hormad. I had known him fairly well in the palace. He was cunning and cruel, but lacked physical courage. He halted his warriors and the ten of them stood facing us.

"You had better surrender," he said, "and come back with me. You have no chance. There are ten of us and only three of you. If you will come quietly, I will say nothing to Ay-mad about this."

I saw that he was anxious to avoid a fight, but in a fight lay our only chance of escape. Once in the palace of Ay-mad, Janai and I would be lost. I pretended to be considering his proposition as I wished to gain a moment's time; and needed but a moment, as presently I saw Tun-gan, Pandar, and Teeaytan-ov closing silently up behind the Governor and his party.

"Now!" I cried, and at my word the three behind them let out a yell that caused the ten to turn simultaneously; then Sytor, Gan Had, and I leaped in with drawn swords. Numerically, the odds were all in their favor; but really they had no chance. The surprise attack disconcerted them, but the factors that gave the greatest advantage were my superhuman strength and my long-sword arm. However, they soon realized that they were fighting for their lives; and, like cornered rats, they fought furiously.

I saw poor Teeaytan-ov go down with a cleft skull and Pandar wounded, but not until he had disposed of one antagonist; Tun-gan accounted for two. Sytor, to my surprise and disappointment, held back, not offering to risk himself; but we did not need him. One after another my long-sword cleft skulls from crown to chin, until the only foe remaining was the Governor who had taken as little part in the brief affair as possible. Now, screaming, he sought to escape; but Tun-gan barred his way. There was a momentary clash of steel, a shriek; and then Tun-gan jerked his blade from the heart of the Governor of the Laboratory Building and wiped it in the hair of his fallen foe.

The corridor was a shambles in which horrible, blood drenched, brainless bodies lunged about. What followed I hate to recall; but it was necessary to destroy them all completely, especially their brains, before we could feel safe in continuing on our way.

Instructing Tun-gan to carry the articles that I had entrusted to Teeaytan-ov, I picked up the motor and led the way to 3–17. I noticed that Sytor walked close to Janai, conversing with her in low tones; but at the moment my mind was too preoccupied with other matters to permit this to assume any particular importance. So far we had been successful. What the future held for us, who could foresee? What means of subsistence there might be on the island, I did not know; nor had I more than the vaguest of plans as to how we might escape from the vicinity of Morbus and from the Great Toonolian Marshes in the event that John Carter failed to return for me. Only his death, I was sure, would prevent that; and I could not conceive that the great Warlord might die. To me, as to many others, he seemed immortal. But suppose he did return and without Ras Thavas? That thought filled me with horror, leaving me no alternative than self-destruction should it prove a true prophesy. Far better death than life in my present hideous and repulsive form. Better death than that Janai should be lost to me forever. Such were my thoughts as we reached the door to 3–17 and, swinging it open, I ushered my party into the chamber.

When Janai saw the body of Vor Daj lying on the cold ersite slab, she voiced an exclamation of horror and turned fiercely upon me. "You have lied to me, Tor-dur-bar," she said, in a suppressed whisper. "All the time you knew that Vor Daj was dead. Why have you done this cruel thing to me?"

"Vor Daj is not dead," I said. "He only awaits the return of Ras Thavas to restore him to life."

"But why didn't you tell me?" she asked.

"Only I knew where the body of Vor Daj was hidden. It would have profited neither you nor him had you known; and the fewer who knew, the safer was the body of Vor Daj. Not even to you, whom I knew that I could trust, would I divulge the secret of his hiding-place. Only now do you and these others know because there was no other avenue of escape from Morbus except through this room where Vor Daj lies. I believe that I can trust you all with this secret, but even so I can promise you that none of you will ever return alive to Morbus while the body of Vor Daj lies here and I remain alive."

Sytor had moved close to the slab where the body lay, and had been examining it rather minutely. I saw him nod his head and a half smile touched his lips as he shot a quick glance in my direction. I wondered if he suspected the truth; but what difference did it make if he did so long as he kept his mouth shut. I did not want Janai to know that the brain of Vor Daj abode in the hideous skull of Tor-dur-bar. Foolishly, perhaps, I thought that were she to know, she might never be able to forget the fact even when my brain was returned to its own body. She seemed immersed in thought for a few moments after I explained to her why I had not told her of the seeming tragedy that had overwhelmed Vor Daj; but presently she turned to me again and spoke kindly. "I am sorry that I doubted you, Tor-dur-bar," she said. "You did well in revealing to no one the whereabouts of Vor Daj's body. It was a wise precaution, and an act of loyalty."

chapter XIX

NIGHT FLIGHT

IT WAS WITH a feeling of relief that I led my little party through the long tunnel to the rocky island off the shore of Morbus. How we were to escape from the island was a problem for the future. There was, of course, uppermost in my mind always the hope that John Carter would return from Helium with a rescuing fleet; but behind this hope lurked the spectre of fear engendered by the doubt as to whether he and Ras Thavas had been able to traverse the hideous wastes of the great Toonolian Marshes and reach his swift flyer that lay hidden beyond Phundahl.

There were birds and rodents on the island, and there grew there trees and shrubs which bore nuts and berries. All these, together with the fish that we were able to catch, furnished us with sufficient food so that we did not suffer from hunger but had an abundance. I had a shelter constructed for Janai so that she might enjoy some privacy; but as the weather was mild, the rest of us slept out.

The little island was hilly, and we made our camp upon the far side away from Morbus so that the hills would hide us from discovery from the city. In this secluded spot, I started construction of two light boats, each capable of carrying three of us and a supply of provisions, one being larger than the other for the purpose of accommodating Vor Daj's body, as I had determined to take it with us in the event that John Carter did not return within a reasonable time and it became necessary for us to attempt the perilous voyage in our frail craft.

During this period, I noticed that Sytor spent much of his leisure time in the company of Janai. He was a personable fellow and a clever conversationalist; so I could not wonder that she found pleasure in his company; yet I must admit that I suffered many pangs of jealousy. Sytor was also very friendly with Pandar, the Phundahlian; so that socially we seemed naturally to split into parties, with Pandar, Sytor and Janai in one, and Gan Had, Tun-gan and I in the other. There was no unpleasantness between any of us; but the division was more or less a natural one. Gan Had was a Toonolian; and Toonol and Phundahl were hereditary enemies, so that Gan Had and Pandar had little or nothing in common. Tun-gan, with the body of a red man and the brain of a hormad, and I, with the body of a hormad, possibly felt drawn to one another because we knew that the others in the secret recesses of their hearts considered us monsters, less human than the lower animals. I can tell you that a hideous body such as mine induces a feeling of inferiority that cannot be overcome; and Tun-gan, while he made a bold front with the body of the assassin of Amhor, must have felt much as I did.

After we had completed the boats, which required several weeks of unremitting labor, enforced idleness weighed heavily upon us, and dissension showed its ugly visage upon us. Sytor insisted that we start out at once, but I wished to wait a little longer as I knew that if John Carter lived and reached Helium, he would return for me. Pandar agreed with Sytor; but Gan Had demurred, as the plan was to try to reach Phundahl where he feared that he would be held prisoner and thrown into slavery. In the many arguments which ensued I had Tun-gan's backing and, to my great satisfaction, that of Janai also when she found that I was determined to wait yet a little longer.

"We should not leave," she said, "unless we can take Vor Daj's body with us, and this Tor-dur-bar refuses to permit until he himself is satisfied that there is no hope of rescue from Helium. I think, however," she said to me, "that you are making a mistake, and that you should bow to the superior judgment and experience of Sytor, who is a red man with a brain of a red man."

Sytor was present during this conversation, and I saw him shoot a quick glance at me; and again I wondered if he suspected that the brain of Vor Daj abode in my hideous head. I hoped he would not impart his suspicions to Janai.

"Sytor may have the brain of a red man," I said, "but it is functioning now only in the interest of Sytor. Mine, however inferior, is imbued with but a single desire, which outweighs every other consideration than the welfare of you and Vor Daj. I shall not leave this island until the return of John Carter, unless I am absolutely forced to do so, until I am convinced that there remains no slightest hope that he will return; nor shall I permit you, Janai, to leave; the others may leave if they please, but I promised Vor Daj that I would protect Janai, and I should not be protecting her if I permitted her to undertake the perilous voyage through the Great Toonolian Marshes toward inhospitable Phundahl until there remains no alternative course to pursue."

"I am my own mistress," retorted Janai, angrily, "and I shall leave if I wish; no hormad may dictate to me."

"Janai is quite right," said Sytor. "You have no right to interfere."

"Nevertheless, I shall interfere," I replied, "and she shall remain here with me even if I have to keep her by force, which, I think you will all admit, I am physically able to do."

Well, things were not very pleasant after that; and Janai, Sytor and Pandar spent more time than ever together, and were often conversing in low tones that could not be overheard. I thought that they were only grumbling among themselves and heaping abuse upon me. Of course, it made me very blue to think that Janai had turned against me; and I was extremely unhappy; but I anticipated no other outcome from their grumblings than this and was quite confident that I should have my own way, which my better judgment convinced me was the safe way.

Sytor and Pandar had found a place to sleep that was quite a distance removed from the spot that Gan Had, Tun-gan, and I had selected, as though they would impress upon us that they had nothing in common with us. This suited me perfectly, as I had come to suspect and dislike both of them.

As I was preparing to retire one night after a day of fishing, Tun-gan came and squatted down beside me. "I overheard something today," he said, "which may interest you. I was dozing beneath a bush down by the beach this afternoon, when Sytor and Janai came and sat down beside the very bush behind which I had been dozing. They had evidently been discussing you, and I heard Janai say 'I am sure that he is really very loyal to Vor Daj and to me. It is only his judgment that is at fault; but what can one expect from the deformed brain of a hormad in such a deformed body?'

"'You are absolutely mistaken,' replied Sytor. 'He has only one idea in mind and that is to possess you for himself. There is something that I have known for a long time, but which I hesitated to tell you because I did not wish to hurt you. The Vor Daj that you knew will never live again. His brain was removed and destroyed, and Tor-dur-bar has hidden and protected his body, awaiting the return of Ras Thavas who will transfer Tor-dur-bar's hormad brain into the skull of Vor Daj. Then he will come to you with this new and beautiful body, hoping to win you; but it will not be Vor Daj who hopes to possess you, but the brain of a hormad in the body of a man.'

"'How horrible!' exclaimed Janai. 'It cannot be true. How can you know such a thing?'

"'Ay-mad told me,' replied Sytor. 'The body of Vor Daj was to be Tor-dur-bar's reward for the services that he had rendered Ay-mad; and to make assurance doubly sure Tor-dur-bar persuaded Ay-mad to have Vor Daj's brain destroyed.'"

"And what did Janai reply?" I asked. "She did not believe him, did she?"

"Yes, she believed him," said Tun-gan, "for she said that it explained many things that hitherto she had been unable to understand, and she now knew why you, a hormad, had evinced such remarkable loyalty toward a red man."

I was disgusted and angry and hurt, and I wondered if such a girl as Janai deserved the love and devotion that I had felt for her, and then my better judgment came to my rescue as I realized that Sytor's statement was, on the face of it, a logical explanation of my attitude toward the girl, for why indeed should a hideous hormad defend a red man whose body he might acquire, while at the same time acquiring a beautiful girl, or at least a reasonable chance of winning her such as his present hideous form would preclude.

"You see that you'll have to watch out for that rat," said Tun-gan.

"I shall not have to for long," I said, "for tomorrow I shall make him eat his words; and I shall tell them the truth, which I think Sytor already suspects, but will surprise Janai."

I lay awake for a long time that night wondering how Janai would react to the truth, what she would say or think or do when I told her that behind this hideous face of mine lay the brain of Vor Daj; but at last I fell asleep, and because I had lain awake so long I slept late the next morning. It was Gan Had of Toonol, who awoke me. He shook me roughly, and when I opened my eyes I saw that he was greatly excited.

"What's the matter, Gan Had?" I demanded.

"Sytor!" he explained. "Sytor and Pandar have taken one of the boats and escaped with Janai."

I leaped to my feet and ran quickly to where we had hidden the boats. One of them was gone; but that was not entirely the worst of it, for a big hole had been hacked in the bottom of the other which was bound to delay pursuit for several days.

So this was my reward for my love, loyalty, and devotion. I was very sick at heart. Now I did not care much whether John Carter returned or not. Life hereafter would be a void empty of all but misery. I turned disconsolately away from the boat. Gan Had laid a hand upon my shoulder.

"Do not grieve," he said. "If she went of her own volition, she is not worth grieving for."

At his words, a hope, a slender hope, just enough to grasp at in desperation came to relieve my mental agony. *If she went of her own volition!* Perhaps she did not go of her own volition. Perhaps Sytor took her away by force. There, at least, was a hope; and I determined to cling to it to the bitter end. I called to Tun-gan, and the three of us set to work to repair the damaged boat. We worked furiously, but it took three full days to make the craft seaworthy again, for Sytor had done an excellent job of demolition.

I guessed that because Pandar was with them, they would go direct to Phundahl where Pandar might succeed in having them received as friends; and so I planned to follow them to Phundahl, no matter what the cost. I felt within me the strength of a hundred men, the power to demolish a whole army single-handed, and to raze the walls of the strongest city.

At last we were ready to depart; but before we left I had one precaution to take. Beneath rocks and brush and dirt, I hid the entrance to the tunnel leading back to the room where Vor Daj's body lay.

Sytor had appropriated the larger boat, which was far more commodious for three people than would have been the smaller, but it was also heavier and there were only two men to paddle it, while in our lighter craft there were three of us. Gan Had, Tun-gan and myself; so notwithstanding the fact that they had three days start of us, I felt that it was within the realm of possibility that we might overtake them before they reached Phundahl. This, however, was only a hope since it would be by the merest chance that we should follow the same course taken by them through the maze of winding waterways that lay between us and our destination. It was entirely possible that we might pass them without being aware of it. Either party might follow some fair-appearing stretch of water only to discover that it came to a blind end, necessitating the retracing of weary miles, for the wastes of the Toonolian Marshes are uncharted and were wholly unfamiliar to every member of both parties. Being accustomed to observing terrain from the air, I had obtained a fair mental picture of the area over which we had flown when the hormads had flown us to Morbus upon the backs of their malagors, and I had no doubt but that Sytor had flown over the district many times. However, I had little reason to believe that these facts would advantage either of us to any great extent, as from the surface of the water one's view was constantly obstructed by the vegetation which grew upon the surface of the marsh and by numerous islands, large and small.

My heart was indeed heavy as I set out in pursuit of Sytor; first, by my doubts as to the loyalty of Janai, and, second, because I was forced to abandon my own body and go into the world in the hideous disguise of a hormad. Why should I pursue Janai, who, listening to Sytor and believing him above me, had deserted me, may only be explained by the fact that I was in love with her, and that love makes a fool of a man.

We set forth after dark that we might escape detection from Morbus. Only Cluros, the smaller and farther moon, was in the sky, but it lighted our way sufficiently; and the stars gave us our direction, my prodigious strength adding at least two more man-power to the paddles. We had determined to push on both by day and by night, each obtaining what sleep he required, by turn, in the bottom of the boat. We had plenty of provisions, and the speed at which we could propel the canoe imbued us with the hope that we could escape the attack of any unfriendly natives who might discover us.

The first day a flock of malagors flew over us, traveling in the direction of Phundahl. We were concealed from them by the overhanging brush of a narrow canal we were traversing; but they were plainly visible to us and we could see that each malagor carried a hormad warrior astride his back.

"Another raiding party," commented Gan Had.

"More likely a searching party that Ay-mad has dispatched in pursuit of us," I said, "for he must have discovered that we have escaped from Morbus."

"But we escaped weeks ago," said Tun-gan.

"Yes," I agreed, "but I have no doubt but that during all this time he has been sending searching parties in all directions."

Gan Had nodded. "Probably you are right. Let us hope that they do not discover any of us, for if they do we shall go to the vats or the incinerator."

On the second day after we had entered a fair-sized lake, we were discovered by savages who dwelt upon its shores. They manned a number of canoes and sallied forth to intercept us. We bent to our paddles, and our little craft fairly skimmed the surface of the water; but the savages had taken off from a point on the shore slightly ahead of us, and it seemed almost a certainty that they would reach us before we could pass them. They were a savage lot; and as they came closer, I saw that they were stark naked, their bushy hair standing out in all directions, their faces and bodies painted to render them more hideous even than Nature had intended them to be. They were armed with crude spears and clubs; but there was nothing crude about the manner in which they handled their long canoes, which sped over the water at amazing speed.

"Faster!" I urged. And now with every stroke our canoe seemed to leave the water, as it sprang ahead like a living thing.

The savages were yelling now in exultation, as it seemed certain that they must overhaul us; but the energy that they put into their savage cries had been better expended on their paddles, for presently we passed their leading boat and commenced to draw away from them. Furious, they hurled spears and clubs at us from the leading boat; but they fell short, and it was soon obvious that we had escaped them and they could not overtake us. They kept on however for a few minutes, and then, with angry imprecations, they turned sullenly back toward shore. It was well for us that they did so, for Gan Had and Tun-gan had reached the limit of their endurance, and both sank exhausted into the bottom of the canoe the moment that the savages gave up the pursuit. I felt no fatigue, and continued to paddle onward toward the end of the lake. Here we entered a winding canal which we followed for about two hours without further adventure. The sun was about to set when we heard the flapping of great wings approaching from ahead of us.

"Malagors," said Tun-gan.

"The searching party returns," remarked Gan Had; "with what success, I wonder."

"They are flying very low," I said. "Come, pull ashore under those bushes. Even so, we shall be lucky if they do not see us."

The bushes grew at the edge of a low, flat island that rose only a few inches above the surface of the water. The malagors passed over us low, and circled back.

"They are going to alight," said Tun-gan. "The hormads do not like to fly at night, for the malagors do not see well after dark, and Thuria, hurtling low above them, frightens and confuses them."

We were all looking up at them as they passed over us, and I saw that three of the malagors were carrying double.

The others noticed it too, and Gan Had said that they had prisoners.

"And I think that one of them is a woman," said Tun-gan.

"Perhaps they have captured Sytor and Pandar, and Janai."

"They are alighting on this island," said Gan Had. "If we wait until it is dark, we can pass them safely."

"First I must know if one of the prisoners is Janai," I replied.

"It will mean death for all of us if we are discovered," said Tun-gan. "We have a chance to escape, and we cannot help Janai by being captured ourselves."

"I must know," I said. "I am going ashore to find out; if I do not return by shortly after dark, you two go on your way, and may good luck attend you."

"And if you find that she is there?" asked Gan Had.

"Then I shall come back to you and we shall set out immediately for Morbus. If Janai is taken back, I must return too."

"But you can accomplish nothing," insisted Gan Had. "You will be sacrificing our lives as well as yours, uselessly. You have no right to do that to us when there is no hope of success. If there were even the slightest hope, it would be different; and I, for one, would accompany you; but as there is no hope, I flatly refuse. I am not going to throw my life away on a fool's errand."

"If Janai is there," I said, "I shall go back, if I have to go back alone. You two may accompany me, or you may remain on this island. That is for you to decide."

They looked very glum, and neither made any reply as I crawled ashore among the concealing bushes. I gave no more thought to Tun-gan and Gan Had, my mind being wholly occupied with the problem of discovering if Janai were one of the prisoners the hormads were bringing back to Morbus. The low shrubs growing upon the island afforded excellent cover, and I wormed my way among them on my belly in the direction from which I heard voices. It was slow work, and it was almost dark before I reached a point from which I could observe the party. There were a dozen hormad warriors and two officers. Presently, creeping closer, I discovered some figures lying down, and immediately recognized the one nearest me as Sytor. He was bound, hand and foot; and by his presence I knew that Janai was there also; but I wished to make sure, and so I moved cautiously to another position from which I could see the other two. One of them was Janai.

I cannot describe the emotions that swept over me, as I saw the woman I loved lying bound upon the ground, again a prisoner of the hideous minions of Ay-mad, and doomed to be returned to him. She was so near to me, yet I could not let her know that I was there seeking a way to serve her as loyally as though she had not deserted me. I lay there a long time just looking at her, and then as darkness fell I turned and crawled cautiously away; but soon, as neither moon was in the heavens at the time, I arose without fear of detection and walked rapidly toward the spot where I had left Gan Had and Tun-gan. I was trying to figure how we might return to Morbus more quickly than we had come; but I knew that it would be difficult to better our speed, and I had to resign myself to the fact that it would be two days before I could reach the City, and in the meantime what might not have happened to Janai? I shuddered as I contemplated her fate; and I had to content myself with the reflection that if I could not rescue her, I might at least avenge her. I hated to think of forcing Tun-gan and Gan Had to return with me; but there was no other way. I needed the strength of their paddles to hasten my return. I could not even offer them the alternative of remaining on the island. Such were my thoughts as I came to the place where I had left the boat. It was gone. Gan Had and Tun-gan had deserted me, taking with them my only means of transportation back to Morbus.

For a moment I was absolutely stunned by the enormity of the misfortune that had overtaken me, for it seemed to preclude any possibility of my being able to be of any assistance whatever to Janai, for after all it was she alone who mattered. I sat down on the edge of the canal and sunk my face in my palms in a seemingly futile effort to plan for the future. I conceived and discarded a dozen mad projects, at last deciding upon the only one which seemed to offer any chance of success. I determined to return to the camp of the hormads and give myself up. At least then I could be near Janai, and once back in Morbus with her some fortunate circumstance might give me the opportunity that I sought, though my better judgment told me that death would be my only reward.

I arose then, and started boldly back toward the camp; but as I approached it, and before I was discovered, another plan occurred to me. Were I to return to Morbus as a prisoner, bound hand and foot, Ay-mad would doubtless have me destroyed while I was still help-less, for he knew my great strength and feared it; but if I could reach Morbus undiscovered I might accomplish something more worth-while; and if I could reach it before Janai was returned to Ay-mad, my chances of saving her from him would be increased a thousandfold; so now I moved more cautiously circling the camp until I came upon the malagors, some resting in sleep, their heads tucked beneath their giant wings, while others moved restlessly about. They were not tethered in any way, for the hormads knew that they would not take flight after dark of their own volition.

Circling still farther, I approached them from the far side of the camp; and as I was a hormad, I aroused no suspicion among them. Walking up to the first one I encountered, I took hold of its neck and led it quietly away; and when I felt that I was far enough away from camp for safety, I leaped to its back. I knew how to control the great bird, as I had watched Teeaytan-ov carefully at the time that I was captured and transported from the vicinity of Phundahl to Morbus; and I had often talked with both officers and hormad warriors about them, thus acquiring all the knowledge that was necessary to control and direct them.

At first the bird objected to taking off and endeavored to fight me, so that I was afraid the noise would attract attention from the camp; and presently it did, for I heard someone shout, "What is going on out there?" And presently, in the light of the farther moon, I saw three hormads approaching.

Once more I sought to urge the great bird to rise, kicking it vio-lently with my heels. Now the hormads were running toward me, and the whole camp was aroused. The bird, excited by my buffetings and by the noise of the warriors approaching behind us, commenced to run away from them; and spreading its great wings, it flapped them vigorously for a moment; and then we rose from the ground and sailed off into the night.

By the stars, I headed it for Morbus; and that was all I that I had to do, for its homing instinct kept it thereafter upon the right course.

The flight was rapid and certain, though the malagor became excited when Thuria leaped from below the horizon and hurtled through the sky.

Thuria, less than six thousand miles from the surface of Barsoom, and circling the planet in less than eight hours, presents a magnificent spectacle as it races through the heavens, a spectacle well calculated to instill terror in the hearts of lower animals whose habits are wholly diurnal. However my bird held its direction, though it flew very low as if it were trying to keep as far away as possible from the giant ball of fire that appeared to be pursuing it.

Ah, our Martian nights! A gorgeous spectacle that never ceases to enthrall the imagination of Barsoomians. How pale and bleak must seem the nights on Earth, with a single satellite moving at a snail's pace through the sky at such a great distance from the planet that it must appear no larger than a platter. Even with the stress under which my mind was laboring, I still could thrill to the magnificent spectacle of this glorious night.

The distance that had required two days and nights of arduous efforts in coming from Morbus was spanned in a few hours by the swift malagor. It was with some difficulty that I forced the creature down upon the island from which we had set forth two days before, as it wished to land in its accustomed place before the gates of Morbus; but at last I succeeded, and it was with a sigh of relief that I slipped from the back of my unwilling mount.

It did not want to take off again, but I forced it to do so, as I could not afford to take the chance that it might be seen if it arose from the island after sunrise, and thus lead my enemies to my only sanctuary when their suspicions were aroused by the tale which I knew the returning searching party would have to tell.

After I had succeeded in chasing it away, I went immediately to the mouth of the tunnel leading back to the Laboratory Building, where I removed enough debris to permit me to crawl through into the tunnel. Before doing so, I tore up a large bush and as I wormed myself backward through the aperture I drew the bush after me, in the hope that it would fill the hole and conceal the opening. Then I hurried through the long tunnel to 3–17.

It was with a feeling of great relief that I found my body still safe in its vault-like tomb. For a moment I stood looking down at it, and I think that with the exception of Janai I had never so longed to possess any other thing. My face and my body may have their faults, but by comparison with the grotesque monstrosity that my brain now directed, they were among the most beautiful things in the world; but there they lay, as lost to me as completely as though they had gone to the incinerator unless Ras Thavas should return.

Ras Thavas! John Carter! Where were they? Perhaps slain in Phundahl; perhaps long since killed by the Great Toonolian Marshes; perhaps the victims of some accident on their return journey to Helium, if they had succeeded in reaching John Carter's flier outside Phundahl. I had practically given up hope that they would return for me, because enough time had elapsed to permit John Carter to have made the trip to Helium and to have returned easily, long before this; yet hope would not die.

chapter XX

THE MIGHTY JED OF GOOLIE

I REALIZED THAT my plans from now on must depend upon the conditions which confronted me. My hope was that I might reach the palace of Ay-mad, undetected, and hide myself in the throne room until Janai was brought before him. I should then attempt to destroy Ay-mad, and if I succeeded, which I had no doubt but that I should, to fight my way with Janai toward liberty. That I should fail seemed quite probable; but at least I should have destroyed her worst enemy, and might even find sufficient following among the hormads, which were always discontented with their rulers, to promise some success in taking over the city and Island of Morbus. This was my dream; but it was doomed never to be realized. I had been reckoning without consideration of Vat Room No. 4.

As I approached the door that opened into the corridor, I thought that I heard sounds beyond the heavy panels; so that it was with the utmost caution that I opened the doors gradually. As I did so, the sound came more plainly to my ears. It was indescribable—a strange surging sound, unlike any other sound in the world, and blending with it were strange human voices mouthing unintelligibly.

Even before I looked out, I knew then what it was; and as I stepped into the corridor I saw at my right and not far from the door a billowing mass of slimy, human tissue creeping gradually toward me. Protruding from it were unrelated fragments of human anatomy—a hand, an entire leg, a foot, a lung, a heart, and here and there a horribly mouthing head. The heads screamed at me, and a hand tried to reach forth and clutch me; but I was well without their reach. Had I arrived an hour later, and opened that door, the whole horrid mass would have surged in upon me and the body of Vor Daj would have been lost forever.

The corridor to the left, leading to the ramp that led to the upper floors, was quite deserted. I realized that the mass in Vat Room No. 4 must have found entrance at the far end of the pits through some unguarded opening below the street level. Eventually it would fill every crevice and make its way up the ramp to the upper stories of the Laboratory Building.

What, I wondered, would be the end? Theoretically, it would never cease to grow and spread unless entirely destroyed. It would spread out of the City of Morbus and across the Great Toonolian Marshes. It would engulf cities; or failing to mount their walls, it would surround and isolate them, condemning their inhabitants to slow starvation. It would roll across the dead sea bottoms to the farmlands of Mars' great canals. Eventually it would cover the entire surface of the planet, destroying all other life. Conceivably, it might grow and grow through all eternity devouring and living upon itself. It was a hideous thing to contemplate, but it was not without probability. Ras Thavas himself had told me as much.

I hastened along the corridor toward the ramp, expecting that I would probably find no other abroad at this time of night, as the discipline and guarding of the Laboratory Building was extremely lax when left to the direction of the hormads, as it had been after I had been demoted; but to my chagrin and consternation I found the upper floors alive with warriors and officers. A veritable panic reigned, and to such an extent that no one paid any attention to me. The officers were trying to maintain some form of order and discipline; but they were failing signally in the face of the terror that was apparent everywhere. From snatches of conversation which I overheard, I learned that the mass from Vat Room No. 4 had entered the palace and that Ay-mad and his court were fleeing to another part of the island outside the city walls. I learned, too, that the mass was spreading through the avenues of the city, and the fear of the hormad warriors was that they would all be cut off from escape. Ay-mad had issued orders that they should remain and attempt to destroy the mass and prevent its further spread through the city. Some of the officers were half-heartedly attempting to enforce the order, but for the most part they were as anxious to flee as the common warriors themselves.

Suddenly one warrior raised his voice above the tumult and shouted to his fellows. "Why should we remain here to die, while Ay-mad escapes with his favorites? There is still one avenue open; come, follow me!"

That was enough. Like a huge wave, the hideous monsters swept the officers to one side, killing some and trampling others, as they bolted for the exit which led to the only avenue of escape left open to them. Nothing could withstand them, and I was carried along in the mad rush for safety.

It was just as well, for if Ay-mad was leaving the City, Janai would not be brought into it.

Once in the avenue, the congestion was relieved, and we moved along in a steady stream toward the outer gate; but the flight did not stop here, as the terrified hormads spread over the Island in an attempt to get as far away from the City as possible; so I found myself standing almost alone in the open space before the City where the malagors landed and from which they took off in their flight. To this spot would the captors of Janai bring her; so here I would remain hoping that some fortunate circumstance might suggest a plan whereby I might rescue her from this city of horrors.

It seemed that I had never before had to wait so long for dawn, and I found myself almost alone on the stretch of open plain that lay between the City gates and the shore of the lake. A few officers and warriors remained at the gate, and scouts were continually entering the City and reporting back the progress of the mass. I thought that they had not noticed me, but presently one of the officers approached me.

"What are you doing here?" he demanded.

"I was sent here by Ay-mad," I replied.

"Your face is very familiar," said the officer. "I am sure that I have seen you before. Something about you arouses my suspicions."

I shrugged. "It does not make much difference," I said, "what you think. I am Ay-mad's messenger, and I carry orders for the officer in command of the party that went in search of the fugitives."

"Oh," he said, "that is possible; still I feel that I know you."

"I doubt it," I replied. "Ever since I was created, I have lived in a small village at the end of the island."

"Perhaps so," he said. "It doesn't make any difference, anyway. What message do you bring to the commander of the search party?"

"I have orders for the commander of the gate, also."

"I am he," said the officer.

"Good," I replied. "My orders are to take the woman, if she has been recaptured, upon a malagor and fly her directly to Ay-mad, and the captain of the gate is made responsible to see that this is done. I feel sorry for you, if there is any hitch."

"There will be no hitch," he said; "but I do not see why there should be."

"There may be, though," I assured him, "for some informer has told Ay-mad that the commander of the search party wishes Janai for himself. In all the confusion and insubordination and mutiny that has followed the abandonment of the city, Ay-mad is none too sure of himself or his power; so he is fearful that this officer may take advantage of conditions to defy him and keep the girl for himself when he learns what has happened here during his absence."

"Well," said the captain of the gate, "I'll see to that."

"It might be well," I suggested, "not to let the officer in command of the party know what you have in mind. I will hide inside the city gates so that he will not see me; and you can bring the girl to me and, later, a malagor, while you engage the officer in conversation and distract his attention. Then, when I have flown away, you may tell him."

"That is a good idea," he said. "You are not such a fool as you look."

"I am sure," I said, "that you will find you have made no mistake in your estimate of me."

"Look!" he said, "I believe they are coming now." And sure enough, far away, and high in the sky, a little cluster of dots were visible which grew rapidly larger and larger, resolving themselves finally into eleven malagors with their burdens of warriors and captives.

As the party came closer and prepared to land, I stepped inside the gate where I could not be observed or recognized by any of them. The captain of the gate advanced and greeted the commander of the returning search party. They spoke briefly for a few moments, and then I saw Janai coming toward the gate; and presently a warrior followed her, leading a large malagor. I scrutinized the fellow carefully as he approached; but I did not recognize him, and so I was sure that he would not know me, and then Janai entered and stood face to face with me.

"Tor-dur-bar!" she exclaimed.

"Quiet," I whispered. "You are in grave danger from which I think I can save you if you will trust me, as evidently you have not in the past."

"I have not known whom to trust," she said, "but I have trusted you more than any other."

The warrior had now reached the gate with the malagor. I tossed Janai to its back and leaped astride the great bird behind her; then we were off. I directed the flight of the bird toward the east end of the island, to make them think I was taking Janai to Ay-mad; but when we had crossed some low hills and they were hidden from my view, I turned back around the south side of the island and headed toward Phundahl.

As we started to fly from the island the great bird became almost unmanageable, trying to return again to its fellows. I had to fight it constantly to keep it headed in the direction I wished to travel. These exertions coming upon top of its long flight tired it rapidly so that eventually it gave up and flapped slowly and dismally along the route I had chosen. Then, for the first time, Janai and I were able to converse.

"How did you happen to be at the gate when I arrived?" she asked. "How is it that you are the messenger whom Ay-mad chose to bring me to him?"

"Ay-mad knows nothing about it," I replied. "It is all a little fiction of my own which I invented to deceive the captain of the gate and the commander of the party that recaptured you."

"But how did you know that I had been recaptured and that I would be returned to Morbus today? It is all very confusing and baffling; I cannot understand it."

"Did you not hear that a malagor was stolen from your camp last night?" I asked.

"Tor-dur-bar!" she exclaimed. "It was you? What were you doing there?"

"I had set out in search of you and was beside the island when your party landed."

"I see," she said. "How very clever and how very brave."

"If you had believed in me and trusted me," I said, "we might have escaped, but I do not believe that I would have been such a fool as to be recaptured, as was Sytor."

"I believed in you and trusted you more than any other," she said.

"Then why did you run away with Sytor?" I demanded.

"I did not run away with Sytor. He tried to persuade me, telling me many stories about you which I did not wish to believe. Finally I told him definitely that I would not go with him, but he and Pandar came in the night and took me by force."

"I am glad that you did not go away with him willingly," I said. I can tell you that it made me feel very good to think that she had not done so; and now I loved her more than ever, but little good it would do me as long as I sported this hideous carcass and monstrously inhuman face.

"And what of Vor Daj?" she asked presently.

"We shall have to leave his body where it is until Ras Thavas returns; there is no alternative."

"But if Ras Thavas never returns?" she asked, her voice trembling.

"Then Vor Daj will lie where he is through all eternity," I replied.

"How horrible," she breathed. "He was so handsome, so wonderful."

"You thought well of him?" I asked. And I was immediately ashamed of myself for taking this unfair advantage of her.

"I thought well of him," she said, in a matter-of-fact tone, a reply which was neither very exciting nor very encouraging. She might have spoken in the same way of a thoat or a calot.

Sometime after noon, it became apparent that the malagor had about reached the limit of its endurance. It began to drop closer and closer toward the marshes, and presently it came to the ground upon one of the largest islands that I had seen. It was a very attractive island, with hill and dale and forest land, and a little stream winding down to the lake, a most unusual sight upon Barsoom. The moment that the malagor alighted, it rolled over upon its side throwing us to the ground, and I thought that it was about to die as it lay there struggling and gasping.

"Poor thing!" said Janai. "It has been carrying double for three days now, and with insufficient food, practically none at all."

"Well, it has at least brought us away from Morbus," I said, "and if it recovers it is going to take us on to Helium."

"Why to Helium?" she asked.

"Because it is the only country where I am sure you will find safe asylum."

"And why should I find safety there?" she demanded.

"Because you are a friend of Vor Daj; and John Carter, Warlord of Barsoom, will see that any friend of Vor Daj is well received and well treated."

"And you?" she asked. I must have shuddered visibly at the thought of entering Helium in this horrible guise, for she said quickly, "I am sure that you will be received well, too, for you certainly deserve it far more than I." She thought for a moment in silence, and then she asked, "Do you know what became of the brain of Vor Daj? Sytor told me that it was destroyed."

I wanted to tell her the truth; but I could not bring myself to it, and so I said, "It was not destroyed. Ras Thavas knows where it is; and if I ever find him, it will be restored to Vor Daj."

"It does not seem possible that we two shall ever find Ras Thavas," she said, sadly.

It did not seem likely to me either, but I would not give up hope. John Carter must live! Ras Thavas must live! And some day I should find them.

But what of my body lying there beneath the Laboratory Building of Morbus? What if the mass from Vat Room No. 4 found its way into 3–17? The very thought made me feel faint; and yet it was not impossible. If the building and the corridor filled with the mass, the great pressure that it would exert might conceivably break down even the massive door of 3–17. Then those horrid heads would devour me; or, if the mass spread from the Island across the marshes, it would be impossible ever to retrieve my body even though it remained forever untouched. It was not a very cheerful outlook, and I found it extremely depressing; but my thoughts were suddenly recalled to other channels by an exclamation from Janai.

"Look!" she cried.

I turned in the direction she was pointing, to see a number of strange creatures coming toward us in prodigious leaps and bounds. That they were some species of human being was apparent, but there were variations which rendered them unlike any other animal on Mars. They had long, powerful legs, the knees of which were always flexed except immediately after the take-off of one of their prodigious leaps, and they had long, powerful tails; otherwise, they seemed quite human in conformation. As they came closer, I noted that they were entirely naked except for a simple harness which supported a short-sword on one side and a dagger on the other. Besides these weapons, each of them carried a spear in his right hand. They quickly surrounded us, remaining at a little distance from us, squatting down with their knees bent as they supported themselves on their broad, flat feet and their tails.

"Who are you, and what are you doing here?" demanded one of them, surprising me by the fact that he possessed speech.

"We were flying over your island," I replied, "when our malagor became tired and was forced to come to ground to rest. As soon as we are able, we shall continue on our way."

The fellow shook his head. "You will never leave Gooli," he said. He was examining me closely. "What are you?" he asked.

"I am a man," I said, stretching the point a little.

He shook his head. "And what is that?" He pointed at Janai.

"A woman," I replied.

Again he shook his head.

"She is only half a woman," he said. "She has no way of rearing her young or keeping them warm. If she had any, they would die as soon as they were hatched."

Well, that was a subject I saw no reason for going into, and so I kept silent. Janai seemed slightly amused, for if she were nothing else she was extremely feminine.

"What do you intend to do with us?" I demanded.

"We shall take you to the Jed, and he will decide. Perhaps he will let you live and work; perhaps he will destroy you. You are very ugly, but you look strong; you should be a good worker. The woman appears useless, if she can be called a woman."

I was at a loss as to what to do. We were surrounded by fully fifty warriors, well though crudely armed. With my terrific strength, I might have destroyed many of them; but eventually I was sure that they would overpower and kill me. It would be better to go with them to their Jed and await a better opportunity for escape. "Very well," I said, "we will go with you."

"Of course you will," he said. "What else could you do?"

"I could fight," I said.

"Ho ho, you would like to fight, would you?" he demanded. "Well, I think that if that is the case, the Jed will accommodate you. Come with us."

They led us back along the stream and up over a little rise of ground beyond which we saw a forest, at the edge of which lay a village of thatched huts.

"That," said the leader, pointing, "is Gooli, the largest city in the world. There, in his great palace, dwells Anatok, Jed of Gooli and all of the Island of Ompt."

As we approached the village, a couple of hundred people came to meet us. There were men, women and children; and when I examined the women I realized why the leader of the party that had captured us thought that Janai was not wholly feminine. These Goolians of the Island of Ompt are marsupials, oviparous marsupials. The females lay eggs which they carry in a pouch on the lower part of their abdomen. In this pouch the eggs hatch, and in it the young live and take shelter until they are able to fend for themselves. It was quite amusing to see the little heads protruding from their mothers' pouches as they surveyed us with wondering eyes. Up to this time I had believed that there was only one marsupial upon Barsoom, and that a reptile; so it seemed quite remarkable to see these seemingly quite human people bearing their young in abdominal pouches.

The creatures that came out from the village to meet us were quite rough with us, pulling and hauling us this way and that as they sought to examine us more closely. I towered above them all and they were a little in awe of me; but they were manhandling Janai quite badly when I interfered, pushing several of them away so forcibly that they were thrown to the ground, whereupon two or three of them drew their swords and came for me; but the party that had captured us acted now as a bodyguard and defended us from attack. After this they kept the rabble at a distance, and presently we were ushered into the village and led to a grass hut much larger than the others. This, I assumed, was the magnificent palace of Anatok. Such it proved to be, and presently the Jed himself emerged from the interior with several men and women and a horde of children. The women were his wives and their attendants, the men were his counselors.

Anatok seemed much interested in us and asked many questions about our capture, and then he asked us from whence we came.

"We came from Morbus," I said, "and we are on our way to Helium."

"Morbus—Helium," he repeated. "I never heard of them. Little villages, no doubt, inhabited by savages. How fortunate we are to live in such a splendid city as Gooli. Don't you think so?" he asked.

"I think you would be very much happier in Gooli than in Morbus, and far more at ease here than in Helium," I replied, truthfully.

"Our countries," I continued, "have never harmed you. We are not at war; therefore you should let us go on our way in peace."

At that he laughed. "What simple people come from other villages!" he exclaimed. "You are my slaves. When you are no longer of service to me you shall be destroyed. Do you think that we want any strangers to go away from Ompt to lead enemies here to destroy our magnificent city and steal our vast riches?"

"Our people would never bother you," I said. "Our country is too far from here. If one of your people should come to our country, he would be treated with kindness. We fight only with our enemies."

"That reminds me," said the leader of the party that had captured us, "this fellow is indeed our enemy by his own words, for he said that he wished to fight us."

"What!" exclaimed Anatok. "Well, if that is so, he shall have his wish. There is nothing that we like better than a good fight. With what weapons would you like to fight?"

"I will fight with anything that my antagonist chooses," I replied.

chapter XXI

Duel to the Death

It soon appeared that a personal combat was a matter of considerable importance to the Goolians. The chief and his advisors held a lengthy discussion relative to the selection of an antagonist for me. The qualities of a number of warriors were discussed, and even their ancestors as far back as the fifth and sixth generation were appraised and compared. It might have been a momentous matter of state, so serious were they. The conference was often interrupted by suggestions and comments from other members of the tribe; but at last they selected a husky young buck, who, impressed by the importance now attached to him, launched into a long and windy speech in which he enumerated his many virtues and those of his ancestors while belittling me and bragging about the short work he would make of me. He finally concluded his harangue by selecting swords as the weapons we were to use; and then Anatok asked me if I had anything to say, for it seemed that this speech-making was a part of the ceremony preceding the duel.

"I have only a question to ask," I replied.

"And what is that?" demanded Anatok.

"What will be my reward if I defeat your warrior?" I asked.

Anatok appeared momentarily confused. "Now that is an outcome that had not occurred to me," he said; "but of course, after all, it is unimportant, as you will not win."

"But it might happen," I insisted, "and if it does, what is to be my reward? Will you grant freedom to my companion and myself?"

Anatok laughed. "Certainly," he said. "I can safely promise you anything you ask for; for when the fight is over you will have lost, and you will be dead."

"Very good," I replied; "but don't forget your promise."

"Is that all you have to say?" demanded Anatok. "Aren't you going to tell us how good you are, and how many men you have killed, and what a wonderful fighter you are? Or aren't you any good?"

"That is something that only the sword may decide," I replied. "My antagonist has done a great deal of boasting, and he might continue to do so indefinitely without drawing any blood or harming me in any way. He has not even frightened me, for I have heard men boast before; and those who boasted the loudest usually have the least to boast about."

"It is evident," said Anatok, "that you know nothing about the warriors of Gooli. We are the bravest people in the world and our warriors are the greatest swordsmen. It is because of these attributes that we are the most powerful nation in the world, which is evidenced by the fact that we have built this magnificent city and protected it for generations, and that we have been able during all this time to safeguard our vast treasures."

I looked around at the mean little village of grass huts and wondered where Anatok's vast treasures might be hidden, and of what they consisted. Perhaps it was a vast store of rare gems and precious metals.

"I see no evidence of great wealth or of any treasure," I said. "Perhaps you are only boasting again."

At this, Anatok flew into a rage. "You dare doubt me, you hideous savage?" he cried. "What do you know of wealth or treasures? Your eyes have probably never rested upon anything that compares with the riches of Gooli."

"Show him the treasure before he dies," cried a warrior. "Then he will understand why we have to be such a brave and warlike people in order to protect and hold it."

"That is not a bad idea," said Anatok. "Let him learn by his own eyes that we of Gooli do not boast about our wealth, just as he will learn by experience that we do not boast about our bravery and swordsmanship. Come, fellow, you shall see the treasures."

He led the way into his palace, and I followed with a score of warriors pressing about me. The interior of the grass hut was bare, except for a litter of dead grass and leaves around the walls which evidently served for beds, some weapons, a few crude cooking utensils, and a large chest that stood in the exact center of the building. To this chest, Anatok conducted me; and, with a grand flourish, raised the lid and exhibited the contents to me as much as to say, "Now there is nothing more in the world for you to see; you have seen everything."

"Here," he said, "are the riches of Gooli."

The chest was about three-quarters filled with marine shells. Anatok and the others watched me closely to note my reaction.

"Where is the treasure?" I asked. "These are nothing but shells."

Anatok trembled with suppressed rage. "You poor, ignorant savage," he cried. "I might have known that you could not appreciate the true value and beauty of the treasure of Gooli. Come, on with the fight; the sooner you are destroyed, the better off the world will be. We Goolians cannot abide ignorance and stupidity; we, who are the most intelligent and wisest people in the world."

"Come on," I said. "The quicker we get it over the better."

It appeared that the preparation for the duel was quite a ceremonious affair. A procession was formed with Anatok and his counselors at the head. Then, following my antagonist, was a guard of honor consisting of about ten warriors. Behind these, I trailed; and would have been alone but for the fact that I took Janai with me, nor did they raise any objections to this. The rest of the tribe, including warriors, women and children, followed behind us. It was a remarkable procession in that it was all procession and no audience. We marched around the palace once and then down the main street and out of the village. The villagers formed a circle, in the center of which were I, my antagonist and his guard of honor. At a word from Anatok I drew my sword; so did my antagonist and the ten warriors with him. Then we advanced toward one another.

I turned to Anatok. "What are those other warriors doing there?" I asked.

"They are Zuki's assistants," he replied.

"Am I supposed to fight all of them?" I demanded.

"Oh, no," replied Anatok. "You will only fight Zuki, and his assistants will only help him if he gets in trouble."

In reality then, I was to fight eleven men.

"Fight, coward!" cried Anatok. "We want to see a good fight."

I turned again toward Zuki and his helpers. They were coming toward me very, very slowly; and they were making faces at me as though in an effort to frighten me. The whole thing struck me as so ridiculous that I could not refrain from laughing; yet I knew that it was serious, for the odds of eleven to one were heavily against me, even though the eleven might be inferior swordsmen.

My face was in itself extremely hideous, and suddenly I twisted it into a horrible grimace and with a wild shout leaped toward them. The reaction was amazing. Zuki was the first to turn and flee, colliding with his fellows, who, in their turn, attempted to escape my onslaught. I did not pursue them; and when they saw that I had not, they stopped and faced me again.

"Is this an example of the vaunted courage of the Goolis?" I asked Anatok.

"You have just witnessed a fine piece of strategy," replied Anatok; "but you are too ignorant to appreciate it."

Once again they came toward me, but still very slowly; and this time they voiced a kind of war whoop while they were making their faces.

I was just about to rush them again when a woman screamed and pointed down the valley. With the others, I turned to see what had attracted her attention, and discovered half a dozen savages such as those which had attacked our boat while Gan Had, Tun-gan, and I had been pursuing Sytor and Janai. At sight of them, a great wail rose from the villagers. The women and children and all but a handful of warriors ran for the woods; and I couldn't tell whether those who remained did so because they were paralyzed with fright and unable to run, or because of a sudden access of courage. Zuki, my late antagonist, was not among them. He and Anatok were racing nip and tuck for the woods in advance of all the others.

"Who are they?" I asked a warrior standing near me.

"The man-eaters," he replied. "After their last raid, we were chosen to be the sacrifice when they should come again."

"What do you mean," I asked, "'the sacrifice'?"

"Yes, it is a sacrifice," he replied. "If we do not willingly give up five warriors to them when they come, they will attack the village and burn it, they will take our treasure, they will steal our women and kill as many of our men as they can find. It is simpler this way; but it is hard on those who are chosen. However, we have no alternative but to obey, for if we did not the tribe would kill us with torture."

"But why give up to them?" I asked. "There are only six, and we are six; let's fight them. We have as good a chance to win as they."

They looked at me in surprise. "But we never fight anyone," they said, "unless we outnumber them ten to one. It would not be good strategy."

"Forget your strategy," I commanded, "and stand up against these men with me."

"Do you suppose we could?" asked one of another.

"It has never been done," was the reply.

"That is no reason why it can't be done now," I snapped. "If you will give me even a little help, we can kill them all."

"Give me a sword," said Janai, "and I will help, too."

"Let us try it," said one of the Goolians.

"Why not?" demanded another. "We are going to die anyway."

The savages had now approached and were quite near us. They were laughing and talking among themselves and casting contemptuous glances at the Goolians. "Come on," said one, "throw down your arms and come with us."

For answer, I leaped forward and clove the fellow from crown to breastbone with a single stroke. The five Goolians came forward slowly. They had no stomach for fighting; but when they saw the success of my first blow they were encouraged; and, in the same measure, the savages were taken aback. I did not stop with the one but pushed on toward the remainder of the savages. I now met with a little competition; but my great reach and my enormous strength gave me an advantage which they could not overcome, with the result that three of them were soon down and the other three running away as fast as they could go.

At sight of the enemy in retreat, something which they had probably seldom seen in their lives, the Goolians became demons of bravery and set out in pursuit of them. They could easily have overtaken them, for they moved in great bounds that carried them fully twenty feet at a time; but they let them escape over the edge of the plateau; and then they came bounding back, their chests stuck out and their expressions radiating self-satisfaction and egotism.

Evidently the encounter had been witnessed by those in hiding in the woods, for now the entire tribe came straggling toward us. Anatok looked a little shame-faced, but his first words belied his expression. "You see the value of our strategy," he said. "By appearing to run away in fright, we lured them on and then destroyed them."

"You are not fooling me or yourself either," I said. "You are a race of braggarts and cowards. I saved the five men that you would have given up as tribute without a single effort to defend them. You permitted six savages to route you and all your warriors. I could kill you all single-handed, and you know it. Now I demand that you reward me for what I have done by permitting me and my companion to remain here in safety until we are able to make plans for continuing our journey. If you refuse, you shall be the first to feel the edge of my sword."

"You don't have to threaten me," he said, trembling. "It was my intention to give you your liberty as a reward for what you have done. You are free to remain with us and to go and come as you please. You may remain as long as you like, if you will fight against our enemies when they come."

THE NEXT DAY Janai and I went to look for our malagor to see if he had recovered; but we could find no trace of him; so I assumed that he had either flown away or been seized by the savages, who, Anatok told me, came from another island some distance from Gooli.

I immediately set to work building a boat, and in this the Goolians helped me a little although they were extremely lazy and tired easily. They were without doubt the most useless race of people I had ever encountered, expending practically all their energies in boasting and little or none in accomplishment. Within a few hours after the encounter with the savages, they were boasting of their great victory and taking all the credit to themselves, Anatok claiming most of it for his marvellous strategy, as he called it. There are lots of people in the world like the Goolians, but some of them are never found out.

I became quite intimate with Zuki in the weeks that followed while we were building the boat. I found him rather above average intelligence and the possessor of a rudimentary sense of humor which the other Goolians seemed to lack entirely. One day I asked him why they considered the shells such a valuable treasure.

"Anatok has to have the treasure," he replied, "in order to give him a feeling of superiority; and it was the same way with the rulers who preceded him, and, in fact, with all of us. It makes us feel tremendously important to have a great treasure; but, being a cautious people, we chose a treasure that nobody else would want; otherwise, warlike people would be coming constantly to steal our treasure from us. Sometimes I think it is a little silly, but I would not dare say so to

Anatok or to any others. All their lives they have heard of the great value of the vast treasure of Gooli; and so they have come to believe in it, and they do not question it because they do not wish to question it."

"And they feel the same way about their vaunted courage and the strategy of Anatok?" I asked.

"Oh, that is different," replied Zuki. "Those things are real. We are really the bravest people in the world, and Anatok the greatest strategist."

Well, his sense of humor had gone the limit in questioning the treasure. It couldn't stand the strain of doubting the valor of the Goolis or the strategy of Anatok. Perhaps the Goolis were better off as they were, for their silly egotism gave them a certain morale that would have been wholly lacking had they admitted the truth.

Janai worked with me in the building of the boat, and so we were much together; but I always had the feeling that I was repulsive to her. She never touched me, if she could avoid it; nor did she often look directly at my face, nor could I blame her; yet I was sure that she was becoming fond of me as one becomes fond of an ugly but faithful dog. It made me wish that I really were a dog, for at least then she would have caressed me; but I was so much uglier than even a calot of Mars that I should always be repulsive to her no matter how kindly she might feel toward me.

These thoughts made me wonder about my poor body. Was it still safely hidden in 3–17, or had the door burst open and the horrid mass from Vat Room No. 4 engulfed and devoured it? Would I ever see it again? Would I ever again possess it, and animate it with this brain of mine which existed solely for Janai without her ever being aware of it? It all seemed very hopeless, and now that we had lost our malagor the trip to Helium seemed little short of an impossibility of accomplishment.

At last the boat was completed, and the Goolians helped me to carry it down to the lake. They stocked it with provisions for me, and they gave me extra spears and a sword and dagger for Janai. They bragged about the building of the boat, telling us that it was the best boat that was ever built and that no one but Goolians could have built it. They bragged about the weapons they gave us and the provisions. Thus we left them still boasting, and set out upon our perilous journey toward the west through the Great Toonolian Marshes.

VAST EXPANSES of the Great Marshes were uninhabitable by man, and for a week we passed through dismal wastes where not even the savage aborigines could live; but we encountered other menaces in the form of great reptiles and gigantic insects, some of the latter being of enormous proportions with a wing-spread well over thirty feet. Equipped with powerful jaws and rapier-like stingers, and sometimes with both, as some of them were, one of these monsters could easily have annihilated us; but fortunately we were never attacked. The smaller reptiles of the Marshes were their natural prey and we witnessed many an encounter in which the insects always came off victorious.

A week after we left Gooli we were paddling one day across one of the numerous lakes that dot the Marshes when, low above the horizon ahead of us, we saw a great battleship moving slowly in our direction. Instantly my heart leaped with joy.

"John Carter!" I cried. "He has come at last. Janai, you are saved."

"And Ras Thavas will be with him," she said, "and we can go back to Morbus and resurrect the body of Vor Daj."

"Once again he will live, and move, and love," I said, carried away by the relief and happiness which this anticipation engendered.

"But suppose it is not John Carter?" she asked.

"It must be, Janai, for what other civilized man would be cruising above this hideous waste?"

We stopped paddling and watched the great airship approach. It was cruising very low, scarcely a hundred feet above the ground and moving quite slowly. As it came nearer, I stood up in the canoe and waved to attract attention, even though I knew that they could not fail to see us for they were coming directly toward us.

The ship bore no insignia to proclaim its nationality, but this is not unusual in Martian navies where a lone vessel is entering into potential enemy country. The lines of the ship, too, were quite unfamiliar to me; that is, I could not identify the vessel. It was evidently one of the older ships of the line, many of which were still in commission on the frontiers of Helium. I could not understand why John Carter had chosen such a craft in preference to one of the swift, new types; but I knew that he must have a very good reason which it was not mine to question.

As the ship drew nearer it dropped still lower; so I knew that we had been observed; and finally it came to rest just above us. Landing tackle was lowered to us through a keel port, and I quickly made it fast to Janai's body so that she could be raised comfortably to the ship. While I was engaged in this, another tackle was lowered for me; and soon we were both being hoisted toward the vessel.

The instant that we were hoisted into the hold of the vessel, and I had a chance to note the sailors who surrounded us, I realized that this was no ship of Helium for the men wore the harness of another country.

Janai turned toward me with frightened eyes. "Neither John Carter nor Ras Thavas are on this ship," she whispered; "it is no ship of Helium, but one of the ships of Jal Had, Prince of Amhor. I should have been as well off in Morbus as I shall be now, if they discover my identity."

"You must not let them know," I said. "You are from Helium; remember that." She nodded in understanding.

The officers and sailors who surrounded us were far more

interested in me than they were in Janai, commenting freely upon my hideousness.

We were immediately taken to the upper deck and before the officer in command. He looked at me in ill-disguised repugnance.

"Who are you?" he demanded. "And where do you come from?"

"I am a hormad from Morbus," I replied, "and my companion is a girl from Helium, a friend of John Carter, Warlord of Mars."

He looked at Janai long and earnestly for a moment. Then a nasty little smile touched his lips. "When did you change your nationality, Janai?" he asked. "You needn't attempt to deny your identity, Janai; I know you. I would know that face anywhere among millions, for your portrait hangs in my cabin as it hangs in the cabin of the commander of every ship of Amhor; and great is to be the reward of him who brings you back to Jal Had, the Prince."

"She is under the protection of the Warlord of Mars," I said. "No matter what reward Jal Had has offered you, John Carter will give you more if you return Janai to Helium."

"Who is this thing?" the commander demanded of Janai, nodding his head toward me. "Weren't you his prisoner?"

"No," she replied. "He is my friend. He has risked his life many times to save me, and he was trying to take me to Helium when you captured us. Please do not take me back to Amhor. I am sure that, if Tor-dur-bar says it is true, John Carter will pay you well if you bring us both to Helium."

"And be tortured to death by Jal Had when I get back to Amhor?" demanded the commander. "No sir! Back to Amhor you go; and I shall probably get an extra reward when I deliver this freak to Jal Had. It will make a valuable addition to his collection, and greatly amuse and entertain the citizens of Amhor. If you behave yourself, Janai, you will be treated well by Jal Had. Do not be such a little fool as you were before. After all, it will not be so bad to be the Princess of Amhor."

"I would as lief mate with Ay-mad of Morbus," said the girl; "and sooner than that, I would die."

The commander shrugged. "That is your own affair," he said. "You will have plenty of time to think the matter over before we reach Amhor, and I advise you to think it over well and change your mind." He then gave instructions that quarters were to be assigned to us and that we were to be carefully watched but not confined if we behaved ourselves.

As we were being conducted toward a companionway that led below, I saw a man dart suddenly across the deck and leap overboard. He had done it so quickly that no one could intercept him; and though the commander had witnessed it no effort was made to save him, and the ship continued on its way. I asked the officer accompanying us who the man was and why he had leaped overboard.

"He was a prisoner who evidently preferred death to slavery in Amhor," he explained.

We were still very low above the surface of the lake, and one of the sailors who had run to the rail when the man had leaped overboard called back that the fellow was swimming toward our abandoned canoe.

"He won't last long in the Great Toonolian Marshes," commented the officer, as we descended toward our quarters.

Janai was given the best cabin on the boat; for they expected that she would be Princess of Amhor, and they wished to treat her well and curry her favor. I was relieved to know that at least until we reached Amhor she would be accorded every courtesy and consideration.

I was taken to a small cabin which accommodated two and was

already occupied by another man. His back was toward me as I entered, as he was gazing out of a porthole. The officer closed the door behind me and departed, and I was left alone with my new companion. As the door slammed, he turned and faced me; and each of us voiced an exclamation of surprise. My roommate was Tun-gan. He looked a little frightened, when he recognized me, as his conscience must have been troubling him because of his desertion of me.

"So it is you?" I said.

"Yes, and I suppose you will want to kill me now," he replied; "but do not blame me too much. Pandar and I discussed it. We did not wish to desert you; but we knew that we should all die if we returned to Morbus, while if he and I went on in the canoe we at least might have a chance to escape."

"I do not blame you," I said. "Perhaps under identical circumstances I should have done the same thing. As it turned out, it was better that you deserted me, for because of it I was able to reach Morbus in a few hours and rescue Janai when she arrived with the party that had captured her; but how do you happen to be aboard this ship?"

"Pandar and I were captured about a week ago; and perhaps it was just as well, for we were being pursued by natives when this ship dropped down, frightening the natives away. We should doubtless have been captured and killed, otherwise; and I for one was glad to come aboard, but Pandar was not. He did not wish to go to Amhor, and slavery. All that he lived for was to get back to Phundahl."

"And where is Pandar now?" I asked.

"He just leaped overboard; I was watching him when you came in. He swam to the canoe, which I presume is the one you were taken from, and he is already paddling along on his way to Phundahl."

"I hope he reaches it," I said.

"He will not," prophesied Tun-gan. "I do not believe that any man alive can pass alone through the horrors of this hellish swamp."

"You have already come a long way," I reminded him.

"Yes, but who knows what lies ahead?"

"And you are not averse to going to Amhor?" I asked.

"Why should I be?" he asked, in turn. "They think I am Gantun Gur, the assassin of Amhor; and they treat me with great respect."

"Amazing!" I exclaimed. "For the moment I had forgotten that you had taken the body of Gantun Gur. Do you think that you can live up to it and continue to deceive them?"

"I think that I can," he replied. "My brain is not as dull as that of most hormads. I have told them that I received a head injury that has made me forget a great deal of my past life; and so far, they have not doubted me."

"They never will doubt you," I said; "because they cannot conceive that the brain of another creature has been grafted into the skull of Gantun Gur."

"Then if you do not tell them, they will never know," he said, "for I certainly shall not tell them; so please remember to call me by my new name. What are you smiling at?"

"The situation is amusing. Neither one of us is himself. I have your body, and you have the body of another man."

"But who were you, whose brain is in my body?" he demanded. "I have often wondered about that."

"Continue to wonder," I replied; "for you may never know."

He looked at me keenly for a long moment. Suddenly his face brightened. "Now I know," he said. "How stupid of me not to have guessed before."

"You know nothing," I snapped; "and if I were you, I should not even guess."

He nodded. "Very well, Tor-dur-bar, it shall be as you wish."

To change the subject, I remarked, "I wonder what this ship from Amhor is doing sailing around alone over the Great Toonolian Marshes?"

"Jal Had, the Prince of Amhor, has a hobby for collecting wild beasts. They say that he has a great number of them, and this ship has been searching the Great Toonolian Marshes for new specimens."

"So they were not searching for Janai, then?"

"No. Was that Janai with you when you were captured? I got only a glimpse of two figures as our ship passed above you."

"Yes, Janai is aboard; and now I am faced with the problem of getting her off the ship before we reach Amhor."

"Well, perhaps you will be able to accomplish it," he said. "They ground the ship occasionally to hunt for new specimens, and the discipline is lax. As a matter of fact, they do not seem to guard us at all. That is why Pandar found it so easy to escape."

But no opportunity for escape was offered us, as the ship turned her nose directly for Amhor the moment that the commander realized that he had Janai aboard; nor did she once touch ground, nor again fly close to it.

Amhor lies about seven hundred and fifty Earth miles directly north of the point at which our capture took place, which distance the ship covered in about seven and a half hours.

During this time I saw nothing of Janai, as she remained in her cabin.

We arrived above Amhor in the middle of the night, and we lay there floating above the city until morning, surrounded by patrol boats as a protection and guard for the precious cargo which we carried. Jal Had was asleep when we arrived, and no one had dared disturb him. I could tell by little things that I overheard that he had a sinister reputation and that everyone was very much afraid of him.

About the second zode a royal craft came along side and took Janai aboard, and I was helpless to prevent it; for they had removed me from Gantun Gur's cabin on our arrival above the city, and locked me in another one in the hold of the ship. I was filled with despondency, for I felt that now I should not only never regain my body, but never again see Janai. I did not care what became of me, and prayed only for death.

chapter XXIV

CAGED

AFTER JANAI WAS TAKEN from the ship, it was lowered to a landing stage and made fast; and shortly thereafter the door of my prison was opened, and I found myself confronted by a detachment of warriors in command of an officer. They carried heavy chains, and with these they manacled my hands. I did not resist, for I no longer cared.

I was then taken out onto the landing stage and, by elevator, to the ground. The warriors who had taken me from the ship were men who had not seen me before. They were very much interested in me, but seemed a little afraid. When we reached the avenue I attracted considerable attention, before I was hustled into a ground flier and whisked off down a broad avenue which led to the palace grounds.

These ground fliers are a common means of private transportation in many Martian cities. They have a ceiling of about one hundred feet and a maximum speed of sixty miles per hour. In Amhor all north and south traffic moves at ground level at intersections, east and west traffic passing above it. East and west traffic is compelled to rise above north and south traffic at each intersection because there is a short runway inclining upward to a height of about ten feet at each intersection, ending in an abrupt drop at the intersection. These inclines force all east and west traffic to rise above the north and south traffic intersections. All vehicular traffic moves in but one direction on any avenue, the direction of flow alternating, so that half the avenues carry traffic in one direction and the other half in the opposite direction. Left turns are made without diminishing speed by the simple expedient of rising above both lanes of traffic. The result is that traffic flows steadily in all directions at an average speed of about fifty miles an hour. Parking accommodations are frequent, and are found inside buildings at a level of about sixty feet above the pavement. North and south pedestrian traffic moves without interruption in either direction on both sides of North and South Streets at the ground level; and, similarly, on East and West Streets through underpasses at street intersections.

I have gone into this matter of traffic control in a Martian city in some detail, and perhaps tediously, because of what John Carter has told me of the congestion and confusion in traffic handling in Earthly cities, and in the hope that the inventors of our sister planet will be encouraged to develop ground fliers similar to those commonly used in the cities of Mars.

The palace grounds, which were our destination, covered an area of about eighty acres. The avenues leading to it were lined with the palaces of the nobility, just beyond which were the better-grade shops and hotels. Amhor is a small city and the only one in the principality which might claim the dignity of such a title, the others being but small and widely scattered villages. The chief business of the principality is the raising of thoats and zitidars, the former the saddle animals and the latter the mammoth draft animals of Mars. Both are also raised for food, and Amhor exports preserved meats, hides, and other by-products to Duhor, Phundahl, and Toonol.

Amhor is the mecca of the stockmen from the country, hard-riding, profane, belligerent men; good spenders, always provided with plenty of money. So it is withal an interesting city, though one may scarcely enjoy it from the inside of a cage in a zoological garden, which is exactly where I landed a few minutes after I was driven through the rear gate of the palace grounds.

Here, upon both sides of an avenue, were cages, pits, and dens containing specimens of a wide variety of Martian animal life, an exhibition of the fauna of a planet which must have been instructive and certainly was entertaining and amusing to the crowds that passed along the avenue daily; for to this part of the palace grounds the public was freely admitted during daylight hours.

A unique feature of the zoological display of Jal Had, Prince of Amhor, was the inclusion of various types of Martian humans. In the cage at my left was a huge green man, with his ivory tusks and four arms; and at my right was a red man from Ptarth. There were thoats and zitidars and the great white apes of Barsoom, fierce, hairy monsters closely resembling man, and, perhaps, the most feared of all Martian beasts. Near me also were two apts, arctic monsters from far Okar. These great beasts are covered with white fur and have six legs, four of which are short and heavy and carry it over snow and ice. The other two grow forward from its shoulders on either side of its long, powerful neck, and terminate in white, hairless hands, with which it seizes and holds its prey. The head and mouth, John Carter has told me, are similar to those of an Earthly hippopotamus, except that from the flat sides of the lower jawbone, two mighty horns curve slightly downward toward the front. Its two huge eyes extend in large oval patches from the center of the top of the cranium down either side of the head to below the roots of the horn, so that these weapons really grow out from the lower part of the eyes, which are composed of several thousand ocelli each. Each ocellus is furnished with its own lid, so that the apt can close as many of the facets of its eyes as it wishes. There were banths, calots, darseens, orluks, siths, soraks, ulsios and many other beasts, insects and men, including even a kaldane, one of the strange spider-men of Bantoom. But when they turned me into my cage, I immediately became the prize specimen of the exhibition.

I must admit that I was by far the most hideous creature in the zoo. Perhaps in time I should have become proud of the distinction, for I attracted far more attention than even the most appalling of the horrid beasts that Jal Had had succeeded in collecting.

Gaping crowds stood in front of my cage, many of them poking sticks at me or throwing pebbles or bits of food. Presently an attendant came with a sign which I had an opportunity to read before he attached it near the top of my cage for the benefit and instruction of the audience: HORMAD FROM MORBUS, A MAN-LIKE MONSTER CAPTURED IN THE WILDS OF THE GREAT TOONOLIAN MARSHES.

I had been in my cage for about two hours when a detachment of the palace guard entered the avenue and chased all the spectators out of the zoo. A few minutes later there was a blare of trumpets at the far end of the avenue, and, looking, I saw a number of men and women approaching.

"What now?" I asked the red man in the cage next to me.

The fellow looked at me as though surprised that I had the power of speech. "Jal Had is coming to look at you," he said. He is going to be very proud of you, because there is nothing else like you in the world."

"He may learn differently in time," I said, "and to his sorrow, for there are millions like me and their leaders are planning to overrun and conquer all Barsoom."

The red man laughed at that, but he would not have laughed if he had known what I knew.

The royal party was approaching, Jal Had walking a few paces ahead of the others. He was a gross-appearing man, with a cruel mouth and shifty eyes. He came and stopped before my cage; and as the others approached and stopped behind him, I saw that Janai was one of them. She looked up at me, and I saw tears forming in her eyes. "Splendid," said Jal Had, after he had examined me minutely for several moments. "I'll wager that there is not another specimen like this anywhere in the world." He turned toward his companions. "What do you think of it?" he demanded.

"It is wonderful," they all replied, practically in unison, that is, all but Janai. She remained silent.

Then Jal Had fixed his gaze upon Janai. "And what do you think of it, my love?" he asked.

"I think a great deal of it," she replied. "Tor-dur-bar is my friend, and I think that it is a cruel shame to cage him up like this."

"You would like to have wild beasts roaming around the city, then?" he demanded.

"Tor-dur-bar is not a wild beast; he is a brave and loyal friend. But for him, I should have been long since dead; and though perhaps I had been better off, I shall never cease to appreciate the dangers and hardships that he endured for me."

"For that, he shall be rewarded, then," said Jal Had, magnanimously. "He shall receive the scraps from the royal table."

Now that was something. I, a noble of Helium, to be fed with the scraps from the table of Jal Had, Prince of Amhor. However, I consoled myself with the thought that scraps from his table would probably be far better fare than that ordinarily served to the beasts of the zoo, and I could easily swallow my pride along with his scraps.

Of course, I had no opportunity to converse with Janai, so I could not learn what had happened to her, nor what the future held for her, if she knew.

"Tell me something about yourself," demanded Jal Had. "Are you just a freak, or are there more like you? What were your father and mother like?"

"I had no father and mother," I replied, "and there are many more like me, millions of us."

"No father and mother?" he demanded. "But some sort of a creature must have laid the egg from which you hatched."

"I came from no egg," I replied.

"Well," said Jal Had, "you are not only the greatest freak I ever saw, but the greatest liar. Perhaps a good beating will teach you better manners than to lie to Jal Had."

"He has not lied," said Janai. "He has told you the truth."

"So you, too," he demanded of her, "you too, think I am a fool? I can have my women beaten, as well as my animals, if they do not behave themselves."

"You are proving definitely that you are a fool," I said, "for you have heard the truth from both of us, and yet do not believe it."

"Silence!" shouted an officer of the guard. "Shall I kill the presumptuous beast, Jal Had?"

"No," replied the Prince. "He is too valuable. Perhaps later I shall have him beaten." I wondered who would have the temerity to enter my cage to beat me, I, who could tear an ordinary man limb from limb.

Jal Had turned and walked away, followed by the members of his party; and when they had left the avenue, the public was once more admitted; and, until dark, I had to endure the gaze and insults of a loud-mouthed rabble. Now I realized with what contempt caged beasts must look upon the human beings which gape and gawk at them.

After the crowds were expelled from the zoo, the animals were fed, for Jal Had had discovered that beasts in captivity thrive better if gaping crowds are not watching them at their food; and so his animals were allowed to feed in peace and in such solitude as their cages afforded. I was not fed with the others, but shortly afterward a slave boy came from Jal Had's palace with a hamper filled with the scraps from his table.

The boy was goggle-eyed with wonderment and awe as he approached my cage and looked at me. There was a small door in the front of my cage near the floor through which the food could be passed to me; but the youth was evidently afraid to open it for fear that I might seize him.

"Do not be afraid," I said. "I shall not harm you. I am not a wild beast."

He came closer then and timidly opened the little door. "I am not afraid," he said; but I knew that he was.

"Where are you from?" I asked.

"From Duhor," he replied.

"A friend of a friend of mine lives there," I said.

"And who might that be?"

"Vad Varo," I replied.

"Ah, Vad Varo! I have seen him often. I was to have taken service in his guard when I finished my training. He married Valla Dia, our Princess. He is a great warrior. And who is your friend that is his friend?"

"John Carter, Prince of Helium, Warlord of Mars," I replied.

Then indeed did his eyes go wide. "John Carter, you know him? Who has not heard of him, the greatest swordsman of all Barsoom? But how could such as you be friend of John Carter?"

"It may seem strange to you," I admitted, "but the fact remains that John Carter is my best friend."

"But what do you know of John Carter?" demanded the red man

in the adjoining cage. "I am from Helium; and there is no creature like you in the entire empire. I think you are a great liar. You lied to me, and you lied to Jal Had, and now you are lying to this young slave. What do you think you can gain by telling so many lies? Have you never heard that Martians pride themselves upon being truthful men?"

"I have not lied," I said.

"You do not even know what John Carter looks like," taunted the red man.

"He has black hair and grey eyes, and a lighter skin than yours," I replied; "and he came from Jasoom, and he is married to Dejah Thoris, Princess of Helium. When he came to Barsoom, he was captured by the green men of Thark. He has fought in Okar, the land of the yellow men in the far north; and he has fought therns in the Valley Dor; the length and breadth of Barsoom, he has fought; and when I saw him last, we were in Morbus together."

The red man looked surprised. "By my first ancestor," he exclaimed, "but you do know a lot about John Carter. Perhaps you are telling the truth after all."

The young slave had looked at me with rapt attention. I could see that he was much impressed; and I hoped that I had won his confidence and that later I might win his friendship, for I wanted a friend in the palace of Jal Had, Prince of Amhor.

"So you have seen John Carter," he said. "You have talked with him, you have touched him. Ah, how wonderful!"

"Some day he may come to Amhor," I said, "and if he does, tell him that you knew Tor-dur-bar, and that you were kind to him; and John Carter will be your friend, too."

"I shall be as kind to you as I can," he said, "and if there is anything that I can do for you, I shall be glad to do it."

"There is something that you can do for me," I said.

"What is it?" he asked.

"Come closer, so that I may whisper it to you." He hesitated. "Do not be afraid; I shall not harm you."

Then he came close to the cage. "What is it?" he asked.

I kneeled and bent my lips close to his ear. "I wish to know all that you can learn about the girl, Janai; I mean, what is happening to her in the palace of Jal Had, and what is going to happen to her."

"I shall tell you all that I can learn," he said; and then he took his empty hamper and went away.

MONOTONOUS DAYS came and went, relieved only by conversation with the red man in the adjoining cage, and by visits twice a day from the young slave from Duhor, whose name was Orm-O.

Quite a friendship developed between the red man from Helium and I. His name was Ur Raj; and when he told me it, I recalled having met him several years before. He was from Hastor, a city on the frontier of the empire, and had been a padwar aboard one of the warships stationed there. I asked him if he remembered an officer named Vor Daj, and he said he remembered him very well.

"Do you know him?" he inquired.

"Intimately," I replied. "In fact, there is nobody in the world whom I know so well."

"But how do you know him?" he demanded.

"He was at Morbus with John Carter," I replied.

"He was a splendid officer," he said. "I recall having a long conversation with him when the grand fleet came to Hastor."

"You and he discussed an invention that you were working upon that would detect and locate enemy ships at a great distance, identifying them by the sound of their motors. You had discovered that no two motors gave forth the same vibrations, and you had developed an instrument that recorded these vibrations accurately at great distances. You also introduced him to a very beautiful young lady whom you hoped to take as your mate."

Ur Raj's eyes went wide in astonishment. "But how in the world could you know of these matters?" he demanded. "You must have been very intimate with him indeed if he narrated to you the gist of conversations that took place years before with a comparative stranger."

"He told neither me nor any other about your invention," I replied, "because he promised you that he would not say anything about it until you had fully developed it and offered it to the navy of Helium."

"But then if he did not tell you, how could you know these things?" he demanded.

"That, you may never know," I replied; "but you may rest assured that Vor Daj never abused your confidence."

I believe that Ur Raj was a little in awe of me after that, believing that I had some supernatural or occult powers. I used to catch him gazing at me intently as he squatted upon the floor of his cage, doubtless trying to fathom what seemed an inexplicable mystery to him.

The slave boy, Orm-O, became quite friendly, telling me all that he could learn about Janai, which was little or nothing. I gathered from him that she was in no immediate danger, as Jal Had's oldest wife had taken her under her protection. Jal Had had several wives; and this first wife he feared above all things on Earth. She had long objected to sharing the affections of Jal Had with other women; and she did not intend that the number should be increased, especially by the acquisition of so beautiful a young woman as Janai.

"It is rumored," said Orm-O, "that she will put Janai out of the way at the first opportunity. She is hesitating now only because of the fear that Jal Had, in his rage, would destroy her if she did so; but she may find a way to accomplish it without bringing suspicion upon herself. In fact, she has several times recently received Gantun Gur, the assassin of Amhor, who recently returned from captivity. I can tell you that I should not like to be Janai, especially if Gantun Gur listens too long to Vanuma and accepts a commission from her."

This information caused me considerable concern for the welfare of Janai. Of course, I felt quite certain that Gantun Gur would not kill her; but that would not keep Vanuma from finding some other means, if she had determined to destroy Janai. I asked Orm-O to warn Janai, and he said that he would if he ever had an opportunity.

The danger threatening Janai was constantly on my mind, and my inability to aid her drove me almost to distraction. If there were only something that I might do. But there was nothing. I seemed to be utterly helpless, and Janai's situation equally hopeless.

Sometimes we had dull days at the zoo; but as a rule there was a steady stream of people passing along the avenue between the cages, and almost always there was a little crowd gathered in front of my cage when the avenue was not jammed by those who came and stood looking at me for hours at a stretch. There were always new faces; but there were those that I had learned to recognize because they came so often; and then one day I saw Gantun Gur in the crowd. He shouldered his way toward me, eliciting much grumbling and some hard words; but when someone recognized him and his name was passed around, the spectators gave way before him, for no one wished to antagonize the assassin of Amhor. What a reputation the original must have gained!

"Kaor, Tor-dur-bar," he said, coming close to the cage.

"Kaor, Gantun Gur," I replied. "It is good to see you again; and I wish that I might speak to you privately."

"I will come back," he said, "after the visitors are expelled. You see, I am something of a privileged character in Amhor and around the palace. No one wishes to antagonize me, not even Jal Had."

I thought that the day would never end, that the visitors would never leave. The hours dragged interminably; but at last the guards drove the public out, and the carts containing food for the beasts were wheeled down the avenue. Then Orm-O came with his hamper of scraps; but there was no sign of Gantun Gur. I wondered if he had again deserted me, or if his boasted privilege was a myth. I was particularly anxious to see him, because I had finally evolved a plan which I thought might prove beneficial for Janai. I asked Orm-O for some word of her, but he only shook his head and said that he had not seen her around the palace for days.

"Perhaps Vanuma has had her destroyed," I suggested, fearfully.

"Perhaps," he said. "The last I heard was that she was not treating Janai so well as she had in the beginning. Some say that she whips her every night now."

I couldn't imagine Vanuma or anyone else whipping Janai, for she was not the type to take a whipping meekly.

It was almost dark and I had given up all hope of Gantun Gur, when I saw him approach my cage. "Kaor, Tor-dur-bar!" he said. "I was delayed; no less a person than Jal Had himself. He came to me in conversation."

"Whom does he wish killed now?" asked Ur Raj.

"He only wished to be certain that I was not planning on killing him," replied Gantun Gur. "Do you know that I would rather be what I am, head of the Assassins' Guild, than to be Prince of Amhor! My power is unlimited; everyone fears me, for, while I am known, all my assassins are not; and even those who might plot against me fear to do so lest my spies learn of it."

"You have come a long way from the Laboratory Building, Gantun Gur," I said, with a smile. "But tell me, does Janai still live? Is she well? Is she safe?"

"She lives and is well, but she is not safe; she never can be safe in Amhor. At least her life will never be safe as long as Vanuma lives. Of course, I do not need to tell you that neither I nor any of my assassins will destroy Janai; but Vanuma may find someone else to do it, or even do it herself in desperation; so I have come to the conclusion that the best thing that I can do is to have Vanuma assassinated."

"No, no," I objected. "The moment Vanuma were out of the way, there would be none to protect Janai from Jal Had."

"That is right," said Gantun Gur, scratching his head. "I had not taken that phase of the matter into consideration. As a matter of fact, it would not be so bad for Janai, for then she would become Princess of Amhor; and from what I have seen of Jal Had's other wife, Janai would rule undisputed queen."

"But she does not wish to marry Jal Had," I said. "Vor Daj loves her. We must save her for him."

"Vor Daj," said Gantun Gur, "lying as one dead in the pits beneath the Laboratory Building of Morbus, certainly surrounded and perhaps long since devoured by the horror that spreads from Vat Room No. 4. No, no, Tor-dur-bar, while I admire your loyalty to Vor Daj, I think that it is wasted. Neither you, nor I, nor Janai will ever see him again."

"Nevertheless, we must do what we can to save Janai for him; for I, for one, have not given up hope that Vor Daj some day will be rescued."

"Well, have you a plan, then?" he asked.

"Yes," I said, "I have."

"What is it?" he demanded.

"Get word to Vanuma, even if you have to tell her yourself, that Jal Had has learned that she is attempting to hire assassins to destroy Janai, and that he has sworn that if Janai dies, no matter what the cause, he will immediately destroy Vanuma."

"Not a bad idea," said Gantun Gur. "I can get that word to her immediately through one of her female slaves."

"I shall breathe more easily when I know that you have done it," I said.

I certainly slept better that night than I had for a long time, because I felt that, temporarily at least, Janai was safe. It was well for my peace of mind that I did not know what the next morning was to bring.

chapter XXVI

THE BITE OF THE ADDER

MY CELL WAS DIVIDED laterally by a partition, the front of the cell being open on the avenue, the rear consisting of a dark compartment in which there was a single, small window and a heavy door in the back wall. This was my bedroom, and my bed was a pile of the moss-like, ochre vegetation that covers the dead sea bottoms of Barsoom. A sliding door, that was raised and lowered by means of a rope passing over a pulley and thence outside the back of the cage, connected the two compartments. When I was in the front compartment, attendants could lower the door and enter the rear compartment for the purpose of cleaning it out, and vice versa, no one venturing to come into either compartment alone with me. I must say for Jal Had, that he had our cages kept reasonably clean; but that was because he realized that he could thus keep us in a more healthy condition and not because of any humanitarian instincts which he possessed.

The morning after Gantun Gur's visit, I was awakened by the beating of drums and the mournful notes of wind instruments producing music that sounded very much like a dirge. Further sleep was impossible; so I crawled out into the daylight of my front compartment where I saw Ur Raj standing with his face pressed against the bars of his cage, looking toward the palace.

"Why the music?" I asked. "Are they celebrating something?"

"Perhaps they are at that," he replied, with a smile, "though that music means that a member of the royal family is dead."

"Let us hope that it is Jal Had," I said.

"Probably no such luck," returned Ur Raj.

The attendants were coming along the avenue, feeding the animals; and when they reached Ur Raj's cage we asked them who was dead; but they told us that it was none of our business, and passed on. Of course, there was no reason why they should not have told us, if they had known; but it seemed to give them a feeling of greater importance if they treated us like wild beasts rather than like men, and wild beasts are not supposed to know anything of the affairs of their masters.

The green man in the adjoining cage had never been a very friendly neighbor. I think he resented the fact that I attracted more attention than he. He never addressed me, and had answered in monosyllables or not at all, the few times that I had spoken to him; but, of course, that might have been because they are naturally a sullen and taciturn race; but now, quite unexpectedly, he spoke to me.

"If Jal Had is dead," he said, "there will be confusion for several days. I have been here a long time, and I have learned much. I have learned that there are several who would like to succeed Jal Had, and if he is dead Amhor may have a civil war on her hands. Then would be a good time for us to try to escape."

"If I had thought that there was any chance of escaping," I said, "I would not have waited for Jal Had to die."

"Until something happens that disrupts the discipline of the guards and throws the city into turmoil," said the green man, "no plan of escape would have a chance of success, but when that happens I have a plan that may succeed."

"What is it?" I asked.

"Come closer to the bars, and I will whisper it to you. I do not wish any to overhear. One man could not accomplish the thing alone, but I believe that I can trust you and the red man next to you. I have watched you both carefully, and I believe that you have the courage and the intelligence to help me carry the plan to a successful conclusion." Then, in a whisper, he explained to me in detail the idea that he had in mind. It was not bad, and perhaps had some element of success. The green man asked me to explain to Ur Raj, and I did so. The red man listened intently and then nodded his head.

"Whether it should fail or succeed," he said, "it is at least better than remaining here in captivity for life."

"I quite agree with you," I said, "and if only my life were at stake, I should be willing to make the attempt at any time; but I must await some opportunity to rescue Janai with me."

"But what can be your interest in the red girl, Janai?" demanded Ur Raj. "She certainly wouldn't give a second glance at anyone as hideous as you."

"I promised Vor Daj that I would protect her," I said; "and so I cannot go without her."

"I see," said Ur Raj; "so inasmuch as no plan of escape will succeed, we might as well plan on taking Janai with us. It won't complicate matters in the least. Fortunately, they cannot keep us from dreaming dreams, Tor-dur-bar; and as that is about all the happiness that we have a right to expect, we might as well make the most of it and dream really worthwhile dreams. I shall dream that we shall be successful; that we destroy Jal Had, and that I become Prince of Amhor. I shall make you one of my dwars, Tor-dur-bar. In fact, I appoint you now." He laughed heartily at his little joke, and I joined in with him.

"But I was an odwar in Morbus," I said.

"Oh, very well, you shall be an odwar here, then. Consider yourself promoted."

The green man saw nothing funny in what we were saying, taking it all literally. They have no sense of humor as we understand it, and never smile or laugh except when witnessing the sufferings of others. I have seen them fairly roll on the ground with laughter while watching the agony of some victim upon which they were reeking the most fiendish tortures. Further conversation between us on this subject was interrupted by the arrival of Orm-O with his hamper of scraps for my breakfast.

"What has happened, Orm-O?" I asked him. "Why the music?"

"Do you mean that you have not heard?" he asked. "Vanuma is dead. One of her slaves told me that there was no doubt but that she had been poisoned; and Jal Had is suspected."

Vanuma dead! What would become of Janai now?

We inmates of the zoo were little affected by what went on in the palace following the death of Vanuma, but for a single circumstance. Until after the funeral, which occurred five days later, the palace grounds were closed to the public, and so we looked forward to a period of what I felt would be a most delightful interlude of peace and quiet; but I soon discovered that it was not as enjoyable as I had anticipated, for I found the monotony of it almost unendurable. Strange as it may seem, I missed the gaping rabble and learned that they afforded us quite as much amusement, entertainment, and distraction as we offered them.

During this time, I learned something from Orm-O which set my mind at rest insofar as Janai was concerned for at least a period of time. He told me that court etiquette required a period of mourning of twenty-seven days, during which the royal family eschewed all pleasures; but he had also told me that immediately following this period Jal Had planned to take Janai in marriage.

Another thing that I learned from him was that the family of Vanuma believed that Jal Had had caused Vanuma to be poisoned.

They were powerful nobles of royal descent, and among them was one who aspired to be Prince of Amhor. This Dur Ajmad was far more popular than Jal Had, his influence with the army, outside of Jal Had's personal troops, being great.

Had it not been for Orm-O, we in the zoo would have known nothing of all this; but he kept us well informed, so that we were able to follow the happenings in the palace and the city quite as well as any of the ordinary citizens of Amhor. As the days passed, I could see that the temper of the people who visited the zoo had changed. They were tense and nervous, and many were the glances cast in the direction of the palace. More people than ever jammed the avenue between the cages, but I felt that they were there more to see what might happen in the palace grounds than to look at us. Whispering groups gathered, paying no attention to us; and they were evidently concerned with more important things than wild beasts.

Then one day near the close of the mourning period, I heard, early in the morning, the humming staccato of Martian firearms; and there were trumpet calls and shouted orders. Guards closed the gates that had just been opened to admit the public; and with the exception of the detail that remained to guard the gate, attendants and warriors alike ran in the direction of the palace.

It was all very exciting; but in the excitement I did not forget what it might mean to me and Janai, nor did I forget the plan that the green man and Ur Raj and I had discussed; and so, when one of the last of the attendants came running down the avenue toward the palace, I threw myself upon the floor of my cage and writhed in apparent agony, as I screamed to him to come to me. I didn't know whether or not the ruse would work, for the man must have wanted to go with the others and see what was happening at the palace; but I banked on the fact that he must realize that if anything happened to one of his charges and especially so valuable a one as I, Jal Had would unquestionably punish him for deserting his post; and Jal Had's punishments were quite often fatal.

The fellow hesitated a moment as he turned and looked in my direction. He started on again toward the palace but after a few steps he turned and ran to my cage. "What is the matter with you, beast?" he cried.

"There is a strange reptile in my sleeping den," I cried. "It has bitten me, and I am going to die."

"Where did it bite you?" he demanded.

"On the hand," I cried. "Come look."

He came close, and when he did so I reached between the bars quickly and seized him by the throat. So quickly and so tightly did I close upon his windpipe that he had no opportunity to make an outcry. Ur Raj and the green man were pressed against the bars of their cages watching me. Only we three saw the guard die.

I dragged the body upward until I could seize the keys that hung upon a ring by his harness. Then I let it drop to the ground. I easily reached the padlock that secured the door in the front of the cage, and in a few seconds I was out on the ground. From there I crawled quickly beneath the cages to the rear where my activities would be hidden from view from any who might pass along the avenue. I released the green man and Ur Raj, and for a moment we stood there discussing the advisability of carrying out in full the plan we had contemplated. It offered considerable risk for us, but we felt that it might create such a diversion that in the ensuing confusion we might have a better chance of escaping.

"Yes," agreed Ur Raj, "the more confusion there is, the better chance we shall have to reach the palace and find your Janai."

I must say that the whole plan was hare-brained and hopeless. It had perhaps one chance in a hundred million of succeeding.

"Very well," I said, "come on."

Back of the cages we found a number of the staves and goads used by the attendants to control the beasts, and armed with these we started toward the lower cages nearest the gate and farthest from the palace. I was also armed with the short-sword and dagger I had taken from the attendant I had killed, but I could not hope that they would be of much use to me in the event that our plans miscarried.

Beginning at the cage nearest the gate, we released the animals, driving them ahead of us along the rear of the cages in the direction of the palace.

I had been fearful that we would be unable to control them and that they would turn upon us and destroy us; but I soon learned that from experience they had become afraid of the sharp goads used by the keepers, with which we threatened and prodded them along. Even the two great apts and the white apes moved sullenly before us. At first there was little noise or confusion, only low growls from the carnivores and the nervous snorting of the herbivorous animals; but as we proceeded and the number and variety of the beasts increased, so did the volume of sounds until the air rang with the bellowing of the zitidars and the squeals of the maddened thoats, and the roars and growls of banths and apts and the scores of other beasts moving nervously ahead of us.

A gate that is always kept closed separates the zoo from the grounds immediately surrounding the palace. This, the attendants in their excitement had left open today, and through it we drove the beasts into the palace grounds without interference.

By now every beast in the horrible pack, excited to a high pitch of nervous tension by this unaccustomed liberty and the voices of their fellows, had joined in the horrid diapason of ferocity so that no one within the palace grounds or, for that matter, for some distance beyond them, could have failed to hear, and now I saw the attendants who had deserted their posts running to meet us. The beasts saw them, too, and some of the more intelligent, such as the great white apes, must have remembered indignities and cruelties heaped upon them during their captivity, for with snarls and growls and roars of rage they sprang forward to meet the keepers, and fell upon them and destroyed them; and then, further incited by this taste of blood and revenge, they moved on toward the soldiers defending the gates, which were being threatened by the troops of Dur Ajmad.

This was precisely what we had hoped for, as it created a diversion which permitted Ur Raj, the green man, and me to enter a side door of the palace unobserved.

At last I had succeeded in entering the palace where Janai was a prisoner; but a plan for turning the situation to our advantage was still as remote as the farther moon. I was in the palace, but where in that great pile was Janai?

THE ROOMS AND CORRIDORS of that portion of the palace which we had entered were deserted, the inmates being either in hiding or defending the gates.

"And now that we are here," demanded Bal Tab, the green man, "what do we do next? Where is the red woman?"

"It is a large palace to search," said Ur Raj. "Even if we meet with no interference, it would take a long time; but certainly before long we shall find warriors barring our way."

"Someone is coming down this corridor," said Bal Tab. "I can hear him."

The corridor curved to the left just ahead of us, and presently around this curve came a youth whom I recognized instantly. It was Orm-O. He ran quickly toward me.

"From one of the upper windows, I saw you enter the palace," he said, "and I hurried to meet you as quickly as I could."

"Where is Janai?" I demanded.

"I will show you," he said; "but if I am found out, I shall be killed. Perhaps you are too late, for Jal Had has gone to visit her in her apartments, even though the period of mourning is not over."

"Hurry," I snapped, and Orm-O set off at a trot along the corridor, followed by Ur Raj, Bal Tab, and me. He led us to the bottom of a spiral ramp and told us to ascend to the third level where we should turn to the right and follow a corridor to its end. There we should find the door leading into Janai's apartments.

"If Jal Had is with Janai, the corridor will be guarded," he said, "and you will have to fight, but you will not have to contend with firearms as Jal Had, fearing assassination, permits no one but himself to carry firearms in the palace."

After thanking Orm-O, the three of us ascended the spiral ramp, and as we reached the third level I saw two warriors standing before a door at the end of a short corridor. Behind that door would be Jal Had and Janai.

The warriors saw us as soon as we saw them, and they came toward us with drawn swords.

"What do you want here?" demanded one of them.

"I wish to see Jal Had," I replied.

"You cannot see Jal Had," he said. "Go back to your cages where you belong."

For answer, Bal Tab felled the warrior with a blow from the metal shod goad that he carried, and almost simultaneously I engaged the other in a duel with swords. The fellow was a remarkably good swordsman, but he could not cope with one who had been a pupil of John Carter and who had the added advantage of an abnormally long reach and great strength.

I finished him quickly as I did not wish to delay much, nor did I wish to add to his sufferings.

Bal Tab was smiling, for it amused him to see men die. "You have a fine sword arm," he said, which was high praise from a green Martian.

Stepping over the body of my antagonist, I threw open the door and entered the room beyond, a small ante-room which was vacant. At the far end of this room was another door, beyond which I could hear the sound of voices raised in anger or excitement. Crossing quickly, I entered the second room where I found Jal Had holding Janai in his arms. She was struggling to escape, and striking at him. His face was red with anger, and I saw him raise his fist to strike her.

"Stop!" I cried, and then they both turned and saw me.

"Tor-dur-bar!" cried Janai, and there was a note of relief in her tone.

When Jal Had saw us he pushed Janai roughly from him and whipped out his radium pistol. I leaped for him, but before I could reach him, a metal shod goad whizzed by my shoulder and passed through the heart of the Prince of Amhor before he could level his pistol or squeeze the trigger. Bal Tab it was who had cast the goad, and to him I probably owed my life.

I think we were all a little surprised and shaken by the suddenness and enormity of the thing that had taken place, and for a moment we stood there in silence looking down at the body of Jal Had.

"Well," said Ur Raj, presently, "he is dead; and now what are we going to do?"

"The palace and the palace grounds are filled with his retainers," said Janai. "If they discover what we have done, we shall all be killed."

"We three should give them a battle they would long remember," said Bal Tab.

"If there were some place where we might hide until after dark," said Ur Raj, "I am sure that we can get out of the palace grounds, and we might even be able to leave the city."

"Do you know any place where we might hide until after dark?" I asked Janai.

"No," she said, "I know of no place where they would not search."

"What is on the level above us?" I asked.

"The royal hangar," she replied, "where Jal Had's private airships are kept."

Involuntarily I voiced an exclamation of relief. "What luck!"

I exclaimed. "Nothing could suit our purpose better than one of Jal Had's fliers."

"But the hangars are well guarded," said Janai. "I have often seen the warriors marching past my door to relieve the hangar guards. There were never less than ten of them."

"There may not be so many today," said Ur Raj, "as Jal Had needed all his force to defend the palace gates."

"If there were twenty," said Bal Tab, "it would make a better fight. Let us hope that there are not too few."

I gave Jal Had's radium pistol to Ur Raj, and then the four of us went out into the corridor and ascended the ramp that led to the hangar on the roof. I sent Ur Raj ahead because he was smaller than either Bal Tab or I, and could reconnoiter with less likelihood of being discovered; also, the fact that he was a red man made it advantageous to use him thus, as he would less quickly arouse suspicion than either Bal Tab or myself. We three trailed a short distance behind him, and when he reached a point where he could get a view of the roof we halted and waited.

Presently he returned to us. "There are but two men on guard," he said. "It will be easy."

"We'll rush them," I suggested. "If we take them by surprise, it may not be necessary to kill them." Although an experienced man who has participated in many conflicts, I still dislike seeing men die and especially by my own hands, if matters can be arranged otherwise; but the chaps who guarded the royal hangar on the roof did not seem to care whether they lived or died for they charged us the moment they saw us; and though I promised not to harm them if they surrendered, they kept on coming until there was nothing for us to do but engage them.

Just before they reached us, one of them spoke quietly to the other, who turned and ran as fast as he could across the roof. Then his valiant companion engaged us; but I caught a glimpse of the second man disappearing through a trap in the roof. Evidently he had gone to summon aid while his fellow sacrificed his life to detain us. The instant that I realized this, I leaped in to close quarters and dispatched the warrior, though I must say that I never before killed a man with less relish. This simple warrior was a hero, if ever there was one; and it seemed a shame to take his life, but it was his or ours.

Knowing that pursuit might develop immediately, I summoned the others to follow me and hastened into the hangar where I quickly selected what appeared to be a reasonably fast flier which would accommodate all of us.

I knew that Ur Raj could pilot a ship; and so I ordered him to the controls, and a moment later we were gliding smoothly out of the hangar and across the roof. As we took off, I looked down into the palace grounds from which rose the cries of the beasts and the shouts of the warriors; and even as I looked I saw the gate fall and the men of Dur Ajmad swarm through to overwhelm the remnants of Jal Had's forces.

As we rose in the air, I saw a patrol boat some distance away turn and head for us. I immediately ordered Bal Tab and Janai below, and after giving some instructions to Ur Raj I followed them so that none of us might be seen by members of the crew of the patrol boat.

The latter approached us rapidly, and when it was in speaking distance asked us who we had aboard and where we were headed. Following my instructions, Ur Raj replied that Jal Had was below and that he had given orders not to divulge our destination. The commander of the patrol boat may have had his doubts as to the veracity of the statement, but evidently he felt that he did not care to take a chance of antagonizing his prince in the event that he were aboard and had given such instructions; so he fell off and let us continue on our way; but presently he started trailing us, and before we had passed beyond the limits of the city I saw at least a dozen fliers in pursuit. The hangar guard who had escaped had evidently raised the alarm. Perhaps, even, they had found the body of Jal Had. In any event, it was quite evident that we were being pursued; and when the other ships overtook the patrol and spoke, it too came after us at full speed.

chapter XXVIII

THE GREAT FLEET

THE FLIER WE HAD commandeered was of about the same speed as the larger vessels that were pursuing us; but the patrol boat was faster, and it was evident that she would eventually overhaul us.

A hasty survey of the boat revealed that there were rifles in their racks below deck and a small gun at bow and astern above. They all fired the ordinary Martian exploding projectiles which have been standard for ages. A single, direct hit in any vital part of the ship might easily disable it, and I knew that as soon as the patrol plane came within range it would commence firing. I had come on deck as soon as I had realized that we were no longer deceiving the Amhorians, and I was standing beside Ur Raj urging him to greater speed.

"She is doing her limit now," he said; "but they are still gaining on us. However, I don't think we need to worry greatly. You may not have noticed it, but the hull of this ship is well protected, probably better armored than the other ships because it was used by Jal Had, personally. Only by scoring a direct hit on the controls or the rudder, can they put us out of commission, unless they are able to get very close and give us a broadside; but with our guns we ought to be able to prevent that."

Janai and Bal Tab had joined me on deck, and we three stood watching the pursuing patrol boat, which was gaining on us steadily.

"There!" said Janai. "They have opened fire."

"It fell short and would have been wide anyway," said Bal Tab.

"But they will soon correct that and get our range," I prophesied.

I told Janai and Bal Tab to go below as there was no sense in risking their lives on deck unnecessarily.

"When we are in rifle range, Bal Tab," I told him, "I shall send for you; and you may bring up two or three rifles from below."

I then went to the stern gun and trained it on the oncoming patrol boat as another shot fell just short of us. Then I trained our gun very carefully and fired.

"Fine!" cried Janai. "You scored a hit the first time." I turned to see both her and Bal Tab kneeling behind me. We were screened by the gun shield, but I still thought it too dangerous; but she would not go below nor either would Bal Tab except only to bring up several rifles and a larger supply of ammunition.

My shot, while a direct hit, had evidently done little or no harm for it neither slowed up the craft nor interfered with its firing.

Presently the patrol boat commenced to veer off slightly to the right with the possible intention of getting into a position from which it could pour broadsides into us.

We were both firing continuously now, and every now and then a shell would strike against the gunshield or the hull and explode.

I cautioned Ur Raj to keep on a straight course, since, if we tried to keep our stern and smallest target always presented to the pursuing enemy, we should have to alter our course and would be driven into a wide curve that would permit the larger vessels to overhaul us. Then we should most certainly be destroyed or captured.

This running fight continued until Amhor lay far behind. We were speeding above vast stretches where once Mars' mighty oceans rolled, now barren waste where only the wild, nomadic green men roved. The patrol boat had steadily gained on us, and the fleet of larger vessels had crept up a little, showing that they were a trifle faster than our flier. The patrol boat was slowly creeping up opposite us but still at a considerable distance. They had ceased firing, and now they signalled us to surrender; but for reply Bal Tab and I turned both the bow and stern guns upon them. They returned our fire, giving us a broadside with all their guns. I dragged Janai down beside me behind the gunshield; but Bal Tab had not been so fortunate. I saw him straighten to his full height and topple backward over the side of the flier.

I regretted the loss of Bal Tab, not only because it reduced our defensive force but because of the loss of a loyal comrade and a fine fighting man. However, he was gone, and mourning would do no good. He had died as he would have wished to die, fighting; and his body lay where he would have wished it to lie, on the ochre moss of a dead sea bottom.

Projectiles were now exploding continually against the armored sides of our craft and the gunshield which was our protection. Ur Raj had ample protection in the pilot's compartment, which was heavily armored.

We three seemed safe enough if we kept behind our protection; but how long the armored side of the flier could withstand this constant bombardment of exploding shells, I did not know.

Attracting Ur Raj's attention, I signalled him to rise and endeavor to get above the patrol boat, for if we could fire down upon her from above, we might disable her.

As we started to rise, Ur Raj called to me and pointed ahead. A sight met my eyes that fairly took my breath away. Approaching, far aloft and already almost above us, was a fleet of great battleships that we had not observed because of our preoccupation with the fight in which we had been engaged.

I was certain from the size and number of them that they were not ships of Amhor; but from our position below them I could not read the insignias upon their bows nor see the colors flying from their superstructures. However, no matter what nation they represented, we would be no worse off in their hands than in the hands of the

Amhorians; so I instructed Ur Raj to continue to set his course for them and to try to get between them and the patrol boat, hoping that the latter would hold its fire rather than take a chance of hitting one of the great ships of the fleet whose big guns could have destroyed it in an instant; nor was I wrong in my conjecture, for the patrol boat ceased firing though it continued to pursue us.

We were now rapidly approaching the leading ship of the fleet. I could see men peering over the sides at us, and presently the great craft slowed down.

As we arose closer to its bow, Ur Raj suddenly cried out in exaltation, "A fleet from Helium!" And then I, too, saw the insignia on the ship's bow, and my heart leaped for I knew that Janai was saved.

Now they hailed us, demanding to know who we were. "Ur Raj of Hastor," I replied, "a padwar in the Navy of Helium, and two of his friends escaping from imprisonment in the City of Amhor."

They ordered us to come aboard, then, and Ur Raj piloted the craft across their rail and set it down on the broad deck of the battleship.

Officers and men looked at me in astonishment as I dropped to the deck and lifted Janai down. Then Ur Raj joined us.

In the meantime, the Amhorian patrol boat had evidently discovered the identity of their fleet, for it turned about and was speeding back toward its sister ships; and soon all those that had been pursuing us were headed back toward Amhor at full speed; for they knew that Ur Raj was from Helium, and they feared reprisals for having held him in captivity.

Janai, Ur Raj, and I were taken before the commanding officer where Ur Raj had no difficulty in convincing them of his identity. "And these other two?" demanded the officer, indicating Janai and me.

"I am a friend of Vor Daj," I replied, "and so is this girl, Janai. I have served John Carter, too, faithfully. He will be glad to know that I am alive and well."

"You are Tor-dur-bar?" asked the officer.

"Yes," I replied, "but how could you know that?"

"This fleet was on its way to Amhor in search of you and the girl, Janai."

"But how in the world could you have known that we were at Amhor?" I asked, amazed.

"It is quite simple," he replied. "The fleet was bringing John Carter and Ras Thavas back to Morbus. Yesterday we were sailing low over the Great Toonolian Marshes when we saw a red man being pursued by savages. Their canoes were about to overtake his when we dropped a bomb among them, dispersing them. Then we dropped lower, and with landing tackle brought the man aboard. He said that his name was Pandar, and that he was escaping from Morbus; and when John Carter questioned him he learned that a flier from Amhor had captured you and the girl, Janai. The fleet was immediately ordered to Amhor to effect your rescue."

"And you arrived none too soon," I said; "but tell me, John Carter and Ras Thavas both live?"

"Yes," he said; "they are aboard the Ruzaar."

I have always prided myself that I have perfect control over my emotions; but with this final proof that John Carter and Ras Thavas both lived, I came as close to breaking down as I ever had in my life. The relief from long months of doubt and uncertainty almost proved my undoing; but I held myself together, and then in a moment another doubt raised its ugly head. John Carter and Ras Thavas lived; but was the body of Vor Daj still in existence? And, if so, was it within the power of man to recover it?

chapter XXIX

BACK TOWARD MORBUS

WE WERE SOON transferred to the Ruzaar, where I received a warm greeting from John Carter and Ras Thavas.

When I told my story, and Ur Raj had assured them that there were no more Heliumetic prisoners in Amhor, John Carter ordered the fleet about; and it headed again toward Morbus.

Ras Thavas was much concerned when I told him about the accident that had occurred in Vat Room No. 4 and its results.

"That is bad," he said, "very bad. We may never be able to stop it. Let us hope that it has not reached the body of Vor Daj."

"Oh, don't suggest such a thing," cried Janai. "Vor Daj must be saved."

"It was to rescue Vor Daj that I returned with this fleet," said John Carter, "and you may rest assured that it will not return without him, unless he has been destroyed."

In fear and trembling, I inquired of John Carter the state of Dejah Thoris's health.

"Thanks to Ras Thavas, she has completely recovered," he replied. "Every great surgeon of Helium had given her up; but Ras Thavas, the miracle worker, restored her to perfect health."

"Did you have any difficulty in returning to Helium from Morbus?" I asked.

"We had little else," he replied. "From Morbus to Phundahl was almost one continuous battle with insects, beasts, reptiles, and savage men. How we survived it and won through is a mystery to me; but Dur-dan and Ras Thavas gave a good account of themselves with sword and dagger, and we came through almost to the flier without the loss of one of our number. Then, just the day before we reached it, Dur-dan was killed in a battle with some wild savages—the last we were to encounter in the Marshes. The journey between Morbus and Phundahl took up most of the time; but then, of course, we had to spend some time in Helium while Dejah Thoris was undergoing treatment. I felt convinced that you would pull through some way. You were powerful, intelligent, and resourceful; but I am afraid that my confidence would have been undermined had I known of what had happened in Vat Room No. 4."

"It is a terrible catastrophe," I said, "perhaps a world catastrophe, and as horrifying a sight as any that you have ever witnessed. There is no combatting it, for even if you cut it to pieces it continues to grow and to spread."

That evening as I was walking on deck, I saw Janai standing alone at the rail. Knowing how repulsive I must be to her I never forced my company upon her; but this time she stopped me.

"Tor-dur-bar," she said, "I wonder if I have ever adequately thanked you for all that you have done for me?"

"I want no thanks," I said. "It is enough that I have been able to serve you and Vor Daj."

She looked at me very closely. "What will it mean to you, Tor-dur-bar, if Vor Daj's body is never recovered?"

"I shall have lost a friend," I said.

"And you will come to Helium to live?"

"I do not know that I shall care to live," I said.

"Why?" she demanded.

"Because there is no place in the world for such a hideous monster as I."

"Do not say that, Tor-dur-bar," she said, kindly. "You are not hideous, because you have a good heart. At first, before I knew you, I thought that you were hideous; but now, my friend, I see only the beauty and nobility of your character."

That was very sweet of her, and I told her so; but it didn't alter the fact that I was so hideous that I knew I should constantly be frightening women and children should I consent to go to Helium.

"Well, I think your appearance will make little difference in Helium," she said, "for I am convinced that you will have many friends; but what is to become of me if Vor Daj is not rescued?"

"You need have no fear. John Carter will see to that."

"But John Carter is under no obligation to me," she insisted.

"Nevertheless, he will take care of you."

"And you will come to see me, Tor-dur-bar?" she asked.

"If you wish me to," I said; but I knew that Tor-dur-bar would never live to go to Helium.

She looked at me in silence and steadily for a moment, and then she said, "I know what is in your mind, Tor-dur-bar. You will never come to Helium as you are; but now that Ras Thavas has returned, why can he not give your brain a new body, as he did for so many other less worthy hormads?"

"Perhaps," I replied; "but where shall I find a body?"

"There is Vor Daj's," she said, in a whisper.

"You mean," I said, "that you would like my brain in the body of Vor Daj?"

"Why not?" she asked. "It is your brain that has been my best and most loyal friend. Sytor told me that Vor Daj's brain had been destroyed. Perhaps it has. If that is true, I know that he lied when he said that you caused it to be destroyed; for I know you better now and know that you would not have so wronged a friend; but if by chance it has been destroyed, what could be better for me than that the brain of my friend animate the body of one whom I so admired?"

"But wouldn't you always say to yourself, 'this body has the brain of a hormad? It is not Vor Daj; it is just a thing that grew in a Vat.'"

"No," she replied. "I do not think that it would make any difference. I do not think that it would be difficult for me to convince myself that the brain and the body belonged together, just as, on the contrary, it has been difficult to conceive that the brain which animates the body of Tor-dur-bar originated in a vat of slimy, animal tissue."

"If Ras Thavas should find me a handsome body," I said, jokingly, "then Vor Daj would have a rival, I can assure you."

She shot me a quizzical look. "I do not think so," she said.

I wondered just what she meant by that and why she looked at me so peculiarly. It was not likely that she had guessed the truth, since it was inconceivable that any man would have permitted his brain to be transferred to the body of a hormad. Could she have meant that Vor Daj could have no successful rival?

It was night when we approached the Great Toonolian Marshes. The great fleet sailed majestically over the City of Phundahl; the lighted city gleamed through the darkness below us, but no patrol boat ventured aloft to question us. Our ships were all lighted and must have been visible for a long time before we passed over the city; but Phundahl, weak in ships, would challenge no strange fleet the size of ours. I could well imagine that the Jed of Phundahl breathed more easily as we vanished into the eastern night.

THE DESOLATE WASTES of the Great Toonolian Marshes over which we passed that night took on a strange, weird beauty and added mystery in the darkness. Their waters reflected the myriad stars which the thin air of Mars reveals; and the passing moons were reflected back from the still lagoons or touched the rocky islets with a soft radiance that transformed them into isles of enchantment. Occasionally, we saw the campfires of savages, and faintly to our ears rose the chanting of barbaric songs and the booming of drums muffled by distance; all punctuated by the scream or bellow of some savage thing.

"The last of the great oceans," said John Carter, who had joined me at the rail. "Its eventual passing will doubtless mark the passing of a world, and Mars will hurtle on through all eternity peopled by not even a memory of its past grandeur."

"It saddens me to think of it," I said.

"And me, too," he replied.

"But you could return to Earth," I reminded him.

He smiled. "I do not think that either of us need worry about the end of Mars; at least, not for another million years, perhaps."

I laughed. "Somehow, when you spoke of it, it seemed as though the end were very near," I said.

"Comparatively speaking, it is," he replied. "Here we have only a shallow marshland to remind us of the mighty oceans which once rolled across the major portion of Barsoom. On Earth, the waters cover three quarters of the globe, reaching a depth of over five miles; yet, eventually the same fate will overtake that planet. The mountains will wash down into the seas; the seas will evaporate; and some day all that will be left to mark their great oceans will be another Toonolian Marsh in some barren waste where the great Pacific Ocean rolls today."

"You make me sad," I said.

"Well, let's not worry about it, then," he laughed. "We have much more important matters to consider than the end of the two worlds. The fate of a friend transcends that of a planet. What shall you do if your body cannot be recovered?"

"I shall never return to Helium with this body," I replied.

"I cannot blame you. We shall have to find you another body."

"No," I said. "I have given the matter a great deal of thought, and I have come to a final decision. If my own body has been destroyed, I shall destroy this body, too, and the brain with it. There are far more desirable bodies than mine, of course; and yet I am so attached to it that I should not care to live in the body of another."

"Do not decide too hastily, Vor Daj."

"Tor-dur-bar, my Prince," I corrected.

"Why carry on the masquerade longer?" he demanded.

"Because she does not know," I said.

He nodded. "You think it might make a difference with her?" he asked.

"I am afraid that she could never forget this inhuman face and body, and that she might always wonder if the brain, too, were not the brain of a hormad, even though it reposed in the skull of Vor Daj. No one knows but you and Ras Thavas and I, my prince. I beg of you that you will never divulge the truth to Janai."

"As you wish," he said; "though I am quite sure that you are making a mistake. If she cares for you, it will make no difference to her; if she does not care for you, it will make no difference to you."

"No," I said. "I want to forget Tor-dur-bar, myself, and I certainly want her to forget him."

"That she will never do," he said, "for, from what she has told me, she entertains a very strong affection for Tor-dur-bar. He is Vor Daj's most dangerous rival."

"Don't," I begged. "The very idea is repulsive."

"It is the character that makes the man," said John Carter, "not the clay which is its abode."

"No, my friend," I replied, "no amount of philosophizing could make Tor-dur-bar a suitable mate for any red woman, least of all, Janai."

"Perhaps you are right," he agreed; "but after the great sacrifice that you have made for her, I feel that you deserve a better reward than death by your own hand."

"Well," I replied, "tomorrow will probably decide the matter for us; and already I see the first streak of dawn above the horizon."

He thought in silence for a few moments, and then he said, "Perhaps the least of the difficulties which may confront us will be reaching 3–17 and the body of Vor Daj. What concerns me more than that is the likelihood that the entire Laboratory Building may be filled with the mass from Vat Room No. 4, in which event it will be practically impossible to reach Ras Thavas's laboratory which contains the necessary paraphernalia for the delicate operation of returning your brain to your own body."

"I anticipated that," I replied; "and on my way out of Morbus, I took everything that was necessary to 3–17."

"Good!" he exclaimed. "My mind is greatly relieved. Ras Thavas and I have both been deeply concerned by what amounted to his practical certainty that we should never be able to reach his laboratory. He believes that it is going to be necessary to destroy Morbus before we can check the growth from Vat No. 4."

It was daylight when we approached Morbus. The ships, with the exception of the Ruzaar, which carried us, were dispatched to circle the island to discover how far the mass from Vat Room No. 4 had spread.

The Ruzaar, dropping to within a few yards of the ground, approached the little island where lay the tunnel leading to 3–17; and, as we approached it, a sight of horror met our eyes. A wriggling, writhing mass of tissue had spread across the water from the main island of Morbus and now completely covered the little island. Hideous heads looked up at us screaming defiance; hands stretched forth futilely to clutch us.

I searched for the mouth of the tunnel; but it was not visible, being entirely covered by the writhing mass. My heart sank, for I felt certain that the mass must have entered the tunnel and found its way to 3–17; for I was sure that it would enter any opening and follow the line of least resistance until it met some impassable barrier.

However, I clung desperately to the hope that I had covered the mouth of the tunnel sufficiently well to have prevented the mass from starting down it. But even so, how could we hope to reach the tunnel through that hideous cordon of horror?

John Carter stood by the rail with several members of his staff. Janai, Ras Thavas, and I were close beside him. He was gazing down with evident horror upon Ras Thavas's creation. Presently he issued instructions to the members of his staff, and two of them left to put them into effect. Then we waited, no one speaking, silenced by the horror surging beneath us, screaming, mouthing, gesticulating.

Janai was standing close to me, and presently she grasped my arm. It was the first time that she had ever voluntarily touched me. "How horrible!" she whispered. "It cannot be possible that Vor Daj's body still exists, for that horrid mass must have spread everywhere through the buildings as well as out beyond the walls of the City."

I shook my head. I had nothing to say. She pressed my arm tightly. "Tor-dur-bar, promise me that you will do nothing rash if the body of Vor Daj is lost."

"Let's not even think of it," I said.

"But we must think of it; and you must promise me."

I shook my head. "You are asking too much," I said. "There can be no happiness for me as long as I retain the body of a hormad." I realized then that I had given myself away, but she did not seem to notice it, but just stood in silence looking down upon the awful thing beneath us.

The Ruzaar was rising now, and it continued to do so until it had gained an altitude of five or six hundred feet. Then it remained stationary again, hanging directly over that part of the little islet where the cave mouth lay. Presently an incendiary bomb fell, and the mass writhed and screamed as it burst, spreading its flaming contents in all directions.

I shall not dwell upon the horror of it, but bomb after bomb was dropped until only a mass of charred and smoking flesh lay within a radius of a hundred feet of the cave opening. Then the Ruzaar dropped closer to the ground, and I was lowered by landing tackle; and following me came Ras Thavas and two hundred warriors, the latter armed with swords and flaming torches with which they immediately attacked the mass that was already creeping back to cover the ground that it had lost.

My heart was in my mouth as I fell to work to remove the earth and stones with which I had blocked the entrance to the tunnel; but as

I worked, I saw no sign that it had been pierced, and presently it lay open before me and I could have shouted with joy, for the mouth of the tunnel was empty.

I cannot describe my feelings as I again traversed that long tunnel back to 3–17. Was my body still there? Was it safe and whole? I conjured all sorts of terrible things that might have happened to it during my long absence. I almost ran through the black tunnel in my haste to learn the truth, and at last with trembling hands I raised the cover of the trap that led from the tunnel up into the chamber. A moment later, I stood in 3–17.

Lying as I had left it was the body of Vor Daj.

Ras Thavas soon joined me; and I could see that he, too, breathed a sigh of relief as he discovered the body and paraphernalia intact.

Without waiting for instructions from Ras Thavas, I stretched myself upon the ersite slab beside my own body; and presently Ras Thavas was bending over me. I felt a slight incision and a little pain, and then consciousness left me.

chapter XXXI

ADVENTURE'S END

I OPENED MY EYES. Ras Thavas was leaning over me. Beside me lay the body of the hormad, Tor-dur-bar. I know that then the tears came to my eyes, tears of such relief and happiness and joy as I had never experienced before in my life, not so much because I had regained my own body but because now I might lay it at the feet of Janai.

"Come, my son," said Ras Thavas. "We have been here a long time. The mass is writhing and screaming in the corridor beyond the door. Let us hope that it has not succeeded in recovering the ground that it lost at the other end of the tunnel."

"Very well," I said, "let us return at once." I stepped from the table and stood again erect upon my own feet. I was just a little stiff, and Ras Thavas noticed it.

"That will pass in a moment," he said. "You have been dead a long time." And he smiled.

I stood for a moment looking down upon the uncouth body of Tor-dur-bar. "It served you well," said Ras Thavas.

"Yes," I assented, "and the best reward that I can offer it is eternal oblivion. We shall leave it here, buried forever in the pits beneath the building where it first felt life. I leave it, Ras Thavas, without a pang of regret."

"It had great strength, and, from what I understand, a good sword arm," commented the Master Mind of Mars.

"Yet I still think that I can endure life without it," I said.

"Vanity, vanity!" exclaimed Ras Thavas. "You, a warrior, would give up enormous strength and an incomparable sword arm for a handsome face."

I saw that he was laughing at me; but the whole world might laugh if it wished, just as long as I had my own body back again.

We hastened back through the tunnel, and when we finally emerged onto the islet again, warriors were still fighting back the insistent growth. Four times the detachment had been relieved since we had descended from the Ruzaar. It had been early morning when we arrived, and now the sun was just about to dip below the far horizon, yet to me it seemed but the matter of a few moments since I had descended from the Ruzaar.

We were quickly hoisted aboard again where we were fairly smothered with congratulations.

John Carter placed a hand upon my shoulder. "I could not have been more concerned over the fate of a son of mine than I have been over yours," he said.

That was all that he said, but it meant more to me than volumes spoken by another. Presently he noted my eyes wandering about the deck, and a smile touched his lips. "Where is she?" I asked.

"She could not stand the strain of waiting," he said, "and she has gone to her cabin to lie down. You had better go and tell her yourself."

"Thank you, sir," I said; and a few moments later I was knocking at the door of Janai's cabin.

"Who knocks?" she asked.

"Vor Daj," I replied, and then without waiting for an invitation I pushed open the door and entered.

She rose and came toward me, her eyes wide with questioning. "It is really you?" she asked.

"It is I," I assured her, and I crossed toward her. I wanted to take her in my arms and tell her that I loved her; but she seemed to anticipate what I had in mind, for she stopped me with a gesture.

"Wait," she said. "Do you realize that I scarcely know Vor Daj?"

I had not thought of that, but it was true. She knew Tor-dur-bar far better. "Answer me one question."

"What is it?" I asked.

"How did Teeaytan-ov die?" she demanded.

It was a strange question. What had that to do with Janai or with me? "Why, he died in the corridor leading to 3–17, struck down by one of the hormad warriors while we were escaping from the Laboratory Building," I replied.

Her white teeth flashed in a sudden smile. "Now what were you going to say to me when I stopped you?"

"I was going to tell you that I loved you," I replied, "and ask you if there was any hope that you might return my love."

"I scarcely knew Vor Daj," she said; "it was Tor-dur-bar that I learned to love; but now I know the truth that for some time I have guessed, and I realize the sacrifice that you were willing to make for me." She came and put her dear arms about my neck, and for the first time I felt the lips of the woman I loved on mine.

For ten days the great fleet cruised high above Morbus, dropping bombs upon the city and the island and the great mass that had started to spread out in all directions to engulf a world; nor would John Carter leave until the last vestige of the horror had been entirely exterminated. At last the bows of the great battleships were turned toward Helium; and with only a brief stop at Phundahl to return Pandar to his native city we cruised on toward home, and for Janai and me, a happiness that we had passed together through horrors to achieve.

As the great towers of the twin cities appeared in the distance, Janai and I were standing together in the bow of the Ruzaar. "I wish you would tell me," I said, "why you asked me that time how Teeaytan-ov died. You knew as well as I."

"Stupid!" she exclaimed, laughing. "Tor-dur-bar, Pandar, and I were the only survivors of that fight who were with the fleet when we returned to Morbus. Of these three, you could have seen only Tor-dur-bar before you saw me. Therefore, when you answered me correctly, I knew that Tor-dur-bar's brain had been transferred to your skull. That was all that I wanted to know, for it was the brain that gave the character and fineness to Tor-dur-bar that I had learned to love; and I do not care, Vor Daj, whose brain it was originally. If you do not care to tell me, I shall never ask; but I suspect that it was your own and that you had it transferred to the head of Tor-dur-bar so that you might better protect me from Ay-mad."

"It is my own brain," I said.

"*Was*, you mean," she laughed; "it is mine now."

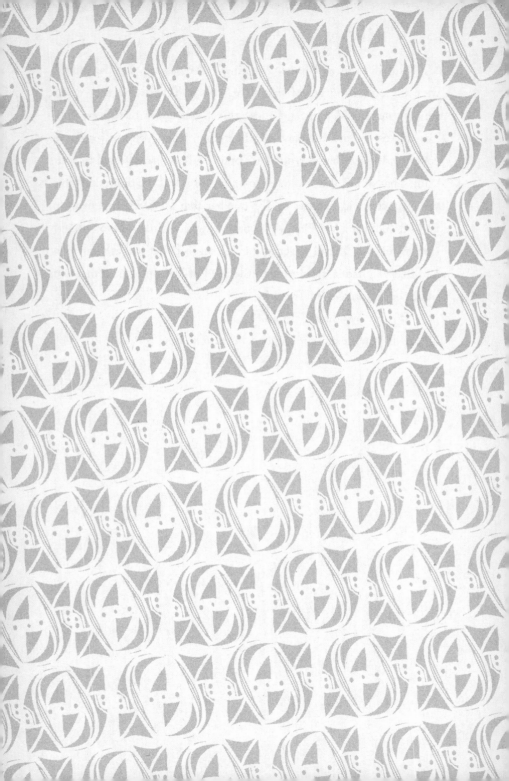

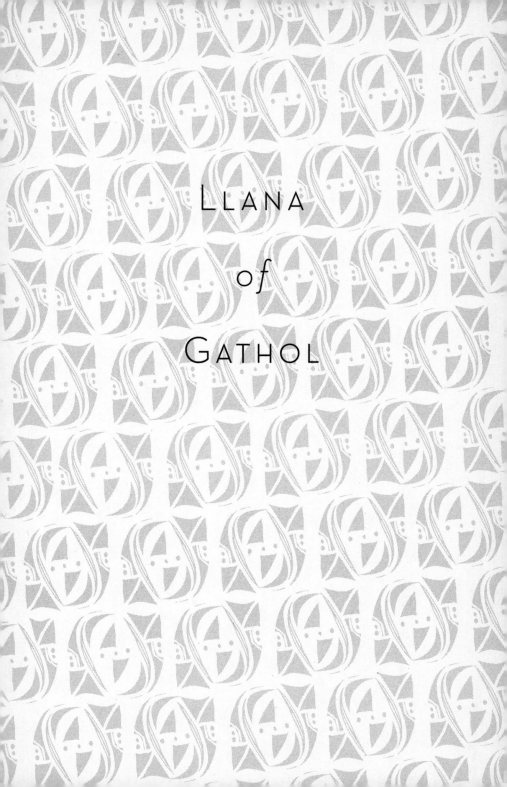

LLANA

of

GATHOL

chapter 1

No MATTER how instinctively gregarious one may be there are times when one longs for solitude. I like people. I like to be with my family, my friends, my fighting men; and probably just because I am so keen for companionship, I am at times equally keen to be alone. It is at such times that I can best resolve the knotty problems of government in times of war or peace. It is then that I can meditate upon all the various aspects of a full life such as I lead; and, being human, I have plenty of mistakes upon which to meditate that I may fortify myself against their recommission.

When I feel that strange urge for solitude coming over me, it is my usual custom to take a one man flier and range the dead sea bottoms and the other uninhabited wildernesses of this dying planet; for there indeed is solitude. There are vast areas on Mars where no human foot has ever trod, and other vast areas that for thousands of years have known only the giant green men, the wandering nomads of the ocher deserts.

Sometimes I am away for weeks on these glorious adventures in solitude. Because of them, I probably know more of the geography and topography of Mars than any other living man; for they and my other adventurous excursions upon the planet have carried me from the Lost Sea of Korus, in the Valley Dor at the frozen South to Okar, land of the black bearded Yellow Men of the frozen North, and from Kaol to Bantoom; and yet there are many parts of Barsoom that I have not visited, which will not seem so strange when there is taken into consideration the fact that although the area of Mars is like more than one fourth that of Earth its land area is almost eight million square miles greater. That is because Barsoom has no large bodies of surface water, its largest known ocean being entirely subterranean. Also, I think you will admit, fifty-six million square miles is a lot of territory to know thoroughly.

Upon the occasion of which I am about to tell you I flew northwest from Helium, which lies 30° south of the Equator which I crossed about sixteen hundred miles east of Exum, the Barsoomian Greenwich. North and west of me lay a vast, almost unexplored region; and there I thought to find the absolute solitude for which I craved.

I had set my directional compass upon Horz, the long deserted city of ancient Barsoomian culture, and loafed along at seventy-five miles an hour at an altitude of five hundred to a thousand feet. I had seen some green men northeast of Torquas and had been forced up to escape their fire, which I did not return as I was not seeking adventure; and I had crossed two thin ribbons of red Martian farm land bordering canals that bring the precious waters from the annually melting ice caps at the poles. Beyond these I saw no signs of human life in all the five thousand miles that lie between Lesser Helium and Horz.

It is always a little saddening to me to look down thus upon a dying world, to scan the endless miles of ocher, mosslike vegetation which carpets the vast areas where once rolled the mighty oceans of a young and virile Mars, to ponder that just beneath me once ranged the proud navies and the merchant ships of a dozen rich and powerful nations where today the fierce banth roams a solitude whose silence is unbroken except for the roars of the killer and the screams of the dying.

At night I slept, secure in the knowledge that my directional compass would hold a true course for Horz and always at the altitude for which I had set it—a thousand feet, not above sea level but above the terrain over which the ship was passing. These amazing little instruments may be set for any point upon Barsoom and at any altitude. If one is set for a thousand feet, as mine was upon this occasion, it will not permit the ship to come closer than a thousand feet to any object, thus eliminating even the danger of collision; and when the ship reaches its objective the compass will stop it a thousand feet above. The pilot whose ship is equipped with one of these directional compasses does not even have to remain awake; thus I could travel day and night without danger.

It was about noon of the third day that I sighted the towers of ancient Horz. The oldest part of the city lies upon the edge of a vast plateau; the newer portions, and they are countless thousands of years old, are terraced downward into a great gulf, marking the hopeless pursuit of the receding sea upon the shores of which this rich and powerful city once stood. The last poor, mean structures of a dying race have either disappeared or are only mouldering ruins now; but the splendid structures of her prime remain at the edge of the plateau, mute but eloquent reminders of her vanished grandeur—enduring monuments to the white-skinned, fair-haired race which has vanished forever.

I am always interested in these deserted cities of ancient Mars. Little is known of their inhabitants, other than what can be gathered from the stories told by the carvings which ornament the exteriors of many of their public buildings and the few remaining murals which have withstood the ravages of time and the vandalism of the green hordes which have overrun many of them. The extremely low humidity has helped to preserve them, but more than all else was the permanency of their construction. These magnificent edifices were built not for years but for eternities. The secrets of their mortars, their cements, and their pigments have been lost for ages; and for countless ages more, long after the last life has disappeared from the face of Barsoom, their works will remain, hurtling through space forever upon a dead, cold planet with no eye to see, with no mind to appreciate. It is a sad thing to contemplate.

At last I was over Horz. I had for long promised myself that some day I should come here, for Horz is, perhaps, the oldest and the greatest of the dead cities of Barsoom. Water built it, the lack of water spelled its doom. I often wonder if the people of Earth, who have water in such abundance, really appreciate it. I wonder if the inhabitants of New York City realize what it would mean to them if some enemy, establishing an air base within cruising radius of the first city of the New World, should successfully bomb and destroy Croton Dam and the Catskill water system. The railroads and the highways would be jammed with refugees, millions would die, and for years, perhaps forever, New York City would cease to be.

As I floated lazily above the deserted city I saw figures moving in a plaza below me. So Horz was not entirely deserted! My curiosity piqued, I dropped a little lower; and what I saw dashed thoughts of solitude from my mind—a lone red man beset by half a dozen fierce green warriors.

I had not sought adventure, but here it was; for no man worthy of his metal would abandon one of his own kind in such a dire extremity. I saw a spot where I might land in a nearby plaza; and, praying that the green men would be too engrossed with their engagement to note my approach, I dove quickly and silently toward a landing.

chapter II

FORTUNATELY I landed unobserved, screened by a mighty tower which rose beside the plaza I had selected. I had seen that they were fighting with long-swords, and so I drew mine as I ran in the direction of the unequal struggle. That the red man lived even a few moments against such odds bespoke the excellence of his swordsmanship, and I hoped that he would hold out until I reached him; for then he would have the best sword arm in all Barsoom to aid him and the sword that had tasted the blood of a thousand enemies the length and breadth of a world.

I found my way from the plaza in which I had landed, but only to be confronted by a twenty-foot wall in which I could perceive no opening. Doubtless there was one, I knew; but in the time that I might waste in finding it my man might easily be killed.

The clash of swords, the imprecations, and the grunts of fighting men came to me distinctly from the opposite side of the wall which barred my way. I could even hear the heavy breathing of the fighters. I heard the green men demand the surrender of their quarry and his taunting reply. I liked what he said and the way he said it in the face of death.

My knowledge of the ways of the green men assured me that they would try to capture him for purposes of torture rather than kill him outright, but if I were to save him from either fate I must act quickly.

There was only one way to reach him without loss of time, and that way was open to me because of the lesser gravitation of Mars and my great Earthly strength and agility. I would simply jump to the top of the wall, take a quick survey of the lay of the land beyond, and then drop down, long-sword in hand, and take my place at the side of the red man.

When I exert myself, I can jump to incredible heights. Twenty feet is nothing, but this time I miscalculated. I was several yards from the wall when I took a short run and leaped into the air. Instead of alighting on the top of the wall, as I had planned, I soared completely over it, clearing it by a good ten feet.

Below me were the fighters. Apparently I was going to land right in their midst. So engrossed were they in their sword play that they did not notice me; and that was well for me; as one of the green men could easily have impaled me on his sword as I dropped upon them.

My man was being hard pressed. It was evident that the green men had given up the notion of capturing him, and were trying to finish him off. One of them had him at a disadvantage and was about to plunge a long-sword through him when I alighted. By rare good luck I alighted squarely upon the back of the man who was about to kill the red man, and I alighted with the point of my sword protruding straight below me. It caught him in the left shoulder and passed downward through his heart, and even before he collapsed I had planted both feet upon his shoulders; and, straightening up, withdrawn my blade from his carcass.

For a moment my amazing advent threw them all off their guard, and in that moment I leaped to the side of the red man and faced his remaining foes, the red blood of a green warrior dripping from my point.

The red man threw a quick glance at me; and then the remaining green men were upon us, and there was no time for words. A fellow swung at me and missed. Gad! what a blow he swung! Had it connected I should have been as headless as a rykor. It was unfortunate for the green man that it did not, for mine did. I cut horizontally with all my Earthly strength, which is great on Earth and infinitely greater on Mars. My long-sword, its edge as keen as a razor and its steel such as only Barsoom produces, passed entirely through the body of my antagonist, cutting him in two.

"Well done!" exclaimed the red man, and again he cast a quick glance at me.

From the corner of my eye I caught an occasional glimpse of my unknown comrade, and I saw some marvellous swordsmanship. I was proud to fight at the side of such a man. By now we had reduced the number of our antagonists to three. They fell back a few steps, dropping their points, just for a breathing spell. I neither needed nor desired a breathing spell; but, glancing at my companion, I saw that he was pretty well exhausted; so I dropped my point too and waited.

It was then that I got my first good look at the man whose cause I had espoused; and I got a shock, too. This was no red man, but a white man if I have ever seen one. His skin was bronzed by exposure to the sun, as is mine; and that had at first deceived me. But now I saw that there was nothing red-Martian about him. His harness, his weapons, everything about him differed from any that I had seen on Mars.

He wore a headdress, which is quite unusual upon Barsoom. It consisted of a leather band that ran around the head just above his brows, with another leather band crossing his head from right to left and a second from front to rear. These bands were highly ornamented with carving and set with jewels and precious metals. To the center of the band that crossed his forehead was affixed a flat piece of gold in the shape of a spearhead with the point up. This, also, was beautifully carved and bore a strange device inlaid in red and black.

Confined by this headdress was a shock of blond hair—a most amazing thing to see upon Mars. At first I jumped to the conclusion that he must be a thern from the far south-polar land; but that thought

I discarded at once when I realized that the hair was his own. The therns are entirely bald and wear great yellow wigs.

I also saw that my companion was strangely handsome. I might say beautiful were it not for the effeminateness which the word connotes, and there was nothing effeminate about the way this man fought or the mighty oaths that he swore when he spoke at all to an adversary. We fighting men are not given to much talk, but when you feel your blade cleave a skull in twain or drive through the heart of a foeman, then sometimes a great oath is wrenched from your lips.

But I had little time then to appraise my companion, for the remaining three were at us again in a moment. I fought that day, I suppose, as I have always fought; but each time it seems to me that I have never fought so well as upon that particular occasion. I do not take great credit for my fighting ability, for it seems to me that my sword is inspired. No man could think as quickly as my point moves, always to the right spot at the right time, as though anticipating the next move of an adversary. It weaves a net of steel about me that few blades have ever pierced. It fills the foeman's eyes with amazement and his mind with doubt and his heart with fear. I imagine that much of my success has been due to the psychological effect of my swordsmanship upon my adversaries.

Simultaneously my companion and I each struck down an antagonist, and then the remaining warrior turned to flee. "Do not let him escape!" cried my comrade-in-arms, and leaped in pursuit, at the same time calling loudly for help, something he had not done when close to death before the points of six swords. But whom did he expect to answer his appeal in this dead and deserted city? Why did he call for help when the last of his antagonists was in full flight? I was puzzled; but having enlisted myself in this strange adventure, I felt that I should see it through; and so I set off in pursuit of the fleeing green man.

He crossed the courtyard where we had been engaged and made for a great archway that opened out into a broad avenue. I was close behind him, having outstripped both him and the strange warrior. When I came into the avenue I saw the green man leap to the back of one of six thoats waiting there, and at the same time I saw at least a hundred warriors pouring from a nearby building. They were yellow-haired white men, garbed like my erstwhile fighting companion, who now joined in the pursuit of the green man. They were armed with bows and arrows; and they sent a volley of missiles after the escaping quarry, whom they could never hope to overtake, and who was soon out of range of their weapons.

The spirit of adventure is so strong within me that I often yield to its demands in spite of the dictates of my better judgment. This matter was no affair of mine. I had already done all, and even more than could have been expected of me; yet I leaped to the back of one of the remaining thoats and took off in pursuit of the green warrior.

chapter III

THERE ARE TWO SPECIES of thoat on Mars: the small, comparatively docile breed used by the red Martians as saddle animals and, to a lesser extent, as beasts of burden on the farms that border the great irrigation canals; and then there are the huge, vicious, unruly beasts that the green warriors use exclusively as steeds of war.

These creatures tower fully ten feet at the shoulder. They have four legs on either side and a broad, flat tail, larger at the tip than at the root, that they hold straight out behind while running. Their gaping mouths split their heads from their snouts to their long, massive necks. Their bodies, the upper portion of which is a dark slate color and exceedingly smooth and glossy, are entirely devoid of hair. Their bellies are white, and their legs shade gradually from the slate color of their bodies to a vivid yellow at the feet, which are heavily padded and nailless.

The thoat of the green man has the most abominable disposition of any creature I have ever seen, not even the green men themselves excepted. They are constantly fighting among themselves, and woe betide the rider who loses control of his terrible mount; yet, paradoxical as it may appear, they are ridden without bridle or bit; and are controlled solely by telepathic means, which, fortunately for me, I learned many years ago while I was prisoner of Lorquas Ptomel, jed of the Tharks, a green Martian horde.

The beast to whose back I had vaulted was a vicious devil, and he took violent exception to me and probably to my odor. He tried to buck me off; and, failing that, reached back with his huge, gaping jaws in an effort to seize me.

There is, I might mention, an auxiliary method of control when these ugly beasts become recalcitrant; and I adopted it in this instance, notwithstanding the fact that I had won grudging approval from the fierce green Tharks by controlling thoats through patience and kindness. I had time for neither now, as my quarry was racing along the broad avenue that led to the ancient quays of Horz and the vast dead sea bottoms beyond; so I laid heavily upon the head and snout of the beast with the flat of my broadsword until I had beaten it into subjection; then it obeyed my telepathic commands, and set out at great speed in pursuit.

It was a very swift thoat, one of the swiftest that I had ever bestrode; and, in addition, it carried much less weight than the beast we sought to overtake; so we closed up rapidly on the escaping green man.

At the very edge of the plateau upon which the old city was built we caught up with him, and there he stopped and wheeled his mount and prepared to give battle. It was then that I began to appreciate the marvellous intelligence of my mount. Almost without direction from me he maneuvered into the correct positions to give me an advantage in this savage duel, and when at last I had achieved a sudden advantage which had almost unseated my rival, my thoat rushed like a mad devil upon the thoat of the green warrior tearing at its throat with his mighty jaws while he tried to beat it to its knees with the weight of his savage assault.

It was then that I gave the *coup de grace* to my beaten and bloody adversary; and, leaving him where he had fallen, rode back to receive the plaudits and the thanks of my newfound friends.

They were waiting for me, a hundred of them, in what had probably once been a public market place in the ancient city of Horz. They were not smiling. They looked sad. As I dismounted, they crowded around me.

"Did the green man escape?" demanded one whose ornaments and metal proclaimed him a leader.

"No," I replied; "he is dead."

A great sigh of relief arose from a hundred throats. Just why they should feel such relief that a single green man had been killed I did not then understand.

They thanked me, crowding around me as they did so; and still they were unsmiling and sad. I suddenly realized that these people were not friendly—it came to me intuitively, but too late. They were pushing against me from all sides, so that I could not even raise an arm; and then, quite suddenly at a word from their leader, I was disarmed.

"What is the meaning of this?" I demanded. "Of my own volition I came to the aid of one of your people who would otherwise have been killed. Is this the thanks I am to receive? Give me back my weapons and let me go."

"I am sorry," said he who had first spoken, "but we cannot—do otherwise. Pan Dan Chee, to whose aid you came, has pleaded that we permit you to go your way; but such is not the law of Horz. I must take you to Ho Ran Kim, the great jeddak of Horz. There we will all plead for you, but our pleas will be unavailing. In the end you will be destroyed. The safety of Horz is more important than the life of any man."

"I am not threatening the safety of Horz," I replied. "Why should I have designs upon a dead city, which is of absolutely no importance to the Empire of Helium, in the service of whose Jeddak, Tardos Mors, I wear the harness of a war lord."

"I am sorry," exclaimed Pan Dan Chee, who had pushed his way to my side through the press of warriors. "I called to you when you mounted the thoat and pursued the green warrior and told you not to return, but evidently you did not hear me. For that I may die, but I shall die proudly. I sought to influence Lan Sohn Wen, who commands this utan, to permit you to escape, but in vain. I shall intercede for you with Ho Ran Kim, the jeddak; but I am afraid that there is no hope."

"Come!" said Lan Sohn Wen; "we have wasted enough time here. We will take the prisoner to the jeddak. By the way, what is your name?"

"I am John Carter, a Prince of Helium and Warlord of Barsoom," I replied.

"A proud title, that last," he said; "but of Helium I have never heard."

"If harm befalls me here," I said, "you'll hear of Helium if Helium ever learns."

I was escorted through still magnificent avenues flanked by beautiful buildings, still beautiful in decay. I think I have never seen such inspiring architecture, nor construction so enduring. I do not know how old these buildings are, but I have heard Martian savants argue that the original dominant race of white-skinned, yellow-haired people flourished fully a million years ago. It seems incredible that their works should still exist; but there are many things on Mars incredible to the narrow, earthbound men of our little speck of dust.

At last we halted before a tiny gate in a colossal, fortress-like edifice in which there was no other opening than this small gate for fifty feet above the ground. From a balcony fifty feet above the gate a sentry looked down upon us. "Who comes?" he demanded, although he could doubtless see who came, and must have recognized Lan Sohn Wen.

"It is Lan Sohn Wen, Dwar, commanding the 1st Utan of The Jeddak's Guard, with a prisoner," replied Lan Sohn Wen.

The sentry appeared bewildered. "My orders are to admit no strangers," he said, "but to kill them immediately."

"Summon the commander of the guard," snapped Lan Sohn Wen, and presently an officer came onto the balcony with the sentry.

"What is this?" he demanded. "No prisoner has ever been brought into the citadel of Horz. You know the law."

"This is an emergency," said Lan Sohn Wen. "I must bring this man before Ho Ran Kim. Open the gate!"

"Only on orders from Ho Ran Kim himself," replied the commander of the guard.

"Then go get the orders," said Lan Sohn Wen. "Tell the Jeddak that I strongly urge him to receive me with this prisoner. He is not as other prisoners who have fallen into our hands in times past."

The officer re-entered the citadel and was gone for perhaps fifteen minutes when the little gate before which we stood swung outward, and we were motioned in by the commander of the guard himself.

"The Jeddak will receive you," he said to the dwar, Lan Sohn Wen.

The citadel was an enormous walled city within the ancient city of Horz. It was quite evidently impregnable to any but attack by air. Within were pleasant avenues, homes, gardens, shops. Happy, care-free people stopped to look at me in astonishment as I was conducted down a broad boulevard toward a handsome building. It was the palace of the Jeddak, Ho Ran Kim. A sentry stood upon either side of the portal. There was no other guard; and these two were there more as a formality and as messengers than for protection, for within the walls of the citadel no man needed protection from another; as I was to learn.

We were detained in an ante-room for a few minutes while we were being announced, and then we were ushered down a long corridor and into a medium size room where a man sat at a desk alone. This was Ho Ran Kim, Jeddak of Horz. His skin was not as tanned as that of his warriors, but his hair was just as yellow and his eyes as blue.

I felt those blue eyes appraising me as I approached his desk. They were kindly eyes, but with a glint of steel. From me they passed to Lan Sohn Wen, and to him Ho Ran Kim spoke.

"This is most unusual," he said in a quiet, well modulated voice. "You know, do you not, that Horzans have died for less than this?"

"I do, my Jeddak," replied the dwar; "but this is a most unusual emergency."

LLANA OF GATHOL / 505

"Explain yourself," said the Jeddak.

"Let me explain," interrupted Pan Dan Chee, "for after all the responsibility is mine. I urged this action upon Lan Sohn Wen."

The Jeddak nodded. "Proceed," he said.

chapter IV

I COULDN'T comprehend why they were making such an issue of bringing in a prisoner, nor why men had died for less, as Ho Ran Kim had reminded Lan Sohn Wen. In Helium, a warrior would have received at least commendation for bringing in a prisoner. For bringing in John Carter, Warlord of Mars, a common warrior might easily have been ennobled by an enemy prince.

"My Jeddak," commenced Pan Dan Chee, "while I was beset by six green warriors, this man, who says he is known as John Carter, Warlord of Barsoom, came of his own volition to fight at my side. From whence he came I do not know. I only know that at one moment I was fighting alone, a hopeless fight, and that at the next there fought at my side the greatest swordsman Horz has ever seen. He did not have to come; he could have left at any time, but he remained; and because he remained I am alive and the last of the six green warriors lies dead by the ancient waterfront. He would have escaped had not John Carter leaped to the back of a great thoat and pursued him.

"Then this man could have escaped, but he came back. He fought for a soldier of Horz. He trusted the men of Horz. Are we to repay him with death?"

Pan Dan Chee ceased speaking, and Ho Ran Kim turned his blue eyes upon me. "John Carter," he said, "what you have done commands

the respect and sympathy of every man of Horz. It wins the thanks of
their Jeddak, but—" He hesitated. "Perhaps if I tell you something of
our history, you will understand why I must condemn you to death."
He paused for a moment, as though in thought.

At the same time I was doing a little thinking on my own account.
The casual manner in which Ho Ran Kim had sentenced me to death
had rather taken my breath away. He seemed so friendly that it didn't
seem possible that he was in earnest, but a glance at the glint in those
blue eyes assured me that he was not being facetious.

"I am sure," I said, "that the history of Horz must be most interesting; but right now I am most interested in learning why I should
have to die for befriending a fighting man of Horz."

"That I shall explain," he said.

"It is going to take a great deal of explaining, your majesty," I
assured him.

He paid no attention to that, but continued. "The inhabitants of
Horz are, as far as we know, the sole remaining remnant of the once
dominant race of Barsoom, the Orovars. A million years ago our ships
ranged the five great oceans, which we ruled. The city of Horz was
not only the capital of a great empire, it was the seat of learning and
culture of the most glorious race of human beings a world has ever
known. Our empire spread from pole to pole. There were other races
on Barsoom, but they were few in numbers and negligible in importance. We looked upon them as inferior creatures. The Orovars owned
Barsoom, which was divided among a score of powerful jeddaks. They
were a happy, prosperous, contented people, the various nations seldom warring upon one another. Horz had enjoyed a thousand years
of peace.

"They had reached the ultimate pinnacle of civilization and

perfection when the first shadow of impending fate darkened their horizon—the seas began to recede, the atmosphere to grow more tenuous. What science had long predicted was coming to pass—a world was dying.

"For ages our cities followed the receding waters. Straits and bays, canals and lakes dried up. Prosperous seaports became deserted inland cities. Famine came. Hungry hordes made war upon the more fortunate. The growing hordes of wild green men overran what had once been fertile farm land, preying upon all.

"The atmosphere became so tenuous that it was difficult to breathe. Scientists were working upon an atmosphere plant, but before it was completed and in successful operation all but a few of the inhabitants of Barsoom had died. Only the hardiest survived—the green men, the red men, and a few Orovars; then life became merely a battle for the survival of the fittest.

"The green men hunted us as we had hunted beasts of prey. They gave us no rest, they showed us no mercy. We were few; they were many. Horz became our last city of refuge, and our only hope of survival lay in preventing the outside world from knowing that we existed; therefore, for ages we have slain every stranger who came to Horz and saw an Orovar, that no man might go away and betray our presence to our enemies.

"Now you will understand that no matter how deeply we must regret the necessity, it is obvious that we cannot let you live."

"I can understand," I said, "that you might feel it necessary to destroy an enemy; but I see no reason for destroying a friend. However, that is for you to decide."

"It is already decided, my friend," said the Jeddak. "You must die."

"Just a moment, O Jeddak!" exclaimed Pan Dan Chee. "Before

you pass final judgment, consider this alternative. If he remains here in Horz, he cannot carry word to our enemies. We owe him a debt of gratitude. Permit him then to live, but always within the walls of the citadel."

There were nods of approval from the others present, and I saw by his quickly darting eyes that Ho Ran Kim had noticed them. He cleared his throat. "Perhaps that is something that should be given thought," he said. "I shall reserve judgment until the morrow. I do so largely because of my love for you, Pan Dan Chee; inasmuch as, because it was due to your importunities that this man is here, you must suffer whatever fate is ordained for him."

Pan Dan Chee was certainly surprised, nor could he hide the fact; but he took the blow like a man. "I shall consider it an honor," he said, "to share any fate that may be meted to John Carter, Warlord of Barsoom."

"Well said, Pan Dan Chee!" exclaimed the Jeddak. "My admiration for you increases as does the bitterness of my sorrow when I contemplate the almost inescapable conviction that on the morrow you die."

Pan Dan Chee bowed. "I thank your majesty for your deep concern," he said. "The remembrance of it will glorify my last hours."

The Jeddak turned his eyes upon Lan Sohn Wen, and held them there for what seemed a full minute. I would have laid ten to one that Ho Ran Kim was about to cause himself further untold grief by condemning Lan Sohn Wen to death. I think Lan Sohn Wen thought the same thing. He looked worried.

"Lan Sohn Wen," said Ho Ran Kim, "you will conduct these two to the pits and leave them there for the night. See that they have good food and every possible comfort, for they are my honored guests."

"But the pits, your majesty!" exclaimed Lan Sohn Wen. "They have never been used within the memory of man. I do not even know that I can find the entrance to them."

"That is so," said Ho Ran Kim, thoughtfully. "Even if you found them they might prove very dirty and uncomfortable. Perhaps it would be kinder to destroy John Carter and Pan Dan Chee at once."

"Wait, majesty," said Pan Dan Chee. "I know where lies the entrance to the pits. I have been in them. They can easily be made most comfortable. I would not think of altering your plans or causing you immediately the deep grief of sorrowing over the untimely passing of John Carter and myself. Come, Lan Sohn Wen! I will lead the way to the pits of Horz!"

chapter V

IT WAS A GOOD THING for me that Pan Dan Chee was a fast talker. Before Ho Ran Kim could formulate any objections we were out of the audience chamber and on our way to the pits of Horz, and I can tell you that I was glad to be out of sight of that kindly and considerate tyrant. There was no telling when some new humanitarian urge might influence him to order our heads lopped off instanter.

The entrance to the pits of Horz was in a small, windowless building near the rear wall of the citadel. It was closed by massive gates that creaked on corroded hinges as two of the warriors who had accompanied us pushed them open.

"It is dark in there," said Pan Dan Chee. "We'll break our necks without a light."

Lan Sohn Wen, being a good fellow, sent one of his men for

some torches; and when he returned, Pan Dan Chee and I entered the gloomy cavern.

We had taken but a few steps toward the head of a rock hewn ramp that ran downward into Stygian darkness, when Lan Sohn Wen cried, "Wait! Where is the key to these gates?"

"The keeper of the keys of some great jeddak who lived thousands of years ago may have known," replied Pan Dan Chee, "but I don't."

"But how am I going to lock you in?" demanded Lan Sohn Wen.

"The Jeddak didn't tell you to lock us in," said Pan Dan Chee. "He said to take us to the pits and leave us there for the night. I distinctly recall his very words."

Lan Sohn Wen was in a quandary, but at last he hit upon an avenue of escape. "Come," he said, "I shall take you back to the Jeddak and explain that there are no keys; then it will be up to him."

"And you know what he will do!" said Pan Dan Chee.

"What?" asked Lan Sohn Wen.

"He will order us destroyed at once. Come, Lan Sohn Wen, do not condemn us to immediate death. Post a guard here at the gates, with orders to kill us if we try to escape."

Lan Sohn Wen considered this for a moment, and finally nodded his head in acquiescence. "That is an excellent plan," he said, and then he detailed two warriors to stand guard; and arranged for their relief, after which he wished us good night and departed with his warriors.

I have never seen such courteous and considerate people as the Orovars; it might almost be a pleasure to have one's throat slit by one of them, he would be so polite about it. They are the absolute opposites of their hereditary enemies, the green men; for these are endowed with neither courtesy, consideration, nor kindness. They are cold, cruel, abysmal brutes to whom love is unknown and whose creed is hate.

Nevertheless, the pits of Horz was not a pleasant place. The dust of ages lay upon the ramp down which we walked. From its end a corridor stretched away beyond the limits of our torchlight. It was a wide corridor, with doors opening from it on either side. These, I presumed, were the dungeons where ancient jeddaks had confined their enemies. I asked Pan Dan Chee.

"Probably," he said, "though our jeddaks have never used them."

"Have they never had enemies?" I asked.

"Certainly, but they have considered it cruel to imprison men in dark holes like this; so they have always destroyed them immediately they were suspected of being enemies."

"Then why are the pits here?" I demanded.

"Oh, they were built when the city was built, perhaps a million years ago, perhaps more. It just chanced that the citadel was built around the entrance."

I glanced into one of the dungeons. A mouldering skeleton lay upon the floor, the rusted irons that had secured it to the wall lying among its bones. In the next dungeon were three skeletons and two magnificently carved, metal bound chests. As Pan Dan Chee raised the lid of one of them I could scarce repress a gasp of astonishment and admiration. The chest was filled with magnificent gems in settings of elaborate beauty, specimens of forgotten arts, the handicraft of master craftsmen who had lived a million years ago. I think that nothing that I had ever seen before had so impressed me. And it was depressing, for these jewels had been worn by lovely women and brave men who had disappeared into an oblivion so complete that not even a memory of them remained.

My reverie was interrupted by the sound of shuffling feet behind me. I wheeled; and, instinctively, my hand flew to where the hilt of a sword should have been but was not. Facing me, and ready to spring upon me, was the largest ulsio I had ever seen.

These Martian rats are fierce and unlovely things. They are many legged and hairless, their hide resembling that of a new-born mouse in repulsiveness. Their eyes are small and close set and almost hidden in deep, fleshy apertures. Their most ferocious and repulsive features, however, are their jaws, the entire bony structure of which protrudes several inches beyond the flesh, revealing five sharp, spadelike teeth in each jaw, the whole suggesting the appearance of a rotting face from which much of the flesh has sloughed away. Ordinarily they are about the size of an Airedale terrier, but the thing that leaped for me in the pits of Horz that day was as large as a small puma and ten times as ferocious.

As the creature leaped for my throat, I struck it a heavy blow on the side of its head and knocked it to one side; but it was up at once and at me again; then Pan Dan Chee came into the scene. They had not disarmed him, and with short-sword he set upon the ulsio.

It was quite a battle. That ulsio was the most ferocious and most determined beast I had ever seen, and it gave Pan Dan Chee the fight of his life. He had knocked off two of its six legs, an ear, and most of its teeth before the ferocity of its repeated attacks abated at all. It was almost cut to ribbons, yet it always forced the fighting. I could only stand and look on, which is not such a part in a fight as I like to take. At last, however, it was over; the ulsio was dead, and Pan Dan Chee looked at me and smiled.

He was looking around for something upon which he might wipe the blood from his blade. "Perhaps there is something in this other chest," I suggested; and, walking to it, I lifted the lid.

The chest was about seven feet long, two and a half wide and two deep. In it lay the body of a man. His elaborate harness was encrusted with jewels. He wore a helmet entirely covered with diamonds, one of the few helmets I had ever seen upon Mars. The scabbards of his long-sword, his short-sword, and his dagger were similarly emblazoned.

He had been a very handsome man, and he was still a handsome corpse. So perfectly was he preserved that, in so far as appearances went, he might still have been alive but for the thin layer of dust overlying his features. When I blew this away he looked quite as alive as you or I.

"You bury your dead here?" I asked Pan Dan Chee, but he shook his head.

"No," he replied. "This chap may have been here a million years."

"Nonsense!" I exclaimed. "He would have dried up and blown away thousands of years ago."

"I don't know about that," said Pan Dan Chee. "There were lots of things that those old fellows knew that are lost arts today. Embalming, I know, was one of them. There is the legend of Lee Um Lo, the most famous embalmer of all time. It recounts that his work was so perfect that not even the corpse, himself, knew that he was dead; and upon several occasions they arose and walked out during the funeral services. The end of Lee Um Lo came when the wife of a great jeddak failed to realize that she was dead, and walked right in on the jeddak and his new wife. The next day Lee Um Lo lost his head."

"It is a good story," I said, laughing; "but I hope this chap realizes that he is dead; because I am about to disarm him. Little could he have dreamed a million years ago that one day he was going to rearm The Warlord of Barsoom."

Pan Dan Chee helped me raise the corpse and remove its harness; and we were both rather startled by the soft, pliable texture of the flesh and its normal warmth.

"Do you suppose we could be mistaken?" I asked. "Could it be that he is not dead?"

Pan Dan Chee shrugged. "The knowledge and the arts of the ancients are beyond the ken of modern man," he said.

"That doesn't help a bit," I said. "Do you think this chap can be alive?"

"His face was covered with dust," said Pan Dan Chee, "and no one has been in these pits for thousands and thousands of years. If he isn't dead, he should be."

I quite agreed, and buckled the gorgeous harness about me without more ado. I drew the swords and the dagger and examined them. They were as bright and fine as the day they had received their first polish, and their edges were keen. Once again, I felt like a whole man, so much is a sword a part of me.

As we stepped out into the corridor I saw a light far away. It was gone almost in the instant. "Did you see that?" I asked Pan Dan Chee.

"I saw it," he said, and his voice was troubled. "There should be no light here, for there are no people."

We stood straining our eyes along the corridor for a repetition of the light. There was none, but from afar there echoed down that black corridor a hollow laugh.

chapter VI

PAN DAN CHEE looked at me. "What," he asked, "could that have been?"

"It sounded very much like a laugh to me," I replied.

Pan Dan Chee nodded. "Yes," he agreed, "but how can there be a laugh where there is no one to laugh?" Pan Dan Chee was perplexed.

"Perhaps the ulsios of Horz have learned to laugh," I suggested with a smile.

Pan Dan Chee ignored my flippancy. "We saw a light and we heard a laugh," he said thoughtfully. "What does that convey to you?"

"The same thing that it conveys to you," I said: "that there is some one down here in the pits of Horz beside us."

"I do not see how that can be possible," he said.

"Let's investigate," I suggested.

With drawn swords we advanced; for we did not know the nature nor the temper of the owner of that laugh, and there was always the chance that an ulsio might leap from one of the dungeons and attack us.

The corridor ran straight for some distance, and then commenced to curve. There were many branches and intersections, but we kept to what we believed to be the main corridor. We saw no more lights, heard no more laughter. There was not a sound in all that vast labyrinth of passageways other than the subdued clanking of our metal, the occasional shuffling of our sandalled feet, and the soft whisperings of our leather harnesses.

"It is useless to search farther," said Pan Dan Chee at last. "We might as well start back."

Now I had no intention of going back to my death. I reasoned that the light and the laugh indicated the presence of man in these pits. If the inhabitants of Horz knew nothing of them; then they must enter the pits from outside the citadel, indicating an avenue of escape open to me. Therefore, I did not wish to retrace our steps; so I suggested that we rest for a while and discuss our future plans.

"We can rest," said Pan Dan Chee, "but there is nothing to discuss.

Our plans have all been made for us by Ho Ran Kim."

We entered a cell which contained no grim reminders of past tragedy; and, after wedging one of our torches in a niche in the wall, we sat
down on the hard stone floor.

"Perhaps your plans have been made for you by Ho Ran Kim," I
said, "but I make my own plans."

"And they are—?" he asked.

"I am not going back to be murdered. I am going to find a way
out of these pits."

Pan Dan Chee shook his head sorrowfully. "I am sorry," he said,
"but you are going back to meet your fate with me."

"What makes you think that?" I asked.

"Because I shall have to take you back. You well know that I cannot let a stranger escape from Horz."

"That means that we shall have to fight to the death, Pan Dan
Chee," I said; "and I do not wish to kill one at whose side I have fought
and whom I have learned to admire."

"I feel the same way, John Carter," said Pan Dan Chee. "I do not
wish to kill you; but you must see my position—if you do not come
with me willingly, I shall have to kill you."

I tried to argue him out of his foolish stand, but he was adamant.
I was positive that Pan Dan Chee liked me; and I shrank from the idea
of killing him, as I knew that I should. He was an excellent swordsman, but what chance would he have against the master swordsman of
two worlds? I am sorry if that should sound like boasting; for I abhor
boasting—I only spoke what is a fact. I am, unquestionably, the best
swordsman that has ever lived.

"Well," I said, "we don't have to kill each other at once. Let's enjoy
each other's company for a while longer."

Pan Dan Chee smiled. "That will suit me perfectly," he said.

"How about a game of Jetan?" I asked. "It will help to pass the time pleasantly."

"How can we play Jetan without a board or the pieces?" he asked.

I opened the leather pocket pouch such as all Martians carry, and took out a tiny, folding Jetan board with all the pieces—a present from Dejah Thoris, my incomparable mate. Pan Dan Chee was intrigued by it, and it *is* a marvellously beautiful piece of work. The greatest artist of Helium had designed the pieces, which had been carved under his guidance by two of our greatest sculptors.

Each of the pieces, such as Warriors, Padwars, Dwars, Panthans, and Chiefs, were carved in the likeness of well-known Martian fighting men; and one of the Princesses was a beautifully executed miniature carving of Tara of Helium, and the other Princess, Llana of Gathol.

I am inordinately proud of this Jetan set; and because the figures are so tiny, I always carry a small but powerful reading glass, not alone that I may enjoy them but that others may. I offered it now to Pan Dan Chee, who examined the figures minutely.

"Extraordinary," he said. "I have never seen anything more beautiful." He had examined one figure much longer than he had the others, and he held it in his hand now as though loath to relinquish it. "What an exquisite imagination the artist must have had who created this figure, for he could have had no model for such gorgeous beauty; since nothing like it exists on Barsoom."

"Every one of those figures was carved from life," I told him.

"Perhaps the others," he said, "but not this one. No such beautiful woman ever lived."

"Which one is it?" I asked, and he handed it to me. "This," I said, "is Llana of Gathol, the daughter of Tara of Helium, who is my daughter. She really lives, and this is a most excellent likeness of her. Of course it cannot do her justice since it cannot reflect her animation nor the charm of her personality."

He took the little figurine back and held it for a long time under the glass; then he replaced it in the box. "Shall we play?" I asked.

He shook his head. "It would be sacrilege," he said, "to play at a game with the figure of a goddess."

I packed the pieces back in the tiny box, which was also the playing board, and returned it to my pouch. Pan Dan Chee sat silent. The light of the single torch cast our shadows deep and dark upon the floor.

These torches of Horz were a revelation to me. They are most ingenious. Cylindrical, they have a central core which glows brightly with a cold light when exposed to the air. By turning back a hinged cap and pushing the central core up with a thumb button, it becomes exposed to the air and glows brightly. The farther up it is pushed and the more of it that is exposed, the more intense the light. Pan Dan Chee told me that they were invented ages ago, and that the lighting results in so little loss of matter that they are practically eternal. The art of producing the central core was lost in far antiquity, and no scientist since has been able to analyze its composition.

It was a long time before Pan Dan Chee spoke again; then he arose. He looked tired and sad. "Come," he said, "let's have it over with," and he drew his sword.

"Why should we fight?" I asked. "We are friends. If I go away, I pledge my honor that I will not lead others to Horz. Let me go, then, in peace. I do not wish to kill you. Or, better still, you come away with me. There is much to see in the world outside of Horz and much to adventure."

"Don't tempt me," he begged, "for I want to come. For the first time in my life I want to leave Horz, but I may not. Come! John Carter. On guard! One of us must die, unless you return willingly with me."

"In which case both of us will die," I reminded him. "It is very silly, Pan Dan Chee."

"On guard!" was his only reply.

There was nothing for me to do but draw and defend myself. Never have I drawn with less relish.

chapter VII

PAN DAN CHEE would not take the offensive, and he offered very little in the way of defense. I could have run him through at any time that I chose from the very instant that I drew my sword. Almost immediately I realized that he was offering me my freedom at the expense of his own life, but I would not take his life.

Finally I backed away and dropped my point. "I am no butcher, Pan Dan Chee," I said. "Come! put up a fight."

He shook his head. "I cannot kill you," he said, quite simply.

"Why?" I asked.

"Because I am a fool," he said. "The same blood flows in your veins and hers. I could not spill that blood. I could not bring unhappiness to her."

"What do you mean?" I demanded. "What are you talking about?"

"I am talking about Llana of Gathol," he said, "the most beautiful woman in the world, the woman I shall never see but for whom I gladly offer my life."

Now, Martian fighting men are proverbially chivalrous to a fault, but this was carrying it much further than I had ever seen it carried before.

"Very well," I said; "and as I don't intend killing you there is no use going on with this silly duel."

I returned my sword to its scabbard, and Pan Dan Chee did likewise.

"What shall we do?" he asked. "I cannot let you escape; but, on the other hand, I cannot prevent it. I am a traitor to my country. I shall, therefore, have to destroy myself."

I had a plan. I would accompany Pan Dan Chee back almost to the entrance to the pits, and there I would overpower, bind, and gag him; then I would make my escape, or at least I would try to find another exit from the pits. Pan Dan Chee would be discovered, and could face his doom without the stigma of treason being attached to his name.

"You need not kill yourself," I told him. "I will accompany you to the entrance to the pits; but I warn you that should I discover an opportunity to escape, I shall do so."

"That is fair enough," he said. "It is very generous of you. You have made it possible for me to die honorably and content."

"Do you wish to die?" I asked.

"Certainly not," he assured me. "I wish to live. If I live, I may some day find my way to Gathol."

"Why not come with me, then?" I demanded. "Together we may be able to find our way out of the pits. My flier lies but a short distance from the citadel, and it is only about four thousand haads from Horz to Gathol."

He shook his head. "The temptation is great," he said, "but until I have exhausted every resource and failed to return to Ho Ran Kim before noon tomorrow I may do nothing else but try."

"Why by noon tomorrow?" I asked.

"It is a very ancient Orovaran law," he replied, "which limits the duration of a death sentence to noon of the day one is condemned to die. Ho Ran Kim decreed that we should die tomorrow. If we do not, we are not in honor bound to return to him."

We set off a little dejectedly for the doorway through which we were expected to pass to our doom. Of course, I had no intention of doing so; but I was dejected because of Pan Dan Chee. I had come to like him immensely. He was a man of high honor and a courageous fighter.

We walked on and on, until I became convinced that if we had followed the right corridor we should long since have arrived at the entrance. I suggested as much to Pan Dan Chee, and he agreed with me; then we retraced our steps and tried another corridor. We kept this up until we were all but exhausted, but we failed to find the right corridor.

"I am afraid we are lost," said Pan Dan Chee.

"I am quite sure of it," I agreed, with a smile. If we were sufficiently well lost, we might not find the entrance before the next noon; in which event Pan Dan Chee would be free to go where he pleased, and I had a pretty good idea of where he pleased to go.

Now, I am no matchmaker; nor neither do I believe in standing in the way to prevent the meeting of a man and a maid. I believe in letting nature take her course. If Pan Dan Chee thought he was in love with Llana of Gathol and wished to go to Gathol and try to win her, I would only have discouraged the idea had he been a man of low origin or of a dishonorable nature. He was neither. The race to which he belonged is the oldest of the cultured races of Barsoom, and Pan Dan Chee had proved himself a man of honor.

I had no reason to believe that his suit would meet with any success. Llana of Gathol was still very young, but even so the swords of some of the greatest houses of Barsoom had been lain at her feet. Like nearly all Martian women of high degree she knew her mind. Like so many of them, she might be abducted by some impetuous suitor; and she would either love him or slip a dagger between his ribs, but she would never mate with a man she did not love. I was more fearful for Pan Dan Chee than I was for Llana of Gathol.

We retraced our steps and tried another corridor, yet still no entrance. We lay down and rested; then we tried again. The result was the same.

"It must be nearly morning," said Pan Dan Chee.

"It is," I said, consulting my chronometer. "It is almost noon."

Of course I didn't use the term *noon*; but rather the Barsoomian equivalent, 25 xats past the 3rd zode, which is 12 noon Earth time.

"We must hurry!" exclaimed Pan Dan Chee.

A hollow laugh sounded behind us; and, turning quickly, we saw a light in the distance. It disappeared immediately.

"Why should we hurry?" I demanded. "We have done the best we could. That we did not find our way back to the citadel and death is no fault of ours."

Pan Dan Chee nodded. "And no matter how much we may hurry, there is little likelihood that we shall ever find the entrance."

Of course this was wishful thinking, but it was also quite accurate thinking. We never did find the entrance to the citadel.

"This is the second time we have heard that laugh and seen that light," said Pan Dan Chee. "I think we should investigate it. Perhaps he who makes the light and voices the laugh may be able to direct us to the entrance."

"I have no objection to investigating," I said, "but I doubt that we shall find a friend if we find the author."

"It is most mystifying," said Pan Dan Chee. "All my life I have believed, as all other inhabitants of Horz have believed, that the pits of Horz were deserted. A long time ago, perhaps ages, some venturesome men entered the pits to investigate them. These incursions occurred at intervals, and none of those who entered the pits ever returned. It was assumed that they became lost, and starved to death. Perhaps they, too, heard the laughter and saw the lights!"

"Perhaps," I said.

chapter VIII

PAN DAN CHEE and I lost all sense of time, so long were we in the pits of Horz without food or water. It could not have been more than two days, as we still had strength; and more than two days without water will sap the strength of the best of men. Twice more we saw the light and heard the laughter. That laugh! I can hear it yet. I tried to think that it was human. I didn't want to go mad.

Pan Dan Chee said, "Let's find it and drink its blood!"

"No, Pan Dan Chee," I counselled. "We are men, not beasts."

"You are right," he said. "I was losing control."

"Let's use our heads," I said. "He knows always where we are, because always he can see the light of our torch. Suppose we extinguish it, and creep forward silently. If he has curiosity, he will investigate. We shall listen attentively, and we shall hear his footfalls." I had it all worked out beautifully, and Pan Dan Chee agreed that it was a perfect plan. I think he still had in mind the drinking of the creature's blood, when we should find it. I was approaching a point when I might have taken a drink myself. God! If you have never suffered from hunger and thirst, don't judge others too harshly.

We extinguished the torch. We each had one, but there was no use in keeping both lighted. The light of one could have been raised to a brilliancy that would have blinded. We crept silently forward in the direction that we had last seen the light. Our swords were drawn. Three times already we had been set upon by the huge ulsios of these ancient pits of Horz, but at these times we had had the advantage of the light of our torch. I could not but wonder how we would come out if one of them attacked us now.

The darkness was total, and there was no sound. We clung to our weapons so that they would not clank against our metal. We lifted our sandalled feet high and placed them gently on the stone flooring. There was no scuffing. There was no sound. We scarcely breathed.

Presently a light appeared before us. We halted, waiting, listening. I saw a figure. Perhaps it was human, perhaps not. I touched Pan Dan Chee lightly on the arm, and moved forward. He came with me. We made no sound—absolutely no sound. I think that we each held his breath.

The light grew brighter. Now I could see a head and shoulder protruding from a doorway at the side of the corridor. The thing had the contour of humanity at least. I could imagine that it was concerned over our sudden disappearance. It was wondering what had become of us. It withdrew within the doorway where it had stood, but the light persisted. We could see it shining from the interior of the cell or room into which the THING had withdrawn.

We crept closer. Here might lie the answer to our quest for water and for food. If the THING were human, it would require both; and if it had them, we should have them.

Silently we approached the doorway from which the light streamed out into the corridor. Our swords were drawn. I was in the lead. I felt that if the THING had any warning of our approach, it would disappear. That must not happen. We must see IT. We must seize IT, and we must force IT to give us water—food and water!

I reached the doorway, and as I stepped into the opening I had a momentary glimpse of a strange figure; and then all was plunged into darkness and a hollow laugh reverberated through the Stygian blackness of the pits of Horz.

In my right hand I held the long-sword of that long dead Orovaran from whose body I had filched it. In my left hand I held the amazing torch of the Horzians. When the light in the chamber was extinguished, I pushed up the thumb button of my torch; and the apartment before me was flooded with light.

I saw a large chamber filled with many chests. There was a simple couch, a bench, a table, bookshelves filled with books, an ancient Martian stove, a reservoir of water, and the strangest figure of a man my eyes had ever rested upon.

I rushed at him and held my sword against his heart, for I did not wish him to escape. He cowered and screamed, beseeching his life.

"We want water," I said; "water and food. Give us these and offer us no harm, and you will be safe."

"Help yourselves," he said. "There is water and food here, but tell me who you are and how you got here to the pits of ancient Horz, dead Horz—dead for countless ages. I have been waiting for ages for some one to come, and now you have come. You are welcome. We shall be great friends. You shall stay here with me forever, as all the countless others have. I shall have company in the lonely pits of Horz." Then he laughed maniacally.

It was evident that the creature was quite mad. He not only looked it, he acted it. Sometimes his speech was inarticulate gibber; often it was broken by meaningless and inopportune laughter—the hollow laugh that we had heard before.

His appearance was most repulsive. He was naked except for the harness which supported a sword and a dagger, and the skin of his malformed body was a ghastly white—the color of a corpse. His flabby mouth hung open, revealing a few yellow, snaggled fangs. His eyes were wide and round, the whites showing entirely around the irises. He had no nose; it appeared to have been eaten away by disease.

I kept my eye on him constantly while Pan Dan Chee drank; then he watched him while I slaked my thirst, and all the while the creature kept up a running fire of senseless chatter. He would take a word like calot, for instance, and keep repeating it over and over just as though he were carrying on a conversation. You could detect an interrogatory sentence by his inflection, as also the declarative, imperative, and exclamatory. All the time, he kept gesturing like a Fourth of July orator.

At last he said, "You seem very stupid, but eventually you may understand. And now about food: You prefer your ulsio raw, I presume; or shall I cook it?"

"Ulsio!" exclaimed Pan Dan Chee. "You don't mean to say that you eat ulsio!"

"A great delicacy," said the creature.

"Have you nothing else?" demanded Pan Dan Chee.

"There is a little of Ro Tan Bim left," said the THING, "but he is getting a bit high even for an epicure like me."

Pan Dan Chee looked at me. "I am not hungry," I said. "Come! Let's try to get out of here." I turned to the old man. "Which corridor leads out into the city?" I asked.

"You must rest," he said; "then I will show you. Lie down upon that couch and rest."

I had always heard that it is best to humor the insane; and as I was asking a favor of this creature, it seemed the wise thing to do. Furthermore, both Pan Dan Chee and I were very tired; so we lay down on the couch and the old man drew up a bench and sat down beside us. He commenced to talk in a low, soothing voice.

"You are very tired," he said, over and over again monotonously, his great eyes fixed first upon one of us and then upon the other. I felt my muscles relaxing. I saw Pan Dan Chee's lids drooping. "Soon you will be asleep," whispered the old man of the pits. "You will sleep and sleep and sleep, perhaps for ages as have these others. You will only awaken when I tell you to or when I die—and I shall never die. You robbed Hor Kai Lan of his harness and weapons." He looked at me as he spoke. "Hor Kai Lan would be very angry were he to awaken and find that you have stolen his weapons, but Hor Kai Lan will not awaken. He has been asleep for so many ages that even I have forgotten. It is in my book, but what difference does it make? What difference does it make who wears the harness of Hor Kai Lan? No one will ever use his swords again; and, anyway, when Ro Tan Bim is gone, maybe I shall use Hor Kai Lan. Maybe I shall use you. Who knows?"

His voice was like a dreamy lullably. I felt myself sinking into pleasant slumber. I glanced at Pan Dan Chee. He was fast asleep. And then the import of the THING'S words reached my reasoning mind. By hypnosis we were being condemned to a living death! I sought to shake the lethargy from me. I brought to bear what remained to me of my will power. Always my mind has been stronger than that of any Martian against whose mind I have pitted it.

The horror of the situation lent me strength: the thought of lying here for countless ages collecting the dust of the pits of Horz, or of being eaten by this snaggled toothed maniac! I put every ounce of my will power into a final, terrific effort to break the bonds that held me. It was even more devastating than a physical effort. I broke out into violent perspiration. I felt myself trembling from head to feet. Would I succeed?

The old man evidently realized the battle I was making for freedom, as he redoubled his efforts to hold me. His voice and his eyes wrapped themselves about me with almost physical force. The THING was sweating now, so strenuous were its endeavors to enthrall my mind. Would it succeed?

chapter IX

I WAS WINNING! I knew that I was winning! And the THING must have known it, too; for I saw it slipping its dagger from the sheath at its side. If it couldn't hold me in the semblance of death, it would hold me in actual death. I sought to wrench myself free from the last weakening tentacles of the THING'S malign mental forces before it could strike the fatal blow that would spell death for me and the equivalent of death for Pan Dan Chee.

The dagger hand rose above me. Those hideous eyes glared down into mine, lighted by the Hellish fires of insanity; and then, in that last instant, I won! I was free. I struck the dagger hand from me and leaped to my feet, the good long-sword of Hor Kai Lan already in my hand.

The THING cowered and screamed. It screamed for help where there was no help, and then it drew its sword. I would not defile the fine art of my swordsmanship by crossing blades with such as this. I recalled its boast that Pan Dan Chee and I would sleep until it awoke us or it died. That alone was enough to determine me—I would be no duelist, but an executioner and a liberator.

I cut once, and the foul head rolled to the stone floor of the pits of Horz. I looked at Pan Dan Chee. He was awakening. He rolled over and stretched; then he sat up and looked at me, questioningly. His eyes wandered to the torso and the head lying on the floor.

"What happened?" he asked.

Before I could reply, I was interrupted by a volley of sound coming from the chamber in which we were and from other chambers in the pits of Horz.

We looked quickly around us. Lids were being raised on innumerable chests, and cries were coming from others the lids of which were held down by the chests on top of them. Armed men were emerging—warriors in gorgeous harness. Women, rubbing their eyes and looking about them in bewilderment.

From the corridor others began to converge upon the chamber, guided by our light.

"What is the meaning of this?" demanded a large man, magnificently trapped. "Who brought me here? Who are you?" He looked around him, evidently bewildered, as though searching for some familiar face.

"Perhaps I can enlighten you?" I said. "We are in the pits of Horz. I have been here only a few hours, but if this dead thing on the floor spoke the truth some of you must have been here for ages. You have been held by the hypnotic power of this mad creature. His death has freed you."

The man looked down at the staring head upon the floor. "Lum

Tar O!" he exclaimed. "He sent for me—asked me to come and see him on an important matter. And you have killed him. You must account to me—tomorrow. Now I must return to my guests."

There was a layer of dust on the man's face and body. By that I knew that he must have been here a long time, and presently my surmise was substantiated in a most dramatic manner.

The awakened men and women were forcing their way from the chests in which they had been kept. Some of those in the lower tiers were having difficulty in dislodging the chests piled on top of them. There was a great clattering and tumult as empty chests toppled to the floor. There was a babel of conversation. There were bewilderment and confusion.

A dusty nobleman crawled from one of the chests. Instantly he and the large man who had just spoken recognized one another. "What is the matter with you?" demanded the latter. "You are all covered with dust. Why did you come down? Come! I must get back to my guests."

The other shook his head in evident bewilderment. "Your guests, Kam Han Tor!" he exclaimed. "Did you expect your guests to wait twenty years for you to return."

"Twenty years! What do you mean?"

"I was your guest twenty years ago. You left in the middle of the banquet and never returned."

"Twenty years? You are mad!" exclaimed Kam Han Tor. He looked at me and then at the grinning head upon the floor, and he commenced to weaken. I could see it.

The other man was feeling his own face and looking at the dust he wiped from it. "You, too, are covered with dust," he said to Kam Han Tor.

Kam Han Tor looked down at his body and harness; then he wiped his face and looked at his fingers. "Twenty years!" he exclaimed, and then he looked down at the head of Lum Tar O. "You vile beast!" he exclaimed. "I was your friend, and you did this to me!" He turned then to me. "Forget what I said. I did not understand. Whoever you may be, permit me to assure you that my sword is always in your service."

I bowed in acknowledgment.

"Twenty years!" repeated Kam Han Tor, as though he still could not believe it. "My great ship! It was to have sailed from the harbor of Horz the day following my banquet—the greatest ship that ever had been built. Now it is old, perhaps obsolete; and I have never seen it. Tell me—did it sail well? Is it still a proud ship?"

"I saw it as it sailed out upon Throxeus," said the other. "It was a proud ship indeed, but it never returned from that first voyage; nor was any word ever heard of it. It must have been lost with all hands."

Kam Han Tor shook his head sadly, and then he straightened up and squared his shoulders. "I shall build another," he said, "an even greater ship, to sail the mightiest of Barsoom's five seas."

Now I commenced to understand what I had suspected but could not believe. It was absolutely astounding. I was looking at and conversing with men who had lived hundreds of thousands of years ago, when Throxeus and the other four oceans of ancient Mars had covered what are now the vast desert wastes of dead sea bottom; when a great merchant marine carried on the commerce of the fair-skinned, blond race that had supposedly been extinct for countless ages.

I stepped closer to Kam Han Tor and laid a hand upon his shoulder. The men and women who had been released from Lum Tar O's malicious spell had gathered around us, listening. "I am sorry to disillusion you, Kam Han Tor," I said; "but you will build no ship, nor will any ship ever again sail Throxeus."

"What do you mean?" he demanded. "Who is to stop Kam Han Tor, brother of the jeddak, from building ships and sailing them upon Throxeus?"

"There is no Throxeus, my friend," I said.

"No Throxeus? You are mad!"

"You have been here in the pits of Horz for countless ages," I explained, "and during that time the five great oceans of Barsoom have dried up. There are no oceans. There is no commerce. The race to which you belonged is extinct."

"Man, you are mad!" he cried.

"Do you know how to get out of these pits?" I asked—"out into the city proper—not up through the—" I was going to say citadel but I recalled that there had been no citadel when these people had been lured to the pits.

"You mean not up through my palace?" asked Kam Han Tor.

"Yes," I said, "not up through your palace, but out toward the quays; then I can show you that there is no longer a Throxeus."

"Certainly I know the way," he said. "Were these pits not built according to my plans!"

"Come, then," I said.

A man was standing looking down on the head of Lum Tar O. "If what this man says is true," he said to Kam Han Tor, "Lum Tar O must have lived many ages ago. How then could he have survived all these ages? How have we survived?"

"You were existing in a state of suspended animation," I said; "but as for Lum Tar O—that is a mystery."

"Perhaps not such a mystery after all," replied the man. "I knew Lum Tar O well. He was a weakling and a coward with the psychological reactions of the weakling and the coward. He hated all who were brave and strong, and these he wished to harm. His only friend was

Lee Um Lo, the most famous embalmer the world had ever known; and when Lum Tar O died, Lee Um Lo embalmed his body. Evidently he did such a magnificent job that Lum Tar O's corpse never realized that Lum Tar O was dead, and went right on functioning as in life. That would account for the great span of years that the thing has existed—not a human being; not a live creature, at all; just a corpse the malign brain of which still functioned."

As the man finished speaking there was a commotion at the entrance to the chamber. A large man, almost naked, rushed in. He was very angry. "What is the meaning of this?" he demanded. "What am I doing here? What are you all doing here? Who stole my harness and my weapons?"

It was then that I recognized him—Hor Kai Lan, whose metal I wore. He was very much excited, and I couldn't blame him much. He forced his way through the crowd, and the moment he laid eyes upon me he recognized his belongings.

"Thief!" he cried. "Give me back my harness and my weapons!"

"I'm sorry," I said; "but unless you will furnish me with others, I shall have to keep these."

"Calot!" he fairly screamed. "Do you realize to whom you are speaking? I am Hor Kai Lan, brother of the jeddak."

Kam Han Tor looked at him in amazement. "You have been dead over five hundred years, Hor Kai Lan," he exclaimed, "and so has your brother. My brother succeeded the last jeddak in the year 27M382J4."

"You have all been dead for ages," said Pan Dan Chee. "Even that calendar is a thing of the dead past."

I thought Hor Kai Lan was going to burst a blood vessel then. "Who are you?" he screamed. "I place you under arrest. I place you all under arrest. Ho! the guard!"

Kam Han Tor tried to pacify him, and at least succeeded in getting him to agree to accompany us to the quays to settle the question of the existence of Throxeus, which would definitely prove or disprove the unhappy truths I had been forced to explain to them.

As we started out, led by Kam Han Tor, I noticed the lid of a chest moving slightly. It was raised little by little, and I could see two eyes peering out through the crack made by the lifting of the lid; then suddenly a girl's voice cried, "John Carter, Prince of Helium! May my first ancestor be blessed!"

chapter X

HAD MY FIRST ancestor suddenly materialized before my eyes, I could not have been more surprised than I was to hear my name from the interior of one of those chests in the pits of Horz.

As I started to investigate, the lid of the chest was thrown aside; and a girl stepped out before me. This was more surprising than my first ancestor would have been, for the girl was Llana of Gathol!

"Llana!" I cried; "what are you doing here?"

"I might ask you the same question, my revered progenitor," she shot back, with that lack of respect for my great age which has always characterized those closest to me in bonds of blood and affection.

Pan Dan Chee came forward rather open-mouthed and goggle-eyed. "Llana of Gathol!" he whispered as one might voice the name of a goddess. The roomful of anachronisms looked on more or less apathetically.

"Who is this person?" demanded Llana of Gathol.

"My friend, Pan Dan Chee of Horz," I explained.

Pan Dan Chee unbuckled his sword and laid it at her feet, an act which is rather difficult to explain by Earthly standards of conduct. It is not exactly an avowal of love or a proposal of marriage. It is, in a way, something even more sacred. It means that as long as life lasts that sword is at the service of him at whose feet it has been laid. A warrior may lay his sword at the feet of a man or a woman. It means lifetime loyalty. Where the object of that loyalty is a woman, the man may have something else in mind. I am sure that Pan Dan Chee did.

"Your friend acts with amazing celerity," said Llana of Gathol; but she stooped and picked up the sword and handed it back to Pan Dan Chee *hilt first!* which meant that she was pleased and accepted his offer of fealty. Had she simply refused it, she would have left the sword lying where it had been placed. Had she wished to spurn his offer, she would have returned his sword to him *point* first. That would have been the final and deadly insult. I was glad that Llana of Gathol had returned Pan Dan Chee's sword hilt first, as I rather liked Pan Dan Chee. I was particularly glad that she had not returned it point first; as that would have meant that I, as the closest male relative of Llana of Gathol available, would have had to fight Pan Dan Chee; and I certainly didn't want to kill him.

"Well," interrupted Kam Han Tor, "this is all very interesting and touching; but can't we postpone it until we have gone down to the quays."

Pan Dan Chee bridled, and laid a hand on the hilt of his sword. I forestalled any unseemly action on his part by suggesting that Kam Han Tor was wholly right and that our private affairs could wait until the matter of the ocean, so vital to all these other people, had been settled. Pan Dan Chee agreed; so we started again for the quay of ancient Horz.

Llana of Gathol walked at my side. "Now you may tell me," I said, "how you came to be in the pits of Horz."

"It has been many years," she began, "since you were in the

kingdom of Okar in the frozen north. Talu, the rebel prince, whom you placed upon the throne of Okar, visited Helium once immediately thereafter. Since then, as far as I have ever heard, there has been no intercourse between Okar and the rest of Barsoom."

"What has all that to do with your being in the pits of Horz?" I demanded.

"Wait!" she admonished. "I am leading up to that. The general belief has been that the region surrounding the North Pole is but sparsely inhabited and by a race of black-bearded yellow men only."

"Correct," I said.

"Not correct," she contradicted. "There is a nation of red men occupying a considerable area, but at some distance from Okar. I am under the impression that when you were there the Okarians themselves had never heard of these people.

"Recently there came to the court of my father, Gahan of Gathol, a strange red man. He was like us, yet unlike. He came in an ancient ship, one which my father said must have been several hundred years old—obsolete in every respect. It was manned by a hundred warriors, whose harness and metal were unknown to us. They appeared fierce and warlike, but they came in peace and were received in peace.

"Their leader, whose name was Hin Abtol, was a pompous braggart. He was an uncultured boor; but, as our guest, he was accorded every courtesy. He said that he was Jeddak of Jeddaks of the North. My father said that he had thought that Talu held that title.

"'He did,' replied Hin Abtol, 'until I conquered his country and made him my vassal. Now I am Jeddak of Jeddaks of the North. My country is cold and bleak outside our glazed cities. I would come south, looking for other lands in which my people may settle and increase.'

"My father told him that all the arable lands were settled and belonged to other nations which had held them for centuries.

"Hin Abtol merely shrugged superciliously. 'When I find what I wish,' he said, 'I shall conquer its people. I, Hin Abtol, take what I wish from the lesser peoples of Barsoom. From what I have heard, they are all weak and effete; not hardy and warlike as are we Panars. We breed fighting men, in addition to which we have countless mercenaries. I could conquer all of Barsoom, if I chose.'

"Naturally, that sort of talk disgusted my father; but he kept his temper, for Hin Abtol was his guest. I suppose that Hin Abtol thought that my father feared him, his kind often believing that politeness is a sign of weakness. I know he once said to my father, 'You are fortunate that Hin Abtol is your friend. Other nations may fall before my armies, but you shall be allowed to keep your throne. Perhaps I shall demand a little tribute from you, but you will be safe. Hin Abtol will protect you.'

"I do not know how my father controlled his temper. I was furious. A dozen times I insulted the fellow, but he was too much of an egotistical boor to realize that he was being insulted; then came the last straw. He told Gahan of Gathol that he had decided to honor him by taking me, Llana of Gathol, as his wife. He had already bragged that he had seven!

"'That,' said my father, 'is a matter that I cannot discuss with you. The daughter of Gahan of Gathol will choose her own mate.'

"Hin Abtol laughed. 'Hin Abtol,' he said, 'chooses his wives— they have nothing to say about it.'

"Well, I had stood about all I could of the fellow; and so I decided to go to Helium and visit you and Dejah Thoris. My father decided that I should go in a small flier manned by twenty-five of his most trusted men, all members of my personal Guard.

"When Hin Abtol heard that I was leaving, he said that he would have to leave also—that he was returning to his own country but that he would come back for me. 'And I hope we have no trouble about it,' he said, 'for it would be too bad for Gathol if she made an enemy of Hin Abtol the Panar, Jeddak of Jeddaks of the North.'

"He left the day before I set out, and I did not change my plans because of his going. As a matter of fact, I had been planning on this visit for some time.

"My ship had covered scarce a hundred haads on the journey toward Helium, when we saw a ship rise from the edge of a sorapus forest ahead of us. It came slowly toward us, and presently I recognized its ancient lines. It was the ship of Hin Abtol the Panar, so-called Jeddak of Jeddaks of the North.

"When we were close enough it hailed us, and its captain told us that something had gone wrong with their compass and they were lost. He asked to come alongside that he might examine our charts and get his bearings. He hoped, he said, that we might repair his compass for him.

"Under the circumstances there was nothing to do but accede to his request, as one does not leave a disabled ship without offering aid. As I did not wish to see Hin Abtol, I went below to my cabin.

"I felt the two ships touch as that of the Panar came alongside, and an instant later I heard shouts and curses and the sounds of battle on the upper deck.

"I rushed up the ladder, and the sight that met my eyes filled me with rage. Nearly a hundred warriors swarmed over our deck from Hin Abtol's ancient tub. I have never seen greater brutality displayed by even the green men. The beasts ignored the commonest ethics of civilized warfare. Outnumbering us four to one, we had not a chance;

but the men of Gathol put up a most noble fight, taking bloody toll of their attackers; so that Hin Abtol must have lost fully fifty men before the last of my brave Guard was slaughtered.

"The Panars threw my wounded overboard with the dead, not even vouchsafing them the *coup de grace*. Of all my crew, not one was left alive.

"Then Hin Abtol swaggered aboard. 'I told you,' he said, 'that Hin Abtol chooses his wives. It would have been better for you and for Gathol had you believed me.'

"'It would have been better for you,' I replied, 'had you never heard of Llana of Gathol. You may rest assured that her death will be avenged.'

"'I do not intend to kill you,' he said.

"'I shall kill myself,' I told him, 'before I shall mate with such an ulsio as you.'

"That made him angry, and he struck me. 'A coward as well as an ulsio,' I said.

"He did not strike me again, but he ordered me below. In my cabin I realized that the ship was again under way, and looking from the port I saw that it was heading north—north toward the frozen land of the Panars.

chapter XI

"EARLY THE following morning, a warrior came to my cabin. 'Hin Abtol commands that you come at once to the control room,' he said.

"'What does he want of me?' I demanded.

"'His navigator does not understand this ship or the instruments,' the fellow explained. 'He would ask you some questions.'

"I thought quickly. Perhaps I might frustrate Hin Abtol's plans if I could have a few minutes with the controls and the instruments, which I knew as well as we know the face of a loved one; so I followed the warrior above.

"Hin Abtol was in the control room with three of his officers. His face was a black scowl as I entered. 'We are off our course,' he snapped, 'and during the night we have lost touch with our own ship. You will instruct my officers as to these silly instruments that have confused them.' With that, he left the control room.

"I looked around the horizon in every direction. The other ship was nowhere in sight. My plan was instantly formed. Had the other ship been able to see us, it could not have succeeded. I knew that if this ship on which I was prisoner ever reached Panar I would have to take my own life to escape a fate worse than death. On the ground I might also meet death, but I would have a better chance to escape.

"'What is wrong?' I asked one of the officers.

"'Everything,' he replied. 'What is this?'

"'A directional compass,' I explained; 'but what have you done to it? It is a wreck.'

"'Hin Abtol could not understand what it was for, which made him very angry; so he started taking it apart to see what was inside.'

"'He did a good job,' I said, '—of taking it apart. Now he, or another of you, should put it together again.'

"'We don't know how,' said the fellow. 'Do you?'

"'Of course not.'

"'Then what are we to do?'

"'Here is an ordinary compass,' I told him. 'Fly north by this, but first let me see what other harm has been done.'

"I pretended to examine all the other instruments and controls, and while I was doing so, I opened the buoyancy tank valves; and then jammed them so that they couldn't be closed.

"'Everything is all right now,' I said. 'Just keep on north by this compass. You won't need the directional compass.' I might have added that in a very short time they wouldn't need any compass as far as navigating this ship was concerned. Then I went down to my cabin.

"I knew that something would happen pretty soon, and sure enough it did. I could see from my porthole that we were losing altitude—just dropping slowly lower and lower—and directly another warrior came to my cabin and said that I was wanted in the control room again.

"Once more Hin Abtol was there. 'We are sinking,' he told me— a fact that was too obvious to need mention.

"'I have noticed that for some time,' I said.

"'Well, do something about it!' he snapped. 'You know all about this ship.'

"'I should think that a man who is thinking of conquering all of Barsoom ought to be able to fly a ship without the help of a woman,' I said.

"He flushed at that, and then he drew his sword. 'You will tell us what is wrong,' he growled, 'or I'll split you open from your crown to your belly.'

"'Always the chivalrous gentleman,' I sneered; 'but, even without your threat, I'll tell you what is wrong.'

"'Well, what is it?' he demanded.

"'In fiddling around with these controls, either you or some equally stupid brute has opened the buoyancy tank valves. All you have to do is close them. We won't sink any lower then, but we'll never go any higher, either. I hope there are no mountains or very high hills between here and Panar.'

"'Where are the valves?' he asked.

"I showed him.

"They tried to close them; but I had made such a good job of jamming them that they couldn't, and we kept right on dropping down toward the ocher vegetation of a dead sea bottom.

"Hin Abtol was frantic. So were his officers. Here they were, thousands of haads from home—twenty-five men who had spent the greater parts of their lives in the glazed, hot-house cities of the North Polar lands, with no knowledge, or very little, of the outside world or what nature of men, beasts, or other menaces might dispute their way toward home. I could scarcely refrain from laughing.

"As we lost altitude, I saw the towers of a city in the distance to the north of us; so did Hin Abtol. 'A city,' he said. 'We are fortunate. There we can find mechanics to repair our ship.'

"'Yes,' I thought; 'if you had come a million years ago, you would have found mechanics. They would have known nothing about repairing a flier, for fliers had not been invented then; but they could have built you a stanch ship wherein you could have sailed the five seas of ancient Barsoom,' but I said nothing. I would let Hin Abtol find out for himself.

"I had never been to Horz; but I knew that those towers rising in the distance could mark only that long dead city, and I wished the pleasure of witnessing Hin Abtol's disappointment after he had made the long and useless trek."

"You are a vindictive little rascal," I said.

"I'm afraid I am," admitted Llana of Gathol; "but, in this instance, can you blame me?"

I had to admit that I could not. "Go on," I urged. "Tell me what happened next."

"Will we never reach the end of these abominable pits!" exclaimed Kam Han Tor.

"You should know," said Pan Dan Chee; "you have said that they were built according to your plans."

"You are insolent," snapped Kam Han Tor. "You shall be punished."

"You have been dead a million years," said Pan Dan Chee. "You should lie down."

Kam Han Tor laid a hand upon the hilt of his long-sword. He was very angry; and I could not blame him, but this was no time to indulge in the pleasure of a duel.

"Hold!" I said. "We have more important things to think of now than personal quarrels. Pan Dan Chee is in the wrong. He will apologize."

Pan Dan Chee looked at me in surprise and disapproval, but he pushed his sword back into its scabbard. "What John Carter, Prince of Helium, Warlord of Barsoom, commands me to do, I do," he said. "To Kam Han Tor I offer my apology."

Well, Kam Han Tor graciously accepted it, and I urged Llana of Gathol to go on with her story.

"The ship dropped gently to the ground without incurring further damage," she continued. "Hin Abtol was undecided at first as whether to take all his men with him to the city or leave some to guard the ship. Finally he concluded that it might be better for them all to remain together in the event they should meet with a hostile reception at the gates of the city. You would have thought, from the way he spoke, that twenty-five Panars could take any city on Barsoom.

"'I shall wait for you here,' I said. 'There is no reason why I should accompany you to the city.'

"'And when I came back, you would be gone,' he said. 'You are a shrewd wench, but I am just a little bit shrewder. You will come with us.'

"So I had to tramp all the way to Horz with them, and it was a very long and tiresome tramp. As we approached the city, Hin Abtol remarked that it was surprising that we saw no signs of life—no smoke, no movement along the avenue which we could see paralleling the plain upon which the city faced, the plain that had once been a mighty ocean.

"It was not until we had entered the city that he realized that it was dead and deserted—but not entirely deserted, as we were soon to discover.

"We had advanced but a short distance up the main avenue when a dozen green warriors emerged from a building and fell upon the Panars. It might have been a good battle, John Carter, had you and two of the warriors of your guard been pitted against the green men; but these Panars are no warriors unless the odds are all on their side. Of course they outnumbered the green men, but the great size and strength and the savage ferocity of the latter gave them the advantage over such weak foemen.

"I saw but little of the fight. The contestants paid no attention to me. They were too engrossed with one another; and as I saw the head of a ramp close by, I dodged into it. The last I saw of the engagement revealed Hin Abtol running at the top of his speed back toward the plain with his men trailing behind him and the green men bringing up the rear. For the sublimation of speed, I accord all honors to the Panars. They may not be able to fight, but they can run."

chapter XII

"**KNOWING THAT** the green men would return for their thoats and that I must, therefore, hide, I descended the ramp," Llana went on. "It led into the pits beneath the city. I intended going in only far enough to avoid discovery from above and to have a head start should the green men come down the ramp in search of me; as I knew they might—they would not quickly forego an opportunity to capture a red woman for torture or slavery.

"I had gone down to the end of the ramp and a short distance along a corridor, when I saw a dim light far ahead. I thought this worth investigating, as I did not wish to be taken unexpectedly from behind and, perhaps, caught between two enemies; so I followed the corridor in the direction of the light, which I presently discovered was retreating. However, I continued to follow it, until presently it stopped in a room filled with chests.

"Looking in, I saw a creature of most horrid mein—"

"Lum Tar O," I said. "The creature I killed."

"Yes," said Llana. "I watched him for a moment, not knowing what to do. A lighted torch illuminated the chamber. He carried another in his left hand. Presently he became alert. He seemed to be listening intently; then he crept from the room."

"That must have been when he first heard Pan Dan Chee and me," I suggested.

"I presume so," said Llana of Gathol. "Anyway, I was left alone in the room. If I went back the way I had come, I might run into the arms of a green man. If I followed the horrid creature I had just seen, I would doubtless be in just as bad a fix. If I only had a place to hide until it would be safe to come out of the pits the way I had entered!

"The chests looked inviting. One of them would provide an excellent hiding place. It was just by the merest chance that the first one I opened was empty. I crept into it and lowered the lid above me. The rest you know."

"And now you are coming out of the pits," I said, as we started up a ramp at the top of which I could see daylight.

"In a few moments," said Kam Han Tor, "we shall be looking upon the broad waters of Throxeus."

I shook my head. "Do not be too disappointed," I said.

"Are you and your friend in league to perpetrate a hoax upon me?" demanded Kan Han Tor. "Only yesterday I saw the ships of the fleet lying at anchor off the quay. Do you think me a fool, that you tell me there is no longer any ocean where an ocean was yesterday, where it has been since the creation of Barsoom? Oceans do not disappear overnight, my friend."

There was a murmur of approval from those of the fine company of nobles and their women who were within earshot. They were loath to believe what they did not wish to believe and what, I realized, must have seemed an insult to their intelligence.

Put yourself in their place. Perhaps you live in San Francisco. You go to bed one night. When you awaken, a total stranger tells you that the Pacific Ocean has dried up and that you may walk to Honolulu or Guam or the Philippines. I'm quite sure that you wouldn't believe him.

As we came up into the broad avenue that led to the ancient sea front of Horz, that assembly of gorgeously trapped men and women looked about them in dumfounded astonishment upon the crumbling ruins of their once proud city.

"Where are the people?" demanded one. "Why is the Avenue of Jeddaks deserted?"

"And the palace of the jeddak!" exclaimed another. "There are no guards."

"There is no one!" gasped a woman.

No one commented, as they pushed on eagerly toward the quay. Before they got there they were already straining their eyes out across a barren desert of dead sea bottom where once the waters of Throxeus had rolled.

In silence they continued on to the Avenue of Quays. They simply could not believe the testimony of their own eyes. I cannot recall ever having felt sorrier for any of my fellow men than I did at that moment for these poor people.

"It is gone," said Kam Han Tor in a scarcely audible whisper.

A woman sobbed. A warrior drew his dagger and plunged it into his own heart.

"And all our people are gone," said Kam Han Tor. "Our very world is gone."

They stood there looking out across that desert waste; behind them a dead city that, in their last yesterday, had teemed with life and youth and energy.

And then a strange thing happened. Before my eyes, Kam Han Tor commenced to shrink and crumble. He literally disintegrated, he and the leather of his harness. His weapons clattered to the pavement and lay there in a little pile of dust that had been Kam Han Tor, the brother of a jeddak.

Llana of Gathol pressed close to me and seized my arm. "It is horrible!" she whispered. "Look! Look at the others!"

I looked about me. Singly, in groups of two or three, the men and women of ancient Horz were returning to the dust from which they had sprung—"Earth to earth, ashes to ashes, dust to dust!"

"For all the ages that they have lain in the pits of Horz," said Pan Dan Chee, "this disintegration has been going slowly on. Only Lum Tar O's obscene powers gave them a semblance of life. With that removed final dissolution came quickly."

"That must be the explanation," I said. "It is well that it is so, for these people never could have found happiness in the Barsoom of today—a dying world, so unlike the glorious world of Barsoom in the full flush of her prime, with her five oceans, her great cities, her happy, prosperous peoples, who, if history speaks the truth, had finally overthrown all the war lords and war mongers and established peace from pole to pole."

"No," said Llana of Gathol, "they could never have been happy again. Did you notice what handsome people they were? and the color of their skins was the same as yours, John Carter. But for their blond hair they might have been from your own Earth."

"There are many blond people on Earth," I told her. "Maybe, after all the races of Earth have intermarried for many ages, we shall develop a race of red men, as has Barsoom. Who knows?"

Pan Dan Chee was standing looking adoringly at Llana of Gathol. He was so obvious that it was almost painful, and I could see that it annoyed Llana even while it pleased her.

"Come," I said. "Nothing is to be gained by standing here. My flier is in a courtyard nearby. It will carry three. You will come with me, Pan Dan Chee? I can assure you a welcome in Helium and a post of some nature in the army of the jeddak."

Pan Dan Chee shook his head. "I must go back to the Citadel," he said.

"To Ho Ran Kim and death," I reminded him.

"Yes, to Ho Ran Kim and death," he said.

"Don't be a fool, Pan Dan Chee," I said. "You have acquitted yourself honorably. You cannot kill me, and I know you would not kill Llana of Gathol. We shall go away, carrying the secret of the forgotten people of Horz with us, no matter what you do; but you must know that neither of us would use our knowledge to bring harm to your people. Why then go back to your death uselessly? Come with us."

He looked straight into the eyes of Llana of Gathol. "Is it your wish that I come with you?" he asked.

"If the alternative means your death," she replied; "then it is my wish that you come with us."

A wry smile twisted Pan Dan Chee's lip, but evidently he saw a ray of hope in her noncommittal answer, for he said to me, "I thank you, John Carter. I will go with you. My sword is yours, always."

chapter XIII

I HAD NO DIFFICULTY in locating the courtyard where I had landed and left my flier. As we approached it, I saw a number of dead men lying in the avenue. They were sprawled in the grotesque postures of death. Some of them were split wide open from their crowns to their bellies. "The work of green men," I said.

"These were the men of Hin Abtol," said Llana of Gathol.

We counted seventeen corpses before we reached the entrance to the courtyard. When I looked in, I stopped, appalled—my flier was not there; but five more dead Panars lay near where it had stood.

"It is gone," I said.

"Hin Abtol," said Llana of Gathol. "The coward abandoned his men and fled in your flier. Only two of his warriors succeeded in accompanying him."

"Perhaps he would have been a fool to remain," I said. "He would only have met the same death that they met."

"In like circumstances, John Carter would have been a fool, then," she shot back.

Perhaps I would, for the truth of the matter is that I like to fight. I suppose it is all wrong, but I cannot help it. Fighting has been my profession during all the life that I can recall. I fought all during the Civil War in the Confederate Army. I fought in other wars before that. I will not bore you with my autobiography. Suffice it to say that I have always been fighting. I do not know how old I am. I recall no childhood. I have always appeared to be about thirty years old. I still do. I do not know from whence I came, nor if I were born of woman as are other men. I have, so far as I know, simply always been. Perhaps I am the materialization of some long dead warrior of another age. Who knows? That might explain my ability to cross the cold, dark void of space which separates Earth from Mars. I do not know.

Pan Dan Chee broke the spell of my reverie. "What now?" he asked.

"A long walk," I said. "It is fully four thousand haads from here to Gathol, the nearest friendly city." That would be the equivalent of fifteen hundred miles—a very long walk.

"And only this desert from which to look for subsistence?" asked Pan Dan Chee.

"There will be hills," I told him. "There will be deep little ravines where moisture lingers and things grow which we can eat; but there may be green men, and there will certainly be banths and other beasts of prey. Are you afraid, Pan Dan Chee?"

"Yes," he said, "but only for Llana of Gathol. She is a woman—it is no adventure for a woman. Perhaps she could not survive it."

Llana of Gathol laughed. "You do not know the women of Helium," she said, "and still less one in whose veins flows the blood of Dejah Thoris and John Carter. Perhaps you will learn before we have reached Gathol." She stooped and stripped the harness and weapons of a dead Panar from his corpse and buckled them upon herself. The act was more eloquent than words.

"Now we are three good sword arms," said Pan Dan Chee with a laugh, but we knew that he was not laughing at Llana of Gathol but from admiration of her.

And so we set out, the three of us, on that long trek toward far Gathol—Llana of Gathol and I, of one blood and two worlds, and Pan Dan Chee of still another blood and of an extinct world. We might have seemed ill assorted, but no three people could have been more in harmony with each other—at least at first.

For five days we saw no living thing. We subsisted entirely upon the milk of the mantalia plant, which grows apparently without water, distilling its plentiful supply of milk from the products of the soil, the slight moisture in the air, and the rays of the sun. A single plant of this species will give eight or ten quarts of milk a day. They are scattered across the dead sea bottoms as though by a beneficent Providence, giving both food and drink to man and beast.

My companions might still have died of thirst or starvation had I not been with them, for neither knew that the quite ordinary looking plants which we occasionally passed carried in their stems and branches this life-giving fluid.

We rested in the middle of the day and slept during the middle portion of the nights, taking turns standing guard—a duty which Llana of Gathol insisted on sharing with us.

When we lay down to rest on the sixth night, Llana had the first watch; and as I had the second, I prepared to sleep at once. Pan Dan Chee sat up and talked with Llana.

As I dozed off, I heard him say, "May I call you my princess?"

That, on Barsoom, is the equivalent of a proposal of marriage on

Earth. I tried to shut my ears and go to sleep, but I could not but hear her reply.

"You have not fought for me yet," she said, "and no man may presume to claim a woman of Helium until he has proved his metal."

"I have had no opportunity to fight for you," he said.

"Then wait until you have," she said, shortly; "and now good-night."

I thought she was a little too short with him. Pan Dan Chee is a nice fellow, and I was sure that he would give a good account of himself when the opportunity arose. She didn't have to treat him as though he were scum. But then, women have their own ways. As a rule they are unpleasant ways, but they seem the proper ways to win men; so I suppose they must be all right.

Pan Dan Chee walked off a few paces and lay down on the other side of Llana of Gathol. We always managed to keep her between us at all times for her greater protection.

I was awakened later on by a shout and a hideous roar. I leaped to my feet to see Llana of Gathol down on the ground with a huge banth on top of her, and at that instant Pan Dan Chee leaped full upon the back of the mighty carnivore.

It all happened so quickly that I can scarcely visualize it all. I saw Pan Dan Chee dragging at the great beast in an effort to pull it from Llana's body, and at the same he was plunging his dagger into its side. The banth was roaring hideously as it tried to fight off Pan Dan Chee and at the same time retain its hold upon Llana.

I sprang close in with my short-sword, but it was difficult to find an opening which did not endanger either Llana or Pan Dan Chee. It must have been a very amusing sight; as the four of us were threshing around on the ground, all mixed up, and the banth was roaring and Pan Dan Chee was cursing like a trooper when he wasn't trying to tell Llana of Gathol how much he loved her.

But at last I got an opening, and drove my short-sword into the heart of the banth. With a final scream and a convulsive shudder, the beast rolled over and lay still.

When I tried to lift Llana from the ground, she leaped to her feet. "Pan Dan Chee!" she cried. "Is he all right? Was he hurt?"

"Of course I'm all right," said Pan Dan Chee; "but you? How badly are you hurt?"

"I am not hurt at all. You kept the brute so busy it didn't have a chance to maul me."

"Thanks be to my ancestors!" exclaimed Pan Dan Chee fervently. Suddenly he turned on her. "Now," he said, "I have fought for you. What is your answer?"

Llana of Gathol shrugged her pretty shoulders. "You have not fought a man," she said, "—just a little banth."

Well, I never did understand women.

Part 2

THE BLACK PIRATES OF BARSOOM

chapter I

IN MY FORMER LIFE on Earth I spent more time in the saddle than I did on foot, and since I have been here on the Planet of Barsoom I have spent much time in the saddle or on the swift fliers of the Navy of Helium; so naturally I did not look forward with any great amount of pleasure to walking fifteen hundred miles. However, it had to be done; and when a thing has to be done the best plan is to get at it, stick to it, and get it over with as quickly as possible.

Gathol is southwest of Horz; but, having no compass and no landmarks, I went, as I discovered later, a little too far to the west. Had I not done so we might have been saved some very harrowing experiences. Although, if my past life is any criterion, we would have found plenty of other adventures.

We had covered some two thousand five hundred haads of the four thousand we had to travel, or at least as nearly as I could compute it, with a minimum of untoward incidents. On two occasions we had been attacked by banths but had managed to kill them before they could harm us; and we had been attacked by a band of wild calots, but fortunately we had met no human beings—of all the creatures of Barsoom the most dangerous. For here, outside of your own country or the countries of your allies, every man is your enemy and bent upon destroying you; nor is it strange upon a dying world the natural resources of which have dwindled almost to the vanishing point and even air and water are only barely sufficient to meet the requirements of the present population.

The vast stretches of dead sea bottom, covered with its ocher vegetation, which we traversed were broken only occasionally by low hills. Here in shaded ravines we sometimes found edible roots and tubers. But for the most part we subsisted upon the milk-like sap of the mantalia bush, which grows on the dead sea bottom, though in no great profusion.

We had tried to keep track of the days, and it was on the thirty-seventh day that we encountered really serious trouble. It was the fourth zode, which is roughly about one P.M. Earth time, that we saw in the distance and to our left what I instantly recognized as a caravan of green Martians.

As no fate can be worse than falling into the hands of these cruel monsters, we hurried on in the hope of crossing their path before we were discovered. We took advantage of what cover the sea bottom afforded us, which was very little; oftentimes compelling us to worm our way along on our bellies, an art which I had learned from the Apaches of Arizona. I was in the lead, when I came upon a human skeleton. It was crumbling to dust, an indication that it must have lain there for many years, for so low is the humidity on Mars that disintegration of bony structures is extremely slow. Within fifty yards I came upon another skeleton and after that we saw many of them. It was a gruesome sight, and what it portended I could not guess. At first I thought that perhaps a battle had once been fought here, but when I saw that some of these skeletons were fresh and well preserved and that others had already started to disintegrate I realized that these men had died many years apart.

At last I felt that we had crossed the line of march of the caravan and that as soon as we had found a hiding place we would be comparatively safe, and just then I came to the edge of a yawning chasm.

Except for the Grand Canyon of the Colorado, I had never seen anything like it. It was a great rift valley that appeared to be about ten miles wide and perhaps two miles deep, extending for miles in either direction.

There were outcroppings of rock at the rim of the rift, and behind these we hid. Scattered about us were more human skeletons than we had seen before. Perhaps they were a warning; but at least they could not harm us, and so we turned our attention to the approaching caravan, which had now changed its direction a little and was coming straight toward us. Hoping against hope that they would again change their direction and pass us, we lay there watching them.

When I had been first miraculously transported to Mars I had been captured by a horde of green men, and I had lived with them for a long time; so that I learned to know their customs well. Therefore, I was quite positive that this caravan was making the quinquennial pilgrimage of the horde to its hidden incubator.

Each adult Martian female brings forth about thirteen eggs each year; and those which reach the correct size, weight and specific gravity are hidden in the recesses of some subterranean vault where the temperature is too low for incubation. Every year these eggs are carefully examined by a counsel of twenty chieftains, and all but about one hundred of the most perfect are destroyed out of each yearly supply. At the end of five years about five hundred almost perfect eggs have been chosen from the thousands brought forth. These are then placed in the almost air-tight incubators to be hatched by the sun's rays after a period of another five years.

All but about one per cent of the eggs hatch, and these are left behind when the horde departs from the incubator. If these eggs hatch, the fate of those abandoned little Martians is unknown. They are not wanted, as their offspring might inherit and transmit the tendency to prolonged incubation and thus upset the system which has been maintained for ages and which permits the adult Martians to figure the proper time for return to the incubator almost to an hour.

The incubators are built in remote fastnesses where there is little or no likelihood of their being discovered by other tribes. The result of such a catastrophe would mean no children in the community for another five years.

The green Martians' caravan is a gorgeous and barbaric thing to see. In this one were some two hundred and fifty enormous three wheeled chariots drawn by huge mastodonian animals known as zitidars, any one of which from their appearance might easily have drawn the entire train when fully loaded.

The chariots themselves were large, commodious and gorgeously decorated; in each was seated a female Martian loaded with ornaments of metal, with jewels and silks and furs; and upon the back of each of the zitidars a young Martian driver was perched on top of gorgeous trappings.

At the head of the caravan rode some two hundred warriors, five abreast; and a like number brought up the rear. About twenty-five or thirty out-riders flanked the chariots on either side.

The mounts of the warriors defy description in earthly words. They towered ten feet at the shoulder, had four legs on either side, a broad flat tail, larger at the tip than at the root, which they held straight out behind while running; a gaping mouth which splits the head from the snout to the long, massive neck.

Like their huge masters, they are entirely devoid of hair, but are a dark slate color and are exceedingly smooth and glossy. Their bellies are white and their legs shaded from the slate of the shoulders and hips to a vivid yellow at the feet. The feet themselves are heavily padded and nailless. Like the zitidars they wear neither bit nor bridle, but are guided entirely by telepathic means.

As we watched this truly magnificent and impressive cortege, it changed direction again; and I breathed a sigh of relief as I saw that they were going to pass us. Evidently, from the backs of their lofty mounts, they had seen the rift and were now moving parallel with it.

My relief was to be short-lived, for as the rear of the caravan was about to pass us one of the flankers spied us.

chapter II

INSTANTLY THE FELLOW wheeled his thoat and, shouting to his companions, came galloping toward us. We sprang to our feet with drawn swords, expecting to die; but ready to sell our lives dearly.

A moment after we had gained our feet, Llana exclaimed, "Look! Here is a trail down into the valley."

I looked around. Sure enough, now that we were standing erect, I could see the head of a narrow, precipitous trail leading down over the edge of the cliff. If we could but reach it, we would be safe, for the great thoats and zitidars of the green men could not possibly negotiate it. It was very possible that the green men were not even aware of the presence of the rift before they had come suddenly upon it, and this is entirely possible; because they build their incubators in uninhabited and unexplored wildernesses sometimes as much as a thousand miles from their own stamping grounds.

As the three of us, Llana, Pan Dan Chee, and I, ran for the trail, I glanced over my shoulder and saw that the leading warrior was almost on top of us and that we could not all reach the trail. So I called to Pan Dan Chee to hurry down it with Llana. They both stopped and turned toward me.

"It is a command," I told them. Reluctantly they turned and continued on toward the end of the trail, while I wheeled and faced the warrior.

He had stopped his thoat and dismounted, evidently intent upon capturing me rather than killing me; but I had no mind to be captured for torture and eventual death. It was far better to die now.

He drew his long-sword as he came toward me and I did likewise. Had there not been six of his fellows galloping up on their huge thoats I should not have worried greatly, for with a sword I am a match for any green Martian that was ever hatched. Even their great size gives them no advantage. Perhaps it handicaps them, for their movements are slow and ponderous by comparison with my earthly agility; and though they are twice my size, I am fully as strong as they. The muscles of earthly man have not contended with the force of gravity since the dawn of humanity for nothing. It has developed and hardened muscles; because every move we make is contested by gravity.

My antagonist was so terribly cock-sure of himself, when facing such a seemingly puny creature as I, that he left himself wide open, as he charged down upon me like a wild bull.

I saw by the way he held his sword that he intended to strike me on the head with the flat of it, rendering me unconscious, so that he could more easily capture me; but when the sword fell I was not there; I had stepped to the right out of his way, and simultaneously I thrust for his heart. I would have punctured it, too, had not one of his four arms happened to swing against the point of my blade before it reached his body. As it was, I gave him a severe wound; and, roaring with rage, he turned and came at me again.

This time he was more careful; but it made no difference; he was doomed, for he was testing his skill against the best swordsman of two worlds.

The other six warriors were almost upon me now. This was no time for the sport of fencing. I feinted once, and ran him through the heart. Then, seeing that Llana was safe, I turned and ran along the edge of the rift; and the six green warriors did just what I had expected them to do. They had probably detached themselves from the rear guard for the sport of catching a red man for torture or for their savage games. Bunched close together they came after me, the nailless, padded feet of their ponderous mounts making no sound upon the ocher, moss-like vegetation of the dead sea bottom. Their spears couched, they came for me, each trying to make the kill or the capture. I felt much as a fox must feel at a fox hunt.

Suddenly I stopped, turned, and ran toward them. They must have thought that I had gone mad with fear, for they certainly couldn't have known what I had in mind and that I had run from them merely to lure them away from the head of the trail leading down into the valley. They were almost upon me when I leaped high into the air and completely over them. My great strength and agility and the lesser gravity of Mars had once again come to my aid in an emergency.

When I alighted, I dashed for the head of the trail. And when the warriors could stop their mounts they turned and raced after me, but they were too late. I can out-run any thoat that was ever foaled. The only trouble with me is that I am too proud to run; but, like the fellow that was too proud to fight, I sometimes have to, as in this case where the safety of others was at stake.

I reached the head of the trail in plenty of time and hurried down after Llana and Pan Dan Chee, whom I found waiting for me when I caught up with them.

As we descended, I looked up and saw the green warriors at the edge of the rift looking at us; and, guessing what would happen, I dragged Llana into the shelter of an overhanging ledge. Pan Dan Chee followed just as radium bullets commenced to explode close to us.

The rifles with which the green men of Mars are armed are of a white metal, stocked with wood; a very light and intensely hard growth much prized on Mars and entirely unknown to us denizens of Earth. The metal of the barrel is an alloy composed principally of aluminum and steel, which they have learned to temper to a hardness far exceeding that of the steel with which we are familiar. The weight of these rifles is comparatively little; and with the small caliber, explosive radium projectiles which they use and the great length of the barrel, they are deadly in the extreme and at ranges which would be unthinkable on Earth.

The projectiles which they use explode when they strike an object, for they have an opaque outer coating which is broken by the impact, exposing a glass cylinder, almost solid, in the forward end of which is a minute particle of radium powder.

(Editor's Note) I have used the word radium in describing this powder because in the light of recent discoveries on Earth I believe it to be a mixture of which radium is the base. In Captain Carter's manuscripts it is mentioned always by the name used in the written language of Helium and is spelled in hieroglyphics which it would be difficult and useless to reproduce.

The moment the sunlight, even though diffused, strikes this powder it explodes with a violence which nothing can withstand. In night battles one notices the absence of these explosions, while the following morning will be filled at sunrise with the sharp detonations of exploding missiles fired the preceding night. As a rule, however, non-exploding projectiles are used after dark.

I felt it safer to remain where we were rather than to expose ourselves by attempting to descend, as I doubted very much that the huge green warriors would follow us down that steep declivity on foot, for the trail was too narrow for their great bodies and they hate going anywhere on foot.

After a few minutes I investigated and found that they apparently had departed. Then we started on down into the valley, not wishing to risk another encounter with that great horde of cruel and ruthless creatures.

chapter III

THE TRAIL WAS STEEP and oftentimes dangerous for it zigzagged down the face of an almost perpendicular cliff. Occasionally on a ledge we would have to step over the skeleton of a man, and we passed three newly dead bodies in various stages of decomposition.

"What do you make of these skeletons and bodies?" asked Pan Dan Chee.

"I am puzzled," I replied; "there must be a great many more who died on the trail than those whose remains we have seen here. You will note that these all lie on ledges where the bodies could have lodged when they fell. Many more must have pitched to the foot of the cliff."

"But how do you suppose they met their death?" asked Llana.

"There might have been an epidemic of disease in the valley," suggested Pan Dan Chee, "and these poor devils died while trying to escape."

"I am sure I haven't the slightest idea of what the explanation can be," I replied. "You see the remains of harness on most of them, but no weapons. I am inclined to think that Pan Dan Chee is right in assuming that they were trying to escape, but whether from an epidemic of sickness or something else we may never know."

From our dizzy footing on that precarious trail we had an excellent view of the valley below. It was level and well watered and the monotony of the scarlet grass which grows on Mars where there is water, was broken by forests, the whole making an amazing sight for one familiar with this dying planet.

There are crops and trees and other vegetation along the canals; there are lawns and gardens in the cities where irrigation is available; but never have I seen a sight like this except in the Valley Dor at the South Pole, where lies the Lost Sea of Korus. For here there was not only a vast expanse of fertile valley but there were rivers and at least one lake which I could see in the distance; and then Llana called our attention to a city, gleaming white, with lofty towers.

"What a beautiful city," she said. "I wonder what sort of people live there?"

"Probably somebody who would love nothing better than to slit our throats," I said.

"We Orovars are not like that," said Pan Dan Chee, "we hate to kill people. Why do all the other races on Mars hate each other so?"

"I don't think that it is hate that makes them want to kill each other," I said. "It is that it has become a custom. Since the drying up of the seas ages ago, survival has become more and more difficult; and in all those ages they have become so accustomed to battling for existence that now it has become second nature to kill all aliens."

"I'd still like to see the inside of that city," said Llana of Gathol.

"Your curiosity will probably never be satisfied," I said.

We stood for some time on a ledge looking down upon that beautiful valley, probably one of the most beautiful sights on all of Mars. We saw several herds of the small thoats used by the red Martians as riding animals and for food. There is a little difference in the saddle and butchering species, but at this distance we could not tell which these were. We saw game animals down there, too, and we who had been so long without good meat were tempted.

"Let's go down," said Llana; "we haven't seen any human beings and we don't need to go near the city; it is a long way off. I should like so much to see the beauties of that valley closer."

"And I would like to get some good red meat," I said.

"And I, too," said Pan Dan Chee.

"My better judgment tells me it would be a foolish thing to do," I said, "but if I had followed my better judgment always, my life would have been a very dull one."

"Anyway," said Llana, "we don't know that it is any more dangerous down on the floor of the valley than it was up on the edge of the rim. We certainly barely missed a lot of trouble up there, and it may still be hanging around."

I didn't think so; although I have known green Martians to hunt a couple of red men for days at a time. Anyway, the outcome of our discussion was that we continued on down to the floor of the valley.

Around the foot of the cliff, where the trail ended, there was a jumble of human bones and a couple of badly mangled bodies—poor devils who had either died on the trail above or fallen to their death here at the bottom. I wondered how and why.

Fortunately for us, the city was at such a distance that I was sure that no one could have seen us from there; and, knowing Martian customs, we had no intention of approaching it; nor would we have particularly cared to had it been safe, for the floor of the valley was so entrancingly beautiful in its natural state that the sights and sounds of a city would have proved a discordant note.

A short distance from us was a little river; and, beyond it, a forest came down to its edge. We crossed to the river on the scarlet sward, close-cropped by grazing herds and starred by many flowers of unearthly beauty.

A short distance down the river a herd of thoats was grazing. They were the beef variety, which is exceptionally good eating; and Pan Dan Chee suggested that we cross the river so that he could take advantage of the concealment of the forest to approach close enough to make a kill.

The river was simply alive with fish, and as we waded across I speared several with my long-sword.

"At least we shall have fish for dinner," I said, "and if Pan Dan Chee is lucky, we shall have a steak."

"And in the forest I see fruits and nuts," said Llana. "What a banquet we shall have!"

"Wish me luck," said Pan Dan Chee, as he entered the forest to work his way down toward the thoats.

Llana and I were watching, but we did not see the young Orovaran again until he leaped from the forest and hurled something at the nearest thoat, a young bull. The beast screamed, ran a few feet, staggered and fell, while the rest of the herd galloped off.

"How did he do that?" asked Llana.

"I don't know," I said, "he did it so quickly that I couldn't see what it was he threw. It was certainly not a spear because he hasn't one, and if it had been his sword we could have seen it."

"It looked like a little stick," said Llana.

We saw Pan Dan Chee cutting steaks from his kill; and presently he was back with us, carrying enough meat for a dozen men.

"How did you kill that thoat?" demanded Llana.

"With my dagger," replied Pan Dan Chee.

"It was marvellous," I said, "but where did you learn it?"

"Dagger throwing is a form of sport in Horz. We are all good at it, but I happen to have won the Jeddak's trophy for the last three years; so I was pretty sure of my ground when I offered to get you a thoat, although I had never before used it to kill game. Very, very rarely is there a duel in Horz; and when there is, the contestants usually choose daggers, unless one of them is far more proficient than the other."

While Pan Dan Chee and I were making fire and cooking the fish and steaks, Llana gathered fruits and nuts; so that we had a delicious meal, and when night came we lay down on the soft sward and slept.

chapter IV

WE SLEPT LATE, for we had been very tired the night before. I speared some fresh fish, and we had fish and steaks and fruit and nuts again for breakfast. Then we started toward the trail that leads out of the valley.

"It is going to be an awful climb," said Pan Dan Chee.

"Oh, I wish we didn't have to make it," said Llana; "I hate to leave this beautiful spot."

My attention was suddenly attracted toward the lower end of the valley.

"Maybe you won't have to leave it, Llana," I said. "Look!"

Both she and Pan Dan Chee turned and looked in the direction I had indicated, to see two hundred warriors mounted on thoats. The men were ebony black, and I wondered if they could be the notorious Black Pirates of Barsoom that I had first met and fought many years ago at the South Pole—the people who called themselves the First Born.

They galloped up and surrounded us; their spears couched, ready for any emergency.

"Who are you?" demanded their leader. "What are you doing in the Valley of the First Born?"

"We came down the trail to avoid a horde of green men," I replied. "We were just leaving. We came in peace; we do not want war, but we are still three swords ready to give a good account of ourselves."

"You will have to come to Kamtol with us," said the leader.

"The city?" I asked. He nodded.

I whipped my sword from its scabbard.

"Stop!" he said. "We are two hundred; you are three. If you come to the city there would be at least a chance that you won't be killed; if you stay here and fight you will be killed."

I shrugged. "It is immaterial to me," I said. "Llana of Gathol wishes to see the city, and I would just as leave fight. Pan Dan Chee, what do you and Llana say?"

"I would like to see the city," said Llana, "but I will fight if you fight. Perhaps," she added, "they will not be unkind to us."

"You will have to give up your arms," said the leader.

I didn't like that and I hesitated.

"It is that or death," said the leader. "Come! I can't stand here all day."

Well, resistance was futile; and it seemed foolish to sacrifice our lives if there were the remotest hope that we might be well received in Kamtol, and so we were taken on the backs of three thoats behind their riders and started for the beautiful white city.

The ride to the city was uneventful, but it gave me an excellent opportunity to examine our captors more closely. They were unquestionably of the same race as Xodar, Dator of the First Born of Barsoom, to give him his full title, who had been first my enemy and then my friend during my strange adventures among the Holy Therns. They are an exceptionally handsome race, clean-limbed and powerful, with intelligent faces and features of such exquisite chiseling that Adonis himself might have envied them. I am a Virginian; and it may seem strange for me to say so, but their black skins, resembling polished ebony, add greatly to their beauty. The harness and metal of our captors was identical with that worn by the Black Pirates whose acquaintance I had made upon the Golden Cliffs above the Valley Dor.

My admiration of these people did not blind me to the fact that they are a cruel and ruthless race and that our life expectancy was reduced to a minimum by our capture.

Kamtol did not belie its promise. It was as beautiful on closer inspection as it had been at a distance. Its pure white outer wall is elaborately carved, as are the facades on many of its buildings. Graceful towers rise above its broad avenues, which, when we entered the city, were filled with people. Among the blacks, we saw a number of red men performing menial tasks. It was evident that they were slaves, and their presence suggested the fate which might await us.

I cannot say that I looked forward with any great amount of enthusiasm to the possibility that John Carter, Prince of Helium, Warlord of Mars, might become a street cleaner or a garbage collector. One thing that I noticed particularly in Kamtol was that the residences could not be raised on cylindrical columns, as is the case in most modern Martian cities, where assassination has been developed to a fine art and where assassins' guilds flourish openly, and their members swagger through the streets like gangsters once did in Chicago.

Heavily guarded, we were taken to a large building and there we were separated. I was taken to an apartment and seated in a chair with my back toward a strange looking machine, the face of which was covered with innumerable dials. A number of heavily insulated cables ran from various parts of the apparatus; metal bands at the ends of these cables were clamped about my wrists, my ankles, and my neck, the latter clamp pressing against the base of my skull; then something like a strait-jacket was buckled tightly around me, and I had a sensation as of countless needles touching my spine for almost its full length. I thought that I was to be electrocuted, but it seemed to me that they took a great deal of unnecessary pains to destroy me. A simple sword thrust would have done it much more quickly.

An officer, who was evidently in charge of the proceedings, came and stood in front of me. "You are about to be examined," he said, "you will answer all questions truthfully;" then he signalled to an attendant who threw a switch on the apparatus.

So I was not to be electrocuted, but examined. For what, I could not imagine. I felt a very gentle tingling throughout my entire body, and then they commenced to hurl questions at me.

There were six men. Sometimes they questioned me singly and sometimes all at once. At such times, of course, I could not answer very intelligently because I could not hear the questions fully. Sometimes they spoke soothingly to me, and again they shouted at me angrily; often they heaped insults upon me. They let me rest for a few moments, and then a slave entered the apartment with a tray of very tempting food which he offered to me. As I was about to take it, it was snatched away; and my tormentors laughed at me. They jabbed me with sharp instruments until the blood flowed, and then they rubbed the wounds with a burning caustic, after which they applied a salve that instantly relieved the pain. Again I rested and again food was offered me. When I made no move to attempt to take it, they insisted; and, much to my surprise, let me eat it.

By this time I had come to the conclusion that we had been captured by a race of sadistic maniacs, and what happened next assured me that I was right, My torturers all left the apartment. I sat there for several minutes wondering at the whole procedure and why they couldn't have tortured me without attaching me to that amazing contraption. I was facing a door in the opposite wall, and suddenly the door flew open and a huge banth leaped into the room with a horrid roar.

This, I thought, is the end, as the great carnivore came racing at me. As suddenly as he had entered the room, he came to a stop a few feet from me, and so instantly that he was thrown to the floor at my feet. It was then that I saw that he was secured by a chain just a little too short to permit him to reach me. I had had all the sensations of impending death—a most refined form of torture. However, if that had been their purpose they had failed, for I do not fear death.

The banth was dragged out of the apartment by his chain and the door closed; then the examining board re-entered smiling at me in the most kindly way.

"That is all," said the officer in charge; "the examination is over."

chapter V

AFTER THE PARAPHERNALIA had been removed from me, I was turned over to my guard and taken to the pits, such as are to be found in every Martian city, ancient or modern. These labyrinthine corridors and chambers are used for storage purposes and for the incarceration of prisoners, their only other tenants being the repulsive ulsio.

I was chained to the wall in a large cell in which there was another prisoner, a red Martian; and it was not long until Llana of Gathol and Pan Dan Chee were brought in and chained near me.

"I see you survived the examination," I said.

"What in the world do they expect to learn from such an examination as that?" demanded Llana. "It was stupid and silly."

"Perhaps they wanted to find out if they could scare us to death," suggested Pan Dan Chee.

"I wonder how long they will keep us in these pits," said Llana.

"I have been here a year," said the red man. "Occasionally I have been taken out and put to work with other slaves belonging to the jeddak, but until someone buys me I shall remain here."

"Buys you! What do you mean?" asked Pan Dan Chee.

"All prisoners belong to the jeddak," replied the red man, "but his nobles or officers may buy them if they wish another slave. I think he is holding me at too high a price, for a number of nobles have looked at me and said that they would like to have me."

He was silent for a moment and then he said, "You will pardon my curiosity, but two of you do not look like Barsoomians at all, and I am wondering from what part of the world you come. Only the woman is typical of Barsoom; both you men have white skin and one of you black hair and the other yellow."

"You have heard of the Orovars?" I asked.

"Certainly," he replied, "but they have been extinct for ages."

"Nevertheless, Pan Dan Chee here is an Orovar. There is a small colony of them that has survived in a deserted Orovar city."

"And you?" he asked; "you are no Orovar, with that black hair."

"No," I said, "I am from another world—Jasoom."

"Oh," he exclaimed, "can it be that you are John Carter?"

"Yes; and you?"

"My name is Jad-han. I am from Amhor."

"Amhor?" I said. "I know a girl from Amhor. Her name is Janai."

"What do you know of Janai?" he demanded.

"You knew her?" I asked.

"She was my sister; she has been dead for years. While I was out of the country on a long trip, Jal Had, Prince of Amhor, employed Gantum Gur, the assassin, to kill my father because he objected to Jal Had as a suitor for Janai's hand. When I returned to Amhor, Janai had fled; and later I learned of her death. In order to escape assassination myself, I was forced to leave the city; and after wandering about for some time I was captured by the First Born. But tell me, what did you know of Janai?"

"I know that she is not dead," I replied. "She is mated with one of my most trusted officers and is safe in Helium."

Jad-han was overcome with happiness when he learned that his sister still lived. "Now," he said, "if I could escape from here and return to Amhor to avenge my father, I would die happy."

"Your father has been avenged," I told him. "Jal Had is dead."

"I am sorry that it was not given to me to kill him," said Jad-han.

"You have been here a year," I said, "and you must know something of the customs of the people. Can you tell us what fate may lie in store for us?"

"There are several possibilities," he replied. "You may be worked as slaves, in which event you will be treated badly, but may be permitted to live for years; or you may be saved solely for the games which are held in a great stadium. There you will fight with men or beasts for the edification of the First Born. On the other hand, you may be summarily executed at any moment. All depends upon the mental vagaries of Doxus, Jeddak of The First Born, who I think is a little mad."

"If the silly examination they gave us is any criterion," said Llana, "they are all mad."

"Don't be too sure of that," Jad-han advised. "If you realized the purpose of that examination, you would understand that it was never devised by any unsound mind. Did you see the dead men as you entered the valley?"

"Yes, but what have they to do with the examination?"

"They took that same examination; that is why they lie dead out there."

"I do not understand," I said. "Please explain."

"The machines to which you were connected recorded hundreds of your reflexes; and automatically recorded your own individual nerve index, which is unlike that of any other creature in the world.

"The master machine, which you did not see and never will, generates short wave vibrations which can be keyed exactly to your individual nerve index. When that is done you have such a severe paralytic stroke that you die almost instantly."

"But why all that just to destroy a few slaves?" demanded Pan Dan Chee.

"It is not for that alone," explained Jad-han. "Perhaps that was one of the initial purposes to prevent prisoners from escaping and spreading word of this beautiful valley on a dying planet. You can imagine that almost any country would wish to possess it. But it has another purpose; it keeps Doxus supreme. Every adult in the valley has had his nerve index recorded, and is at the mercy of his jeddak. You don't have to leave the valley to be exterminated. An enemy of the jeddak might be sitting in his own home some day, when the thing would find him out and destroy him. Doxus is the only adult in Kamtol whose index has not been recorded; and he and one other man, Myr-lo, are the only ones who know exactly where the master machine is located, or how to operate it. It is said to be very delicate and that it can be irreparably damaged in an instant—and can never be replaced."

"Why couldn't it be replaced?" asked Llana.

"The inventor of it is dead," replied Jad-han. "It is said that he hated Doxus because of the purpose to which the jeddak had put his invention and that Doxus had him assassinated through fear of him. Myr-lo, who succeeded him, has not the genius to design another such machine."

chapter VI

THAT NIGHT, after Llana had fallen asleep, Jad-han, Pan Dan Chee, and I were conversing in whispers; so as not to disturb her.

"It is too bad," said Jad-han, who had been looking at the sleeping girl; "it is too bad that she is so beautiful."

"What do you mean?" asked Pan Dan Chee.

"This afternoon you asked me what your fate might be; and I told you what the possibilities might be, but those were the possibilities for you two men. For the girl—" He looked sorrowfully at Llana and shook his head; he did not need to say more.

The next day a number of the First Born came down into our cell to examine us, as one might examine cattle that one purposed buying. Among them was one of the jeddak's officers, upon whom developed the duty of selling prisoners into slavery for the highest amounts he could obtain.

One of the nobles immediately took a fancy to Llana and made an offer for her. They haggled over the price for some time, but in the end the noble got her.

Pan Dan Chee and I were grief-stricken as they led Llana of Gathol away, for we knew that we should never see her again. Although her father is Jed of Gathol, in her veins flows the blood of Helium; and the women of Helium know how to act when an unkind Providence reserves for them the fate for which we knew Llana of Gathol was intended.

"Oh! to be chained to a wall and without a sword when a thing like this happens," exclaimed Pan Dan Chee.

"I know how you feel," I said; "but we are not dead yet, Pan Dan Chee; and our chance may come yet."

"If it does, we will make them pay," he said.

Two nobles were bidding for me, and at last I was knocked down to a dator named Xaxak. My fetters were removed, and the jeddak's agent warned me to be a good and docile slave.

Xaxak had a couple of warriors with him, and they walked on either side of me as we left the pits. I was the object of considerable curiosity, as we made our way toward Xaxak's palace, which stood near that of the jeddak. My white skin and grey eyes always arouse comment in cities where I am not known. Of course, I am bronzed by exposure to the sun, but even so my skin is not the copper red of the red men of Barsoom.

Before I was to be taken to the slaves' quarters of the palace, Xaxak questioned me. "What is your name?" he asked.

"Dotar Sojat," I replied. It is the name given me by the green Martians who captured me when I first came to Mars, being the names of the first two green Martians I had killed in duels; and is in the nature of an honorable title. A man with one name, an o-mad, is not considered very highly. I was always glad that they stopped with two names, for had I had to assume the name of every green Martian warrior I had killed in a duel it would have taken an hour to pronounce them all.

"Did you say dator?" asked Xaxak. "Don't tell me that you are a prince!"

"I said Dotar," I replied. I hadn't given my real name; because I had reason to believe that it was well known to the First Born, who had good reason to hate me for what I had done to them in the Valley Dor.

"Where are you from?" he asked.

"I have no country," I said; "I am a panthan."

As these soldiers of fortune have no fixed abode, wandering about from city to city offering their services and their swords to whomever will employ them, they are the only men who can go with impunity into almost any Martian city.

"Oh, a panthan," he said. "I suppose you think you are pretty good with a sword."

"I have met worse," I replied.

"If I thought you were any good, I would enter you in the lesser games," he said; "but you cost me a lot of money, and I'd hate to take the chance of your being killed."

"I don't think you need worry about that," I told him.

"You are pretty sure of yourself," he said. "Well, let's see what you can do. Take him out into the garden," he directed the two warriors. Xaxak followed us out to an open patch of sand.

"Give him your sword," he said to one of the warriors; and, to the other, "Engage him, Ptang; but not to the death;" then he turned to me. "It is not to the death, slave, you understand. I merely wish to see how good you are. Either one of you may draw blood, but don't kill."

Ptang, like all the other Black Pirates of Barsoom whom I have met, was an excellent swordsman—cool, quick, and deadly. He came toward me with a faint, supercilious smile on his lips.

"It is scarcely fair, my prince," he said to Xaxak, "to pit him against one of the best swordsmen in Kamtol."

"That is the only way in which I can tell whether he is any good at all, or not," replied Xaxak. "If he extends you, he will certainly be good enough to enter in the Lesser Games. He might even win his price back for me."

"We shall see," said Ptang, crossing swords with me.

Before he realized what was happening, I had pricked him in the shoulder. He looked very much surprised, and the smile left his lips.

"An accident," he said; "it will not occur again;" and then I pinked him in the other shoulder. Now, he made a fatal mistake; he became angry. While anger may stiffen a man's offense, it weakens his defense. I have seen it happen a thousand times, and when I am anxious to dispatch an antagonist quickly I always try to make him angry.

"Come, come! Ptang," said Xaxak; "can't you make a better showing than that against a slave?"

With that, Ptang came for me with blood in his eye, and I didn't see anything there that looked like a desire to pink—Ptang was out to kill me.

"Ptang!" snapped Xaxak; "don't kill him."

At that, I laughed; and drew blood from Ptang's breast. "Have you no real swordsmen in Kamtol?" I asked, tauntingly.

Xaxak and his other warrior were very quiet. I caught glimpses of their faces occasionally, and they looked a bit glum. Ptang was furious, and now he came for me like a mad bull with a cut that would have lopped off my head had it connected. However, it didn't connect; and I ran him through the muscles of his left arm.

"Hadn't we better stop," I asked Xaxak, "before your man bleeds to death?"

Xaxak did not reply; but I was getting bored with the whole affair and wanted to end it; so I drew Ptang into a lunge and sent his sword flying across the garden.

"Is that enough now?" I asked.

Xaxak nodded. "Yes," he said, "that is enough."

Ptang was one of the most surprised and crestfallen men I have ever seen. He just stood there staring at me, making no move to retrieve his blade. I felt very sorry for him.

"You have nothing to be ashamed of, Ptang," I told him. "You are a splendid swordsman, but what I did to you I can do to any man in Kamtol."

"I believe it," he said. "You may be a slave, but I am proud to have crossed swords with you. The world has never seen a better swordsman."

"I am convinced of that," said Xaxak, "and I can see where you are going to make a lot of money for me, Dotar Sojat."

chapter VII

XAXAK TREATED ME much as a wealthy horse owner on Earth would treat a prospective Derby winner. I was quartered in the barracks of his personal guard, where I was treated as an equal. He detailed Ptang to see that I had the proper amount of exercise and sword play; and also, I presume, to see that I did not try to escape. And now my only concern was the fate of Llana of Gathol and Pan Dan Chee, of whose whereabouts and state I was totally ignorant.

Somewhat of a friendship developed between Ptang and myself. He admired my swordsmanship, and used to brag about it to the other warriors. At first they had been inclined to criticize and ridicule him because he had been bested by a slave; so I suggested that he offer to let his critics see if they could do any better with me.

"I can't do that," he said, "without Xaxak's permission; for if anything happened to you, I should be held responsible."

"Nothing will happen to me," I told him; "no one should know that better than you."

He smiled a bit ruefully. "You are right," he said, "but still I must ask Xaxak;" and this he did the next time that he saw the dator.

In order to win Ptang's greater friendship, I had been teaching him some of the finer points of swordsmanship which I had learned in two worlds and in a thousand duels and battles; but by no means did I teach him all of my tricks, nor could I impart to him the strength and agility which my earthly muscles give me on Mars.

Xaxak was watching us at swordplay when Ptang asked him if I might take on some of his critics. Xaxak shook his head. "I am afraid that Dotar Sojat might be injured," he said.

"I will guarantee that I shall not be," I told him.

"Well," he said; "then I am afraid that you may kill some of my warriors."

"I promise not to. I will simply show them that they cannot last as long as Ptang did."

"It might be good sport," said Xaxak. "Who are those who criticized you, Ptang?"

Ptang gave him the names of five warriors who had been particularly venomous in their ridicule and criticism, and Xaxak immediately sent for them.

"I understand," said Xaxak, when they had assembled, "that you have condemned Ptang because he was bested in a duel with this slave. Do any of you think that you could do better than Ptang did? If so, here is your chance."

They assured him, almost in chorus, that they could do very much better.

"We shall see," he said, "but you must all understand that no one is to be killed and that you are to stop when I give the word. It is an order."

They assured him that they would not kill me, and then the first of them swaggered out to meet me. One after another, in rapid succession, I pinked each in the right shoulder and disarmed him.

I must say they took it very decently; all except one of them—a fellow named Ban-tor, who had been Ptang's most violent critic.

"He tricked me," he grumbled. "Let me at him again, my dator; and I will kill him." He was so angry that his voice trembled.

"No," said Xaxak; "he has drawn your blood and he has disarmed you, demonstrating that he is the better swordsman. If it were due to a trick, it was a trick of swordsmanship which you might do well to master before you attempt to kill Dotar Sojat."

The fellow was still scowling and grumbling as he walked away with the other four; and I realized that while all of these First Born were my nominal enemies, this fellow, Ban-tor, was an active one. However, I gave the matter little thought as I was too valuable to Xaxak for anybody to risk his displeasure by harming me; nor could I see that there was any way in which the fellow could injure me.

"Ban-tor has always disliked me," said Ptang, after they had all left us. "He dislikes me; because I have always bested him in swordsmanship and feats of strength; and, in addition to this, he is a natural born trouble maker. If it were not for the fact that he is related to Xaxak's wife, the dator would not have him around."

Since I have already compared myself to a prospective Derby winner, I might as well carry out the analogy by describing their Lesser Games as minor race meets. They are held about once a week in a stadium inside the city, and here the rich nobles pit their warriors or their slaves against those of other nobles in feats of strength, in boxing, in wrestling, and in dueling. Large sums of money are wagered, and the excitement runs high. The duels are not always to the death, the nobles deciding beforehand precisely upon what they will place their bets. Usually it is for first blood or disarming; but there is always at least one duel to the death, which might be compared to the feature race of a race meet, or the main event of a boxing tournament.

Kamtol has a population of about two hundred thousand, of which possibly five thousand are slaves. As I was allowed considerable freedom, I got around the city quite a bit; though Ptang always accompanied me, and I was so impressed with the scarcity of children that I asked Ptang what accounted for it.

"The Valley of the First Born will only comfortably support about two hundred thousand population," he replied; "so only sufficient children are permitted to replace the death losses. As you may have guessed, by looking at our people, the old and otherwise unfit are destroyed; so that we have about sixty-five thousand fighting men and about twice as many healthy women and children. There are two factions here, one of which maintains that the number of women should be greatly decreased; so that the number of fighting men may be increased, while the other faction insists that, as we are not menaced by any powerful enemies, sixty-five thousand fighting men are sufficient.

"Strange as it may seem, most of the women belong to the first faction; notwithstanding the fact that this faction which believes in decreasing the number of females would do so by permitting a far greater number of eggs to incubate, killing all the females which hatched and as many of the adult women as there were males in the hatching. This is probably due to the fact that each woman thinks that she is too desirable to be destroyed and that that fate will fall to some other woman. Doxus believes in maintaining the *status quo*; but some future jeddak may believe differently; and even Doxus may change his mind, which, confidentially, is most vacillating."

My fame as a swordsman soon spread among the sixty-five thousand fighting men of Kamtol, and opinion was most unevenly divided as to my ability. Perhaps a dozen men of Kamtol had seen my swordplay; and they were willing to back me against anyone; but all the remainder of the sixty-five thousand felt that they could best me in individual combat; for this is a race of fighting men, all extremely proud of their skill and their valor.

I was exercising in the garden with Ptang one day, when Xaxak came with another dator, whom he called Nastor. When Ptang saw them coming, he whistled. "I never saw Nastor here before," he said in a low tone of voice. "Xaxak has no use for him, and he hates Xaxak. Wait!" he exclaimed; "I have an idea why he is here. If they ask for swordplay, let me disarm you. I will tell you why, later."

"Very well," I said, "and I hope it will do you some good."

"It is not for me," he said; "it is for Dator Xaxak."

As the two approached us, I heard Nastor say, "So this is your great swordsman! I should like to wager that I have men who could best him any day."

"You have excellent men," said Xaxak; "still, I think my man would give a good account of himself. How much of a wager do you want to lay?"

"You have seen my men fight," said Nastor, "but I have never seen this fellow at work. I would like to see him in action; then I shall know whether to ask or give odds."

"Very well," said Xaxak, "that is fair enough," then he turned to us. "You will give the Dator Nastor an exhibition of your swordsmanship, Dotar Sojat; but not to the death—you understand?"

Ptang and I drew our swords and faced one another. "Don't forget what I asked of you," he said, and then we were at it.

I not only remembered what he had asked, but I now realized why he had asked it; and so I put up an exhibition of quite ordinary swordsmanship, just good enough to hold my own until I let Ptang disarm me.

"He is an excellent swordsman," said Nastor, knowing that he was lying, but not knowing that we knew it; "but I will bet even money that my man can kill him."

"You mean a duel to the death?" demanded Xaxak. "Then I shall demand odds; as I did not desire my man to fight to the death the first time he fought."

"I will give you two to one," said Nastor; "are those odds satisfactory?"

"Perfectly," said Xaxak. "How much do you wish to wager?"

"A thousand tanpi to your five hundred," replied Nastor. A tanpi is equivalent to about $1 in United States money.

"I want to make more than enough to feed my wife's sorak," replied Xaxak.

Now, a sorak is a little six-legged, cat-like animal, kept as a pet by many Martian women; so what Xaxak had said was equivalent to telling Nastor that we didn't care to fight for chicken feed. I could see that Xaxak was trying to anger Nastor; so that he would bet recklessly, and I knew then that he must have guessed that Ptang and I were putting on a show when I let Ptang disarm me so easily.

Nastor was scowling angrily. "I did not wish to rob you," he said; "but if you wish to throw your money away, you may name the amount of the wager."

"Just to make it interesting," said Xaxak, "I'll bet you fifty thousand tanpi against your hundred thousand."

This staggered Nastor for a moment; but he must have got to thinking how easily Ptang had disarmed me, for eventually he rose to the bait. "Done!" he said; "and I am sorry for both you and your man," with which polite hypocrisy he turned on his heel and left without another word.

Xaxak looked after him with a half smile on his lips; and when he had gone, turned to us. "I hope you were just playing a little game," he said, "for if you were not you may have lost me fifty thousand tanpi."

"You need not worry, my prince," said Ptang.

"I shall not worry unless Dotar Sojat worries," replied the dator.

"There is always a gamble in such an enterprise as this," I replied; "but I think that you got very much the best of the bargain, for the odds should have been the other way."

"At least you have more faith than I have," said Xaxak the dator.

chapter VIII

PTANG TOLD ME that he had never known more interest to be displayed in a duel to the death than followed the announcement of the wager between Xaxak and Nastor. "No common warrior is to represent Nastor," he said. "He has persuaded a dator to fight for him, a man who is considered the best swordsman in Kamtol. His name is Nolat. I have never before known of a prince fighting a slave; but they say that Nolat owes Nastor a great deal of money and that Nastor will cancel the debt if Nolat wins, which Nolat is sure that he will—he is so sure that he has pledged his palace to raise money to bet upon himself."

"Not such a stupid thing for him to do, after all," I said; "for if he loses he won't need a palace."

Ptang laughed. "I hope he doesn't need it," he said; "but don't be over-confident, for he is rated the best swordsman among the First Born; and there are supposed to be no better swordsmen in all Barsoom."

Before the day arrived that I was to fight Nolat, Xaxak and Ptang grew more and more nervous; as did all of Xaxak's warriors, who seemed to feel a personal interest in me—that is, with the exception of Ban-tor, whose enmity I had aroused by disarming him.

Ban-tor had placed a number of wagers against me; and he kept bragging about this, insisting that I was no match for Nolat and that I should be killed in short order.

I slept in a small room by myself on old, discarded furs, as befitted a slave. My room connected with that occupied by Ptang; and had only one door, which opened into Ptang's room. It was on the second floor of the palace and overlooked the lower end of the garden.

The night before the encounter I was awakened by a noise in my room, and as I opened my eyes I saw a man leap out of the window with a sword in his hand; but, as neither of Mars' two moons was in the sky, it was not light enough for me to be sure that I could recognize him; yet there was something very familiar about him.

The next morning I told Ptang about my nocturnal visitor. Neither of us, however, could imagine why anyone would want to enter my room in stealth, as I had nothing to steal.

"It might have been an assassin who wanted to stop the fight," suggested Ptang.

"I doubt that," I said; "for he had plenty of opportunity to kill me, as I didn't awaken until he was leaping through the window."

"You missed nothing?" asked Ptang.

"I had nothing to miss," I replied, "except my harness and weapons, and I am wearing them now."

Ptang finally suggested that the fellow may have thought that a female slave slept in the room; and when he found out his error, took his departure; and with that we dropped the matter from our minds.

We went to the stadium about the fourth zode, and we went in style—in fact it was a regular pageant. There were Xaxak and his wife, with her female slaves, and Xaxak's officers and warriors. We were all mounted on gaily caparisoned thoats; pennants waved above us, and mounted trumpeters preceded us. Nastor was there with the same sort of retinue. We all paraded around the arena to the accompaniment of "Kaors!" and growls—the kaors were applause and the growls were boos. I received a great many more growls than kaors, for after all I was a slave pitted against a prince, a man of their own blood.

There were some wrestling and boxing matches and a number of duels for first blood only, but what the people were waiting for was the duel to the death. People are very much alike everywhere. On Earth, they go to boxing matches hoping for blood and a knockout; they go to the wrestling matches hoping to see someone thrown out of the ring and crippled; and when they go to automobile races they hope to see somebody killed. They will not admit these things, but without the element of danger and the risk of death these sports wouldn't draw a hatful of people.

At last the moment came for me to enter the arena, and I did so before a most distinguished audience. Doxus, Jeddak of the First Born, was there with his Jeddara. The loges and boxes were crowded with the nobility of Kamtol. It was a gorgeous spectacle; the harnesses of the men and women were resplendent with precious metals and jewels, and from every vantage point flew pennants and banners.

Nolat was escorted to the jeddak's box and presented; then to the box of Xaxak, where he bowed; and last of all to the box of Nastor, for whom he was fighting a stranger to the death.

I, being a slave, was not presented to the jeddak; but I was taken before Nastor; so that he could identify me as the individual against whom he had placed his wagers. It was, of course, a mere formality; but in accordance with the rules of the Games.

I had caught only a brief glimpse of Nastor's entourage as we had paraded around the arena; as they had been behind us; but now I got a good look at them, as I stood in the arena before Nastor, and I saw Llana of Gathol sitting there beside the dator. Now, indeed, would I kill Nastor's man!

Llana of Gathol gasped and started to speak to me; but I shook my head, for I was afraid she would call me by name, which might, here among the First Born, have been the equivalent of a death sentence. It was always a surprise to me that none of these men recognized me; for my white skin and grey eyes make me a marked man, and if any of them had been in the Valley Dor when I was there they must have remembered me. I was to learn later why none of these Black Pirates of Barsoom knew me.

"Why did you do that, slave?" demanded Nastor.

"Do what?" I asked.

"Shake your head," he replied.

"Perhaps I am nervous," I said.

"And well you may be, slave, for you are about to die," he snapped, nastily.

I was taken then to a point in the arena opposite the jeddak's box. Ptang was with me, as a sort of a second, I suppose. They let us stand there alone for several minutes, presumably to shake my nerves; then Nolat approached, accompanied by another noble dator. There was a fifth man; possibly he might have been called a referee; although he didn't have much to do besides giving the signal for the duel to commence.

Nolat was a large, powerful man; and built like a fighter. He was a very handsome man, but with a haughty, supercilious expression. Ptang had told me that we were supposed to salute each other with our swords before we engaged; and as soon as I got in position, I saluted; but Nolat merely sneered and said, "Come, slave! You are about to die."

"You made a mistake, Nolat," I said, as we engaged.

"What do you mean?" he demanded, lunging at me.

"You should have saluted your better," I said, parrying his lunge. "Now it will go harder with you—unless you would like to stop and salute me as you should have at first."

"Insolent calot!" he growled, and thrust viciously at me.

For reply, I cut a gash in his left cheek. "I told you you should have saluted," I mocked.

Nolat became furious then, and came at me with the evident intention of ending the encounter immediately. I sliced him along the other cheek, then; and a moment later I carved a bloody cross upon his left breast, a difficult maneuver requiring exceptional agility and skill, since his right side was always presented to me; or always should have been had he been quick enough to follow my foot work.

That audience was as silent as a tomb, except for the kaors from Xaxak's contingent. Nolat was bleeding profusely, and he had slowed down considerably.

Suddenly somebody shouted, "Death!" Then other voices took it up. They wanted the kill; and as it was quite evident that Nolat couldn't kill me, I assumed that they wished me to kill him. Instead, I disarmed him, sending his blade flying half way across the arena. The referee ran after it; at last I had given him something to do.

I turned to Nolat's second. "I offer the man his life," I said in a tone of voice loud enough to have been heard in any part of the stadium.

Immediately there were shouts of "Kaor!" and "Death!" The "Deaths" were in the majority.

"He offers you your life, Nolat," said the second.

"But the wagers must be paid precisely as though I had killed you," I said.

"It is to the death," said Nolat. "I shall fight."

Well, he was a brave man; and because of that I hated to kill him.

His sword was returned to him by now, and we fell to it again. This time Nolat did not smile nor sneer, and he had no nasty remarks to make to me. He was in deadly earnest, fighting for his life like a cornered rat. He was an excellent swordsman; but I do not think that he was the best swordsman among the First Born; for I had seen many of them fight before, and I could have named a dozen who could have killed him offhand.

I could have killed him myself any time that I had wished to, but somehow I couldn't bring myself to do it. It seemed a shame to kill such a good swordsman and such a brave man; so I pricked him a few times and disarmed him again. I did the same thing three more times; and then, while the referee was running after Nolat's sword again, I stepped to the jeddak's loge and saluted.

"What are you doing here, slave?" demanded an officer of the jeddak's guard.

"I come to ask for the life of Nolat," I replied. "He is a good swordsman and a brave man—and I am not a murderer; and it would be murder to kill him now."

"It is a strange request," said Doxus; "the duel was to the death; it must go on."

"I am a stranger here," I said, "but where I come from if a contestant can show fraud or chicanery he is awarded the decision without having to finish the contest."

"Do you mean to imply that there has been fraud or chicanery on the part of either the Dator Nastor or the Dator Nolat?" demanded Doxus.

"I mean to say that a man entered my room last night while I slept, took my sword, and left a shorter one in the scabbard. This sword is several inches shorter than Nolat's; I noticed it when we first engaged. It is not my sword, as Xaxak and Ptang can testify if they will examine it."

Doxus summoned Xaxak and Ptang and asked them if they could identify the sword. Xaxak said that he could only identify it as coming from his armory; that he did not know the sword that had been issued to me, but that Ptang did; then Doxus turned to Ptang.

"Is this the sword that was issued to the slave, Dotar Sojat?" he demanded.

"No; it is not," replied Ptang.

"Do you recognize it?"

"I do."

"To whom did it belong?"

"It is the sword of a warrior named Ban-tor," replied Ptang.

chapter IX

THERE WAS NOTHING for Doxus to do but award the contest to me; and he also ordered that all bets be paid, just as though I had killed Nolat. That didn't set very well with Nastor, nor did the fact that

Doxus made him pay over to Xaxak one hundred thousand tanpi in the jeddak's presence; then he sent for Ban-tor.

Doxus was furious; for the First Born hold their honor as fighting men very high, and the thing that had been done was a blot upon the escutcheons of them all.

"Is this the man who entered your room last night?" he asked me.

"It was dark; and I only saw his back; there was something familiar about the fellow, but I couldn't identify him positively."

"Did you lay any wagers on this contest?" he asked Ban-tor.

"A few little ones, Jeddak," replied the man.

"On whom?"

"On Nolat."

Doxus turned to one of his officers. "Summon all those with whom Ban-tor wagered on this contest."

A slave was sent around the arena, shouting out the summons; and soon there were fifty warriors gathered before Doxus' loge. Ban-tor appeared most unhappy; as, from each of the fifty, Doxus gleaned the information that Ban-tor had wagered large sums with each, in some instances giving extremely big odds.

"You thought that you were betting on a sure thing, didn't you?" demanded Doxus.

"I thought that Nolat would win," replied Ban-tor; "there is no better swordsman in Kamtol."

"And you were sure that he would win against an antagonist with a shorter sword. You are a disgrace; you have dishonored the First Born. For punishment you will fight now with Dotar Sojat;" then he turned to me. "You may kill him; and before you engage him, I, myself, will see that your sword is as long as his; although it would be only fair were he to be compelled to fight with the shorter sword he gave to you."

"I shall not kill him," I replied, "but I shall put a mark upon him that he will carry through life to remind all men that he is a knave."

As we started to take our places before the loge of the jeddak, I heard bets being offered with odds as high as a hundred to one that I would win, and later I learned that even a thousand to one was offered without any takers; then, as we faced one another, I heard Nastor shout, "I will lay no wager, but I'll give Ban-tor fifty thousand tanpi if he kills the slave." It appeared that the noble dator was wroth at me.

Ban-tor was no mean antagonist; for he was not only a good swordsman, but he was fighting for his life and fifty thousand tanpi. He didn't try any rushing tactics this time; but fought carefully, mostly on the defensive, waiting for me to make one little false move that would give him an opening; but I do not make false moves. It was he who made the false move; he thrust, following a feint, thinking to find me off balance.

I am never off balance. My blade moved twice with the swiftness of light, leaving an X cut deep in the center of Ban-tor's forehead; then I disarmed him.

Without even glancing at him again, I walked to Doxus' loge. "I am satisfied," I said. "To bear the scar of that cross through life is punishment enough. To me, it would be worse than death."

Doxus nodded assent; and then caused the trumpets to be blown to announce that the Games were over, after which he again turned to me.

"What country are you from?" he asked.

"I have no country; I am a panthan," I replied; "my sword is for sale to the highest bidder."

"I shall buy you, and thereby acquire your sword also," said the jeddak. "What did you pay for this slave, Xaxak?"

"One hundred tanpi," replied my owner.

"You got him too cheap," said Doxus; "I shall give you fifty tanpi for him." There is nothing like being a jeddak!

"It is my pleasure to present him to you," said Xaxak, magnanimously; I had already netted him a hundred thousand tanpi, and he must have realized that it would be impossible ever to get another wager placed against me.

I welcomed this change of masters; because it would take me into the palace of the jeddak, and I had been harboring a hare-brained scheme to pave the way for our eventual escape, that could only be successful if I were to have entry to the palace—that is, if my deductions were correct.

So John Carter, Prince of Helium, Warlord of Barsoom, came into the palace of Doxus, Jeddak of the First Born, as a slave; but a slave with a reputation. The warriors of the jeddak's guard treated me with respect; I was given a decent room; and one of Doxus' trusted under-officers was made responsible for me, just as Ptang had been in the palace of Xaxak.

I was at something of a loss to know why Doxus had purchased me. He must have known that he couldn't arrange a money duel for me, for who would be fool enough to place a man or a wager against one who had made several of the best swordsmen of Kamtol look like novices?

The next day I found out. Doxus sent for me. He was alone in a small room when I was escorted in, and he immediately dismissed the warrior who had accompanied me.

"When you entered the valley," he commenced, "you saw many skeletons, did you not?"

"Yes," I replied.

"Those men died trying to escape," he said. "It would be impossible for you to succeed any better than they. I am telling you this so that you won't make the attempt. You might think that by killing me you might escape in the confusion which would ensue; but you could not; you can never escape from the Valley of the First Born. However, you may live on here in comfort, if you wish. All that you have to do is teach me the tricks of swordsmanship with which you bested the finest swordsman of all the First Born. I wish you to make me that, but I wish the instruction given in secret and no word of it ever to pass your lips on pain of instant death—and a most unpleasant death, I can assure you. What do you say?"

"I can promise the utmost discretion," I said, "but I cannot promise to make you the greatest swordsman among the First Born; the achievement of that will depend somewhat upon your own native ability. I will instruct you, however."

"You do not talk much like a poor panthan," he said. "You speak to me much as would a man who had been accustomed to speaking with jeddaks—and as an equal."

"You may have much to learn about being a swordsman," I said, "but I have even more to learn about being a slave."

He grunted at that, and then arose and told me to follow him. We passed through a little door behind the desk at which he had been sitting, and down a ramp which led to the pits below the palace. At the foot of the ramp we entered a large, well lighted room in which were filing cases, a couch, several benches, and a table strewn with writing materials and drawing instruments.

"This is a secret apartment," said Doxus. "Only one person other than myself has access to it. We shall not be disturbed here. This other man of whom I spoke is my most trusted servant. He may come in occasionally, but he will not divulge our little secret. Let us get to work. I can scarcely wait until the day that I shall cross swords with some of those egotistical nobles who think that they are really great swordsmen. Won't they be surprised!"

chapter X

Now, I HAD NO INTENTION of revealing all of my tricks of swordsmanship to Doxus; although I might have as far as any danger to myself was concerned, for he could never equal me; because he could never match my strength or agility.

I had been practicing him in disarming an opponent, when a door opposite that from which we had entered the room opened; and a man came in. During the brief time that the door remained open, I saw beyond it a brilliantly lighted room; and caught a glimpse of what appeared to be an amazingly complicated machine. Its face was covered with dials, buttons, and other gadgets—all reminiscent of the machine to which I had been attached during the weird examination I had received upon entry to the city.

At sight of me, the newcomer looked surprised. Here was I, a total stranger and evidently a slave, facing the Jeddak of the First Born with a naked blade in my hand. Instantly, the fellow whipped out a radium pistol; but Doxus forestalled a tragedy.

"It is all right, Myr-lo," he said. "I am just taking some instruction in the finer points of swordsmanship from this slave. His name is Dotar Sojat; you will see him down here with me daily. What are you doing down here now? Anything wrong?"

"A slave escaped last night," said Myr-lo.

"You got him, of course?"

"Just now. He was about half way up the escarpment, I think."

"Good!" said Doxus. "Resume, Dotar Sojat."

I was so full of what I had just heard and seen and what I thought that it all connoted that I had hard work keeping my mind on my work; so that I inadvertently let Doxus prick me. He was as pleased as Punch.

"Wonderful!" he exclaimed. "In one lesson I have been so improved that I have been able to touch you! Not even Nolat could do that. We will stop now. I give you the freedom of the city. Do not go beyond the gates." He went to the table and wrote for a minute; then he handed me what he had written. "Take this," he said; "it will permit you to go where you will in all public places and return to the palace."

He had written:

> Dotar Sojat, the slave, is granted the freedom of the
> palace and the city.
>
> > Doxus,
> >
> > Jeddak.

As I returned to my quarters, I determined to let Doxus prick me every day. I found Man-lat, the under-officer who had been detailed to look after me, alone in his room, which adjoined mine.

"Your duties are going to be lessened," I told him.

"What do you mean?" he asked.

I showed him the pass.

"Doxus must have taken a liking to you," he said. "I never knew before of a slave being given that much freedom, but don't try to escape."

"I know better than to try that. I saw the skeletons from the top to the bottom of the escarpment."

"We call them Myr-lo's babies," said Man-lat; "he's so proud of them."

"Who is Myr-lo?" I asked.

"Somebody you'll probably never see," replied Man-lat. "He sticks to his pots and his kettles, his lathes and drills and his drawing instruments."

"Does he live in the palace?" I asked.

"Nobody knows where he lives, unless it be the jeddak. They say he has a secret apartment in the palace, but I don't know about that. What I do know is that he's the most powerful man in Kamtol, next to Doxus; and that he has the power of life and death over every man and woman in the Valley of the First Born. Why, he could strike either one of us dead right while we are sitting here talking; and we'd never see what killed us."

I was even more convinced now than I had been before that I had found what I had hoped to in that secret room beneath the palace—but how to utilize the knowledge!

I immediately took advantage of my freedom to go out into the city, only a part of which I had seen during the short time that I had been out with Ptang. The guards at the palace gate were as surprised when they read my pass as Man-lat had been. Of course, pass or no pass, I was still an enemy and a slave—a person to be viewed with suspicion and contempt; but in my case the contempt was tempered by the knowledge that I had bested their best at swordsmanship. I doubt that you can realize in what high esteem a great swordsman is held everywhere on Mars. In his own country he is worshipped, as might be a Juan Belmonte in Spain or a Jack Dempsey in America.

I had not gone far from the palace, when I chanced to look up; and, to my surprise, saw a number of fliers dropping down toward the city.

The First Born I had seen in the Valley Dor had all been flying men; but I had not before seen any fliers over the valley, and I had wondered.

Martian aeroplanes, being lighter than air, or in effect so; because of the utilization of that marvellous discovery, the ray of repulsion, which tends to push them away from the planet, can land vertically in a space but little larger in area than themselves; and I saw that the planes I was watching were coming down into the city at no great distance from the palace.

Fliers! I think that my heart beat a little faster at the sight of them. Fliers! a means of escape from the Valley of the First Born. It might take a great deal of scheming; and would certainly entail enormous risks; but if all went well with the other part of my plan, I would find a way—and a flier.

I made my way toward the point at which I had seen the fliers disappear behind the roofs of the buildings near me, and at last my search was rewarded. I came to an enormous building some three stories high, on the roof of which I could just see a part of a flier. Practically all hangars to Barsoom are on the roofs of buildings, usually to conserve space in crowded, walled cities; so I was not surprised to find a hangar in Kamtol thus located.

I approached the entrance to the building, determined to inspect it and some of the ships if I could get in. As I stepped through the entrance, a warrior barred my way with drawn sword.

"Where do you think you're going, slave?" he demanded.

I showed him my pass.

He looked equally as surprised as the others had who had read it. "This says the freedom of the palace and the city," he said; "it doesn't say the freedom of the hangars."

"They're in the city, aren't they?" I demanded.

He shook his head. "They may be in the city, but *I* won't admit you. I'll call the officer."

He did so, and presently the officer appeared. "So!" he exclaimed, when he saw me; "you're the slave who could have killed Nolat, but spared his life. What do you want here?"

I handed him my pass. He read it carefully a couple of times. "It doesn't seem possible," he said, "but then your swordsmanship didn't seem possible either. It is hard for me to believe it yet. Why, Nolat was considered the best swordsman in Kamtol; and you made him look like an old woman with one leg. Why do you want to come in here?"

"I want to learn to fly," I said, naïvely.

He slapped his thighs and laughed at that. "Either you are foolish, or you think we First Born are, if you have an idea that we would teach a slave to fly."

"Well, I'd like to come in and look at the fliers anyway," I said. "That wouldn't do any harm. I've always been interested in them."

He thought a moment; then he said, "Nolat is my best friend; you might have killed him, but you refused. For that I am going to let you come in."

"Thank you," I said.

The first floor of the building was largely given over to shops where fliers were being built or repaired. The second and third floors were packed with fliers, mostly the small, swift ones for which the Black Pirates of Barsoom are noted. On the roof were four large battleships; and, parked under them, were a number of small fliers for which there was evidently no room on the floors below.

The building must have covered several acres; so there were an enormous number of planes hangared there. I could see them now, as I had seen them years before, swarming like angry mosquitoes over the

Golden Cliffs of the Holy Therns; but what were they doing here? I had supposed that the First Born lived only in the Valley Dor, although the majority of Barsoomians still believe that they come from Thuria, the nearer moon. That theory I had seen refuted the time that Xodar, a Black Pirate, had nearly succumbed from lack of oxygen when I had flown too high while escaping from them, that time that Thuvia and I had escaped the Therns, during their battle with the Black Pirates. If a man can't live without oxygen, he can't fly back and forth between Thuria and Barsoom in an open flier.

The officer had sent a warrior along with me, as a precaution against sabotage, I suppose; and I asked this fellow why I had seen no ships in the air since I had come, except the few I had seen this day.

"We fly mostly at night," he replied, "so that our enemies cannot see where we take off from, nor where we land. Those that you saw coming in a few minutes ago were visitors from Dor. That may mean that we are going to war, and I hope so. We haven't raided any cities for a long time. If it's to be a big raid, those from Dor and from Kamtol band together."

Some Black Pirates from the Valley Dor! Now, indeed, I might be recognized.

chapter XI

As I WALKED AWAY from the hangar building, I turned and looked back, studying every detail of the architecture; then I walked around the entire building, which covered a whole square, with avenues on all four sides. Like nearly all Martian buildings, this one was highly ornamented with deep carvings. It stood in a rather poor section of the city, although not far from the palace; and was surrounded by small and modest homes. They were probably the homes of the artisans employed around the hangar. A little farther from the hangar a section of small shops began; and as I passed along, looking at the wares displayed, I saw something which brought me to a sudden stop, for it suggested a new accessory to my rapidly formulating plans for escape from the Valley of the First Born—from which none ever escaped. It is sometimes well not to be too greatly constrained by precedent.

I entered the shop and asked the proprietor the price of the article I wished. It was only three teepi, the equivalent of about thirty cents in United States money; but with the information came the realization that I had none of the money of the First Born.

The medium of exchange upon Mars is not dissimilar to our own, except that the coins are oval; and there are only three; the pi, pronounced pī; worth about one cent; the teepi, ten cents; and the tanpi, one dollar. These coins are oval; one of bronze, one of silver, and one of gold. Paper money is issued by individuals, much as we write a check, and is redeemed by the individual twice yearly. If a man issues more than he can redeem, the government pays his creditors in full; and the debtor works out the amount upon the farms, or in the mines, which are government owned.

I had with me money of Helium to the value of some fifty tanpi, and I asked the proprietor if he would accept a larger amount than the value of the article in foreign coin. As the value of the metal is equal to the value of the coin, he gladly accepted one dollar in gold for what was worth thirty cents in silver; and I placed my purchase in my pocket pouch and departed.

As I approached the palace, I saw a white-skinned man ahead of me carrying a heavy burden on his back. Now, as far as I knew, there was only one other white-skinned man in Kamtol; and that was Pan Dan Chee; so I hastened to overtake him.

Sure enough, it was the Orovar from Horz; and when I came up behind him and called him by name, he almost dropped his burden, so surprised was he.

"John Carter!" he exclaimed.

"Hush!" I cautioned; "my name is Dotar Sojat. If the First Born knew that John Carter was in Kamtol I hate to think what would happen to him. Tell me about yourself. What has happened to you since I last saw you?"

"I was purchased by Dator Nastor, who has the reputation of being the hardest master in Kamtol. He is also the meanest; he bought me only because he could buy me cheap, and he made them throw in Jad-han for good measure. He works us day and night, and feeds us very little—and poor food at that. Since he lost a hundred thousand tanpi to Xaxak, it has been almost like working for a maniac.

"By my first ancestor!" he exclaimed suddenly; "so it was you who defeated Nolat and caused Nastor to lose all that money! I didn't realize it until just now. They said the slave who won the contest was named Dotar Sojat, and that meant nothing to me until now—and I was a little slow in getting it, at that."

"Have you seen Llana of Gathol?" I asked him. "She was in Nastor's loge at the Games; so I presume she was purchased by him."

"Yes, but I have not seen her," replied Pan Dan Chee; "however, I have heard gossip in the slaves' quarters; and I am much worried by what is being whispered about the palace."

"What have you heard? I felt that she was in danger when I saw her in Nastor's loge. She is too beautiful to be safe."

"She was safe enough at first," said Pan Dan Chee, "as she was originally purchased by Nastor's principal wife. Everything was comparatively well for her until Nastor got a good look at her at the Games; then he tried to buy her from his wife. But she, Van-tija, refused to sell. Nastor was furious, and told Van-tija that he would take Llana anyway; so Van-tija has locked her in an apartment at the top of the tower of her own part of the palace, and has placed her personal guards at the only entrance. There is the tower, there," he said, pointing; "perhaps Llana of Gathol is looking down at us now."

As I looked up at the tower, I saw that it rose above a palace which stood directly across the large central plaza from that of the jeddak; and I saw something else—I saw the windows of Llana's apartments were not barred.

"Do you think that Llana is in any immediate danger?" I asked.

"Yes," he replied, "I do. It is rumored in the palace that Nastor is going to lead warriors to Van-tija's section of the palace and attempt to take the tower by storm."

"Then we have no time to lose, Pan Dan Chee. We must act tonight."

"But what can we two slaves do?" he demanded. "Even if we succeeded in getting Llana out of the tower, we could never escape from the Valley of the First Born. Do not forget the skeletons, John Carter."

"Trust me," I said, "and don't call me John Carter. Can you get out of the palace of Nastor after dark?"

"I think so; they are very lax; because assassination and theft are practically unknown here, and the secret machine of the jeddak makes escape from the valley impossible. I am quite sure that I can get out. In fact, I have been sent out on errands every night since I was purchased."

"Good!" I said. "Now listen carefully: Come out of the palace and loiter in the shadows near Nastor's palace at about twenty-five xats after the eighth zode.* Bring Jad-han with you, if he wishes to escape. If my plan succeeds, a flier will land here in the plaza near you; run for it and climb aboard. It will be piloted by a Black Pirate, but don't let that deter you. If you and Jad-han can arm yourselves, do so; there may be fighting. If the flier does not come, you will know that I have failed; and you can go back to your quarters and be no worse off. If I do not come, it will be because I am dead, or about to die."

"And Llana?" he asked. "What of her?"

"My plans all center around the rescue of Llana of Gathol," I assured him. "If I fail in that, I fail in all; for I will not leave without her."

"I wish you could tell me how you expect to accomplish the impossible," he said. "I should feel very much surer of the outcome, I know, if you would tell me at least something of your plans."

"Certainly," I said. "In the first place—"

"What are you two slaves doing loitering here?" demanded a gruff voice behind us. I turned to see a burly warrior at my shoulder. For answer, I showed him my pass from the jeddak.

Even after he read it, he looked as though he didn't believe it; but presently he handed it back to me and said, "That's all right for you, but how about this other one? Has he got a pass from the jeddak, too?"

"The fault is mine," I said. "I knew him before we were captured, and I stopped him to ask how he was faring. I am sure that if the jeddak knew, he would say that it was all right for me to talk with a friend. The jeddak has been very kind to me." I was trying to impress

---

*Midnight, Earth time.

the fellow with the fact that his jeddak was very kindly disposed toward me. I think that I succeeded.

"Very well," he said, "but get on your way now—the Great Plaza is no place for slaves to visit with one another."

Pan Dan Chee picked up his burden and departed, and I was about to leave when the warrior detained me. "I saw you defeat Nolat and Ban-tor at the Games," he said. "We were talking about it a little while ago with some of our friends from the Valley Dor. They said that there was once a warrior came there who was just such a marvellous swordsman. His name was John Carter, *and he had a white skin and grey eyes!* Could your name, by any chance, be John Carter?"

"My name is Dotar Sojat," I replied.

"Our friends from the Valley Dor would like to get hold of John Carter," he said; and then, with a rather nasty little smile, he turned on his heel and left me.

chapter XII

Now INDEED was the occasion for haste increased a hundredfold. If one man in Kamtol suspected that I might be John Carter, Prince of Helium, I should be lost by the morrow at the latest—perhaps before the morrow. Even as I entered the palace I feared arrest, but I reached my room without incident. Presently Man-lat came in; and at sight of him I expected the worst, for he had never visited me before. My sword was ready to leap from its scabbard, for I had determined to die fighting rather than let them arrest and disarm me. Even now, if Man-lat made a false move, I could kill him; and there might still be a chance that my plan could move on to successful fruition.

But Man-lat was in a friendly, almost jovial mood. "It is too bad that you are a slave," he said, "for there are going to be great doings in the palace tonight. Doxus is entertaining the visitors from Dor. There will be much to eat and much to drink, and there will be entertainment. Doxus will probably have you give an exhibition of sword play with one of our best swordsmen—not to the death, you understand, but just for first blood. Then there will be dancing by slave girls; the nobles will enter their most beautiful. Doxus has commanded Nastor to bring a new purchase of his whose beauty has been the talk of Kamtol since the last games. Yes, it is too bad that you are not a First Born; so that you might enjoy the evening to the full."

"I am sure I shall enjoy the evening," I said.

"How's that?" he demanded.

"Didn't you say that I was going to be there?"

"Oh, yes; but only as an entertainer. You will not eat nor drink with us, and you will not see the slave girls. It is really too bad that you are not a First Born; you would have been a credit to us."

"I feel that I am quite the equal of any of the First Born," I said, for I was pretty well fed up with their arrogance and conceit.

Man-lat looked at me in pained surprise. "You are presumptuous, slave," he said. "Do you not know that the First Born of Barsoom, sometimes known to you lesser creatures as The Black Pirates of Barsoom, are of the oldest race on the planet. We trace our lineage, unbroken, direct to the Tree of Life which flourished in the Valley Dor twenty-three million years ago.

"For countless ages the fruit of this tree underwent the gradual changes of evolution, passing by degrees from the true plant life to a combination of plant and animal. In the first stages of this phase, the fruit of the tree possessed only the power of independent muscular action, while the stem remained attached to the parent plant; later, a brain developed in the fruit; so that, hanging there by their long stems, they thought and moved as individuals.

"Then, with the development of perceptions, came a comparison of them; judgments were reached and compared, and thus reason and the power to reason were born upon Barsoom.

"Ages passed. Many forms of life came and went upon the Tree of Life, but still all were attached to the parent plant by stems of varying lengths. In time the fruit upon the tree consisted of tiny plant men, such as we now see reproduced in such huge dimensions in the Valley Dor; but still hanging to the limbs and branches of the Tree by the stems which grew from the tops of their heads.

"The buds from which the plant men blossomed resembled large nuts about a sofad* in diameter, divided by double partition walls into four sections. In one section grew the plant man; in another a sixteen-legged worm; in the third the progenitor of the white ape; and in the fourth, the primeval black man of Barsoom.

"When the bud burst, the plant man remained dangling at the end of his stem; but the three other sections fell to the ground, where the efforts of their imprisoned occupants to escape sent them hopping about in all directions.

"Thus, as time went on, all Barsoom was covered by these impris-oned creatures. For countless ages they lived their long lives within their hard shells, hopping and skipping about the broad planet; falling into rivers, lakes, and seas to be still farther spread about the surface of the new world.

"Countless billions died before the first black man broke through

---

*11.17 Earth inches.

his prison walls into the light of day. Prompted by curiosity, he broke open other shells; and the peopling of Barsoom commenced.

"The pure strain of the blood of this first black man has remained untainted by admixture with that of other creatures; but from the sixteen legged worm, the first white ape, and renegade black men has sprung every other form of life upon Barsoom."

I hoped he was through, for I had heard all this many times before; but, of course, I didn't dare tell him so. I wished he would go away—not that I could do anything until after dark, but I just wanted to be alone and re-plan every minutest detail of the night's work that lay before me.

At last he went; and at long last night came, but I must still remain inactive until about two hours before the time that I had told Pan Dan Chee to be prepared to climb aboard a flier piloted by a Black Pirate. I was betting that he was still puzzling over that.

The evening wore on. I heard sounds of revelry coming from the first floor of the palace through the garden upon which my window opened—the jeddak's banquet was in full swing. The zero hour was approaching—and then malign Fate struck. A warrior came, summoning me to the banquet hall!

I should have killed him and gone on about my business, but suddenly a spirit of bravado possessed me. I would face them all, let them see once more the greatest swordsman of two worlds, and let them realize, when I had escaped them, that I was greater in all ways than the greatest of the First Born. I knew it was foolish; but now I was following the warrior toward the banquet hall; the die was cast, and it was too late to turn back.

No one paid any attention to me as I entered the great room—I was only a slave. Four tables, forming a hollow square, were filled with men and women, gorgeously trapped. They were talking and laughing; and wine was flowing, and a small army of slaves was bearing more food and more wine. Some of the guests were already a little bit high, and it was evident that Doxus was holding his own with the best of them. He had his arm about his wife, on one side; but he was kissing another man's wife on the other.

The warrior who had fetched me went and whispered in the jeddak's ear, and Doxus banged a huge gong for silence. When they had quieted down, he spoke to them: "For long the First Born of the Valley Dor have boasted of their swordsmanship; and, in contests, I admit that they have proved that they possess some slight superiority over us; but I have in my palace a slave, a common slave, who can best the best swordsman from Dor. He is here now to give an exhibition of his marvellous ability in a contest with one of my nobles; not to the death, but for first blood only—unless there be one from Dor who believes that he can best this slave of mine."

A noble arose. "It is a challenge," he said. "Dator Zithad is the best swordsman here from Dor tonight; but if he will not meet a slave, I will for the honor of Dor. We have heard of this slave since we arrived in Kamtol, how he bested your best swordsmen; and I for one shall be glad to draw his blood."

Then Zithad arose, haughty and arrogant. "I have never sullied my sword with the blood of a slave," he said, "but I shall be glad to expunge the shame of Kamtol. Where is the knave?"

Zithad! He had been Dator of the Guards of Issus at the time of the revolt of the slaves and the overthrow of Issus. He had good reason to remember me and to hate me.

When we faced each other in the center of that hollow square in the banquet hall of Doxus, Jeddak of the First Born of Kamtol, he looked puzzled for a moment, and then stepped back. He opened his mouth to speak.

"So, you are afraid to meet a slave!" I taunted him. "Come! they want to see you spill my blood; let's not disappoint them." I touched him lightly with my point.

"Calot!" he growled, and came for me.

He was a better swordsman than Nolat, but I made a monkey of him. I backed him around the square, keeping him always on the defensive; but I drew no blood—yet. He was furious—and he was afraid. The audience sat in breathless silence.

Suddenly he screamed: "Fools! Don't you know who this slave is? He is—" Then I ran him through the heart.

Instantly pandemonium reigned. A hundred swords sprang from their scabbards, but I waited to see no more—I'd seen plenty! With drawn sword, I ran straight for the center of one of the tables; a woman screamed. In a single bound I cleared the table and the diners, and bolted through the door behind them into the garden.

Of course, they were after me instantly; but I dodged into the shrubbery, and made my way to a point beneath my window at the lower end of the garden. It was scarcely a fifteen foot jump to the sill; and a second later I had passed through my room and down a ramp to the floor below.

It was dark, but I knew every inch of the way to my goal. I had prepared for just some such eventuality. I reached the room in which Doxus had first interviewed me, and passed through the doorway behind the desk and down the ramp to the secret chamber below.

I knew that no one would guess where I had gone; and as Myr-lo was doubtless at the banquet, I should be able to accomplish with ease that which I had come here to do.

As I opened the door into the larger room, Myr-lo arose from the couch and faced me.

"What are you doing here, slave?" he demanded.

chapter XIII

HERE WAS A PRETTY PASS! Everything seemed to be going wrong; first, the summons to the banquet hall; then Zithad; and now Myr-lo. I hated to do it, but there was no other way.

"Draw!" I said. I am no murderer; so I couldn't kill him unless he had a sword in his hand; but Myr-lo was not so ethical—he reached for the radium pistol at his hip. Fatal error! I crossed the intervening space in a single bound; and ran Myr-lo, the inventor of Kamtol, through the heart.

Without even waiting to wipe the blood from my blade, I ran into the smaller room. There was the master mechanism that held two hundred thousand souls in thrall, the hideous invention that had strewn the rim of the great rift with mouldering skeletons.

I looked about and found a heavy piece of metal; then I went for that insensate monster with all the strength and enthusiasm that I possess. In a few minutes it was an indescribable jumble of bent and broken parts—a total wreck.

Quickly I ran back into the next room, stripped Myr-lo's harness and weapons from his corpse and removed my own; then from my pocket pouch I took the article that I had purchased in the little shop. It was a jar of the ebony black cream with which the women of the First Born are wont to conceal the blemishes upon their glossy skins.

In ten minutes I was as black as the blackest Black Pirate that ever broke a shell. I donned Myr-lo's harness and weapons; and, except for my grey eyes, I was a noble of the First Born. I was glad now that Myr-lo had not been at the banquet, for his harness would help to pass me through the palace and out of it, an ordeal that I had not been looking forward to with much relish; for I had been wearing the harness of the commonest of common warriors, and I very much doubted that they passed in and out of the palace late at night without being questioned—and I had no answers.

I got through the palace without encountering anyone, and when I approached the gate I commenced to stagger. I wanted them to think that a slightly inebriated guest was leaving early. I held my breath as I approached the warriors on guard; but they only saluted me respectfully, and I passed out into the avenues of Kamtol.

My plan had been to climb the façade of the hangar building, which I could have done because of the deep carving of its ornamentation; but that would probably have meant a fight with the guard on the roof as I clambered over the cornice. Now, I determined to try another, if no less hazardous, plan.

I walked straight to the entrance. There was but a single warrior on guard there. I paid no attention to him, but strode in. He hesitated; then he saluted, and I passed on and up the ramp. He had been impressed by the gorgeous trappings of Myr-lo, the noble.

My greatest obstacle to overcome now was the guard on the roof, where I had no doubt but that I should find several warriors. It might be difficult to convince them that even a noble would go flying alone at this time of night, but when I reached the roof there was not a single warrior in sight.

It took me but a moment to find the flier I had selected for the adventure when I had been there before, and but another moment to climb to its controls and start the smooth, silent motor.

The night was dark; neither moon was in the sky, and for that I was thankful. I rose in a steep spiral until I was high above the city; then I headed for the tower of Nastor's palace where Llana of Gathol was imprisoned.

The black hull of the flier rendered me invisible, I was sure, from the avenues below on a dark night such as this; and I came to the tower with every assurance that my whole plan had worked out with amazing success, even in spite of the untoward incidents that had seemed about to wreck it in its initial stages.

As I drew slowly closer to the windows of Llana's apartment, I heard a woman's muffled scream and a man's voice raised in anger. A moment later the prow of my ship touched the wall just below the window; and, seizing the bow line, I leaped across the sill into the chamber, Myr-lo's sword in my hand.

Across the room, a man was forcing Llana of Gathol back upon a couch. She was striking at him, and he was cursing her.

"Enough!" I cried, and the man dropped Llana and turned toward me. It was Nastor, the dator.

"Who are you?" he demanded. "What are you doing here?"

"I am John Carter, Prince of Helium," I replied; "and I am here to kill you."

He had already drawn, and our swords crossed even as I spoke.

"Perhaps you will recall me better as Dotar Sojat, the slave who cost you one hundred thousand tanpi," I said; "the prince who is going to cost you your life."

He commenced to shout for the guard, and I heard the sound of running footsteps which seemed to be coming up a ramp outside the door. I saw that I must finish Nastor quickly; but he proved a better swordsman than I had expected, although the encounter quickly developed into a foot race about the chamber.

The guard was coming closer when Llana darted to the door and pushed a heavy bolt into place; and not a moment too soon, for almost immediately I heard pounding on the door and the shouts of the warriors outside; and then I tripped upon a fur that had fallen from the couch during the struggle between Llana and Nastor, and I went down upon my back. Instantly Nastor leaped for me to run me through the heart. My sword was pointed up toward him, but he had all the advantage. I was about to die.

Only Llana's quick wit saved me. She leaped for Nastor from the rear and seized him about the ankles. He pitched forward on top of me, and my sword went through his heart, two feet of the blade protruding from his back. It took all my strength to wrest it free.

"Come, Llana!" I said.

"Where to?" she asked. "The corridor is full of warriors."

"The window," I said. "Come!"

As I turned toward the window, I saw the end of my line, that I had dropped during the fight, disappear over the edge of the sill. My ship had drifted away, and we were trapped.

I ran to the window. Twenty-five feet away, and a few feet below the level of the sill, floated escape and freedom, floated life for Llana of Gathol, for Pan Dan Chee, for Jad-han, and for me.

There was but a single hope. I stepped to the sill, measured the distance again with my eyes—and jumped. That I am narrating this adventure must assure you that I landed on the deck of that flier. A moment later it was beside the sill again, and Llana was aboard.

"Pan Dan Chee!" she said. "What has become of him? It seems cruel to abandon him to his fate."

Pan Dan Chee would have been the happiest man in the world could he have known that her first thought was for him, but I knew that the chances were that she would snub or insult him the first opportunity she had—women are peculiar that way.

I dropped swiftly toward the plaza. "Where are you going?" demanded Llana. "Aren't you afraid we'll be captured down there?"

"I am going for Pan Dan Chee," I said, and a moment later I landed close to Nastor's palace, and two men dashed from the shadows toward the ship. They were Pan Dan Chee and Jad-han.

As soon as they were aboard, I rose swiftly; and headed for Gathol. I could feel Pan Dan Chee looking at me. Finally he could contain himself no longer. "Who are you?" he demanded; "and where is John Carter?"

"I am now Myr-lo, the inventor," I said; "a short time ago I was Dotar Sojat the slave; but always I am John Carter."

"We are all together again," he said, "and alive; but for how long? Have you forgotten the skeletons on the rim of the rift?"

"You need not worry," I assured him. "The mechanism that laid them there has been destroyed."

He turned to Llana. "Llana of Gathol," he said, "we have been through much together; and there is no telling what the future holds for us. Once again I lay my heart at your feet."

"You may pick it up," said Llana of Gathol; "I am tired and wish to sleep."

Part 3

ESCAPE ON MARS

chapter 1

THERE WERE FOUR OF US aboard the flier I had stolen from the hangar at Kamtol to effect our escape from The Valley of the First Born: Llana of Gathol; Pan Dan Chee of Horz; Jad-han, the brother of Janai of Amhor; and I, John Carter, Prince of Helium and Warlord of Barsoom.

It was one of those startlingly gorgeous Martian nights that fairly take one's breath away. In the thin air of the dying planet, every star stands out in scintillant magnificence against the velvet blackness of the firmament in splendor inconceivable to an inhabitant of Earth.

As we rose above the great rift valley, both of Mars' moons were visible, and Earth and Venus were in conjunction, affording us a spectacle of incomparable beauty. Cluros, the farther moon, moved in stately dignity across the vault of heaven but fourteen thousand miles away, while Thuria, but four thousand miles distant, hurtled through the night from horizon to horizon in less than four hours, casting ever changing shadows on the ground below us which produced the illusion of constant movement, as though the surface of Mars was covered by countless myriads of creeping, crawling things. I wish that I might convey to you some conception of the weird and startling strangeness of the scene and of its beauty; but, unfortunately, my powers of description are wholly inadequate. But perhaps some day you, too, will visit Mars.

As we rose above the rim of the mighty escarpment which bounds the valley, I set our course for Gathol and opened the throttle wide, for I anticipated possible pursuit; but, knowing the possibilities for speed of this type of flier, I was confident that, with the start we had, nothing in Kamtol could overhaul us if we had no bad luck.

Gathol is supposed by many to be the oldest inhabited city on Mars, and is one of the few that has retained its freedom; and that despite the fact that its ancient diamond mines are the richest known and, unlike practically all the other diamond fields, are today apparently as inexhaustible as ever.

In ancient times the city was built upon an island in Throxeus, mightiest of the five oceans of old Barsoom. As the ocean receded, Gathol crept down the sides of the mountain, the summit of which was the island on which she had been built, until today she covers the slopes from summit to base, while the bowels of the great hill are honeycombed with the galleries of her mines.

Entirely surrounding Gathol is a great salt marsh, which protects it from invasion by land, while the rugged and oft-times vertical topography of the mountain renders the landing of hostile airships a precarious undertaking.

Gahan, the father of Llana, is jed of Gathol, which is very much more than just a single city, comprising, as it does, some one hundred forty thousand square miles, much of which is fine grazing land where run their great herds of thoats and zitidars. It was to return Llana to her father and mother, Tara of Helium, that we had passed through so many harrowing adventures since we had left Horz. And now Llana was almost home; and I should soon be on my way to Helium and my incomparable Dejah Thoris, who must long since have given me up for dead.

Jad-han sat beside me at the controls, Llana slept, and Pan Dan

Chee moped. Moping seems to be the natural state of all lovers. I felt sorry for Pan Dan Chee; and I could have relieved his depression by telling him that Llana's first words after I had rescued her from the tower of Nastor's palace had been of him—inquiring as to his welfare—but I didn't. I wished the man who won Llana of Gathol to win her by himself. If he gave up in despair while they both lived and she remained unmated; then he did not deserve her; so I let poor Pan Dan Chee suffer from the latest rebuff that Llana had inflicted upon him.

We approached Gathol shortly before dawn. Neither moon was in the sky, and it was comparatively dark. The city was dark, too; I saw not a single light. That was strange, and might forebode ill; for Martian cities are not ordinarily darkened except in times of war when they may be threatened by an enemy.

Llana came out of the tiny cabin and crouched on the deck beside me. "That looks ominous," she said.

"It does to me, too," I agreed; "and I'm going to stand off until daylight. I want to see what's going on before I attempt to land."

"Look over there," said Llana, pointing to the right of the black mass of the mountain; "see all those lights."

"The camp fires of the herdsmen, possibly," I suggested.

"There are too many of them," said Llana.

"They might also be the camp fires of warriors," said Jad-han.

"Here comes a flier," said Pan Dan Chee; "they have discovered us."

From below, a flier was approaching us rapidly. "A patrol flier doubtless," I said, but I opened the throttle and turned the flier's nose in the opposite direction. I didn't like the looks of things, and I wasn't going to let any ship approach until I could see its insigne. Then came a hail: "Who are you?"

"Who are you?" I demanded in return.

"Stop!" came the order; but I didn't stop; I was pulling away from him rapidly, as my ship was much the faster.

He fired then, but the shot went wide. Jad-han was at the stern gun. "Shall I let him have it?" he asked.

"No," I replied; "he may be Gatholian. Turn the searchlight on him, Pan Dan Chee; let's see if we can see his insigne."

Pan Dan Chee had never been on a ship before, nor ever seen a searchlight. The little remnant of the almost extinct race of Orovars, of which he was one, that hides away in ancient Horz, has neither ships nor searchlights; so Llana of Gathol came to his rescue, and presently the bow of the pursuing flier was brightly illuminated.

"I can't make out the insigne," said Llana, "but that is no ship of Gathol."

Another shot went wide of us, and I told Jad-han that he might fire. He did and missed. The enemy fired again; and I felt the projectile strike us, but it didn't explode. He had our range; so I started to zigzag, and his next two shots missed us. Jad-Han's also missed, and then we were struck again.

"Take the controls," I said to Llana, and I went back to the gun. "Hold her just as she is, Llana," I called, as I took careful aim. I was firing an explosive shell detonated by impact. It struck her full in the bow, entered the hull, and exploded. It tore open the whole front of the ship, which burst into flame and commenced to go down by the bow. At first she went slowly; and then she took the last long, swift dive—a flaming meteor that crashed into the salt marsh and was extinguished.

"That's that," said Llana of Gathol.

"I don't think it's all of that as far as we are concerned," I retorted; "we are losing altitude rapidly; one of his shots must have ripped open a buoyancy tank."

I took the controls and tried to keep her up; as, with throttle wide open, I sought to pass that ring of camp fires before we were finally forced down.

chapter II

THAT WAS A GOOD LITTLE SHIP—staunch and swift, as are all the ships of The Black Pirates of Barsoom—and it carried us past the farthest camp fires before it finally settled to the ground just at dawn. We were close to a small forest of sorapus trees, and I thought it best to take shelter there until we could reconnoiter a bit.

"What luck!" exclaimed Llana, disgustedly, "and just when I was so sure that we were practically safe and sound in Gathol."

"What do we do now?" asked Pan Dan Chee.

"Our fate is in the hands of our ancestors," said Jad-han.

"But we won't leave it there," I assured them; "I feel that I am much more competent to direct my own fate than are my ancestors, who have been dead for many years. Furthermore, I am much more interested in it than they."

"I think perhaps you are on the right track there," said Llana, laughing, "although I wouldn't mind leaving my fate in the hands of my living ancestors—and now, just what is one of them going to do about it?"

"First I am going to find something to eat," I replied, "and then I am going to try to find out who were warming themselves at those fires last night; they might be friends, you know."

"I doubt it," said Llana; "but if they are friends, then Gathol is in the hands of enemies."

"We should know very shortly; and now you three remain here while I go and see if anything edible grows in this forest. Keep a good lookout."

I walked into the forest, looking for roots or herbs and that life giving plant, the mantalia, the milk-like sap of which has saved me from death by thirst or starvation on many an occasion. But that forest seemed to be peculiarly barren of all forms of edible things, and I passed all the way through it and out upon the other side without finding anything that even a starving man would try to eat.

Beyond the forest, I saw some low hills; and that gave me renewed hope, as in some little ravine, where moisture might be held longest, I should doubtless find something worth taking back to my companions.

I had crossed about half the distance from the forest to the hills when I heard the unmistakable clank of metal and creaking of leather behind me; and, turning, saw some twenty red men mounted on riding thoats approaching me at a gallop, the nailless, padded feet of their mounts making no sound on the soft vegetation which covered the ground.

Facing them, I drew my sword; and they drew rein a few yards from me. "Are you men of Gathol?" I asked.

"Yes," replied one of them.

"Then I am a friend," I said.

The fellow laughed. "No Black Pirate of Barsoom is any friend of ours," he shot back.

For the moment I had forgotten the black pigment with which I had covered every inch of my face and body as a disguise to assist me in effecting my escape from The Black Pirates of the Valley of the First Born.

"I am not a Black Pirate," I said.

"Oh, no!" he cried; "then I suppose you are a white ape." At that they all laughed. "Come on now, sheathe your sword and come along with us. We'll let Gan Hor decide what is to be done with you, and I can tell you right now that Gan Hor doesn't like Black Pirates."

"Don't be a fool," I said; "I tell you I am no Black Pirate—this is just a disguise."

"Well," said the fellow, who thought he was something of a wit, "isn't it strange that you and I should meet?—I'm really a Black Pirate disguised as a red man." This simply convulsed his companions. When he could stop laughing at his own joke, he said, "Come on now, no more foolishness! Or do you want us to come and take you?"

"Come and take me!" I replied. In that, I made a mistake; but I was a little sore at being laughed at by these stupid fools.

They started circling me at a gallop; and as they did so, they uncoiled the ropes they use to catch thoats. They were whirling them about their heads now and shouting. Suddenly a dozen loops spun through the air at me simultaneously. It was a beautiful demonstration of roping, but I didn't really appreciate it at the moment. Those nooses settled around me from my neck to my heels, rendering me absolutely helpless as they yanked them taut; then the dozen whose ropes had ensnared me rode away all in the same direction, jerking me to the ground; nor did they stop there—they kept on going, dragging me along the ground.

My body rolled over and over in the soft ocher vegetation, and my captors kept riding faster and faster until their mounts were at a full run. It was a most undignified situation for a fighting man; it is like me that I thought first of the injury to my pride, rather than to the injury to my body—or the fact that much more of this would leave me but a bloody corpse at the ends of twelve rawhide ropes.

They must have dragged me half a mile before they finally stopped, and only the fact that the moss-like vegetation which carpets most of Mars *is* soft found me alive at the end of that experience.

The leader rode back to me, followed by the others. He took one look at me, and his eyes were wide. "By my first ancestor!" he exclaimed; "he is no Black Pirate—the black has rubbed off!"

I glanced at myself; sure enough, much of the pigment had been rubbed off against the vegetation through which I had been dragged, and my skin was now a mixture of black and white streaks smeared with blood.

The man dismounted; and, after disarming me, took the nooses from about me. "He isn't a Black Pirate and isn't even a red man," he said to his companions; "he's white and he has grey eyes. By my first ancestor, I don't believe he's a man at all. Can you stand up?"

I came to my feet. I was a little bit groggy, but I could stand. "I can stand," I said, "and if you want to find out whether or not I'm a man, give me back my sword and draw yours," and with that I slapped him in the face so hard that he fell down. I was so mad that I didn't care whether he killed me or not. He came to his feet cursing like a true pirate from the Spanish main.

"Give him his sword!" he shouted. "I was going to take him back to Gan Hor alive, but now I'll leave him here dead."

"You'd better take him back alive, Kor-an," advised one of his fellows. "We may have captured a spy; and if you kill him before Gan Hor can question him, it won't go so well for you."

"No man can strike me and live," shouted Kor-an; "where is his sword?"

One of them handed me my long-sword, and I faced Kor-an. "To the death?" I asked.

"To the death!" replied Kor-an.

"I shall not kill you, Kor-an," I said; "and you cannot kill me, but I shall teach you a lesson that you will not soon forget." I spoke in a loud tone of voice, that the others might hear.

One of them laughed, and said, "You don't know who you're talking to, fellow. Kor-an is one of the finest swordsmen in Gathol. You will be dead in five minutes."

"In one," said Kor-an, and came for me.

I went to work on Kor-an then, after trying to estimate roughly how many bleeding cuts and scratches I had on my body. He was a furious but clumsy fighter. In the first second I drew blood from his right breast; then I cut a long gash in his right thigh. Again and again I touched him, drawing blood from cuts or scratches. I could have killed him at any time, and he could touch me nowhere.

"It has been more than a minute, Kor-an," I said.

He did not reply; he was breathing heavily, and I could tell from his eyes that he was afraid. His companions sat in silence, watching every move.

Finally, after I had cut his body from forehead to toe, I stepped back, lowering my point. "Have you had enough, Kor-an?" I asked, "or do you want me to kill you?"

"I chose to fight to the death," he said, courageously; "it is your right to kill me—and I know that you can. I know that you could have killed me any time from the moment we crossed swords."

"I have no wish to kill a brave man," I said.

"Call the whole thing off," said one of the others; "you are up against the greatest swordsman anyone ever saw, Kor-an."

"No," said Kor-an, "I should be disgraced, if I stopped before I killed him or he killed me. Come!" He raised his point.

I dropped my sword to the ground and faced him. "You now have your chance to kill me," I told him.

"But that would be murder," he said; "I am no assassin."

"Neither am I, Kor-an; and if I ran you through, even while you carried your sword, I should be as much a murderer as you, were you to kill me now; for even with a sword in your hand you are as much unarmed against me as I am now against you."

"The man is right," spoke up one of the Gatholians. "Sheathe your sword, Kor-an; no one will hold it against you."

Kor-an looked at the others, and they all urged him to quit. He rammed his sword into its scabbard and mounted his thoat. "Get up behind me," he said to me. I mounted and they were off at a gallop.

chapter III

AFTER ABOUT HALF AN HOUR they entered another grove of sorapus, and presently came to a cluster of the rude huts used by the warrior-herdsmen of Gathol. Here was the remainder of the troop to which my captors belonged. These herdsmen are the warriors of Gathol, being divided into regular military units. This one was a utan of a hundred men commanded by a dwar, with two padwars, or lieutenants under him. They remain on this duty for one month, which is equivalent to about seventy days of Earth time; then they are relieved and return to Gathol city.

Gan Hor, the dwar, was sitting in front of one of the shelters playing jetan with a padwar when I was taken before him by Kor-an. He looked us both up and down for a full minute. "In the name of Issus!" he exclaimed, "what have you two been doing—playing with a herd of banths or a tribe of white apes? And who is this? He is neither red nor black."

"A prisoner," said Kor-an; then he explained quite honestly why we were in the condition we were.

Gan Hor scowled. "I'll take this matter up with you later, Kor-an," he said; then he turned to me.

"I am the father of Tara of Helium," I said, "the princess of your jed."

Gan Hor leaped to his feet, and Kor-an staggered as though he had been struck; I thought he was going to fall.

"John Carter!" exclaimed Gan Hor. "The white skin, the grey eyes, the swordsmanship of which Kor-an has told me. I have never seen John Carter, but you could be no other;" then he wheeled upon Kor-an. "And you dragged the Prince of Helium, Warlord of Barsoom for half a mile at the ends of your ropes!" He was almost screaming. "For that, you die!"

"No," I said. "Kor-an and I have settled that between us; he is to be punished no further."

These warrior-herdsmen of Gathol live much like our own desert nomads, moving from place to place as the requirements of pasturage and the presence of water dictate. There is no surface water in Gathol other than the moisture in the salt marsh that encircles the city; but in certain places water may be found by sinking wells, and in these spots they make their camps, as here in the sorapus grove to which I had been brought.

Gan Hor had water brought for me; and while I was washing away the black pigment, the dirt, and the blood, I told him that Llana of Gathol and two companions were not far from the spot where Kor-an had captured me; and he sent one of his padwars with a number of warriors and three extra thoats to bring them in.

"And now," I said, "tell me what is happening to Gathol. The fact that we were attacked last night, coupled with the ring of camp fires encircling the city, suggests that Gathol is besieged by an enemy."

"You are right," replied Gan Hor; "Gathol is surrounded by the troops of Hin Abtol, who styles himself Jeddak of Jeddaks of the North. He came here some time ago in an ancient and obsolete flier, but as he came in peace he was treated as an honored guest by Gahan. They say that he proved himself an egotistical braggart and an insufferable boor, and ended by demanding that Gahan give him Llana as a wife—he already had seven, he boasted.

"Of course, Gahan told him that Llana of Gathol would choose her own mate; and when Llana refused his proposition, he threatened to come back and take her by force. Then he went away, and the next day our Princess started out for Helium on a ship with twenty-five members of her personal guard. She never reached Helium, nor has she been seen or heard of since, until you just told me that she is alive and has returned to Gathol.

"But we soon heard from Hin Abtol. He came back with a large fleet of the most ancient and obsolete fliers that I have ever seen; some of his ships must be over a hundred years old. Hin Abtol came back, and he demanded the surrender of Gathol.

"His ships were crammed with warriors, thousands of whom leaped overboard and descended upon the city with equilibrimotors. There was fighting in the avenues and upon the roofs of buildings all of one day, but we eventually destroyed or made prisoners of all of them; so, finding that he could not take the city by storm, Hin Abtol laid siege to it.

"He has sent all but a few of his ships away, and we believe that they have returned to the frozen north for reinforcements. We who were on herd duty at the beginning of the investment are unable to return to the city, but we are continually harassing the warriors of Hin Abtol who are encamped upon the plain."

"So they are using equilibrimotors," I said; "it seems strange that any peoples from the frozen north should have these. They were absolutely unknown in Okar when I was there."

The equilibrimotor is an ingenious device for individual flying. It consists of a broad belt, not unlike the life belt used aboard passenger ships on Earth; the belt is filled with the eighth Barsoomian ray, or ray of propulsion, to a sufficient degree to equalize the pull of gravity and thus to maintain a person in equilibrium between that force and the opposite force exerted by the eighth ray. Attached to the back of the belt is a small radium motor, the controls for which are on the front of the belt; while rigidly attached to and projecting from the upper rim of the belt is a strong, light wing with small hand levers for quickly altering its position. I could understand that they might prove very effective for landing troops in an enemy city by night.

I had listened to Gan Hor with feelings of the deepest concern, for I knew that Gathol was not a powerful country and that a long and persistent siege must assuredly reduce it unless outside help came. Gathol depends for its food supplies upon the plains which comprise practically all of its territory. The far northwest corner of the country is cut by one of Barsoom's famous canals; and here the grains, and vegetables, and fruits which supply the city are raised; while upon her plains graze the herds that supply her with meat. And enemy surrounding the city would cut off all these supplies; and while Gahan doubtless had reserves stored in the city, they could not last indefinitely.

In discussing this with Gan Hor, I remarked that if I could get hold of a flier I'd return to Helium and bring a fleet of her mighty war ships and transports with guns and men enough to wipe Hin Abtol and his Panars off the face of Barsoom.

"Well," said Gan Hor, "your flier is here; it came with Hin Abtol's fleet. One of my men recognized it and your insigne upon it the moment he saw it; and we have all been wondering how Hin Abtol acquired it; but then, he has ships from a score of different nations, and has not bothered to remove their insignia."

"He found it in a courtyard in the deserted city of Horz," I explained; "and when he was attacked by green men, he made off in it with a couple of his warriors, leaving the others to be killed."

Just then the padwar who had gone to fetch Llana, Pan Dan Chee, and Jad-han returned with his detachment—and three riderless thoats!

"They were not there," he said; "though we searched everywhere, we could not find them; but there was blood on the ground where they had been."

chapter IV

So Llana of Gathol was lost to me again! That she had been captured by Hin Abtol's warriors, there seemed little doubt. I asked Gan Hor for a thoat, that I might ride out and examine the spot at which the party had been taken; and he not only acceded to my request, but accompanied me with a detachment of his warriors.

There had evidently been a fight at the place that I had left them; the vegetation was trampled, and there was blood upon it; but so resilient is this mosslike carpeting of the dead sea bottoms of Mars, that, except for the blood, the last traces of the encounter were fast disappearing; and there was no indication of the direction taken by Llana's captors.

"How far are their lines from here?" I asked Gan Hor.

"About nine haads," he replied—that is not quite three Earth miles.

"We might as well return to your camp," I said; "we haven't a sufficiently strong force to accomplish anything now. I shall return after dark."

"We can make a little raid on one of their encampments tonight," suggested Gan Hor.

"I shall go alone," I told him; "I have a plan."

"But it won't be safe," he objected. "I have a hundred men with whom I am constantly harassing them; we should be glad to ride with you."

"I am going only for information, Gan Hor; I can get that better alone."

We returned to camp, and with the help of one of Gan Hor's warriors I applied to my face and body the red pigment that I always carry with me for use when I find it necessary to disguise myself as a native born red man—a copper colored ointment such as had first been given me by the Ptor brothers of Zodanga many years ago.

After dark I set out on thoatback, accompanied by Gan Hor and a couple of his warriors; as I had accepted his offer of transportation to a point much nearer the Panar lines. Fortunately the heavens were temporarily moonless, and we came quite close to the enemy's first fires before I dismounted and bid my new friends good-by.

"Good luck!" said Gan Hor; "and you'll need it."

Kor-an was one of the warriors who had accompanied us. "I'd like to go with you, Prince," he said; "thus I might atone for the thing I did."

"If I could take anyone, I'd take you, Kor-an," I assured him. "Anyway, you have nothing to atone for; but if you want to do something for me, promise that you will fight always for Tara of Helium and Llana of Gathol."

"On my sword, I swear it," he said; and then I left them and made my way cautiously toward the Panar camp.

Once again, as upon so many other occasions, I used the tactics of another race of red warriors—the Apaches of our own Southwest—worming my way upon my belly closer and closer toward the lines of the enemy. I could see the forms of warriors clustered about their fires, and I could hear their voices and their rough laughter; and, as I drew nearer, the oaths and obscenities which seem to issue most naturally from the mouths of fighting men; and when a gust of wind blew from the camp toward me, I could even smell the sweat and the leather mingling with the acrid fumes of the smoke of their fires.

A sentry paced his post between me and the fires; when he came closest to me, I flattened myself upon the ground. I heard him yawn. When he was almost on top of me, I rose up before him; and before he could voice a warning cry, I seized him by the throat. Three times I drove my dagger into his heart. I hate to kill like that; but now there was no other way, and it was not for myself that I killed him—it was for Llana of Gathol, for Tara of Helium, and for Dejah Thoris, my beloved princess.

Just as I lowered his body to the ground, a warrior at a nearby fire arose and looked out toward us. "What was that?" he asked his fellows.

"The sentry," one of them replied; "there he is now." I was slowly pacing the post of the departed, hoping none would come to investigate.

"I could have sworn I saw two men scuffling there," said the first speaker.

"You are always seeing things," said a third.

I walked the post until they had ceased to discuss the matter and had turned their attention elsewhere; then I knelt beside the dead man and removed his harness and weapons, which I immediately donned. Now I was, to outward appearances anyway, a soldier of Hin Abtol, a Panar from some glazed, hot-house city of the frozen North.

Walking to the far end of my post, I left it and entered the camp at some distance from the group which included the warrior whose suspicions I had aroused. Although I passed close to another group of warriors, no one paid any attention to me. Other individuals were wandering around from fire to fire, and so my movements attracted no notice.

I must have walked fully a haad inside the lines away from my point of entry before I felt that it would be safe to stop and mix with the warriors. Finally I saw a lone warrior sitting beside a fire, and approached him.

"Kaor!" I said, using the universal greeting of Barsoom.

"Kaor!" he replied. "Sit down. I am a stranger here and have no friends in this dar." A dar is a unit of a thousand men, analogous to our Earthly regiment. "I just came down today with a fresh contingent from Pankor. It is good to move about and see the world again, after having been frozen in for fifty years."

"You haven't been away from Pankor for fifty years!" I exclaimed, guessing that Pankor was the name of the Arctic city from which he hailed, and hoping that I was guessing right.

"No," he said; "and you! How long were you frozen in?"

"I have never been to Pankor," I said; "I am a panthan who has just joined up with Hin Abtol's forces since they came south." I thought this the safest position to take, since I should be sure to arouse suspicion were I to claim familiarity with Pankor, when I had never been there.

"Well," said my companion, "you must be crazy."

"Why?" I asked.

"Nobody but a crazy man would put himself in the power of Hin Abtol. Well, you've done it; and now you'll be taken to Pankor after this war is over, unless you're lucky enough to be killed; and you'll be frozen in there until Hin Abtol needs you for another campaign. What's your name?"

"Dotor Sojat," I replied, falling back on that old time name the green Martian horde of Thark had given me so many years before.

"Mine is Em-tar; I am from Kobol."

"I thought you said you were from Pankor."

"I'm a Kobolian by birth," he explained. "Where are you from?"

"We panthans have no country," I reminded him.

"But you must have been born somewhere," he insisted.

"Perhaps the less said about that the better," I said, attempting a sly wink.

He laughed. "Sorry I asked," he said.

Sometimes, when a man has committed a political crime, a huge reward is offered for information concerning his whereabouts; so, as well as changing his name, he never divulges the name of his country. I let Em-tar think that I was a fugitive from justice.

"How do you think this campaign is going?" I asked.

"If Hin Abtol can starve them out, he may win," replied Em-tar; "but from what I have heard he could never take the city by storm. These Gatholians are great fighters, which is more than can be said for those who fight under Hin Abtol—our hearts aren't in it; we have no feeling of loyalty for Hin Abtol; but these Gatholians now, they're fighting for their homes and their jed; and they love 'em both. They say that Gahan's Princess is a daughter of The Warlord of Barsoom. Say, if he hears about this and brings a fleet and an army from Helium, we might just as well start digging our graves."

"Are we taking many prisoners?" I asked.

"Not many. Three were taken this morning; one of them was the daughter of Gahan, the Jed of Gathol; the other two were men."

"That's interesting," I said; "I wonder what Hin Abtol will do with the daughter of Gahan."

"That I wouldn't know," replied Em-tar, "but they say he's sent her off to Pankor already. You hear a lot of rumors in an army, though; and most of them are wrong."

"I suppose Hin Abtol has a big fleet of fliers," I said.

"He's got a lot of old junk, and not many men capable of flying what he has got."

"I'm a flier," I said.

"You'd better not let 'em know it, or they'll have you on board some old wreck," advised Em-tar.

"Where's their landing field here?"

"Down that way about a haad"; he pointed in the direction I had been going when I stopped to talk with him.

"Well, good-by, Em-tar," I said, rising.

"Where are you going?"

"To fly for Hin Abtol of Pankor," I said.

chapter V

I MADE MY WAY through the camp to where a number of fliers were lined up; it was an extremely ragged, unmilitary line, suggesting inefficiency; and the ships were the most surprising aggregation of obsolete relics I have ever seen; most of them were museum pieces.

Some warriors were sitting around fires nearby; and, assuming that they were attached to the flying service, I approached them.

"Where is the flying officer in command?" I asked.

"Over there," said one of the men, pointing at the largest ship on the line. "Why—do you want to see him?"

"Yes."

"Well, he's probably drunk."

"He *is* drunk," said another.

"What's his name?" I asked.

"Odwar Phor San," replied my informant. Odwar is about the same as general, or brigadier general. He commands ten thousand men in the army and a fleet in the navy.

"Thanks," I said; "I'll go over and see him."

"You wouldn't, if you knew him; he's as mean as an ulsio."

I walked over to the big ship. It was battered and weatherbeaten, and must have been at least fifty years old. A boarding ladder hung down amidships, and at its foot stood a warrior with drawn sword.

"What do you want?" he demanded

"I have a message for Odwar Phor San," I said.

"Who is it from?"

"That is none of your business," I told him; "send word to the odwar that Dotor Sojat wishes to see him on an important matter."

The fellow saluted with mock elaborateness. "I didn't know we had a jedwar among us," he said. "Why didn't you tell me?"

Now, jedwar is the highest rank in a Barsoomian army or navy, other than that of jed or jeddak or Warlord, a rank created especially for me by the jeddaks of five empires. That warrior would have been surprised could he have known that he had conferred upon me a title far inferior to my own.

I laughed at his little joke, and said, "One never knows whom one is entertaining."

"If you really have a message for the old ulsio, I'll call the deck watch; but, by Issus, you'd better have a message of importance."

"I have," I assured him; and I spoke the truth, for it was of tremendous importance to me; so he hailed the deck watch and told him to tell the odwar that Dotor Sojat had come with an important message for him.

I waited about five minutes, and then I was summoned aboard and conducted to one of the cabins. A gross, slovenly man sat before a table on which was a large tankard and several heavy, metal goblets. He looked at me scowlingly out of bleary eyes.

"What does that son of a calot want now?" he demanded.

I guessed that he referred to a superior officer, and probably to Hin Abtol. Well, if he thought I bore a message from Hin Abtol, so much the better.

"I am to report to you as an experienced flier," I said.

"He sent you at this time of night to report to me as a flier?" he almost shouted at me.

"You have few experienced fliers," I said. "I am a panthan who has flown every type of ship in the navy of Helium. I gathered that you would be glad to get me before some other commander snapped me up. I am a navigator, and familiar with all modern instruments; but if you don't want me, I shall then be free to attach myself elsewhere."

He was befuddled by strong drink, or I'd probably never have gotten away with such a bluff. He pretended to be considering the matter seriously; and while he considered it, he poured himself another drink, which he swallowed in two or three gulps—what didn't run down his front. Then he filled another goblet and pushed it across the table toward me, slopping most of its contents on the table top.

"Have drink!" he said.

"Not now," I said; "I never drink when I am on duty."

"You're not on duty."

"I am always on duty; I may have to take a ship up at any moment."

He pondered this for several minutes with the assistance of another drink; then he filled another goblet and pushed it across the table toward me. "Have drink," he said.

I now had two full goblets in front of me; it was evident that Phor San had not noticed that I had failed to drink the first one.

"What ship shall I command?" I asked; I was promoting myself rapidly. Phor San paid no attention to my question, being engaged in what was now becoming a delicate and difficult operation—the pouring of another drink; most of it went on the table, from where it ran down into his lap.

"What ship did you say I was to command?" I demanded.

He looked bewildered for a moment; then he tried to draw himself together with military dignity. "You will command the Dusar, Dwar," he said; then he filled another goblet and pushed it toward me. "Have drink, Dwar," he said. My promotion was confirmed.

I walked over to a desk covered with an untidy litter of papers, and searched until I found an official blank; on it I wrote:

> To Dwar Dotor Sojat:
>
> You will immediately take over command of ship Dusar.
>
> By order of
>
> Odwar Commanding

After finding a cloth and wiping the liquor from the table in front of him, I laid the order down and handed him a pen.

"You forgot to sign this, Odwar," I said. He was commencing to weave, and I saw that I must hurry.

"Sign what?" he demanded, reaching for the tankard.

I pushed it away from him, took his hand, and placed the pen point at the right place on the order blank. "Sign here," I ordered.

"Sign here," he repeated, and laboriously scrawled his name; then he fell forward on the table, asleep. I had been just in time.

I went on deck; both moons were now in the sky, Cluros just above the horizon, Thuria a little higher; by the time Cluros approached zenith, Thuria would have completed her orbit around Barsoom and passed him, so swift her flight through the heavens.

The deck watch approached me. "Where lies the Dusar?" I asked.

He pointed down the line. "About the fifth or sixth ship, I think," he said.

I went overside; and as I reached the ground, the sentry there asked, "Was the old ulsio as drunk as ever?"

"He was perfectly sober," I replied.

"Then some one had better send for the doctor," he said, "for he must be sick."

I walked along the line, and at the fifth ship I approached the sentry at the foot of its ladder. "Is this the Dusar?" I asked.

"Can't you read?" he demanded, impudently.

I look up then at the insigne on the ship's bow; it was the Dusar. "Can you read?" I asked, and held the order up in front of him.

He snapped to attention and saluted. "I couldn't tell by your metal," he said, sullenly. He was quite right; I was wearing the metal of a common warrior.

I looked the ship over. From the ground it hadn't a very promising appearance—just a disreputable, obsolete old hulk. Then I climbed the ladder and stepped to the deck of my new command; there was no boatswain's call to pipe the side; there was only one man on watch; and he was curled up on the deck, fast asleep.

I walked over and poked him with the toe of a sandal. "Wake up, there!" I ordered.

He opened an eye and looked up at me; then he leaped to his feet. "Who are you?" he demanded. "What are you doing here? What do you mean by kicking me in the ribs and waking me up?"

"One question at a time, my man," I said. "I shall answer your first question, and that will answer the others also." I held the order out to him.

As he took it, he said, "Don't call me my man, you—" But he stopped there; he had read the order. He saluted and handed the order back to me, but I noticed just the suggestion of a grin on his face.

"Why did you smile?" I asked.

"I was thinking that you probably got the softest job in Hin Abtol's navy," he said.

"What do you mean?"

"You won't have anything to do; the Dusar is out of commission— she won't fly."

So! Perhaps Odwar Phor San was not as drunk as I had thought him.

chapter VI

THE DECK OF THE DUSAR was weatherbeaten and filthy; everything was in disorder, but what difference did that make if the ship wouldn't fly?

"How many officers and men comprise her complement?" I asked.

The fellow grinned and pointed to himself. "One," he said, "or, rather, two, now that you are here."

I asked him his name, and he said that it was Fo-nar. In the United States he would have been known as an ordinary seaman, but the Martian words for seaman and sailor are now as obsolete as the oceans with which they died, almost from the memory of man. All sailors and soldiers are known as *thans*, which I have always translated as *warriors*.

"Well, Fo-nar," I said; "let's have a look at our ship. What's wrong with her? Why won't she fly?"

"It's the engine, sir," he said; "it won't start any more."

"I'll have a look over the ship," I said, "and then we'll see if we can't do something about the engine."

I took Fo-nar with me and went below. Everything there was filthy and in disorder. "How long has she been out of commission?" I asked.

"About a month."

"You certainly couldn't have made all this mess by yourself in a month," I said.

"No, sir; she was always like this even when she was flying," he said.

"Who commanded her? Whoever he was, he should be cashiered for permitting a ship to get in this condition."

"He won't ever be cashiered, sir," said Fo-nar.

"Why?" I asked.

"Because he got drunk and fell overboard on our last flight," Fo-nar explained, with a grin.

I inspected the guns, there were eight of them, four on a side beside smaller bow and stern guns on deck; they all seemed to be in pretty fair condition, and there was plenty of ammunition. The bomb racks in the bilge were full, and there was a bomb trap forward and another aft.

There were quarters for twenty-five men and three officers, a good galley, and plenty of provisions. If I had not seen Odwar Phor San, I could not have understood why all this material—guns, ammunition, provisions, and tackle—should have been left on a ship permanently out of commission. The ship appeared to me to be about ten years old—that is, after a careful inspection; superficially, it looked a hundred.

I told Fo-nar to go back on deck and go to sleep, if he wished to; and then I went into the dwar's cabin and lay down; I hadn't had much sleep the night before, and I was tired. It was daylight when I awoke, and I found Fo-nar in the galley getting his breakfast. I told him to prepare mine, and after we had both eaten I went to have a look at the engine.

It hurt me to go through that ship and see the condition its drunken skipper had permitted it to get into. I love these Barsoomian fliers, and I have been in the navy of Helium for so many years that ships have acquired almost human personalities for me. I have designed them; I have superintended their construction; I have developed new ideas in equipment, engines, and armament; and several standard flying and navigating instruments are of my invention. If there is anything I don't know about a modern Martian flier; then nobody else knows it.

I found tools and practically dismantled the engine, checking every part. While I was doing this, I had Fo-nar start cleaning up the ship. I told him to start with my cabin and then tackle the galley next. It would have taken one man a month or more to put the Dusar in even fair condition, but at least we would make a start.

I hadn't been working on the engine half an hour before I found what was wrong with it—just dirt! Every feed line was clogged; and that marvellous, concentrated, Martian fuel could not reach the motor.

I was appalled by the evidence of such stupidity and inefficiency, though not entirely surprised; drunken commanders and Barsoomian fliers just don't go together. In the navy of Helium, no officer drinks while on board ship or on duty; and not one of them drinks to excess at any time.

If an officer were ever drunk on board his ship, the crew would see to it that he was never drunk again; they know that their lives are in the hands of their officers, and they don't purpose trusting them to a drunken man—they simply push the officer overboard. It is such a well established custom, or used to be before drinking on the part of officers practically ceased, that no action was ever taken against the warrior who took discipline into his own hands, even though the act were witnessed by officers. I rather surmised that this time honored custom had had something to do with the deplorable accident that had robbed the Dusar of her former commander.

The day was practically gone by the time I had cleaned every part of the engine thoroughly and reassembled it; then I started it; and the sweet, almost noiseless and vibrationless, hum of it was music to my ears. I had a ship—a ship that would fly!

One man can operate such a ship, but of course he can't fight it. Where, however, could I get men? I didn't want just any men; I wanted good fighting men who would just as lief fight against Hin Abtol as not.

Pondering this problem, I went to my cabin to clean up; it looked spick-and-span. Fo-nar had done a good job; he had also laid out the harness and metal of a dwar—doubtless the property of the late commander. Bathed and properly garbed, I felt like a new man as I stepped out onto the upper deck. Fo-nar snapped to attention and saluted.

"Fo-nar," I said, "are you a Panar?"

"I should say not," he replied with some asperity. "I am from Jahar originally, but now I have no country—I am a panthan."

"You were there during the reign of Tul Axtar?" I asked.

"Yes," he replied; "it was on his account that I became an exile—I tried to kill him, and I got caught; I just barely escaped with my life. I cannot go back so long as he is alive."

"You can go back, then," I said; "Tul Axtar is dead."

"How do you know, sir?"

"I know the man who killed him."

"Just my luck!" exclaimed Fo-nar; "now that I might go back, I can't."

"Why can't you?"

"For the same reason, sir, that where ever you are from you'll never go back, unless you are from Panar, which I doubt."

"No, I am not from Panar," I said; "but what makes you think I won't go back to my own country?"

"Because no one upon whom Hin Abtol gets his hands ever escapes, other than through death."

chapter VII

"OH, COME, FO-NAR," I said; "that is ridiculous. What is to prevent either one of us from deserting?"

"If we deserted here," he replied, "we would immediately be picked up by the Gatholians and killed; after this campaign is over, we will not make a landing until we reach Panar; and from Panar there is no escape. Hin Abtol's ships never stop at a friendly city, where one might find an opportunity to escape; for there are no cities friendly to Hin

Abtol. He attacks every city that he believes he can take, sacks it, and flies away with all the loot he can gather and with as many prisoners as his ships will carry—mostly men; they say he has a million now, and that he plans eventually to conquer Helium and then all of Barsoom. He took me prisoner when he sacked Raxar on his way down from Panar to Gathol; I was serving there in the army of the jed."

"You would like to return to Jahar?" I asked.

"Certainly," he replied. "My mate is there, if she still lives; I have been gone twenty years."

"You feel no loyalty toward Hin Abtol?"

"Absolutely none," he replied; "why?"

"I think I can tell you. I have the same power that all Barsoomians have of being able to read the mind of another when he happens to be off guard; and a couple of times, Fo-nar, your subconscious mind has dropped its guard and permitted me to read your thoughts; I have learned several things about you. One is that you are constantly wondering about me—who I am and whether I am to be trusted. For another thing, I have learned that you despise the Panars. I also discovered that you were no common warrior in Jahar, but a dwar in the jeddak's service—you were thinking about that when you first saw me in the metal and harness of a dwar."

Fo-nar smiled. "You read well," he said; "I must be more careful. You read much better than I do, or else you guard your thoughts more jealously than I; for I have not been able to obtain even the slightest inkling of what is passing in your mind."

"No man has ever been able to read my mind," I said, and that is very strange, too, and quite inexplicable. The Martians have developed mind reading to a point where it is a fine art, but none has ever been able to read my mind. Perhaps that is because it is the mind of an Earth man, and may account for the fact that telepathy has not advanced far on our planet.

"You are fortunate," said Fo-nar; "but please go on and tell me what you started to."

"Well," I said, "in the first place, I have repaired the engine—the Dusar can now fly."

"Good!" exclaimed Fo-nar. "I said you were no Panar; they are the stupidest people in the world. No Panar could ever have repaired it; all they can do is let things go to wrack and ruin. Go on."

"Now we need a crew. Can we find from fifteen to twenty-five men whom we can trust and who can fight—men who will follow me anywhere I lead them to win their freedom from Hin Abtol?"

"I can find you all the men you need," replied Fo-nar.

"Get busy, then," I said; "you are now First Padwar of the Dusar."

"I am getting up in the world again," said Fo-nar, laughing. "I'll start out immediately, but don't expect a miracle—it may take a little time to find the right men."

"Have them report to the ship after dark, and tell them to be sure that no one sees them. What can we do about that sentry at the foot of the ladder?"

"The one who was on duty when you came aboard is all right," said Fo-nar; "he'll come with us. He's on from the eighth to the ninth zodes, and I'll tell the men to come at that time."

"Good luck, padwar!" I said, as he went overside.

The remainder of the day dragged slowly. I spent some time in my cabin looking through the ship's papers. Barsoomian ships keep a log just as Earth ships do, and I occupied several hours looking through the log of the Dusar. The ship had been captured four years before while on a scientific expedition to the Arctic, since then, under Panar commanders, the log had been very poorly kept. Some times there were no entries for a week, and those that were made were unprofessional and sloppy; the more I learned about the Panars the less I liked them—and to think that the creature who ruled them aspired to conquer a world!

About the end of the seventh zode Fo-nar returned. "I had much better luck than I anticipated," he said; "every man I approached knew three or four he could vouch for; so it didn't take long to get twenty-five. I think, too, that I have just the man for Second Padwar. He was a padwar in the army of Helium, and has served on many of her ships."

"What is his name?" I asked. "I have known many men from Helium."

"He is Tan Hadron of Hastor," replied Fo-nar.

Tan Hadron of Hastor! Why, he was one of my finest officers. What ill luck could have brought him to the navy of Hin Abtol?

"Tan Hadron of Hastor," I said aloud; "the name sounds a little familiar; it is possible that I knew him." I did not wish anyone to know that I was John Carter, Prince of Helium; for if it became known, and I was captured, Hin Abtol could have wrested an enormous ransom from Tardos Mors, Jeddak of Helium and grandfather of my mate, Dejah Thoris.

Immediately after the eighth zode, warriors commenced to come aboard the Dusar. I had instructed Fo-nar to immediately send them below to their quarters, for I feared that too much life on the deck of the Dusar might attract attention; I had also told him to send Tan Hadron to my cabin as soon as he came aboard.

About half after the eighth zode someone scratched on my door; and when I bade him enter, Tan Hadron stepped into the cabin. My red skin and Panar harness deceived him, and he did not recognize me.

"I am Tan Hadron of Hastor," he said; "Padwar Fo-nar instructed me to report to you."

"You are not a Panar?" I asked.

He stiffened. "I am a Heliumite from the city of Hastor," he said, proudly.

"Where is Hastor?" I asked.

He looked surprised at such ignorance. "It lies directly south of Greater Helium, sir; about five hundred haads. You will pardon me," he added, "but I understood from Padwar Fo-nar that you knew many men from Helium, and so I imagined that you had visited the empire; in fact he gave me to understand that you had served in our navy."

"That is neither here nor there," I said. "Fo-nar has recommended you for the post of Second Padwar aboard the Dusar. You will have to serve me faithfully and follow where ever I lead; your reward will consist of your freedom from Hin Abtol."

I could see that he was a little bit skeptical about the whole proposition now that he had met me—a man who had never heard of Hastor couldn't amount to much; but he touched the hilt of his sword and said that he would follow me loyally.

"Is that all, sir?" he asked.

"Yes," I said; "for the time being. After the men are all aboard I shall have them mustered below deck, and at that time I shall name the officers; please be there."

He saluted, and turned to go.

"Oh, by the way," I called to him, "how is Tavia?"

At that he wheeled about as though he had been shot, and his eyes went wide. "What do you know of Tavia, sir?" he demanded. Tavia is his mate.

"I know that she is a very lovely girl, and that I can't understand why you are not back in Hastor with her; or are you stationed in Helium now?"

He came a little closer, and looked at me intently. As a matter of fact, the light was not very good in my cabin, or he would have recognized me sooner. Finally his jaw dropped, and then he unbuckled his sword and threw it at my feet. "John Carter!" he exclaimed.

"Not so loud, Hadron," I cautioned; "no one here knows who I am; and no one must, but you."

"You had a good time with me, didn't you, sir?" he laughed.

"It has been some time since I have had anything to laugh about," I said; "so I hope you will forgive me; now tell me about yourself and how you got into this predicament."

"Perhaps half the navy of Helium is looking for Llana of Gathol and you," he said. "Rumors of the whereabouts of one or the other of you have come from all parts of Barsoom. Like many another officer I was scouting for you or Llana in a one man flier. I had bad luck, sir; and here I am. One of Hin Abtol's ships shot me down, and then landed and captured me."

"Llana of Gathol and I, with two companions, were also shot down by one of Hin Abtol's ships," I told him. "While I was searching for food, they were captured, presumably by some of Hin Abtol's warriors, as we landed behind their lines. We must try to ascertain, if possible, where Llana is; then we can plan intelligently. Possibly some of our recruits may have information; see what you can find out."

He saluted and left my cabin. It was good to know that I had such a man as Tan Hadron of Hastor as one of my lieutenants.

chapter VIII

SHORTLY AFTER Tan Hadron left my cabin, Fo-nar entered to report that all but one of the recruits had reported and that he had the men putting the flier in shipshape condition. He seemed a little bit worried about something, and I asked him what it was.

"It's about this warrior who hasn't reported," he replied. "The man who persuaded him to join up is worried, too. He said he hadn't known him long, but since he came aboard the Dusar he's met a couple of men who know the fellow well; and they say he's an ulsio."

"Well, there's nothing we can do about it now," I said. "If this man talks and arouses suspicion, we may have to take off in a hurry. Have you assigned each man to his station?"

"Tan Hadron is doing that now," he replied. "I think we have found a splendid officer in that man."

"I am sure of it," I agreed. "Be sure that four men are detailed to cut the cables instantly, if it becomes necessary for us to make a quick getaway."

When on the ground, the larger Martian fliers are moored to four deadmen, one on either side at the bow and one on either side at the stern. Unless a ship is to return to the same anchorage, these deadmen are dug up and taken aboard before she takes off. In the event of forced departure, such as I anticipated might be necessary in our case, the cables attached to the deadmen are often cut.

Fo-nar hadn't been gone from my cabin five minutes before he came hurrying in again. "I guess we're in for it, sir," he said; "Odwar Phor San is coming aboard! That missing recruit is with him; he must have reported all he knew to Phor San."

"When the odwar comes aboard, bring him down to my cabin; and then order the men to their stations; see that the four men you have detailed for that duty stand by the mooring cables with axes; ask Tan Hadron to start the engine and stand by to take off; post a man outside my cabin door to pass the word to take off when I give the signal; I'll clap my hands twice."

Fo-nar was gone only a couple of minutes before he returned. "He won't come below," he reported; "he's storming around up there like a mad thoat, demanding to have the man brought on deck who gave orders to recruit a crew for the Dusar."

"Is Tan Hadron at the controls ready to start the engine?" I asked.

"He is," replied Fo-nar.

"He will start them, then, as soon as I come on deck; at the same time post your men at the mooring cables; tell them what the signal will be."

I waited a couple of minutes after Fo-nar had left; then I went on deck. Phor San was stamping up and down, evidently in a terrible rage; he was also a little drunk.

I walked up to him and saluted. "Did you send for me, sir?" I asked.

"Who are you?" he demanded.

"Dwar commanding the Dusar, sir," I replied.

"Who said so?" he yelled. "Who assigned you to this ship? Who assigned you to any ship?"

"You did, sir."

"I?" he screamed. "I never saw you before. You are under arrest. Arrest him!" He turned to a warrior at his elbow—my missing recruit, as I suspected—and started to speak to him again.

"Wait a minute," I said; "look at this; here's a written order over your own signature assigning me to the command of the Dusar." I held the order up where he could read it in the bright light of Mars' two moons.

He looked surprised and a little crestfallen for just a moment; then he blustered, "It's a forgery! Anyway, it didn't give you authority to recruit warriors for the ship." He was weakening.

"What good is a fighting ship without warriors?" I demanded.

"You don't need warriors on a ship that won't fly, you idiot," he came back. "You thought you were pretty cute, getting me to sign that order; but I was a little cuter—I knew the Dusar wouldn't fly."

"Well, then, why all the fuss, sir?" I asked.

"Because you're plotting something; I don't know what, but I'm going to find out—getting men aboard this ship secretly at night! I rescind that order, and I place you under arrest."

I had hoped to get him off the ship peaceably, for I wanted to make sure of Llana's whereabouts before taking off. One man had told me that he had heard that she was on a ship bound for Pankor, but that was not definite. I also wished to know if Hin Abtol was with her.

"Very well, Phor San," I said; "now let me tell you something. I am in command of this ship, and I intend to stay in command. I'll give you and this rat here three seconds to get over the side, for the Dusar will take off in three seconds," and then I clapped my hands twice.

Phor San laughed a sneering laugh. "I told you it wouldn't fly," he said; "now come along! If you won't come quietly, you'll be taken;" he pointed overside. I looked, and saw a strong detachment of warriors marching toward the Dusar; at the same time, the Dusar rose from the ground.

Phor San stood in front of me, gloating. "What are you going to do now?" he demanded.

"Take you for a little ride, Phor San," I replied, and pointed overside.

He took one look, and then ran to the rail. His warriors were looking up at him in futile bewilderment. Phor San shouted to the padwar commanding them, "Order the Okar to pursue and take this ship!" The Okar was his flagship.

"Perhaps you'd like to come down to my cabin and have a little drink," I suggested, the liquor of the former commander being still there. "You go with him," I ordered the recruit who had betrayed us; "you will find liquor in one of the cabinets;" then I went to the bridge. On the way, I sent a warrior to summon Fo-nar. I told Tan Hadron to circle above the line of ships; and when Fo-nar reported, I gave him his orders, and he went below.

"We can't let them take to the air," I told Tan Hadron; "this is not a fast ship, and if several of them overhauled us we wouldn't have a chance."

Following my orders, Tan Hadron flew low toward the first ship on the line; it was the Okar, and she was about to take off. I signalled down to Fo-nar, and an instant later there was a terrific explosion aboard the Okar—our first bomb had made a clean hit! Slowly we moved down the line, dropping our bombs; but before we had reached the middle of it, ships at the lower end were taking off and projectiles were bursting around us from the ground batteries.

"It's time we got out of here," I said to Tan Hadron. He opened the throttle wide then, and the Dusar rose rapidly in a zigzag course.

Our own guns were answering the ground batteries, and evidently very effectively, for we were not hit once. I felt that we had come out of the affair so far very fortunately. We hadn't disabled as many ships as I had hoped that we I might, and there were already several in the air which would doubtless pursue us; I could see one ship on our tail already, but she was out of range and apparently not gaining on us rapidly, if at all.

I told Tan Hadron to set his course due North, and then I sent for Fo-nar and told him to muster all hands on deck; I wanted a chance to look over my crew and explain what our expedition involved. There was time for this now, while no ships were within range of us, which might not be true in a short time.

The men came piling up from below and from their stations on deck. They were, for the most part, a hardbitten lot, veterans, I should say, of many a campaign. As I looked them over, I could see that they were sizing me up; they were probably wondering more about me than I was about them, for I was quite sure what they would do if they thought they could get the upper hand of me—I'd "fall" overboard, and they would take over the ship; then they'd quarrel among themselves as to what they would do with it and where they would fly it; in the end, half a dozen of the hardiest would survive, make for the nearest city, sell the Dusar, and have a wild orgy—if they didn't wreck her before.

I asked each man his name and his past experience; there were, among the twenty-three, eleven panthans and twelve assassins; and they had fought all over the world. Seven of the panthans were from Helium, or had served in the Helium navy. I knew that these men were accustomed to discipline. The assassins were from various cities, scattered all over Barsoom. I didn't need to ask them, to be quite sure that each had incurred the wrath of his Guild and been forced to flee in order to escape assassination himself; they were a tough lot.

"We are flying to Pankor," I told them, "in search of the daughter of the jed of Gathol, who has been abducted by Hin Abtol. There may be a great deal of fighting before we get her; if we succeed and live, we will fly to Helium; there I shall turn the ship over to you, and you can do what you please with it."

"You're not flying me to Pankor," said one of the assassins; "I've been there for twenty-five years, and I'm not going back."

This was insubordination verging on mutiny. In a well disciplined navy, it would have been a very simple thing to handle; but here, where there was no higher authority than I, I had to take a very different course from a commander with a powerful government behind him. I stepped up to the man and slapped him as I had slapped Kor-an; and, like Kor-an, he went down.

"You're flying wherever I fly you," I said; "I'll have no insubordination on this ship."

He leaped to his feet and whipped out his sword, and there was nothing for me to do but draw also.

"The penalty for this, you understand, is death," I said, "—unless you sheathe your sword immediately."

"I'll sheathe it in your belly, you calot!" he cried, making a terrific lunge at me, which I parried easily and then ran him through the right shoulder. I knew that I would have to kill him, for the discipline of the ship and perhaps the fate of Llana of Gathol might hinge on this question of my supremacy and my authority; but first I must give an exhibition of swordplay that would definitely assure the other members of the crew that the lethal thrust was no accident, as they might have thought had I killed him at once.

So I played with him as a cat plays with a mouse, until the other members of the crew, who had stood silent and scowling at first, commenced to ridicule him.

"I thought you were going to sheathe your sword in his belly," taunted one.

"Why don't you kill him, Gan-ho?" demanded another. "I thought you were such a great swordsman."

"I can tell you one thing," said a third: "you are not going to fly to Pankor, or anywhere else. Good-by, Gan-ho! you are dead."

Just to show the other men how easily I could do it, I disarmed Gan-ho, sending his blade rattling across the deck. He stood for a moment glaring at me like a mad beast; then he turned and ran across the deck and dove over the rail. I was glad that I did not have to kill him.

I turned to the men gathered before me. "Is there any other who will not fly to Pankor?" I asked, and waited for a reply.

Several of them grinned sheepishly; and there was much scuffing of sandals on the deck, but no one replied.

"I had you mustered here to tell where we were flying and why; also that Fo-nar is First Padwar, Tan Hadron is Second Padwar, and I am your Dwar—we are to be obeyed. Return to your stations."

chapter IX

SHORTLY AFTER the men dispersed, Phor San and his satellite appeared on deck; they were both drunk. Phor San came toward me and stopped in front of me waving an erratic finger at me. He stunk of the liquor he had been drinking.

"In the name of Hin Abtol, Jeddak of Jeddaks of the North," he declaimed, "I order you to turn over the command of this ship to me, or suffer the full consequences of your crime of mutiny."

I saw the men on deck eyeing the two banefully. "You'd better go below," I said; "you might fall overboard."

Phor San turned to some of the crew members. "I am Odwar Phor San," he announced, "commander of the fleet; put this man in irons and return the ship to the air field!"

"I think you have gone far enough, Phor San," I said; "if you continue, I shall have to assume that you are attempting to incite my crew to mutiny, and act accordingly. Go below!"

"You trying to give me orders on one of my ships?" he demanded. "I'll have you understand that I am Phor San—"

"Commander of the fleet," I finished for him, "Here," I said to a couple of warriors standing near, "take these two below, and if they don't behave themselves, tie them up."

Fuming and blustering, Phor San was dragged below. His companion went quietly; I guess he knew what was good for him.

The one ship was still hanging onto our tail and not gaining perceptibly, but there were two just behind her which were overhauling both of us.

"That doesn't look so good," I said to Tan Hadron, who was standing at my side.

"Let's show them something," he said.

"What, for instance?" I asked.

"Do you remember that maneuver of yours the last time Helium was attacked by an enemy fleet, where you got the flag ship and two other ships that thought you were running from them?"

"All right," I said, "we'll try it." Then I sent for Fo-nar and gave him full instructions. While we were talking, I heard a series of piercing screams, gradually diminishing in the distance; but my mind was so occupied with this other matter, that I scarcely gave them a thought. Presently I got an "all's ready" report from Fo-nar, and told Tan Hadron to go ahead with the maneuver.

The Dusar was going full speed ahead against a strong head wind, and when he brought her about she sped toward the oncoming ships like a racing thoat. Two of them were in position to open up on us when we came within range; however, they commenced firing too soon. We quite properly held our fire until it was effective. We were all firing our bow guns—the only ones that could be brought to bear; and no one was doing much damage.

As we drew closer to the leading ship, I saw considerable confusion on her deck; I imagine they thought we were going to ram them. Just then our gunner succeeded in putting her bow gun out of commission, which was fortunate indeed for us; then Tan Hadron elevated the Dusar's nose, and we rose above the leading ship. As we passed over her, there was a terrific explosion on her deck and she burst into flame. Tan Hadron turned to port so fast that the Dusar lay over on her side, and we on deck had to hang to anything we could get hold of to keep from going overboard; by this maneuver, he crossed over the second ship; and the bombers in the bilge of the Dusar dropped a heavy bomb on her deck. With the detonation of the bomb, she turned completely over, and then plummeted toward the ground, four thousand feet below. The explosion must have burst all her buoyancy tanks.

Only one ship now remained in our immediate vicinity; and as we made for her, she turned tail and ran, followed by the cheers of our men. We now resumed our course toward the north, the enemy having abandoned the chase.

The first ship was still burning, and I directed Tan Hadron to approach her to learn if any of the crew remained alive. As we came closer, I saw that she was hanging bow down, the whole after part of the ship being in flames. The bow was not burning, and I saw a number of men clinging to holds upon the tilted deck.

My bow gunner thought that I was going to finish them off, and trained his piece on them; but I stopped him just in time; then I hailed them. "Can you get at your boarding harness?" I shouted.

"Yes," came back the answer.

"I'll pull in below you and take you off," I called, and in about fifteen minutes we had taken off the five survivors, one of which was a Panar padwar.

They were surprised that I hadn't either finished them off when I had them at such a disadvantage, or let them hang there and burn. The padwar was sure that we had some ulterior motive in taking them off the burning ship, and asked me how I intended to have them killed.

"I don't intend to kill you at all," I said, "unless I have to."

My own men were quite as surprised as the prisoners; but I heard one of them say, "The Dwar's been in the Helium navy—they don't kill prisoners of war in Helium." Well, they don't kill them in all Martian countries, except that most do kill their prisoners if they find it difficult or impossible to take them home into slavery without endangering their own ships.

"What are you going to do with us?" asked the padwar.

"I'll either land as soon as it is convenient, and set you free; or I'll let you enlist and come with us. You must understand, however, that I am at war with Hin Abtol."

All five decided to cast their lot with us, and I turned them over to Fo-nar to assign them to watches and prescribe their duties. My men were gathered amidships discussing the engagement; they were as proud as peacocks.

"We destroyed two ships and put a third to flight without suffering a casualty," one was saying.

"That's the kind of a Dwar to fly under," said another. "I knew he was all right when I saw him handle Gan-ho. I tell you there's a man to fight for."

After overhearing this conversation and a lot more like it, I felt much more assured as to the possible success of the venture, for with a disloyal crew anything may happen except success.

A little later, as I was crossing the deck, I saw one of the warriors who had taken Phor San and his companion below; and I hailed him and asked him if the prisoners were all right.

"I am sorry to report, sir," he said, "that they both fell overboard."

"How could they fall overboard when they were below?" I demanded.

"They fell through the after bomb trap, sir," he said, without cracking a smile.

chapter X

NATURALLY I WAS a little suspicious of the dependability of Gor-don, the Panar padwar we had taken off the disabled Panar ship. He was the only Panar aboard the Dusar, and the only person aboard who might conceivably owe any allegiance to Hin Abtol. I cautioned Fo-nar and Tan Hadron to keep an eye on the fellow, although I really couldn't imagine how he could harm us.

As we approached the North Polar region, it was necessary to issue the warm fur clothing which the Dusar carried in her stores— the white fur of Apts for the warriors, and the black and yellow striped fur of orluks for the three officers; and to issue additional sleeping furs to all.

I was quite restless that night with a perfectly baseless premonition of impending disaster, and about the 9th zode (1:12 A.M. E.T.) I arose and went on deck. Fo-nar was at the wheel, for as yet I didn't know any of the common warriors of the crew well enough to trust them with this important duty.

There was a group of men amidships, whispering among themselves. As they were not members of the watch, they had no business there at that time of night; and I was walking toward them to order them below, when I saw three men scuffling farther aft. This infraction of discipline requiring more immediate attention than the gathering on the deck, I walked quickly toward the three men, arriving just as two of them were about to hurl the third over the rail.

I seized the two by their collars and dragged them back; they dropped their victim and turned on me; but when they recognized me, they hesitated.

"The Panar was falling overboard," said one of the men, rather impudently.

Sure enough, the third man was Gor-don, the Panar. He had had a mighty close call. "Go below, to my cabin," I told him; "I will talk with you there later."

"He won't talk too much, if he knows what's good for him," one of the men who had tried to throw him overboard shouted after him as he walked away.

"What is the meaning of this?" I demanded of the two men, whom I recognized as assassins.

"It means that we don't want any Panars aboard this ship," replied one.

"Go to your quarters," I ordered; "I'll attend to you later." It was my intention to immediately have them put in irons.

They hesitated; one of them moved closer to me. There is only one way to handle a situation like that—be first. I swung a right to the fellow's chin, and as he went down I whipped out my sword and faced them.

"I'll run you both through if you lay a hand on a weapon," I told them, and they knew that I meant it. I made them stand against the rail then, with their backs toward me, and disarmed them. "Now go below," I said.

As they walked away, I saw the men in the group amidships watching us, and as I approached them they moved away and went below before I could order them to do so. I went forward and told Fo-nar of what had happened, cautioning him to be constantly on the lookout for trouble.

"I am going below to talk to Panar," I said; "I have an idea that there was more to this than just the wish to throw him overboard; then I'll have a talk with some of the men. I'm going to rouse Tan Hadron first and instruct him to have those two assassins put in irons at once. I'll be back on deck shortly; the three of us will have to keep a close watch from now on. Those men weren't on deck at this hour in the night just to get fresh air."

I went below then and awakened Tan Hadron, telling him what had occurred on deck and ordering him to take a detail of men and put the two assassins in irons; after that, I went to my cabin. Gor-don arose from a bench and saluted as I entered.

"May I thank you, sir," he said, "for saving my life."

"Was it because you are a Panar that they were going to throw you overboard?" I asked.

"No, sir, it was not," he replied. "The men are planning to take over the ship—they are afraid to go to Pankor—and they tried to get me to join with them, as none of them can navigate a ship and I can; they intended killing you and the two padwars. I refused to join them, and tried to dissaude them; then they became afraid that I would report their plans to you, as I intended doing; so they were going to throw me overboard. You saved my life, sir, when you took me off that burning ship; and I am glad to offer it in the defense of yours—and you're going to need all the defense you can get; the men are determined to take over the ship, though they are divided on the question of killing you."

"They seemed very contented to serve under me immediately after our engagement with your three ships," I said; "I wonder what could have changed them."

"Fear of Hin Abtol as the ship drew nearer to Pankor," replied Gor-don; "they are terrified at the thought that they might be frozen in there again for years."

"Pankor must be a terrible place," I said.

"For them, it would be," he replied.

I saw to it that he was armed, and then I told him to follow me on deck. There would be at least four of us, and I hoped that some of the crew might be loyal. Tan Hadron of Hastor and I could give a good account of ourselves; as to Fo-nar and Gor-don, I did not know.

"Come," I said to the Panar, and then I opened my cabin door and stepped into the arms of a dozen men, waiting there, who fell upon me and bore me to the deck before I could strike a blow in defense; they disarmed both the Panar and me and bound our hands behind our backs. It was all done very expeditiously and quietly, the plan had been admirably worked out, and it won my approbation—anyone who can take John Carter as easily as that deserves praise.

They took us on deck, and I could not but notice that many of them still treated me with deference. Those who immediately surrounded me were all panthans. On deck, I saw that both Fo-nar and Tan Hadron were prisoners.

The men surrounded us, and discussed our fate. "Overboard with the four of them!" cried an assassin.

"Don't be a fool," said one of the panthans; "we can't navigate the ship without at least one of them."

"Keep one of them, then; and throw the others over the rail—over with the dwar first!"

"No!" said another panthan; "he is a great fighting man, a good commander who led us to victory; I will fight before I will see him killed."

"And I!" shouted several others in unison.

"What do you want to do with them, then?" demanded still another assassin. "Do you want to take them along so that we'll all have our heads lopped off at the first city we stop at where they can report us to the authorities?"

"Keep two to pilot the ship," said a man who had not spoken before; "and ground the other two, if you don't want to kill them."

Several of the assassins were still for killing us; but the others prevailed, and they had Tan Hadron bring the Dusar to ground. Here, as they put us off the ship, Gor-don and I, they gave us back our weapons over the protest of several of the assassins.

As I stood there on the snow and ice of the Arctic and saw the Dusar rise in the air and head toward the south, I thought that it might have been kinder had they killed us.

chapter XI

NORTH OF US rose a range of rocky hills, their wind swept granite summits, flecked with patches of snow and ice, showed above their snow covered slopes like the backbone of some dead monster. To the south stretched rough, snow covered terrain as far as the eye could reach—to the north, a frozen wilderness and death; to the south, a frozen wilderness and death. There seemed no alternative.

But it was the south that called me. I could struggle on until death claimed me, but I would never give up while life remained.

"I suppose we might as well be moving," I said to Gor-don, as I started toward the south.

"Where are you going?" he asked; "only death lies in that direction for a man on foot."

"I know that," I replied; "death lies in any direction we may go."

The Panar smiled. "Pankor lies just beyond those hills," he said.

"I have hunted here many times on this side of them; we can be in Pankor in a couple of hours."

I shrugged. "It doesn't make much difference to me," I said, "as I shall probably be killed in Pankor," and I started off again, but this time toward the north.

"You can come into Pankor safely," said Gor-don, "but you will have to come as my slave. It is not as I would have it, sir; but it is the only way in which you will be safe."

"I understand," I said, "and I thank you."

"We shall have to say that I took you prisoner; that the crew of my ship mutinied and grounded us," he explained.

"It is a good story, and at least founded on fact," I said. "But, tell me: will I ever be able to escape from Pankor?"

"If I get another ship, you will," he promised. "I am allowed a slave on board, and I'll take you along; the rest we shall have to leave to fate; though I can assure you that it is no easy thing to escape from Hin Abtol's navy."

"You are being very generous," I said.

"I owe you my life, sir."

Life is strange. How could I have guessed a few hours before that my life would be in the hands of one of Hin Abtol's officers, and safe? If ever a man was quickly rewarded for a good deed, it was I now for the rescuing of those poor devils from the burning ship.

Gor-don led the way with confidence over that trackless waste to a narrow gorge that split the hills. One unfamiliar with its location could have passed along the foot of the hills within a hundred yards of its mouth without ever seeing it, for its ice- and snow-covered walls blended with the surrounding snow to hide it most effectively.

It was rough going in that gorge. Snow covered broken ice

and rocks, so that we were constantly stumbling and often falling. Transverse fissures crossing the gorge formed a labyrinth of corridors in which a man might be quickly lost. Gor-don told me this was the only pass through the hills, and that if an enemy ever got into it he would freeze to death before he found his way out again.

We had plodded on for about half an hour, when, at a turn, our way was blocked by one of the most terrible creatures that inhabit Mars. It was an apt, a huge, white furred creature with six limbs, four of which, short and heavy, carry it swiftly over the snow and ice; while the other two, growing forward from its shoulders on either side of its long, powerful neck, terminate in white, hairless hands, with which it seizes and holds its prey.

Its head and mouth are more nearly similar in appearance to those of a hippopotamus than to any other earthly animal, except that from the sides of the upper jawbone two mighty horns curve slightly downward toward the front.

Its two huge eyes inspire one's greatest curiosity. They extend in two vast oval patches from the center of the top of the cranium down either side of the head to below the roots of the horns, so that these weapons really protrude from the lower part of the eyes, which are composed of several thousand ocelli each.

This eye structure has always seemed remarkable to me in a beast whose haunts were on a glaring field of ice and snow, and though I found upon minute examination of the eyes of several that Thuvan Dihn and I killed, that time that we passed through the carrion caves, that each ocellus is furnished with its own lid, and that the animal can, at will, close as many of the facets of its huge eyes as it wishes, yet I am sure that nature has thus equipped him because much of his life is spent in dark, subterranean recesses.

The moment that the creature saw us, it charged; and Gor-don and I whipped out our radium pistols simultaneously, and commenced firing. We could hear the bullets exploding in its carcass and see great chunks of flesh and bone being torn away, but still it came on. One of my bullets found a thousand faceted eye and exploded there, tearing the eye away. For just a moment the creature hesitated and wavered; then it came on again. It was right on top of us now, and our bullets were tearing into its vitals. How it could continue to live, I cannot understand; but it did, and it reached out and seized Gor-don with its two horrible, white, hairless hands and dragged him toward its massive jaws.

I was on its blind side; and realizing that our bullets would not bring death in time to save Gor-don, I drew my long-sword; and, grasping the hilt in both hands, swung it from low behind my right shoulder and brought the keen blade down onto the beast's long neck. Just as the jaws were about to close on Gor-don, the apt's head rolled upon the icy floor of the gorge; but its mighty fingers still clung to the Panar, and I had to hack them off with my short-sword before the man was freed.

"That was a close call," I said.

"Once again you have saved my life," said Gor-don; "how can I ever repay you?"

"By helping me find Llana of Gathol, if she is in Pankor," I told him.

"If she is in Pankor, I'll not only help you find her; but I'll help you get her away, if it is humanly possible to do so," he replied. "I am an officer in Hin Abtol's navy," he continued, "but I feel no loyalty toward him. He is a tyrant, hated by all; how he has been able to rule us for more than a hundred years, without being found by the assassin's dagger or poison, is a miracle."

As we talked, we continued on through the gorge; and presently came out upon a snow covered plain upon which rose one of those amazing, glass covered, hot-house cities of Barsoom's North Polar region.

"Pankor," said Gor-don; presently he turned and looked at me and commenced to laugh.

"What is it?" I asked.

"Your metal," he said; "you are wearing the insigne of a dwar in Hin Abtol's service; it might appear strange that you, a dwar, are the prisoner and slave of a padwar."

"That might be difficult to explain," I said, as I removed the insigne and threw it aside.

At the city gate, it was our good fortune to find one of Gor-don's acquaintances in command of the guard. He heard Gor-don's story with interest and permitted us to enter, paying no attention whatever to me.

Pankor was much like Kadabra, the capital city of Okar, only much smaller. Though the country around it and up to its walls was clothed in snow and ice, none lay upon the great crystal dome which roofed the entire city; and beneath the dome a pleasant, springlike atmosphere prevailed. Its avenues were covered with the sod of the mosslike ocher vegetation which clothes the dead sea bottoms of the red planet, and bordered by well kept lawns of crimson Barsoomian grass. Along these avenues sped the noiseless traffic of light and airy ground fliers with which I had become familiar in Marentina and Kadabra long years before.

The broad tires of these unique fliers are but rubberlike gas bags filled with the eighth Barsoomian ray, or ray of propulsion—that remarkable discovery of the Martians that has made possible the great fleets of mighty airships that render the red man of the outer world supreme. It is this ray which propels the inherent and reflected light of suns and planets off into space, and when confined gives to Martian craft their airy buoyancy.

Hailing a public flier, Gor-don and I were driven to his home, I sitting with the driver, as befitted a slave. Here he was warmly greeted by his mother, father, and sister; and I was conducted to the slaves' quarters by a servant. It was not long, however, before Gor-don sent for me; and when the servant who had brought me had departed, Gor-don explained to me that he had told his parents and his sister that I had saved his life, and that they wished to express their gratitude. They were most appreciative.

"You shall be my son's personal guard," said the father, "and we shall not look upon you here in this home as a slave. He tells me that in your own country you are a noble." Gor-don had either guessed at that, or made up the story for effect; as I certainly had told him nothing of my status at home. I wondered how much more he had told them; I did not wish too many people to know of my search for Llana. When next we were alone, I asked him; and he assured me that he had told them nothing.

"I trust them perfectly," he said, "but the affair is not mine to speak of." At least there was one decent Panar; I presume that I had come to judge them all by Hin Abtol.

Gor-don furnished me with harness and insignia which definitely marked me as a slave of his household and rendered it safe for me to go about the city, which I was anxious to do on the chance that I might pick up some word regarding Llana; for Gor-don had told me that in the market place, where slaves gathered to buy and sell for their owners, all the gossip of the city was discussed daily.

"*If it has happened or is going to happen, the market place knows it*, is an old saying here," he told me; and I found this to be true.

As Gor-don's bodyguard, I was permitted to wear weapons, the insignia on my harness so denoting. I was glad of this, as I feel lost without arms—much as an Earth man would feel walking down the street without his pants.

The day after we arrived, I went alone to the market place.

chapter XII

I GOT INTO CONVERSATIONS with a number of slaves, but I didn't learn anything of value to me; however, being there, put me in the way of learning something that was of value to me. I was talking with another slave, when we saw an officer coming through the market place, touching first one slave and then another, who immediately fell in behind him.

"If he touches you, don't ask any questions; but go along," said the slave with whom I was talking and whom I had told I was a newcomer to Pankor.

Well, the officer did tap me on the shoulder as he passed; and I fell in behind him with fifteen or twenty other slaves. He led us out of the market place and along an avenue of poorer shops, to the city wall. Here, beside a small gate, was a shed in which was a stock of apt-fur suits. After we had each donned one of these, in accordance with the officer's instructions, he unlocked the small gate and led us out of the city into the bitter cold of the Arctic, where such a sight met my eyes as I hope I may never see again. On row after row of racks which extended as far as I could see hung frozen human corpses, thousands upon thousands of them hanging by their feet, swinging in the biting wind.

Each corpse was encased in ice, a transparent shroud through which their dead eyes stared pleadingly, reproachfully, accusingly, horribly. Some faces wore frozen grins, mocking Fate with bared teeth.

The officer had us cut down twenty of the bodies, and the thought of the purpose for which they seemed obviously intended almost nauseated me. As I looked upon those endless lines of corpses hanging heads down, I was reminded of winter scenes before the butcher shops of northern cities in my native country, where the bodies of ox and bear and deer hung, frozen, for the gourmet to inspect.

It took the combined strength of two red men to lift and carry one of these ice encrusted bodies; and as the officer had tapped an odd number of slaves, I was left without a partner to carry a corpse with me; so I waited for orders.

The officer saw me standing idle, and called to me. "Hey, you!" he cried; "don't loaf around doing nothing; drag one of them over to the gate."

I stooped and lifted one of the bodies to my shoulder, carrying it alone to the gate. I could see that the officer was astounded, for what I had done would have been an impossible feat of strength for a Martian. As a matter of fact, it was not at all remarkable that I was able to do it; because my unusually great strength, combined with the lesser gravity of Mars, made it relatively easy for me.

All the time I was carrying my grisly burden, I was thinking of the roast we had had at the meal I had eaten at Gor-don's house—and wondering! Was it possible that civilized human beings could be so depraved? It seemed incredible of such people as Gor-don and his family. His sister was a really beautiful girl. Could she—? I shuddered at the implication.

We carried the corpses into a large building across the avenue from the little gate. Here were row upon row and tier upon tier of ersite topped tables; and when, at the officer's direction, we laid the bodies upon some of them, the place looked like a morgue.

Presently a number of men entered the room; they carried heavy knives. These are the butchers, I thought. They attached hoses to hydrants, and each one of them stood over a corpse and sprayed it with warm water, at the same time chipping away the ice with his knife. It took some little time.

When the first corpse was entirely released from its icy winding sheet I wanted to look away, but I couldn't—I was fascinated by the horror of it as I waited to see the butcher wield his knife; but he didn't. Instead, he kept on spraying the body with warm water, occasionally massaging it. Finally, he took a hypodermic syringe from his pocket pouch and injected something into the arm of the cadaver; then the most horrifying thing of all occurred: the corpse rolled its head to and fro and opened its eyes!

"Stand by, slaves!" commanded the officer; "some of them may be a little wild at first—be ready to seize them."

The first corpse sat up and looked around, as others of them showed signs of life. Soon they were all either sitting up or standing staring about them in a confused sort of way. Now they were each given the harness of a slave; and when a detachment of warriors came to take charge of them, we other slaves were dismissed. Now I recalled and understood that oft repeated reference of the warriors of Hin Abtol to being "frozen in." I had thought that they merely meant being confined in an Arctic city surrounded by ice and snow.

As I was leaving the building, the officer accosted me. "Who are you, slave?" he demanded.

"I am the slave and bodyguard of Padwar Gor-don," I replied.

"You are a very strong man," he said; "what country are you from?"

"Virginia," I replied.

"I never heard of it; where is it?"

"Just south of Maryland."

"Well, never mind—let's see how strong you are; can you lift one end of that ersite table alone?"

"I don't know."

"Try it," he ordered.

I picked up the entire table and held it above my head. "Incredible!" exclaimed the officer. The warriors were standing looking at me in open mouthed astonishment.

"What is your name?" demanded the officer.

"Dotor Sojat."

"Very good," he said; "you may go now."

When I returned to Gor-don's home, he told me that he had become apprehensive because of my long absence. "Where have you been all this time?" he asked. "I was worried."

"Thawing out corpses," I told him, laughing. "Before I saw them start coming to life, I thought you Panars ate them. Tell me; what is the idea?"

"It is a part of Hin Abtol's mad scheme to conquer all of Barsoom and make himself Jeddak of Jeddaks and Warlord of Barsoom. He has heard of the famous John Carter, who holds these titles; and he is envious. He has been at the preserving of human beings by freezing for fully a hundred years. At first it was only a plan by which he might have great numbers of slaves available at any time without the expense of feeding them while they were idle. After he heard of John Carter and the enormous wealth of Helium and several other empires, this grandiose scheme of conquest commenced taking form.

"He had to have a fleet; and as no one in Pankor knew how to build airships, he had to acquire them by trickery and theft. A few crossed the ice barrier from some of the northern cities; these were lured to land by signals of friendship and welcome; then their crews were captured and all but one or two of them frozen in. Those who were not had promised to train Panars in the handling of the ships. It has been a very slow process of acquiring a navy; but he has supplemented it by visiting several of the northern cities, pretending friendship, and then stealing a ship or two, just as he pretended friendship for Gahan of Gathol and then stole his daughter.

"His present attack on Gathol is merely a practice campaign to give his officers and warriors experience and perhaps at the same time acquire a few more ships."

"How many of those frozen men has he?" I asked.

"He has accumulated fully a million in the last hundred years," replied Gor-don; "a very formidable army, if he had the ships to transport them."

On this dying planet, the population of which has been steadily decreasing for probably a million years, an army of a million warriors would indeed be formidable; but led by Hin Abtol and officered by Panars, *two* million disloyal warriors would be no great menace to such a power as Helium.

"I am afraid Hin Abtol's dream will never come true," I said.

"I hope not. Very few Panars are in sympathy with it. Life here is easy, and we are content to be left alone and leave others alone. By the way, did you learn anything about the whereabouts of Llana of Gathol while you were away?"

"Not a thing; did you?"

"No," he replied; "but I haven't made any direct inquiries yet. I am waiting until I can talk with some of my friends who are stationed in the palace. I do know, however, that Hin Abtol has returned from Gathol and is in his palace."

As we talked, a slave came to announce that an officer had come from the Jeddak and wished to speak to Gor-don.

"Bring him here," said my master; and a moment later a gorgeously trapped man entered the room, by which time I was standing behind Gor-don's chair, as a well trained slave and bodyguard should do.

The two men greeted each other by name and title; and then the visitor said, "You have a slave named Dotor Sojat?"

"Yes," replied Gor-don; "my personal bodyguard, here."

The officer looked at me. "You are the slave who lifted the ersite table alone today in the resuscitating house?" he inquired.

"Yes."

He turned again to Gor-don. "The Jeddak will honor you by accepting this slave as a gift," he said.

Gor-don bowed. "It is a great pleasure as well as an honor to present the slave, Dotor Sojat, to my jeddak," he said; and then, as the officer looked away from him to glance again at me, Gor-don winked at me. He knew how anxious I had been to get into the palace of Hin Abtol.

Like a dutiful slave, I left the home of Gor-don, the padwar, and followed the jeddak's officer to the palace of the jeddak.

chapter XIII

A HIGH WALL encloses the grounds where stands the palace of Hin Abtol in the city of Pankor at the top of the world, and guards pace this wall night and day. At the gates are a full utan of a hundred men; and within, at the grand entrance to the palace itself, is another utan. No wonder that it has been difficult to assassinate Hin Abtol, self-styled Jeddak of Jeddaks of the North.

At one side of the palace, on an open scarlet sward, I saw something which made me start with astonishment—it was my own flier! It was the flier that Hin Abtol had stolen from me in the deserted city of Horz; and now, as I learned later, he had it on exhibition here as proof of his great courage and ability. He bragged that he had taken it single handed from The Warlord of Barsoom after defeating him in a duel. The fact that there could be no doubt but that it was my personal flier lent color to the story; my insigne was there for everyone to read, plain upon the bow. They must have towed it through one of the gates; and then flown it to its present resting place; as, of course, no airship could land inside Pankor's great dome.

I was left in the guard-room just inside the entrance to the palace, where some of the warriors of the guard were loafing; two of them were playing Jetan, the Martian chess game, while others played Yano. They had all risen when the officer entered the room with me; and when he left I sat down on a bench at one side, as the others seated themselves and resumed their games.

One of them looked over at me, and scowled. "Stand up, slave!" he ordered. "Don't you know better than to sit in the presence of Panar warriors?"

"If you can prove that you are a better man than I," I said, "I'll stand." I was in no mood to take anything like that meekly; as a matter of fact, I was pretty well fed up on being a slave.

The warrior leaped to his feet. "Oh, insolent, too!" he said; "well, I'll teach you a lesson."

"You'd better go slow there, Ul-to," warned one of his companions; "I think this fellow was sent for by the jeddak. If you muss him up, Hin Abtol may not like it."

"Well, he's got to be taught a lesson," snarled Ul-to; "if there's one thing I can't stand, its an impudent slave," and he came toward me. I did not rise, and he grabbed me by the harness and attempted to drag me to my feet; at the same time, he struck at me.

I parried his blow, and seized hold of his harness; then I stood up and lifted him above my head. I held him there for a moment, and then I tossed him across the room. "That will teach you," I called to him, "to be more respectful to your betters."

Some of the other guardsmen were scowling at me angrily; but many were laughing at Ul-to, who now scrambled to his feet, whipped out his long-sword, and came for me. They had not yet disarmed me; and I drew mine; but before we could engage, a couple of Ul-to's companions seized him and held him. He was cursing and struggling to free himself and get at me, when the officer of the guard, evidently attracted by the disturbance, entered the room.

When he heard what had happened, he turned angrily on me. "You ought to be flogged," he said, "for insulting and attacking a Panar warrior."

"Perhaps you would like to try to flog me," I said.

At that, he turned purple and almost jumped up and down, he was so furious. "Seize him!" he shouted to the warriors, "and give him a good beating."

They all started toward me, and I drew my sword. I was standing with my back to a wall, and there would have been several dead Panars scattered about that room in a few minutes if the officer who had brought me there had not come in just then.

"What's the meaning of this?" he demanded.

The guard officer explained, making me appear wholly in the wrong.

"He lies," I said to the officer; "I was attacked without provocation."

He turned to the guard officer. "I don't know who started this," he said, "but it's a good thing for your neck that nothing happened to this man;" then he disarmed me and told me to follow him.

He led me out of the palace again and to the side of the building where my flier stood. I noticed that it was not moored, there being no danger of winds beneath that great dome; and I wished that it were out in the open so that I could fly it away if I were able to find Llana of Gathol; it would have been a Heaven sent opportunity for escape had it not been for that enclosing dome.

He took me out to the center of an expanse of well kept lawn, facing a number of people who had gathered beside the building. There were both men and women, and more were coming from the palace. At last there was a fanfare of trumpets; and the Jeddak came, accompanied by courtiers and women.

In the meantime, a large man had come out on the lawn beside me; he was a warrior wearing metal that denoted him a member of Hin Abtol's bodyguard.

"The Jeddak has heard tales of your great strength," said the officer who had brought me there, "and he wishes to see a demonstration of it. Rab-zov, here, is supposed to be the strongest man in Pankor—"

"I *am* the strongest man in Pankor, sir," interrupted Rab-zov; "I am the strongest man on Barsoom."

"He must be pretty strong," I said. "What is he going to do to me?"

"You are going to wrestle to amuse the Jeddak and his court.

Rab-zov will demonstrate how easily he can throw you to the ground and hold you there. Are you ready, Rab-zov?"

Rab-zov said he was ready, and the officer signed us to start. Rab-zov swaggered toward me, taking occasional quick glances at the audience to see if all were looking at him. They were; looking at him and admiring his great bulk.

"Come on, fellow!" said Rab-zov; "put up the best fight you can; I want to make it interesting for the Jeddak."

"I shall hope to make it interesting for you, Rab-zov," I said.

He laughed loudly at that. "You won't feel so much like joking when I'm through with you," he said.

"Come on, wind bag!" I cried; "you talk too much."

He was leaning forward, reaching for a hold, when I seized one of his wrists, turned quickly and threw him over my shoulder. I purposely let him fall hard, and he was still a little groggy when he came to his feet. I was waiting, very close; and I seized him by the harness and lifted him over my head; then I commenced to whirl with him. He was absolutely helpless; and when I thought he was befuddled enough, I carried him over and threw him down heavily in front of Hin Abtol. Rab-zov was down—and out.

"Have you no strong men in Pankor?" I asked him, and then I saw Llana of Gathol standing beside the Jeddak. Almost with the suddenness of a revelation a mad scheme came to me.

"Perhaps I had better send two men against you," said Hin Abtol, rather good-naturedly; he had evidently enjoyed the spectacle.

"Why not a swordsman?" I asked. "I am quite good with a sword," and I wanted a sword very much right then—I needed a sword to carry out my plan.

"Do you want to be killed, slave?" demanded Hin Abtol; "I have the best swordsmen in the world in my guard."

"Bring out your best, then," I said; "I may surprise him—and somebody else," and I looked straight at Llana of Gathol, and winked. Then, for the first time, she recognized me through my disguise.

"Who were you winking at?" demanded Hin Abtol, looking around.

"Something got in my eye," I said.

Hin Abtol spoke to an officer standing near him. "Who is the best swordsman in the guard?" he asked.

"There is none better than Ul-to," replied the officer.

"Fetch him!"

So! I was to cross swords with my old friend, Ul-to. That would please him—for a few moments.

They brought Ul-to; and when he found that he was to fight me, he beamed all over. "Now, slave," he said, "I will teach you that lesson that I promised you."

"Again?" I asked.

"It will be different this time," he said.

We crossed swords.

"To the death!" I said.

"To the death, slave!" replied Ul-to.

I fought on the defensive mostly at first, seeking to work my man around in the position in which I wanted him; and when I had him there, I pressed him; and he fell back. I kept backing him toward the audience, and to make him more amenable to my directions, I started carving him—just a little. I wanted him to acquire respect for my point and my ability. Soon he was covered with blood, and I was forcing him to go wherever I wished him.

I backed him into the crowd, which fell back; and then I caught

Llana's eye, and motioned her with my head to step to one side; then I pressed close to her. "At the kill," I whispered, "run for the flier and start the engine."

I backed Ul-to away from the crowd then, and I saw Llana following, as though she was so much interested in the duel that she did not realize what she was doing.

"Now! Llana!" I whispered, and I saw her walking slowly backward toward the flier.

In order to attract the crowd's attention from Llana, I pressed Ul-to to one side with such an exhibition of swordplay as I knew would hold every eye; then I turned him around and had him almost running backward, carrying me nearer my ship.

Suddenly I heard Hin Abtol cry, "The girl! Get her! She's gone aboard that flier!"

As they started forward, I ran Ul-to through the heart and turned and ran for my ship. At my heels came a dozen warriors with drawn swords. The one who started first, and who was faster than the others, overtook me just as I had to pause a moment at the side of the flier to make assurance doubly sure that she was not moored in any way. I wheeled and parried a vicious cut; my blade moved once more with the swiftness of light, and the warrior's head rolled from his shoulders.

"Let her go!" I cried to Llana, as I leaped to the deck.

As the ship rose, I hastened to the controls, and took over.

"Where are we going, John Carter?" asked Llana.

"To Gathol," I replied.

She looked up at the dome above us. "How—?" she started, but she saw that I had turned the nose of the flier upward at an angle of forty-five degrees and opened the throttle—that was her answer.

The little ship, as sweet and fast a flier as I have ever flown, was streaking through the warm air of Pankor at tremendous speed. We both huddled close to the deck of the little cockpit—and hoped.

The flier shuddered to the terrific impact; broken glass showered in every direction—and then we were out in the cold, clear air of the Arctic.

I levelled off then, and headed for Gathol at full speed; there was danger of our freezing to death if we didn't get into a warmer climate soon, for we had no furs.

"What became of Pan Dan Chee and Jad-han?" I asked.

"I haven't seen them since we were all captured in Gathol," replied Llana. "Poor Pan Dan Chee; he fought for me, and he was badly wounded; I am afraid that I shall never see him again," and there were tears in her voice.

I greatly deplored the probable fate of Pan Dan Chee and Jad-han, but at least Llana of Gathol was at last safe. Or was this a masterpiece of overstatement? She was at least safe from Hin Abtol, but what lay in the future? Immediately she was in danger of freezing to death should any mishap delay our flight before we reached a warmer latitude, and there were innumerable other hazards in the crossing of the wastelands of this dying planet.

But, being an incorrigible optimist, I still felt that Llana was safe; and so did she. Perhaps because no conceivable danger could have been greater than that which had threatened her while she lay in the power of Hin Abtol.

Presently I noticed that she was laughing, and I asked her what amused her. "More than any other man on Barsoom, Hin Abtol feared you," she said, "and he had you in his power and did not know it. And he pitted against you, the greatest swordsman of two worlds, a clumsy oaf, when he might have loosed upon you a full utan and destroyed you. Though he would doubtless have lost half his utan. I only pray that some day he may know the opportunity he missed when he permitted John Carter, Warlord of Barsoom to escape him."

"Yes," I said, "it is amusing. So is that hole we left in the roof of his hot-house city; but I am afraid that Hin Abtol's sense of humor will not be equal to the task of appreciating it."

We sped swiftly toward the south and warmer climes, happy in our miraculous escape from the tyrant of Panar; and, fortunately, unaware of what lay in our future.

Llana of Gathol was safe—but for how long? When would we see Gathol again, or Helium?

chapter I

YES, LLANA OF GATHOL was safe at last. I had brought her from captivity in the Arctic city of Pankor, stolen her from under the very nose of Hin Abtol, the self-styled Jeddak of Jeddaks of the North; and we were speeding through the thin air of dying Mars in my own fast flier toward Gathol. I was very contented with what I had achieved, but I was also very cold.

"You said that you were taking me to Gathol," said Llana, after we had left Pankor far behind. "Nothing would make me happier than to return to my father, my mother, and my native city; but how may we hope to make a landing there while Gathol is surrounded by the warriors of Hin Abtol?"

"The Panars are a stupid, inefficient lot," I replied; "most of Hin Abtol's warriors are unwilling conscripts who have no heart in waging war for their tyrannical master. These poor frozen men only endure it because they know there is no escape and prefer life and consciousness to being returned to Pankor and frozen in again until Hin Abtol needs their swords for a future war."

"'Frozen men'!" ejaculated Llana; "what do you mean by that?"

"You heard nothing of them while you were a prisoner in Pankor?" I asked, surprised.

"Nothing," Llana assured me; "tell me about them."

"Just outside the walls of the hot-house city there are rows upon rows of racks in the biting cold and bitter wind of the North Polar region. On these racks, like beef in a cold storage warehouse, thousands of warriors hang by their feet, frozen solid and in a state of suspended animation. They are captives whom he had taken on numerous raids during a period of fully a hundred years. I have talked with some who had been frozen in over fifty years.

"I was in the resuscitating room when a number of them were thawed out; after a few minutes they don't seem to be any worse for their experience, but the whole idea is revolting."

"Why does he do it?" demanded Llana. "Why thousands of them?"

"Better say thousands upon thousands," I said; "one slave told me that there were at least a million. Hin Abtol dreams of conquering all of Barsoom with them."

"How grotesque!" exclaimed Llana.

"Were it not for the navy of Helium, he might go far along the road toward the goal of his grandiose ambition; and you may thank your revered ancestors, Llana, that there is a navy of Helium. After I return you to Gathol, I shall fly to Helium and organize an expedition to write finis to Hin Abtol's dreams."

"I wish that before you do that we might try to find out what has become of Pan Dan Chee and Jad-han," said Llana; "the Panars separated us shortly after we were captured."

"They may have been taken to Pankor and frozen in," I suggested.

"Oh, no!" exclaimed Llana; "that would be too terrible."

"You are very fond of Pan Dan Chee, aren't you?" I asked.

"He has been a very good friend," she replied, a little stiffly. The stubborn minx wouldn't admit that she was in love with him—and possibly she wasn't; you never can tell anything about a woman. She had treated him abominably when they were together; but when they were separated and he was in danger, she had evinced the greatest concern for his safety.

"I don't know how we can learn anything about his fate," I said, "unless we can inquire directly of the Panars; and that might prove rather dangerous. I should like to know what has become of them and Tan Hadron of Hastor as well."

"Tan Hadron of Hastor? Where is he?"

"The last I saw of him, he was on board the Dusar, the Panar ship I stole from their line outside Gathol; and he was the prisoner of the mutinous crew that took it from me. There were a lot of assassins among them, and these were determined to kill Tan Hadron as soon as he had taken the ship to whatever destination they had decided upon; you see, none of the crew knew anything about navigation."

"Tan Hadron of Hastor," said Llana again; "his mother was a royal princess of Gathol and Tan Hadron himself one of the greatest fighting men of Barsoom."

"A splendid officer," I added.

"Steps must be taken to save him, too."

"If it is not too late," I said; "and the only chance of saving any of them lies in my reaching Helium in time to bring a fleet to Gathol before Hin Abtol succeeds in reducing it, and then on to Pankor, if we do not find these three among Hin Abtol's prisoners at Gathol."

"Perhaps we had better fly direct to Helium," suggested Llana. "A fleet from Helium could accomplish something, while we two, alone, might accomplish no more than getting ourselves captured again by the Panars—and it would go hard with you, John Carter, if Hin Abtol ever got his hands on you again, after what you did in Pankor today." She laughed. "I shall never forget what you did to Rab-zov, 'the strongest man in Pankor.'"

"Neither will Rab-zov," I said.

"Nor Hin Abtol. And the hole you made in the glass dome covering the city, when you drove the flier right through it! I'll wager they all had chills before they got that patched up. No, Hin Abtol will never forget you."

"But he never knew who I really was," I reminded Llana; "with my disguise removed, I was no longer a red man; and he might never guess that he had once had John Carter in his power."

"The results would be the same as far as you are concerned," said Llana; "I think it would be death in either event."

Before we had come far from Pankor I decided that our wisest course would be to proceed directly to Helium and enlist the aid of Tardos Mors, the jeddak. While I hold the titles of Jeddak of Jeddaks and Warlord of Barsoom, conferred upon me by the jeddaks of five nations, I have always considered them largely honorary, and have never presumed to exercise the authority implicit in them, except in times of war when even the great Jeddak of Helium has graciously served under me.

Having reached the decision to fly to Helium rather than Gathol, I turned toward the southeast. Before us lay a journey half the distance around the planet, and we were absolutely without water or provisions. Soon the towers and stately ruins of Horz were visible, reminding us both of the circumstances under which we had met Pan Dan Chee, and I thought that Llana looked down a little sadly on that long dead city from which her lost lover had been self-exiled because of us. It was here that she had escaped from Hin Abtol, and it was here that Hin Abtol had stolen this very flier of mine that I had found and recovered in his Polar capital. Yes, Horz held many memories for both of us; and I was glad when it lay behind us, this dead monument to a dead past.

Far ahead lay Dusar where water and provisions might be obtained, but the friendliness of Dusar was open to question. It had not been so many years since Carthoris, the Prince of Helium, had almost been done to death there by Astok, son of Nutus, the jeddak of Dusar; and there had been no intercourse between Helium and Dusar since that time. Beyond Dusar was no friendly city all the way to Helium.

I decided to give Dusar a wide berth, and in doing so we flew over country with which I was entirely unfamiliar. It was a hilly country; and in the long, deep valley I saw one of those rarest of all sights on Mars, a splendid forest. Now, to me a forest means fruits and nuts and, perhaps, game animals; and we were hungry. There would doubtless be mantilia plants too, the sap of which would quench our thirst; and so I decided to land. My best judgment told me that it was a risky thing to do, and subsequent events proved that my judgment was wholly correct.

chapter II

I LANDED ON LEVEL GROUND close to the forest, and telling Llana to remain aboard the flier ready to take off at a moment's notice, I went in search of food. The forest consisted principally of skeel, sorapus, and sompus trees. The first two are hardwood trees bearing large, delicious nuts, while the sompus trees were loaded with a citrus-like fruit with a thin red rind. The pulp of this fruit, called somp, is not unlike grapefruit, though much sweeter. It is considered a great delicacy among Barsoomians, and is cultivated along many of the canals. I had never seen any, however, as large as these, growing wild; nor had I ever seen trees on Mars of the size of many of those growing in this hidden forest.

I had gathered as much of the fruit and as many nuts as I could carry, when I heard Llana calling me. There was a note of excitement and urgency in her voice, and I dropped all that I had gathered and ran in the direction of the flier. Just before I came out of the forest I heard her scream; and as I emerged, the flier rose from the ground. I ran toward it as fast as I can run, and that is extremely fast under the conditions of lesser gravity which prevail on Mars. I took forty or fifty feet in a leap, and then I sprang fully thirty feet into the air in an effort to seize the rail of the flier. One hand touched the gunwale; but my fingers didn't quite close over the rail, and I slipped back and fell to the ground. However, I had had a glimpse of the deck of the flier, and what I saw there filled me with astonishment and, for some reason, imparted that strange sensation to my scalp as though each separate hair were standing erect—Llana lay on the deck absolutely alone, and there was no one at the controls!

"A noble endeavor," said a voice behind me; "you can certainly jump."

I wheeled about, my hand flying to the hilt of my sword. There was no one there! I looked toward the forest; there was no sign of living thing about me. From behind me came a laugh—a taunting, provocative laugh. Again I wheeled. As far as I could see there was only the peaceful Martian landscape. Above me, the flier circled and disappeared beyond the forest—flown with no human hand at the controls by some sinister force which I could not fathom.

"Well," said a voice, again behind me, "we might as well be on our way. You realize, I presume, that you are our prisoner."

"I realize nothing of the sort," I retorted. "If you want to take me, come and get me—come out in the open like men; if you are men."

"Resistance will be futile," said the voice; "there are twenty of us and only one of you."

"Who are you?" I demanded.

"Oh, pardon me," said the voice, "I should have introduced myself. I am Pnoxus, son of Ptantus, jeddak of Invak; and whom have I had the honor of capturing?"

"You haven't had the honor of capturing me yet," I said. I didn't like that voice—it was too oily and polite.

"You are most unco-operative," said the voice named Pnoxus. "I should hate to have to adopt unpleasant methods with you." The voice was not so sweet now; there was just a faint ring of steel in it.

"I don't know where you're hiding," I said; "but if you'll come out, all twenty of you, I'll give you a taste of steel. I have had enough of this foolishness."

"And I've had enough," snapped the voice. Somehow it sounded like a bear trap to me—all the oily sweetness had gone out of it. "Take him, men!"

I looked quickly around for the men, but I was still alone—just I and a voice were there. At least that is what I thought until hands seized my ankles and jerked my feet from beneath me. I fell flat on my face, and what felt like half a dozen heavy men leaped on my back and half a dozen hands ripped my sword from my grasp and more hands relieved me of my other weapons. Then unseen hands tied my own behind my back and others fastened a rope around my neck, and the voice said, "Get up!"

I got up. "If you come without resistance," said the voice named Pnoxus, "it will be much easier for you and for my men. Some of them are quite short tempered, and if you make it difficult for them you may not get to Invak alive."

"I will come," I said, "but where? For the rest, I can wait."

"You will be led," said Pnoxus, "and see that you follow where you're led. You've already given me enough trouble."

"You won't know what trouble is until I can see you," I retorted.

"Don't threaten; you have already stored up enough trouble for yourself."

"What became of the girl who was with me?" I demanded.

"I took a fancy to her," said Pnoxus, "and had one of my men, who can fly a ship, take her on to Invak."

I cannot tell you what an eerie experience it was being led through that forest by men that I could not see and being talked to by a voice that had no body; but when I realized that I was probably being taken to the place that Llana of Gathol had been taken, I was content, nay, anxious, to follow docilely where I was led.

I could see the rope leading from my neck out in front of me; it fell away in a gentle curve as a rule and then gradually vanished, vignette-like; sometimes it straightened out suddenly, and then I would feel a jerk at the back of my neck; but by following that ghostly rope-end as it wound among the trees of the forest and watching the bight carefully, so as to anticipate a forthcoming jerk by the straightening of the curve, I learned to avoid trouble.

In front of me and behind I continually heard voices berating other voices: "Sense where you're going, you blundering idiot," or, "Stop stepping on my heels, you fool," or "Who do you think you're bumping into, son-of-a-calot!" The voices seemed to be constantly getting in one another's way. Serious as I felt my situation might be, I could not help but be amused.

Presently I felt an arm brush against mine, or at least it felt like an arm, the warm flesh of a bare arm; it would touch me for an instant only to be taken away immediately, and then it would touch me again in a measured cadence, as might the arms of two men walking out of step side by side; and then a voice spoke close beside me, and I knew that a voice was walking with me.

"We are coming to a bad place," said the voice; "you had better take my arm."

I groped out with my right hand and found an arm that I could not see. I grasped what felt like an upper arm, and as I did so *my right hand disappeared!* Now, my right arm ended at the wrist, or at least it appeared to do so; but I could feel my fingers clutching that arm that I could not see. It was a most eerie sensation. I do not like situations that I cannot understand.

Almost immediately we came to an open place in the forest, where no trees grew. The ground was covered with tiny hummocks, and when I stepped on it it sank down a few inches. It was like walking on coil springs covered with turf.

"I'll guide you," said the voice at my side. "If you should get off the trail here alone you'd be swallowed up. The worst that can happen to you now would be to get one leg in it, for I can pull you out before it gets a good hold on you."

"Thank you," I said; "it is very decent of you."

"Think nothing of it," replied the voice. "I feel sorry for you; I am always sorry for strangers whom Fate misguides into the forest of Invak. We have another name for it which, I think, better describes it—The Forest of Lost Men."

"It is really so bad to fall into the hands of your people?" I asked.

"I am afraid that it is," replied the voice; "there is no escape."

I had heard that one before; so it didn't impress me greatly. The lesser peoples of Barsoom are great braggarts; they always have the best swordsmen, the finest cities, the most outstanding culture; and once you fall into their hands, you are always doomed to death or a life of slavery—you can never escape them.

"May I ask you a question?" I inquired.

"Certainly," said the voice.

"Are you always only a voice?"

A hand, I suppose it was his right hand, seized my arm and squeezed it with powerful, though invisible, fingers; and whatever it was that walked beside me chuckled. "Does that feel like only a voice?" it asked.

"A stentorian voice," I said. "You seem to have the physical attributes of a flesh and blood man; have you a name?"

"Most assuredly; it is Kandus; and yours?" he asked politely.

"Dotar Sojat," I told him, falling back upon my well-worn pseudonym.

We had now successfully crossed the bog, or whatever it was; and I removed my hand from Kandus's arm. Immediately I was wholly visible again, but Kandus remained only a voice. Again I walked alone, I and a rope sticking out in front of me and apparently defying the law of gravity. Even the fact that I surmised that the other end of it was fastened to a voice did not serve to make it seem right; it was a most indecent way for a rope to behave.

"'Dotar Sojat,'" repeated Kandus; "it sounds more like a green man's name."

"You are familiar with the green men?" I asked.

"Oh, yes; there is a horde which occasionally frequents the dead sea bottoms beyond the forest; but they have learned to give us a wide berth. Notwithstanding their great size and strength, we have a distinct advantage over them. As a matter of fact, I believe that they are very much afraid of us."

"I can well imagine so; it is not easy to fight voices; there is nothing one may get one's sword into."

Kandus laughed. "I suppose you would like to get your sword into me," he said.

"Absolutely not," I said; "you have been very decent to me, but I don't like that voice which calls itself Pnoxus. I wouldn't mind crossing swords with it."

"Not so loud," cautioned Kandus. "You must remember that he is the jeddak's son. We all have to be very nice to Pnoxus—no matter what we may privately think of him."

I judged from that that Pnoxus was not popular. It is really amazing how quickly one may judge a person by his voice; this had never been so forcibly impressed upon me before. Now, I had disliked the Pnoxus voice from the first, even when it was soft and oily, perhaps because of that; but I had liked the voice named Kandus—it was the voice of a man's man, open and without guile; a good voice.

"Where are you from, Dotar Sojat?" asked, Kandus.

"From Virginia," I said.

"That is a city of which I have never heard. In what country is it?"

"It is in the United States of America," I replied, "but you never heard of that either."

"No," he admitted; "that must be a far country."

"It is a far country," I assured him, "some forty-three million miles from here."

"You can talk as tall as you jump," he said. "I don't mind your joking with me," he added, "but I wouldn't get funny with Pnoxus, nor with Ptantus, the jeddak, if I were you; neither one of them has a sense of humor."

"But I was not joking," I insisted. "You have seen Jasoom in the heavens at night?"

"Of course," he replied.

"Well, that is the world I come from; it is called Earth there, and Barsoom is known as Mars."

"You look and talk like an honorable man," said Kandus; "and, while I don't understand, I am inclined to believe; however, you'd better pick out some place on Barsoom as your home when anyone else in Invak questions you; and you may soon be questioned—here we are at the gates of the city now."

chapter III

INVAK! The city in the Forest of Lost Men. At first only a gate was visible, so thickly set were the trees that hid the city wall—the trees and the vines that covered the wall.

I heard a voice challenge as we approached the gate, and I heard Pnoxus' voice reply, "It is Pnoxus, the prince, with twenty warriors and a prisoner."

"Let one advance and give the countersign," said the voice.

I was astonished that the guard at the gate couldn't recognize the jeddak's son, nor any of the twenty warriors with him. I suppose that one of the voices advanced and whispered the countersign, for presently a voice said, "Enter, Pnoxus, with your twenty warriors and your prisoner."

Immediately the gates swung open, and beyond I saw a lighted corridor and people moving about within it; then my rope tightened and I moved forward toward the gate; and ahead of me, one by one, armed men suddenly appeared just beyond the threshold of the gateway; one after another they appeared as though materialized from thin air and continued on along the lighted corridor. I approached the gate apparently alone, but as I stepped across the threshold there was a warrior at my side where the voice of Kandus had walked.

I looked at the warrior, and my evident amazement must have

been written large upon my face, for the warrior grinned. I glanced behind me and saw warrior after warrior materialize into a flesh and blood man the moment that he crossed the threshold. I had walked through the forest accompanied only by voices, but now ten warriors walked ahead of me and nine behind and one at my side.

"Are you Kandus?" I asked this one.

"Certainly," he said.

"How do you do it?" I exclaimed.

"It is very simple, but it is the secret of the Invaks," he replied. "I may tell you, however, that we are invisible in daylight, or rather when we are not illuminated by these special lamps which light our city. If you will notice the construction of the city as we proceed, you will see that we take full advantage of our only opportunity for visibility."

"Why should you care whether other people can see you or not?" I asked. "Is it not sufficient that you can see them and yourselves?"

"Unfortunately, there is the hitch," he said. "We can see you, but we can't see each other any more than you can see us."

So that accounted for the grumbling and cursing I had heard upon the march through the forest—the warriors had been getting in each other's way because they couldn't see one another any more than I could see them.

"You have certainly achieved invisibility," I said, "or are you hatched invisible from invisible eggs?"

"No," he replied, "we are quite normal people; but we have learned to make ourselves invisible."

Just then I saw an open courtyard ahead of us, and as the warriors passed out of the lighted corridor into it they disappeared. When Kandus and I stepped out, I was walking alone again. It was most uncanny.

The city was spotted with these courtyards which gave ventilation to the city which was, otherwise, entirely roofed and artificially lighted by the amazing lights which gave complete visibility to its inhabitants. In every courtyard grew spreading trees, and upon the city's roof vines had been trained to grow; so that, built as it was in the center of the Forest of Lost Men, it was almost as invisible from either the ground or the air as were its people themselves.

Finally we halted in a large courtyard in which were many trees wherein iron rings were set with chains attached to them, and here invisible hands snapped around one of my ankles a shackle that was fastened to the end of one of these chains.

Presently a voice whispered in my ear, "I will try to help you, for I have rather taken a liking to you—you've got to admire a man who can jump thirty feet into the air; and you've got to be interested in a man who says he comes from another world forty-three million miles from Barsoom."

It was Kandus. I felt that I was fortunate in having even the suggestion of a friend here, but I wondered what good it would do me. After all, Kandus was not the jeddak; and my fate would probably rest in the hands of Ptantus.

I could hear voices crossing and recrossing the courtyard. I could see people come down the corridors or streets and then fade into nothingness as they stepped out into the courtyard. I could see the backs of men and women appear quite as suddenly in the entrances to the streets as they left the courtyard. On several occasions voices stopped beside my tree and discussed me. They commented upon my light skin and grey eyes. One voice mentioned the great leap into the air that one of my captors had recounted to its owner.

Once a delicate perfume stopped near me, and a sweet voice said, "The poor man, and he is so handsome!"

"Don't be a fool, Rojas," growled a masculine voice. "He is an enemy, and anyway he's not very good-looking."

"I think he is very good-looking," insisted the sweet voice, "and how do you know he's an enemy?"

"I was not an enemy when I brought my ship down beside the forest," I said, "but the treatment I have received is fast making one of me."

"There, you see," said the sweet voice; "he was not an enemy. What is your name, poor man?"

"My name is Dotar Sojat, but I am not a 'poor man,'" I replied with a laugh.

"That may be what you think," said the masculine voice. "Come on, Rojas, before you make any bigger fool of yourself."

"If you'll give me a sword and come out of your cowardly invisibility, I'll make a fool of you, calot," I said.

An invisible, but very material, toe kicked me in the groin. "Keep your place, slave!" growled the voice.

I lunged forward and, by chance, got my hands on the fellow; and then I held him by his harness for just long enough to feel for his face, and when I had located it I handed him a right upper-cut that must have knocked him half way across the courtyard.

"That," I said, "will teach you not to kick a man who can't see you."

"Did Motus kick you?" cried the sweet voice, only it wasn't so sweet now; it was an angry voice, a shocked voice. "You looked as though you were hitting him—I hope you did."

"I did," I said, "and you had better see if there is a doctor in the house."

"Where are you, Motus?" cried the girl.

There was no response; Motus must have gone out like a light. Pretty soon I heard some lurid profanity, and a man's voice saying, "Who are you, lying around here in the courtyard?" Some voice had evidently stumbled over Motus.

"That must be Motus," I said in the general direction from which the girl's voice had last come. "You'd better have him carried in."

"He can lie there until he rots, for all I care," replied the voice as it trailed away. Almost immediately I saw the slim figure of a girl materialize in the entrance to one of the streets. I could tell from her back that she was an angry girl, and if her back were any criterion she was a beautiful girl—anyway, she had had a beautiful voice and a good heart. Perhaps these Invaks weren't such bad people after all.

chapter IV

"THAT WAS A BEAUTY that you handed Motus," said a voice behind me.

I wasn't going to bother even to turn around. What was the use of turning around and seeing no one there? But when the voice said, "I'll bet he's out for a week, the dirty Invak calot," I did turn around, for I knew no Invak had made a remark like that.

Chained to a tree near me, I saw another red man (it is strange that I should always think of myself as a red man here on Barsoom; and yet, perhaps, not so strange after all. Except for my color, I *am* a red man—a red man in thought and feeling to the marrow of my bones. I no longer ever think of myself as a Virginian, so ingrained has become my love for this world of my adoption.)

"Well, where did *you* come from?" I demanded. "Are you one of the invisibles?"

"I am not," replied the man. "I have been here all along. When you were first brought I must have been asleep behind my tree, but the people stopping to comment on you awoke me. I heard you tell the girl that your name is Dotar Sojat. That is a strange name for a red man. Mine is Ptor Fak; I am from Zodanga."

Ptor Fak! I recalled him now; he was one of the three Ptor brothers who had befriended me that time that I had wished to enter Zodanga in search of Dejah Thoris. At first I hesitated to tell him who I really was; but then, knowing him to be an honorable man, I was about to when he suddenly exclaimed, "By the mother of the nearer moon! Those eyes, that skin!"

"S-h-h!" I cautioned. "I don't know the nature of these people yet, and so I thought it wiser to be Dotar Sojat."

"If you're not Dotar Sojat, who are you?" demanded a voice at my elbow. That's the trouble with this invisibility business—a man can sneak up on you and eavesdrop, and you haven't the slightest idea that there is anyone near you.

"I am the Sultan of Swat," I said, that being the first name that popped into my head.

"What's a sultan?" demanded the voice.

"A jeddak of jeddaks," I replied.

"In what country?"

"In Swat."

"I never heard of Swat," said the voice.

"Well, now that it's out, you had better tell your jeddak that he's got a sultan chained up here in his back yard."

The voice must have gone away, for I heard it no more. Ptor Fak was laughing. "I can see that things are going to brighten up a bit now that you are here," he said. "My deepest reverence for whichever one of your ancestors gave you a sense of humor. This is the first laugh I have had since they got me."

"How long have you been here?"

"Several months. I was trying out a new motor that we have developed in Zodanga and was trying to establish a record for a circumnavigation of Barsoom at the Equator, and of course this place had to be on the Equator and right under me when my motor quit. How did you get here?"

"I had just escaped from Pankor with Llana, daughter of Gahan of Gathol, and we were on our way to Helium to bring back a fleet to teach Hin Abtol a lesson. We had neither food nor water on our flier; so I landed beside this forest to get some. While I was in the forest, one of these Invaks, invisible of course to Llana, climbed aboard the flier and took off with her; and twenty more of them jumped on me and took me prisoner."

"A girl was with you! That is too bad. They may kill us, but they'll keep her."

"Pnoxus said that he had taken a fancy to her," I said, bitterly.

"Pnoxus is a calot and the son of a calot and the grandson of a calot," said Ptor Fak, illuminatingly. Nothing could have evaluated Pnoxus more concisely.

"What will they do with us?" I asked. "Will we have any opportunity to escape that might also give me an opportunity to take Llana away?"

"Well, as long as they keep you chained to a tree, you can't escape; and that's what they've done with me ever since I've been here. I think they intend to use us in some sort of Games, but just what they are I don't know. Look!" he exclaimed, pointing and laughing.

I looked in the direction he indicated and saw two men carrying the limp form of a third down one of the streets.

"That must be Motus," said Ptor Fak. "I am afraid that may get you into trouble," he added, suddenly sobered.

"Whatever trouble it gets me into, it was worth it," I said. "Think of kicking a blind man, and that's what it amounted to. The girl was as mad about it as I; she must be a good sort. Rojas—that's rather a pretty name."

"The name of a noblewoman," said Ptor Fak.

"You know her?" I asked.

"No, but you can tell by the endings of their names whether or not they are noble and by the beginnings and endings of their names if they're royal. The names of the noblemen end in us and the names of noblewomen in as. The names of royalty end the same way but always begin with two consonants, like Pnoxus and Ptantus."

"Then Motus is a nobleman," I said.

"Yes; that is what is going to make it bad for you."

"Tell me," I said; "how do they make themselves invisible?"

"They have developed something that gives them invisibility for perhaps a day; it is something they take internally—a large pill. I understand that they take one every morning, so as to be sure that they will be invisible if they have to go outside the city. You see it takes about an hour for the stuff to work, and if the city were attacked by an enemy they'd be in a bad way if they had to go out and fight while visible."

"What enemies can they have around here?" I asked. "Kandus told me that even the green men are afraid of them."

"There is another city in the forest inhabited by an offshoot of this tribe," explained Ptor Fak; "it is called Onvak, and its people also possess the secret of invisibility. Occasionally the Onvaks come and attack Invak, or lie in wait for the Invak hunting parties when they go out into the forest."

"I should think it might be rather difficult to fight a battle in which one could see neither foe nor friend," I suggested.

"Yes; I understand that there's never very much damage done, though occasionally they capture a prisoner. The last battle they had the Invaks took two prisoners, and when they got them into the city they discovered that they were both their own men. They never know how many of their own people they kill; they just go slashing about them with their swords, and Issus help whoever gets in the way."

Just as Ptor Fak finished speaking I felt hands doing something to the shackles about my ankles and presently they were unlocked and removed.

"Come, slave," said the voice. Then someone took me by the arm and led me toward the entrance to one of the streets.

The moment we entered I could see a warrior at my side and there were others in front and behind me. They conducted me along this street through two other courtyards in which, of course, they immediately became invisible and I seemed to be walking alone with only the pressure of a hand upon my arm to indicate that I was not. They took me to a large room in which a number of people were standing about in front of and on either side of a desk at which there sat a scowling, fierce visaged man.

I was led up to the desk and halted there and the man behind it surveyed me in silence for several seconds. His harness was extremely elaborate, the leather being beautifully carved and studded with precious stones. The hilt of his sword which I could just see above the desk was apparently of gold and it too was studded with those rare and beautiful gems of Barsoom which defy description in words of earthly origin. Encircling his brow was a diadem of carved leather upon the front of which the Barsoomian hieroglyphs which spelled jeddak were emblazoned in precious stones. So this was Ptantus, jeddak of Invak. I felt that Llana and I could not have fallen into much worse hands.

chapter V

Ptantus looked at me so ferociously that I was sure he was attempting to frighten me. It seems to be a way that tyrants and bullies have of attempting to break down the morale of a victim before they destroy him; but I was not greatly impressed; and, impelled by a rather foolish desire to annoy him, I stopped looking at him. I guess that got his goat for he thumped the desk with his fist and leaned forward across it.

"Slave!" he almost roared at me, "pay attention to me."

"You haven't said anything yet," I reminded him. "When you say anything worth listening to I shall listen, but you don't have to yell at me."

He turned angrily to an officer. "Don't ever dare to bring a prisoner before me again," he said, "until he has been instructed how to behave in the presence of a jeddak."

"I know how to behave in the presence of a jeddak," I told him. "I have been in the presence of some of the greatest jeddaks on Barsoom, and I treat a jeddak just as I treat any other man—as he deserves. If he is a nobleman at heart he has my deference, if he is a boor he does not."

The inference was clear, and Ptantus colored. "Enough of your insolence," he said. "I understand that you are a troublesome fellow, that you gave Pnoxus, the prince, a great deal of trouble after your capture and that you struck and badly injured one of my nobles."

"That man may have a title," I said, "but he is no noble; he kicked me while he was invisible—it was the same as kicking a blind man."

"That is right," said a girlish voice a little way behind me and at one side. I turned and looked. It was Rojas.

"You saw this thing done, Rojas?" demanded Ptantus.

"Yes, Motus insulted me; and this man, Dotar Sojat, berated him for it. Then Motus kicked him."

"Is this true, Motus?" asked Ptantus, turning his head and looking past me on the other side. I turned and glanced in that direction and saw Motus with his face swathed in bandages; he was a sorry looking sight.

"I gave the slave what he deserves," he growled; "he is an insolent fellow."

"I quite agree with you," said Ptantus, "and he shall die when the time comes. But I did not summon him here to conduct a trial. I, the jeddak, reach my decisions without testimony or advice. I sent for him because an officer said he could leap thirty feet into the air; and if he can do that it may be worth keeping him a while for my amusement."

I couldn't help but smile a little at that for it had been my ability to jump that had probably preserved my life upon my advent to Barsoom so many years ago, when I had been captured by the green hordes of Thark, and Tars Tarkas had ordered me to *sak* for the edification of Lorquas Ptomel, the jed, and now it was going to give me at least a short reprieve from death.

"Why do you smile?" demanded Ptantus. "Do you see anything funny in that? Now jump, and be quick about it."

I looked up at the ceiling. It was only about fifteen feet from the floor. "That would be only a hop," I said.

"Well hop, then," said Ptantus.

I turned and looked behind me. For about twenty feet between me and the doorway men and women were crowded thickly together. Thanking my great agility and the lesser gravity of Mars, I easily jumped completely over them. I could have made a bolt for the door then, leaped to the roof of the city and made my escape; and I should have done it had it not been that Llana of Gathol was still a prisoner here.

Exclamations of surprise filled the room at this, to them, marvellous feat of agility; and when I leaped back again there was almost a ripple of applause.

"What else can you do?" demanded Ptantus.

"I can make a fool out of Motus with a sword," I said, "as well as with my fists, if he will meet me under the lights where I can see him."

Ptantus actually laughed. "I think I shall let you do that sometime when I am through with you," he said, "for Motus will most certainly kill you. There is probably not a better swordsman on all Barsoom than the noble Motus."

"I shall be delighted to let him try it," I said, "and I can promise you that I shall still be able to jump after I have killed Motus. But, if you really want to see some jumping," I continued, "take me and the girl who was captured with me out into the forest, and we will show you something worthwhile." If I could only get outside the gates with Llana I knew that we should be able to get away, for I could outdistance any of them even if I had to carry her.

"Take him back and lock him up," said Ptantus; "I have seen and heard enough for today"; so they took me back into the courtyard and chained me to my tree.

"Well," said Ptor Fak, after he thought the guards had left, "how did you get along?"

I told him all that had transpired in the jeddak's presence; and he said he hoped that I would get a chance to meet Motus, as Ptor Fak well knew my reputation as a swordsman.

After dark that night, a voice came out and sat down beside me. It was Kandus.

"It's a good thing you jumped for Ptantus today," he said, "the old devil thought Pnoxus had been lying to him and after it had been demonstrated that you could not jump Ptantus was going to have you destroyed immediately in a very unpleasant way he has of dealing with those who have aroused his anger or resentment."

"I hope I can keep on amusing him for a while," I said.

"The end will be the same eventually," said Kandus, "but if there is anything I can do to make your captivity easier for you I shall be glad to do it."

"It would relieve my mind if you could tell me what has become of the girl who was captured at the same time that I was."

"She is confined in the quarters of the female slaves. It's over on that side of the city beyond the palace," and he nodded in that direction.

"What do you think is going to happen to her?" I asked.

"Ptantus and Pnoxus are quarreling about her," he replied; "they are always quarreling about something; they hate each other. Because Pnoxus wants her Ptantus doesn't want him to have her; and so, for the time being at least, she is safe. I must go now," he added a moment later, and I could tell from the direction of his voice that he had arisen. "If there is anything I can do for you be sure to let me know."

"If you could bring me a piece of wire," I said, "I would appreciate it."

"What do you want of wire?" he asked.

"Just to pass the time," I said; "I bend them around in different shapes and make little figures of them to amuse myself. I am not accustomed to being chained to a tree, and time is going to hang very heavy on my hands."

"Certainly," he said, "I'll be glad to bring you a piece of wire; I'll be back with it in just a moment, and until then good-by."

"You are fortunate to have made a friend here," said Ptor Fak; "I've been here several months and I haven't made one."

"I think it was my jumping," I said; "it has served me in good stead before and in many ways."

It was not long before Kandus returned with the wire. I thanked him and he left immediately.

It was night now and both moons were in the sky. Their soft light illuminated the courtyard, while the swift flight of Thuria across the vault of heaven swept the shadows of the trees into constantly changing movement across the scarlet sward, turned purple now in the moonlight.

Ptor Fak's chain and mine were sufficiently long to just permit us to sit side by side, and I could see that his curiosity was aroused by my request for a piece of wire by the fact that he kept watching it in my hand. Finally he could contain himself no longer. "What are you going to do with that wire?" he asked.

"You'd be surprised," I said; and then I paused for I felt a presence near me, "at the clever things one may do with a piece of wire."

chapter VI

WERE I TO LIVE HERE in Invak the rest of my life I am sure I could never accustom myself to these uncanny presences, or to the knowledge that someone might always be standing close to me listening to everything that I said to Ptor Fak.

Presently I felt a soft hand upon my arm, and then that same sweet voice that I had heard before said, "It is Rojas."

"I am glad that you came," I said. "I wished an opportunity to thank you for the testimony you gave in my behalf before Ptantus today."

"I'm afraid it didn't do you much good," she replied; "Ptantus doesn't like me."

"Why should he dislike you?" I asked.

"Pnoxus wanted me as his mate and I refused him; so, though Ptantus doesn't like Pnoxus, his pride was hurt; and he has been venting his spleen on my family ever since." She moved closer to me, I could feel the warmth of her arm against mine as she leaned against me. "Dotar Sojat," she said, "I wish that you were an Invak so that you might remain here forever in safety."

"That is very sweet of you, Rojas," I said, "but I am afraid that Fate has ordained it otherwise."

The soft arm stole up around my shoulders. The delicate perfume which had first announced her presence to me that afternoon, filled my nostrils and I could feel her warm breath upon my cheek. "Would you like to stay here, Dotar Sojat," she paused, "—with me?"

The situation was becoming embarrassing. Even Ptor Fak was embarrassed and there were no soft invisible arms about his neck. I knew that he was embarrassed because he had moved away from us the full length of his chain. Of course he couldn't see Rojas any more than I could but he must have heard her words; and, being a gentleman, he had removed himself as far as possible; and now he sat there with his back toward us. Being made love to by a beautiful girl in a moonlit garden may be romantic, but if the girl is wholly invisible it is like being made love to by a ghost; though I can assure you that Rojas didn't feel like a ghost at all.

"You have not answered me, Dotar Sojat," she said.

I have never loved but one woman—my incomparable Dejah Thoris; nor do I, like some men, run around pretending love for other women. So, as you say in America, I was on the spot. They say that all is fair in love and war; and as far as I was concerned I, personally, was definitely at war with Invak. Here was an enemy girl whose loyalty I could win or whose bitter hatred I could incur by my reply. Had I had only myself to consider I should not have hesitated; but the fate of Llana of Gathol outweighted all other considerations, and so I temporized.

"No matter how much I should like to be with you always, Rojas," I said, "I know that is impossible. I shall be here only subject to the whims of your jeddak and then death will separate us forever."

"Oh, no, Dotar Sojat," she cried, drawing my cheek close to hers, "you must not die—for I love you."

"But Rojas," I expostulated, "how can you love a man whom you have known for only a few hours and seen but for a few minutes?"

"I knew that I loved you the moment that I set eyes upon you," she replied, "and I've seen you for a great many more than a few minutes. I have been almost constantly in the courtyard since I first saw you, watching you. I know every changing expression of your face. I have seen the light of anger, and of humor, and of friendship in your eyes. Had I known you all my life I could not know you better. Kiss me, Dotar Sojat," she concluded. And, then I did something for which I shall probably always be ashamed. I took Rojas in my arms and kissed her.

Did you ever hold a ghost in your arms and kiss her? It humiliates me to admit that it was not an unpleasant experience. But Rojas clung to me so tightly and for so long that I was covered with confusion and embarrassment.

"Oh, that we could be always thus," sighed Rojas.

Personally I thought that however pleasant, it might be a little inconvenient. However, I said, "Perhaps you will come often again, Rojas, before I die."

"Oh, don't speak of death," she cried.

"But you know yourself that Ptantus will have me killed—unless I escape."

"Escape!" She scarcely breathed the word.

"But I suppose there will be no escape for me," I added, and I tried not to sound too hopeful.

"Escape," she said again, "Escape! ah if I could but go with you."

"Why not?" I asked. I had gone this far and I felt that I might as well go all the way if by so doing I could release Llana of Gathol from captivity.

"Yes, why not?" repeated Rojas, "but how?"

"If I could become invisible," I suggested.

She thought that over for a moment and then said, "It would be treason. It would mean death, a horrible death, were I apprehended."

"I couldn't ask that of you," I said, and I felt like a hypocrite for that I knew that I could ask it of her if I thought that she would do it. I would willingly have sacrificed the life of every person in Invak, including my own, if thereby I could have liberated Llana of Gathol. I was desperate, and when a man is desperate he will resort to any means to win his point.

"I am most unhappy here," said Rojas, in a quite natural and human attempt at self-justification. "Of course, if we were successful," continued Rojas, "it wouldn't make any difference who knew what I had done because they could never find us again. We would both be invisible, and together we could make our way to your country." She was planning it all out splendidly.

"Do you know where the flier is that brought the girl prisoner?" I asked.

"Yes, it was landed on the roof of the city."

"That will simplify matters greatly," I said. "If we all become invisible we can reach it and escape with ease."

"What do you mean 'all'?" she demanded.

"Why I want to take Ptor Fak with me," I said, "and Llana of Gathol who was captured the same time I was."

Rojas froze instantly and her arms dropped from about me. "Not the girl," she said.

"But, Rojas, I must save her," I insisted. There was no reply. I waited a moment and then I said, "Rojas!" but she did not answer, and a moment later I saw her slim back materialize in the entrance to one of the streets opposite me. A slim back surmounted by a defiantly held head. That back radiated feminine fury.

chapter VII

AFTER ROJAS LEFT I was plunged almost into the depths of despair. Had she but waited I could have explained everything and the four of us might have escaped. I will admit that I have never been able to fathom the ways of women, but I felt that Rojas would never return. I presume that my conviction was influenced by those lines from The Mourning Bride, "Heaven has no rage like love to hatred turned, nor hell a fury like a woman scorned."

However, I did not give up hope entirely—I never do. Instead of repining, I went to work on the lock of my shackle with the bit of wire that Kandus had brought me. Ptor Fak moved over to watch me. I sat facing my tree, close to it, and bending over my work; and Ptor Fak leaned close and bent over it too. We were trying to hide from preying eyes the thing that I was attempting to do; and as it was now late at night we hoped that there would be no one in the courtyard other than ourselves.

At last I found the combination and after that it took me only a few seconds to unlock Ptor Fak's shackle. Then a voice behind us spoke.

"What are you doing?" it demanded; "why are you not asleep?"

"How can we sleep with people constantly annoying us?" I asked, hiding the wire beneath me.

"Stand up," said the voice, and as we stood up the shackles fell away from our ankles.

"I thought so," said the voice. Then I saw the piece of wire rise from the ground and disappear. "You are very clever, but I don't think Ptantus will appreciate your cleverness when he hears about this. I shall set a guard to watch you two constantly hereafter."

"Everything is going wrong," I said to Ptor Fak a moment later, after I saw a warrior enter one of the streets, hoping that it was he who had spoken to us and that there were no others around.

"It seems hopeless, doesn't it?" said Ptor Fak.

"No," I snapped, "not while I still live."

The following afternoon Kandus' voice came and sat down beside me. "How goes it?" he asked.

"Terrible," I said.

"How is that?" he asked.

"I can't tell you," I said, "because there is probably a guard standing right here listening to everything that I say."

"There is no one here but us," said Kandus.

"How do you know?" I asked; "your people are as invisible to you as they are to me."

"We learn to sense the presence of others," he explained; "just how, I can't tell you."

"How you do it is immaterial," I said, "as long as you are sure there is no one here listening to us. I will be perfectly frank with you, I succeeded in removing Ptor Fak's shackle and my own. Someone caught me at it and took the piece of wire away from me." I did not tell Kandus that I had broken the wire he had given me in two and that I still had the other half of it in my pocket pouch. There is no use in telling even a friend everything that you know.

"How in the world could you have hoped to escape even if you could remove your shackles?" he asked.

"It was only the first step," I told him. "We really had no plan, but we knew that we certainly could not escape as long as we were shackled."

Kandus laughed. "There is something in that," he said, and then he was silent for a moment. "The girl who was captured with you," he said presently.

"What of her?" I asked.

"Ptanus has given her to Motus," he replies; "it was all done very suddenly. Why, no one seems to know, because Ptantus hasn't any particular love for Motus."

If Kandus didn't know why, I thought that I did. I saw Rojas's hand and a green-eyed devil in it—jealousy is a heartless monster. "Will you do something more for me, Kandus?" I asked.

"Gladly, if I can," he replied.

"It may seem like a very silly request," I said, "but please don't ask me to explain. I want you to go to Rojas and tell her that Llana of Gathol, the girl that Ptantus has given to Motus, is the daughter of my daughter." It may seem strange to you denizens of Earth that Rojas could have become infatuated with a grandfather, but you must remember that Mars is not Earth and that I am unlike all other Earth-men. I do not know how old I am. I recall no childhood. It seems to me that I have just always been, and I have always been the same. I look now as I did when I fought with the Confederate army during the Civil War—a man of about thirty. And here on Barsoom, where the natural span of life is around a thousand years and people do not commence to show the ravages of old age until just shortly before dissolution, differences in age do not count. You might fall in love with a beautiful girl on Barsoom; and, as far as appearances were concerned, she might be seventeen or she might be seven hundred.

"Of course I don't understand," said Kandus, "but I'll do what you ask."

"And now another favor," I said. "Ptantus half promised me that he would let me duel with Motus and he assured me that Motus would kill me. Is there any possible way of arranging for that duel to be fought today?"

"He will kill you," said Kandus.

"That is not what I asked," I said.

"I don't know how it could be done," said Kandus.

"Now if Ptantus has any sporting blood," I suggested, "and likes to lay a wager now and then, you bet him that if Motus will fight me while Motus is still visible, that he cannot kill me but that I can kill him whenever I choose."

"But you can't do it," said Kandus. "Motus is the best swordsman on Barsoom. You would be killed and I should lose my money."

"How can I convince you?" I said. "I know that I can kill Motus in a fight. If I had anything of value, I would give it to you as security for your wager."

"I have something of value," said Ptor Fak, "and I would wager it and everything that I could scrape together on Dotar Sojat." He reached into his pocket pouch and drew forth a gorgeous jewelled medallion. "This," he said to Kandus, "is worth a jeddak's ransom—take it as security and place its value on Dotar Sojat."

A second later the medallion disappeared in thin air, and we knew that Kandus had reached out his hand and taken it.

"I'll have to go inside and examine it," said Kandus' voice, "for of course I cannot see it now that it has become invisible. I'll not be gone long."

"That is very decent of you, Ptor Fak," I said, "that medallion must be almost invaluable."

"One of my remote ancestors was a jeddak," explained Ptor Fak; "that medallion belonged to him, and it has been in the family for thousands of years."

"You must be quite certain of my swordsmanship," I said.

"I am," he replied; "but even had I been less certain, I should have done the same."

"That is friendship," I said, "and I appreciate it."

"It is priceless," said a voice at my side, and I knew that Kandus had returned. "I will go at once and see what can be done about the duel."

"Don't forget what I asked you to tell Rojas," I reminded him.

chapter VIII

AFTER KANDUS LEFT US, time dragged heavily. The afternoon wore on and it became so late that I was positive that he had failed in his mission. I was sitting dejectedly thinking of the fate that was so soon to overtake Llana of Gathol. I knew that she would destroy herself, and I was helpless to avert the tragedy. And, while I was thus sunk in the depths of despair, a hand was placed on mine. A soft hand; and a voice said, "Why didn't you tell me?"

"You didn't give me a chance," I said; "you just ran out on me without giving me a chance to explain."

"I am sorry," said the voice, "and I am sorry for the harm I have done Llana of Gathol; and now I have condemned you to death."

"What do you mean?" I asked.

"Ptantus has commanded Motus to fight you and kill you."

I threw my arms around Rojas and kissed her. I couldn't help it, I was so happy. "Good!" I exclaimed. "Though neither of us realized it at the time, you have done me a great favor."

"What do you mean?" she demanded.

"You have given me the chance to meet Motus in a fair fight; and now I know that Llana of Gathol will be safe—as far as Motus is concerned."

"Motus will kill you," insisted Rojas.

"Will you be there to see the duel?" I asked.

"I do not wish to see you killed," she said, and clung to me tightly.

"You haven't a thing to worry about, I shall not be killed; and Motus will never have Llana of Gathol or any other woman."

"You can tell his friends to start digging his grave immediately," said Ptor Fak.

"You are that sure?" said Rojas.

"We have the princess," said Ptor Fak, which is the same as saying in America "It is in the bag." The expression derives from the Barsoomian chess game, jetan, in which the taking of a princess decides the winner and ends the game.

"I hope you are right," said Rojas. "At least you have encouraged me to believe, and it is not so difficult to believe anything of Dotar Sojat."

"Do you know when I am to fight Motus?" I asked.

"This evening," replied Rojas, "before the whole Court in the throne room of the palace."

"And after I have killed him?" I asked.

"That is to be feared, too," said Rojas, "for Ptantus will be furious. He will not only have lost a fighting man but all the money he has wagered on the duel. But it will soon be time," she added, "and I must go now." I saw her open my pocket pouch and drop something into it, and then she was gone.

I knew from the surreptitious manner in which she had done it that she did not wish anyone to know what she had put in my pocket pouch, or in fact that she had put anything into it; and so I did not investigate immediately, fearing that someone may have been watching and had their suspicions aroused. The constant strain of feeling that unseen eyes may be upon you, and that unseen ears may be listening to your every word was commencing to tell upon me; and I was becoming as nervous as a cat with seven kittens.

After a long silence Ptor Fak said, "What are you going to do with her?"

I knew what he meant; because the same question had been worrying me. "If we succeed in getting out of this," I said, "I am going to take her back to Helium with me and let Dejah Thoris convince her that there are a great many more charming men than I there." I had had other women fall in love with me and this would not be the first time that Dejah Thoris had unscrambled things for me. For she knew that no matter how many women loved me, she was the only woman whom I loved.

"You are a brave man," said Ptor Fak.

"You say that because you do not know Dejah Thoris," I replied; "it is not that I am a brave man, it is that she is a wise woman."

That started me off again thinking about her, although I must confess that she is seldom absent from my thoughts. I could picture her now in our marble palace in Helium, surrounded by the brilliant men and women who crowd her salons. I could feel her hand in mine as we trod the stately Barsoomian dances she loves so well. I could see her as though she were standing before me this minute, and I could see Thuvia of Ptarth, and Carthoris, and Tara of Helium, and Gahan of Gathol. That magnificent coterie of handsome men and beautiful women bound together by ties of love and marriage. What memories they evoked!

A soft hand caressed my cheek and a voice, tense with nervousness said, "Live! Live for me! I shall return at midnight and you must be here"; then she was gone.

For some reason or other which I cannot explain, her words quieted my nerves. They gave me confidence that at midnight I should be free. Her presence reminded me that she had dropped something into my pocket pouch and I opened it casually and put my hand into it. My fingers came in contact with a number of spheres, about the size of marbles, and I knew that the secret of invisibility was mine. I moved close to Ptor Fak; and once again with the remaining bit of wire I picked the lock of his shackle, and then I handed him one of the spheres that Rojas had given me.

I leaned very close to his ear. "Take this," I whispered; "in an hour you will be invisible. Go to the far end of the courtyard and wait. When I return I too shall be invisible and when I whistle thus, answer me." I whistled a few of the opening notes of the national anthem of Helium, a signal that Dejah Thoris and I had often used.

"I understand," said Ptor Fak.

"What do you understand?" demanded a voice.

Doggonit! there was that invisibility nemesis again and now all our plans might be knocked into a cocked hat. How much had the fellow heard? What had he seen? I trembled inwardly, fearing the answer. Then I felt hands at my ankle and saw my shackle fall open.

"Well," repeated the voice peremptorily, "what was it that you understood?"

"I was just telling Ptor Fak," I said, "how I was going to kill Motus, and he said he understood perfectly."

"So you think you are going to kill Motus, do you?" demanded the voice. "Well, you are going to be very much surprised for a few minutes, and after that you will be dead. Come along with me; the duel is about to take place."

I breathed a sigh of relief. The fellow had evidently seen or heard nothing of any importance.

"I'll see you later, Ptor Fak," I said.

"Good-by and good luck," he replied. And then, accompanied by the warrior, I entered a city street on my way to the throne room of Ptantus, jeddak of Invak.

chapter IX

"So you think you're pretty good with the sword," said the warrior walking at my side and who was now visible to me.

"Yes," I replied.

"Well, you're going to get a lesson in swordsmanship tonight. Of course it won't do you much good because after it is all over you will be dead."

"You are very encouraging," I said, "but if you are fond of Motus,

I suggest that you save your encouragement for him. He is going to need it."

"I am not fond of Motus," said the warrior; "no one is fond of Motus. He is a calot and I apologize to calots for the comparison. I hope that you kill him but of course you won't. He always kills his man, but he is tricky. Watch out for that."

"You mean he doesn't fight fair?" I asked.

"No one ever taught him the word," said the warrior.

"Well, thank you for warning me," I said; "I hope you stay to see the fight, maybe you will be surprised."

"I shall certainly stay to see it," he said. "I wouldn't miss it for the world. But I am not going to be surprised; I know just what will happen. He will play with you for about five minutes and then he'll run you through; and that won't please Ptantus for he likes a long drawn out duel."

"Oh, he does does he?" I said. "Well, he shall have it." That fitted in perfectly with my plans. I had swallowed one of the invisibility spheres just before the warrior unshackled me, and I knew that it would take about an hour for it to effect perfect invisibility. It might be difficult to drag the duel out for an hour, but I hoped to gain a little time by stalling up to the moment that we crossed swords. And I accomplished it now by walking slowly to kill as much time as possible, and twice I stopped to tighten the fastenings of my sandals.

"What's the matter?" demanded the warrior. "Why do you walk so slow? Are you afraid?"

"Terrified," I replied. "Everyone has told me how easily Motus is going to kill me. Do you think that a man wants to run to his death?"

"Well, I don't blame you much," said the warrior, "and I won't hurry you."

"A lot of you Invaks are pretty good fellows," I remarked.

"Of course we are," he said. "What made you think anything different?"

"Pnoxus, Motus, and Ptantus," I replied.

The warrior grinned. "I guess you are a pretty shrewd fellow," he said, "to have sized them up this quickly."

"Everybody seems to hate them," I said; "why don't you get rid of them? I'll start you off by getting rid of Motus tonight."

"You may be a good swordsman," said the warrior, "but you are bragging too much; I never knew a braggart yet who could 'take the princess.'"

"I am not bragging," I said; "I only state facts." As a matter of fact, I often realize that in speaking of my swordsmanship, it may sound to others as though I were bragging but really I do not feel that I am bragging. I know that I am the greatest swordsman of two worlds. It would be foolish for me to simper, and suck my finger, and say that I was not. I am, and everyone who has seen me fight knows that I am. Is it braggadocio to state a simple fact? It has saved a number of lives, for it has kept no end of brash young men from challenging me. Fighting has been, you might say, my life's work. There is not a lethal weapon in the use of which I do not excel, but the sword is my favorite. I love a good blade and I love a good fight and I hoped that tonight I should have them both. I hoped that Motus was all that they thought him. The thought might have obtruded on the consciousness of some men that perhaps he was, but no such idea ever entered my head. They say that overconfidence often leads to defeat, but I do not think that I am ever overconfident. I am merely wholly confident, and I maintain that there is all the difference in the world there.

At last we came to the throne room. It was not the same room in which I had first seen Ptantus; it was a much larger room, a more ornate room; and at one side of it was a raised dais on which were two thrones. They were empty now, for the jeddak and the jeddara had not yet appeared. The floor of the room was crowded with nobles and their women. Along three sides of the room were several tiers of benches, temporary affairs, which had evidently been brought in for the occasion. They were covered with gay cloths and cushions; but they were still empty, for, of course, no one could sit until the jeddak came and was seated.

As I was brought into the room, a number of people called attention to me and soon many eyes were upon me.

In my well-worn fighting harness, I looked rather drab in the midst of this brilliant company with their carved leather harness studded with jewels. The Invaks, like most of the red nations of Barsoom, are a handsome people and those in the throne room of this tiny nation, hidden away in the Forest of Lost Men, made a brave appearance beneath the strange and beautiful lights which gave them visibility.

I heard many comments concerning me. One woman said, "He does not look like a Barsoomian at all."

"He is very handsome," said a sweet voice, which I immediately recognized; and for the second time I looked Rojas in the face. As our eyes met I could see her tremble. She was a beautiful girl, by far the most beautiful of all the women in the room, I am sure.

"Let's talk with him," she said to a woman and two men standing with her.

"That would be interesting," said the woman, and the four of them walked toward me.

Rojas looked me square in the eye. "What is your name?" she asked, without a flicker of recognition.

"Dotar Sojat," I replied.

"The Sultan of Swat," said one of the men, "whatever a sultan is and wherever Swat may be." I could scarcely repress a smile.

"Where is Swat?" inquired the woman.

"In India," I replied.

"I think the fellow is trying to make fools of us," snapped one of the men. "He is just making up those names. There are no such places on Barsoom."

"I didn't say they were on Barsoom," I retorted. "They are forty-three million miles from Barsoom."

"If they're not on Barsoom, where are they?" demanded the man.

"On Jasoom," I replied.

"Come," said the man, "I have had enough of this slave's insolence."

"I find him very interesting," said the woman.

"So do I," said Rojas.

"Well, enjoy it while you may," said the man, "for in a few minutes he will be dead."

"Have you laid a wager on that?" I asked.

"I couldn't find anyone to bet against Motus," he growled. "Kandus was the only fool to do that and the jeddak covered his entire wager."

"That is too bad," I said; "someone is losing an opportunity to make some money."

"Do you think you will win?" asked Rojas, trying to conceal the eagerness in her voice.

"Of course I shall win," I replied. "I always do. You look like a very intelligent girl," I said, "if I may speak to you alone I will tell you a little secret."

She saw that I had something that I wished to say to her in private, but I will admit that I had put her in rather an embarrassing position. However, the other woman helped me out."

"Go ahead, Rojas," she urged. "I think it would be fun to hear what he has to say."

Thus encouraged Rojas took me to one side. "What is it?" she asked.

"Llana of Gathol," I said. "How are we to get her?"

She caught her breath. "I never thought of that," she said.

"Could you get one of those invisibility spheres to her right away?" I asked.

"For you, yes," she said. "For you I would do anything."

"Good; and tell her to come out into the courtyard by the quarters of the slave women. A little after midnight she will hear me whistle. She will recognize the air. She must answer and then wait for me. Will you do that for me, Rojas?"

"Yes, but what excuse am I to make for leaving my friends?"

"Tell them you are going to get some money to wager on me," I said.

Rojas smiled. "That is a splendid idea," she said. And a moment later she had made her explanations to her friends and I saw her leave the throne room.

chapter X

THE CROWD WAS growing restless waiting for the jeddak, but I was more than pleased by this delay as it would shorten the time that I should have to wait before I could achieve invisibility.

It seemed now that everything had been nicely arranged; and when I saw Rojas return to the throne room and she gave me a quick fleeting smile, I was convinced that almost the last of my worries were over. There was really only one doubt remaining in my mind, and that was as to what might happen to me after I had killed Motus. I had no doubt but that Ptantus would be furious; and being a tyrant with the reactions of a tyrant, he might order my immediate death. Anticipating this, however, I had decided to make a run for the nearest courtyard; and if sufficient time had elapsed since I had taken the invisibility sphere, I would only have to step out into the open to elude them. And, once in one of the courtyards, and invisible, I knew that I could escape.

Suddenly trumpets blared and the people fell back to each side of the throne room. Then, preceded by the trumpeters, Ptantus and his jeddara entered the throne room accompanied by a band of gorgeously trapped courtiers.

I glanced at the great clock on the wall. It was exactly the 8th zode which is the equivalent of 10:48 P.M. Earth time. By midnight Llana of Gathol would have achieved invisibility—if Rojas had given her the sphere. That was the question. Yet I felt that Rojas had not failed me. I firmly believed that she had done her part.

The royal pair made their way slowly across the room to the dais and seated themselves upon their thrones, whereat the nobles and their women found their places on the benches.

From somewhere Motus had appeared; and he, and a noble who accompanied him, and I, and my warrior guard, were alone upon the floor. A fifth man then appeared who I later discovered was what you might call a referee, or umpire. He summoned me forward, and the five of us advanced and stopped before the throne.

"I bring you the noble Motus," he said addressing Ptantus, "and Dotar Sojat, the Sultan of Swat, who are to duel to the death with long-swords."

The jeddak nodded. "Let them fight," he said, "and see that you fight fair," he added, glaring directly at me.

"And, I suppose that Motus does not have to fight fair," I said; "but that is immaterial to me. I shall kill him however he fights."

The referee was almost beside himself with embarrassment. "Silence, slave!" he whispered. He carried an extra sword which he handed to me and then motioned us to cross swords.

Instead of adhering to this honorable custom, Motus lunged for my heart.

"That was unwise, Motus," I said, as I parried the thrust; "I am going to make you suffer a little more for that."

"Silence, slave," demanded the referee.

"Silence yourself, calot," I replied, "and get out of my way. I am not supposed to be fighting two men," I pricked Motus on the right breast and brought blood, "but I shall be glad too if you will draw."

Motus came at me again, but he was wary and he was a good swordsman.

"Your face is all black and swollen, Motus," I said; "it looks as if someone had hit you, for that is what a son-of-a-calot is apt to get when he kicks a blind man."

"Silence," screamed the referee.

I fought on the defensive at first with one eye on the great clock. It had been over half an hour since I had taken the invisibility sphere, and I planned on letting Motus live another half hour so as to be quite sure that I had gained potential invisibility before I finished him off.

By fighting on the defensive, I compelled Motus to do all the work; and by repeatedly side-stepping his most vicious lunges, letting them slip off my blade so that he had to leap quickly back, I subjected him to considerable nervous as well as physical strain, so that presently the sweat was streaming down his body. And, now I commenced to touch him here and there; and blood mixed with the sweat until he was a sorry looking spectacle, although nowhere had he received a severe wound.

The crowd was all on Motus's side; that is, all who were vocal. I knew of two at least who hoped that I would win, and I guess that there were many others who disliked Motus but who dared not cheer on an alien and a slave.

"You are tiring, Motus," I said to him; "hadn't you better finish me off now before you become wholly exhausted?"

"I'll finish you off all right, slave," he came back, "if you'll stand still and fight."

"It is not time to kill you yet, Motus," I said, glancing up at the clock, "when the hand points to eleven xats past the 8th zode, I shall kill you."

"Silence," screeched the referee.

"What is the slave saying?" demanded Ptantus in stentorian tones.

"I said," I shouted back at him, "that I should kill Motus at exactly 8 zodes, 11 xats. Watch the clock, Ptantus, for at that instant you are going to lose your wager, and Motus his life."

"Silence," commanded the jeddak.

"Now, Motus," I whispered, "I am going to show you how easily I can kill you when the time comes," and with that I disarmed him and sent his sword clattering across the floor.

A mighty gasp arose from the audience, for now under the rules of a duel of this nature, I was at liberty to run Motus through the heart; but instead I rested my point upon the floor and turned to the referee.

"Go and fetch Motus's sword," I said, "and return it to him."

Motus was trembling a little. I could see his knees shake though almost imperceptibly. I knew then what I had suspected before— Motus was yellow.

While the referee was retrieving Motus' sword, a little ripple of applause ran through the stands. But Ptantus only sat and scowled more fiercely; I fear that Ptantus did not like me.

When Motus' sword was returned to him, he came for me furiously; and I knew perfectly well what was in his mind; he was going to finish me off immediately. I disarmed him again; and again I lowered my point, while the referee without waiting to be told ran after the blade.

Now Motus was more wary. I could see that he was trying to work me around to some position in which he wished to have me. I noticed presently that the referee was not within my range of vision, and a quick glance told me he was standing directly behind me; it was not intuition that told me why, for I had seen that trick played before by crooked swordsmen with an accomplice. I heard a few groans from the stands; and then I knew that I was right, for no honorable person could witness such a thing without voicing his disapproval.

When Motus next lunged, hoping to force me back, the referee would "accidentally" be close behind me; I would bump into him, and Motus would have me at his mercy. It is a despicable trick; and Ptantus must have seen it coming, but he made no move to prevent it.

I watched Motus' eyes and they telegraphed his intention to me an instant before he lunged, throwing all his weight behind it. I had slightly crouched in anticipation of this and my earthly muscles carried me to one side, and Motus's sword drove to the hilt through the body of the referee.

For a moment pandemonium reigned in the throne room. The entire audience stood up in the stands and there were cheers and groans, and something told me that the cheers were for me and the groans for Motus and the referee.

Motus was a terribly unstrung and rattled man as he jerked his blade from the body of the dead man, but now I gave him no respite. I went after him in earnest, though not yet for the kill. I cut a deep gash across his swollen jaw. "You will not make a good looking corpse now, Motus," I said, "and before I am through with you, you are going to look a great deal worse."

"Calot!" he snapped, and then he rushed me, cutting and thrusting violently. I parried every cut and thrust and wove a net of steel around him, and every time he missed I brought blood from some new spot on his body.

"You have three xats to live, Motus," I said; "you had better make the best of them."

He rushed at me like a madman; but I sidestepped him and as he turned I took off one of his ears as neatly as a surgeon could have done it—I thought he was going to faint, for his knees seemed to give beneath him and he staggered about for a moment.

I waited for him to recover control of himself, and then I went to work on him again. I tried to carve my initials on his breast, but by this time there was not a whole place large enough; from the waist up he looked like a plate of raw hamburger.

The floor was covered with his blood by now; and as he rushed me again furiously, he slipped and fell. He lay there for a moment glaring at me, for I am sure he expected that I would finish him off then; but instead I said, "You have a xat and a half to live yet, Motus."

He staggered to his feet and tried to throw himself upon me, screaming imprecations as he came. I think that by this time Motus had gone quite mad from pain and terror. I felt no sympathy for him—he was a rat; and now he was fighting like a cornered rat.

"The floor is too slippery here," I said to him; "let's go over by the jeddak's throne—I am sure that he would like to see the finish."

I maneuvered him around into position and backed him across

the floor until we stood directly in front of Ptantus.

It is seldom that I have ever punished a man as I punished Motus; but I felt that he deserved it, and I was the plaintiff, prosecuting attorney, jury, and judge; I was also the executioner.

Motus was gibbering now and making futile passes at me with his blade. Ptantus was glaring at me, and the audience was tense with breathless expectancy. I saw many an eye glance quickly at the clock.

"One more tal, Motus," I said. A tal is about eight tenths of an earthly second.

At that Motus turned suddenly and ran screaming toward the great doorway that led from the throne room; and again the audience rose to its feet, and there were groans and cries of "Coward!"

The fight was to have been to the death and Ptantus had wagered that I would not kill Motus. If I did not kill him, I feared that Ptantus would then claim the money; so I risked everything on an art I had often practiced for my own amusement. I carried my sword hand far behind my right shoulder and then brought it forward with all my strength, releasing the blade point first. It flew like a sped arrow and drove through Motus' body below the left shoulder blade at exactly 11 xats past the 8th zode.

chapter XI

I TURNED AND BOWED to Ptantus, now having no sword with which to salute him. He should have acknowledged this customary courtesy but he did nothing of the sort, he merely glared at me and stood up. The jeddara arose too; and, with the trumpeters before them and the courtiers behind, the two stalked out of the throne room, making a wide detour to avoid the blood and the two corpses.

After they had left, the warrior who had brought me from the courtyard came and touched me on the arm. "Come," he said. "All you get out of this is to be chained to your tree again."

"I got a great deal more than that out of it," I replied, as I accompanied him across the throne room; "I had the satisfaction of avenging a cowardly kick."

As we crossed toward the doorway, someone started cheering and then practically the entire audience took it up. "That is an unusual demonstration," said the warrior, "but you deserve it. No one on Barsoom ever saw such swordplay as you showed us tonight—and I thought you were boasting!" He laughed.

I knew that it would be necessary for us to cross a couple of courtyards before we reached the one in which I had been confined; and I realized that if I suddenly disappeared before the warrior's eyes, he would know that I had obtained invisibility spheres; and while of course he couldn't have found me, it would certainly have started an investigation and would have upset our plans for escape. If they knew that I was at large and invisible, one of the first things that they would most naturally have done would have been to place a guard over my flier.

If, however, they merely thought that I had escaped, and was not invisible, they would feel that they need only search for me to find me very quickly. Of course, they might still place a guard over the flier; but such a guard would not be so on the alert, and we still might board the ship and get away before they were aware of our presence.

As we approached the first courtyard, I suddenly broke away from my guard and ran ahead with all my earthly speed. The warrior shouted for me to halt, and broke into a run. As I reached the entrance to the courtyard I pretended to dodge around the corner, which would of course have hidden me from him.

I must confess that in that short sprint my heart had been in my mouth, for of course I could not know whether or not I should become invisible.

However, the moment that I left the lighted corridor I absolutely disappeared; I could not see any part of my body—it was the strangest sensation that I have ever experienced.

I had made my plans, and now I ran to the far end of the courtyard and leaped lightly to the roof of the city.

I could hear the warrior guard rushing about calling to me; my disappearance must certainly have mystified him, for having no idea that I could become invisible, there was really no way in which he could account for it except on the theory that I had run into the entrance to another street. However, he was probably confident that I did not have time to do this.

Well, I did not bother much about him or what he was thinking; instead I took off across the roof in search of the courtyard where Ptor Fak was awaiting me and where I expected to meet Rojas at midnight; and it was pretty close to what we call midnight then, the Barsoomian midnight occurring twenty-five xats after the eighth zode.

A Martian day is divided into ten zodes, there being four tals to a xat, or two hundred to a zode. The dials of their clocks are marked with four concentric circles; between the inner circle and the next outer one the Zodes are marked from one to ten; in the next circle, the xats are marked from one to fifty between each two zodes; and in the outer circle two hundred tals are marked between the radii which pass through the zode numbers and extend to the outer periphery of the dial. Their clock has three different colored and different length hands, one indicating the zode, the second one the xat, and the longest one the tal.

(Editor's note: I have before me the diagram of the dial of a Martian clock drawn for me by John Carter many years ago.)

I had no difficulty in finding the courtyard in which I had been confined; and when I reached it I whistled, and Ptor Fak answered. I dropped down into it and whistled again, and when Ptor Fak answered I groped around until I bumped into him.

"How well you look," he said, and we both laughed. "It took you much longer to dispose of Motus than I had anticipated," he continued.

"I had to drag it out so that I would be sure to be invisible when I had returned here," I explained.

"And now what?" asked Ptor Fak.

I found his head and placed my lips close to one of his ears. "After Rojas comes," I whispered, "we'll cross the roof to the quarters of the slave women and get Llana of Gathol. In the meantime, you climb this tree which overhangs the roof and wait for us up there."

"Whistle when you come up," he said, and left me.

Invisibility I discovered was most disconcerting; I could see no part of my body; I was only a voice without visible substance—a voice standing in an apparently deserted courtyard which might be filled with enemies, as far as I knew. I couldn't even have heard them had there been any there, for the Invaks have taken the precaution of covering all the metal parts of their accouterments so that there is not the usual clank of metal upon metal when they move about.

Knowing as I did that a search for me must have been instituted, I felt positive that there must be Invak warriors in the courtyard, notwithstanding the fact that I neither heard nor saw anyone.

As I waited for Rojas, I took the precaution of not moving about lest I inadvertently bump into someone who might require me to identify myself; but I could not prevent someone from bumping into me, and that is exactly what happened. Hands were laid upon me and a gruff voice demanded, "Who are you?"

Here was a pretty kettle of fish. What was I to do? I doubted that

I could pass myself off as an Invak—I knew too little about them to do that successfully; so, I did the next best thing that occurred to me.

"I am the ghost of Motus," I said, in a sepulchral voice. "I am searching for the man who killed me, but he is not here."

The hands relinquished their hold upon me; I could almost feel the fellow shrink away from me, and then another voice said, "Ghost of Motus nothing—I recognize that voice—it is the voice of the slave who killed Motus. Seize him!"

I jumped to one side but I jumped into the arms of another voice, and it seized me. "I have him!" cried the voice. "How did you achieve the secrets of invisibility, slave?"

With my left hand I groped for the hilt of the fellow's sword; and when I found it, I said, "You have made a mistake," and drove his sword through the heart of the voice.

There was a single piercing scream, and I was free. Holding my sword point breast high, I turned and ran for the tree by which Ptor Fak had mounted to the roof. One of my shoulders brushed a body, but I reached the tree in safety.

As I climbed carefully to a lower branch so as not to reveal my presence by the shaking of the foliage, I heard a low whistle. It was Rojas.

"Who whistled?" demanded a voice somewhere in the courtyard. There was no reply.

Rojas could not have come at a worse time; I did not answer her; I did not know what to do, but Ptor Fak evidently thought that he did, for he answered the whistle. He must have thought that it was I who was signalling to him.

"They're on the roof!" cried a voice. "Quick! up that tree!"

Now the only tree that overhung the roof was the one that I was in, and if I remained there I was sure to be discovered. There was only one thing for me to do and that was to go up on the roof myself, and I did so as quickly as I could.

I hadn't taken half a dozen steps after I arrived, before I bumped into someone. "Zodanga?" I whispered. I didn't wish to speak Ptor Fak's name, but I knew that he would understand if I spoke the name of the country from which he came.

"Yes," he replied.

"Find the flier and stay near it until I come." He pressed my arm to show that he understood, and was gone.

I could see the tree up which I had come shaking violently; so I knew that a number of warriors were climbing up in pursuit of me, though how in the world they expected to find me, I don't know.

It was a most amazing situation; there must have been at least a dozen men on the roof and possibly still others down in the courtyard where I knew Rojas to be, yet both the roof and the courtyard were apparently deserted—neither the eye nor the ear could perceive any living thing; only when someone spoke was the illusion dispelled, and presently I heard a voice a short distance away. "He has probably gone this way—the city wall lies nearest in this direction. Spread out and comb the roof right to the city wall."

"It's a waste of time," said another voice. "If someone has given him the secret of invisibility, we can never find him."

"I do not think it was he, anyway," said a third voice; "there is no way in which he could have become invisible—it was unquestionably the ghost of Motus that spoke."

By this time the voices were dwindling in the distance, and I felt that it was safe to assume that all the warriors had gone in search of me; so I walked to the edge of the roof and jumped down into the courtyard. I stood there a moment concentrating all my mental powers in an endeavor to sense the presence of others near me, as Kandus had said that he was able to do, but I got no reaction. This might mean either that I failed to sense the presence of others or that there was no one there—at least near me; so I took the chance and whistled again. An answer came from the other side of the courtyard; I waited. Presently I heard a low whistle much nearer, and I replied—a moment later Rojas' hand touched mine.

I did not speak again for fear of attracting other pursuers, but I led her to the tree and helped her to clamber to the roof.

"Where is my flier?" I whispered.

She took me by the arm and led me in a direction at right angles to that which my pursuers had taken. The outlook appeared brighter immediately.

Rojas and I walked hand in hand so as not to lose one another. Presently I saw my flier standing there in the light of the farther moon, and it certainly looked good to me.

"The quarters of the slave women are near by, are they not?" I asked in a whisper.

"Right there," she said, and I suppose she pointed; then she led me to the edge of the roof overlooking a courtyard.

chapter XII

ROJAS AND I STOOD hand in hand at the edge of the roof looking down into a seemingly deserted courtyard. "You gave Llana of Gathol the invisibility sphere?" I asked.

"Yes," replied Rojas, "and she must be invisible by this time." She pressed my hand. "You fought magnificently," she whispered.

"Everyone knew that you could have killed Motus whenever you wished; but only I guessed why you did not kill him sooner. Ptantus is furious; he has ordered that you be destroyed immediately."

"Rojas," I said, "don't you think that you should reconsider your decision to come with me? All of your friends and relatives are here in Invak, and you might be lonesome and unhappy among my people."

"Wherever you are, I shall be happy," she said. "If you do not take me with you I shall kill myself."

So that was that. I had involved myself in a triangle which bid fair to prove exceedingly embarrassing and perhaps tragic. I felt sorry for Rojas, and I was annoyed and humiliated by the part that I was forced to play. However, there had been no other way; it had been a question of Rojas' happiness or of Llana's life, and the lives of Ptor Fak and myself. I knew that I had chosen wisely, but I was still most unhappy.

Motivated by the habits of a lifetime, I strained my eyes in search of Llana of Gathol, who perhaps was down there somewhere in the courtyard; and then, realizing the futility of looking for her, I whistled. There was an immediate response from below and I sprang down from the roof. It did not take us long to locate one another; and as we were not challenged, I assumed that we were fortunate enough to be alone.

Llana touched my hand. "I thought that you would never come," she said. "Rojas told me about the duel that you were to fight; and while I had no doubts about your swordsmanship, I realized that there is always the danger of an accident or trickery. But at last you are here; how strange it is not to be able to see you. I was really quite frightened when I stepped out here into the courtyard and discovered that I could not even see myself."

"It is the miracle of invisibility that will save us," I said, "And only a miracle could have saved us. Now I must get you to the roof."

There was no overhanging tree in this courtyard, and the roof was fifteen feet above the ground. "You are about to have an experience, Llana," I said.

"What do you mean?" she asked.

"I am going to toss you up onto the roof," I told her, "and I hope you land on your feet."

"I am ready," she said.

I could see the roof all right, but I couldn't see Llana; all I could do was pray that my aim would be true. "Keep your whole body perfectly rigid," I said, "until I release you; then draw your feet up beneath you and relax. You may get a bad fall, but I don't think that it can hurt you much; the roof is heavily padded with vines."

"Let's get it over," said Llana.

I grasped one of her legs at the knee with my right hand and cradled her body on my left forearm; then I swung her back and forth a couple of times, and tossed her high into the air.

Llana of Gathol may have been invisible, but she was also definitely corporeal. I heard her land on the roof with anything but an invisible thud, and I breathed a sigh of relief. To spring lightly after her was nothing for my earthly muscles, and soon a low whistle brought the three of us together. I cautioned the girls to silence, and we walked hand in hand in the direction of the flier.

This was the moment that aroused my greatest apprehension, as I realized that the flier might be surrounded by invisible warriors; and, as far as I knew, the only sword among us was the one I had taken from the warrior I had killed in the courtyard; but perhaps Rojas had one.

"Have you a sword, Rojas?" I whispered.

"Yes," she said; "I brought one."

"Can you use it?" I asked.

"I never have used one," she replied.

"Then give it to Llana of Gathol; she can use if it necessary, and very effectively too."

We approached to within about a hundred feet of the flier and stopped. This was the crucial moment; I was almost afraid to whistle, but I did. There was an immediate answer from the vicinity of the flier. I listened a moment for voices that might betray the presence of the enemy, but there were none.

We advanced quickly then, and I helped the girls over the rail. "Where are you, Ptor Fak?" I asked. "Are you alone?"

"On deck," he said, "and I don't think there is anyone around."

"All the warriors of Invak could be here now," I said, as I reached the controls and started the motor.

A moment later the little ship rose gracefully into the air, and almost immediately from below us, we heard shouts and imprecations. The Invaks had seen the ship, but too late to prevent our escape. We were safe. We had accomplished what a few hours before would have seemed impossible, for then Ptor Fak and I were chained to trees and Llana of Gathol was a captive in another part of the city.

"We owe Rojas a great debt of gratitude," I said.

"A debt," she replied, "which it will be very easy, and I hope pleasant, for you to repay."

I winced at that; I saw a bad time ahead for me. I would rather face a dozen men with my sword than one infuriated or heartbroken woman. Before we reached Helium, I would have to tell her; but I decided to wait until we had regained visibility.

Perhaps it would have been easier to tell her while we were both invisible, but it seemed a cowardly way to me.

"You are going on to Helium, John Carter?" asked Llana.

"Yes," I said.

"What will they think of a flier coming in by itself with no one on board?" she asked.

"We will have to wait until we become visible before we approach the city," I replied. "We must not take any more of the invisibility spheres."

"Who is John Carter?" asked Rojas. "Is there another here of whom I did not know?"

"I am John Carter," I replied. "Dotar Sojat is merely a name that I assumed temporarily."

"Then you are not the Sultan of Swat?" demanded Rojas.

"No," I replied, "I am not."

"You have deceived me."

"I am sorry, Rojas," I said; "I was not trying to deceive you—about my name; as a matter of fact I never told you I was the Sultan of Swat; I told some warrior who questioned me." If she were angry about my deceiving her concerning my name and status, how was she going to take the fact that I did not love her, and that I already had a mate! I was as unhappy as a live eel in a frying pan; then of a sudden I decided to take the bull by the horns and get the whole thing over with. "Rojas," I began, "though I did not deceive you about my name, I did deceive you in a much more important matter."

"What is that?" she asked.

"I used your—ah—friendship to gain freedom for Llana of Gathol. I pretended to love you when I did not; I already have a mate."

I waited for the explosion, but no explosion came; instead there was a faint, tinkling, little laugh. I continued to wait; no one spoke; the silence became oppressive. Momentarily I expected a dagger to be slipped into me; or that Rojas would leap overboard; but neither of these things occurred, and I sat there at the controls wondering about that laugh. Perhaps the shock of my avowal had unbalanced Rojas' mind. I wished that I could see her, and at the same time I was glad that I could not—and I was certainly glad that no one could see me, for I felt like a fool.

I couldn't think of anything to say, and I thought the silence was going to last forever, but finally Llana of Gathol broke it. "How long will we remain invisible?" she asked.

"A little more than ten zodes from the time you took the sphere," said Rojas. "I shall become visible first, and then probably either John Carter or Ptor Fak, as I imagine that they took the spheres about the same time; you will be the last to regain visibility." Her voice was perfectly normal; there was no trace of nervousness nor bitterness in it. I couldn't make the girl out.

Perhaps she was the type that would bide its time until it could wreak some terrible revenge. I'll tell you that I had plenty to think about on that trip to Helium.

chapter XIII

SHORTLY AFTER DAWN, I saw a most amazing phenomenon—I saw just a suggestion of the outline of a shadowy form beside me; it took shape slowly: Rojas was materializing! The effects of the invisibility compound were disappearing, and as they disappeared Rojas appeared. There she sat gazing out across the Martian landscape, the shadow of a happy smile upon her lips; somehow she reminded me of a cat which had just swallowed a canary.

"Kaor!" I said, which is the Barsoomian equivalent of Good

Morning, Hello, or How do you do?—in other words, it is a Barsoomian greeting.

Rojas looked in my direction but of course she could not see me.

"Kaor," she replied, smiling. "You must be very tired, John Carter; you have had no sleep all night."

"When Llana of Gathol awakens, I shall sleep," I replied; "she can handle the controls quite as well as I."

"I have never been beyond the forests of Invak before," said Rojas. "What a drab, lonely world this is."

"You will find the twin cities of Helium very beautiful," I said. "I hope that you will like it there, Rojas."

"I am sure that I shall," she said; "I am looking forward to being in Helium with you, John Carter."

I wondered what she meant by that. The girl was an enigma; and I gave up trying to find a solution for her, and when Llana of Gathol spoke a moment later, and I knew that she was awake, I asked her to take the controls.

"We will cruise around outside of Helium," I said, "until we have all regained visibility," and then I lay down and fell asleep.

It was late that night before we had all regained visibility, and the next morning I approached Helium. A patrol boat came up to meet us, and recognizing my flier, it came alongside. The officer in command, and, in fact, the whole crew were overjoyed to see both Llana of Gathol and myself, alive and safe. The patrol boat escorted us to the hangar on the roof of my palace, where we received a tremendous welcome, as we had both been given up for dead long since.

Ptor Fak, Llana, and Rojas were behind me when I took Dejah Thoris in my arms; then I turned and presented Rojas and Ptor Fak to her.

"Had it not been for Rojas," I told Dejah Thoris, "none of us would have been here," and then I told her very briefly of our capture and incarceration in Invak.

I watched Rojas very closely as Dejah Thoris took both her hands in hers and kissed her on the forehead; and then, to my surprise, Rojas threw her arms about her and kissed her squarely on the mouth; the girl was absolutely bewildering.

After we had all breakfasted together Dejah Thoris asked me what my plans were now. "I shall see Tardos Mors immediately," I replied, "and after I have arranged for the dispatch of a fleet for Gathol, I shall fly there myself, alone, to reconnoiter."

"Why alone?" demanded Dejah Thoris; "But why should I ask? It has always been your way to do things alone."

I saw Tardos Mors and made the necessary arrangements for the dispatch of a fleet to Gathol; and then I returned to my palace to bid Dejah Thoris good-by; and as I passed through the garden, I saw Rojas sitting there alone.

"Come here a moment, John Carter," she said; "I have something to say to you."

Here it comes, I thought; well, it would have to be gotten over sooner or later, and it would be a relief to get it over at once.

"You deceived me, John Carter," she said.

"I know I did," I replied.

"I am so glad that you did," she said, "for I deceived you. I admired you, John Carter, tremendously; but I never loved you. I knew that you had come to Invak in a flier; and I knew that if you could be helped to escape in it, you might be persuaded to take me with you. I hate Invak; I was most unhappy there; I would have sold my very soul to have escaped, and so I tried to make you love me so that you would take me away. I thought I had succeeded, and I was very much ashamed of myself. You can never know how relieved I was when I found that I had failed, for I admired you too much to wish to bring unhappiness to you."

"But why did you pretend to be so jealous of Llana of Gathol?" I asked.

"To make my love seem more realistic," she said.

"You have lifted a great weight from my conscience, Rojas. I hope that you will like it here and that you will be very happy."

"I shall love it," she said, "for I already love Dejah Thoris, and she has asked me to stay here with her."

"Now I know that you will be happy here," I told her.

"I am sure of it, John Carter—I have seen some very handsome men already, and they can't all have mates."

The flight to Gathol was uneventful. I had taken an invisibility sphere some time before leaving Helium, and before I reached Gathol I had completely disappeared.

As I approached the city, I could see Hin Abtol's army drawn up around it; there were many more than there had been when I escaped in the Dusar; and on the line from which I had stolen the ship were at least a hundred more fliers, many of them large fighting ships, with some transports.

Presently several patrol boats rose to meet me. I was flying no colors, and when they hailed me I made no response. A couple of them ranged alongside me, and I could hear the exclamations of astonishment when they discovered that there was no one aboard the ship and no pilot at the controls.

I think they were rather frightened, for no one attempted to board me; and they let me fly on without interfering.

I dropped down to the Panar line, and set my flier down beside the last ship in it. One of the patrol ships landed also, and was soon surrounded by a crowd of officers and warriors, who approached my ship with every sign of curiosity written on their faces.

"This ship is piloted by Death," I said in a loud voice; "it is death to approach too close or to try to board it."

The men stopped then, and most of them fell back. I dropped to the ground and wandered about at will, my purpose being to gather what information I could from conversations among the officers. These men, however, were so interested in my ship that I gained no information from them; and so I wandered away and walked down the line to the flagship, which I boarded, passing the sentry at the foot of the ladder and the watch on deck. It seemed strange to walk there among the enemy, unseen; all that I had to do was to avoid contact with any of them, and I was safe from detection.

I went to the cabin of the commander of the fleet. He was sitting there with several high ranking officers, to whom he was giving instructions.

"As soon as Hin Abtol arrives from Pankor," he was saying, "we are to take up several thousand men equipped with equilibrimotors and drop them directly into the city; and then, with Gathol as a base, we shall move on Helium with fully a million men."

"When will Hin Abtol arrive?" asked one of the officers.

"Tonight or tomorrow morning," replied the commander. "He is coming with a large fleet."

Well, at last I had learned something; and my plans were formulated instantly. I left the flagship and returned to my flier, which was being examined by a considerable number of officers and men, but from a safe distance.

I had difficulty in finding an opening through which I could pass without touching any of them; but at last I succeeded, and I was soon at the controls of my flier.

As it rose from the ground apparently without human guidance, exclamations of awe and astonishment followed it. "It is Death," I heard a man cry; "Death is at the controls."

I circled low above them. "Yes, it is Death at the controls," I called down to them; "Death, who has come to take all who attack Gathol;" then I zoomed swiftly aloft and turned the nose of my ship toward Pankor.

I only went far enough from Gathol to be out of sight of Hin Abtol's forces; and then I flew in wide circles at considerable altitudes, waiting for Hin Abtol's fleet.

At long last I saw it in the distance. With it was the man who, with the enormous number of his conscripts, would surely take Gathol and sack it, were he not stopped.

I spotted Hin Abtol's flagship immediately and dropped down alongside it. My little flier evoked no alarm, as it would have been helpless in the midst of this great fleet; but when those aboard the flagship saw that the flier was maneuvering without human control, their curiosity knew no bounds, and they crowded to the rail to have a better look.

I circled the ship, drawing nearer and nearer. I could see Hin Abtol on the bridge with a number of officers, and I saw that they were as much intrigued as were the warriors on deck.

Hin Abtol was leaning far out over the rail to have a better look at me; I moved in closer; the side of the flier touched the bridge lightly.

Hin Abtol was peering down at the deck and into the little control room. "There is no one aboard this ship," he said; "some one had discovered the means of flying it by remote control."

I had set the wheel to hold the flier tightly against the bridge; then I sprang across the deck, seized Hin Abtol by his harness, and dragged him over the rail onto the deck of the flier. An instant later still holding Hin Abtol, I was at the controls; the flier nosed down and dove beneath the flagship at full speed. I heard shouts of astonishment mingled with cries of rage and fear.

A number of small craft took after me; but I knew that they could not overtake me, and that they would not dare fire on me for fear of killing Hin Abtol.

Hin Abtol lay trembling at my side, almost paralyzed with terror. "What are you?" he finally managed to stammer. "What are you going to do with me?"

I did not reply; I thought that that would terrify him the more; and I know that it did, for after a while he implored me to speak.

We flew back, high over Gathol, which was now safe from attack. Early the next morning I saw a great fleet coming out of the south-east—it was the fleet from Helium that Tardos Mors was bringing to relieve Gathol.

As I was approaching it, the effects of the invisibility sphere diminished rapidly; and I materialized before the astounded gaze of Hin Abtol.

"Who are you? What are you?" he demanded.

"I am the man whose flier you stole at Horz," I replied. "I am the man who took it from beneath your nose in Pankor, and with it Llana of Gathol—I am John Carter, Prince of Helium; have you ever heard of me?"

Nearing the fleet, I broke out my colors—the colors of the Prince of Helium; and a great cheer rose from the deck of every ship that could distinguish them.

The rest is history now—how Helium's great fleet destroyed Hin

Abtol's fleet, and the army of Helium routed the forces which had for so long invested Gathol.

When the brief war was over, we set free nearly a million of the frozen men of Panar; and I returned to Helium and Dejah Thoris, from whom I hope never to be separated again.

I had brought with me Jad-han and Pan Dan Chee, whom we had found among the prisoners of the Panars; and though I was not present at the meeting between Pan Dan Chee and Llana of Gathol, Dejah Thoris has assured me that the dangers and vicissitudes he had suffered for love of the fair Gatholian had not been in vain.

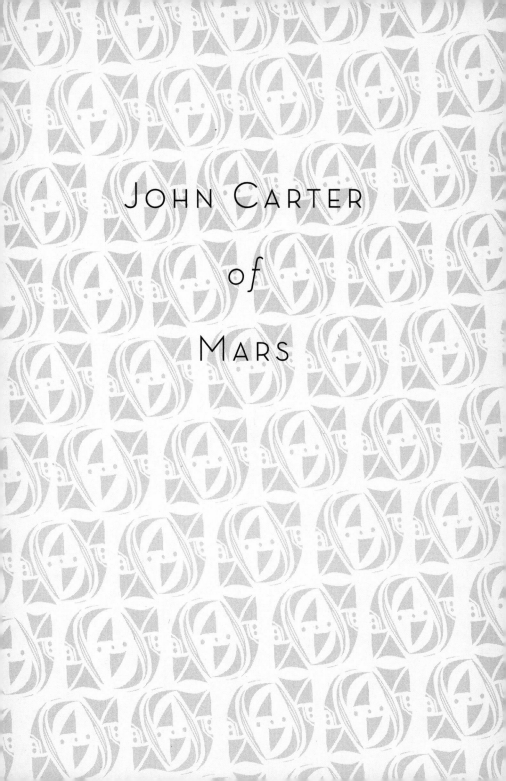

John Carter

of

Mars

Part 1

John Carter and the Giant of Mars

chapter 1

Abduction

The moons of Mars looked down upon a giant Martian thoat as it raced silently over the soft mossy ground. Eight powerful legs carried the creature forward in great, leaping strides.

The path of the mighty beast was guided telepathically by the two people who sat in a huge saddle that was cinched to the thoat's broad back.

It was the custom of Dejah Thoris, Princess of Helium, to ride forth weekly to inspect part of her grandfather's vast farming and industrial kingdom.

Her journey to the farm lands wound through the lonely Helium Forest where grow the huge trees that furnish much of the lumber supply to the civilized nations of Mars.

Dawn was just breaking in the eastern Martian sky, and the jungle was dark and still damp with the evening dew. The gloom of the forest made Dejah Thoris thankful for the presence of her companion, who rode in the saddle in front of her. Her hands rested on his broad, bronze shoulders, and the feel of those smooth, supple muscles gave her a little thrill of confidence. One of his hands rested on the jewel-encrusted hilt of his great long-sword; and he sat his saddle very straight, for he was the mightiest warrior on Mars.

John Carter turned to gaze at the lovely face of his princess.

"Frightened, Dejah Thoris?" he asked.

"Never, when I am with my chieftain," Dejah Thoris smiled.

"But what of the forest monsters, the arboks?"

"Grandfather has had them all removed. On the last trip, my guard killed the only tree reptile I've ever seen."

Suddenly Dejah Thoris gasped, clutched vainly at John Carter to regain her balance. The mighty thoat lurched heavily to the mossy ground. The riders catapulted over his head. In an instant the two had regained their feet; but the thoat lay very still.

Carter jerked his long-sword from its scabbard and motioned Dejah Thoris to stay at his back.

The silence of the forest was abruptly shattered by an uncanny roar directly above them.

"An arbok!" Dejah Thoris cried.

The tree reptile launched itself straight for the hated man-things. Carter lifted his sword and swung quickly to one side, drawing the monster's attention away from Dejah Thoris who crouched behind the fallen thoat.

The earthman's first thrust sliced harmlessly through the beast's outer skin. A huge claw knocked him off balance, and he found himself lying on the ground with the great fangs at his throat.

"Dejah Thoris, get the atom gun from the thoat's back," Carter called hoarsely to the girl. There was no answer.

Calling upon every ounce of his great strength, Carter drove his sword into the arbok's neck. The creature shuddered. A stream of blood gushed from the wound. The man wriggled from under the dead body and sprang to his feet.

"Dejah Thoris! Dejah Thoris!"

Wildly Carter searched the ground and trees surrounding the

dead thoat and arbok. There was no sign of Dejah Thoris. She had utterly vanished.

A shaft of light from the rising sun filtering through the foliage glistened on an object at the earthman's feet. Carter picked up a large shell, a shell recently ejected from a silent atom gun.

Springing to the dead thoat, he examined the saddle trappings. The atom gun that he had told Dejah Thoris to fire was still in its leather boot!

The earthman stooped beside the dead thoat's head. There was a tiny, bloody hole through its skull. That shot and the charging arbok had been part of a well conceived plan to abduct Dejah Thoris, and kill him!

But Dejah Thoris—how had she disappeared so quickly, so completely?

Grimly, Carter set off at a run back to the forest toward Helium.

Noon found the earthman in a private audience-chamber of Tardos Mors, Jeddak of Helium, grandfather of Dejah Thoris.

The old jeddak was worried. He thrust a rough piece of parchment into John Carter's hand. Crude, bold letters were inscribed upon the parchment; and as Carter scanned the note his eyes burned with anger: It read:

"I, Pew Mogel, the most powerful ruler on Mars, have decided to take over the iron works of Helium. The iron will furnish me with all the ships I need to protect Helium and the other cities of Barsoom from invasion. If you have not evacuated all your workers from the iron mines and factories in three days, then I will start sending you the fingers of the Royal Princess of Helium. Hurry, because I may decide to send her tongue, which wags too much of John Carter. Remember, obey Pew Mogel, for he is all-powerful."

Tardos Mors dug his nails into the palms of his hands.

"Who is this upstart who calls himself the most powerful ruler of Mars?"

Carter looked thoughtfully at the note.

"He must have spies here," he said. "Pew Mogel knew that I was to leave this morning with Dejah Thoris on a tour of inspection."

"A spy it must have been," Tardos Mors groaned. "I found this note pinned to the curtains in my private audience-chamber. But what can we do? Dejah Thoris is the only thing in life that I have left to love—" His voice broke.

"All Helium loves her, Tardos Mors, and we will all die before we return to you empty-handed."

Carter strode to the visiscreen and pushed a button.

"Summon Kantos Kan and Tars Tarkas." He spoke quickly to an orderly. "Have them come here at once."

Soon after, the huge, green warrior and the lean, red man were in the audience-chamber.

"It is fortunate, John Carter, that I am here in Helium on my weekly visit from the plains." Tars Tarkas, the green thark, gripped his massive sword with his powerful four hands. His great, giant body loomed majestically above the others in the room.

Kantos Kan laid his hand on John Carter's shoulder.

"I was on my way to the palace when I received your summons. Already, word of our princess' abduction has spread over Helium. I came immediately," said the noble fellow, "to offer you my sword and my heart."

"I have never heard of this Pew Mogel," said Tars Tarkas. "Is he a green man?"

Tardos Mors grunted, "He's probably some petty outlaw or criminal who has an overbloated ego."

Carter raised his eyes from the ransom note.

"No, Tardos Mors. I think he is more formidable than you imagine. He is clever, also. There must have been an airship, with a silent motor, at hand to carry Dejah Thoris away so quickly—or perhaps some great bird! Only a very powerful man who is prepared to back up his threats would kidnap the Princess of Helium and even hope to take over the great iron works.

"He probably has great resources at his command. It is doubtful, however, if he has any intention of returning the princess or he would have included more details in his ransom note."

Suddenly the earthman's keen eyes narrowed. A shadow had moved in the adjoining room.

With a powerful leap, Carter reached the arched doorway. A furtive figure melted away into the semi-gloom of the passageway, with Carter close behind.

Seeing escape impossible, the stranger halted, sank to one knee and leveled a ray-gun at the approaching figure of the earthman. Carter saw his finger whiten as he squeezed the trigger.

"Carter!" Kantos Kan shouted, "throw yourself to the floor."

With the speed of light, Carter dropped prone. A long blade whizzed over his head and buried itself to the hilt in the heart of the stranger.

"One of Pew Mogel's spies," John Carter muttered as he rose to his feet. "Thank you, Kantos Kan."

Kantos Kan searched the body but found no clue to the man's identity.

Back in the audience-chamber, the men set to work with fierce resolve.

They were bending over a huge map of Barsoom when Carter spoke.

"Cities for miles around Helium are now all friendly. They would have warned us of this Pew Mogel if they had known of him. He has probably taken over one of the deserted cities in the dead sea bottom east or west of Helium. It means thousands of miles to search; but we will go over each mile."

Carter seated himself at a table and explained his plan.

"Tars Tarkas, go east and contact the chiefs of all your tribes. I'll cover the west with air scouts. Kantos Kan will stay in Helium as contact man. Be ready night and day with the entire Helium air force. Whoever discovers Dejah Thoris first will notify Kantos Kan of his position. Naturally, we can only communicate to each other through Kantos Kan. The wave length will be constant and secret, 2000 kilocycles."

Tardos Mors turned to the earthman.

"Every resource in my kingdom is at your command, John Carter."

"We leave at once, your majesty; and if Dejah Thoris is alive on Barsoom, we shall find her," replied John Carter.

WITHIN THREE HOURS, John Carter was standing on the roof of the Royal Airdrome giving last-minute instructions to a fleet of twenty-four fast, one-man scouts.

"Cover all the territory in your district thoroughly. If you discover anything, don't attempt to handle it by yourself. Notify Kantos Kan immediately." Carter surveyed the grim faces before him and knew that they would obey him.

"Let's go." Carter jerked a thumb over his shoulder to the ships.

The men scattered and soon their planes were speeding away from Helium.

Carter stayed on the roof long enough to check with Kantos Kan. He adjusted the earphones around his head and then signalled on 2000 kilocycles. The dots and dashes of Kantos Kan's reply began coming in immediately.

"Your signal comes in perfectly. Tars Tarkas is just leaving the city. The air fleet is mobilizing. The entire air force will stand by to come to your aid. Kantos Kan signing off."

Night found Carter cruising about five hundred miles from Helium. He was very tired. The search of several ruined cities and canals had been fruitless. The buzzing of the microset aroused him again.

"Kantos Kan reporting. Tars Tarkas has organized a complete ground search east to south; other air scouts west to south report nothing. Will acquaint you with any news that might come in. Await orders. Will stand by. Signing off."

"No orders. No news. Carter signing off."

Wearily he let the ship drift. No need to look further until the moons came up. The earthman fell into a fitful sleep.

It was midnight when the speaker sounded, jerking Carter to wakefulness. Kantos Kan was signalling again, excitedly.

"Tars Tarkas has found Dejah Thoris. She is held in a deserted city on the banks of the dead sea at Korvas." Kantos Kan gave the exact latitude and longitude of the spot.

"Further instructions from Tars Tarkas request the greatest secrecy in your movements. He will be at the main bridge leading into the City. Kantos Kan signing off. Come in, John Carter."

John Carter signed off with Kantos Kan, urging him to stand by constantly to be ready with the Helium Air Fleet. Now he set his gyro-compass, a device that would automatically steer him to his destination.

Several hours later, the earthman flew over a low range of hills and saw below him an ancient city on the banks of the Dead Sea. He circled his plane and dropped to the bridge where he had been instructed to meet Tars Tarkas. Long, black shadows filled a dry gully below him.

Carter climbed out of his plane, keeping to the shadows, and made his way to the towering ruins of the city. It was so quiet that a lonely bat swooping from a tower sounded like a falling airship.

Where was Tars Tarkas? The green man should have appeared at the bridge.

At the entrance to the city, Carter stepped into the black shadow of a wall and waited. No sound broke the stillness of the quiet night. The city was like a tomb. Diemos and Phobos, the two fast-moving moons of Mars, whirled across the heavens.

Carter stopped breathing to listen. To his keen ears came the faint sound of steps—strange, shuffling steps dragging closer.

Something was coming along the wall. The earthman tensed, ready to spring away to his ship. Now he could hear other steps all around him. Inside the ruins something dragged against the fallen rocks.

Then a great, heavy body dropped on John Carter from the wall above. Hot, fetid breath burned his neck. Huge, shaggy arms smothered him in their fierce embrace.

The thing hurled him to the rough cobblestones. Huge hands clutched at his throat. Carter turned his head and saw above him the face of a great, white ape.

Three of the creature's fellows were circling around Carter, striving to tie his feet with a piece of rope while the other choked him into insensibility with his four mighty hands.

Carter wriggled his feet under the belly of the ape with whom he was grappling. One mighty heave sent the creature into the air to fall, groaning and helpless, to the ground.

Like a cornered banth,* Carter was on his feet, crouched against the wall, awaiting the attacking trio, with drawn sword.

They were mighty beasts, fully eight feet tall with long, white hair covering their great bodies. Each was equipped with four muscular arms that ended in tremendous hands armed with sharp, hooked claws. They were baring their fangs and growling viciously as they came toward the earthman.

Carter crouched low; and as the beasts sprang in, his earthly muscles sent him leaping high into the air over their heads. The earthman's heavy blade backed by all the power of his muscles, smacked down upon one ape's head, splitting the skull wide open.

---

*A banth is the huge, eight-legged lion of Mars.—ED.

Carter hit the ground and, turning, was ready when the two apes remaining flew at him again. There was a hideous, hair-raising shriek as this time the earthman's sword sank deep into a savage heart.

As the monster sprawled to the ground, the earthman jerked free his sword.

Now the other beast turned and slunk away in fright, his eyes gleaming at Carter in the darkness as it fled down a long corridor in the adjacent building. The earthman could have sworn that he heard his own name coming from the ape's throat and mingling with its sullen growl as it fled away.

The earthman had just seized his sword when he felt a rush of air above his head. There was a blur of motion as something came down toward him.

Now he felt himself clutched about the waist; then he was jerked fifty feet into the air. Struggling for breath, Carter clutched at the thing encircling his body. It was as horny as the skin of an arbok. It had hairs as large as tree roots bristling from the horny scales.

It was a giant hand!

chapter III

JOOG, THE GIANT

JOHN CARTER found himself looking into a monstrous face.

From top of shaggy head to bottom of its hairy chin, the head measured fully fifteen feet.

A new monstrosity had come to life on Mars. Judging by the adjacent buildings, the creature must have been a hundred and thirty feet tall!

The giant raised Carter high over his head and shook him; then he threw back his face. Hideous, hollow laughter rumbled out of his pendulous lips revealing teeth like small mountain crags.

He was dressed in an ill-fitting, baggy tunic that came down in loose folds over his hips but which allowed his arms and legs to be free.

With his other hand he beat his mighty chest.

"I, Joog. I, Joog," he kept repeating as he continued to laugh and shake his helpless victim. "I can kill! I can kill!"

Joog, the giant, commenced to walk. Carefully he stepped along the barren streets, sometimes going around a building that was too high to step over.

Finally he stopped before a partially ruined palace. The ravages of time had only dimmed its beauty. Huge masses of moss and vines trailed through the masonry, hiding the shattered battlements. With a sudden thrust, Joog, the giant, shoved John Carter through a high window in the palace tower.

When Carter felt the giant's hold releasing upon him he relaxed completely. He hit the stone floor in a long roll, protecting his head with his arms. As he lay in the deep darkness of the place where he had fallen, the earthman listened while he regained his breath.

No sound came to his ears for some time; then he began to hear the heavy breathing of Joog outside his window. Once more Carter's earthly muscles, reacting to the lesser gravity of Mars, sent him leaping twenty feet to the sill of the narrow window. Here he clung and looked once again into the hairy, hideous face of the giant.

"I, Joog. I, Joog," he mumbled. "I can kill! I can kill!" The giant's breath swept over Carter like a blast from a sulphur furnace. There would be no escape from that window!

Once more he dropped down into his cell. This time he commenced a slow circuit of the room, groping his way along the polished ersite slabs that formed the wall. The cobblestone floor was thick with debris. Once, Carter heard the sinister hiss of a Martian spider as he brushed its web.

How long he groped his way around the walls, there was no way of knowing. It seemed hours. Then, suddenly, the deathly silence was shattered by a woman's scream coming from somewhere in the building.

John Carter could feel his skin grow cold. Could that have been the voice of Dejah Thoris?

Once again John Carter leaped toward the faint light that marked the window ledge. Cautiously, he looked down. Joog lay on his back on the flagstones below, breathing as though he were asleep, his great chest rising five feet with every breath.

Quietly he started to edge his way along a ledge that ran from the window and disappeared into the shadow of an adjoining tower. If he could make that shadow without awakening Joog!

He had almost gained his objective when Joog growled hoarsely.

He had opened one great eye. Now he reached up and, grabbing Carter by the leg, hurled him into the tower window again.

Wearily, the earthman crawled to the wall of his dark cell and there slumped down against it. That scream haunted his memory. He was tormented by the thought that Dejah Thoris might be in danger.

And where was Tars Tarkas? Pew Mogel must have captured him, too. Carter suddenly sprang to his feet.

One of the ersite slabs at his back had moved! He waited. Nothing came out. Cautiously, he approached the rock and shoved it with his foot. The slab moved slightly inward. Now Carter shoved the stone with all his tremendous strength. Inch by inch he moved it until finally there was room for him to squeeze his body through.

He was still in utter darkness, but his groping fingers revealed to him that he was in a corridor between two walls. Perhaps this was the way out of his prison!

Carefully he shoved the stone back into position, leaving no trace of his disappearance from the room. The corridor in which he found himself was so low that he was forced to crawl on hands and knees. The low corridor had the stench of age, as if it had been unused for a long time.

Gradually the tunnel sloped more and more downward. Many little side-passages branched off from the main tunnel. There was no light, no noise. Only a faint, pungent odor beginning to fill the air.

Now it was growing lighter. The earthman realized that he must be in the subterranean caverns of the palace. The dim light was caused by the phosphorescent radium glow that is used on all Mars for radiation.

The source of this faint light the earthman suddenly discovered. It was shining through a cleft in the wall ahead. Pushing aside another loose stone, John Carter crawled forth into a chamber. He drew in his breath sharply.

Facing him was a warrior with drawn sword, the point of which was almost touching the breast of the earthman!

John Carter leaped back with the speed of lightning, whipped out his own sword and struck at the other's weapon.

The arm of the red man fell from his body to the floor where it dissolved into dust. The ancient sword clattered on the cobblestones.

Carter could see now that the warrior had been leaning against the wall, balanced there precariously for ages, his sword arm extending in front of him just as it had stiffened long ago in death. The loss of the arm overbalanced the torso which toppled to the floor and there dissolved into a heap of ash-like dust!

In an adjoining chamber there were a score of women, beautiful girls, chained together by collars of gold around their necks. They sat at a table where they had been eating, and the food was still before them. They had been the prisoners, the slaves of the rulers of the long-dead city. The dry, motionless air combined with some gaseous secretion from the walls and dungeons had preserved their beauty through the ages.

The earthman had traversed some little distance down a musty corridor when he became aware of something scraping behind him. Whirling into a side corridor he looked back. Gleaming eyes were coming toward him. They followed him as he backed into the tunnel.

Now again came the scraping, repeated this time farther ahead in the tunnel. Other eyes shone ahead of him.

John Carter ran forward, his sword-point extended. The eyes

ahead retreated, but those in back of him started to close in.

It was very dark now, but far ahead the earthman could see a faint gleam of light filtering into the tunnel.

He ran toward the light. Fighting the things where he could see them would be a lot easier than stumbling around in a dark corridor.

Carter entered the room and in the dim light came face to face with the creature whose eyes he had seen ahead of him in the tunnel. It was a species of the huge three-legged Martian rat!

Its yellow fangs were bared hideously in a vicious snarl, as it backed slowly away from Carter to the far end of the small room.

Now behind him came the other rat, and together the two beasts started to close in upon the earthman.

Carter smiled grimly as he gripped his sword.

"I am the proverbial cornered rat now," he muttered as he swung his blade at the nearest creature.

It ducked the blow and scurried toward him.

But the earthman's sword was ready. The charging rat lunged full upon the waiting sword-point.

The momentum of the beast carried Carter back five feet; but he still retained a hold on his sword, the point of which had plunged through the animal's single shoulder and pierced its wild heart.

When Carter had jerked free his sword and turned to meet his other antagonist an exclamation of dismay escaped his lips.

The room was half filled with rats!

The creatures had entered through another opening and had formed a circle around him, waiting to attack.

For half an hour, Carter battled furiously for his life in the lonely dungeon beneath the palace in the ancient city of Korvas.

The carcasses of the dead rats were piled high around him, but still they came and eventually they overpowered him by their very numbers.

John Carter went down by a terrific blow to his head from a snake-like tail.

He was half stunned, but he still clung tenaciously to his sword as he felt himself seized by the arms and dragged away into the darkness of an adjoining tunnel.

chapter IV

THE CITY OF RATS

JOHN CARTER RECOVERED fully when he was dragged through a pool of muddy water. He heard the rats greedily drinking, saw their green eyes gleaming in the darkness. The smell of freshly dug earth reached his nostrils and he realized that he was in a burrow far under the subterranean vaults of the palace.

Several rats on either side of him had hold of his arms by their forepaws as they dragged him along. It was very uncomfortable, and he wondered how much longer the journey would last.

Nor had he long to wait. The strange company finally came out into a huge underground cavern. Light from the outside filtered down through various openings in the ceiling above, its rays reflecting on thousands of gleaming stalactites of red sand stone. Massive stalagmites, huge sedimentary formations of grotesque shape, rose up from the floor of the cavern.

Among these formations on the floor were numerous dome-shaped mud huts.

As Carter was dragged by, he stared at a hut that several rats were constructing. The framework was composed of white sticks of various shapes plastered with mud from an underground stream bed. The white sticks were very irregular in length and size. One of the rats stopped work to gnaw at a stick. It looked like a bone.

As he was dragged closer, he saw that the stick was a human thigh bone!

The mud huts were studded with bones and skulls, upon some of which were still dangling hideously the vestiges of hair and skin.

Carter noticed that the tops of all the skulls had been removed, neatly sliced off.

The earthman was dragged to a clearing in the center of the cavern. Here, upon a mound of skulls, sat a rat half again as large as the others.

The baleful, pink eyes of the creature glared at Carter as he was dragged up on top of the mound.

The beasts released their hold upon the earthman and descended to the bottom of the mound, leaving Carter alone with the large rat.

The long whiskers of the monster were constantly twitching as the thing sniffed at the man. It had lost one ear in some battle long ago and the other was bright with scar-tissue.

Its little pink eyes surveyed Carter for a long time while it fondly caressed its long, hairless tail with its one claw-like paw.

This, evidently, was the King of the Rats.

"Lord of the Underworld," Carter thought, trying to hold his breath. The stench in the cavern was overwhelming.

Without taking his eyes from Carter's, the rat reached down and picked up a skull beside him and put it in front of Carter. This he repeated, picking up a skull from the other side and placing it beside the first. By repeating this, he eventually formed a little ring of topless heads in front of the earthman.

Now, very judiciously, he climbed inside the circle of skulls and picking one of them up tossed it to Carter. The earthman caught it and tossed it back at the king.

This seemed to annoy his royal highness. He made no effort to catch the skull and it flew past him and went bouncing down the mound.

Instead, the king leaped up and down inside the little circle of skulls, at the same time emitting angry squeals.

This was all very puzzling to the earthman. As he stood there, he became aware of two circles of rats forming at the base of the mound, each circle consisting of about a thousand animals. They began a weird dance, moving around the raised dais of bones counter-clockwise. The tail of each rat was gripped in the mouth of the following beast, thus forming a continuous chain.

There was no doubt that the earthman was in the center of a weird ritual. While he was ignorant of the exact nature of the ceremony, he had little doubt as to its final outcome. The countless barren skulls, the yellowed ones that filled the cavern were mute, horrible evidence of his final fate.

Where did the rats get all the bodies from which the skulls were obtained and why were the tops of those skulls missing? The City of Korvas, as every Martian schoolboy knew, had been deserted for a thousand years; yet many of the skulls and bones were recently picked clean of their flesh. Carter had seen no evidence in the city of any life other than the great white apes and the mysterious giant, and the rats themselves.

However, there had been the woman's scream that he had heard earlier. This thought accentuated his ever-present anxiety over Dejah Thoris's safety and whereabouts.

This delay was tormenting. As the circles of rats closed in about him, the earthman's eyes eagerly searched for some avenue of escape.

The rats circled slowly, watching their king who rose to his hind legs stamping his feet, thumping his tail. The mound of skulls echoed hollowly.

Faster danced the king and faster moved the circles of rats drawing ever closer to the mound.

The closer rats shot hungry glances at the earthman. Carter smiled grimly and gripped his sword more tightly. Strange that they should let him retain it.

More than one of the beasts would die before he was overcome, and the king would be the first to go. There was no doubt that he was to be sacrificed to furnish a gastronomic orgy.

Suddenly the king stopped his wild gyrations directly in front of Carter. The dancers halted instantly, watching, waiting.

A strange, growling squeal started deep in the king's throat and grew in volume to an ear-piercing shriek. The King of Rats stepped over the ring of skulls and advanced slowly toward Carter.

Once again the earthman glanced about seeking some means of escape from the mound. This time he looked up. The ceiling was at least fifty feet away. No native-born Martian would even consider escaping in that direction.

But John Carter had been born on the planet Earth, and he had brought with him to Mars all the strength and agility of a trained athlete.

It was upon this, combined with the lesser gravity of Mars, that the earthman made his quick plan for the next moment.

Tensely he waited for his opportunity. The ceremony was nearly concluded. The king was baring his fangs not a foot from Carter's neck.

The earthman's hand tightened on his sword-hilt; then the blade streaked from its scabbard. There was a blur of motion and a sickening smack. The king's head flew into the air and then rolled away, bouncing down the mound.

The other beasts beneath were stunned into silence, but only momentarily. Now, squealing wildly, they swarmed up the mound intent on tearing the earthman to pieces.

John Carter crouched and with a mighty leap his earthly muscles sent him shooting fifty feet up into the air.

Desperately he clutched and held to a hanging stalactite. Soon he was swinging on the hanging moss to the vast upper reaches of the cavern.

Once he looked down to see the rats milling and squealing in confusion beneath. One other fact he noted, also. Apparently there was only one means of entrance or exit into the dungeon that formed the rats' underground city, the same tunnel through which he had first been dragged.

Now, however, the earthman was intent upon finding some means of exit in the ceiling above.

At last he found a narrow opening; and plunging through a heavy curtain of moss Carter swung into a cave.

There were several tunnels branching off into the darkness, most of them thickly hung with the sticky webs of the great Martian spider. They were evidently parts of a vast underground network of tunnels that had been fashioned long ages ago by the ancients who once inhabited Korvas.

Carter was ready with his blade for any encounter with man or beast that might come his way; and so he started off up the largest tunnel.

The perpetually burning radium light that had been set in the wall when the tunnel was constructed furnished sufficient illumination for the earthman to see his way quite clearly.

Carter halted before a massive door set into the end of a tunnel. It was inscribed with hieroglyphics unfamiliar to the earthman. The subdued drone of what sounded like many motors seemed to come from somewhere beyond the door.

He pushed open the unbarred door and halted just beyond, staring unbelievingly at the tremendous laboratory in which he found himself.

Great motors pumped oxygen through low pipes into rows of glass cages that lined the walls and filled the antiseptically white chamber from end to end. In the center of the laboratory were several operating tables with large searchlights focused down upon them from above.

But the contents of the glass cages immediately absorbed the earthman's attention.

Each cage contained a giant white ape, standing upright inside, apparently lifeless.

The top of each hairy head was swathed in bandages. If these beasts were dead, why then the oxygen tubes running to their cages?

Carter moved across the room to examine the cases at closer range. Halfway to the farther wall he came upon a low, glassed dome that covered a huge pit set in the floor.

He gasped. The pit was filled with dead bodies, red warriors with the tops of their heads neatly sliced off!

chapter V

CHAMBER OF HORRORS

FAR BELOW, in the pit, John Carter could see forms moving in and about the bodies of the dead red men.

They were rats; and as he watched, the earthman could see them dragging bodies off into adjoining tunnels. These tunnels probably entered the main one which ran into the rats' underground city.

So this was where the beasts got the skulls and bones with which they constructed their odorous, underground dwellings!

Carter's eyes scanned the laboratory. He noted the operating tables, the encased instruments above, the anesthetics. Everything pointed to some grisly experiment, conducted by some insane scientist.

Within a glass case were many books. One ponderous volume was inscribed in gold letters: PEW MOGEL, HIS LIFE AND WONDERFUL WORKS.

The earthman frowned. What was the explanation? Why this well-equipped laboratory buried in an ancient lost city, a city apparently deserted except for apes, rats, and a giant man?

Why the cages about the wall containing the mute, motionless bodies of apes with bandaged heads? And the red men in the pit—why were their skulls cut in half, their brains removed?

From whence came the giant, the monstrous creature whose likeness had existed only in Barsoomian folklore?

One of the books in a case before Carter bore the name "Pew Mogel." What connection had Pew Mogel with all this and who was the man?

But more important, where was Dejah Thoris, the Princess of Helium?

John Carter reached for Pew Mogel's book. Suddenly the room fell silent. The generators that had been humming out their power, stopped.

"Touch not that book, John Carter," came the words echoing through the laboratory.

Carter's hand dropped to his sword. There was a moment's pause; then the hidden voice continued.

"Give yourself up, John Carter, or your princess dies." The words were apparently coming from a concealed loudspeaker somewhere in the room.

"Through the door to your right, earthman, the door to your right."

Carter immediately sensed a trap. He crossed to the door. Warily, he pushed it open with his foot.

Upon a gorgeous throne at the far end of a huge dome-shaped chamber sat a hideous, misshapen man. A tiny, bullet head squatted upon massive shoulders.

Everything about the creature seemed distorted. His torso was crooked, his arms were not equal in length; one foot was larger than the other.

The face in the diminutive head leered at John Carter. A thick tongue hung partly out over yellowed teeth.

The hulking body was encased in gorgeous trappings of platinum and diamonds. One claw-like hand stroked the bare head.

From head to foot there was apparently not a hair on his body!

At the man's feet crouched a great, four-armed shaggy brute— another white ape. Its little red eyes were fixed steadily upon the earthman as he stood at the far end of the chamber.

The man on the throne idly fingered the microphone with which he had summoned Carter to the room.

"I have trapped you at last, John Carter!" Beady, cocked eyes glared with hatred. "You cannot cope with the great brain of Pew Mogel!"

Pew Mogel turned to a television screen studded with dials and lights of various colors.

His face twisted into a smile. "You honor my humble city, John Carter. It is with the greatest interest I have watched your progress through the many chambers of the palace with my television machine." Pew Mogel patted the machine.

"This little invention of my good teacher, Ras Thavas," continued Pew Mogel, "which I acquired from him, has been an invaluable aid to me in learning of your intended search for my unworthy person. It was unfortunate that you should suspect the honorable intentions of my agent that afternoon in the Jeddak's chambers.

"Fortunately, however, he had already completed his mission; and through an extension upon this television set, concealed cleverly behind a mirror in the Jeddak's private throne room, I was able to see and hear the entire proceedings."

Pew Mogel laughed vacantly, his little unblinking eyes staring steadily at Carter who remained motionless at the other end of the room.

The earthman could see nothing in the chamber that indicated a trap. The walls and floor were all of grey, polished ersite slabs. Carter stood at one end of a long aisle leading to Pew Mogel's throne.

Slowly he advanced toward Pew Mogel, his hand grasping his sword, the muscles of his arm etched bands of steel.

Half way down the aisle, the earthman halted. "Where is Dejah Thoris?" His words cut the air.

The microcephalic* head of Pew Mogel cocked to one side. Carter waited for him to speak.

In spite of having the features of a man, Pew Mogel did not look quite human. There was something indescribably repulsive about him, the thin lips, the hollow cheeks, the close-set eyes.

Then Carter realized that those eyes were unblinking. There were no eyelids. The man's eyes could never close.

Pew Mogel spoke coldly. "I am greatly indebted to you for this visit. I was fortunate enough to be able to entertain your princess and your best friend; but I hardly dared to hope you would honor me, too."

Carter's face was expressionless. Slowly he repeated. "Where is Dejah Thoris?"

Pew Mogel leered mockingly.

The earthman advanced toward the throne. The white ape at Pew Mogel's feet growled, the hairs on its neck bristling upright as Pew Mogel flinched slightly.

Again the twisted smile passed over his face as he raised his hand toward John Carter and drawled.

"Have patience, John Carter, and I will show you your princess; but first, perhaps you will be interested in seeing the man who, last night, told you to meet him at the main bridge outside the city."

* * *

---

*A microcephalic head is one possessing a very small brain capacity. It is the opposite of megacephalic, which means a large brain capacity. Generally microcephalia is a sign of idiocy, although in the case of Pew Mogel, the condition did not mean idiocy, but extreme craftiness, and madness, which might indicate that, since Pew Mogel was an artificial, synthetic product of Ras Thavas, one of Mars's most famous scientists, his microcephalia was either caused by a disease, or by inability of the brain to adapt itself to a foreign, ill-fitting cranial cavity. Pew Mogel's head was obviously too small for his body, or for his brain. —Ed.

Pew Mogel hooked one of his fingers over a lever projecting from the golden arm of his throne and slipped it toward himself. A pillar to the left of his throne, half set in the wall, began to revolve slowly.

A giant green man appeared, chained to the pillar. His four mighty arms were strapped securely; and for Pew Mogel's additional safety, several steel chains were wrapped around his body and cinched with massive padlocks. His neck and ankles were also secured with bands of steel, also padlocked.

"Tars Tarkas!" Carter exclaimed.

"Kaor, John Carter," there was a grim smile on Tars Tarkas' face as he replied. "I see our friend here trapped us both the same way; but it took a giant fifteen times my size to hold me while they trussed me in these chains."

"The message you sent me last night—" In a flash, Carter realized the truth. Pew Mogel had faked the messages from Kantos Kan and Tars Tarkas, trapping them both in the city the night before.

"Yes, I sent you both identical messages," said Pew Mogel, "each message apparently from the other. The proper broadcasting length I ascertained from listening to the concealed microphone I had planted in the Jeddak's throne room. Clever, eh?"

Pew Mogel's left eye suddenly popped out of its socket and dangled on his cheek. He took no notice of it, but continued to speak, glancing first at Carter and then at Tars Tarkas with the other eye.

"You have both met Joog," stated Pew Mogel. "One hundred and thirty feet tall, he is all muscle, a product of science, the result of my great brain.

"With my own hands I created him from living flesh, the greatest fighting monster that Barsoom has ever seen.

"I modeled him from the organs, tissues, and bones of ten thousand red men and white apes."

Pew Mogel, becoming aware of his left eye, quickly shoved it back into place.

Tars Tarkas laughed one of his rare laughs.

"Pew Mogel," he said, "you are falling apart. As you claim to have created your giant, so you yourself have been made.

"Unless I miss my guess, John Carter," continued Tars Tarkas, "this freak before us who calls himself a king has, himself, crawled out of a tissue vat!"

Pew Mogel's pallid countenance turned even paler as he leaped to his feet. He struck Tars Tarkas a vicious blow on the face.

"Silence, green man!" he shrieked.

Tars Tarkas only smiled at this insult, ignoring the pain. John Carter's face was a frozen mask. One more blow at his defenseless friend would have sent him at Pew Mogel's throat.

Better to bide his time, he knew, until he learned where Dejah Thoris was hidden.

Pew Mogel sank back upon his throne. The white ape, who had risen, once more squatted down at his master's feet.

Presently Pew Mogel smiled again.

"So sorry, he drawled, "that I lost my temper. Sometimes I forget that my present appearance reveals the nature of my origin.

"You see, soon I shall have trained one of my apes in the intricate procedure of transferring my marvellous brain into a suitable, handsome body; then no one will guess that I am not like any other normal man on Barsoom.

John Carter smiled grimly at Pew Mogel's words.

"Then you *are* one of Ras Thavas' synthetic men?"

"YES, I AM A SYNTHETIC MAN," answered Pew Mogel slowly. "My brain was the greatest achievement of all the Master Mind's creations.

"For years I was a devoted pupil of Ras Thavas in his laboratories at Morbus. I learned all that the Master could teach me of the secrets of creating living tissue. When I learned from him all that I thought necessary to pursue my plans, I left Morbus. With a hundred synthetic men I escaped over the Great Toonolian Marshes on the backs of malagors, the birds of transport.

"I brought with me all the intricate equipment that I could steal from his laboratories. The rest, I have fashioned here in this ancient deserted city where we finally landed."

John Carter was studying Pew Mogel intently.

"I was tired of being a slave," continued Pew Mogel. "I wanted to rule; and by Issus, I have ruled; and some day I shall rule all Barsoom!"

Pew Mogel's eyes gleamed.

"It was not long before red men gathered in our city, escaped and exiled criminals. Since their faces would only lead them to capture and execution in other civilized cities on Barsoom, I persuaded them to allow me to transfer their brains in the bodies of the stupid white apes that overran this city.

"I promised to later restore their brains into the bodies of other red men, provided they would help me in my conquests."

Carter recalled the apes with the bandaged heads in the adjoining laboratory, and the red men with their skulls sliced off in the chamber of the rats. He began to understand a little; then he remembered Joog.

"But the giant?" asked John Carter. "Whence came he?"

Pew Mogel was silent for a minute; then he spoke.

"Joog I have built, piece by piece, during several years, from the bones, tissues and organs of a thousand red men and white apes who came voluntarily to me or whom I captured.

"Even his brain is the synthesis of the brains of ten thousand red men and white apes. Into Joog's veins I have pumped a serum that makes all tissues self-repairing.

"My giant is practically indestructible. No bullet or cannon-shot made can stop him!"

Pew Mogel smiled and stroked his hairless chin.

"Think how powerful my ape soldiers will be," he purred, "each one armed with the great strength of an ape. With their four arms they can hold twice as many weapons as ordinary men, and inside their skulls will function the cunning brains of human beings.

"With Joog and my army of white apes, I can go forth and become master of all Barsoom." Pew Mogel paused and then added, "—provided I acquire more iron for even greater weapons than I already have."

Now Pew Mogel had risen from his throne in his great excitement.

"I preferred to conquer peacefully by first acquiring the Helium iron works as payment for Dejah Thoris's safe return. But the Jeddak and John Carter force me into other alternatives—

"However, I'll give you one more chance to settle peacefully," he said.

Pew Mogel's hand moved toward the right arm of his throne, as he pulled a duplicate lever. A beautiful woman swung into view.

It was Dejah Thoris!

At the sight of his princess chained to the other pillar before him, John Carter grew very pale. He sprang forward to free her.

His earthly muscles could have easily covered the distance in one leap; but halfway there in his spring, Dejah Thoris and Tars Tarkas saw the earthman sprawl in mid-air as though he had struck full force against some invisible barrier. Half-stunned, he crumpled to the floor.

Dejah Thoris gave a little cry. Tars Tarkas strained at his bonds. Slowly, the earthman rose to his feet, shaking his body like some majestic animal. With his sword he reached down and felt the barrier that stood between him and the throne.

Pew Mogel laughed harshly.

"You are trapped, John Carter. The invisible glass partition that you struck is another invention of the great Ras Thavas that I acquired. It is invulnerable.

"From there, you may watch the torture of your princess, unless she sees fit to sign a note to her grandfather demanding the surrender of Helium to me."

The earthman looked at his princess not ten feet from him. Dejah Thoris held her head proudly high, which was answer enough to Pew Mogel's demands that she betray her people.

Pew Mogel saw, and angrily issued a command to the ape. The white brute rose and ambled over to Dejah Thoris. Grabbing her hair with one paw, he forced her head back until he could see her face. His hideous, grinning face was not two inches from hers.

"Demand Helium's surrender," hissed Pew Mogel, "and you shall have your freedom!"

"Never!" the word shot back at him.

Pew Mogel flung another command to the ape.

The creature planted his great, pendulous lips on those of the princess. Dejah Thoris went limp in his embrace, while Tars Tarkas surged vainly at the steel chains. The girl had fainted.

The earthman again hurled himself futilely against the barrier that he could not see.

"Fool," yelled Pew Mogel, "I gave you your chance to retain your princess by turning over to me the Helium iron works; but you and the Jeddak thought you could thwart me and regain Dejah Thoris without paying me the price I asked for her safe return. For that mistake, you all die."

Pew Mogel again reached over to the instrument board beside his throne. He began to turn several dials, and Carter heard a strange, droning noise that increased steadily in volume.

Suddenly the earthman turned and raced for the door through which he came.

But before he had covered fifteen feet, another barrier had closed down. Escape through the door was impossible.

There was a window over on the wall to his right. He leaped for it. He struck another glass barrier.

There was another window on the left side of the room. He had nearly reached it when he was met by another wall of invisible glass.

In a flash he became acutely conscious of his predicament. The walls were moving in upon him. He could see now that the glass barriers had moved out from cleverly concealed slits in the adjoining walls.

The two side barriers, however, were fastened to horizontal pistons in the ceiling. These pistons were moving together, bringing the glass walls toward each other, and would eventually crush the earthman between them.

Upon John Carter's finger was a jeweled ring. Set in the center of the ring was a large diamond.

Diamonds can cut glass!

Here was a new type of glass, but the chances were it was not as hard as the diamond on Carter's finger!

The earthman clenched his fist, pressed the diamond ring against the barrier in front of him and quickly made a large circular scratch in the glass surface.

Then he crashed his body with all his strength against the area of glass enclosed by the scratch.

The section broke out neatly at the blow, and the earthman found himself face to face with Pew Mogel.

Dejah Thoris had regained consciousness, a set, intent expression on her beautiful face. A grim smile had settled over Tars Tarkas's lips when he saw that his friend was no longer impeded by the invisible barriers.

Pew Mogel shrank back on his throne and gasped in a cracked voice.

"Seize him, Gore, seize him!" Little beads of sweat stood forth on his brow.

Gore, the white ape, released his hold on Dejah Thoris and, turning, saw the earthman advancing toward them. Gore snarled viciously, revealing jagged, mighty fangs. He crouched low, so that his four massive fists supported his weight on the floor. His little, beady, blood-shot eyes gleamed hatred, for Gore hated all men save Pew Mogel.

chapter VII

THE FLYING TERROR

AS GORE, the great white ape with a man's brain crouched to meet John Carter, he was fully confident of overcoming his puny man opponent.

But to make assurance doubly sure, Gore drew the great blade at his side and rushed madly at his foe, hacking and cutting viciously.

The momentum of the brute's attack forced Carter backward a few steps as he deftly warded off the mighty blows.

But the earthman saw his chance. Quickly, surely, his blade streaked. There was a sudden twist and Gore's sword went hurtling across the room.

Gore, however, reacted with lightning speed. With his four huge hands he grasped the naked steel of the earthman's sword.

Violently he jerked the blade from Carter's grasp and, raising it overhead, snapped the strong steel in two as if it had been a splinter of wood.

Now, with a low growl, Gore closed in; and Carter crouched.

Suddenly the man leaped over the ape's head; but again with uncanny speed the monster shot out a hairy hand and grasped the earthman's ankle.

Gore held John Carter in his four hands, drawing the man closer and closer to the drooling jowls and gleaming fangs.

But with a surge of his mighty muscles, the earthman jerked free his arm and sent a terrific blow crashing full into Gore's face.

The ape recoiled, dropping John Carter, and staggered back toward the huge window on the right wall by Pew Mogel's throne.

Here the beast tottered; and the earthman, seeing his chance, once again leaped into the air, but this time flew feet foremost toward the ape.

At the moment of contact with the ape's chest, Carter extended his legs violently; and so, as his feet struck Gore, this force was added to the hurtling momentum of his body.

With a bellowing cry, Gore hurtled out through the window and his screams ended only when he landed with a sickening crunch in the courtyard far below.

Dejah Thoris and Tars Tarkas, chained to the pillars, had watched the short fight, fascinated by the earthman's sure, quick actions.

But when Carter did not succumb instantly to Gore's attack, Pew Mogel had grown frightened. He began jerking dials and switches; and then spoke swiftly into the little microphone beside him.

So now, as the earthman regained his feet and advanced slowly toward Pew Mogel, he did not see the black shadow that obscured the window behind him.

Only when Dejah Thoris screamed a warning did the earthman turn.

But he was too late!

A giant hand, fully three feet across, closed about his body. He was lifted from the floor and pulled out quickly through the window.

To Carter's ears came the hopeless cry of his princess mingled with the cruel, hollow laugh of Pew Mogel.

Carter did not need the added assurance of his eyes to know that he was being held in the grasp of Pew Mogel's synthetic giant. Joog's fetid breath blasting across his face was ample evidence.

Joog held Carter several feet from his face and contracted his features in the semblance of a grin, exposing his two great rows of cracked, stained teeth the size of sharp boulders.

Hoarse, gurgling sounds emanated from Joog's throat as he held the earthman before his face.

"I, Joog. I, Joog," the monster finally managed. "I can kill! I can kill!"

Then he shook his victim until the man's teeth rattled.

But quite suddenly the giant was quiet, listening; then Carter became aware of muffled words coming, apparently, from Joog's ear.

Then John Carter realized that the command was coming from Pew Mogel, transmitted by short wave to a receiving device attached to one of Joog's ears.

"To the arena," repeated the voice. "Fasten him over the pit!"

The pit—what new form of devilish torture was this? Carter tried vaguely to ease the awful pressure that was crushing him.

But his arms were pinned to his sides by the giant's grasp. All the man could do was breathe laboriously and hope that Joog's great strides would soon bring them to his destination, whatever that might be.

The giant's tremendous pace, stepping over tall, ancient edifices or across wide, spacious plazas in single, mighty strides, soon brought them to a large, crowded amphitheatre on the outskirts of the city.

The amphitheatre apparently was fashioned from a natural crater. Row upon row of circular tiers had been carved within the inner wall of the crater, forming a series of levels upon which sat thousands of white apes.

In the center of the arena was a circular pit about fifty feet across. The pit contained what appeared to be water whose level was about fifteen feet from the top of the pit.

Three iron-barred cages hung suspended over the center of the pit by means of three heavy ropes, one attached to the top of each cage and running up through a pulley in the scaffolding built overhead and down to the edge of the pit where it was anchored.

Joog climbed partly over the edge of the coliseum and deposited Carter on the brink of the pit. Five great apes held him there while another ape lowered one of the cages to ground level.

Then he reached out with a hooked pole and swung the cage over the edge. He unlocked the cage door with a large key.

The keeper of the key was a short, heavy-set ape with a bull neck and exceedingly cruel, close-set eyes.

This brute now came up to Carter; and although the captive was being held by five other apes, he grabbed him cruelly by the hair and jerked Carter into the cage, at the same time kicking him viciously.

The cage door was slammed immediately, its padlock bolted closed. Now Carter's cage was pulled up over the pit and the rope end anchored to a davit at the edge.

It was not long before Joog returned with Dejah Thoris and Tars Tarkas. Their chains had been removed.

They were placed in the other two cages that hung over the pit next to that of John Carter.

"Oh, John Carter, my chieftain!" cried Dejah Thoris, when she saw him in the cage next to hers. "Thank Issus you are still alive!" The little princess was crying softly.

John Carter reached through the bars and took her hand in his. He tried to speak reassuring words to her; but he knew, as did Tars Tarkas, who sat grim-faced in the other cage beside his, that Pew Mogel had ordained their deaths—but in what manner they would die, Carter, as yet, was uncertain.

"John Carter," spoke Tars Tarkas softly, "do you notice that all these thousands of apes gathered here in the arena apparently are paying no attention to us?"

"Yes, I noticed," replied the earthman. "They are all looking into the sky toward the city."

"Look," whispered Dejah Thoris. "It's the same thing upon which the ape rode when he captured me in the Helium Forest after shooting our thoat!"

There appeared in the sky, coming from the direction of the city, a great, lone bird upon whose back rode a single man.

The earthman's keen eyes squinted for an instant. "The bird is a malagor. Pew Mogel is riding it."

The bird and its rider circled directly overhead.

"Open the east gate," Pew Mogel commanded, his voice ringing out through a loudspeaker somewhere in the arena. The gates were thrown open and there began pouring out into the arena wave after wave of malagors exactly like the bird Pew Mogel rode.

As the malagors came out, column after column of apes were waiting at the entrance to vault onto the birds' backs. As each bird was mounted, it rose into the air by telepathic command to join a constantly growing formation circling high overhead.

The mounting of the birds must have taken nearly two hours, so great were the number of Pew Mogel's apes and birds. Carter noticed that upon each ape's back was strapped a rifle and each bird itself carried a varying assortment of military equipment, including ammunition supplies, small cannon; and a sub-machine gun was carried by each flight platoon.

At last all was ready and Pew Mogel descended down over the cages of his three captives.

"You see, now, Pew Mogel's mighty army," he cried, "with which he will first conquer Helium and then all Barsoom." The man seemed very confident, for his crooked, misshapen body sat very straight upon his feathered mount.

"Before you are chewed to bits by the reptiles in the rising water below you," he said, "you will have a few moments to consider the fate that awaits Helium within the next forty-eight hours. I should have preferred to conquer peacefully; but you interfered. For that, you die, slowly and horribly."

Pew Mogel turned to the only ape that was left in the arena, the keeper of the key to the cages.

"Open the flood-gate!" was his single command before he rose up to lead his troops off toward the north.

Accompanying the weird, flying army in a sling carried by a hundred malagors rode Joog, the synthetic giant. A hollow, mirthless laugh peeled like thunder from the giant's throat as he was borne away into the sky.

AS THE LAST BIRD in Pew Mogel's fantastic army flapped out of sight behind the rim of the crater, John Carter turned to Tars Tarkas in the cage hanging beside him. He spoke softly, so that Dejah Thoris would not hear.

"Those creatures will make Helium a formidable enemy," he said. "Kantos Kan's splendid airfleet and infantry will be hard pressed against those thousands of apes equipped with human brains and modern armament, mounted upon fast birds of prey!"

"Kantos Kan and his airfleet are not even in Helium to protect the city," announced Tars Tarkas grimly. "I heard Pew Mogel bragging that he had sent Kantos Kan a false message, supposedly from you, urging that all Helium's fleet, as well as all ships of the searching party, be dispatched to your aid in the Great Toonolian Marshes."

"The Toonolian Marshes!" Carter gasped. "They're a thousand miles from Helium in the other direction."

A little scream from Dejah Thoris brought the men's attention to their own, immediate fate.

The ape beside the pit had pulled back a tall, metal lever. There was a gurgle of bubbles as air blasted up from the water in the pit below the three captives; and the water at the same time commenced to rise slowly.

The guard now unfastened the rope on each cage and lowered them so that the cage tops were a little below the surface of the ground inside the pit; then he refastened the ropes and stood for some time on the brink looking down at the helpless captives.

"The water rises slowly," he sneered thickly; "and so I shall have time now for a little sleep."

It was uncanny to hear words issuing from the mouth of the beast. They were barely articulate, for although the human brain in the ape's skull directed the words, the muscles of the larynx in the creature's throat were normally unequipped for the specialized task of human speech.

The guard lay down on the brink and stretched his massive, squat body.

"Your death cries will awaken me," he mumbled pleasantly, "when the water begins to envelop your feet and the reptiles start clawing at you through the bars of your cages." Whereupon, the ape rolled over and began snoring.

It was then that the three captives saw the slanting, evil eyes, the rows of flashing teeth, in a dozen hideous, reptilian faces staring greedily up at them from the rising waters below.

"Quite ingenious," remarked Tars Tarkas, his stoic face giving no more evidence of fear than did that of the earthman. "When the water partly submerges us, the reptiles will reach in with their claws and begin tearing us to pieces—if there is any life left in us, the rising water will drown it out when it submerges the tops of our cages."

"How horrible!" gasped Dejah Thoris.

John Carter's eyes were fastened on the brink of the pit. From his cage he could just see one of the guard's feet as the fellow lay asleep at the edge of the pit.

Cautioning the others to silence, Carter began swinging his body back and forth while he held fast to the bars of his cage. If he could just get his cage to swinging!—

* * *

The water had risen to about ten feet below their cages.

It seemed an eternity before he could get the heavy cage to even moving slightly. Nine feet to the water surface and those hideous, staring eyes and those gleaming teeth!

The cage was swinging now a little more, in rhythm to the earthman's constantly swaying body.

Eight feet, seven feet, six feet came the water. There were about ten reptiles in the water below the captives—ten pairs of narrow, evil eyes fixed steadily to their prey.

The cage was swinging faster.

Five feet, four feet. Tars Tarkas and Dejah Thoris could feel the hot breath of the reptiles!

Three, two feet! Only two more feet to go before the steadily swinging cage would cut into the water and slow down again to a standstill.

But the iron prison, swinging pendulum-like, would reach the brink on its next swing; so this time as the cage moved toward the brink on which lay the sleeping guard, John Carter knew he must act and act quickly!

As the bars of the cage smacked against the cement wall of the pit, John Carter's arms shot out with the quickness of a striking snake.

His fingers closed in a grip of steel about the ankle of the sleeping guard.

An ear-piercing shriek rang out across the arena, echoing dismally in the hollow crater, as the ape felt himself jerked suddenly from his slumbers.

Back swung the cage. Carter regrasped the shrieking ape with his other hand through the bars as they swung out over the water. The reptiles had to lower their heads as the cage moved over them so close had the water risen.

"Good work, John Carter," came Tars Tarkas's tense words as he reached out and grabbed hold of the ape with his four mighty hands. At the same time, Carter's cage splashed to a sudden stop. It had hit the water's surface.

"Hold him, Tars Tarkas, while I pull the key off the scoundrel's neck— there, I've got it!"

The water was flowing over the bottom of the cages. One of the reptiles had reached a horny arm into Dejah Thoris's cage and was attempting to snag her body with its sharp, hooked claws.

Tars Tarkas flung the ape's body with all the force of his giant thews straight at the reptile beside the girl's cage.

"Quickly, John Carter," cried Dejah Thoris. "Save yourself while they are fighting over the ape's body."

"Yes," echoed Tars Tarkas, "unlock your cage and get out while there is still time."

A half-smile lifted the corner of Carter's mouth as he swung open his prison door and leaped to the top of Dejah Thoris's cage.

"I'd sooner stay and die with you both," the earthman said, "than desert you now."

Carter soon had the princess' prison door unlocked; but as he reached down to lift the girl up, a reptile darted forward into the cage with the princess.

In a quick second, Carter was inside the girl's cage, already knee-deep in water; and he had hurled himself onto the back of the reptile. A steely arm was clamped tightly around the creature's neck. The head was jerked back just in time, for the heavy jaws snapped closed only an inch from the girl's body.

"Climb out, Dejah Thoris—to the top of the cage!" ordered Carter. When the girl had obeyed, Carter dragged the flopping, helpless reptile to the cage door, as other slimy monsters started in. Using its body as a shield before him, the earthman forced his way to the door.

In an instant he had released his hold and vaulted up on top of the cage with the girl.

A moment later he had unlocked Tars Tarkas's cage door. After the green man had swung up beside them without mishap, the three climbed the ropes to the scaffolding above and then lowered themselves down to the ground beside the pit.

"Thank Issus," breathed the girl as they sat down to regain their breaths. Her beautiful head was cushioned upon Carter's shoulder, and he stroked her lovely black hair reassuringly.

Presently the earthman rose to his feet. Tars Tarkas had motioned him across the arena.

"There are some malagors left inside here," Tars Tarkas called from the entrance to the cavern inside the crater from where had come Pew Mogel's mounts.

"Good!" exclaimed Carter. "There may be a chance yet to reach and help Helium."

A moment later they had caught two of the birds and had risen over the ancient city of Korvas.

They spotted their planes on the outskirts of the city where they had left them the night they were tricked into being captured by Pew Mogel.

But to their disappointment, the controls had been destroyed irreparably, so that they were forced to continue their journey on the backs of the malagors.

However, the malagors proved speedy mounts. By noon the next day the trio had reached the City of Thark, inhabited by a hundred thousand green warriors over whom Tars Tarkas ruled.

Gathering the warriors together in the marketplace, Tars Tarkas and John Carter explained the peril that confronted Helium and asked for their support in marching to their allies' aid.

As one man, the mighty warriors shouted their approval. The next day dawned upon a long caravan of thoat-mounted soldiers streaming out from the city gates toward Helium.

A messenger was sent on a malagor to the Toonolian Marshes in an attempt to locate Kantos Kan and urge him to return home with his fleet to aid in the defense of Helium.

Tars Tarkas had abandoned his malagor to this messenger, in favor of a thoat upon which he rode at the head of his warriors. Directly above him, mounted on the other malagor, rode Dejah Thoris and John Carter.

chapter IX

ATTACK ON HELIUM

JOHN CARTER and Dejah Thoris, mounted upon their malagor, were scouting far ahead of the main column of advancing warriors when they first came into sight of the besieged City of Helium.

It was bright moonlight. The princess voiced a little, disappointed cry when she looked out across the spacious valley toward Helium. Her grandfather's city was completely surrounded by the besieging troops of Pew Mogel.

"My poor city!" The girl was crying softly, for in the bright moonlight below could be easily discerned the terrific gap in the ramparts and the many crushed and shattered buildings of the beautiful metropolis.

John Carter telepathically commanded the malagor to land upon a high peak in the mountains overlooking the Valley of Helium.

"Listen," cautioned John Carter. Pew Mogel's light entrenched cannon and small arms were commencing to open fire again by moonlight. "They are getting ready for an air attack."

Suddenly, from behind the low foothills between the valley and the towering peaks, there rose the vast, flying army of Pew Mogel.

"They are closing in from all sides," Dejah Thoris cried.

The great winged creatures and their formidable ape riders were swooping down relentlessly upon the city. Only a few of Helium's airships rose to give battle.

"Kantos Kan must have taken nearly all Helium's fleet with him," the earthman remarked. "I am surprised Helium has withstood the attack as long as this."

"You should know my people by now, John Carter," replied the princess.

"The infantry and anti-aircraft fire entrenched in Helium are doing well," Carter replied. "See those birds plummet to the ground."

"They can't hold out much longer, though," the girl replied. "Those apes are dropping bombs squarely into the city, as they swoop over, wave after wave of them—oh, John Carter, what can we do?"

John Carter's old fighting smile, usually present at times of personal danger, had given way to a stern, grave expression.

He saw below him the oldest and most powerful city on Mars being conquered by Pew Mogel's forces. Armed with Helium's vast resources, the synthetic man would go forth and conquer all civilized nations on Mars.

Fifty thousand years of Martian learning and culture wrecked by a power-mad maniac—himself the synthetic product of civilized man!

"Is there nothing we can do to stop him, John Carter?" came the girl's repeated question.

"Very little, I'm afraid, my princess," he replied sadly. "All we can do is station Tars Tarkas's green warriors at advantageous points in preparation for a counterattack and trust to fate that our messenger reached Kantos Kan in time that he may return and aid us.

"Without supporting aircraft, our green warriors, heroic fighters that they are, can do little against Pew Mogel's superior numbers in the air."

When John Carter and Dejah Thoris returned to Tars Tarkas, they reported what they had seen.

The great Thark agreed that his warriors could avail but little in a direct attack against Pew Mogel's air force. It was decided that half their troops be concentrated at one point and at dawn attempt to rush through into the City.

The remaining half of the warriors would scatter into the

mountains in smaller groups and engage the enemy in guerrilla warfare.

Thus they hoped to forestall the fate of Helium until Kantos Kan returned with his fleet of speedy air fighters.

"Helium's fleet of trim, metal fighting craft will furnish Pew Mogel's feathered bird brigade a worthy enemy," remarked Tars Tarkas.

"Provided, of course," added Carter, "Kantos Kan's fleet reaches Helium before Pew Mogel has entrenched himself in the City and returned his own anti-aircraft guns upon them."

All that night in the mountains, under cover of semi-darkness, John Carter and Tars Tarkas reorganized and restationed their troops. By dawn all was ready.

John Carter and Tars Tarkas would lead the advance half of the Tharks in a wild rush toward the gates of Helium; the other half would remain behind, covering their comrades' assault with long-range rifles.

Much against the earthman's will, Dejah Thoris insisted she would ride into the city beside him upon their malagor.

It was just commencing to grow brighter.

"Prepare to charge," Carter ordered. Tars Tarkas passed the word down by his orderly to his unit commanders.

"Prepare to charge! Prepare to charge!" echoed down and across the battalions of magnificent, four-armed, green fighters astride their eight-legged, massive, restless thoats.

The minutes dragged by as the troop lines swung around. Steel swords were drawn from scabbards. Hammers, on short, deadly ray-pistols, clicked back as they cocked over saddle pommels.

John Carter looked around at the girl sitting so straight and steady behind him.

"You are very brave, my princess," he said.

"It's easy to be brave," she replied, "when I'm so close to the greatest warrior on Mars."

"Charge!" came Carter's terse, sudden order.

Down the mountain and across the plain toward Helium streaked the savage horde of Tharks. Out ahead raced Tars Tarkas, his sword held high.

Far ahead and above, on speedy wings, streaked the malagor carrying John Carter and the Princess of Helium.

"John Carter, thank Issus!" Dejah Thoris cried in relief, and pointed toward the far mountain skyline.

"The Helium Fleet has returned," shouted John Carter. "Our messenger reached Kantos Kan in time!" Over the mountains, with flying banners streaming, sailed the mighty Helium Fleet.

There was a moment's silence in the entrenched guns of the enemy. They had seen the charging Tharks and the Helium Fleet simultaneously.

A great cry of triumph rose from the ranks of the charging warriors at sight of the Helium Fleet streaking to their aid.

"Listen," cried Dejah Thoris to Carter, "the bells of Helium are tolling our victory song!" Then it seemed as though all of Pew Mogel's guns broke loose at once; and from behind the protecting hills rose his flying legions of winged malagors. Upon their backs rode the white apes with men's brains.

Down upon the legions of Tharks came wave after wave of Pew Mogel's feathered squadrons. In true blitzkrieg fashion, the birds would swoop down just out of sword's reach over the green warriors. As each bird pulled out of its dive, the ape on its back would empty its death-dealing atomgun into the mass of warriors beneath.

The carnage was terrific. Only after Tars Tarkas and John Carter had led their warriors into the first lines of entrenched apes did the Tharks find an enemy with whom they could fight effectively.

Here, the four-armed green soldiers of Thark fought gloriously against the great white apes of Pew Mogel's ghastly legions.

But never for a second did the horrible death-diving squadrons cease their attacks from above. Like angry hornets, the thousands dove, killed, climbed, dove, and killed again—always killing.

John Carter masterfully controlled his frightened bird while he issued orders and directed attacks from his vantage point immediately above the center of battle.

Bravely, efficiently, the Princess of Helium protected her chieftain against countless side and rear attacks from the air. The barrel of her radium pistol was red-hot with constant firing; and many were the charging birds and shrieking apes she sent catapulting into the melee below.

Suddenly a hoarse shout rose again from Pew Mogel's legions on ground and in air.

"What is it, my chieftain?" cried the girl. "Why are the enemy shouting in triumph?"

John Carter looked toward the advancing ships now over the mountains only a half mile away; then his blood ran cold.

"The giant—Joog, the giant!"

The creature had risen up from behind the shelter of a low hill, as the ships approached above him. The giant grasped a huge tree trunk in his mighty hand.

Even from where they were, John Carter could discern the head of a man sitting in an armor-enclosed, steel howdah strapped to the top of Joog's helmet.

From the giant's lips there suddenly issued a thunderous, shrieking roar that echoed in the mountains and across the plain.

Then he clambered swiftly to the top of a small hill. Before the astonished Heliumites could swerve their speeding craft, the giant struck out mightily with the great tree trunk.

The great, synthetic muscles of Pew Mogel's giant swung the huge weapon full into the advancing craft.

The vanguard of twenty ships, the pride of Helium's airfleet met the blow head-on—went smashing and shattering against the mountain-side, carrying their crews to swift, crushing death!

KANTOS KAN'S FLAGSHIP narrowly escaped annihilation at the first blow of the giant. The creature's club only missed the leading ship by a few feet.

From their position on the malagor, John Carter and Dejah Thoris could see many of the airships turning back toward the mountains. Others, however, were not so fortunate.

Caught in the wild rush of air resulting from the giant's swinging club, the craft pitched and tossed crazily out of control.

Again and again the huge tree trunk split through the air as the giant swung blow after blow at the helpless ships.

"Kantos Kan is re-forming his fleet," John Carter shouted above the roar of battle as the fighting on the ground was once more resumed with increased zeal.

"The ships are returning again," cried the princess, "toward that awful creature!"

"They are spreading out in the air," the earthman relied. "Kantos Kan is trying to surround the giant!"

"But why?"

"Look, they are giving him some of Pew Mogel's own medicine!"

Helium's vast fleet of airships was darting in from all sides. Others came zooming down from above. As they approached within range of their massive target, the gunners would pour out a veritable hail of bullets and rays into the giant's body.

Dejah Thoris sighed in relief.

"He can't stand that much longer!" she said.

John Carter, however, shook his head sadly as the giant began to strike down the planes with renewed fury.

"I'm afraid it's useless. Not only those bullets but the ray-guns as well are having no effect upon the creature. His body has been imbued with a serum that Ras Thavas discovered. The stuff spreads throughout the tissue cells and makes them grow immediately with unbelievable speed to replace all wounded or destroyed flesh."

"You mean," Dejah Thoris asked, horror-stricken, "the awful monster might never be destroyed?"

"It is probable that he will live and grow forever," replied the earthman, "unless something drastic is done to destroy him—"

A sudden fire of determination flared in the earthman's steel grey eyes.

"There may be a way yet to stop him, my princess, and save our people—"

A weird, bold plan had formulated itself in John Carter's mind. He was accustomed to acting quickly on sudden impulse. Now he ordered his malagor down close over Tars Tarkas's head.

Although he knew the battle was hopeless, the green man was fighting furiously on his great thoat.

"Call your men back to the mountains," shouted Carter to his old friend. "Hide out there and reorganize—wait for my return!"

The next half hour found John Carter and the girl beside Kantos Kan's flagship. The great Helium Fleet had once more retreated over the mountains to take stock of its losses and re-form for a new attack.

Every ship's captain must have known the futility of further battle against this indomitable element; yet they were all willing to fight to the last for their nation and for their princess, who had so recently been rescued.

After the earthman and the girl boarded the flagship, they freed the great malagor that had so faithfully served them. Kantos Kan joyously greeted the princess on bended knee and then welcomed his old friend.

"To know you two are safe again is a pleasure that even outweighs the great sadness of seeing our City of Helium fall into the enemy's hands," stated Kantos Kan sincerely.

"We have not lost yet, Kantos Kan," said the earthman. "I have a plan that might save us—I'll need ten of your largest planes manned by only a minimum crew."

"I'll wire orders for them to break formation and assemble beside the flagship immediately," replied Kantos Kan, turning to an orderly.

"Just a minute," added Carter. "I'll want each plane equipped with *two hundred parachutes!*"

"Two hundred parachutes?" echoed the orderly. "Yes, sir!"

Almost immediately there were ten large aircraft, empty troop ships, drifting in single file formation beside Kantos Kan's flagship. Each had a minimum crew of ten men and two hundred parachutes, two thousand parachutes in all!

Just before he boarded the leading ship, John Carter spoke to Kantos Kan.

"Keep your fleet intact," he said, "until I return. Stay near Helium and protect the city as best you can. I'll be back by dawn."

"But that monster," groaned Kantos Kan. "Look at him—we must do something to save Helium."

The enormous creature, standing one hundred and thirty feet tall, dressed in his ill-fitting, baggy tunic, was tossing boulders and bombs into Helium, his every action dictated through short wave by Pew Mogel, who sat in the armored howdah atop the giant's head.

John Carter laid his hand on Kantos Kan's shoulder.

"Don't waste further ships and men uselessly in fighting the creature," he warned; "and trust me, my friend. Do as I say—at least until dawn!"

John Carter took Dejah Thoris's hand in his and kissed it.

"Good-by, my chieftain," she whispered, tears filling her eyes.

"You'll be safer here with Kantos Kan, Dejah Thoris," spoke the earthman; and then, "Good-by, my princess," he called and vaulted lightly over the craft's rail to the deck of the troop ship alongside. It pained him to leave Dejah Thoris; yet he knew she was in safe hands.

Ten minutes later, Dejah Thoris and Kantos Kan watched the ten speedy craft disappear into the distant haze.

When John Carter had gone, Kantos Kan unfurled Dejah Thoris's personal colors beside the nation's flag; so that all Helium would know that their princess had been found safe and the people be heartened by her close presence.

During his absence, Kantos Kan and Tars Tarkas followed the earthman's orders, refraining from throwing away their forces in hopeless battle. As a result, Pew Mogel's fighters had moved closer and closer to Helium; while Pew Mogel himself was even now preparing Joog to lead the final assault upon the fortressed city.

Exactly twenty-four hours later, John Carter's ten ships returned.

As he approached Helium, the earthman took in the situation at a glance. He had feared that he would be too late, for his secret mission had occupied more precious time than he had anticipated.

But now he sighed with relief. There was still time to put into execution his bold plan, the plan upon which rested the fate of a nation.

chapter XI

A DARING PLAN

FEARING THAT Pew Mogel might somehow intercept any shortwave signal to Kantos Kan, John Carter sought out the flagship and hove to alongside it.

The troop ships that had accompanied him on his secret mission were strung out behind their leader.

Their captains awaited the next orders of this remarkable man from another world. In the last twenty-four hours they had seen John Carter accomplish a task that no Martian would have even dreamed of attempting.

The next four hours would determine the success or failure of a plan so fantastic that the earthman himself had half-smiled at its contemplation.

Even his old friend, Kantos Kan, shook his head sadly when John Carter explained his intentions a few minutes later in the cabin of the flagship.

"I'm afraid it's no use, John Carter," he said. "Even though your plan is most ingeniously conceived, it will avail naught against that horrible monstrosity.

"Helium is doomed, and although we shall all fight until the last to save her, it can do no good."

As he talked, Kantos Kan was looking down at Helium far below. Joog the giant could be seen on the plain hurling great boulders into the city.

Why Pew Mogel had not ordered the giant into the city itself by this time, Carter could not understand—unless it was because Pew

Mogel actually enjoyed watching the destructive effect of the boulders as they crashed into the buildings of Helium.

Actually, Joog, however frightful in appearance, could best serve his master's purpose by biding his time, for he was doing more damage at present than he could possibly accomplish within the city itself.

But it was only a matter of time before Pew Mogel would order a general attack upon the city.

Then his entrenched forces would dash in, scaling the walls and crashing the gates. Overhead would swoop the supporting apes on their speedy mounts, bringing death and destruction from the air.

And finally Joog would come, adding the final coup to Pew Mogel's victory.

The horrible carnage that would then fall upon his people made Kantos Kan shudder.

"There is no time to lose, Kantos Kan," spoke the earthman. "I must have your assurance that you will see that my orders are followed to the letter."

Kantos Kan looked at the earthman for some time before he spoke.

"You have my word, John Carter," he said, "even though I know it will mean your death, for no man, not even you, can accomplish what you plan to do!"

"Good!" cried the earthman. "I shall leave immediately; and when you see the giant raise and lower his arm three times, that will be your signal to carry out my orders!"

Just before he left the flagship, John Carter knocked at Dejah Thoris's cabin door.

"Come," he heard her reply from within. As he threw open the door, he saw Dejah Thoris seated at a table. She had just flicked off the visiscreen upon which she had caught the vision of Kantos Kan. The girl rose, tears filling her eyes.

"Do not leave again, John Carter," she pleaded. "Kantos Kan has just told me of your rash plan—it cannot possibly succeed, and you will only be sacrificing yourself uselessly. Stay with me, my chieftain, and we shall die together!"

John Carter strode across the room and took his princess in his arms—perhaps for the last time. She pillowed her head on his broad chest and cried softly. He held her close for a brief moment before he spoke.

"Upon Mars," he said, "I have found a free and kindly people whose civilization I have learned to cherish. Their princess is the woman I love.

"She and her people to whom she belongs are in grave danger. While there is even a slight chance for me to save you and Helium from the terrible catastrophe that threatens all Mars, I must act."

Dejah Thoris straightened a little at his words and smiled bravely as she looked up at him.

"I'm sorry, my chieftain," she whispered. "For a minute, my love for you made me forget that I belong also to my people. If there is any chance of saving them, I would be horribly selfish to detain you; so go now and remember, if you die the heart of Dejah Thoris dies with you!"

A moment later John Carter was seated behind the controls of the fastest, one-man airship in the entire Helium Navy.

He waved farewell to the two forlorn figures who stood at the rail of the flagship.

Then he opened wide the throttle of the quiet, radium engine. He could feel the little craft shudder for an instant as it gained speed. The earthman pointed its nose upward and rose far above the battleground.

Then he nosed over and dove down. The wind whistled shrilly off the craft's trim lines as its increased momentum sped it, comet-like, downward—straight toward the giant!

chapter XII

THE FATE OF A NATION

NEITHER PEW MOGEL nor the giant Joog had yet seen the lone craft diving toward them from overhead. Pew Mogel, seated inside the armored howdah that was attached to Joog's enormous helmet, was issuing attack orders to his troops by shortwave.

A strip of glass, about three feet wide, completely encircled the howdah, enabling Pew Mogel to obtain complete, unrestricted vision of his fighting forces below.

Perhaps if Pew Mogel had looked up through the circular glass skylight in the dome of his steel shelter, he would have seen the earth-man's speedy little craft streaking down on him from above.

John Carter was banking his life, that of the woman he loved and the survival of Helium upon the hope that Pew Mogel would *not* look up.

John Carter was driving his little craft with bullet speed—straight toward that circular opening on top of Pew Mogel's sanctuary.

Joog was standing still now, shoulders hunched forward. Pew Mogel had ordered him to be quiet while he completed his last-minute command to his troops.

The giant was on the plain between the mountains and the city. Not until he was five hundred feet above the little round window did Carter pull back on the throttle.

He had gained his great height to avoid discovery by Pew Mogel. His speed was for the same purpose.

Now, if he were to come out alive himself, he must slow down his hurtling craft. That impact must occur at exactly the right speed.

If he made the crash too fast, he might succeed only in killing himself, with no assurance that Pew Mogel had died with him.

On the other hand, if the speed of his ship were too slow it would never crash through the tough glass that covered the opening. In that case, his crippled plane would bounce harmlessly off the howdah and carry Carter to his death on the battlefield below.

One hundred feet over the window!

He shut off the motor, a quick glance at the speedometer—too fast for the impact!

His hands flew over the instrument panel. He jerked back on three levers. Three little parachutes whipped out behind the craft. There was a tug on the plane as its speed slowed down.

Then the ship's nose crashed against the little window!

There was a crunch of steel, a splinter of wood, as the ship's nose collapsed; then a clatter of glass that ended in a dull, trembling thud as the craft bore through the window and lodged part way into the floor of Pew Mogel's compartment.

The tail of the craft was protruding out of the top of the howdah, but the craft's door was inside the compartment.

John Carter sprang from his ship, his blade gleaming in his hand.

Pew Mogel was still spinning around crazily in his revolving chair from the tremendous impact. His earphones and attached microphone, with which he had directed Joog's actions as well as his troop formations, had been knocked off his head and lay on the floor at his feet.

When his foolish spin finally stopped, Pew Mogel remained seated. He stared incredulously at the earthman.

His small, lidless eyes bulged. He opened his crooked mouth

several times to speak. Now his twisted fingers worked spasmodically.

"Draw your sword, Pew Mogel!" spoke the earthman so low that Pew Mogel could hardly hear the words.

The synthetic man made no move to obey.

"You're dead!" he finally croaked. It was like the man was trying to convince himself that what he saw confronting him with naked sword was only an ill-begotten hallucination. So hard, in fact, did Pew Mogel continue to stare that his left eye behaved as Carter had seen it do once before in Korvas when the creature was excited.

It popped out of its socket and hung down on his cheek.

"Quickly, Pew Mogel, draw your weapon—I have no time to waste!"

Carter could feel the giant below him growing restless, shifting uneasily on his enormous feet. Apparently he did not yet suspect the change of masters in the howdah strapped to his helmet; yet he had jumped perceptibly when Carter's craft had torn into his master's sanctuary.

Carter reached down and picked up the microphone on the floor.

"Raise your arm," he shouted into the mouthpiece.

There was a pause; then the giant raised the right arm high over his head.

"Lower arm," Carter commanded again. The giant obeyed.

Twice more, Carter gave the same command and the giant obeyed each time. The earthman half smiled. He knew Kantos Kan had seen the signal and would follow the orders he had given him earlier.

Now Pew Mogel's hand suddenly shot down to his side. It started back up with a radium gun.

There was a blinding flash as he pulled the trigger; then the gun flew miraculously from his hand.

Carter had leaped to one side. His sword had crashed against the weapon knocking it from Pew Mogel's grasp.

Now the man was forced to draw his sword.

There, on top of the giant's head, fighting furiously with a synthetic man of Mars, John Carter found himself in one of the weirdest predicaments of his adventurous life.

Pew Mogel was no mean swordsman. In fact, so furious was his first attack that he had the earthman backing around the room hard-pressed to parry the swift torrent of blows that were aimed indiscriminately at every inch of his body from head to toe.

It was a ghastly sensation, fighting with a man whose eye hung down the side of his face. Pew Mogel had forgotten that it had popped out. The synthetic man could see equally well with either eye.

Now Pew Mogel had worked the earthman over to the window. Just for an instant he glanced out.

An exclamation of surprise escaped his lips.

chapter XIII

PANIC

JOHN CARTER'S EYES followed those of Pew Mogel. What he saw made him smile, renewed hope surging over him.

"Look, Pew Mogel," he cried. "Your flying army is disbanding!"

The thousands of malagors that had littered the sky with their hairy riders were croaking hoarsely as they scattered in all directions. The apes astride their backs were unable to control their wild fright. The birds were pitching off their riders in wholesale lots, as their great wings flapped furiously to escape that which had suddenly appeared in the sky among them.

The cause of their wild flight was immediately apparent.

The air was filled with parachutes!—and dangling from each falling parachute was a three-legged Martian rat—every Martian bird's hereditary foe!

In the quick glance that he took, Carter could see the creatures tumbling out of the troop ships into which he had loaded them during his absence of the last twenty-four hours.

His orders were being followed implicitly.

The rats would soon be landing among Pew Mogel's entrenched troops.

Now, however, John Carter's attention returned to his own immediate peril.

Pew Mogel swung viciously at the earthman. The blade nicked his shoulder, the blood flowed down his bronzed arm.

Carter stole another glance down. Those rats would need support when they landed in the trenches.

Good! Tars Tarkas's green warriors were again racing out of the hills, unhindered now by scathing fire from an enemy above.

True, the rats when they landed would attack anything in their path; but the green Tharks were mounted on fleet thoats—the apes had no mounts. No malagor would stay within sight of its most hated enemy.

Pew Mogel was backing up now once more near the window. Out of the corner of his eye, Carter caught sight of Kantos Kan's air fleet zooming down toward Pew Mogel's ape legions far below.

Pew Mogel suddenly reached down with his free hand.

His fingers clutched the microphone that Carter had dropped when Pew Mogel had first rushed at him.

Now the creature held it to his lips and before the earthman could prevent he shouted into it.

"Joog!" He cried. "Kill! Kill! Kill!"

The next second, John Carter's blade had severed Pew Mogel's head from his shoulders.

The earthman dived for the microphone as it fell from the creature's hands; but he was met by Pew Mogel's headless body as it lunged blindly around the room still wielding its gleaming weapon.

Pew Mogel's head rolled about the floor, shrieking wildly as Joog charged forward to obey his master's last command to kill!

Joog's head jerked back and forth with each enormous stride. John Carter was hurled roughly about the narrow compartment with each step.

Pew Mogel's headless body floundered across the floor, still striking out madly with the sword in its hand.

"You can't kill me. You can't kill me," shrieked Pew Mogel's head, as it bounced about. "I am Ras Thavas's synthetic man. I never die. I never die!"

The narrow entrance door to the howdah had flopped open as some flying object hit against its bolt.

Pew Mogel's body walked vacantly through the opening and went hurtling down to the ground far below.

Pew Mogel's head saw and shrieked in dismay; then Carter managed to grab it by the ear and hurl the head out after the body.

He could hear the thing shrieking all the way down; then its cries ceased suddenly.

Joog was now fighting furiously with the weapon he had just uprooted.

"I kill! I kill!" he bellowed as he smacked the huge club against the Helium planes as they drove down over the trenches.

Although the howdah was rocking violently, Carter clung to the window. He could see the rats landing now by the scores, hurling themselves viciously at the apes in the trenches.

And Tars Tarkas's green warriors were there now, also. They were fighting gloriously beside their great, four-armed leader.

But Joog's mighty club was mowing down a hundred fighters at a time as he swept it close above the ground.

Joog had to be stopped somehow!

John Carter dove for the microphone that was sliding around the floor. He missed it, dove again. This time his fingers held it.

"Joog—stop! Stop!" Carter shouted into the microphone. Panting and growling, the great creature ceased his ruthless slaughter. He stood hunched over, the sullen, glaring hatred slowly dying away in his eyes, as the battle continued to rage at his feet.

The apes were now completely disbanded. They broke over the trenches and ran toward the mountains, pursued by the vicious, snarling rats and the green warriors of Tars Tarkas.

John Carter could see Kantos Kan's flagship hovering near Joog's head.

Fearing that Joog might aim an irritated blow at the craft with its precious cargo, the earthman signalled the ship to remain aloof.

Then his command once again rang into the microphone.

"Joog, lie down. Lie down!"

Like some tired beast of prey, Joog settled down on the ground amid the bodies of those he had killed.

John Carter leaped out of the howdah onto the ground. He still retained hold of the microphone that was turned to the shortwave receiving set in Joog's ear.

"Joog!" shouted Carter again. "Go to Korvas. Go to Korvas."

The monster glared at the earthman, not ten feet from his face, and snarled.

chapter XIV

ADVENTURE'S END

ONCE AGAIN the earthman repeated his command to Joog the giant. Now the snarl faded from his lips and from the brute's chest came a sound not unlike a sigh as he rose to his feet once again.

Turning slowly, Joog ambled off across the plain toward Korvas.

It was not until ten minutes later after the Heliumite soldiers had stormed from their city and surrounded the earthman and their princess that John Carter, holding Dejah Thoris tightly in his arms, saw Joog's head disappear over the mountains in the distance.

"Why did you let him go, John Carter?" asked Tars Tarkas, as he wiped the blood from his blade on the hide of his sweating thoat.

"Yes, why," repeated Kantos Kan, "when you had him in your power?"

John Carter turned and surveyed the battlefield.

"All the death and destruction that has been caused here today was due not to Joog but to Pew Mogel," replied John Carter.

"Joog is harmless, now that his evil master is dead. Why add his death to all those others, even if we could have killed him—which I doubt?"

Kantos Kan was watching the rats disappear into the far mountains in pursuit of the great, lumbering apes.

"Tell me, John Carter," finally he said, a queer expression on his face, "how did you manage to capture those vicious rats, load them into those troop ships and even strap parachutes on them?"

John Carter smiled. "It was really simple," he said. "I had noticed in Korvas, when I was a prisoner in their underground city, that there was only one means of entrance to the cavern in which the rats live—a single tunnel that continued back for some distance before it branched, although there were openings in the ceiling far above; but they were out of reach.

"I led my men down into that tunnel and we built a huge smoke fire with debris from the ground above. The natural draft carried the smoke into the cavern.

"The place became so filled with smoke that the rats passed out by the scores from lack of oxygen, for they couldn't get by the fire in the tunnel—their only means of escape. Later, we simply went in and dragged out as many as we needed to load into our troop ships."

"But the parachutes!" exclaimed Kantos Kan. "How did you manage to get those on their backs or keep them from tearing them off when the creatures finally became conscious?"

"They did not regain consciousness until the last minute," replied the earthman. "We kept the inside cabin of each troop ship filled with enough smoke to keep the rats unconscious all the way to Helium. We had plenty of time to attach the parachutes to their backs. The rats came to in mid-air after my men shoved them out of the ships."

John Carter nodded toward the disappearing creatures in the mountains. "They were very much alive and fighting mad when they hit the ground, as you saw," added the earthman. "They simply stepped out of their parachute harnesses when they landed, and leaped for anyone in sight.

"As for the malagors," he concluded, "they are birds—and birds on both Earth and Mars have no love for snakes or rats. I knew those malagors would prefer other surroundings when they saw and smelled their natural enemies in the air around them!"

Dejah Thoris looked up at her chieftain and smiled.

"Was there ever such a man before?" she asked. "Could it be that all earthman are like you?"

That night all Helium celebrated its victory. The streets of the city surged with laughing people. The mighty, green warriors of Thark mingled in common brotherhood with the fighting legions of Helium.

In the royal palace was staged a great feast in honor of John Carter's service to Helium.

Old Tardos Mors, the jeddak, was so choked with feeling at the miraculous delivery of his city from the hands of their enemy and the safe return of his granddaughter that he was unable to speak for some time when he arose at the dining table to offer the kingdom's thanks to the earthman.

But when he finally spoke, his words were couched with the simple dignity of a great ruler. The intense gratitude of these people deeply touched the earthman's heart.

Later that night, John Carter and Dejah Thoris stood alone on a balcony overlooking the royal gardens.

The moons of Mars circled majestically across the heavens, causing the shadows of the distant mountains to roll and tumble in an ever-changing fantasy over the plain and the forest.

Even the shadows of the two people on the royal balcony slowly merged into one.

chapter 1

BETRAYED

I AM NO SCIENTIST. I am a fighting man. My most beloved weapon is the sword, and during a long life I have seen no reason to alter my theories as to its proper application to the many problems with which I have been faced. This is not true of the scientists. They are constantly abandoning one theory for another one. The law of gravitation is about the only theory that has held throughout my lifetime—and if the earth should suddenly start rotating seventeen times faster than it now does, even the law of gravitation would fail us and we would all go sailing off into space.

Theories come and theories go—scientific theories. I recall that there was once a theory that Time and Space moved forward constantly in a straight line. There was also a theory that neither Time nor Space existed—it was all in your mind's eye. Then came the theory that Time and Space curved in upon themselves. Tomorrow, some scientist may show us reams and reams of paper and hundreds of square feet of blackboard covered with equations, formulae, signs, symbols, and diagrams to prove that Time and Space curve out away from themselves. Then our theoretic universe will come tumbling about our ears, and we shall have to start all over again from scratch.

Like many fighting men, I am inclined to be credulous concerning matters outside my vocation; or at least I used to be. I believed whatever the scientists said. Long ago, I believed with Flammarion that Mars was habitable and inhabited; then a newer and more reputable school of scientists convinced me that it was neither. Without losing hope, I was yet forced to believe them until I came to Mars to live. They still insist that Mars is neither habitable nor inhabited, but I live here. Fact and theory seem to be opposed. Unquestionably, the scientists appear to be correct in theory. Equally incontrovertible is it that I am correct in fact.

In the adventure that I am about to narrate, fact and theory will again cross swords. I hate to do this to my long-suffering scientific friends; but if they would only consult me first rather than dogmatically postulating theories which do not meet with popular acclaim, they would save themselves much embarrassment.

Dejah Thoris, my incomparable princess, and I were sitting upon a carved ersite bench in one of the gardens of our palace in Lesser Helium when an officer in the leather of Tardos Mors, Jeddak of Helium, approached and saluted.

"From Tardos Mors to John Carter, kaor!" he said. "The jeddak requests your immediate presence in the Hall of Jeddaks in the imperial palace in Greater Helium."

"At once," I replied.

"May I fly you over, sir?" he asked. "I came in a two-seater."

"Thanks," I replied. "I'll join you at the hangar in a moment." He saluted and left us.

"Who was he?" asked Dejah Thoris. "I don't recall ever having seen him before."

"Probably one of the new officers from Zor, whom Tardos Mors has commissioned in the Jeddak's Guard. It was a gesture of his, made to assure Zor that he has the utmost confidence in the loyalty of that city and as a measure for healing old wounds."

Zor, which lies about three hundred eighty miles southeast of Helium, is one of the more recent conquests of Helium and had given us a great deal of trouble in the past because of treasonable acts instigated by a branch of its royal family led by one Multis Par, a prince. About five years before the events I am about to narrate occurred, this Multis Par had disappeared; and since then Zor had given us no trouble. No one knew what had become of the man, and it was supposed that he had either taken the last, long voyage down the river Iss to the Lost Sea of Korus in the Valley Dor or had been captured and murdered by members of some horde of savage Green men. Nor did anyone appear to care—just so he never returned to Zor, where he was thoroughly hated for his arrogance and cruelty.

"I hope that my revered grandfather does not keep you long," said Dejah Thoris. "We are having a few guests for dinner tonight, and I do not wish you to be late."

"A few!" I said. "How many? Two hundred or three hundred?"

"Don't be impossible," she said, laughing. "Really, only a few."

"A thousand, if it pleases you, my dear," I assured her as I kissed her. "And now, good-by! I'll doubtless be back within the hour." That was a year ago!

As I ran up the ramp toward the hangar on the palace roof, I had, for some then unaccountable reason, a sense of impending ill; but I attributed it to the fact that my tête-à-tête with my princess had been so quickly interrupted.

The thin air of dying Mars renders the transition from day to night startlingly sudden to an earthman. Twilight is of short duration owing to the negligible refraction of the sun's rays. When I had left

Dejah Thoris, the sun, though low, was still shining; the garden was in shadow, but it was still daylight. When I stepped from the head of the ramp to that part of the roof of the palace where the hangar was located which housed the private fliers of the family, dim twilight partially obscured my vision. It would soon be dark. I wondered why the hangar guard had not switched on the lights.

In the very instant that I realized that something was amiss, a score of men surrounded and overpowered me before I could draw and defend myself. A voice cautioned me to silence. It was the voice of the man who had summoned me into this trap. When the others spoke, it was in a language I had never heard before. They spoke in dismal, hollow monotone—expressionless, sepulchral.

They had thrown me face down upon the pavement and trussed my wrists behind my back. Then they jerked me roughly to my feet. Now, for the first time, I obtained a fairly good sight of my captors. I was appalled. I could not believe my own eyes. These things were not men. They were human skeletons! Black eye sockets looked out from grinning skulls. Bony, skeletal fingers grasped my arms. It seemed to me that I could see every bone in each body. Yet the things were alive! They moved. They spoke. They dragged me toward a strange craft that I had not before noticed. It lay in the shadow of the hangar— long, lean, sinister. It looked like an enormous projectile, with rounded nose and tapering tail.

In the first brief glance I had of it, I saw fins forward below its median line, a long, longitudinal aileron (or so I judged it to be) running almost the full length of the ship, and strangely designed elevator and rudder as part of the empennage assembly. I saw no propellors; but then I had little time for a close examination of the strange craft, as I was quickly hustled through a doorway in its metal side. The interior was pitch dark. I could see nothing other than the faint light of the dying day visible through long, narrow portholes in the ship's side.

The man who had betrayed me followed me into the ship with my captors. The door was closed and securely fastened; then the ship rose silently into the night. No light showed upon it, within or without. However, I was certain that one of our patrol ships must see it; then, if nothing more, my people would have a clew upon which to account for my disappearance; and before dawn a thousand ships of the navy of Helium would be scouring the surface of Barsoom and the air above it in search of me, nor could any ship the size of this find hiding place wherein to elude them.

Once above the city, the lights of which I could see below us, the craft shot away at appalling speed. Nothing upon Barsoom could have hoped to overhaul it. It moved at great speed and in utter silence. The cabin lights were switched on. I was disarmed and my hands were freed. I looked with revulsion, almost with horror, upon the twenty or thirty creatures which surrounded me.

I saw now that they were not skeletons, though they still closely resembled the naked bones of dead men. Parchmentlike skin was stretched tightly over the bony structure of the skull. There seemed to be neither cartilage nor fat underlying it. What I had thought were hollow eye sockets were deep set brown eyes showing no whites. The skin of the face merged with what should have been gums at the roots of the teeth, which were fully exposed in both jaws, precisely as are the teeth of a naked skull. The nose was but a gaping hole in the center of the face. There were no external ears—only the orifices—nor was there any hair upon any of the exposed parts of their bodies nor upon their heads. The things were even more hideous than the hideous kaldanes of Bantoom—those horrifying spider men into whose toils fell

Tara of Helium during that adventure which led her to the country of The Chessmen of Mars; they, at least, had beautiful bodies, even though they were not their own.

The bodies of my captors harmonized perfectly with their heads—parchmentlike skin covered the bones of their limbs so tightly that it was difficult to convince one's self that it was not true bone that was exposed. And so tightly was this skin drawn over their torsos that every rib and every vertebra stood out in plain and disgusting relief. When they stood directly in front of a bright light, I could see their internal organs.

They wore no clothing other than a G string. Their harness was quite similar to that which we Barsoomians wear, which is not at all remarkable, since it was designed to serve the same purpose—supporting a sword, a dagger, and a pocket pouch.

Disgusted, I turned away from them to look down upon the moon bathed surface of my beloved Mars. But where was it! Close to port was Cluros, the farther moon! I caught a glimpse of its surface as we flashed by. Fourteen thousand five hundred miles in a little more than a minute! It was incredible.

The red man who had engineered my capture came and sat down beside me. His rather handsome face was sad. "I am sorry, John Carter," he said. "Perhaps, if you will permit me to explain, you will at least understand why I did it. I do not expect that you will ever forgive me."

"Where is this ship taking me?" I demanded.

"To Sasoom," he said.

Sasoom! That is the Barsoomian name for Jupiter three hundred and forty-two million miles from the palace where my Dejah Thoris awaited me!

chapter II
U DAN

FOR SOME TIME I sat in silence, gazing out in the inky black void of space, a Stygian backdrop against which stars and planets shone with intense brilliancy, steady and untwinkling. To port or starboard, above, below, the heavens stared at me with unblinking eyes—millions of white hot, penetrating eyes. Many questions harassed my mind. Had I been especially signalled out for capture? If so, why? How had this large ship been able to enter Helium and settle upon my landing stage in broad daylight? Who was this sad-faced, apologetic man who had led me into such a trap? He could have nothing against me personally. Never, before he had stepped into my garden, had I seen him.

It was he who broke the silence. It was as though he had read my thoughts. "You wonder why you are here, John Carter," he said. "If you will bear with me, I shall tell you. In the first place, let me introduce myself. I am U Dan, formerly a padwar in the guard of Zu Tith, the Jed of Zor who was killed in battle when Helium overthrew his tyrannical reign and annexed the city.

"My sympathies were all upon the side of Helium, and I saw a brilliant and happy future for my beloved city once she was a part of the great Heliumetic empire. I fought against Helium; because it was my sworn duty to defend the jed I loathed—a monster of tyranny and cruelty—but when the war was over, I gladly swore allegiance to Tardos Mors, Jeddak of Helium.

"I had been raised in the palace of the jed in utmost intimacy with the members of the royal family. I knew them all well, especially Multis Par, the prince, who, in the natural course of events, would have succeeded to the throne. He was of a kind with his father, Zu Tith—arrogant, cruel, tyrannical by nature. After the fall of Zor, he sought to foment discord and arouse the people to revolt. When he failed, he disappeared. That was about five years ago.

"Another member of the royal family whom I knew well was as unlike Zu Tith and Multis Par as day is unlike night. Her name is Vaja. She is a cousin of Multis Par. I loved her and she loved me. We were to have been married, when, about two years after the disappearance of Multis Par, Vaja mysteriously disappeared."

I did not understand why he was telling me all this. I was certainly not interested in his love affairs. I was not interested in him. I was still less interested, if possible, in Multis Par; but I listened.

"I searched," he continued. "The governor of Zor gave me every assistance within his power, but all to no avail. Then, one night, Multis Par entered my quarters when I was alone. He wasted no time. He came directly to the point.

"'I suppose,' he said, 'that you are wondering what has become of Vaja.'

"I knew then that he had been instrumental in her abduction; and I feared the worst, for I knew the type of man he was. I whipped out my sword. 'Where is she?' I demanded. 'Tell me, if you care to live.'

"He only laughed at me. 'Don't be a fool,' he said. 'If you kill me you will never see her again. You will never even know where she is. Work with me, and you may have her back. But you will have to work fast, as I am becoming very fond of her. It is odd,' he added reminiscently, 'that I could have lived for years in the same palace with her and have been blind to her many charms, both mental and physical—especially physical.'

"'Where is she?' I demanded. 'If you have harmed her, you beast—'

"'Don't call names, U Dan,' he said. 'If you annoy me too greatly I may keep her for myself and enlist the services of some one other than you to assist me with the plan I had come to explain to you. I thought you would be more sensible. You used to be a very sensible man; but then, of course, love plays strange tricks upon one's mental processes. I am commencing to find that out in my own case.' He gave a nasty little laugh. 'But don't worry,' he continued. 'She is quite safe—so far. How much longer she will be safe depends wholly upon you.'

"'Where is she?' I demanded.

"'Where you can never get her without my help,' he replied.

"'If she is anywhere upon all Barsoom, I shall find her,' I said.

"'She is not on Barsoom. She is on Sasoom.'

"'You lie, Multis Par,' I said.

"He shrugged, indifferently. 'Perhaps you will believe her,' he said, and handed me a letter. It was indeed from Vaja. I recall its message word for word:

"'Incredible as it may seem to you, I am a prisoner on Sasoom. Multis Par has promised to bring you here to me if you will perform what he calls a small favor for him. I do not know what he is going to ask of you; but unless it can be honorably done, do not do it. I am safe and unharmed.'"

"What is it you wish me to do?" I asked.

"I shall not attempt to quote his exact words; but this, in effect, is what he told me: Multis Par's disappearance from Zor was caused by his capture by men from Sasoom. For some time they had been coming to this planet, reconnoitering, having in mind the eventual conquest of Barsoom.

"I asked him for what reason, and he explained that it was simply because they were a warlike race. Their every thought was of war, as it had been for ages until the warlike spirit was as compelling as the urge for self-preservation. They had conquered all other peoples upon Sasoom and sought a new world to conquer.

"They had captured him to learn what they could of the armaments and military effectiveness of various Barsoomian nations, and had decided that as Helium was the most powerful, it would be Helium upon which they would descend. Helium once disposed of, the rest of Barsoom would, they assumed, be easy to conquer."

"And where do I come in in this scheme of theirs?" I asked.

"I am coming to that," said U Dan. "The Morgors are a thoroughgoing and efficient people. They neglect no littlest detail which might affect the success or failure of a campaign. They already have excellent maps of Barsoom and considerable data relative to the fleets and armament of the principal nations. They now wish to check this data and obtain full information as to the war technique of the Heliumites. This they expect to get from you. This they will get from you."

I smiled. "Neither they nor you rate the honor and loyalty of a Heliumite very highly."

A sad smile crossed his lips. "I know how you feel," he said. "I felt the same way—until they captured Vaja and her life became the price of my acquiescence. Only to save her did I agree to act as a decoy to aid in your capture. The Morgors are adepts in individual and mass psychology as well as in the art of war."

"These things are Morgors?" I asked, nodding in the direction of some of the repulsive creatures. U Dan nodded. "I can appreciate the position in which you have been placed," I said, "but the Morgors have no such hold on me."

"Wait," said U Dan.

"What do you mean?" I demanded.

"Just wait. They will find a way. They are fiends. No one could have convinced me before Multis Par came to me with his proposition that I could have been forced to betray a man whom I, with all decent men, admire as I have admired you, John Carter. Perhaps I was wrong, but when I learned that Vaja would be tortured and mutilated after Multis Par had had his way with her and even then not be allowed to die but kept for future torture, I weakened and gave in. I do not expect you to forgive, but I hope that you will understand."

"I do understand," I said. "Perhaps, under like circumstances, I should have done the same thing." I could see how terribly the man's conscience tortured him. I could see that he was essentially a man of honor. I could forgive him for the thing that he had done for an innocent creature whom he loved, but could he expect me to betray my country, betray my whole world, to save a woman I had never seen. Still, I was bothered. Frankly, I did not know what I should do when faced with the final decision. "At least," I said, "should I ever be situated as you were, I could appear to comply while secretly working to defeat their ends."

"It was thus that I thought," he said. "It is still the final shred by which I cling to my self-respect. Perhaps, before it is too late, I may still be able to save both Vaja and yourself."

"Perhaps we can work together to that end and to the salvation of Helium," I said; "though I am really not greatly worried about Helium. I think she can take care of herself."

He shook his head. "Not if a part, even, of what Multis Par has told me is true. They will come in thousands of these ships, invisible to the inhabitants of Barsoom. Perhaps two million of them will invade Helium and overrun her two principal cities before a single inhabitant is aware that a single enemy threatens their security. They will come with lethal weapons of which Barsoomians know nothing and which they cannot, therefore, combat."

"Invisible ships!" I exclaimed. "Why I saw this one plainly after I was captured."

"Yes," he said. "It was not invisible then, but it was invisible when it came in broad daylight under the bows of your patrol ships and landed in one of the most prominent places in all Lesser Helium. It was not invisible when you first saw it; because it had cast off its invisibility, or, rather, the Morgors had cast it off so that they might find it again themselves, for otherwise it would have been as invisible to them as to us."

"Do you know how they achieve this invisibility?" I asked.

"Multis Par has explained it to me," replied U Dan. "Let me see; I am not much of a scientist, but I think that I recall more or less correctly what he told me. It seems that on some of the ocean beaches on Sasoom there is a submicroscopic, magnetic sand composed of prismatic crystals. When the Morgors desire invisibility for a ship, they magnetize the hull; and then from countless tiny apertures in the hull, they coat the whole exterior of the ship with these prismatic crystals. They simply spray them out, and they settle in a cloud upon the hull, causing light rays to bend around the ship. The instant that the hull is demagnetized, these tiny particles, light as air, fall or are blown off; and instantly the ship is visible again."

Here, a Morgor approached and interrupted our conversation. His manner was arrogant and rude. I could not understand his words, as he spoke his own language in the hollow, graveyard tones I had previously noticed. U Dan replied in the same language but in a less lugubrious tone of voice; then he turned to me.

"Your education is to commence at once," he said, with a wry smile.

"What do you mean?" I asked.

"During this voyage you are to learn the language of the Morgors," he explained.

"How long is the voyage going to last?" I asked. "It takes about three months to learn a language well enough to understand and make yourself understood."

"The voyage will take about eighteen days, as we shall have to make a detour of some million miles to avoid the Asteroids. They happen to lie directly in our way."

"I am supposed to learn their language in eighteen days?" I asked.

"You are not only supposed to, but you will," replied U Dan.

chapter III

THE MORGORS OF SASOOM . . .

MY EDUCATION COMMENCED. It was inconceivably brutal, but most effective. My instructors worked on me in relays, scarcely giving me time to eat or sleep. U Dan assisted as interpreter, which was immensely helpful to me, as was the fact that I am exceedingly quick in picking up new languages. Some times I was so overcome by lack of sleep that my brain lagged and my responses were slow and inaccurate. Upon one such occasion, the Morgor who was instructing me slapped my face. I had put up with everything else; because I was so very anxious to learn their language—a vital necessity if I were ever to hope to cope with them and thwart their fantastic plan of conquest. But I could not put up with that. I hit the fellow a single blow that sent him entirely across the cabin, but I almost broke my hand against his unpadded, bony jaw.

He did not get up. He lay where he had fallen. Several of his fellows came for me with drawn swords. The situation looked bad, as I was unarmed. U Dan was appalled. Fortunately for me, the officer in command of the ship had been attracted by the commotion and appeared at the scene of action in time to call his men off. He demanded an explanation.

I had now mastered sufficient words of their language so that I could understand almost everything that was said to me and make myself understood by them, after a fashion. I told the fellow that I had been starved and deprived of sleep and had not complained, but that no man could strike me without suffering the consequences.

"And no creature of a lower order may strike a Morgor without suffering the consequences," he replied.

"What are you going to do about it?" I asked.

"I am going to do nothing about it," he relied. "My orders require me to bring you alive to Eurobus. When I have done that and reported your behavior, it will lie wholly within the discretion of Bandolian as to what your punishment shall be"; then he walked away, but food was brought me and I was allowed to sleep; nor did another Morgor strike me during the remainder of the voyage.

While I was eating, I asked U Dan what Eurobus was. "It is their name for the planet Sasoom," he relied.

"And who is Bandolian?"

"Well, I suppose he would be called a jeddak on Barsoom. I judge this from the numerous references I have heard them make concerning him. Anyhow, he seems to be an object of fear if not veneration."

After a long sleep, I was much refreshed. Everything that I had been taught was clear again in my mind, no longer dulled by exhaustion. It was then that the commander took it upon himself to examine me personally. I am quite sure that he did so for the sole purpose of finding fault with me and perhaps punishing me. He was extremely nasty and arrogant. His simplest questions were at first couched in sarcastic language; but finally, evidently disappointed, he left me. I was given no more instruction.

"You have done well," said U Dan. "You have, in a very short time, mastered their language well enough to suit them."

This was the fifteenth day. During the last three days they left me alone. Travelling through space is stupifyingly monotonous. I had scarcely glanced from the portholes for days. This was, however, principally because my time was constantly devoted to instruction; but now, with nothing else to do, I glanced out. A most gorgeous scene presented itself to my astonished eyes. Gorgeous Jupiter loomed before me in all his majestic immensity. Five of his planets were plainly visible in the heavens. I could even see the tiny one closest to him, which is only thirty miles in diameter. During the ensuing two days, I saw, or at least I thought I saw, all of the remaining five moons. And Jupiter grew larger and more imposing. We were approaching him at the very considerable speed of twenty-three miles per second, but were still some two million miles distant.

Freed from the monotony of language lessons, my mind was once more enslaved to my curiosity. How could life exist upon a planet which one school of scientific thought claimed to have a surface temperature of two hundred and sixty degrees below zero and which another school was equally positive was still in a half molten condition and so hot that gases rose as hot vapor into its thick, warm atmosphere to fall as incessant rain? How could human life exist in an atmosphere made up largely of ammonia and methane gases? And what of the effect of the planet's terrific gravitational pull? Would my legs be able to support my weight? If I fell down, would I be able to rise again?

Another question which presented itself to my mind, related to the motive power which had been carrying us through space at terrific speeds for seventeen days. I asked U Dan if he knew.

"They utilize the eighth Barsoomian Ray, what we know as the ray of propulsion, in combination with the highly concentrated gravitational forces of all celestial bodies within the range of whose attraction the ship passes, and a concentration of Ray L (cosmic rays) which are collected from space and discharged at high velocities from propulsion tubes at the ship's stern. The eighth Barsoomian Ray helps to give the ship initial velocity upon leaving a planet and as a brake to its terrific speed when approaching its landing upon another. Gravitational forces are utilized both to accelerate speed and to guide the ship. The secret of their success with these inter-planetary ships lies in the ingenious methods they have developed for concentrating these various forces and directing their tremendous energies."

"Thanks, U Dan," I said, "I think I grasp the general idea. It would certainly surprise some of my scientific friends on Earth."

My passing reference to scientists started me to thinking of the vast accumulation of theories I was about to see shattered when I landed on Jupiter within the next twenty-four hours. It certainly must be habitable for a race quite similar to our own. These people had lungs, a heart, kidneys, a liver, and other internal organs similar to our own. I knew this for a fact, as I could see them every time one of the Morgors stood between me and a bright light, so thin and transparent was the parchmentlike skin that stretched tightly over their frames. Once more the scientists would be wrong. I felt sorry for them. They have been wrong so many times and had to eat humble pie. There were those scientists, for instance, who clung to the Ptolemaic System of the universe; and who, after Galileo had discovered four of the moons of Jupiter in 1610, argued that such pretended discoveries were absurd, their argument being that since we have seven openings in the head— two ears, two eyes, two nostrils, and a mouth, there could be in the heavens but seven planets. Having dismissed Galileo's absurd pretensions in this scientific manner, they caused him to be thrown into jail.

When at a distance of about five hundred thousand miles from Jupiter, the ship began to slow down very gradually in preparation for a landing; and some three or four hours later we entered the thick cloud envelope which surrounds the planet. We were barely crawling along now at not more than six hundred miles an hour.

I was all eagerness to see the surface of Jupiter; and extremely impatient of the time that it took the ship to traverse the envelope, in which we could see absolutely nothing.

At last we broke through, and what a sight was revealed to my astonished eyes! A great world lay below me, illuminated by a weird red light which seemed to emanate from the inner surface of the cloud envelope, shedding a rosy glow over mountain, hill, dale, plain, and ocean. At first I could in no way account for this all-pervading illumination; but presently, my eyes roving over the magnificent panorama lying below me, I saw in the distance an enormous volcano, from which giant flames billowed upward thousands of feet into the air. As I was to learn later, the crater of this giant was a full hundred miles in diameter and along the planet's equator there stretched a chain of these Gargantuan torches for some thirty thousand miles, while others were dotted over the entire surface of the globe, giving both light and heat to a world that would have been dark and cold without them.

As we dropped lower, I saw what appeared to be cities, all located at a respectful distance from these craters. In the air, I saw several ships similar to that which had brought me from Mars. Some were very small; others were much larger than the one with which I had become so familiar. Two small ships approached us, and we slowed down almost to a stop. They were evidently patrol ships. From several ports guns were trained on us. One of the ships lay at a little distance; the other came alongside. Our commander raised a hatch in the upper surface of the ship above the control room and stuck his head out. A door in the side of the patrol ship opened, and an officer appeared. The two exchanged a few words; then the commander of the patrol ship saluted and closed the door in which he had appeared. We were free to proceed. All this had taken place at an altitude of some five thousand feet.

We now spiraled down slowly toward a large city. Later, I learned that it covered an area of about four hundred square miles. It was entirely walled, and the walls and buildings were of a uniform dark brown color, as were the pavements of the avenues. It was a dismal, repellent city built entirely of volcanic rock. Within its boundaries I could see no sign of vegetation—not a patch of sward, not a shrub, not a tree; no color to relieve the monotony of somber brown.

The city was perfectly rectangular, having a long axis of about twenty-five miles and a width of about sixteen. The avenues were perfectly straight and equidistant, one from the other, cutting the city into innumerable, identical square blocks. The buildings were all perfect rectangles, though not all of either the same size or height—the only break in the depressing monotony of this gloomy city.

Well, not the only break: there were open spaces where there were no buildings—perhaps plazas or parade grounds. But these I did not notice until we had dropped quite low above the city, as they were all paved with the same dark brown rock. The city was quite as depressing in appearance as is Salt Lake City from the air on an overcast February day. The only relief from this insistent sense of gloom was the rosy light which pervaded the scene, the reflection of the flames of the great volcanoes from the inner surface of the cloud envelope; this and the riotous growth of tropical verdure beyond the city's walls—weird, unearthly growths of weird unearthly hues.

Accompanied by the two patrol ships, we now dropped gently into a large open space near the center of the city, coming to rest close to a row of hangars in which were many craft similar to our own.

We were immediately surrounded by a detail of warriors; and, much to my surprise, I saw a number of human beings much like myself in appearance, except that their skins were purple. These were unarmed and quite naked except for G strings, having no harness such as is worn by the Morgors. As soon as we had disembarked, these people ran the ship into the hangar. They were slaves.

There were no interchanges of greetings between the returning Morgors and those who had come out to meet the ship. The two commanding officers saluted one another and exchanged a few routine military brevities. The commander of our ship gave his name, which was Haglion, the name of his ship, and stated that he was returning from Mars—he called it Garobus. Then he detailed ten of his own men to accompany him as guards for U Dan and me. They surrounded us, and we walked from the landing field in the wake of Haglion.

He led us along a broad avenue filled with pedestrian and other traffic. On the sidewalks there were only Morgors. The purple people walked in the gutters. Many Morgors were mounted on enormous, repulsive looking creatures with an infinite number of legs. They reminded me of huge centipedes, their bodies being jointed similarly, each joint being about eighteen inches long. Their heads were piscine and extremely ugly. Their jaws were equipped with many long, sharp teeth. Like nearly all the land animals of Jupiter, as I was to learn later, they were ungulate, hoofs evidently being rendered necessary by the considerable areas of hardened lava on the surface of the planet, as well as by the bits of lava rock which permeate the soil.

These creatures were sometimes of great length, seating as high as ten or twelve Morgors on their backs. There were other beasts of burden on the avenue. They were of strange, unearthly forms; but I shall not bore you by describing them here.

Above this traffic moved small fliers in both directions. Thus the avenue accommodated a multitude of people, strange, dour people who seldom spoke and, as far as I had seen, never laughed. They might have, as indeed they looked, risen from sad graves to rattle their bones in mock life in a cemetery city of the dead.

U Dan and I walked in the gutter, a guard on the sidewalk close beside each of us. We were not good enough to walk where the Morgors walked! Haglion led us to a large plaza surrounded by buildings of considerable size but of no beauty. A few of them boasted towers—some squat, some tall, all ugly. They looked as though they had been built to endure throughout the ages.

We were conducted to one of these buildings, before the entrance to which a single sentry stood. Haglion spoke to him, and he summoned an officer from the interior of the building, after which we all entered. Our names and a description of each of us were entered in a large book. Haglion was given a receipt for us, after which he and our original escort left.

Our new custodian issued instructions to several warriors who were in the room, and they hustled U Dan and me down a spiral stairway to a dim basement, where we were thrown into a gloomy cell. Our escort locked the door on us and departed.

chapter IV

. . . AND THE SAVATORS

ALTHOUGH I HAD often wondered about Jupiter, I had never hoped nor cared to visit it because of the inhospitable conditions which earthly scientists assure us pertain to this great planet. However, here I was, and conditions were not at all as the scientists had described. Unquestionably, the mass of Jupiter is far greater than that of Earth or Mars, yet I felt the gravitational pull far less than I had upon Earth. It was even less than that which I had experienced upon Mars. This was due, I realized, to the rapid revolution of the planet upon its axis. Centrifugal force, tending to throw me off into space, more than outweighed the increased force of gravitation. I had never before felt so light upon my feet. I was intrigued by contemplation of the height and distances to which I might jump.

The cell in which I found myself, while large, precluded any experiments along that line. It was a large room of hard, brown lava rock. A few white lights set in recesses in the ceiling gave meager illumination. From the center of one wall a little stream of water tinkled into a small cavity in the floor, the overflow being carried off by a gutter through a small hole in the end wall of the cell. There were some grass mats on the floor. These constituted the sole furnishings of the bleak prison.

"The Morgors are thoughtful hosts," I remarked to U Dan. "They furnish water for drinking and bathing. They have installed sewage facilities. They have given us whereon to lie or sit. Our cell is lighted. It is strong. We are secure against the attacks of our enemies. However, as far as the Morgors are concerned, I—"

"S-s-sh!" cautioned U Dan. "We are not alone." He nodded toward the far end of the cell. I looked, and for the first time perceived what appeared to be the figure of a man stretched upon a mat.

Simultaneously, it arose and came toward us. It was, indeed a man. "You need have no fear of me," he said. "Say what you please of the Morgors. You could not possibly conceive any terms of opprobrium in which to describe them more virulent than those which I have long used and considered inadequate."

Except that the man's skin was a light blue, I could not see that he differed materially in physical appearance from U Dan and myself. His body, which was almost naked, was quite hairless except for a heavy growth on his head and for eyebrows and eyelashes. He spoke the same language as the Morgors. U Dan and I had been conversing in the universal language of Barsoom. I was surprised that the man had been able to understand us. U Dan and I were both silent for a moment.

"Perhaps," suggested our cell mate, "you do not understand the language of Eurobus—eh?"

"We do," I said, "but we were surprised that you understood our language."

The fellow laughed. "I did not," he said. "You mentioned the Morgors, so I knew that you were speaking of them; and then, when your companion discovered me, he warned you to silence; so I guessed that you were saying something uncomplimentary about our captors. Tell me—who are you? You are no Morgors, nor do you look like us Savators."

"We are from Barsoom," I said.

"The Morgors call it Garobus," explained U Dan.

I have heard of it," said the Savator. "It is a world that lies far above the clouds. The Morgors are going to invade it. I suppose they have captured you either to obtain information from you or to hold you as hostages."

"For both purposes, I imagine," said U Dan. "Why are you imprisoned?"

"I accidentally bumped into a Morgor who was crossing an avenue at an intersection. He struck me and I knocked him down. For that, I shall be destroyed at the graduation exercises of the next class."

"What do you mean by that?" I asked.

"The education of the Morgor youth consists almost wholly of subjects and exercises connected with the art of war. Because it is spectacular, because it arouses the blood lust of the participants and the spectators, personal combat winds up the exercises upon graduation day. Those of the graduating class who survive are inducted into the warrior caste—the highest caste among the Morgors. Art, literature, and science, except as they may pertain to war, are held in contempt by the Morgors. They have been kept alive upon Eurobus only through the efforts of us Savators; but, unfortunately, to the neglect of offensive military preparation and training. Being a peace loving people, we armed only for defense." He smiled ruefully and shrugged. "But wars are not won by defensive methods."

"Tell us more about the graduating exercises," said U Dan. "The idea is intriguing. With whom does the graduating class contend?"

"With criminals and slaves," replied the Savator. "Mostly men of my race," he added; "although sometimes there are Morgor criminals of the worst types sentenced to die thus. It is supposed to be the most shameful death that a Morgor can die—fighting shoulder to shoulder with members of a lower order against their own kind."

"Members of a lower order!" I exclaimed. "Do the Morgors consider you that?"

"Just a step above the dumb beasts, but accountable for our acts because we are supposed to be able to differentiate between right and wrong—wrong being any word or act or facial expression adversely critical of anything Morgorian or that can be twisted into a subversive act or gesture."

"And suppose you survive the graduating contest," I asked. "Are you then set at liberty?"

"In theory, yes," he replied; "but in practice, never."

"You mean they fail to honor terms of their own making?" demanded U Dan.

The Savator laughed. "They are entirely without honor," he said, "yet I do not know that they would not liberate one who survived the combat; because, insofar as I know, no one ever has. You see, the members of the class outnumber their antagonists two to one."

This statement gave me a still lower estimate of the character of the Morgors than I had already inferred from my own observation of them. It is not unusual that a warlike people excel in chivalry and a sense of honor; but where all other characteristics are made subservient to brutality, finer humanistic instincts atrophy and disappear.

We sat in silence for some time. It was broken by the Savator. "I do not know your names," he said. "Mine is Zan Dar."

As I told him ours, a detail of Morgor warriors came to our cell and ordered U Dan and me to accompany them. "Good-by!" said Zan Dar. "We probably shall never meet again."

"Shut up, thing!" admonished one of the warriors.

Zan Dar winked at me and laughed. The Morgor was furious. "Silence, creature!" he growled. I thought for a moment that he was going to fall upon Zan Dar with his sword, but he who was in charge of the detail ordered him out of the cell. The incident was but another proof of the egomaniac arrogance of the Morgors. However, it helped to crystallize within me an admiration and liking for the Savator that had been growing since first he spoke to us.

U Dan and I were led across the plaza to a very large building the entrance to which was heavily guarded. The hideous, grinning, skull-like heads of the warriors and their skeletal limbs and bodies, together with the dark and cavernous entrance to the building suggested a grisly fantasia of hell's entrance guarded by the rotting dead. It was not a pleasant thought.

We were held here for quite some time, during which some of the warriors discussed us as one might discuss a couple of stray alley cats. "They are like the Savators and yet unlike them," said one.

"They are quite as hideous," said another.

"One of them is much darker than the other."

Now, for the first time, I was struck by the color of these Morgors. Instead of being ivory color, they were a pink or rosy shade. I looked at U Dan. He was a very dark red. A glance at my arms and hands showed that they, too, were dark red; but not as dark a red as U Dan. At first I was puzzled; then I realized that the reflection of the red glare of the volcanoes from the inner surface of the cloud envelope turned our reddish skins a darker red and made the yellow, parchment-like skins of the Morgors appear pink. As I looked around, I realized that this same reddish hue appeared upon everything within sight. It reminded me of a verse in the popular song I heard some time ago on one of my visits to Earth. It went, I think: "I am looking at the world through rose colored glasses, and everything is rosy now." Well, everything wasn't rosy with me, no matter how rosy this world looked.

Presently an officer came to the entrance and ordered our escort to bring us in. The interior of the building was as unlovely as its exterior. Although this was, as I later learned, the principal palace of the Morgor ruler, there was absolutely no sign of ornamentation. No art relieved the austerity of gloomy, lava-brown corridors and bare, rectangular chambers. No hangings softened the sharp edges of openings; no rugs hid even a part of the bare, brown floors. The pictureless walls frowned down upon us. I have seldom been in a more depressing environment. Even the pits beneath the deserted cities of Barsoom often had interesting vaulted ceilings, arched doorways, elaborate old iron grill work, attesting the artistic temperaments of their designers. The Morgors, like death, were without art.

We were led to a large, bare chamber in which a number of Morgors were clustered about a desk at which another of the creatures was seated. All Morgors look very much alike to me, yet they do have individual facial and physical characteristics; so I was able to recognize Haglion among those standing about the desk. It was Haglion who had commanded the ship that had brought me from Mars.

U Dan and I were halted at some distance from the group, and as we stood there two other red Martians were brought into the room— a man and a girl. The girl was very beautiful.

"Vaja!" exclaimed U Dan, but I did not need this evidence to know who she was. I was equally certain that the man was Multis Par, Prince of Zor. He appeared nervous and downcast, but even so the natural arrogance of the man was indelibly stamped upon his features.

At U Dan's exclamation, one of those guarding us whispered, "Silence, thing!" Vaja's eyes went wide in incredulity as she recognized my companion; and she took an impulsive step toward him, but a warrior seized her arm and restrained her. The faint shadow of a malicious smile touched the thin lips of Multis Par.

The man seated at the desk issued an order, and all four of us were brought forward and lined up in front of him. The fellow differed in appearance not at all from other Morgors. He wore no ornaments. His harness and weapons were quite plain but evidently serviceable. They were marked with a hieroglyph that differed from similar markings on the harness and weapons of the other Morgors, as those of each of the others differed from all the rest. I did not know then what they signified; but later learned that each hieroglyph indicated the name, rank, and title of him who wore it. The hieroglyph of the man at the desk was that of Bandolian, Emperor of the Morgors.

Spread upon the desk before Bandolian was a large map, which I instantly recognized as that of Barsoom. The man and his staff had evidently been studying it. As U Dan and I were halted before his desk with Vaja and Multis Par, Bandolian looked up at the Prince of Zor.

"Which is he," he asked, "who is called Warlord of Barsoom?" Multis Par indicated me, and Bandolian turned his hollow eyes upon me. It was as though Death had looked upon me and singled me out as his own. "I understand that your name is John Carter," he said. I nodded in affirmation. "While you are of a lower order," he continued, "yet it must be that you are endowed with intelligence of a sort. It is to this intelligence that I address my commands. I intend to invade and conquer Barsoom (he called it Garobus), and I command you to give me all the assistance in your power by acquainting me and my staff with such military information as you may possess relative to the principal powers of Garobus, especially that one known as the Empire of Helium. In return for this your life will be spared."

I looked at him for a moment, and then I laughed in his face. The faintest suggestion of a flush overspread the pallor of his face. "You dare laugh at me, thing!" he growled.

"It is my answer to your proposition," I said.

Bandolian was furious. "Take it away and destroy it!" he ordered.

"Wait, Great Bandolian!" urged Multis Par. "His knowledge is almost indispensable to you, and I have a plan whereby you may make use of it."

"What is it?" demanded Bandolian.

"He has a mate whom he worships. Seize her and he will pay any price to protect her from harm."

"Not the price the Morgor has asked," I said to Multis Par, "and if she is brought here it will be the seal upon your death warrant."

"Enough of this," snapped Bandolian. "Take them all away."

"Shall I destroy the one called John Carter?" asked the officer who commanded the detail that had brought us to the audience-chamber.

"Not immediately," replied Bandolian.

"He struck a Morgor," said Haglion; "one of my officers."

"He shall die for that, too," said Bandolian.

"That will be twice," I said.

"Take it away!" snapped Bandolian.

As we were led away, Vaja and U Dan gazed longingly at one another.

chapter V

I Would Be a Traitor

Zan Dar, the Savator, was surprised to see us returned to the cell in so short a time. "In fact," he said, "I did not expect ever to see you again. How did it happen?"

I explained briefly what had occurred in the audience-chamber, adding, "I have been returned to the cell to await death."

"And you, U Dan?" he asked.

"I don't know why they bothered to take me up there," replied U Dan. "Bandolian paid no attention to me whatever."

"He had a reason, you may rest assured. He is probably trying to break down your morale by letting you see the girl you love, in the belief that you will influence John Carter to accede to his demands. John Carter lives only because Bandolian hopes to eventually break down his resistance."

Time dragged heavily in that cell beneath the Morgor city. For that matter, there would have been none had we been above ground, for there are no nights upon Jupiter. It is always day. The sun, four hundred eighty-three million miles away, would shed but little light upon the planet even were it exposed to the full light of the star that is the center of our solar system; but that little light is obscured by the dense cloud envelope which surrounds this distant world. What little filters through is negated by the gigantic volcanic torches which bathe the entire planet in perpetual daylight. Although Jupiter rotates upon its axis in less than ten hours, its day is for eternity.

U Dan and I learned much concerning conditions on the planet from Zan Dar. He told us of the vast warm seas which seethed in constant tidal agitation resulting from the constantly changing positions of the four larger moons which revolve about Jupiter in forty-two hours, eighty-five hours, one hundred seventy-two hours, and four hundred hours respectively while the planet spins upon its axis, making a complete revolution in nine hours and fifty-five minutes. He told us of vast continents and enormous islands; and I could well imagine that such existed, as a rough estimate indicated that the area of the planet exceeded twenty-three billion square miles.

As the axis of Jupiter is nearly perpendicular to the plane of its motion, having an inclination of only about 3°, there could be no great variety of seasons; so over this enormous area there existed an equable climate, warm and humid, perpetually lighted and heated by the innumerable volcanoes which pit the surface of the planet. And here was I, an adventurer who had explored two worlds, cooped up in a subterranean cell upon the most amazing and wonderful planet of our entire solar system. It was maddening.

Zan Dar told us that the continent upon which we were was the largest. It was the ancestral home of the Morgors, from which they had, over a great period of time, sallied forth to conquer the remainder of the world. The conquered countries, each of which was ruled by what might be called a Morgor Governor-General, paid tribute to the Morgors in manufactured goods, foodstuffs, and slaves. There were still a few areas, small and considered of little value by the Morgors, which retained their liberty and their own governments. From such an area came Zan Dar—a remote island called Zanor.

"It is a land of tremendous mountains, thickly forested with trees of great size and height," he said. "Because of our mountains and our forests, it is an easy land to defend against an air borne enemy."

When he told me the height of some of the lofty peaks of Zanor, it was with difficulty that I could believe him: to a height of twenty miles above sea level rose the majestic king of Zanor's mountains.

"The Morgors have sent many an expedition against us," said Zan Dar. "They get a foothold in some little valley; and there, above them and surrounding them in mountain fastnesses that are familiar to us and unknown to them, we have had them at our mercy, picking them off literally one by one until they are so reduced in numbers that they dare remain no longer. They kill many of us, too; and they take prisoners. I was taken thus in one of their invasions. If they brought enough ships and enough men, I suppose they could conquer us; but our land is scarcely worth the effort, and I think they prefer to leave us as we are to give their recruits practice in actual warfare."

I don't know how long we had been confined when Multis Par was brought to our cell by an officer and a detachment of warriors. He came to exhort me to cooperate with Bandolian.

"The invasion and conquest of Barsoom are inevitable," he said. "By assisting Bandolian you can mitigate the horror of it for the inhabitants of Barsoom. You will thus be serving our world far better than by stupidly and stubbornly refusing to meet Bandolian half way."

"You are wasting your time," I told him.

"But our own lives depend upon it," he cried. "You and U Dan, Vaja and I shall die if you refuse. Bandolian's patience is almost worn out now." He looked pleadingly at U Dan.

"We could not die in a better cause," said U Dan, much to my surprise. "I shall be glad to die in atonement for the wrong that I did John Carter."

"You are two fools!" exclaimed Multis Par, angrily.

"At least we are not traitors," I reminded him.

"You will die, John Carter," he growled; "but before you die, you shall see your mate in the clutches of Bandolian. She has been sent for. Now, if you change your mind, send word by one of those who bring your meals."

I sprang forward and knocked the creature down. I should have killed him then had not the Morgors dragged him from the cell.

So they had sent for Dejah Thoris—and I was helpless. They would get her. I knew how they would get her—by assuring her that only through her co-operation could my immediate death be averted. I wondered if they would win. Would I, in the final test, sacrifice my beloved princess or my adopted country? Frankly, I did not know; but I had the example of U Dan to guide me. He had placed patriotism above love. Would I?

Time dragged on in this gloomy cell where there was no time. We three plotted innumerable futile plans of escape. We improvised games to help mitigate the monotony of our dull existence. More profitably, however, U Dan and I learned much from Zan Dar concerning this great planet. And Zan Dar learned much of what lay beyond the eternal cloud envelope which hides from the view of the inhabitants of Jupiter the sun, the other planets, the stars, and even their own moons. All that Zan Dar knew of them was the little he had been able to glean from remarks dropped by Morgors of what had been seen from their interplanetary ships. Their knowledge of astronomy was only slightly less than their interest in the subject, which was practically non-existent. War, conquest, and bloodshed were their sole interests in life.

At last there came a break in the deadly monotony of our lives: a new prisoner was thrown into the cell with us. And he was a Morgor! The situation was embarrassing. Had our numbers been reversed, had there been three Morgors and one of us, there would have been no doubt as to the treatment that one would have received. He would have been ostracized, imposed upon, and very possibly abused. The Morgor expected this fate. He went into a far corner of the cell and awaited what he had every reason to expect. U Dan, Zan Dar, and I discussed the situation in whispers. That must have been a trying time for the Morgor. We three finally decided to treat the creature simply as a fellow prisoner until such time as his own conduct should be our eventual guide. Zan Dar was the first to break the ice. In a friendly manner he asked what mischance had brought the fellow to this pass.

"I killed one who had an influential relative in the palace of Bandolian," he replied, and as he spoke he came over closer to us. "For that I shall die, probably in the graduating exercises of the next class. We shall doubtless all die together," he added with a hollow laugh. He paused. "Unless we escape," he concluded.

"Then we shall die," said Zan Dar.

"Perhaps," said the Morgor.

"One does not escape from the prisons of the Morgors," said Zan Dar.

I was interested in that one word "perhaps." It seemed to me fraught with intentional meaning. I determined to cultivate this animated skeleton. It could do no harm and might lead to good. I told him my name and the names of my companions; then I asked his.

"Vorion," he replied; "but I need no introduction to you, John Carter. We have met before. Don't you recognize me?" I had to admit that I did not. Vorion laughed. "I slapped your face and you knocked me across the ship. It was a noble blow. For a long time they thought that I was dead."

"Oh," I said, "you were one of my instructors. It may please you to know that I am going to die for that blow."

"Perhaps not," said Vorion. There was that "perhaps" again. What did the fellow mean?

Much to our surprise, Vorion proved not at all a bad companion. Toward Bandolian and the powerful forces that had condemned him to death and thrown him into prison he was extremely bitter. I learned from him that the apparent veneration and loyalty accorded Bandolian by his people was wholly a matter of disciplined regimentation. At heart, Vorion loathed the man as a monster of cruelty and tyranny. "Fear and generations of training hold our apparent loyalty," he said.

After he had been with us for some time, he said to me, "You three have been very decent to me. You could have made my life miserable here; and I could not have blamed you had you done so, for you must hate us Morgors."

"We are all in the same boat," I said. "We could gain nothing by fighting among ourselves. If we work together—perhaps—" I used his own perhaps.

Vorion nodded. "I have been thinking that we might work together," he said.

"To what end?" I asked.

"Escape."

"Is that possible?"

"Perhaps."

U Dan and Zan Dar were eager listeners. Vorion turned to the latter. "If we should escape," he said, "you three have a country to which you might go with every assurance of finding asylum, while I could expect only death in any country upon the face of Eurobus. If you could promise me safety in your country—" He paused, evidently awaiting Zan Dar's reaction.

"I could only promise to do my best for you," said Zan Dar; "but I am confident that if you were the means of my liberation and return to Zanor, you would be permitted to remain there in safety."

Our plotting was interrupted by the arrival of a detail of warriors. The officer in command singled me out and ordered me from the cell. If I were to be separated from my companions, I saw the fabric of my dream of escape dissolve before my eyes.

They led me from the building and across the plaza to the palace of Bandolian, and after some delay I found myself again in the audience-chamber. From behind his desk, the hollow eyes of the tyrant stared at me from their grinning skull. "I am giving you your last chance," said Bandolian; then he turned to one of his officers. "Bring in the other," he said. There was a short wait, and then a door at my right opened and a guard of warriors brought in the "other." It was Dejah Thoris! My incomparable Dejah Thoris!

What a lovely creature she was as she crossed the floor surrounded by hideous Morgors. What majestic dignity, what fearlessness distinguished her carriage and her mien! That such as she should be sacrificed even for a world! They halted her scarce two paces from me. She gave me a brave smile, and whispered, "Courage! I know now why I am here. Do not weaken. Better death than dishonor."

"What is she saying?" demanded Bandolian.

I thought quickly. I knew that the chances were that not one of them there understood the language of Barsoom. In their stupid arrogance they would not deign to master the tongue of a lower order.

"She but pleads with me to save her," I said. I saw Dejah Thoris smile. Evidently they had taught her the language of the Morgors on the long voyage from Mars.

"And you will be wise to do so," said Bandolian, "otherwise she will be given to Multis Par and afterward tortured and mutilated many times before she is permitted to die."

I shuddered in contemplation of such a fate for my princess, and in that moment I weakened once again. "If I aid you, will she be returned unharmed to Helium?" I asked.

"Both of you will—after I have conquered Garobus," replied Bandolian.

"No! No!" whispered Dejah Thoris. "I should rather die than return to Helium with a traitor. No, John Carter, you could never be that even to save my life."

"But the torture! The mutilation! I would be a traitor a thousand times over to save you from that, and I can promise you that no odium would be attached to you: I should never return to Barsoom."

"I shall be neither tortured nor mutilated," she said. "Sewn into my harness is a long, thin blade."

I understood and I was relieved. "Very well," I said. "If we are to die for Barsoom, it is no more than thousands of her brave warriors have done in the past; but we are not dead yet. Remember that, my princess; and do not use that long, thin blade upon yourself until hope is absolutely dead."

"While you live, hope will live," she said.

"Come, come," said Bandolian. "I have listened long enough to your silly jabbering. Do you accept my proposition?"

"I am considering it," I said, "but I must have a few more words with my mate."

"Let them be few," snapped the Morgor.

I turned to Dejah Thoris. "Where are you imprisoned?" I asked.

"On the top floor of a tower at the rear of this building at the corner nearest the great volcano. There is another Barsoomian with me—a girl from Zor. Her name is Vaja."

Bandolian was becoming impatient. He drummed nervously on his desk with his knuckles and snapped his grinning jaws together like castanets. "Enough of this!" he growled. "What is your decision?"

"The matter is one of vast importance to me," I replied. "I cannot decide it in a moment. Return me to my cell so that I may think it over and discuss it with U Dan, who also has much at stake."

"Take it back to its cell," ordered Bandolian; and then, to me: "You shall have time, but not much. My patience is exhausted."

I HAD NO PLAN. I was practically without hope, yet I had gained at least a brief reprieve for Dejah Thoris. Perhaps a means of escape might offer itself. Upon such unsubstantial fare I fed the shred of hope to which I clung.

My cell mates were both surprised and relieved when I was returned to them. I told them briefly of what had occurred in the audience-chamber of Bandolian. U Dan showed real grief when he learned that Dejah Thoris was in the clutches of the Morgors, and cursed himself for the part he had taken in bringing her and me to a situation in which we faced the alternatives of death or dishonor.

"Vain regrets never got anyone anywhere," I said. "They won't get us out of this cell. They won't get Dejah Thoris and Vaja out of Bandolian's tower. Forget them. We have other things to think about." I turned to Vorion. "You have spoken of the possibility of escape. Explain yourself."

He was not accustomed to being spoken to thus peremptorily by one of the lower orders, as the Morgors considered us; but he laughed, taking it in good part. The Morgors cannot smile. From birth to death they wear their death's head grin—frozen, unchangeable.

"There is just a chance," he said. "It is just barely a chance. Slender would be an optimistic description of it, but if it fails we shall be no worse off than we are now."

"Tell us what it is," I said.

"I can pick the lock of our cell door," he explained. "If luck is with us, we can escape from this building. I know a way that is little used, for I was for long one of the prison guard."

"What chance would we have once we were in the streets of the city?" demanded U Dan. "We three, at least, would be picked up immediately."

"Not necessarily," said Vorion. "There are many slaves on the avenues who look exactly like Zan Dar. Of course, the color of the skin of you men from Garobus might attract attention; but that is a chance we shall have to take."

"And after we are in the streets?" asked Zan Dar. "What then?"

"I shall pretend that I am in charge of you. I shall treat you as slaves are so often treated that it will arouse no comment nor attract any undue attention. I shall have to be rough with you, but you will understand. I shall herd you to a field where there are many ships. There I shall tell the guard that I have orders to bring you to clean a certain ship. In this field are only the private ships of the rich and powerful among us, and I well know a certain ship that belongs to one who seldom uses it. If we can reach this ship and board it, nothing can prevent us from escaping. In an hour from now, we shall be on our way to Zanor—if all goes well."

"And if we can take Vaja and Dejah Thoris with us," I added.

"I had forgotten them," said Vorion. "You would risk your lives for two females?"

"Certainly," said U Dan.

Vorion shrugged. "You are strange creatures," he said.

"We Morgors would not risk a little finger for a score of them. The only reason that we tolerate them at all is that they are needed to replenish the supply of warriors. To attempt to rescue two of yours may easily end in disaster for us all."

"However, we shall make the attempt," I said. "Are you with us, Zan Dar?" I asked the Savator.

"To the end," he said, "whatever it may be."

Again Vorion shrugged. "As you will," he said, but not with much enthusiasm; then he set to work on the lock, and in a very short time the door swung open and we stepped out into the corridor. Vorion closed the door and relocked it. "This is going to give them food for speculation," he remarked.

He led us along the corridor in the opposite direction from that in which we had been brought to it and from which all those had come who had approached our cell since our incarceration. The corridor became dark and dusty the farther we traversed it. Evidently it was little used. At its very end was a door, the lock to which Vorion quickly picked; and a moment later we stepped out into a narrow alleyway.

So simple had been our escape up to now that I immediately apprehended the worst: such luck could not last. Even the alley which we had entered was deserted: no one had seen us emerge from the prison. But when we reached the end of the alley and turned into a broad avenue, the situation was very different. Here were many people—Morgors upon the sidewalks, slaves in the gutters, strange beasts of burden carrying their loads of passengers upon the pavement.

Now, Vorion began to berate and cuff as we walked in the gutter and he upon the sidewalk. He directed us away from the central plaza and finally into less frequented avenues, yet we still passed too many Morgors to suit me. At any minute one of them might notice the unusual coloration of U Dan's skin and mine. I glanced at Zan Dar to note if the difference between his coloration and ours was at all startling, and I got a shock. Zan Dar's skin had been blue. Now it was purple! It took me a moment to realize that the change was due to the rosy light of the volcano's flames turning Zan Dar's natural blue to purple.

We had covered quite a little distance in safety, when a Morgor, passing, eyed us suspiciously. He let us go by him; then he wheeled and called to Vorion. "Who are those two?" he demanded. "They are not Savators."

"They have been ill," said Vorion, "and their color has changed." I was surprised that the fellow could think so quickly.

"Well, who are you?" asked the fellow, "and what are you doing in charge of slaves while unarmed?"

Vorion looked down at his sides in simulated surprise. "Why, I must have forgotten them," he said.

"I think that you are lying to me," said the fellow. "Come along with me, all of you."

Here seemed an end of our hopes of escape. I glanced up and down the street. It appeared to be a quiet, residential avenue. There was no one near us. Several small ships rested at the curb in front of drear, brown domiciles. That was all. No eyes were upon us. I stepped close to the fellow who had thus rashly presented himself as an obstacle in the way of Dejah Thoris' rescue. I struck him once. I struck him with all my strength. He dropped like a log.

"You have killed him," exclaimed Vorion. "He was one of Bandolian's most trusted officers. If we are caught now, we shall be tortured to death."

"We need not be caught," I said. "Let's take one of these ships standing at the curb. Why take the time and the risk to go farther?"

Vorion shook his head. "They wouldn't do," he said. "They are only for intramural use. They are low altitude ships that would never get over even a relatively small mountain range; but more important still, they cannot be rendered invisible. We shall have to go on to the field as we have planned."

"To avoid another such encounter as we have just experienced," I said, "we had better take one of these ships at least to the vicinity of the field."

"We shall be no worse off adding theft to murder," said Zan Dar.

Vorion agreed, and a moment later we were all in a small ship and sailing along a few yards above the avenue. Keenly interested, I carefully noted everything that Vorion did in starting the motor and controlling the craft. It was necessary for me to ask only a few questions in order to have an excellent grasp of the handling of the little ship, so familiar was I with the airships of two other worlds. Perhaps I should never have the opportunity to operate one of these, but it could do no harm to know how.

We quitted the flier a short distance from the field and continued on foot. As Vorion had predicted, a guard halted us and questioned him. For a moment everything hung in the balance. The guard appeared skeptical, and the reason for his skepticism was largely that which had motivated the officer I had killed to question the regularity of Vorion's asserted mission—the fact that Vorion was unarmed. The guard told us to wait while he summoned an officer. That would have been fatal. I felt that I might have to kill this man, too; but I did not see how I could do it without being observed, as there were many Morgors upon the field, though none in our immediate vicinity.

Vorion saved the day. "Come! Come!" he exclaimed in a tone of exasperation. "I can't wait here all day while you send for an officer. I am in a hurry. Let me take these slaves on and start them to work. The officer can come to the ship and question me as well as he can question me here."

The guard agreed that there was something in this; and, after ascertaining the name and location of the ship which we were supposed to clean, he permitted us to proceed. I breathed an inward sigh of relief. After we had left him, Vorion said that he had given him the name and location of a different ship than that which we were planning to steal. Vorion was no fool.

The ship that Vorion had selected, was a slim craft which appeared to have been designed for speed. We lost no time boarding her; and once again I watched every move that Vorion made, questioning him concerning everything that was not entirely clear to me. Although I had spent some eighteen days aboard one of these Morgorian ships, I had learned nothing relative to their control, as I had never been allowed in the control room or permitted to ask questions.

First, Vorion magnetized the hull and sprayed it with the fine sands of invisibility; then he started the motor and nosed up gently. I had explained my plan to him, and once he had gained a little altitude he headed for the palace of Bandolian. Through a tiny lens set in the bow of this ship the view ahead was reflected upon a ground glass plate, just as an image is projected upon the finder of a camera. There were several of these lenses, and through one of them I presently saw the square tower at the rear of the palace, the tower in which Dejah Thoris and Vaja were confined.

"When I bring the ship up to the window," said Vorion, "you will have to work fast, as the moment that we open the door in the ship's hull, part of the interior of the ship will be visible. Some one in the palace or upon the ground may notice it, and instantly we shall be surrounded by guard and patrol ships."

"I shall work fast," I said.

I must admit that I was more excited than usual as Vorion brought the craft alongside the tower window, which we had seen was wide open and unbarred. U Dan and Zan Dar stood by to open the door so that I could leap through the window and then to close it immediately after I had come aboard with the two girls. I could no longer see the window now that the craft was broadside to it; but at a word from Vorion, U Dan and Zan Dar slid the door back. The open window was before me, and I leaped through it into the interior of the tower room.

Fortunately for me, fortunately for Dejah Thoris, and fortunately for Vaja, it was the right room. The two girls were there, but they were not alone. A man held Dejah Thoris in his arms, his lips searching for hers. Vaja was striking him futilely on the back, and Dejah Thoris was trying to push his face from hers.

I seized the man by the neck and hurled him across the room, then I pointed to the window and the ship beyond and told the girls to get aboard as fast as they could. They needed no second invitation. As they ran across the room toward the window, the man rose and faced me. It was Multis Par! Recognizing me, he went almost white; then he whipped out his sword and simultaneously commenced to shout for the guard.

Seeing that I was unarmed, he came for me. I could not turn and run for the window: had I, he could have run me through long before I could have reached it; so I did the next best thing. I charged straight for him. This apparently suicidal act of mine evidently confused him, for he fell back. But when I was close to him, he lunged for me. I parried the thrust with my forearm. I was inside his point now, and an instant later my fingers closed upon his throat. Like a fool, he dropped his sword then and attempted to claw my fingers loose with his two hands. He could have shortened his hold on it and run me through the heart, but I had had to take that chance.

I would have finished him off in a moment had not the door of the room been then thrown open to admit a dozen Morgor warriors. I was stunned! After everything had worked so well, to have this happen! Were all our plans to be thus thwarted? No, not all.

I shouted to U Dan: "Close the door and take off! It is a command!"

U Dan hesitated. Dejah Thoris stood at his side with one hand outstretched toward me and an indescribable expression of anguish on her face. She took a step forward as though to leap from the ship back into the room. U Dan quickly barred her way, and then the ship started to move away. Slowly the door slid closed, and once again the craft was entirely invisible.

All this transpired in but a few seconds while I still clung to Multis Par's throat. His tongue protruded and his eyes stared glassily. In a moment more he would have been dead; then the Morgor warriors were upon me, and I was dragged from my prey.

My captors handled me rather roughly and, perhaps, not without reason, for I had knocked three of them unconscious before they overpowered me. Had I but had a sword! What I should have done to them then! But though I was battered and bruised as they hustled me down from the tower, I was smiling; for I was happy. Dejah Thoris had been snatched from the clutches of the skeleton men and was, temporarily at least, safe. I had good cause for rejoicing.

I was taken to a small, unlighted cell beneath the tower; and here I was manacled and chained to the wall. A heavy door was slammed shut as my captors left me, and I heard a key turn in a massive lock.

IN SOLITARY CONFINEMENT unrelieved by even a suggestion of light, one is thrown entirely upon the resources of one's thoughts for mitigation of absolute boredom—such boredom as sometimes leads to insanity for those of weak wills and feeble nerves. But my thoughts were pleasant thoughts. I envisaged Dejah Thoris safely bound for a friendly country in an invisible ship which would be safe from capture, and I felt that three of those who accompanied her would be definitely friendly and that one of them, U Dan, might be expected to lay down his life to protect her were that ever necessary. As to Vorion, I could not even guess what his attitude toward her would be.

My own situation gave me little concern. I will admit that it looked rather hopeless, but I had been in tight places before and yet managed to survive and escape. I still lived, and while life is in me I never give up hope. I am a confirmed optimist, which, I think, gives me an attitude of mind that more often than not commands what we commonly term the breaks of life.

Fortunately, I was not long confined in that dark cell. I slept once, for how long I do not know; and I was very hungry when a detail of warriors came to take me away, hungry and thirsty, for they had given me neither food nor water while I had been confined.

I was not taken before Bandolian this time, but to one of his officers—a huge skeleton that continually opened and closed its jaws with a snapping and grinding sound. The creature was Death incarnate. From the way he questioned me, I concluded that he must be the lord high inquisitor. In silence, he eyed me from those seemingly hollow sockets for a full minute before he spoke; then he bellowed at me.

"Thing," he shouted, "for even a small part of what you have done you deserve death—death after torture."

"You don't have to shout at me," I said; "I am not deaf."

That enraged him, and he pounded upon his desk. "For impudence and disrespect it will go harder with you."

"I cannot show respect when I do not feel respect," I told him. "I respect only those who command my respect. I surely could not respect a bag of bones with an evil disposition."

I do not know why I deliberately tried to infuriate him. Perhaps it is just a weakness of mine to enjoy baiting enemies whom I think contemptible. It is, I admit, a habit fraught with danger; and, perhaps, a stupid habit; but I have found that it sometimes so disconcerts an enemy as to give me a certain advantage. In this instance I was at least successful in part: the creature was so furious that for some time it remained speechless; then it leaped to its feet with drawn sword.

My situation was far from enviable. I was unarmed, and the creature facing me was in an uncontrollable rage. In addition to all this, there were four or five other Morgors in the room, two of whom were holding my arms—one on either side. I was as helpless as a sheep in an abattoir. But as my would-be executioner came around the end of his desk to spit me on his blade, another Morgor entered the room.

The newcomer took in the situation at a glance, and shouted. "Stop, Gorgum!" The thing coming for me hesitated a moment then he dropped his point.

"The creature deserves death," Gorgum said, sullenly. "It defied and insulted me—me, an officer of the Great Bandolian!"

"Vengeance belongs to Bandolian," said the other, "and he has different plans for this insolent worm. What has your questioning developed?"

"He has been so busy screaming at me that he has had no time to question me," I said.

"Silence, low one!" snapped the newcomer. "I can well understand," he said to Gorgum, "that your patience must have been sorely tried; but we must respect the wishes of the Great Bandolian. Proceed with the investigation."

Gorgum returned his sword to its scabbard and reseated himself at his desk. "What is your name?" he demanded.

"John Carter, Prince of Helium," I replied. A scribe at Gorgum's side scribbled in a large book. I supposed that he was recording the question and the answer. He kept this up during the entire interview.

"How did you and the other conspirators escape from the cell in which you were confined?" Gorgum asked.

"Through the doorway," I replied.

"That is impossible. The door was locked when you were placed in the cell. It was locked at the time your absence was discovered."

"If you know so much, why bother to question me?"

Gorgum's jaws snapped and ground more viciously than ever. "You see, Horur," he said angrily, turning to the other officer, "the insolence of the creature."

"Answer the noble Gorgum's question," Horur snapped at me. "How did you pass through a locked door?"

"It was not locked."

"It *was* locked," shouted Gorgum.

I shrugged. "What is the use?" I asked. "It is a waste of time to answer the questions of one who knows more about the subject than I, notwithstanding the fact that he was not there."

"Tell me, then, in your own words how you escaped from the cell," said Horur in a less irritating tone of voice.

"We picked the lock."

"That would have been impossible," bellowed Gorgum.

"Then we are still in the cell," I said. "Perhaps you had better go and look."

"We are getting nowhere," snapped Horur.

"Rapidly," I agreed.

"I shall question the prisoner," said Horur. "We concede that you did escape from the cell."

"Rather shrewd of you."

He ignored the comment. "I cannot see that the means you adopted are of great importance. What we really wish to know is where your accomplices and the two female prisoners are now. Multis Par says that they escaped in a ship—probably one of our own which was stolen from a flying field."

"I do not know where they are."

"Do you know where they planned to go?"

"If I did, I would not tell you."

"I command you to answer me, on pain of death."

I laughed at the creature. "You intend to kill me anyway; so your threat finds me indifferent."

Horur kept his temper much better than had Gorgum, but I could see that he was annoyed. "You could preserve your life if you were more co-operative," he said. "Great Bandolian asks but little of you. Tell us where your accomplices intended going and promise to aid Great Bandolian in his conquest of Helium, and your life will be spared."

"No," I said.

"Wait," urged Horur. "Bandolian will go even further. Following our conquest of Helium, he will permit you and your mate to return to that country and he will give you a high office in the new government he intends to establish there. If you refuse, you shall be destroyed; your mate will be hunted down and, I promise you, she will be found. Her fate will be infinitely worse than death. You had better think it over."

"I do not need to think over such a proposition. I can give you a final answer on both counts—my irrevocable answer. It is—never!"

If Horur had had a lip, he would doubtless have bitten it. He looked at me for a long minute; then he said, "Fool!" after which he turned to Gorgum. "Have it placed with those who are being held for the next class," then he left the room.

I was now taken to a building located at some distance from those in which I had previously been incarcerated, and placed in a large cell with some twenty other prisoners, all of whom were Savators.

"What have we here?" demanded one of my fellow prisoners after my escort had left and locked the door. "A man with a red skin! He is no Savator. What are you, fellow?"

I did not like the looks of him, nor his tone of voice. I was not seeking trouble with those with whom I was to be imprisoned and with whom I was probably destined to die; so I walked away from the fellow and sat down on a bench in another part of the chamber, which was quite large. But the fool followed me and stood in front of me in a truculent attitude.

"I asked you what you were," he said, threateningly; "and when Pho Lar asks you a question, see that you answer it—and quickly. I am top man here." He looked around at the others. "That's right, isn't it?" he demanded of them.

There were some sullen, affirmative grunts. I could see at once that the fellow was unpopular. He appeared a man of considerable muscular development; and his reception of me, a newcomer among them, testified to the fact that he was a bully. It was evident that he had the other prisoners cowed.

"You seem to be looking for trouble, Lo Phar," I said; "but I am not. I am already in enough trouble."

"My name is Pho Lar, fellow," he barked.

"What difference does it make? You would stink by any name." The other prisoners immediately took interested notice. Some of them grinned.

"I see that I shall have to put you in your place," said Pho Lar, advancing toward me angrily.

"I do not want any trouble with you," I said. "It is bad enough to be imprisoned, without quarrelling with fellow prisoners."

"You are evidently a coward," said Pho Lar; "so, if you will get down on your knees and ask my pardon, I shall not harm you."

I had to laugh at that, which made the fellow furious; yet he hesitated to attack me. I realized then that he was a typical bully—yellow at heart. However, to save his face, he would probably attack me if he could not bluff me. "Don't make me angry," he said. "When I am angry I do not know my own strength. I might kill you."

"I wonder if this would make you angry," I said, and slapped him across the cheek with my open palm. I slapped him so hard that he nearly fell down. I could have slapped him harder. This staggered him more than physically. The blood rushed to his blue face until it turned purple. He was in a spot. He had started something; and if he were to hold his self-appointed position as top man, as he had described himself, he would have to finish it. The other prisoners had now all arisen and formed a half circle about us. They looked alternately at Pho Lar and at me in eager anticipation.

Pho Lar had to do something about that slap in the face. He rushed at me and struck out clumsily. As I warded off his blows, I realized that he was a very powerful man; but he lacked science, and

I was sure that he lacked guts. I determined to teach him a lesson that he would not soon forget. I could have landed a blow in the first few seconds of our encounter that would have put him to sleep, but I preferred to play with him.

I countered merely with another slap in the face. He came back with a haymaker that I ducked; then I slapped him again—a little harder this time.

"Good work!" exclaimed one of the prisoners.

"Go to it, red man!" cried another.

"Kill him!" shouted a third.

Pho Lar tried to clinch; but I caught one of his wrists, wheeled around, bent over, and threw him over my shoulder. He lit heavily on the lava flooring. He lay there for a moment, and as he scrambled to his feet I put a headlock on him and threw him again. This time he did not get up; so I picked him up and hit him on the chin. He went down for a long count. I was through with him, and went and sat down.

The prisoners gathered around me. I could see that they were pleased with the outcome of the fight. "Pho Lar's had this coming to him for a long time," said one.

"He sure got it at last!"

"Who are you, anyway?"

"My name is John Carter. I am from Garobus."

"I have heard of you," said one. I think we all have. The Morgors are furious at you because you tricked them so easily. I suppose they have sent you here to die with us. My name is Han Du." He held out a hand to me. It was the first time that I had seen this friendly gesture since leaving the earth. The Martians place a hand upon your shoulder. I took his hand.

"I am glad to know you, Han Du," I said. "If there are many more here like Pho Lar, I shall probably need a friend."

"There are no more like him," said Han Du, "and he is finished."

"You intimated that you are all doomed to die," I said. "Do you know when or how?"

"When the next class graduates, we shall be pitted against twice our number of Morgors. It will be soon, now."

PHO LAR was unconscious for a long time. For a while, I thought that I might have killed him; but finally he opened his eyes and looked about. Then he sat up, felt of his head, and rubbed his jaw. When his eyes found me, he dropped them to the floor. Slowly and painfully he got to his feet and started for the far side of the room. Four or five of the prisoners immediately surrounded him.

"Who's top man now?" demanded one of them and slapped his face. Two more struck him. They were pushing him around and buffeting him when I walked among them and pushed them away.

"Leave him alone," I said. "He has had enough punishment for a while. When he has recovered, if one of you wishes to take him on, that will be all right; but you can't gang up on him."

The biggest of them turned and faced me. "What have *you* got to say about it?" he demanded.

"This," I replied and knocked him down.

He sat up and looked at me. "I was just asking," he said, and grinned a sickly grin; then everybody laughed and the tension was over. After this, we got along famously—all of us, even Pho Lar; and I found them all rather decent men. Long imprisonment and the knowledge that they were facing death had frayed their nerves; but what had followed my advent had cleared the air, much as a violent electrical storm does. After that there was a lot of laughing and talking.

I inquired if any of them were from Zan Dar's country—Zanor; but none of them was. Several of them knew where it was, and one scratched a rough map of part of Jupiter on the wall of our cell to show me where Zanor was located. "But much good it will do you to know," he said.

"One never can tell," I replied.

They had told me what I was to expect at the graduating exercises, and I gave the subject considerable thought. I did not purpose attending a Morgor commencement in the role of a willing sacrifice.

"How many of you men are expert swordsmen?" I asked.

About half of them claimed to be, but it is a failing of fighting men to boast of their prowess. Not of all fighting men, but of many—usually those with the least to boast of. I wished that I had some means of determining which were really good.

"Of course we can't get hold of any swords," I said, "but if we had some sticks about the length of swords, we could soon find out who were the best swordsmen among us."

"What good would that do us?" asked one.

"We could give those Morgors a run for their money," I said, "and make them pay for their own graduation."

"The slave who brings our food is from my country," said Han Du. "I think he might smuggle a couple of sticks in to us. He is a good fellow. I'll ask him when he comes."

Pho Lar had said nothing about his swordsmanship; so, as he had proved himself a great boaster, I felt that he was not a swordsman at all. I was sorry, as he was by far the most powerful of all the Savator prisoners; and he was tall, too. With a little skill, he should have proved a most formidable swordsman. Han Du never boasted about anything; but he said that in his country, the men were much given to sword play; so I was counting on him.

Finally, Han Du's compatriot smuggled in a couple of wooden rods about the length of a long-sword; and I went to work to ascertain how my fellow prisoners stacked up as swordsmen. Most of them were good; a few were excellent; Han Du was magnificent; and, much to everyone's surprise, Pho Lar was superb. He gave me one of the most strenuous workouts I have ever had before I could touch him. It must have taken me nearly an hour to disarm him. He was one of the greatest swordsmen I had ever faced.

Since our altercation upon my induction to their company, Pho Lar had kept much to himself. He seldom spoke, and I thought he might be brooding and planning on revenge. I had to find out just where he stood, as I could not take any chances on treachery or even half-hearted co-operation.

I took Pho Lar aside after the passage with the wooden sticks. I put my cards squarely on the table. "My plan," I said, "requires as many good swordsmen as I can get. You are one of the finest I have ever met, but you may think that you have reason to dislike me and therefore be unwilling to give me your full support. I cannot use any man who will not follow me and obey me even to death. How about it?"

"I will follow wherever you lead," he said. "Here is my hand on it—if you will take my hand in friendship."

"I am glad to do it."

As we grasped hands, he said, "If I had known a man like you years ago, I should not have been the fool that I have been. You may count on me to my last drop of blood, and before you and I die we shall have shown the Morgors something that they will never forget. They think that they are great swordsmen, but after they have seen you in action they will have their doubts. I can scarcely wait for the time."

I was impressed by Pho Lar's protestations. I felt that he was sincere, but I could not disabuse my mind of my first impression of him that he was at heart an arrant coward. But perhaps, facing death, he would fight as a cornered rat fights. If he did, and didn't lose his head, he would wreak havoc on the Morgors.

There were twenty of us in that cell. No longer did time drag heavily. It passed quickly in practice with our two wooden rods. Han Du, Pho Lar, and I, acting as instructors, taught the others what tricks of swordsmanship we knew until we were twenty excellent swordsmen. Several were outstanding.

We discussed several plans of action. We knew that, if custom prevailed, we should be pitted against forty young Morgor cadets striving to win to the warrior caste. We decided to fight in pairs, each of our ten best swordsmen being paired with one of the ten less proficient; but this pairing was to follow an initial charge by the first ten, with our team mates close behind us. We hoped thus to eliminate many of the Morgors in the first few moments of the encounter, thus greatly reducing the odds against us. Perhaps we of the first ten overestimated our prowess. Only time would tell.

There was some nervousness among the prisoners, due, I think, to the uncertainty as to when we should be called upon to face those unequal odds. Each knew that some of us would die. If any survived, we had only rumor to substantiate our hope that they would be set free; and no man there trusted the Morgors. Every footfall in the corridor brought silence to the cell, with every eye fixed upon the door.

At long last our anxiety was relieved: a full company of warriors came to escort us to the field where we were to fight. I glanced quickly around at the prisoners' faces. Many were smiling and there were sighs of relief. I felt greatly encouraged.

We were taken to a rectangular field with tiers of seats on each of its four sides. The stands were crowded. Thousands of eyes stared from the hollow sockets of grinning skulls. It might have been a field day in Hell. There was no sound. There were no bands. There were no flying flags—no color. We were given swords and herded together at one end of the field. An official gave us our instructions.

"When the cadets come on the field at the far end, you will advance and engage them." That was all.

"And what of those of us who survive?" I asked.

"None of you will survive, creature," he replied.

"We understand that those who survive would be given their freedom," I insisted.

"None of you will survive," he repeated.

"Would you like to place a little bet on that?"

"None of your impudence, creature!" The fellow was getting angry.

"But suppose one of us should survive?" I demanded.

"In that case his life would be spared and he would be allowed to continue in slavery, but none has ever survived these exercises. The cadets are on the field!" he cried. "Go to your deaths, worms!"

"To your stations, worms!" I commanded. The prisoners laughed as they took their allotted positions: the first ten in the front line, each with his partner behind him. I was near the center of the line. Han Du and Pho Lar were on the flanks. We marched forward as we had practiced it in our cell, all in step, the men in the rear rank giving the cadence by chanting, "Death to the Morgors!" over and over. We kept intervals and distance a little greater than the length of an extended sword arm and sword.

It was evident that the Morgors had never seen anything like that at a commencement exercise, for I could hear the hollow sound of their exclamations of surprise arising from the stands; and the cadets advancing to meet us were seemingly thrown into confusion. They were spread out in pairs in a line that extended almost all the way across the field, and it suddenly became a very ragged line. When we were about twenty-five feet from this line, I gave the command, "Charge!"

We ten, hitting the center of their line, had no odds against us: the Morgors had spread their line too thin. They saw swordsmanship in those first few seconds such as I'll warrant no Morgor ever saw before. Ten Morgors lay dead or dying on the field, as five of our first ten wheeled toward the right, followed by our partners; and our remaining ten men wheeled to the left.

As we had not lost a man in the first onslaught, each ten was now pitted against fifteen of the enemy. The odds were not so heavily against us. Taking each half of the Morgor line on its flank, as we now were, gave us a great advantage; and we took heavy toll of them before those on the far flanks could get into action, with the result that we were presently fighting on an almost even footing, our partners having now come into action.

The Morgors fought with fanatic determination. Many of them were splendid swordsmen, but none of them was a match for any of our first ten. I caught an occasional glimpse of Pho Lar. He was magnificent. I doubt that any swordsman of any of the three worlds upon which I had fought could have touched Pho Lar, Han Du, or me with his point; and there were seven more of us here almost as good.

Within fifteen minutes of the start of the engagement, all that remained was the mopping up of the surviving Morgors. We had lost ten men, all of the first ten swordsmen having survived. As the last of the Morgors fell, one could almost feel the deathly silence that had settled upon the audience.

The nine gathered around me. "What now?" asked Pho Lar.

"How many of you want to go back to slavery?" I asked.

"No!" shouted nine voices.

"We are the ten best swords on Eurobus," I said. "We could fight our way out of the city. You men know the country beyond. What chance would we have to escape capture?"

"There would be a chance," said Han Du. "Beyond the city, the jungle comes close. If we could make that, they might never find us."

"Good!" I said, and started at a trot toward a gate at one end of the field, the nine at my heels.

At the gateway, a handful of foolish guardsmen tried to stop us. We left them behind us, dead. Now we heard angry shouts arising from the field we had left, and we guessed that soon we should have hundreds of Morgors in pursuit.

"Who knows the way to the nearest gate?" I demanded.

"I do," said one of my companions. "Follow me!" and he set off at a run.

As we raced through the avenues of the drear city, the angry shouts of our pursuers followed us; but we held our distance and at last arrived at one of the city gates. Here again we were confronted by armed warriors who compelled us to put up a stiff battle. The cries of the pursuing Morgors grew louder and louder. Soon all that we had gained would be lost. This must not be! I called Pho Lar and Han Du to my side and ordered the remaining seven to give us room, for the gateway was too narrow for ten men to wield their blades within it advantageously.

"This time we go through!" I shouted to my two companions as we rushed the surviving guardsmen. And we went through. They hadn't a chance against the three best swordsmen of three worlds.

Miraculous as it may seem, all ten of us won to freedom with nothing more than a few superficial scratches to indicate that we had been in a fight; but the howling Morgors were now close on our heels.

If there is anything in three worlds that I hate, it is to run from a foe; but it would have been utterly stupid to have permitted several hundred angry Morgors to have overtaken me. I ran.

The Morgors gave up the chase before we reached the jungle. Evidently they had other plans for capturing us. We did not stop until we were far into the tropical verdure of a great forest; then we paused to discuss the future and to rest, and we needed rest.

That forest! I almost hesitate to describe it, so weird, so unearthly was it. Almost wholly deprived of sunlight, the foliage was pale, pale with a deathlike pallor, tinged with rose where the reflected light of the fiery volcanoes filtered through. But this was by far its least uncanny aspect: the limbs of the trees moved like living things. They writhed and twined—myriad, snakelike things. I had scarcely noticed them until we halted. Suddenly one dropped down and wrapped itself about me. Smiling, I sought to disentwine it. I stopped smiling: I was as helpless as a babe encircled by the trunk of an elephant. The thing started to lift me from the ground, and just then Han Du saw and leaped forward with drawn sword. He grasped one of my legs, and at the same time sprang upward and struck with the keen edge of his blade, severing the limb that had seized me. We dropped to the ground together.

"What the devil!" I exclaimed. "What is it? and why did it do that?"

Han Du pointed up. I looked. Above me, at the end of a strong stem, was a huge blossom—a horrible thing! In its center was a large mouth armed with many teeth, and above the mouth were two staring, lidless eyes.

"I had forgotten," said Han Du, "that you are not of Eurobus. Perhaps you have no such trees as these in your world."

"We certainly have not," I assured him. "A few that eat insects, perhaps, like Venus's-flytrap; but no maneaters."

"You must always be on your guard when in one of our forests," he warned me. "These trees are living, carnivorous animals. They have a nervous system and a brain, and it is generally believed that they have a language and talk with one another."

Just then a hideous scream broke from above us. I looked up, expecting to see some strange, Jupiterian beast above me, but there was nothing but the writhing limbs and the staring eyes of the great blossoms of the mantrees.

Han Du laughed. "Their nervous systems are of a low order," he said, "and their reactions correspondingly slow and sluggish. It took all this time for the pain of my sword cut to reach the brain of the blossom to which that limb belongs."

"A man's life would never be safe for a moment in such a forest," I commented.

"One has to be constantly on guard," admitted Han Du. "If you ever have to sleep out in the woods, build a smudge. The blossoms don't like smoke. They close up, and then they cannot see to attack you. But be sure that you don't oversleep your smudge."

Vegetable life on Jupiter, practically devoid of sunlight, has developed along entirely different lines from that on Earth. Nearly all of it has some animal attributes and nearly all of it is carnivorous, the smaller plants devouring insects, the larger, in turn, depending upon the larger animals for sustenance on up to the maneaters such as I had encountered and those which Han Du said caught and devoured even the hugest animals that exist upon this strange planet.

We posted a couple of guards, who also kept smudges burning; and the rest of us lay down to sleep. One of the men had a chronometer, and this was used to inform the men on guard when to awaken their reliefs. In this way, we all took turns watching and sleeping.

When all had slept, the smudges were allowed to burn more brightly, the men cut limbs from the living trees, sliced them and roasted them. They tasted much like veal. Then we talked over our plans for the future. It was decided that we should split up into parties of two or three and scatter; so that some of us at least might have a chance to escape recapture. They said that the Morgors would hunt us down for a long time. I felt that we would be much safer remaining together as we were ten undefeatable sword-arms; but as the countries from which my companions came were widely scattered; and, as naturally, each wished if possible to return to his own home, it was necessary that we separate.

It chanced that Han Du's country lay in the general direction of Zanor, as did Pho Lar's; so we three bid good-by to the others and left them. How I was to reach faraway Zanor on a planet of twenty-three billion square miles of area, I was at some loss to conceive. So was Han Du. He told me that I would be welcome in his country—if we were fortunate enough to reach it; but I assured him that I should never cease to search for Zanor and my mate.

chapter IX

TO ZANOR!

I SHALL NOT BORE YOU with an account of that part of my odyssey which finally brought me to one of the cities of Han Du's country. We kept as much to cover as we could, since we knew that if Morgors were searching for us, they would be flying low in invisible ships. Forests offered us our best protection from discovery, but there were wide plains to cross, rivers to swim, mountains to climb.

In this world without night, it was difficult to keep account of time; but it seemed to me that we must have traveled for months. Pho Lar remained with us for a great deal of the time, but finally he had to turn away in the direction of his own country. We were sorry to lose him, as he had developed into a splendid companion; and we should miss his sword, too.

We had met no men, but had had several encounters with wild beasts—creatures of hideous, unearthly appearance, both powerful and voracious. I soon realized the inadequacy of our swords as a sole means of defense; so we fashioned spears of a bamboolike growth that seemed wholly vegetable. I also taught Han Du and Pho Lar how to make bows and arrows and to use them. We found them of great advantage in our hunting of smaller animals and birds for food. In the forests, we subsisted almost wholly on the meat of the mantree.

At last Han Du and I came within sight of an ocean. "We are home," he said. "My city lies close beside the sea." I saw no city.

We had come down out of some low hills, and were walking across a narrow coastal plain. Han Du was several yards to my right, when I suddenly bumped into something solid—solid as a brick wall; but there was nothing there! The sudden collision had caused me to step back. I stretched out my hands, and felt what seemed to be a solid wall barring my way, yet only a level expanse of bare ground, but the ground was not entirely bare. It was dotted, here and there, with strange plants—a simple, leafless stock a foot or two tall bearing a single fuzzy blossom at its top.

I looked around for Han Du. He had disappeared! He had just vanished like a punctured soap bubble. All up and down the shore there was no place into which he could have vanished, nothing behind which he would have hidden, no hole in the ground into which he might have darted. I was baffled. I scratched my head in perplexity, as I started on again toward the beach only to once more bump into the wall that was not there.

I put my hands against the invisible wall and followed it. It curved away from me. Foot by foot, I pursued my tantalizing investigation. After a while I was back right where I had started from. It seemed that I had run into an invisible tower of solid air. I started off in a new direction toward the beach, avoiding the obstacle which had obstructed my way. After a dozen paces I ran into another; then I gave up—at least temporarily.

Presently I called Han Du's name aloud, and almost instantly he appeared a short distance from me. "What kind of a game is this?" I demanded. "I bump into a wall of solid air and when I look for you, you are not anywhere, you have disappeared."

Han Du laughed. "I keep forgetting that you are a stranger in this world," he said. "We have come to the city in which I live. I just stepped into my home to greet my family. That is why you could not see me." As he spoke, a woman appeared beside him, and a little child. They seemed to materialize out of thin air. Had I come to a land of disembodied spirits who had the power to materialize? I could scarcely believe it, as there was nothing ghostly nor ethereal about Han Du.

"This is O Ala, my mate," said Han Du. "O Ala, this is John Carter, Prince of Helium. To him we owe my escape from the Morgors."

O Ala extended her hand to me. It was a firm, warm hand of flesh and blood. "Welcome, John Carter," she said. "All that we have is yours."

It was a sweet gesture of hospitality; but as I looked around, I could not see that they had anything. "Where is the city?" I asked.

They both laughed. "Come with us," said O Ala. She led the way, apparently around an invisible corner; and there, before me, I saw an open doorway in thin air. Through the doorway, I could see the interior of a room. "Come in," invited O Ala, and I followed her into a commodious, circular apartment. Han Du followed and closed the door. The roof of the apartment was a dome perhaps twenty feet high at its center. It was divided into four rooms by sliding hangings which could be closed or drawn back against the wall.

"Why couldn't I see the house from the outside?" I asked.

"It is plastered on the outside with sands of invisibility which we find in great quantities along the beach," explained Han Du. "It is about our only protection against the Morgors. Every house in the city is thus protected, a little over five hundred of them."

So I had walked into a city of five hundred houses and seen only an expanse of open beach beside a restless sea. "But where are the people?" I asked. "Are they, too, invisible?"

"Those who are not away, hunting or fishing are in their homes," explained O Ala. "We do not venture out any more than is necessary, lest Morgors be cruising around in their invisible ships and see us; thus discovering our city."

"If any of us should be thus caught out," said Han Du, "he must run away from the city as fast as he can, for if he entered a house, the Morgors would immediately know that there was a city here. It is the sacrifice that each of us is in honor bound to make for the safety of all, for he who runs is almost invariably caught and carried away, unless he chooses to fight and die."

"Tell me," I said to Han Du, "how in the world you found your house, when you could not see it or any other house."

"You noticed the umpalla plants growing throughout the city?" he asked.

"I noticed some plants, but I saw no city."

They both laughed again. "We are so accustomed to it that it does not seem at all strange to us," said O Ala, "but I can understand that it might prove very confusing to a stranger. You see, each plant marks the location of a house. By long experience, each of us has learned the exact location of every house in the city in relation to every other house."

I remained for what may have been five or six days of Earth time in the home of Han Du and O Ala. I met many of their friends, all of whom were gracious and helpful to me in every way that they could be. I was furnished with maps of considerable areas of the planet, parts of which, I was told, were still unexplored even by the Morgors. Of greatest value to me was the fact that Zanor appeared on one of the maps, which also showed that a vast ocean lay between me and the country in which I believed Dejah Thoris to be. How I was to cross this ocean neither I nor my new found friends could offer a suggestion, other than the rather mad scheme I envisioned of building a sail boat and trusting myself to the mad caprices of an unknown sea perhaps swarming with dangerous reptiles. But this I at last decided was the only hope I had for being again reunited with my princess.

There was a forest several miles along the coast from the city, where I might hope to find trees suitable for the construction of my craft. My friends tried their best to dissuade me; but when they found that I was determined to carry out my plan, they loaned me tools; and a dozen of them volunteered to accompany me to the forest and help me build my boat.

At last all was in readiness; and, accompanied by my volunteer helpers, I stepped from the house of Han Du to start the short march to the forest.

Scarcely were we in the open when one of my companions cried, "Morgors!" Whereupon the Savators scattered in all directions away from their city.

"Run, John Carter!" shouted Han Du, but I did not run.

A few yards distant, I saw the open doorway in the side of an invisible ship; and I saw six or seven Morgors emerge from it. Two rushed toward me; the others scattered in pursuit of the Savators. In that instant a new plan flashed across my mind. Hope, almost extinct, leaped to life again.

I whipped my sword from its scabbard and leaped forward to meet the first of the oncoming Morgors, thanking God that there were only two of them, as delay might easily wreck my hopes. There was no finesse in my attack: it was stark, brutal murder; but my conscience did not bother me as I drew my sword from the heart of the first Morgor and faced the second.

The second fellow gave me a little more trouble, as he had been forewarned by the fate of his companion; and, too, he presently recognized me. That made him doubly wary. He commenced to howl to the others, who were pursuing the Savators, to come back and help him, bellowing that here was the creature from Garobus who had led the slaughter at the graduating exercises. From the corner of an eye, I saw that two of them had heard and were returning. I must hurry!

The fellow now fought wholly on the defensive in order to gain time for the others to join him. I had no mind to permit this, and I pressed him hard, often laying myself wide open—a great swordsman could have killed me easily. At last I reached him with a mighty cut that almost severed his head from his body; then, with only a quick glance behind me to see how close the others were, I leaped toward the open doorway of the otherwise invisible ship, a Morgor close upon my heels.

With naked blade still in my hand, I sprang aboard and closed the door behind me; then I wheeled to face whatever of their fellows had been left aboard to guard the craft. The fools had left no one. I had the ship all to myself; and as I ran to the controls I heard the Morgors beating upon the door, angrily demanding that I open it. They must have taken me for a fool, too.

A moment later the ship rose into the air, and I was away upon one of the strangest adventures of my life—navigating an unknown planet in an invisible craft. And I had much to learn about navigation on Jupiter. By watching Vorion, I had learned how to start and stop a Morgor ship, how to gain or lose altitude, and how to cloak the ship in invisibility; but the instruments upon the panel before me were all entirely meaningless to me. The hieroglyphs of the Morgors were quite unintelligible. I had to work it all out for myself.

Opening all the ports, I had a clear field of vision. I could see the shore I had just left, and I knew the direction of the coast line. Han Du had explained this to me. It ran due north and south at that point. The ocean lay to the west of it. I found an instrument which might easily have been a compass; when I altered the course of the ship, I saw that it was a compass. I now had my bearings as closely as it was possible for me to get them. I consulted my map and discovered that Zanor lay almost exactly southeast; so out across that vast expanse of ocean I turned the prow of my ship.

I was free. I had escaped the Morgors unharmed. In Zanor, Dejah Thoris was safe among friends. That I should soon be with her, I had no doubt. We had experienced another amazing adventure. Soon we should be reunited. I had not the slightest doubt of my ability to find Zanor. Perhaps it is because I am always so sure of myself that I so often accomplish the seemingly impossible.

How long I was in crossing that dismal ocean, I do not know. With Jupiter whirling on its axis nearly three times as fast as Earth, and with no sun, moon, nor stars, I could not measure time.

I saw no ship upon that entire vast expanse of water, but I did see life—plenty of it. And I saw terrific storms that buffeted my craft, tossing it about like a feather. But that was nothing compared with what I saw below me as the storms at the height of their fury lashed the surface of the waters. I realized then how suicidal would have been my attempt to cross that terrible ocean in the frail craft that I had planned to build. I saw waves that must have measured two hundred feet from trough to crest—waves that hurled the mighty monsters of the deep as though they had been tiny minnows. No ship could have lived in such seas. I realized then why I saw no shipping on this great Jupiterian ocean.

But at last I sighted land ahead—and what land! Zan Dar had told me of the mighty mountains of Zanor rearing their forested heads twenty miles above the level of the sea, and it was such mountains that lay ahead of me. If I had reckoned accurately, this should be Zanor;

and these breath-taking mountains assured me that I had not gone wrong.

I knew from Zan Dar's explanation, just where to search for the stamping grounds of his tribe—a wild mountain and at an altitude of only about ten miles, or meadows and ravines on the east slope of the highest mountain and at an altitude of only about ten miles, or about halfway to the summit. Here the air is only slightly thinner than at sea level, as the cloud envelope retains the atmosphere of Jupiter as though it were held in a bag, permitting none of it to escape, while the rapid revolution of the planet tends to throw the atmosphere far up from the surface.

Most fortunate was I in coming upon the village of Zan Dar with little or no difficulty. Entirely invisible, I hovered above it, dropping down slowly. I knew that the moment they saw a Morgor ship, they would disappear into the forests that surrounded the village, waiting there to rush upon any Morgors who might be foolish enough to leave the ship after landing.

There were people in plain view of me in the village as I dropped to within fifty feet of the ground. I stopped the ship and hung there, then I demagnetized the hull; and, as the ship became instantly visible, I leaped to the door and pushed it open; so that they could see that I was no Morgor. I waved to them and shouted that I was a friend of Zan Dar, and asked permission to land.

They called to me to do so, and I brought the ship slowly toward the ground. My lonely voyage was over. I had surmounted seemingly unsurmountable obstacles and I had reached my goal. Soon my incomparable Dejah Thoris would be again in my arms.